I0636325

SOLAR WINDS

PROVIDENCE ENDS

BRYAN G. SHEWMAKER

Printed in the United States of America
Line edited by Kristen Corrects, Inc.
Cover art design by Lance Buckley
Appendix edited by Kingsman Editing Services

Hardback edition published 2021
Second edition published 2025

ISBN: 978-0-9989606-8-5

SOLAR WINDS

PROVIDENCE ENDS

PROLOGUE

NEAR THE CENTER OF the Virgo Cluster lay the Hourglass Galaxy, epicenter of tensions between the Solar Empire and the Interstellar Combine. A spiral galaxy of six arms, the Hourglass was not named for its shape. Instead, it took its name from the unusual passage of time within its influence. To both the newly arrived Empire and the long-resident Combine, the source of the galaxy's chronological anomalies was a mystery.

For Solar colonies within the Hourglass' Auchard arm, every second that passed equated to nine of Interstellar Coordinated Time. The closer one approached the core of the galaxy, the more intense this dilation became. Eventually one reached the Void Zone, a region around the center of the galaxy where time was so dilated as to be at a virtual standstill.

At random intervals, ripples would emerge from the Void Zone and spread through the galaxy. To those with the ability to warp space-time and achieve faster-than-light travel, doing so made these ripples imperceptible. But for those not so protected, time was altered. Each ripple was itself a distortion of space-time, carrying with it the dilation of its source as it moved in an ever-accelerating wave until becoming imperceptible at the galaxy's perimeter. Since its arrival, the Empire had sought to unlock the secrets of this mystery of the universe, an endeavor for which the Combine had a long head start.

The border between the Combine and the Hourglass Strategic Allies, now satellite states of the Empire, was formed by a line separating the galactic disc from the arm named Auchard. A lone ship crossed this border, passing beyond the Neutral Zone, and was now on its way deep into Combine space. Too small to be a true warship, it was a vessel more expensive than a flotilla of armed destroyers. Remaining undetected in the vacuum of space against the most advanced sensors was an expensive prospect. This ship and those like it were so secret, they had no names.

Within the vessel, the light of hologram displays cast an amber glow over the pall of smoke swirling through the cockpit. With a nearly unobstructed view of space, a single occupant sat with an arm draped over his lap. Whiskey-voiced, he sang along with the music while chewing on a fresh cigar.

Panzer glared down at his left arm and carefully unfurled a weave of polymer bandages to reveal a hand that had been split in two. The thumb, index, and middle fingers along with most of the palm were gone. As his gaze focused on the wounded hand, his eyes scanned the characters that only he could see. The Neural-Optic Display enabled an individual to exert control of the nanites inhabiting every cell of their body. Data from the nanites was conveyed to those in his brain, creating the digital images in his vision as surely as if his eyes scanned a computer screen. While he flexed his remaining fingers, the nanites in his arm fed his NOD a constant stream of data about the ongoing process to heal his limb.

He did not have time for the nanites to finish the job normally, and with his other hand he laid a box marked by a white cross on his lap. From its side he deployed a long wire ending in a needle. He bit harder into his cigar and jammed the needle into the remains of his palm. The two fingers of the wounded hand curled involuntarily as energy and nutrients were forced into his flesh, supercharging the nanites. He watched as bone jutted from the wound before it was surrounded by soft tissue.

In only a few minutes his hand had been restored, the only sign of the prior injury found in the nearly albino shade of the new skin. A few eye movements in his NOD later, and the new skin matched the old. He removed the needle from his palm and poked each of his fingertips to ensure sensation before returning the med kit to its slot beneath his chair.

"Colonel."

A female voice interrupted his music.

"We are ten minutes to intercept. Will you be ready by then?"

"Plenty of time," he answered, his eyes twitching to change screens in his NOD before his chair descended into a narrow corridor.

"Colonel, you have not rested since the encounter on Yuros. Are you sure this is wise without your auxiliaries?"

"I'm sure."

"Colonel, I must advise you—"

"We lose Solnus and our only connection to the Sovari Soma is gone. We don't have time for me to take a nap."

"Yes sir."

Companion AIs were unwaveringly loyal to their masters, but even those owned by soldiers were known for being extremely protective. Doors parted ahead of his stride until he came to the pair he sought. On the reinforced doors, red letters spelled out *COL. ROBERT PANZER*. The doors parted to reveal a library of armaments and a small pit at the armory's center. A black film formed in the pit as he stepped down and held out his arms. Additional nanites scaled his body to form the nanoskin, the first layer. When they reached his neck, the horde of machines stopped, and with an annoyed sigh he shrugged his shoulders to encourage them to continue. Only then did a fatigued mind realize that they waited for him to remove the obstruction in order to complete a hermetic seal. Spitting out the cigar, he took a breath as the machines enveloped him completely.

From above, a quilted suit lined in luminescent wires descended to cinch tight around him, forming the second layer. Still motionless, Panzer waited as copper-tone coils of wire affixed themselves to the quilting. Actuators, artificial muscles to augment his own considerable strength. The last layer came as metal plates attaching themselves to the actuators. Together they formed an obsidian shell broken only where the luminescent wires of the inner quilt were allowed to shine through. Finally a helmet descended, hissing as it closed around his head. Three sensors formed a triangle over his left eye, with an upright prism opposite and both above a large respirator.

Several markings adorned the armor, runes cast into the metal upon its creation. But the markings within the metal were of an alien language, not those of humanity. Such identifying markings rarely mattered. Few enemies survived an encounter with a commando unless they were permitted to do so. The Commando Corps prided itself on handling missions at which other intelligence and special forces services balked. In an empire that drew men from an intergalactic population, there were fewer than 50,000 who qualified for membership. They were veteran soldiers and gifted metapsions able to wield telepathy, telekinesis, and other more esoteric abilities. For the Commando Corps, the unofficial mantra had long been, "Send an army, or send a commando."

"Close quarters," he whispered to himself. "Keep it light."

He scanned the walls, letting his gaze rest for a moment on a conspicuously empty spot. There a placard read: *A warrior should not have a favorite weapon*. With a grumble, he moved on.

"RA-117Co."

At his command, one of the many racks of guns rotated, bringing the desired weapon into view. Extending an arm, he called it to his grasp before drawing a box of magazines from the same rack. Thirty power cores to a magazine, ten shots per core; he drew five. With a shrug he drew more, a dozen in all. He had never heard of the man who lost a fight due to an excess of ammunition. The first magazine he jammed into the rifle before pressing the rest against his breastplate where they adhered in the silhouette of a bandolier.

"GL Mark-46."

The large pistol moved into his hand before it and a company of magazines was adhered to his thigh. He debated if he would need more as he drew a large knife from the wall and affixed it to his other thigh.

"That should do it," he remarked, turning to leave before reversing and calling up another pair of magazines. Upon exiting the armory, his new weight brought a ring to the deck with every step.

"I am decelerating for interception," Andira announced. "I have the target in my scope."

"What do you see?"

"The ships are hiding in the rings of a Class-9 ice giant. One of the ships matches the silhouette of the vessel from Yuros. Both ships are powered down to avoid detection. I am unable to match engine harmonics at this time."

"It's them. Full stealth," Panzer ordered. "Get me alongside."

"Yes sir. I can get you within 200 kilometers. Any closer and we risk detection."

"Close enough."

"Colonel, a dilation wave is approaching," she warned. "It will reach our position in approximately thirty-two minutes."

"Amplitude?"

"I estimate a forty-seven second interval."

"Understood. Keep me updated."

"Yes sir, I am bringing us alongside now." Her voice now came from within his helmet as she wrote a copy of her program to the armor's mainframe.

Focusing in his NOD, he gazed through his ship's sensors to observe the pair of vessels. Both resembled simple cylinders bundling a ring of engines opposite a blunt nose. The two were joined by a pair of pylons as the larger ship refueled the smaller. More proof that this was the ship he sought—they had left so quickly that their fuel supply was exhausted before making it home.

"I'm exiting now," he said. "Have the deep fryer on standby, and be ready to pick me up."

"Yes sir."

Craning his head slightly, he sent the command through his NOD and sparks danced over his armor a moment before he was rendered transparent. The airlock depressurized as the doors parted and he stepped out to drift in the vacuum. Thrusters on his back and ankles fired together to orient him toward his target before he was propelled forward. Ten G's of acceleration made the trip a short one. In the emptiness, the only sounds were the whine of his thrusters, and the pieces of ice that shattered against his armor.

The distance closed and he rotated to bring his feet toward the larger ship, throttling his thrusters to decelerate. A dull thump radiated through his armor as his boots made contact, adhering to the hull. From his belt he produced a small disc and knelt to affix it to the ship. There was no downside to knowing from where this tanker had come. Content with this small bit of intel gathering, he turned toward his real objective. Carefully he laid a foot on one of the pylons connecting the ships, checking that it adhered before adding the second and descending to the smaller vessel. With his foot on the hull, he scanned for an airlock and found it near the rear of the ship as a sine wave in his NOD indicated the presence of a wireless network.

"Interrogating network," Andira announced. "Network is defended by AIIC. Attempting to circumvent."

He crossed his arms while he waited for Andira to do her work. Artificial-Intelligence Interface Controls were AIs dedicated to the sole task of controlling access to a network. While he waited, Andira was attempting to convince the ship that she was merely the tanker trying to reestablish a dropped connection. Combine network designers were not fools—no vital system was accessible via remote—but a connection to the ship could still prove useful. Though the task took longer than he expected, he did not worry. Andira's knowledge and skills could surpass those of any Combine AI.

"Access enabled."

With her work finished, he turned to the airlock and pointed two fingers to the doors. Spreading his fingers, he coaxed the doors to move and quickly slipped inside before they slammed shut behind him. With luck, if the pilot noticed, it would appear as no more than an instrumentation glitch. Next, he forced the inner doors apart and made his way into the ship while shouldering his rifle. Once confident that no one was coming to investigate the noise, he made his way toward the cockpit. He followed the rounding of the corridor, found his destination, and glanced inside.

His hand flexed on the grip of his rifle as he glared at the cockpit's lone occupant. Though Panzer was a man of enormous stature, the alien on whom he spied dwarfed him. A fairly typical example of the species, the Vaar stood some three and a half meters tall. The warrior was relaxed; in one seven-digit hand it held the leg of an animal. Multiple rows of serrated teeth shredded the flesh and bone while the warrior dined. With each of its subtle movements, the massive muscles responsible for moving the Vaar's iron skeleton rippled beneath a carapace of black plates that grew out of the skin more resilient than diamond.

For a moment, Panzer hesitated. He knew that all males of the species bore a large crest where the plates covering their skull grew together into a fan. This warrior's fan was quite small—he was barely an adult. Unfortunately, he was still the enemy, and had to be dealt with accordingly.

As soon as he laid eyes on the Vaar, his NOD had overlain a silhouette of the alien's internal anatomy. In most circumstances, this aided in his ability to aim for vital organs. But it was of little help against the Vaar, with an anatomy so redundant and so decentralized that there were few places to hit that could prove lethal.

The ship's internal sensors would detect a gunshot, so with one hand, Panzer rested the butt of his rifle on the deck. The other hand he extended into the cockpit, his eyes focused on the anatomy chart in his vision while he pinched two fingers together.

Almost immediately the warrior knew something was wrong, and shook his head. A moment later, he held a hand to his neck as the pressure on his arteries mounted.

By the time the warrior realized he was under attack, it was too late. The Vaar sprang from his chair as the increasing torque on his arteries caused them to split, and it let out a pained gasp before falling to the deck with a loud thud.

With the arteries of its neck torn, the Vaar could only lay twitching. Its lungs emptied and the air whistled between its teeth in a death gasp. Panzer stared at the warrior's eyes as it lay dying, frantically scanning for the assassin. Five pupils formed a pentagon around a sixth, and all dilated together as the corpse stilled.

Panzer turned to be sure none had come to investigate the sound of the warrior's body hitting the floor. Satisfied, he stepped into the cockpit. For a moment, he glanced down at its crest. Silver runes inlaid in the small fan indicated he was a lieutenant. For a Vaar to reach that rank at such a young age meant he had been somebody—until today.

"Opening network connections," he said, turning his attention to the controls.

"I have root access," Andira answered.

"Download the ship's database. Once you're finished, go dark."

"Understood. T-minus twenty-two minutes to dilation wave."

The lights flickered for a moment before fading as Andira sent the ship's systems into diagnostic mode. With his rifle ready, Panzer left the cockpit behind, blips in his NOD serving to guide his movement through the corridors. Ahead he could hear the growling between two Vaar as they inquired of each other about the lack of light. Hugging the wall, Panzer approached the room's entrance, where inside several bunks lined a crowded barracks. Twelve Vaar lay in slumber, while two more sat up in their beds. A third was on the intercom, unaware that he was speaking to Andira.

Panzer extended his arm into the room and concentrated on the conscious warriors. As he attempted to manipulate more objects, the difficulty rose at a geometric rate. With triple-redundant arteries in each neck, all encased in iron bone, there was much to focus on. The three who were awake soon fell silent, the two in their beds slumping over while the third fell toward the deck. Subconsciously Panzer extended a foot, catching the falling warrior in a psionic embrace. Carefully and quietly, he laid the corpse down.

The rest remained asleep, leading him to sling his rifle upon entering the room. Out came the knife, a silver kukri-style blade that even with armored hands he gripped carefully. A Vaar skull housed two brains, resting atop one other. One was the seat of knowledge, reason, and emotions while the other handled autonomic functions. The most reliable way to assure a Vaar was dead was to destroy both. The rest of their body was simply too decentralized, and their capacity to regenerate too great.

Reichsylvannian steel was easily the strongest material known to Solar science, forming Panzer's helmet, the trauma plates of his armor, and the blade in his hand. The blade bit easily through the carbon plates of the first Vaar before slipping through the iron of its skull to the brains within. The sleeping warrior's body jerked as Panzer worked the blade before withdrawing it. Even a Vaar's brain could heal through regeneration if allowed to do so. To prevent this, Panzer dragged the knife over its neck to open the arteries. He gave the same treatment to each of the others as he worked his way through the room.

"T-minus fifteen minutes to dilation wave."

A similar pattern repeated itself as Panzer worked his way through the ship's berths. Upon completing the third room, only eleven life signs remained on his NOD, and his device indicated they were centered on the rear of the ship. He approached the final room cautiously and glared inside.

"T-minus two minutes to dilation wave."

Thick chains hung from the ceiling to connect to bolts in the floor. Implements of torture were arrayed across bloodstained walls. At the rear of the room, a single Vaar was splayed between two chains, suspended by bolts driven through his limbs. The plates had been torn from his body to lie in pools of blood below.

There would be no quiet way to clear this room. Aside from the victim, all the Vaar here were garbed in form-fitting armor the color of ash. Were he to attempt a telepathic or psionic attack, the 4CM systems in their armor would engage to thwart him while alerting the wearer of the attack.[1] It was time to go loud.

His hands brought the rifle to his shoulder as he selected the anti-personnel setting in his NOD and targeting markers formed in his vision. His aggression fell first on a warrior who sat on a cabinet, drinking from a flask with one hand, chewing meat with the other, all the while laughing with the others. Panzer angled the muzzle toward the targeting marker, where the overlap of the warrior's brains was greatest, and fired.

Five warp pulses streamed out of the weapon, each an incredibly intense distortion of space-time. In a flash of static discharge, five holes opened in the warrior's helmet as the warp pulses dragged flesh, bone, and armor along their path. Panzer knew that less than 0.01% of this displaced matter was drawn into the very core of each pulse, where atoms were shredded into light, electricity, and radiation.[2] The warp pulses did their job, perforating

---

[1] While the exact nature of metapsionics is not understood, it is known that they in some way manipulate space-time. 4CM is an adaptation of anti-gravity technology and is capable of inhibiting metapsionic abilities to varying degrees.

[2] Warp weapons, also known as disrupters, are an adaptation of the same technology used to warp space-time that allows for faster-than-light travel. These weapons create an intense pulse of highly warped space-time that drags all matter it encounters along its line of travel. The nature of their operation renders many material properties such as hardness, melting point, and tensile

the warrior's head. With a pained gasp, the Vaar went rigid and fell to the deck. The remaining Vaar flinched, holding up their hands to protect their eyes as the oscillating warp pulses showered them with pieces of their friend, lighting up their shield systems.

They glared at their fallen comrade for only a moment before a lifetime of training took over. While they drew their weapons Panzer strafed into the room, firing two bursts to drop the nearest pair. The passage of a warp pulse registered in his NOD as it flew past his head, and falling to a knee, he returned fire. His first burst tore into the offending warrior's chest, and the Vaar writhed in electric shock before a second burst put him down.

With a chirp in his ears, Andira cracked their communications, allowing him to listen to their helmet-to-helmet broadcasts. This flooded his brain with a stream of growls and hisses that she routed through a translator.

"Spread out!" their leader shouted. "Overlapping fire!"

The others spread to two of the walls, and Panzer ducked as they swept the room, cutting the chains as they used their shots to scan for him. Holding out an arm, he focused on one of the cut chains, ripping it from its mooring in the floor. He propelled it toward the nearest pair with a sweep of his arm. He was careful not to push it fast enough to activate their shields and used it as a tripwire, taking the pair from their feet. Seizing on the vulnerability, he dashed through the gap in the field of fire and offered disrupter pulses to their helmets. Four remained, on opposite corners of the room.

"Shoot the chains!"

At their leader's command, the Vaars' fire rose to the ceiling, and Panzer used the opportunity to attack the pair in the far corner. His hasty aim was low, drilling holes through the chest of each, and severing the arm of one. The pair was barely fazed despite the gaping holes that had been torn in their bodies. One continued to fire while the other knelt to recover his weapon from the bleeding limb on the deck. Focusing on the stooped warrior, Panzer fired another burst into his helmet, putting him down. His aim returned to the other while Panzer's rifle merely let out a click while the ammo counter in his NOD read *ERR*.

He held the rifle with a hand on the fore grip, while his other hand went for his knife. He pulled the defective magazine with his mind, letting it drop while drawing a replacement from his chest and simultaneously unsheathing the blade. While his mind drove the magazine home, his arm launched the knife toward the Vaar. The warrior emitted a scream as the blade pierced the relatively soft sensor over his eye, and sank into the tissue.

The knife stopped at its hilt, failing to penetrate deeply enough to reach the warrior's brains.

---

strength largely moot. This allows disrupters to defeat defenses that would otherwise require far more powerful weapons that would entail far greater collateral damage.

Still holding his rifle, the massive warrior used one hand to grab the knife, and jerk it free. But with the jam in his weapon cleared, Panzer took aim and put disrupter pulses through the other eye.

The final pair of Vaar had stopped firing on the chains, and each produced a silver sphere in their hands. One threw high, the other threw low. At the room's center the spheres burst, throwing out a cloud of glowing filaments. The glowing strands clung to the floor, to the ceiling, to those chains still taut…and to Panzer.

"Concentrate fire!"

In an instant, warp pulses were slamming into him as the two Vaar parted, one dashing to an opposite corner. With their opponent visible, they were free to focus their fire, and Panzer's armor shook as his shield generators spooled up to resist the attack.

Their focused attack allowed a warp pulse aimed for his chest to pierce his shields and strike his rifle, splitting the stock. Discarding the broken weapon, Panzer dropped a hand for his pistol while lurching to the side. His thrusters fired, propelling him toward the wall to give a brief reprieve. But covered in filaments as he was, the enemies' shots quickly followed as he took aim at the closest Vaar. The first shot drilled through the warrior's visor, but even with a 14mm hole through his brainpan, the warrior merely let out a pained gasp and staggered back. As warp pulses returned to his shields, Panzer fired again, touching off a three-round burst to put the Vaar down.

But their attacks had disabled his cloak, leaving him plainly visible to the final warrior.

Panzer turned to the sound of a snarl. The final Vaar had realized that his one rifle was not up to the job, dropped it, and was now charging him while brandishing a long rod. Amid the warrior's battle cry, the Vaar's weapon extended out, taking the form of a glowing axe. A lonely chain exploded in the blade's arc as it vaporized a path toward Panzer.

To defend himself, Panzer instinctively blocked with the only weapon left. He stumbled as the axe cleaved the barrel of his pistol in two. The Vaar brought the battle-axe around, spinning with perfect form to deliver another strike.

Panzer shuffled away, narrowly escaping the blade that had sought his neck.

The warrior was well practiced; he kept the heavy weapon moving at all times, never letting his foe know for sure when the next swing was coming. Panzer squared himself with the Vaar, and braced his legs as the axe came in again. As the thickest part of his armor, he offered his chest to the weapon, and when it struck he quickly grabbed hold. Though he had allowed himself to be struck with the intent to take the weapon away, the Vaar was not so cooperative. With a roar, the ugly warrior charged forward, driving Panzer back to the wall.

Panzer's armor began to glow, turning incandescent as it worked to radiate the heat being forced into it by the weapon. He was eye level with the Vaar's waist as the alien bore down on him, trying to force the blade through his armor. Panzer's skin tingled as energy coursed through his nanites, augmenting his own strength as the actuators in his armor did the same. The Vaar let out a frustrated growl as Panzer slowly overpowered the immense creature and forced the blade away.

Suddenly the warrior turned, spinning on its heel and using Panzer's grip on the axe to hurtle him toward the rear of the room. Airborne, Panzer caught hold of one of the remaining chains dangling from the ceiling and slid to the ground.

Panzer's eyes scanned for his knife, and he found it where it was dropped. He called it to his hand.

To create a distraction, the warrior kicked a downed chain toward him before charging again. On reflex, Panzer cut the chain before elevating his blade.

"Dilation wave imminent."

As Andira completed the words, the warrior's axe came down, and Panzer's knife embedded itself in the blade before everything stopped and the world turned red.

The charging Vaar, the bits of metal carved from his axe, all were frozen in place. The world became a crimson reflection of itself as Panzer's perceptions were stilted and everything seemed to fall beneath a red fog.

One of the few things not halted by the dilation was the mind of a metapsion. The same did not apply to their equipment, or to their body. Unlike the Vaar, Panzer remained conscious and aware, but like the Vaar, he was unable to move until the wave had passed. He took the opportunity to focus his mind, calming the rush of battle.

The feeling of pressure slowly returned as the Vaar began to move, and Panzer drew in a deep breath. In slow motion, his free hand opened as he focused his mind on the warrior's chest.

As the dilation wave passed, the red pall faded and the full force of the Vaar came down on him, Panzer's hand extended. The air between them rippled, compressing under his mind before erupting in a sonic boom. The Vaar's shout turned to a gurgle as the psionic wave struck. Overtaxed 4CM generators in the warrior's armor exploded before the Vaar was sent careening away to slam against the wall.

Panzer fell to a knee, shaking his head and letting pass the disorientation of pushing a psionic strike through an active 4CM field.

The Vaar slid out of the indentation his bulk had left in the wall, and fell on his hands and knees. That kind of impact would have rendered most aliens into a bloody paste, yet despite broken bones and ruptured arteries, the Vaar returned to his feet.

Still dizzy, Panzer charged forward before leaping to bring his blade to the warrior's helmet. But the Vaar still had the reach advantage, and intercepted him with a punch that cost the warrior a few fingers but sent Panzer tumbling away. The Vaar was unable to capitalize, falling prone when he attempted to charge.

While Panzer returned to his feet the Vaar was already on his knees, relying heavily on his axe to stand.

Panzer circled the Vaar, measuring for his next strike before moving forward. This time he aimed for the warrior's axe, which came to intercept him, and the Vaar screamed as both his axe and his hand were bisected.

Panzer took a step closer and lifted the blade, grasping it with both hands before driving down into the warrior's skull. The Vaar let out a wheeze as Panzer forcefully twisted the blade before ripping it free, and stepping away as the alien collapsed.

With a relieved sigh, Panzer returned the blade to his thigh, and turned to the Vaar still dangling at the back of the room. He scanned intently, lowering his head as only flat lines filled his NOD. He grabbed one of the chains to hoist himself up and reached for one of the fist-sized eyes. There he gently pried the eyelid open, revealing a single large pupil surrounded by a pentagon of five smaller. They did not react to the light, or even when he poked the soft tissue.

"I'm sorry, Solnus," he whispered, closing the eye. "I got here as quick as I could. Andira, is there anything we can do for him?"

"Unlikely, brain activity is zero, and he has lost too much blood for autonomic functions. Information death is already underway."

"Damn." He bowed his head before looking back to Solnus. He would have to do this the hard way.

Providence was the rarest and most coveted of metapsionic traits. Even among the Commando Corps it was rare, and one of the primary reasons he had been accepted into their ranks. It was the ability to extend one's consciousness beyond the moment-to-moment progression, and see through space-time. Only the strongest metapsions demonstrated this ability, and only through great effort.

Roars of agony filled his ears, and blurred pictures crept beneath his closed eyelids. Images formed in his mind, covered by the red haze, static in a faint signal. He witnessed the final moments of a life ended by heinous torture. It lasted for hours; they had rendered medical aid so they could continue the process. When they did not receive answers, frustration only fueled their depravity. Finally it grew so extreme that it had taken Solnus' life.

"Traitor." The word had been spoken over and over again between each cut, each puncture, and every plate torn from the flesh. "Coward. Defector."

He strained to look harder, to see further back through the final hours. The question was heard, but Solnus had refused to answer. With each silent answer a new piece of flesh was violated, a new bone broken. Yet for hours he did not answer. Not when they took his fingers, not when they took his teeth, not even when they took his genitals. He did not lie, for they would know; instead, he kept silent.

Instead of answering, Solnus had concentrated on fond memories of his childhood, thwarting their attempts to scan his memory. Finally, Panzer heard the question once more, the first time it had been asked.

"Where is the Sovari Soma?"

With three words, Solnus had answered.

"Safe—from you."

Panzer lowered himself back to the deck, and drew in a long breath as he returned himself to the moment. Upon collecting himself, he looked back to the dead Vaar.

"I'll find him, Solnus," he whispered. "I promise. And they will know what you endured for them. Andira, dock and pick us up. We hit Avalon to refuel, then it's straight to Acheron."

CHAPTER
1A

I N THE KNOWN UNIVERSE, there was no nation larger than the Solar Empire. From its founding in the Solar Galaxy, it had spread to all of its neighbors in the Local Group. From there it had continued to grow, expanding out into the local supercluster. Without the aid of the astranet, intergalactic travel was accomplished via the wormhole-generating transpatial drive.

In his command chair, Robert Panzer sat up as the glow of the wormhole faded. He could not wormhole directly to his destination, as sensors for light years around would detect it.

He had arrived on the edge of the Solar Galaxy, and with the intergalactic voyage complete, the interstellar voyage began. Through the open cockpit, he saw the light of the distant stars flicker as the Massless Impulse Drive spooled up.[3] To the ship's nose, space-time was compressed, while at the rear it was dilated. Within the resulting warp envelope, the ship traveled a mere 1,000 meters per second. But to the universe beyond the envelope, the ship was now moving at four million c.

One of the great mysteries in the Solar Empire was the location of the fabled home base of the Solar Commandos. Curious private citizens, vengeful enemies, and foreign intelligence services had tried to find it without success. So secret was the location that many believed it did not truly exist, and was merely a fable to lure intelligence services into wasting their time. In truth, Acheron was not hidden—except in plain sight.

Acheron appeared on every star chart as SG-RP-119. Yet none took an interest in this small body of rock and ice. Acheron was a rogue planet, not bound to any star. Alone in the night, it wandered through the galaxy on its own path. The small planet thus left little reason for anyone to care about it.

Here, the Solar Commando Corps had made its headquarters, where the Empire's most elite were supplied and organized. Yet even knowing the truth of the planet was not enough to give one access. The caverns carved

---

3   The Massless Impulse Drive is named for its ability to warp space-time without having to resort to the application of huge quantities of gravity and the requisite mass that would entail.

throughout the rock and ice were not accessible from the surface. To gain entry required the precise use of the technology to warp space-time, a function nominally carried out by the Solar Astranet, the all-encompassing array of information relays, wormhole gates, and other features that made the modern intergalactic civilization possible. But Acheron had its own network, only detectable by those who knew how to use it and only accessible by those who carried the necessary identification code in the nanites of their brain.

Panzer had made his way through the bowels of his cloaked ship, which was now skimming the galactic core. He stood in a small recess in the floor, making a final check on his attire. The Corps was a clandestine service, and outside of formal events or efforts to blend in, its members were expected to cultivate a distinctly non-military appearance. Blood-red hair was worn swept back to the shoulders, save for the flanks of his scalp where two thick braids were held in place by golden bands etched in Nordic patterns.

Irises as black as the pupils they surrounded darted around as he accessed his Neural-Optic Display. Through it he transmitted the code, and Acheron's network answered. A moment later, a sphere of light encircled him, and he emerged in a cavern carved from the glacial ice. Now he stood outside a metal door labeled *Office of the commandant*. Panzer checked his attire once more—simple brown trousers and shirt, hopefully pedestrian enough. At the door he held up a hand to allow its security sensor to scan him.

An automated voice greeted him. "You may enter."

The doors parted and he stepped into a dark room, the only light cast by holograms a few steps away. Panzer was quiet as he approached the chair at the room's center, waiting to be acknowledged. He would wait patiently, however long it took. In a society where medical technology allowed humans to regularly live well into the quadruple digits, the term "old" took on a new meaning. Someone old enough to carry the title of Elder carried an aura of respect, even reverence, for all they had seen and experienced.[4]

The commandant of the Solar Commandos, Nicolae Espada, was such an Elder. He was respected, feared by those whose mission it was to put fear in others. The long years had drained the color from his body. For more than 2,000 years he had been a commando, and for several centuries the Corps' leader. For decades at a time, the commandant would remain in his chair, watching, guiding, dispatching, and always abreast of developments within the Empire and beyond. Unfortunately someone as old as an Elder often had a…different sense of time.

By the clock in his NOD, Panzer knew he had waited for two hours before the commandant's chair swiveled to bring a pair of red eyes toward

---

4   The exact age of Elder varies by race; in the case of Solar humans, those who live beyond the age of 3,000 may use it as a courtesy title.

him. He braced himself; the mind of a metapsion Elder was not something to be endured lightly, or at all by those unprepared.

"Thank you for coming, Colonel."

The metal walls rang, shedding frost as they resonated with the commandant's words. The result of a telepathic voice so strong it bled over into the psionic. The commandant's face was largely obscured by the breath mask he wore as part of the ensemble that allowed him to long remain in his chair.

"Of course, sir," Panzer answered with his mouth rather than his mind. He hoped that subtle nudge would encourage the commandant to continue the conversation verbally.

"You know why I've called you?"

Panzer blinked as his vision blurred.

"I have my suspicions, sir."

"I've reviewed your report." The words seemed to cut at Panzer's brow. *"Do you have anything you would like to add?"*

"No sir, I do not."

The ringing in the walls grew louder with the annoyed tone of the commandant's thoughts.

"Colonel, I have given you a great deal of latitude in this investigation. You promised me results. Where are they?"

"As my report shows, I managed to track one of the Sovari Soma's operatives, but he was killed before he could pass on any information."

"I assume you attempted to read his memories?"

Panzer nodded.

"I tried, but he was too far gone when I found him. But I did see that they questioned him about the Sovari Soma before his death."

"Colonel, you have expended a great deal of time and resources on this. I fail to see how the Empire or the Corps has profited. Your peers are complaining that your investigation is appropriating resources they require for their own missions."

"Sir, I have been working with almost no assistance, and often in competition with the projects of other—"

"I do not accept excuses from a commando." The commandant's rebuke struck so hard that his body was staggered. *"You were told the last time you stood in this office that you had one last chance to produce your wayward defector. Have you? Or have you failed to do so?"*

"I…." Panzer grit his teeth. "I have not done so."

"Then the discussion is over. I am reassigning you."

"Sir." He hesitated. "Even if I have not produced the Sovari Soma, I have still killed three warlords and several dozen members of DOS. It will take the Vaar years to recover."

"Battle is not for the sake of inflicting casualties. I would expect someone of your breeding and education to understand that. The death of three Vaar warlords is an accomplishment for which you should be proud, but it has not accomplished your objective.

I am convinced that the Vaar are only throwing warlords at this because we have assigned a commando. If the Sovari Soma wishes to defect, he will find his way to us. You are forbidden from expending further Corps assets on this matter. Am I clear?"

"Sir"—he struggled not to let the anger carry in his voice—"if I'm right, we're going to have a full scale war on our hands."

"Your words would mean more if you had proven yourself when you had the chance. You aren't the only provident in the Empire. I have seen nothing that suggests more than border skirmishes."

"I have. I've shown you what I've seen."

"And I do not concur with your assessment. It will be many years before any real peace is reached with the Combine. Skirmishes will happen, and some, I have no doubt, will be intense. But I've seen nothing to suggest these battles you have seen are anything else."

"Sir—"

"I have no intention of explaining myself to you further, Colonel. You will be reassigned, or you will find a new career. Understood?"

The commandant's chair turned again as he swiveled back to face the flood of holograms and audio input.

"As to your new assignment, the emperor is planning a trip to the Knox Vault soon. You will accompany him."

Panzer cursed under his breath.

"Yes sir."

"None of us enjoy that duty, but it is our responsibility to perform."

"Yes sir."

"Afterward, you will remain in the Cathedral. The emperor tells me a part of the Imperial Family will be making a trip soon. I expect you will attend to that as well."

When Panzer did not answer, the commandant turned to him.

"Problem, Colonel?"

"No sir, I just do not think I've done anything to merit punishment."

"The emperor requested you by name. I would think you of all people would be anxious to attend vanguard duty. Or should I tell His Majesty that you are otherwise occupied?"

Panzer's posture straightened.

"No sir. I will attend to it."

"Good, it would be unfortunate if you bit the hand that feeds you." The commandant eyed him, briefly grasping at Panzer's mind but unable to read the thoughts within.

No one had ever been able to read his thoughts, not even a metapsion as old and powerful as the commandant. Panzer was long certain that was one of several reasons the commandant had never liked nor fully trusted him.

"You are dismissed."

Panzer wanted to say more, but he stopped himself. Instead, he nodded and quietly left the chamber to return to his ship. There he looked to his NOD, pulling up a map of the Empire's galaxies.

"Andira, I'm going to the Cathedral. We're ahead of schedule, but go ahead and take the ship in for service. Might as well have the engines and stealth system overhauled before we leave the Empire again."

"Yes sir, I will inform you as soon as the ship is ready. Also, you wanted me to remind you that the emperor requested you be in full dress uniform on your next visit to the Cathedral."

He rolled his eyes.

"Guess I'll go pretty up."

CHAPTER 1B

THE SOLAR CATHEDRAL SERVED as the capital of the Empire, no mere space station but an artificial world. From a distance, the light of the Cathedral could have easily been mistaken for a distant star. Nothing about the Cathedral was practical, as first and foremost it served to inspire awe. Entire planets had been mined out for the resources to supply its construction. Entirely new disciplines of engineering had emerged to make it possible. All to create a spectacle unrivaled in the known universe.

As one drew closer, the Cathedral took on the appearance of a golden sphere, out of which twelve obelisk arms sprang to emulate the rays of a sun. Larger than any inhabited planet, the surface of the sphere was covered in a forest of arcologies surrounding artificial oceans. At 32,000 kilometers in diameter, with more than two trillion cubic kilometers of livable volume, some five hundred quadrillion people called the Cathedral their home. The northernmost obelisk served as the Imperial Palace, the largest residence of a head of state in the known universe.

In one of the palace's high chambers, Simmonne Mandrake awoke with a yawn. She looked to the corner of her NOD, beckoning the lights to switch on dimly. Slipping from beneath the sheets, she donned her robe before rubbing her eyes. She approached the windows to her bedchambers and gave a small wave. The heavy security shutters opened, the arcologies far below. Rising on her toes, she stretched her arms before curling her fingers.

"Chilled milk."

The astranet answered, and from the nearest kitchen the glass formed in her grasp.

"Good morning, milady."

Simmonne turned and nodded to her friend. Jenna had been her handmaiden since the beginning. To Simmonne she had always been something between a friend and an older sister. Most in public knew her as little more than the princess' servant, going quietly wherever she led. In bare feet, Simmonne was slightly shorter than Jenna, who would walk so quietly that her high heels made no sound on a stone floor. No matter how early or late Simmonne woke, Jenna required only seconds to show herself.

When walking together they were contrasting images. Jenna's hair was the color of coal, often worn in a wave of loose curls to frame her brown eyes. Despite dedicating so much time to other people, Jenna somehow found a way to always look her best.

"You're up early," Jenna remarked. "Is everything all right?"

"Glorious." Simmonne smiled, tossing her glass for the astranet to whisk away before it struck the soft carpet. "I believe we have a busy day."

"A meeting with the Elyur Fing, a meet and greet with a group of M'gah delegates. And round two of Miss Empire this evening."

Simmonne closed her eyes with a shudder, now wanting to slip back into bed. But she would not; she would do as she was delegated. And she would do it with the seductive, gleeful poise expected of the *Imperial Rose*.

"The Twins are using the grand bath at the moment. Would you care to join them?"

"I suppose I have to if I want to bathe before breakfast."

Jenna followed her lady down a short hallway before stepping into a large room where they were greeted by a veil of steam. The floor was dominated by the large sunken tub and the warm water within. The stone bath was a dark red, obscured by the layer of bubbles undulating through the circulating water.

"Good morning," two voices greeted in unison.

At the tub's far end, two women sat with only their heads above the water. Two years Simmonne's senior, they were known as the Katyusha Twins. Jennifer and Julie, wards of the Imperial Family, adopted by the emperor the day they were born. It had long been the policy of the court to surround Simmonne with attractive women, the logic being that the only way to make the most attractive woman more so was to surround her with additional beautiful women.

Physically the Twins shared much in common with her, almost enough for Simmonne to be mistaken as a third sister. Slightly shorter, they did not wear their blonde hair as long, while their eyes were a much darker shade of blue. On most days they would wear their hair wrapped around their heads, its length dangling over one shoulder. This proved the easiest way to tell them apart, as Jennifer would wear her hair to the right, and Julie to the left. Though once in a while, they would switch, giggling if anyone were able to tell.

While they gossiped, they were attended by four blue-haired lantai, two grooming their hair, while another pair attended to their nails. The lantai occupied a unique place in the Empire, the only race recognized as a slave race. These four were a gift from the Rhinegrave Family, the principal owners of all lantai. For the wealthy, they were a status symbol, granting the prestige of a living being to carry out work that would otherwise be handled by machines. It was an arrangement the lantai did not mind; to have their purpose in life being destroyed by being freed was enough to drive most lantai to suicide. The matter caused no shortage of scholarly debate about applying slavery, even to a willing people.

Lantai resembled smaller, leaner humans, and indeed some aliens found it difficult to tell the two races apart. The most visible differences were in the hair and eye colors, which were quite unnatural for a human. Their ears bore three distinct points, one at the end of a long lobe sweeping back with their hair, with two smaller below. Scholar and scientist alike debated if somehow the two races shared a common ancestor. Genetics practically demanded a link, but the fact the lantai were first encountered millions of light years from Earth cast doubt on this conclusion. Even so, humans and lantai could reproduce with each other. What were the odds if no common ancestor existed?

Jenna removed her shoes before helping Simmonne out of her robe and into the water. Once she was seated, Jenna held out a hand, calling her tools to her grasp. From there she went about scrubbing, treating, and brushing. This ritual was one of several that occurred without fail, for the Imperial Rose could never been seen in public unless her appearance was perfect.

"Anything in the news?" Simmonne asked.

"Same as yesterday." Jennifer shrugged. "Things are happening in the Hourglass; no one knows anything."

"Well," Jenna said around the comb between her teeth, "the Combine is accusing us of supplying weapons to quant refugees."

Simmonne tilted her head back and glared into the virtual world, her NOD connecting to the astranet so that she could view her own news feeds. With her eyes on the virtual world, she could see the transparent screens over the Twins' faces as they viewed their own media. While Jenna attended her hair, Simmonne focused on stories about the quants, the unfortunate people driven from their homes by Vaar occupation. She had almost returned to slumber when Jenna gave her hair a gentle tug.

"Almost finished."

Upon opening her eyes she realized the Twins had already left, and looking to her NOD she realized the time. Daddy always insisted that the family eat together when possible, and did not abide tardiness. When Jenna finished, Simmonne rose to her feet and looked back to her NOD. There she moved through the options before settling on the default labeled *PRIME STYLE*.

Her scalp tingled as her hair moved into the predefined shape, a style that had become her trademark. Her hair came to assume the shape of a cross, with ends flaring like a fleur de lis. Meanwhile her bangs flared upward to twin apexes before falling outward to her shoulders to frame her face. Many chose to imitate it, but whenever someone wore their hair in that pattern, it was clearly done to emulate her.

Simmonne walked through a blast of hot air as she followed Jenna to the dressing room. Jenna glossed over the garments in the shifting closet.

Each had come from the finest designers, most of which had offered them for free in the hopes that she would wear it in public. In the closet's center a new dress hung from a rack, demanding her attention. Most of the cloth was sheer and covered by gold embroidery. There was a time she found such revealing attire invasive, until she realized how beneficial it was to command every eye in a room.

"Did you make this one, Jenna?" Simmonne asked, touching the soft material.

"Yes, I thought you might wear it tonight."

"Very nice. We should keep it fresh until then. Find me something heavy; Daddy always keeps the dining room so cold."

"How about this one?" Jenna held up a garment that signaled the message had not been received.

"A little heavier?"

"This one?"

"Heavier please."

Finally agreeing on one, Simmonne raised her arms so that Jenna could apply the outfit. Since the public would not see her this morning, she could at least enjoy the warmth of something that actually covered her. With the dress in place, she continued to wait as Jenna saddled her with adornments. Jenna stood on a small stool to apply her crown, a tiara formed by gold strands and sapphires sewn into her hair with golden thread. Finally eight rings were added to her hair, two of the hand-span halos taking position front and rear to the flaring tips of her hair. Even she found such ornaments gaudy, but such frivolous use of things such as anti-gravity helped to demonstrate Solar technological supremacy. The eight rings gave off an azure glow as they came to life, completing her ensemble.

Only after all of this could she exit her domicile with Jenna close behind. The mansions of her twenty-six elder siblings were guarded by the menacing presence of delta arens. Simmonne was a special case; her entourage was made up of gammas. Arens bridged a gap between organics and autonomous machines. Genetically engineered from human templates, they were broken into breeds specializing in particular functions. Alpha arens by and large were military officers, arguably the most human and specializing in leadership responsibilities. Emotionless and coldly logical betas were rank and file, often serving alongside enlisted soldiers. Delta arens were massive, well over two meters tall and packed with hundreds of pounds of muscle. They were sergeants, military police, and bodyguards. Gamma arens were the only female variant, normally employed as living computer interfaces specialized in multitasking functions. Yet Simmonne's were different; her gammas were special.

Her guards were part of a unique brood, genetic sisters designed with the sole purpose of protecting the Imperial Rose. Each stood slightly taller than her with vibrant yellow eyes. Unlike other imperial guards who always wore power armor, her guards appeared unarmed. This was of course an illusion; their gowns concealed a rather impressive armament if such a need arose.

"How are you today?"

"We are well, Majesty," their leader answered. Isis held the only distinguishing traits in her silver eyes. Her hair was as green as that of the rest. "To where are we escorting you?"

"Just to breakfast."

As the Twins exited their rooms, they stepped past the guards who then formed two lines to escort them. Between the gammas was a no-man's-land that only a few were allowed to enter. While her guards appeared frail compared to the larger deltas, they remained highly trained soldiers. Less than a week ago, she had watched Isis take down a grown man with a single punch. The star-struck individual had made the mistake of trying to push through the guards to touch her while she signed autographs. Despite having to jump to reach his jaw, Isis had left his mouth toothless. Simmonne shuddered as she cleared the memory. It was time to start the day.

At the long hall's end, Simmonne stepped into a recessed ring in the floor and the lights around her dimmed briefly. She and her entourage reached a new corridor. The presence of delta arens through the hall indicated that her father had already arrived. Each of the two and a half meter soldiers stood completely encased in gilded power armor, bearing weapons that upright would stand taller than her. As she passed between the warriors, each stood at attention before she rounded the corner into the dining room.

Her father, the emperor sat at the head of a long table carved from sapphire. As she walked past, she kissed him lightly on the cheek. An Elder, he had waited until quite late in his life to have children. Perhaps he simply knew he should. Mason Mandrake was destined to be recorded as one of the greatest emperors. Long ago, he lost the vanity to combat the gray that had conquered his hair and beard, and eyes once green had turned blue on their way toward losing all color. But those eyes saw things others did not. Among the reasons for his success was his gift for providence. Perhaps it was not fair to compare him to other emperors; so few of them could see the future, even if it were only in glimpses.

"Over here," her mother's mind called to her while tapping the chair at her side.

"Mother, this is Raymond's seat," Simmonne whispered as she sat. The Twins sat to her left, while Jenna stood quietly behind.

"We have a guest," she answered with a smile. *"No one has their regular seats today."*

Her mother turned to face Simmonne's father, who was now looking over. Their eyes moved, their expressions changed, but no words were spoken. Of all the metapsions in the family, as a mere empath, Simmonne was by far the weakest. All of her siblings were powerful telepaths and pisonics, and both of her parents gifted providents. Her mother had told her the story so many times of how the two married almost as soon as they met, each having seen visions of their life together long before their actual introduction. For that she envied them, as she doubted that she would be so fortunate as to have the right man simply fall into her life.

"Who is joining us?" she asked when she was certain their conversation was finished.

"A commando," her father answered before turning to the door expectantly.

A commando? Simmonne's heel tapped the floor apprehensively. Like any Solar, she knew of them, but only through half-truths and dubious depictions in media. She had never met one in person—at least, not while knowing who they were. Her eyes snapped to the door as an alpha aren joined them. At least, from his height that's what she took him for at first glance. Only one service in the Empire wore black uniforms with a white jacket—the Solar Commandos.

"Colonel Panzer." The emperor held out his hand.

Simmonne realized the rest of her family had risen to their feet and quickly did the same as their guest shook his father's hand.

"Thank you for the invitation," he answered in a deep, almost thronging voice.

Robert Panzer…she knew this name, spoken from the lips of her parents. Was this really him? Daddy did not shake hands with just anyone; he preferred to maintain the etiquette of the court wherein most citizens bowed and soldiers saluted. He knew this man, respected him—it was him.

"Vi…Robert." Simmonne's brother Steven smiled and shook the stranger's hand next. "They didn't tell me you were coming."

"I try to keep a low profile," the colonel answered.

"Nice job," her brother quipped, flicking one of the numerous medals on Panzer's chest.

The colonel simply scoffed before they sat, he now directly across from her. He was huge, taller even than Steven. But what called out to her were his medals. She knew very little about military affairs, but knew that a pin in a medal's ribbon indicated a multiple recipient. Nearly all of his medals bore multiple pins. But most significant was the one around his neck.

The Solar Cross was the highest award conveyed by the Empire, most often posthumously. A white crucifix framed in gold rested over a galaxy beneath a bar etched with the word *Valor*. Stars sparkled on a red ribbon around the neck, amid other instruments. But what truly shocked her was the galaxy pin on the ribbon—he was not a Solar Cross recipient, he was a multiple recipient. Even more, his bore every instrument that could be conferred.[5]   This man…he was not simply a hero, he was a legend in his own time. No wonder Daddy respected him, if he had awarded him this medal twice.

USER JULIE INVITES YOU TO CHAT.

Focusing on the message in her NOD, she opened a new screen, where the Twins were already gushing.

JULIE: That guy is huge!

JENNIFER: You think the rest of him is too?

JULIE: His voice is so deep.

Simmonne tried not to giggle. The Twins were boy crazy and had been for some time, particularly in regard to large men. But their curiosity was understandable.

SIMMONNE: Down, girls.

She checked that the Twins had their own 4CM systems up. The colonel was obviously a powerful metapsion, and did not need to know the Twins were already undressing him in their minds.

JULIE: Ask him!

JENNIFER: You ask him!

"Colonel?" Julie spoke up as soon as there was a lull in the conversation between him and Steven.

"Yes?" He turned to them.

"How tall are you?"

"Two point two-three meters," he answered. "Depending on gravity."

With a giggle, the two returned to their NOD chat, while Simmonne continued to eye every detail about his uniform. Roman numeral X on his risen collar indicated that he was considered a master at some part of his occupation. Swords crossed over a shield on his shoulder boards nominated a colonel, somewhat unusual for such a young man.[6] Yet there was no patch on his upper arm to indicate membership of a noble house.

"So what brings you to the Cathedral?" Steven inquired as lantai began serving their food.

---

5   The Solar Cross can be awarded denoting circumstances pertaining to the awarding of the medal. Diamonds in the arms of the cross indicate individuals who died receiving the medal but were successfully reanimated. Rubies denote those who were killed and could not be revived. Swords flanking the valor bar are conferred when the medal is awarded to someone serving in a leadership capacity. Stars in the ribbon are conferred on those who perform additional acts of valor that do not individual merit the awarding of an additional Solar Cross. Only 15% of recipients are awarded the medal without diamonds or rubies.

6   With the exception of the commandant, all commando officers are colonels. As agents of the emperor, they are accorded rank making them superior to all military personnel barring flag officers, who are agents of the crown.

"The three of us will get into that later," her father quickly answered.

Simmonne glanced to her father and back to the colonel. Curiosity wrestled with prudence in her mind. She had to do it.

She was not a telepath, but she was among the strongest of empaths able to sense, feel, and even project emotions in others. In that regard, she had never met her equal. While the colonel conversed with Steven she focused, scanning the room. Pure, unadulterated lust—that would be the Twins. Reverence—the feeling flowed from her mother. Pride—from her father. Restrained excitement—Steven. Curiosity—her other siblings around the table. Continuing, she found the feelings of every person in the room— except the colonel's.

She took a moment to compose herself. She did not sense any 4CM; he was not jamming her empathy, at least not in any way she could detect. Perhaps he had some secret piece of Solar Commando tech? That would not stop her; only the strongest 4CM systems could impede her, and she sensed nothing like that at work here. Her legs curled behind those of her chair, and the noise of the room fell away as she focused more intently. In her mind's eye, every consciousness in the room was a pillar of light, but there was only shadow in the colonel's chair.

She flinched as he turned toward her, and her body froze. His eyes seemed to draw her own into the gaze of irises as black as the pupils they surrounded. In her chest her heart seemed to stop, and her breath was still. Trying to raise her arms, she found her body paralyzed, even as it felt as though a hand had closed firmly around her neck. The world around her dimmed further until there was nothing but those cold eyes glaring in the darkness.

Mercifully he looked away, and she drew in a gasp before sitting upright.

"Are you all right?" She heard her mother's voice in her head.

"I'm fine." It took her a moment to compose the breath for a whisper.

JULIE: What's wrong?

JENNIFER: What's wrong?

SIMMONNE: Nothing, I'm all right.

Looking down at her plate, she continued breathing heavily. What was that? Had he touched her mind? He couldn't have, the 4CM field of her tiara would have stopped him...wouldn't it? She had heard stories of Solar Commandos, and tales from her father about this man. She had always written much of it off as exaggeration and embellished storytelling. But now, she was not sure. By the time she had fully recovered, most of her siblings had excused themselves to attend their day's errands. Only she and Steven remained of the Imperial scions.

"Milady, we should be going," Jenna whispered in her ear.

Willing herself upright, she rose from the table.

"If I may be excused." She turned to her father. "I have a full day."

"Of course." He nodded. "We'll talk later."

"Pleased to meet you, Colonel."

She was unsure if he had answered, but her thoughts turned to guiding her feet out of the room, the memory of those eyes in the darkness still at the forefront of her mind.

CHAPTER
1C

AN OLD PROVERB MAINTAINED that the journey of a thousand miles begins with a single step. A journey between stars was somewhat more complicated. Few civilizations had the means to bridge the gulf between systems and achieve interstellar travel. Only a handful could cross the exponentially larger distance between galaxies. Among them only the Solar Empire had the means to travel not just to other galaxies, but the tens of millions of light years separating galaxy clusters.

Jonathan Clearwater was at the end of that journey, riding a small shuttle through an alien atmosphere. Of all the colonies in the Hourglass Galaxy disputed by the Combine, none was more contentious than this one. To the Empire it was simply HG-ND-31; no proper name had yet been assigned, yet the Combine, for reasons they would not explain, called this world Origin.

The sky of every world was unique, but to Clearwater the night curtain of this planet was particularly alien. Surrounded on all sides by the Auchard Nebula, it received no light from the other stars of the galaxy. With no moon, the sky was filled only by the faint and distant amber glow of the great nebula.

"Touchdown in five minutes, Lieutenant," the pilot announced.

"Thank you, Major," he answered, checking once more to ensure his possessions remained on the skid with which he shared the cargo bay. The brown uniform of a Solar Legionnaire was still new, broadening his shoulders when its fabric met his skin. Thick brown hair once worn long was now shaved into a regulation flattop. His chin could not sport a beard if he tried. Eyes as dark as his hair darted constantly across his uniform while he checked and rechecked that the few commendations awarded during training were all in their proper place.

The start of training felt like so long ago. With the availability of automatech, arens, kurai, kodaz, and other races of greater physical ability and disposition, it was no small feat for a human to earn a place in the Solar Armed Forces. Automation had long ago replaced not only the bulk of the civilian workforce, but most of the military's personnel as well. Organic troops were partly a redundancy, but their core function was to ensure that machines with the power to kill were not without organic supervision. Competition for those seeking a spot in the military was beyond fierce. A man could only wear a uniform if he demonstrated the leadership qualities expected of an officer.

Like all but those prestigious few admitted to the great academies, one could only enter Legionnaire Officer Training after passing the selection process known as Hell's Gate. Twenty-one months of testing, conditioning, and reinforcement had swallowed his life. Before attending, he had shrugged off the stories of Hell's Gate's brutality, before struggling to survive it for himself.

After graduation and six months of training, he endured another six months of augmentation. The nanites with which he was born were systematically stripped from every cell in his body before they were replaced with military-grade systems. Every bone in his body had been replaced by cybernetics, with corresponding changes to his musculature, replacement of his nerves, and a reconstruction of his circulatory system. Every soldier underwent the same process before receiving additional augmentation appropriate to their area of expertise—a process that was far from painless for those who endured it.

The shuttle bucked as the pilot decelerated to make his final approach, prompting Clearwater to peer out the window once more. The small colony of Twilight was now in view, a burgeoning city still comprised primarily of prefabricated buildings. Such cities were carried by explorer ships and deployed from orbit so as to rapidly claim and settle habitable worlds. The prefabs were arrayed in clearly demarcated districts across a giant disc some 10 kilometers in diameter. Just beyond the disk he could see a darker ring, the security cordon ready to be raised into a protective wall should the need arise.

The town held his attention briefly before his eyes were drawn to a nearby hill. Atop the hill, a single rotunda glowered as it reflected the light of the town, sparkling as the closest thing to a star in this planet's night. Through the sparkling light he could make out large runes etched into the stone, no doubt meaningful to whatever civilization had erected the structure.

Lightning flashed on the horizon as the shuttle moved to the town's southern demarcation where the Legionnaires had established their garrison. A full platoon had been assigned to this colony, over 1,000 personnel, with ten times their number in automatech. He would soon join them; on the right chest of his uniform rested a silver badge in the shape of a spear's head. Astride its edges were the words *Armored to the Core*, the icon of the Solar Legionnaires Armored Infantry.

The deck shook as the shuttle touched down and the interior lights engaged.

"You're good to disembark, Lieutenant."

"Disembarking now. Thanks for the ride."

On his feet, Clearwater motioned for his sled to follow. He descended the boarding ramp to be met by the first drops of rain on the wind. Outside of the astranet, shuttles and ships were the way to get around. Now he stood at the Legionnaire barracks, a two-story armored box where the metal plates amplified the sounds of the increasing rain.

He donned his cap, holding it tight against a gust of wind. He watched the shuttle ascend before turning its nose up and rocketing through the sky. He turned to his skid, dominated by a sealed container more than double his height before motioning for it to follow. With each step he scanned the surrounding area, committing the instillation layout to memory. Right of the barracks the platoon's armored vehicles were sheltered by a fortified garage. He could not help himself, and stopped to admire one in particular.

The warmech stood on heavily built legs and cloven feet. A bullet-shaped nose jutted out from massive shoulders supporting missile racks above cannons that formed its arms. The Brutus-class warmech was a mainstay of the Legionnaires armored forces. When he applied to wear the brown, it had been with the hope of piloting such a machine. But that was something for the future. Every legionnaire was required to put in a minimum of five years as light or armored infantry before they were eligible for other roles.

His attention was stolen by the bellow of a delta aren leading a section of betas through the rain. Beta arens were by far the most numerous biological personnel in the Solar Armed Forces. Though shorter than most non-gamma arens at two meters, no one would mistake physiques so unnaturally toned for human.

The armored doors of the barracks parted, allowing him to escape the rain only to enter an acrid fog. His eyes darted briefly to the *No Smoking* sign that obviously carried no authority. Four men and two arens sat on several couches watching a hologram of two species he did not recognize in a boxing ring. Patiently he waited for the break between rounds before approaching.

"Excuse me. I'm looking for First Lieutenant Brower."

"Yo!" A man only slightly older than Clearwater raised his hand.

He approached, having to remind himself not to salute indoors and merely stood at attention.

"Third Lieutenant Jonathan Clearwater." He offered his hand. "You are First Lieutenant Brower?"

"Well, if not, he'll be wanting his face back." The man chuckled, shaking Clearwater's hand. "Jason Brower."

"Good to meet you, sir. Reporting for duty."

"Orders?"

"Yes sir." He nodded, giving a firm blink of his eyes to send the data from his NOD to Brower's.

"I ask for a new CO for Third Section, and they send you," Brower scoffed, his eyes moving as he read.

"Is there a problem, sir?"

"I'm wondering that myself. Third Section is a veteran unit, most experienced in the platoon. I was certain they'd send a Second Lieutenant to take over for 'em. But, we'll give you a shot. If you screw up too bad I can always transfer you to a different unit later."

Brower scanned the couches for a moment before vocalizing.

"Sergeant Dolph!"

"Sir!" a delta's voice bellowed as the aren jumped to his feet and approached, forcing Clearwater to look up to meet his gaze. Though surprised to find a sergeant in the officer's lounge, he elected to say nothing on the matter.

"This is First Sergeant Dolph; I've asked him to serve as your section sergeant until you, you know, cut your teeth a little."

"Good to meet you." Clearwater extended his hand to the delta. The aren's face was pieced together between thick patches of scar tissue, and his mouth seemed to hold a permanent sneer.

"Likewise, sir," the aren answered, shaking his hand in an almost too-firm grip.

"Brower to Parsons. Please send Doctor Gilyard; her DE is here. While we wait, let's get your inspection out of the way."

"Yes sir." Clearwater nodded, leading Brower and Dolph back to the skid. With a wave of his hand, the enormous box moved to the floor before splitting open. Armored Infantry formed a niche between light infantry and armored vehicles in suits that blurred the line between powered armor and warmech.

The Myrmidon-class Armored Infantry Combatant's Exosuit was the icon by which most knew the Armored Infantry. In their inferiority complex toward the Legionnaires, the Army often referred to these suits and those who wore them as "footers." A nod to the large expanding feet required for three meters of bond-forged titanium to operate in open ground without sinking.[7]

Boxy shoulders protruded out from its wedge-like body over heavily built legs. Four-barrel rotary guns jutted from armored housings in each arm below two missile racks retracted behind the shoulders. Like most Legionnaire assets, it was painted in earthen brown.

---

7   Bond forging is a process by which synthetically generated particles are used to replace protons, neutrons, and electrons in atoms. Bond particles create the exotic forces X, Y, and Z and can exponentially strengthen a material. Titanium has a melting point of 1940 K, and a tensile strength of 434 MPa. Bond forged titanium has a melting point of 16 MK, and a tensile strength of 778 TPa.

Bidding the machine open, he climbed in from behind. His feet found the control pedals while his hands closed around the sticks and the neural interface engaged. The armored plates closed in a hermetic seal and his NOD was filled with the data from the machine's sensors as he turned to face Brower through the one-way transparency of the frontal armor.

Scanning him, Brower paused to make a few notes.

"Raise the right arm," Brower ordered. "Your other right, Clearwater."

Grimacing, he lowered the left arm and raised the right.

"Good, raise the right foot. Now the left. Good. Full turn."

He turned a full circle, heavy feet thumping with each step.

"Interface looks good. Network presence looks good. Weapons check out. Good. Take care of your AICES and it takes care of you."

"Yes sir."

"All right, come on out."

He extricated himself from the machine before returning it to the case and the accompanying skid.

"You link up to back-net?" Brower inquired.

"Not yet sir."

The senior Lieutenant's face turned stern.

"Do it now," he spoke firmly. "They should have taught you that at the gate. First thing you do at a new post is link to back-net. That way if some asshole blows your head off, we don't have to explain to your family why we couldn't bring you back."

"Yes sir."

His eyes moved through his NOD, forming the new connection. A moment later his face twitched and his vision blurred. From the gray matter to the nanites to the network, his memories were uploaded, encrypted, and stored on the barracks' network. An insurance policy, so that the essence of the person could be restored in the face of overwhelming damage to their bodies.[8]

As his vision cleared, his eyes were drawn to a young woman entering the lounge.

"Over here, Doctor." Brower motioned for her to approach. "Clearwater, this is Doctor Taula Gilyard; she will be your designated civilian during your time here."[9]

"Pleased to meet you," she said with a smile, extending her hand. He was careful not to apply any pressure. Still acclimating to his post-training

---

8   Solar law recognizes a person as the brain with which they were born, and the memories of their lifetimes. If both of these can be saved, that person can be reanimated and still considered the same entity as that which was killed.

9   While in potentially dangerous areas, garrisoning legionnaires will often be assigned a designated civilian, who can call upon them to perform various functions involving potential dangers.

strength, he hoped to avoid the first impression of crushing her bones to a fine powder. Thus while she gave a firm handshake, his own hand remained limp.

One point eight meters made Clearwater short for a Solar man, especially a legionnaire. Her high heels almost brought her eyes level with his. His eyes quickly moved to her hair, an almost shimmering black traced by streaks of blue. Her eyes were an emerald green and as she lowered her hand, he noticed three faint points in her ears. Putting the streaks and points together, he realized that one of her parents was certainly lantai. Unfortunately her buttoned lab coat did not allow him to evaluate her figure as well as he would have liked.

"My pleasure, Doctor."

"Taula." She smiled.

"Okay." He grinned nervously.

"Your section is on maneuvers until midnight," Brower explained. "You've had a long trip. Catch some REM and you can meet them in the morning."

"Yes sir."

"As soon as you're available, give me a call," Taula remarked as her number appeared in his vision. "I'll get you up to speed on my work and schedule."

"Okay."

"Well, see you tomorrow."

As he watched her leave, he heard Brower's voice just above a whisper.

"My DC is a kodaz who smells of wet dog at twenty meters, and you get her."

"Hey Brower, why does the new guy get her?" one of the other officers called.

"Shut up Clancy, I don't like it any more than you do," Brower fired back before turning to Clearwater. "Sometimes life just isn't fair. Welcome to the Iron Brows."

CHAPTER
1D

THE DISTANT STARLIGHT MIXED with the glow of the streets below to form a gentle twilight beyond the windows. Looking down to the arcologies, Prince Steven Mandrake sipped quietly from a tall glass. Some alien excuse for music filled the halls, making the alcohol in his glass all the more enticing. His first wife Jasmine lay strung out on a fur couch, her nude form obscured by the smoke of a hookah sitting on the floor nearby. She sang along with the music, so far off key it would be funny were he not forced to hear it every night.

He leaned against the window and glared at her while she inhaled the fumes. Marvat was a powerful narcotic often laced into high-end cigarettes. In levels considered appropriate for normal consumption, it merely caused a sense of serenity for short periods. In its pure form, it obliterated a person's inhibitions for hours on end, even bringing forth hallucinations. While the hallucinations would last only so long as the drug was strong in the bloodstream, the psychological impact of repeated use and its effect on inhibition was much more profound. Any human's nanotech could easily repair the damage, but only if that person did not become so loyal to the high that they turned off their nanotechs' cleansing and repair algorithms.

Steven did not mind that she indulged so heavily; in fact, he preferred it. She did not love him, and never had—he knew this from the beginning. It was the privilege of the lifestyle her wedding ring provided that she loved. When they first met, she was the worst stereotype of a woman of the Elysian Commonwealth. Bossy, manipulative, convinced of her own intellectual superiority, and completely unwilling to ever...*ever* shut up. All traits that were subordinate to an unquenchable resentment toward the other half of the species.

There was no doubt that she was attractive, with a girlish figure, a caramel tan, hair the color of night, and vibrant blue eyes. But physical attraction simply could not make up for such an abrasive personality. That was why he introduced her to pure marvat, its removal of inhibitions, and its rushes of euphoria. Over time, the drug had replaced the intolerable shrew with a submissive lapdog prone only to the occasional outburst of her former personality. Whenever he watched the silver smoke emerge from her mouth, he could not help but be pleased with himself. She was the most manipulative and self-important person he had ever known. He had not simply won the battle of wills—he had conquered.

While Jasmine lay on one of the thirty couches below the vaulted ceilings of his sitting room, his second wife—his real wife—Natalie lay curled up on another. With hair like the red sails before a rain-filled morning and hazel eyes bearing their own glint, she was in his eyes the more attractive of the two. She sat quietly, her eyes moving as she read some piece of fiction in her NOD.

She rarely spoke to him, to Jasmine, or to anyone. Jasmine's drive to satisfy her own selfish desires had led her into his grasp, but with Natalie things were different. Lacking the will and ego Jasmine once had, she would have never been drawn the same way. He had known her since childhood, daughter of wealthy parents who often did business that required words with the emperor. Though he would not admit it in those days, he had always carried a flame for her, and for many years did so in darkness.

The day she announced her wedding was the most painful in his life. When her would-be husband was murdered the night before their union, it was his finest hour. The killer was found, but of course he resisted arrest, and was killed by the authorities. In her moment of weakness he swept in, gently reminding her of how he had always been there. Pouring a tonic of love in her ear, he drew her in, binding her to him a year later with a ring—a ring far grander than any that could have been provided by the poor artist who tried to steal her.

Like Jasmine, her heart did not throb to the sound of his name, but that was fine too. He had her, and through her meek nature he ensured she would always be bound to him. If he could not have her love, her compliant presence would suffice.

Refilling his glass, he walked toward Natalie and sat down beside her. She did not react but continued reading from her ARAND. He held up a hand to call a glass of wine to him and offered it to her.

"Here." He held the glass in front of her eyes.

"No thanks," she whispered with a smile.

Steven released the glass so that it hovered in the air. He snaked an arm around her shoulders before pulling her to him, and offering the glass again. She sighed and took the wine, sipping lightly before resting her head on his shoulder.

"Is something wrong?" She had long ago learned that a metapsion as strong as him could read her thoughts with little effort.

He shook his head, rubbing his eyes.

"End music!" He sighed happily when the racket faded.

"Hey!" Jasmine remarked, too intoxicated to realize that she had spilled her wine on herself.

"Listen on your NOD or go to bed, Jasmine."

"Alone?" she mewed.

"Jasmine…"

"Okay." She huffed, laying back on the couch and rolling onto her side.

"So what's wrong?" Natalie said.

"I was just thinking. Father should have named a successor by now. He keeps giving me administrative work while sending Raymond and Joseph on PR assignments. I think he's going to choose one of them."

"Raymond isn't as smart as you," she answered. *"And Joseph is a weakling. But people like them, maybe he is giving you administrative work to prepare you for running the Empire."*

"I don't think so. He's always believed relations with the people come first, and the administration should be delegated to people who don't have the charisma. I think he's going to pick Raymond."

"He wouldn't do that. Your dad knows Raymond isn't smart enough to run the Empire. He's cute, he's funny, and people like him. But he doesn't have your mind; he doesn't have what it takes to make the important decisions. Your dad knows that; just give him time. Maybe he's testing you."

"Testing me?"

"He's always talking about how emperors must do what needs to be done without complaint or doubt. Maybe he's giving you that work to see if you'll do it without complaining."

"Maybe." He nodded. His hand moved down to open the buttons of her dress before she lay back to rest her head in his lap. Stretching out, Natalie relaxed as his hand found her bare skin. So long as he had a hand on her, he could relax. She could return to her reading while he returned to his thoughts. Taking another drink, he contemplated his rivals while tracing his fingertips over her silky skin.

"Natalie. Do you really think I'd make a good emperor? I don't mean better than Raymond or Joseph. I mean an actual, good emperor. Someone people would respect?"

"Steven." She waited for him to make contact, and actually spoke the words. "Do you think Raymond or Joseph worry about it half as much as you do?"

"I don't know." He shrugged. "I doubt it. I think they're both so busy trying to get themselves chosen that they don't think beyond it."

"Don't you see?" She smiled. "That's the difference. They worry about how to become emperor. You worry about how to be a good one."

"You always know just what to say." He smiled back. "No wonder it's easy to love you."

She simply smiled in return, before returning her focus to her reading. She never said it back; she didn't even think it.

"I guess what bothers me most is what I'll do if he doesn't choose me. I don't want to go administer some backwater. I don't want to go back to the Armadas. I did my bit; I shut down the damn pillagers. I gave my service; I don't want to make a life out of it."

Thoughts moved through her mind as she tried to think of something to comfort him, but drew a blank.

"I don't know."

"Steven," she whispered again, laying her hands on his. "If you keep worrying about it, you won't live long enough to be emperor."

Forcing a smile, he nodded.

"What are you reading?"

"*Fall's Pendulum.* Simmonne convinced me to read it."

"Sylvia Stockholm?"

She nodded.

"Why bother, I can sum up the plot."

"*Don't.*"

"What? Men are evil and will hurt you, and you can only love them if you accept that."

Rolling her eyes, she shifted before he began to rise.

"*Where are you going?*" She inquired a moment before he reached down to slide his arms under her and whisk her off the couch.

"To be evil."

CHAPTER
1E

I N A LARGE LABORATORY deep beneath the Vaar home world, two beings stood watch over those at work. Among the pair was Hahk'xess, Grand Warlord of the Interstellar Combine. Tall even for a Vaar, he stood in gilded armor, grasping two halves of a broken pole arm. From his mouth came the quiet sound of metal scraping against metal. As the head of state for the Combine, he was merely a figurehead, but as supreme commander of its military, his power was very real.

The alien standing beside him had never been seen; he could not be seen. Through the six pupils of their eyes, Vaar could see across the electromagnetic spectrum from radio waves to gamma rays. Six nostrils contained more than a billion sensory cells to detect by scent those that could hide from sight. Electrosensory organs in the mouth could pick up on the magnetic fields in many creatures' bodies. Yet none of these senses allowed him to observe the alien directly, nor did the Combine have access to any sensor that proved more capable in this regard.

He was seen only when he wished to be, but never directly. Whatever means he used to hide, he would distort slightly to give away his presence. When the alien did so, Hahk'xess could see only the faint outline of an otherwise hollow figure. The being was certainly no Vaar, as it was too short, yet it was much taller than a Viss.

Together they watched as the six-armed pods of flesh known as qorim scurried over a scaffold to complete their work. Within the metal framework, light reflected off the bronze shine of a new warmech. In normal circumstances, a Vaar warrior would pilot it, but this was not an ordinary circumstance.

"You seem nervous, Hahk'xess."

The Vaar turned to the hollow one, all twelve pupils contracting together.

"Divest my mind of your presence," Hahk'xess growled. "You have the ability to make words. Use them."

"I grow weary of your hostility." The hollow one spoke in a voice no less unsettling than telepathic intrusion. With each word, four voices seemed to speak as one, assailing his ears with a quartet of bass that caused the exposed plates of Hahk'xess' face to reverberate.

"What troubles you, Hahk'xess?" the hollow one continued.

"You know very well," he answered, shifting the dilation of his pupils in vain effort to see through the hollow one's cloak.

"You do not think he has earned a second chance?"

Hahk'xess snarled for a moment before turning his gaze back to the machine.

"Do not speak of our rituals as if you deserve an opinion. Those who have gone to the Void are not meant to be returned."

"The council disagrees."

Hahk'xess ground his teeth together more firmly, now in anger rather than apprehension.

"The council is full of brutes, too many who earned the position through no more than killing. Too few who achieved merit through guile and foresight. They are easily misled."

The hollow one's figure shifted as he turned to face Hahk'xess.

"From someone of lesser stature, such talk would be sedition."

Hahk'xess bore his teeth before sneering.

"Do not toy with me, Indorai." He spoke in a murmur that whistled between the gaps of his fangs. "And do not converse with me unneeded."

"I do not understand why you bear me such hostility, Hahk'xess, after all I've done for your people. You still doubt my benevolence?"

Hahk'xess took a step closer, closing one eye to glare with the other in a Vaar expression of contempt.

"You are not benevolent." He articulated each word carefully. "With technology you paint yourself as an ally. But being the enemy of my enemy does not make you my friend. You come and go as you please, you tell us nothing about who you serve, our weapons cannot harm you, and you never reveal yourself. All the while you appeal to greed and glory, promising wealth and conquest. You may have lured the other warlords into your confidence, but do not take me for the fool."

The hollow image shifted as Indorai moved closer, seeming to grow until the two creatures looked face to face.

"That you cannot perceive me is purely your own limitations. When the Crossroads returns, would you prefer the Empire have it? Today, your people have the strength that, with its help, you can drive them away, perhaps even bend them to your mercy. You know what will happen if you do not. They will conquer you. Not through force of arms, but they will conquer you all the same."

Indorai took a step back.

"The Viss will be especially prone. They will fall in love with the Empire and its consumer culture, bathing them in better goods than your own at prices that would bankrupt your producers. Your children will fall in love with its technology, its automation, its power. With your females and children coveting its culture, they will begin to emulate it until they are enthralled by it. And by the time you realize you have been conquered, it will be too late."

Hahk'xess' jaw quivered, anger bubbling over from emotional energy to physical.

"Using females and children to appeal to one's fears is a low tactic."

"I speak only the truth, Hahk'xess, and you know it. As the black market for Imperial goods grows, you see it already. I see it, a particular Viss… You saw it in your daughter's jewelry."

"Stay out of my mind, creature!"

The qorim on the scaffold paused their work, turning their eyestalks toward the shout as Indorai stepped away, answering calmly.

"The only thing that stands between your people and eventual consumption by the Empire is the Crossroads. The only reason you know to prepare for it is me. Try to keep that in mind, Hahk'xess, and perhaps show a little gratitude."

Four Vaar in the iridescent armor of a burial detail joined them in the chamber. Their leader bore a metal cylinder wrapped in fine cloth. Straightening his posture, Hahk'xess lowered his head in reverence to the deceased.

"Let us be done with this."

With the cylinder in hand, the four approached the mech to ascend the scaffolding toward its neck. There, two opened a pair of armored panels, while the one bearing the cylinder placed it near the gap they had created. The fourth gave the cylinder's head a twist before peeling back the casing to reveal a transparent vat of fluid and the overlapping brains within. The cylinder was placed into the recess where it began to rise toward the head, and the armored panels closed.

"Move away," Hahk'xess ordered as machinery within the mech began to spool up. The qorim and the burial detail quickly departed the scaffolding as the mech began to move. The machine resembled the form of the Vaar who designed it, but with the finest metal for plates, and a dozen small sensors in place of eyes.

"Where am I?" The voice of an old warrior came from the machine's facsimile of a Vaar mouth. "Why do I feel so strange?"

The multitude of sensors rotated in their sockets to scan the room before the entire collection zeroed in on its center.

"Hahk'xess? Where am I? What is happening?"

"You're safe, Oul'sor." Hahk'xess raised a hand. "You are on Prithone."

Oul'sor's gaze moved down his new body, focusing on his hand as he flexed his new fingers.

"Why am I in this body? What happened?"

Hahk'xess' mouth twitched, hesitant to speak the news it fell to him to deliver.

"You were sent to Yuros to catch the traitor, and to await the Imperials coming for him."

Oul'sor nodded slowly, shakily stepping out of the scaffolding with footfalls that sent tremors through the metal floor.

"I remember…we ambushed them at the mine." The column of light from his glowing eyes narrowed. "Crykeeper—"

"You fell in battle, Oul'sor," Hahk'xess continued. "But your brains were saved. The council has chosen to grant you vek'thim."

Oul'sor's giant head dipped as he glared down.

"I…appreciate the council's overture," Oul'sor answered. "But I had a good death against a worthy foe. I do not see it as…an…."

His sensors had come to rest on the broken pole arm in Hahk'xess' hand.

"What is that you carry?" Oul'sor's tone shifted as his sensors began to scan the room. "Hahk'xess, where is Vil'sor? Where is my son?"

Hahk'xess said nothing, and quietly held the broken weapon over his head for Oul'sor to see. The scaffolding howled in protest as Oul'sor tore himself free of the cables binding him to it, and approached. The entire lab shook as the machine fell to its knees, and Oul'sor leaned down to glare at the broken weapon.

"Vil'sor…"

"We believe the Crykeeper followed them from Yuros to recover their prisoner." Hahk'xess laid the broken weapon in Oul'sor's giant palm. "We found this in the wreckage of the ship."

"No," Oul'sor whispered, his hand closing on the weapon.

His mechanized mouth opened in a roar that shook the chamber, then transitioned into a wail that forced Hahk'xess to cover his ears. To the side he watched the hollow one raise an arm and though Oul'sor continued his cry, the sound of it faded from the chamber. Hesitantly Hahk'xess lowered his arms as Indorai spoke.

"Oul'sor. It was the Crykeeper who killed your son. And I can give him to you."

Oul'sor's head turned quickly to Indorai, who lowered his arm and continued.

"His name is Robert Panzer, the emperor's favorite commando, and he has just been given a new mission. Do as I instruct, and you will have your right of vengeance."

Silence returned to the room as Oul'sor leaned closer and finally spoke.

"Tell me everything, Indorai," Oul'sor whispered. "*Everything.*"

CHAPTER
2A

EMPEROR MASON MANDRAKE HAD chosen an unusual office for himself, converting one of the palace's many parks into his workplace. When questioned about the choice, he said only that the serenity helped curtail rash decisions.

Panzer strode on a walkway of gold bricks as he approached a grove of cherry blossoms. Within a clearing a single great willow stood, and beneath it lay the emperor's desk. Many chairs and tables were present throughout, but uncharacteristically they were empty. The emperor sat at his desk, manipulating a hologram map with his hands while two members of the Imperial Guard stood at each side of his chair. The four deltas took notice of his approach, turning their golden visors toward him.

"Sorry to make you wait, Colonel," the emperor greeted. "Have a seat and I will be with you shortly."

With a nod Panzer sat at a jeweled table. While he waited, a lantai emerged from the cherry blossoms to offer a drink. Fortunately they did not bring him the wretched, puss-capped bile most people called coffee. Instead the lantai offered a cold beer before setting a platter of cheeses on the table. Panzer sampled both as he waited, and eventually the emperor joined him at the table.

"Apologies, busy day," the old man remarked, sitting across from Panzer.

"No apologies necessary."

"So how go things in the Corps? Old man Espada still as crotchety as ever?"

Chewing on a piece of red windsor, Panzer contemplated the best answer.

"I suppose that's one word to describe it."

The emperor smiled while taking a piece of cheese for himself.

"He speaks highly of your work."

Panzer shrugged before selecting a piece of weisslacker.

"I wouldn't expect otherwise. The commandant only speaks ill of a subordinate when speaking to them."

"A wise way to lead, wouldn't you agree?"

"Yes sir. So, the commandant led me to believe you would provide details of my next assignment?"

"Yes. We will be visiting the vault tonight. Are you ready?"

"I will be by then."

"I'll be bringing Steven."

Panzer cocked an eyebrow.

"Does he know what we're going to see?"

"No, he will learn tonight. That's why I asked for you specifically. As to the other matter…"

Both glanced up as they sensed additional minds joining them in the park. Panzer followed the emperor's lead to rise to his feet amid the sound of approaching footsteps. The Imperial Rose walked at the head of her entourage, her eyes turned while conversing with her handmaidens.

"Only ten minutes late," the emperor admonished as they approached.

Panzer watched her head turn as she intended to answer, and she was cut short, stopping abruptly when she saw him. She quickly averted her eyes before walking to her father.

"I am sorry." She bowed her head slightly. "I was delayed with the M'gah."

"Have a seat," the emperor directed, before motioning to the Katyusha Twins to do the same.

The princess kept her eyes averted as she took a seat on one side of the table, with the Twins on the other sharing a single large chair. He turned, giving a nod as one of the Twins gave a little wave. In his peripheral vision, he noted the death glare this elicited from Jenna.

"Now that we are all here," the emperor began once all parties were seated, "Colonel Panzer: You will be serving as vanguard for Simmonne."

Even through the 4CM field of her tiara, Panzer could sense the sudden discomfort in the princess' mind when she heard the words.

"Vanguard?" She glared at her father. "Where am I going?"

"Right now," the emperor began, "we are seeing millions of refugees flooding into our space within the Hourglass colony zone. Until the astranet in that region is fully operational, we have them corralled on Avalon. I want a member of the Imperial Family there to greet these unfortunate souls, then, once the astranet is online, see them shepherded back to the Empire proper. That will be your job."

The princess glanced to her father, to her friends, and back.

"Avalon?" The protest was apparent in her voice. "Daddy, that's right next to the Combine."

"Yes."

"Daddy, I don't want to go to a war zone."

The emperor shot a glance at Panzer before looking back to his daughter.

"It's not a war zone, Simmonne, but it is near to one. Exactly why I want these people to see a member of the Imperial Family there to greet them. I want them to know that we are inviting them as friends into our home, and not treating them like a burden. I think you would be perfect for that."

"But Daddy…"

While the princess continued to protest, Panzer's attention was diverted to the foot rubbing against his shin. His glance turned to the side and saw the Twins eyeing him. Julie, if he remembered correctly based on how she wore her hair, was pawing with her foot while Jennifer stared at him, her chin resting on her palm.

USER: *JENNIFER KATYUSHA INVITES YOU TO CHAT.*

He waited to answer the request, while reaching for a piece of cheese. In a huff from her father's words, the princess had done the same. His pulse began to race; the words still being spoken seemed to draw out. The gentle breeze of the park seemed to fade. His eyes lowered as time seemed to slow around him.

A provident moment was beginning, a red haze like misting blood flooded through his vision. His eyes did not see it, only his mind's eye, as the red haze washed the world away.

He was in a dimly lit room, and he was not alone. Someone's wrists were held firmly in his hand. A beautiful lantai sat in his lap, apricot eyes filled with apprehension while he held her wrists above a mane of orange hair. She was nervous, worried about something she had done. He realized it was no lantai in his lap—it was the Imperial Rose, and she was in disguise. Her arms were pulling at the grasp of his fingers; he was not going to let her go. Of course he wasn't, she belonged to him now—

"Are you all right, Colonel?"

The world spun back toward him, coming to settle as he glared down at his hand. For a moment he was still, waiting for the red haze to lift so that he would know the moment had ended. He realized that his thumb and forefinger had closed on the princess' wrist. The grasp of his two fingers alone was too strong for her to pull away, and wide eyed, she stared at him fearfully. Jenna stood close behind, her pistol half drawn from a concealed holster below her bust line.

"My apologies," he remarked, releasing the princess' hand.

The emperor broke the silence by softly laughing, turning to his daughter.

"Never come between Colonel Panzer and his cheese."

The room relaxed. Jenna closed the flap of her dress, concealing her pistol, and the gammas of the princess' guard returned to their previous distance.

"Provident moment, Colonel?"

How much of a lie to tell? A father was not likely to take information on that vision in stride. Particularly when the context was unknown.

"Apologies. A vision of nothing important."

"Hate when that happens," the emperor answered before returning to his words. "So Colonel, what do you think of my little girl going to Avalon?"

Panzer took a minute to compose himself, distracted slightly by the return of a foot to his shin.

"Well sir, you know my feelings on the situation with the Combine. I'd recommend against any member of the Imperial Family going to the Hourglass."

"You don't think the Combine would try anything, do you?" the emperor pressed.

"No sir, not without a declaration of war. But if a shooting war were to start, I'd prefer that royalty be here, where they are safely beyond the Combine's reach."

The emperor nodded.

"Exactly why I want you for this assignment. The commandant tells me you've spent more time in the Hourglass, and know the Vaar better than anyone. Her bodyguards and Miss Prideaux can handle any deranged individuals. If a bigger threat shows itself, you will be there. Since Admiral Aetius feels much the same way as you, you will be happy to know I've approved his request to take another flotilla to the Hourglass."

"A flotilla?" Panzer questioned. "It's better than nothing, sir."

"Exactly Aetius' reaction. But I think it will be enough to show we are not to be trifled with, without being a large enough force to provoke an immediate response. The *Hurricane* is currently at Galaxy Staryards finishing up its ten-year overhaul. So the two of you will travel to Reichsylvannia, and Aetius will ferry you to Avalon."

"Daddy—" the princess began.

With a telepathic message the emperor cut her off, and for a moment she glanced at Panzer before turning back.

"But Daddy—"

USER: JULIE KATYUSHA INVITES YOU TO CHAT.

The two were persistent if nothing else. He kept his eye on the emperor and the Imperial Rose. Someone of his abilities could always tell when a telepathic conversation was ongoing, almost like hearing a whisper too quiet to understand its words. Though in this case he could only perceive one side, as the emperor projected, read his daughter's mind, and projected again. He fought the temptation to eavesdrop, and waited quietly for more than a minute. Finally the princess bowed her head, pouting as the emperor turned back to Panzer.

"So," the emperor continued, "after Miss Empire concludes, to Avalon you go. I expect you will behave yourself."

Still pouting, the Imperial Rose nodded and the emperor turned to the Twins.

"Yes sir," they answered his thoughts together.

"Good." He clapped his hands together. "Well if you will excuse us, Colonel Panzer and I must speak in private."

The princess said nothing as she rose from her chair and briskly walked away. The Twins moved to join her. For a moment Jenna remained, glaring at Panzer.

"Touch her again, I'll kill you."

Panzer smirked at her threat, her eyes boring into his until the emperor's hand caught her attention. Turning to him, she nodded, taking something in her palm as he offered it to her. Whatever it was, she pocketed it quickly and shot Panzer another glare before jogging to catch up with the others.

He shook his head, returning to the matter at hand once they were out of earshot.

"Sir, you know I'd never question you in front of others," Panzer began, "but I must ask that you give this assignment to someone else."

The emperor eyed him before biting into a fresh piece of cheese.

"The commandant told me of your search for the Sovari Soma," the emperor began. "He tells me it has been a waste."

"He is entitled to his opinion," Panzer returned. "But I'm the one who has been in the Hourglass. I'm the one who has seen what is going on. The Vaar are preparing for war. For the first time, they are allowing other races into their military. They are bankrupting their economy building weapons, and making technological leaps in their capabilities that should be impossible. New techs are going from prototype to mature technology without any of the evolutionary steps in between."

"Even my most pessimistic advisers assure me that the Combine must see that any war with the Empire would be unwinnable."

"But they're preparing all the same." Panzer stared directly into the old man's eyes. "The changes they're making…they're too big to simply be a cold war. Sooner or later, they're going to attack."

"And you believe the Sovari Soma can tell you why?" The emperor crossed his arms before leaning back in his chair. "I'm still unclear on exactly who or what he is. The intelligence services can't seem to agree."

"In several Vaar languages, Sovari means 'memories,'" Panzer explained. "Individuals with this title have sat on the Council of Warlords since before the Vaar had space travel. It is my understanding that, somehow, every Sovari has the memories of each of his predecessors. They use that wisdom to advise the warlords. At least they did, until their people turned against them in some cultural revolution before we arrived in the Hourglass. The Sovari Soma is the last one."

He paused, collecting his thoughts.

"With the technological progress the Vaar are making, they have to be getting help from somewhere. He would have to know from whom. Even if he doesn't, he sat on the Council of Warlords for centuries. Think of all the secrets he could tell us."

The emperor stroked his chin as he contemplated.

"Colonel, do you know for a fact that he is still alive?"

Panzer began to speak, but stopped himself; this man had done too much for him to hear lies from his mouth.

"I have a strong reason to believe he is."

"But you don't know?"

He sighed.

"No, I don't know it for certain."

"And you believe war is inevitable?"

"I've seen it."

The emperor leaned forward, resting an elbow on the table, staring at the cheese platter.

"When you glimpse the future, Colonel, do you act on what you see?"

"I try to. Doesn't seem to make much of a difference."

"But you do try?"

"Yes, sir."

The emperor glanced up at him and smiled.

"Me too."

The emperor rose to his feet, prompting Panzer to do the same.

"Now I must take my leave; I have much to do."

Panzer suspiciously eyed him for a moment before nodding and turning to leave. The old man was holding something back, but if he was, he had his reasons. Panzer would not question them.

"Colonel."

"Sir?"

"Take care of her," the emperor spoke just above a whisper.

"I will," he answered before making his way out of the park.

CHAPTER
2B

S IMMONNE SAT ON A small throne within one of the Cathedral's many auditoriums. Her position allowed her to look down on the grand stage where Miss Empire was taking place. To her left sat the Twins, while her brother Steven sat to the right with an arm around her. Together they were four of the event's two hundred judges.

Citizenship in the Empire was something that very few were born with. A person had birthright citizenship only within the nation of their birth. Solar Citizenship had to be earned through military or community service.

A few other avenues existed, one of which was Miss Empire. Of all the nations in the Empire, none was larger, wealthier, or more powerful than the Reichsylvannian Dominion. Beauty pageants were common there, and their influence had allowed such pageants to expand beyond their borders. Within a nation where women were property of their husbands, such pageants were primarily a means for young ladies to audition for the role of trophy wife.

Unlike its Reichsylvannian inspiration, Miss Empire judged not only beauty, laughingly referred to as fitness. It also judged knowledge in civics, politics, and law. Simmonne did not mind judging the beauty aspects; a beautiful body was a beautiful body. She only wished that those who organized the event would acknowledge that like its predecessors, it was merely a larger audition for future trophy wives of noblemen. That said, the winner would gain Solar Citizenship, and with it the right to vote for members of the senate—or even run for it themselves.[10]

STEVEN: You're not smiling.

SIMMONNE: Sorry.

She glanced away from the message in her NOD, and smiled while focusing on the stage. There, an overweight man serving as the master of ceremonies continued to prattle on. Simmonne noticed he was a strange man, with a curious habit of pausing between almost every word he spoke.

---

10 Solar Citizenship as a reward for victory in Miss Empire was first conferred by Empress Lana Mandrake II. Most historians suspect it was a deliberate effort to annoy the Reichsylvannians, with whom she had a contentious relationship throughout her reign.

After eliciting a cheer from the crowd, the MC turned to look up at the balcony where Simmonne sat.

"Our next question, is for, Miss Elysium, the beautiful, the witty, Emily Skinner. This question, will go, to her Majesty, Princess Simmonne."

Leaning away from Steven, Simmonne looked down on the thin brunette who awaited the question.

"Miss Skinner," she began. "We are all aware of the tensions with the Interstellar Combine. If you could speak directly to the leaders of both the Empire and the Combine, what would you say about this issue?"

"An excellent, question, from the Imperial Rose!" the MC blustered before motioning to Miss Skinner. "And, your answer?"

"Your Majesty," the young woman began, trying a little too hard to smile while talking. "The Combine is one of the oldest powers in known space, and I feel we have encroached on their territory. If I were to speak to our leaders, I would urge them to remember that the Combine was in the Hourglass first. We are new neighbors in their territory and we should act the part. I would also suggest that we consider paying a lease on the disputed planets we have colonized."

STEVEN: Typical pacifist Elysian answer.

Simmonne suppressed a laugh.

"Suppose the Combine were offered such a proposal and rejected it, what then would you say?"

The contestant thought a moment before answering.

"I would say, Majesty, that peace is its own reward and we should do whatever is necessary for it."

"Thank you, Miss Skinner; that is all I have for you."

The MC moved on while Simmonne marked her score for the answer and the contest resumed.

SIMMONNE: Did you talk to Dad?

Her brother shifted uncomfortably.

STEVEN: I tried, but he seems pretty intent on your going.

SIMMONNE: But I don't want to go to the Combine!

STEVEN: I know, but you know how he is when he decides someone is going to do something. But hey, this could be a good thing.

SIMMONNE: How do you figure?

STEVEN: Well, you said you wanted to try some more serious work. This could be that opportunity. And hey, who knows, away from the Cathedral for a while. You could meet a guy.

She blushed as he hugged her with his looping arm. The momentary giggle was hushed as the image of Colonel Panzer raced into her thoughts, and the memory of his hand on her wrist.

STEVEN: You okay?

SIMMONNE: I'm fine. I was just thinking about my vanguard.

STEVEN: Ah, you and Victor.

SIMMONNE: Who?

STEVEN: I meant Robert, you won't be seeing that much of him. He's been my vanguard several times. He's a good guy. You just…have to get to know him. Besides, he does anything to my little sister, I'll kick his ass.

She smiled—always the protective big brother. Her attention was drawn back to the stage; the part she had been waiting for was here. The talent portion of the event.

"Many of you, have been, waiting for this!" the MC was practically shouting. "You know her, as the Human Railgun, from the tropical paradise, of Tortuga Salona, Miss Dominion, Annabelle Chriss!"

Like most of the Reichsylvannian contestants, the petite blonde wore what could almost be considered a dress. As one of the shortest contestants, something about her made her seem larger, bolder. She walked with a gait that came only from raw confidence. The MC continued.

"For those unfamiliar, with psionic strength, it is, measured, on the P-Scale, with, two numbers. The first number, is, the force number."

He paused to hold up a metal sphere for the audience to see.

"The second number, is simply, the quantity, how many objects, they can manipulate, at once. Now me…"

He dropped the sphere from his hand, which simply clattered on the ground.

"I think, I, might be P-Negative."

Simmonne chuckled with the audience as the MC turned up toward her and Steven.

"I understand, our, very own, Prince Steven, is fairly high, on the P-scale, yes?"

Steven unfurled his arm from around her as he leaned forward.

"I would say I am a fair ways up there," he answered.

"Would his, Majesty, care to share with us?"

"My T-Score is 6/12, and my P-Score is 5/10."

"Wow," the MC answered. "That would mean, you could, exert, a kilonewton, and manipulate, up to, ten objects. Very impressive, but, I think I know someone, who can do better! What do you say, Miss Chriss, shall we, find out?"

The crowd fell into utter silence, and a pair of roliams approached carrying a basket. The two aliens walked cautiously toward her. Metapsionics were unknown outside of humanity, and more than a few aliens were awed, even frightened by the abilities. The small insectoids gently sat the basket at her feet before retreating.

Simmonne watched, spellbound as Miss Chriss approached the basket to bring her hands out and her palms up. Annabelle wiggled her fingers, and one of the silver spheres within the basket rose to orbit her right hand. Playing to the crowd, she extended her arm away, keeping the sphere in its relative position. As she pulled her arm back, she called more from the basket, until three orbited each wrist and twenty others circled her waist in concentric rings.

Simmonne watched from the edge of her seat. As an empath she knew no equal, but no matter how hard she tried, she had never been able to read another person's thoughts. Nor even push the lightest of objects with her own mind. So little was known about metapsionics, even after ages of research. To Simmonne, it might as well have been magic.

She eyed Annabelle intently; she was beautiful but also so confident, as if the entire world was hers. Emerald eyes were almost hungry in their gaze, as if she were feasting on the adoration of the crowd. Perhaps she was—as a psionic, she obviously bore the full spectrum of telepathic abilities. Simmonne held her breath, her heart fluttering as Annabelle glanced up at her and gave a wink. Suddenly the psion turned, and with a loud whistle one of the spheres left the orbit of her waist to be caught by a force field at the stage's far edge.

Within the field, a hologram target was alight, now flashing where she had struck the bull's-eye. Above her hologram number read 209. She took a step forward while launching another sphere, eliciting cheers as the numbers flashed 422. Simmonne's heels clicked on the floor as she leered at Annabelle, and, the numbers rising each time, she launched another sphere. The MC paused to quiet the crowd before the final sphere was launched, and the numbers shifted to 11,617.

The MC took a step toward her as Annabelle fell to her knees, but quickly she rose before bowing to the crowd. Despite her composure, Simmonne could sense that she was ready to collapse again.

"Eleven point six kilometers per second!" the MC shouted. "That, ladies and gentlemen, is why, she is, the Human Railgun! The judges, are tabulating, she manipulated twenty-six objects in tandem. With, that final velocity, her score comes to…P-6/26!"

Simmonne was the first to rise, applauding as Annabelle bowed to the crowd. Before she turned away, the lithe woman glanced up at Simmonne again. She shuddered as the contestant winked at her before making her way off stage.

CHAPTER
2C

I N THE EARLY MORNING, Clearwater cried out in a combination of pain and shock—the result of that strange reflex to strike out at whatever dared wake one from a peaceful slumber, even if it were the NOD buried in their own face. With a grimace he sat up in bed, holding his palm to his now tender cheek.

He staggered to the bathroom and found the shower. Careful not to linger, he bathed quickly before half dressing and making way to the kitchenette of his quarters.

"Let's see…print me twelve pieces of bacon, eight sausage links, nine eggs—make that scrambled eggs with cheddar cheese—milk, juice, and think I'll go for red goo today. Oh, and six pieces of buttered toast."[11]

Hell's Gate had more than tripled his muscle mass, increasing the number, size, and density of the cells. One result was a change in his eating habits to ensure that he consumed enough protein that the new muscles did not shrivel away, and enough goo to maintain his military-grade nanotech. He took a seat at the table and waited until the meal rose from the center before proceeding to eat.

With an eye to the time in his NOD, he tore through the meal before pushing the empty dishes back to the receptacle at the table's center. After donning the rest of his uniform, he made for the door. He had spent most of his life on a world with a twenty-one hour day, before he had to adjust to Hell's Gate's thirty-one-hour day. ND-31's nineteen-hour day was doing him no favors. He was halfway out the door before he realized he had almost forgotten the day's most important task.

He quickly brushed the crumbs from his shirt and stood upright.

"Begin recording."

"Happy birthday, Ryan," he said with a smile. "If I time it right, this message will be waiting for you when you wake up. Sorry I can't be there in

11 Goo is a colloquial term for a variety of compounds consumed by Solars which serve the function of helping to maintain their nanites. Most goo is flavored in such a way as to be used as a garnish or condiment in conjunction with normal food intake.

person; they still don't have the local astranet up. Soon, I hope. Today's a big day for you; your age is no longer measured in single digits. Means you're getting closer to being a man."

He paused, concentrating on keeping a happy face.

"If you go to my room and look in the old chest, you'll find tickets to the Cornal Brothers. Should be enough there for David, your sisters, and all your friends. I couldn't get you front row, but it's pretty close. Melanie has my account number. You make sure she buys you some merchandise while you're there. Don't let her be a tightwad about it; it's your birthday. Be good for Nana, and take care of everyone. While I'm gone, you're the man of the house. I'll call live as soon as I can. Happy birthday. Save message, and transmit."

It would take a few days. Long-wave carriers from the local stellar com would relay the message to Avalon, which would then broadcast it to the astranet buoys that had been relayed across the intergalactic void. Once it hit the astranet, it would reach its destination almost immediately.

With a yawn he donned his jacket and exited his quarters before following the stairs out of the officer's barracks. The sun struck his eyes, reminding him to go back for his cap. He then made his way to the parade field. There he stopped in his tracks, spying Sergeant Dolph standing at the head of a section of troops. He hesitated for a moment before approaching and returning Sarge's salute.

"Got them up early, I see," Clearwater remarked.

"Legionnaires wait for their commander; commanders don't wait for their legionnaires, sir."

With a nod Clearwater turned to the section and took a breath. Ten squads of ten men stood in rows, ahead of ten times their number in military automatech. Most of the organics in his section were beta arens, the majority sharing identical features. But several kurai filled out the ranks of the section's sergeants. The kurai could be mistaken for humans at a great distance were it not for their blood-red skin. Two pair of eyes moved together within each eye socket, and their faces bore no nose. Instead horizontal slits underlining their cheek bones fulfilled the nasal function.

"Section Sergeant." Clearwater turned back to Dolph. "Is this unit ready for inspection?"

"Sir, this unit is ready for inspection."

Clearwater began to walk the ranks. Each legionnaire stood in Class-B dress uniform, and Clearwater took note of the many ribbons on their chests. As he inspected the third squad he stopped, spotting a particular ribbon on the uniform of its kurai sergeant. Larger than the others, this sergeant's ribbon was positioned above them, a red field marked by two stars flanking a golden cross. It was the ribbon of the Solar Cross, highest of military orders. Clearwater's heels snapped together and he elevated his own arm in salute.

"Sergeant ahn Culan, I presume?"

"Yes sir," the kurai answered after reciprocating the salute and returning to attention.

"Sergeant, I want you to know I'm honored to have you as part of my first command."

"Sir," the kurai answered flatly.

Clearwater continued on, and turned his eyes to the AICES that stood behind each legionnaire. From afar, the machines had appeared immaculate, almost sparkling. But up close, they whispered of their history. A fresh coat of paint here and there, a few parts more worn than others. These machines had seen combat more than once.

He finished by examining the Spartoi-class automatech at the formation's rear. The man-sized machines had been designed with intimidation in mind. Red sensors glared out of skull-like heads. Their jagged bodies were covered in armored plates that seemed hewn together from razor blades. Like the AICES ahead of them, close inspection showed signs of previous battles.

He returned to the front of the formation, and faced Sarge.

"I find no fault with this unit."

"Good to hear, sir. Do you have any words for your new section?"

Clearwater opened his mouth, but his mind went blank. Cursing to himself, he brought up the prepared notes in his NOD, and tried to read without moving his eyes.

"I went through Hell's Gate to become a Legionnaire officer—to command people like you in whatever battle, wherever the need. I learned the skills of a legionnaire, and how to teach them to subordinates. When I received the file for this unit, I realized I wouldn't be doing a lot of teaching. It is very humbling that such a veteran unit is my first command, and I imagine there will be a lot of learning on my end."

He paused to make a scripted smile.

"At the same time, it is reassuring to know that if I screw up, my legionnaires can handle anything."

While the emotionless betas made no sound, the remark drew a laugh from the kurai.

"This unit has seen combat on over a hundred different worlds. I've no doubt that is why you are here on ND-31. The powers that be know that if the Combine should consider taking leave of its senses, they'll hesitate knowing warriors like you are here to greet them. Blood and Stars, legionnaires."

"*Blood and Stars!*" the section answered in unison.

"Sergeant?"

"Yes sir?"

"You may proceed with daily drills."

"Yes sir. You heard the lieutenant! Two minutes to utility uniform, then asses in the PT field!"

While the legionnaires dashed for their barracks, Clearwater realized Sarge was eyeing him.

"Fine speech, sir. Come up with that yourself?"

"No." Clearwater chuckled. "My sister helped me write it."

"Sounds like a smart girl."

"Oh very much so."

"Will you be attending morning drill, sir?"

"No, I have a full plate for the next few days."

"I'll make sure they're up to snuff, sir."

Sarge offered a new salute, and once it was returned he dashed away to join the legionnaires.

CHAPTER
2D

STEVEN YAWNED AS HIS NOD impelled him to open his eyes. He had set the alarm with no knowledge of what unholy reason his father had for a meeting at this time of night. He rubbed his eyes with a free arm before glancing down and grimacing. Jasmine lay with her head on his chest, drooling in her drunken stupor. With a hand on her forehead he deftly pushed her off before leaning over to Natalie. As carefully as he could, he removed his arm from beneath her, then delicately extricated himself from the bed.

After pulling the covers up to Natalie's shoulders, he dressed quickly and made his way out of the abode. The delta arens who formed his guards joined him on the path to the nearest router. There he input the coordinates for their meeting and stepped into the recess. The Knox Vault was situated in the heart of the Cathedral, a near fabled place to most of the Empire. Named for some legendary treasure vault on Earth, it was where many of the Empire's greatest treasures were safeguarded.

The router deposited him in the narrow corridor of the main entrance, and while his guards followed single file, he proceeded forward. For reasons he did not know, his heart fluttered and a tremble reverberated through his arm. He had never demonstrated a gift for providence, but he had learned to trust these feelings when they came.

"Not like Father to be late," he thought aloud as he arrived in the waiting area.

As if reading his mind, he was quickly joined by two others: his father and Robert Panzer. The smile with which he greeted them faded against the solemn expressions they wore.

"Vic, didn't know you'd be coming," he remarked.

"Colonel Panzer joins us because he must," his father explained. "There will be few moments in your lifetime more serious than this one, Steven."

"You're uh"—he forced a chuckle—"scaring me a little."

The emperor did not laugh, but nodded to Panzer, who proceeded forward onto a small walkway.

"We're going to cell eighty-eight, Steven."

"The forbidden cell?" Steven whispered. "Does that mean you've—"

"No. But it behooves the Empire to be sure that more than one person in the family knows what is in there."

The emperor turned to the deltas.

"We will proceed alone from here."

"Yes sir," one of them answered.

"No guards?" Steven inquired.

"They are not permitted. Only the reigning emperor and specific guests may visit that cell. When I step down, I will no longer be permitted. I may enter with only one other member of the Imperial Family, and only with the escort of a commando."

"What the hell is in that cell?" Steven questioned as a hovering tram came to Panzer's summons. The three sat down inside before the emperor answered.

"You always enjoyed history, didn't you, Steven?"

"Yes." He nodded. "We repeat the same mistakes so many times; I've learned you can predict the future if you study the past."

"Well, forget everything you were taught about the Therican War."

Steven eyed him.

"What do you mean?"

"Steven, other races follow humanity because they see us as natural leaders. We are so successful as a people that we have time and effort to spare helping others achieve their own success. We have cultivated this narrative over the generations for everyone's well being, but it is not completely true.

"What you learned about the Thericans coming out of the Andromeda Galaxy and butchering everyone in their path is correct. What is not correct is the story that the Interstellar Confederacy bravely fought the good fight against them, and emerged victorious, resulting in the creation of the Empire."

Steven's eyes lowered as the old man began popping his knuckles, something he only did when he was nervous.

"The Thericans only targeted the most powerful races. The Intergalactic Confederacy did not have much of a military when the war began. The Thericans had nearly destroyed half of it before the Confederacy could mount anything resembling effective resistance. The Thericans were thousands of years beyond us technologically; they had a hundred times our population if not more.

"The Confederacy fought the Thericans with their allies for years, but I can only assume they knew they were doomed. Humans were the most populous race in the Confederacy, so the Thericans took a special interest in exterminating us. The first Commando Corps was created by the Confederacy as part of a desperate bid to save us from extinction. They succeeded when they learned of the Common Control Organism, but it was not the hive mind that many believe it was. It was a sort of overriding sapience, defining the morality and controlling the impulses of the Thericans. They were utterly enthralled by it. When the commandos found the CCO, they hijacked a Therican ship and crashed it into the planet.

"They won the war for us. The Thericans had grown so dependent on the CCO that they could not function without it. Their society imploded as they turned on each other, or were driven insane. Others quit caring, like lantai without masters; they quit eating, and died of starvation or exposure.

"The Solar Commandos had won the war, but only after a terrible price. Only a handful of the galaxy's races survived the war, with most reduced to mere shadows of their former selves. With humanity, the Thericans had gone to great lengths to ensure that even if we somehow defeated them, we would perish. They went out of their way to kill as many women as possible. Less than ten percent of the human race survived the war. Of the survivors, only one out of every 144 were women. Women thus became the rarest, and most fought over of resources, which only added to the chaos that ensued.

"The Confederacy fell; a representative government cannot survive anarchy. The Twelve Families came together and founded the Empire. Women were not the only resource we were short of. Food, clean water, shelter, energy—all were in critical supply. So while we told those who could to focus on breeding, our ancestors put as many men as possible under arms. We begged the few races that had been spared to help us; we pleaded with them. None did. They just waited for us to die, so they could pick over our remains.

"The Conquest Wars were not fought to bring peace and prosperity to the Solar Galaxy. They were fought so that we could take what we needed to survive. All the prosperity that followed was simply a side effect. Three hundred years later, we had crushed all opposition and stood as the lone power in our home galaxy. A thousand years later, the whole of Andromeda was beneath our flag. Fortunately, by that time, we had begun the transition into the Empire of today."

Steven tapped his fingers on his knees, enthralled with the lesson.

"So, what does that have to do with cell eighty-eight?"

His father popped his knuckles again.

"Many years after the war, we sent expeditions to the Therican home world. There they discovered that part of the CCO had survived. Deep in the planet's crust, it had endured and lived in dormancy. Since Earth was a field of smoking craters, it was taken to Mars, and once fed, it began speaking to the scientists. It called itself the Encephalon, and in recognition of our conquest, it began sharing some of its knowledge."

Steven's pupils narrowed as he glared at his father.

"It *survived?*"

The emperor nodded.

"Over time, it was noticed that those in regular contact with the creature began to…change. They suffered psychological trauma; many were driven to madness. Emperor Christopher began to worry about the secret of its survival leaking. So the studies ended, and the creature has been kept under the tightest security ever since. Now he remains only as an occasional adviser to emperors."

"An adviser?" Steven scoffed. "That's…insane."

"If the Encephalon is to be believed, he is beyond ancient, from a time before life ever existed in our home galaxy. It has been able to give us insights about the universe, warning us of other races, threats, long before we encounter them. When we were struck by the Scythian Plaque and faced extinction a second time, it was the Encephalon who suggested the solution through nanotechnology. Thus came about the nanosingularity, where homo sapien became homo solaris, and forevermore nanites became a part of our biology. Today, we will ask the Encephalon about the Combine."

"I…" Steven shook his head. "I don't know what to say."

The emperor turned to Panzer.

"Not long after the nanosingularity, the first telepaths were confirmed to exist. It was soon learned that they could protect those speaking to the Encephalon, serving as a buffer against his mind and sparing them the madness that exposure would otherwise inevitably lead to. The Corps has thus always provided the telepath."

"So you knew about this?" Steven looked to Panzer, who merely nodded.

"If you haven't decided to pick me, why are you telling me this?"

"Someone needs to know. Your own mother does not know what is in that cell, nor will she ever. If anything happens to me, you become emperor by default. If I should choose another and something happen to them, the knowledge of what lies within that cell must remain with the Imperial Family."

His father leaned closer.

"Listen to me, Steven. This is the greatest secret in the Empire. If I select you, you must never tell any more than two of your potential heirs. If I choose someone else, you must carry this secret to your grave."

He nodded, swallowing dryly.

"Swear it to me, Steven."

"I swear."

The emperor nodded as the tram came to a halt. Directly ahead, a series of stairs led to a large door. Astride the stairs stood thirty delta arens in full power armor—vault sentries, who would spend their entire lives within its confines, protecting the secrets and treasures within.

"Those guards"—the emperor pointed—"they don't know what they're guarding, and they were born with no other purpose. Wait here and make no movements. If there is a breach in protocol, they *will* kill all three of us."

Steven nodded and remained seated as Panzer and his father exited the tram and approached the guards. On the second stair, the emperor motioned to one of the arens, and leaned close to whisper. Panzer ascended the highest stair and whispered to another guard. Once both arens had nodded, the emperor motioned for Steven to join them.

A section of the floor lowered on the highest stair, revealing a new router. The emperor produced a key from a necklace hidden under the collar of his shirt. Panzer removed a badge from his pocket. On opposite sides of the door, they held their passes to sensors and the router lit up.

"Not the door?" Steven questioned his father.

"The door is a decoy. Anyone trying to break through it will find himself going through several kilometers of kilosteel. This standalone router is the only way in or out."

Panzer was the first into the router, and he vanished with a flash.

"After you," his father directed.

With a hesitant step, Steven placed his foot on the router, and was transported to a dark room with his father following.

"Put this on," Panzer's voice directed as a metal halo was pressed into his hands.

Steven placed the device on his head.

"Do not take it off," Panzer directed.

"All right."

"Seriously," Panzer pressed. "I'm supposed to shoot you, if you do."

"Good to know," Steven answered, pulling the device down more firmly on his brow. He felt a knot in his stomach, and a wave of disorientation passed through him. He realized he had just donned a powerful 4CM system, and his own telepathy had just been nullified. The emperor donned his own halo, and the lights came on. He realized the three of them were in a room no larger than a closet.

From a rack on the wall Panzer took a segmented helmet and placed it on his head, concealing his face behind an opaque mask.

"Ready?" Panzer asked, and the emperor nodded.

A small door opened and Panzer led the way into the next room.

Immediately Steven recoiled as a cloud of red mist swirled through the chamber.

"What is that?"

"Only a telepath can see it," the emperor explained.

"What is it?"

"We don't really know." The emperor smiled. "He's never told us, and we've never been able to figure it out. Some scientists think it's metapsionic static, like that a provident sees in a premonition. In this case, a result of the Encephalon's current, damaged form. All we know for sure is that it does things to telepaths. Hence the halo. Colonel, whenever you are ready."

The swirl of mist seemed to intensify at their intrusion but a shadow at the epicenter of the room was visible through the mist. Panzer held out an arm and with a psionic push, he parted the mist to reveal a pair of chairs that faced a pedestal. Silently he motioned for them to sit. Atop the pedestal, several force fields glowed around a metal cylinder, flanged at its upper and lower caps where hoses interfaced.

Steven watched as Panzer glanced back to be sure they were seated before looking back to the cylinder. Hesitantly he extended his hand, and spoke.

"Encephalon, you have visitors."

Steven trembled at the reply, like a hundred flanging voices speaking together. They seemed to come from all around, and he realized that they came from the mist.

"Ah, you have returned." Every word was spoken without inflection. *"I trust you brought the fool."*

"I did not come to be insulted, Encephalon," the emperor retorted. "We have questions, and you will answer."

"Do not take a tone with me, little emperor. I am older than the star that gave birth to your home world. No matter what your thralls call you, you are no more to me than a chain of chemical reactions. I will answer your questions if it suits me."

"You will answer the questions, Encephalon," Panzer spoke more forcefully.

"Of course, what would you like to know?"

"What do you know of a species called the Vaar?" the emperor questioned.

Steven shuddered as the voices answered.

"You have reached far to find them."

"What do you know?" the emperor repeated.

"Far more than you, and less than I will tell you. Your scientists are aware that they are an engineered species?"

"Yes," the emperor answered impatiently. "Their natural defenses are far too potent to have resulted from natural evolution. Obviously it was long ago, but we do not know who created them or why. What do you know?"

Silence reigned, and Steven exchanged glances with his father as they waited for an answer.

"Encephalon?" the emperor pressed.

"Ask other questions."

Steven watched his father grind his teeth in irritation.

"What do you know of a planet called Origin?"

"Even for you that is a profoundly stupid question. Do you have any idea how many species call their home world by that name?"

"As it pertains to the Vaar, Encephalon," Panzer spoke. "What do you know?"

"There is a planet in a galaxy neighboring the one which the Vaar call their home. If you have not already, you will find it quite uninhabited. But if you ask, then you have found it already."

"What do you know about it?" Panzer pressed.

"You must go there."

"Me?" Panzer's tone was incredulous.

"It is the only way you will understand."

"What will I understand if I go?"

"Everything."

"That's…helpful." Panzer scoffed.

"That's not good enough, Encephalon," the emperor spat. "What is so important about that planet? Why would the Vaar dispute colonization there?"

Steven blinked as silence returned, and a chill washed over his skin. He realized that Panzer was not moving, even breathing—nor was his father.

"What the—"

"Steven." A single voice spoke to him now, so deep it felt as though thousands of insects were creeping over his flesh.

His gaze was forced back to the cylinder, his eyes compelled by the words spoken to him.

"It is time, Steven."

"T-time?" he stammered. "Time for what?"

"For you."

He had never seen a light so bright as that which erupted from the cylinder. His eyes, his flesh, everything on his body felt as if it had been set aflame. His breath became a wheeze, and forcing his eyes closed, he tried to scream. But no sound came out.

"I have waited a long time for you."

"W-what?" He managed to speak the words before the sounds of pain escaped his lips.

"Open your eyes, Steven."

"No, I…I can't."

"Become more than what you are."

His body did not obey. His strength was gone. What little remained he used to force his eyelids apart and screamed at the flood of scarlet light. Agony ripped through his eyes, his face, and through the rest of his flesh while he remained unable to move. His breath ceased, and his heart stilled with a sudden hard beat. His vision began to darken, and he knew that he would die.

Everything seemed to fall away before a new world was lit before him. He was seated; men were kneeling at his feet. Something heavy was atop his head, and reaching up, he took it in hand to bring to his eyes…the Solar Halo. The largest and most ornamental of emperors' crowns.

The world faded away again, and all that surrounded him was the red mist. His eyes found a shape there, a phantasm, a hollow silhouette standing with a hand out toward him. As he reached out for the hand, he drew in a desperate gasp of air. He was back in the vault, Panzer stood ahead of him, his father sat to his side, both still motionless.

"Your time will come soon," the Encephalon said as the world seemed to restart. *"I have nothing more to say."*

"Come on," his father whispered with a disgusted tone.

Steven's knees wobbled as he rose to his feet and began to follow. For a moment the thought came to say something, but a part of him knew not to. He followed his father toward the door with Panzer tailing them. Only when they were back in the closet and the door closed did he lower his arm.

"Unfortunately," the emperor began, "he's not always in the mood to be helpful."

"You look like hell," Panzer remarked to Steven. "You okay?"

This was the time to say something, if he was going to. But he could not find the words, nor the will. But the crown...the crown was in his hands, on his brow. He had to suppress a smile.

"Yeah," he whispered. "It's...just a lot to take in."

"I had the same reaction," Panzer replied. "I think it would be wise for all of us to get some rest."

"I concur." The emperor nodded. "Let's go."

"Steven."

Hearing the words, he turned back, but he was the only one. With a shudder, he turned about and stepped onto the router.

CHAPTER
2E

SETTLED ON THE HIGHEST peak of Prithone's most savage mountain range, the Hall of Warlords was gathering its members to session. In the society of the Vaar, and by extension the Combine, there was no separation between military and government. No distinction between the state and business. The same police that handled military discipline enforced civilian law. The same engineers that designed the mighty warships laid out the plans for the dams and cities. The same leaders who commanded the military governed the population.

Among the Vaar, *warlord* was an antiquated term, one that had evolved over time into new meanings. Warlords were no longer generals with private armies. Instead they were the military's best, the most capable people in their fields no matter what those might be. The one thing that every warlord shared was the trait of being the best at what they did.

With the Sovari and their ilk cast down, Oul'sor was the eldest member of the Council. But today he did not stand before them as a senior governor, but rather as a petitioner. His bronzed body sparkled in the light from above. The chamber stood for ten levels, hosting thousands of platforms for the warlords and their staff. At the northern point of the circular room a high podium stood for the grand warlord, flanked by the twenty-two chairs for the most senior members. This included his own, which was now empty.

A ray of light descended from above to call attention to the grand podium, where Hahk'xess rose to speak.

"Oul'sor." His friend gazed down at him from above. "You are here to contest the orders of this council. Is this correct?"

The sensors that formed his eyes scanned the chamber, picking out the figures of every warlord in the shadows. His metal mouth worked, creating a scraping of metal that echoed through the hall before he answered.

"For six hundred years, I have served our people faithfully. I have fought in six different fields of combat, from infantry to fleet command, to deniable operations. I have shed more of my blood, and more of my enemies' blood, than any who sit within this hall. I have fathered many children who have grown their plates as orphans while I carried out the will of our nation. I have embodied the finest virtues of our culture, and until now I have done so with abject humility. And, in service to this council, I was sent to the Void."

His gaze returned to Hahk'xess.

"Yes, Grand Warlord. I contest the orders of this council. But more, I demand to know why I have been returned to this life, yet denied the vek'thim that is cause for my continued days."

His sensors moved as a new light descended from above, highlighting Gal'ta. One of the few Viss on the council, she was known as the Grand Master of Logistics. She was a fairly typical female, less than half the size of a male with her only plates covering her forehead.

"There are none in these halls who do not revere your accomplishments, Oul'sor," she began, "but not even you are permitted to make demands of this council."

"Be silent in darkness, Gal'ta!" Hahk'xess growled. "Oul'sor was making ash of our enemies before your grandfather grew his plates."

Oul'sor watched as the light around her faded, plunging her to the shadows again. He had always hated the ageism that plagued the council, but if it helped him now, he would not complain.

"As to you, Oul'sor." Hahk'xess turned to him. "Be mindful of your words. This council tolerates and extends no credit to disrespect, even to one as you."

Gears whirred in his neck as he nodded.

"If it pleases the council, I will craft my challenge with different words, but the interrogative remains. I contest my orders. I was brought back for vek'thim. Why do I now see the bridges to that final destination drawn?"

A light was cast on one of the senior chairs. There sat Dolum, warlord of the clandestine.

"Oul'sor," Dolum began, "your complaints are valid, as your anger is just. Your dispute is with me. It was at my behest that you were brought back, and at my insistence that you were given the orders you challenge now."

Were his jaw organic it would have lowered, but without the conscious effort on his part the metal of his imitation teeth remained together. It could not have been Dolum. Surely someone counted so many years among his friends could not be at fault for this terrible resurrection.

"You?" Oul'sor asked. "Why? Why would you do something so disreputable?"

"I am master of the clandestine," Dolum answered. "Honesty in word and deed are luxuries not often afforded me. You have sat more years on this council than any other in its number. You know as I that there come times that we must bring hollow justification for actions that serve greater purpose."

"Greater purpose?" Oul'sor repeated. "Tell me, old friend. What greater purpose is served by using my son's murder as cause to bring me back from death well-fought, and then to deny me my rightful vengeance?"

Dolum's eyes alternated in blinking, a disconcerted expression.

"You have spoken no false words to the ears of this council. All you claim for yourself is true. You know as we do that you are a hero to our people. That when young warriors are given a figure to emulate, and a face to associate with grand action, yours is chosen. We can ill afford your death to come now."

"You brought me back as a figurehead?" The rise of his tone echoed off the walls. "To hoist me up like a flag for the endless masses?"

"Yes." Dolum nodded. "You know, Oul'sor, the future that races toward us. When the Crossroads returns, and war begins, when the time comes that our warriors march into the jaws of the human war machine, when mothers weep on the ashes of their sons, and all the resources of our civilization are subordinated to the effort of victory that shall be only costly won…the eyes of our people will seek a hero. Their hearts will cry out for the symbol of one who carries with him the promise of victory. When they look for these things, they will look for you. Should we have been forced to hide your death, or share it, it would pour water upon the fighting spirit when it must burn brightest."

Oul'sor's sensors scanned the shadows. Dolum could not have done this alone. The council had to agree. How could they do this? So many he called his friends—how could they do this to him?

"When I wore the plates of my younger self, I would have rushed to meet such a call. But not today, Dolum. I was returned for vek'thim, and it must be granted. What shining symbol do you expect me to be when I cannot wield my soul in the battles I fight?"

"Oul'sor, my plates crack that after you have done so much, I must ask you to do yet more. But such is the burden to be carried. We all weep for the death of your son, but an entire war will grant you time to secure his vengeance. But for now, we must have your symbolism in the conflict's opening days."

"Not good enough!" Oul'sor shouted. "I—"

His voice was suddenly silent, even as his facsimile mouth moved and he tried to form the words. Equally quiet were all in the chamber, as if sound itself had faded from the universe. Their eyes were drawn to the floor where, by Oul'sor's feet, the hollow one had taken shape.

"If the council might hear my words"—Indorai's quadraphonic voice rose unopposed—"my will wishes to present them."

The hollow one lowered his arm, and all in the chamber glared down at him.

"Indorai, this gathering is solely for warlords. You have no voice to wield in this hall."

The hollow one's posture shifted, perhaps crossing his arms.

"I would never dishonor the walls of this hall, nor those who line them. But in all I have done for your people, have my actions extended no credit, that your ears are indebted to pay?"

Those in the chamber turned to Hahk'xess, awaiting his decision.

"Very well, Indorai; you may speak."

"I wish to add my voice to Oul'sor's, that it may strengthen the weight of his challenge. There is more to be gained by granting his vek'thim than through any gains by withholding."

Oul'sor suspiciously glared down at Indorai, following his movements. He always inserted himself into critical matters. How did this apply? How could one warrior's revenge be an issue of galaxy-spanning import?

"Your support is noted," Hahk'xess answered. "Are there any others who wish to speak on this matter?"

When silence echoed, Hahk'xess nodded.

"Then the elder members will consider now the merits of your challenge."

Every light in the chamber went out. Why? Why was it still dark?

A single light came from above, and Hahk'xess stood in it once more. Inwardly Oul'sor smiled, knowing that at least this one friend would never abandon him. He briefly glanced up to the empty chairs of the Sovari. Traitors though they were, he could have at least counted on their support here. Another light came to life, followed by another, and more after. When Hahk'xess panned his head to take stock of the lights, he turned back to Oul'sor.

"The Elders have decided. Your challenge shall be heard, Oul'sor. As you are conflicted by personal matters, who do you wish to speak your desires with their words?"

"I choose you, Grand Warlord."

Hahk'xess nodded. "I accept."

"If it pleases the council," Indorai said again. "I too wish to speak in this matter, that the council may see why it is a matter of such great importance."

Oul'sor growled quietly. This was none of Indorai's affair. But his gifts had won the hearts of many on the council. He could not turn the help away.

"Very well." Hahk'xess nodded. "This council is at rest. When we gather again to these halls, we shall hear the merits of your challenge."

The lights dimmed once more, and the warlords began their exit from the hall. Oul'sor cast his gaze down to Indorai, who remained where he had first appeared.

"Be at ease, Oul'sor. What it is owed you shall be yours."

"I do not need your help, hollow one."

"Oh but you do, more than you know," Indorai answered before his image faded to the ether.

CHAPTER
3A

TWO DAYS HAD PASSED since the trip to the vault, and Panzer was wide awake. He sat within a well-appointed lounge in luxury quarters. He had not slept; it would be days before he would be able. Though he had left the red mist behind, he still saw it in the corner of his eye, in the periphery of his vision, behind closed eyelids. As if every moment was provident, the haze lingered.

This was only the sixth time he had to face the Encephalon, and with the task finished he kept himself isolated for as long as he could. The exposure…did things to his mind, especially when forcing himself to shield the emperor. He had to keep the strange one's mind under control, allowing no more strength than the weakest of telepaths to pass through him on the way to their minds. But as a result of doing so, his own mind would be stilted for days. The greatest effect was an increase in his aggression.

He did not know why. Every scan in his NOD showed his body to be functioning normally. There was no chemical imbalance, no source of pain. Nothing to explain why every cell in his body cried out for a fight. But even with no cause the effect was there, it always was.

If only there was someone here it was okay to kill, he could try to work it out early. Instead he would have to find other ways to burn off the energy. In his NOD he watched a news feed and listened to the talking heads discussing events in the Hourglass. How little they knew, how little they all knew—how blissful they must be. While he should be out searching for proof of the imminent war, he was here.

The news feed moved on to a recap of Miss Empire's conclusion. Annabelle Chriss, media darling, the Human Railgun. A lightweight in the psionic world. A P-Score of six could impress the masses, people who might meet only one, perhaps two psionics in their lifetime. But it was far below the minimum thresholds for an organization like the Commando Corps.

He exhaled and closed his eyes, still watching the news behind his eyelids. His mind stretched across the room. A dining set moved toward him before rising from the ground, followed by the table. He moved the furniture into an orbit over his head, and began to add more. Pillows from a nearby couch, blankets from its back, knickknacks lost within, the couch itself.

From another table, an ashtray moved into an orbit around one of his wrists, while the ashes within moved to orbit the other. He took his first metapsionics test at age five, annihilating old records, and had only gone up from there. Specialty nanotech and proprietary cyberware further enhanced his abilities.

There were a handful of those in the Corps stronger than him. Yet of those few with scores higher than his, the one thing they shared in common was that they were all many centuries his senior. There were none his age or younger who had ever approached his scores. A P-6 was nothing to mock, but no doubt Miss Chriss owed her fame as much to her pretty face and lithe figure as she did her psionics.

The orbiting objects came to a halt as the feed opened up to show the Imperial Rose as she moved to present Miss Chriss with the crown. His eyes opened narrowly, almost as if he were aiming. Why couldn't he get away from her? The part of him that was a red-blooded male had found her beautiful as long as she had been famous. Like any man, he'd thought of her more than once in late nights. But since meeting her, she seemed to have made a home in his thoughts. Looking at her with that perfect hair, flawless skin, immaculate clothing, it was almost as though she was not real.

His heartbeat intensified, his thoughts turning. How satisfying it would be to feel her writhe in his grasp. He'd have to be careful—too much force and he would tear her apart before she knew what was happening. Before he could enjoy the sensation of her fear. To take hold of that elaborate hair, and hear her cry out at a hard tug. To feel her trying to struggle against someone who could rip her apart like wet paper. He would not kill her; there were better ways a woman could serve as a sink for aggression.

He shook his head. That was the exposure talking, wasn't it? He did not even hear the furniture shattering around him as he unconsciously compressed the items in his psionic grasp.

It would be so easy to overpower her, so satisfying to feel her wrists held in his grasp. Or to close a hand around her neck, making her realize she could only so much as breathe because he allowed it. She was already frightened of him. A wild look filled his eyes as he smiled, remembering how just a bit of pressure from his mind had utterly paralyzed her. A mere empath poking at a commando's mind. So defenseless, prey poking at a sleeping predator. Did she think that little tiara would protect her against someone who could not even be measured on the scale it was calibrated against? Perhaps it was a challenge to see what he was capable of. She was fortunate that he did not show her.

Why stop with her? It would be rude to leave her friends out of the game. He could take his time, keeping them leashed with his mind while he had his way with them. The things he could do with them. The things he could make them do with each other, or to each other. The way the Twins looked at him, he could probably charm them into whatever he wanted. Her guard dog Jenna might present a bit of an inconvenience, but he doubted she would pose any real threat. Annihilating her in a storm of psionics would no doubt be an effective demonstration to ensure the obedience of the others.

The objects slipped from the grasp of his mind to crash on the floor as he brought his hands to his eyes. He had to get this under control; it was almost time to leave. He shouldn't have done that to her; she had just been curious. Like every other metapsion he met, she wanted to know why she could not sense him. All he wanted was for her to stop distracting him, drawing his attention with her scans while he attempted to converse with an old friend.

It served her right. Trying to force her way into the feelings of someone she had just met. Spoiled little girl, probably accustomed to ordering men around and treating them like disposable tools. Used to getting away with almost anything solely because she was pretty. He lowered his hands, his mind flashing back to the vision in the emperor's office. Somehow, at some point in the future, she would be truly at his mercy. But why was she in disguise, and how did they end up alone together?

"She's not safe with me," he whispered.

Why should she be? He was no bodyguard. His job was to kill people and break their stuff, not run around looking for boogeymen on behalf of the Imperial Guard.

"Are you all right, Colonel?" Andira questioned from a device on his forearm.

"I'm fine."

"Your vitals do not concur with your statement."

"Not now, Andira."

"Yes sir."

He looked at the time—0600. She was probably waking up now, preparing for her trip. He lit a cigarette and held it to his mouth, only to realize one was already there. With a shrug he puffed on both.

This was not good. This adolescent infatuation with a pretty face, and the Encephalon's touch on his mind. It would be days until one of them went away. He needed someone to kill. Someone to beat to death with his bare hands. No martial arts, no form or finesse, merely the tactile sensation of feeling bones shattering under his fists. To hit them so hard his own bones broke, giving him enough pain to know he was *really* hitting them. Someone, anyone would do. Something to work out the aggression before it found other outlets.

"Andira, page the emperor. I need to be reassigned."

"Sir, the emperor is paging you."

"What?"

He had failed to notice the message in his NOD.

HM: Reminder, router room 100, in one hour.

He cursed to himself. He had forgotten the time difference. It was early morning here, but where they were going, midday was approaching.

"Should I let the emperor know you wish to speak with him?" Andira inquired.

"No," he whispered, snuffing his cigarettes. He could control this. He would control it.

CHAPTER
3B

THOSE BORN WITH THE benefits of the astranet often took it for granted, but there was no wonder in the Empire that could compare. The all-encompassing network of communications systems, transport routers, navigation aids, and more enabled Solar civilization to exist. Lag-free intergalactic communication, the ability to send people or goods across the void of space without the need of a ship, so many things were possible.

In a private chamber of the Cathedral, Simmonne stood by a long-range router. The simple appearance of metal framework and dangling circuitry belied the sophistication of the device. With Jenna and the Twins at her side, Simmonne waited while automatech loaded her luggage on the risen platform.

"Your Majesty, we will be ready for the first transmission in five minutes."

Simmonne nodded to the window near the ceiling, and to the gamma who had addressed her.

"We will be ready," she answered, pulling tighter at the robe that shielded her from the room's chill. She turned from the router to face her parents who stood together. She could see the parental worry, sense that special feeling any parent felt when a baby left the nest.

"The High King will have quite the greeting ready," her father remarked. "I trust you will behave yourself?"

"Yes Daddy." She laughed, but his expression remained stern.

"You will of course make sure." He turned to Jenna.

"Yes, Majesty," she answered with a short bow.

"Oh, lighten up, dear," the empress remarked.

They turned as the door behind opened, and Colonel Panzer joined them in the chamber.

"On time as always, Colonel," her father greeted.

"I have few virtues," Panzer answered as she watched him swagger in. "But I do try to be punctual."

Her eyes moved to the floor as he glanced at her.

"Princess," he greeted, moving to stand beside her.

"Colonel," she whispered in reply. The sight of his eyes at the table flashed in her mind, causing her to shudder.

"We'd better go," the emperor said. "Busy day."

"Be safe," her mother whispered, kissing her cheek.

"I will."

Her father bent to kiss her other cheek.

"Remember, the dignity of the family walks in your footsteps."

He waited for her to make eye contact and smiled at her before walking with her mother out of the chamber. As they turned he laced an arm around his wife, and they smiled as the doors closed.

Simmonne took a breath before nodding to the Twins and pulling the strings that held her cloak together, allowing Jenna to remove it. Jenna had slaved on this outfit since being informed of the trip, and now it was time for it to be seen. Simmonne stood in shoes plated from gold, with tall heels formed by upright rings. Her body was barely covered in a scant garment of blue and pink. Two strips of fur covered her bust, suspended from a jeweled collar by gold chains and joined to each other by a large ring.

A small thong of fur was shaped into a heart. A veil of fur hung from her waist down the backs of her legs, gradually widening to her ankles. String-thin chains of gold tied into bows held the front and back together. On her thighs, silver garters in a floral pattern held her stockings in place. Should she find a chill, the rear of her collar suspended into a translucent shawl. Despite covering so little, the outfit felt quite weighty from its gems and precious metals. It was the pahri, the prime attire of young women in the Reichsylvannian Dominion. Thousands of variations of the outfit existed but all retained the same basic form. A young woman to dress more modestly was seen as a sign of poor self-esteem. Such was an image the Imperial Rose simply could not convey.

The Twins were dressed almost identically, but having no title of their own, their pahris were made of silk, with chains of silver. Jenna had chosen to wear a corisse. The corset-like outfit exposed her sides with gaps from her arms to her hips. Such was the preferred dress of more middle-aged women, or those wanting something more conservative than the pahri without wearing the full dresses that were a privilege of children and elderly women.

For a moment Simmonne felt an inkling of resentment looking at Jenna. She had at least fully covered her own buttocks when designing her corrise. No doubt Simmonne's own outfit would be more substantial had Jenna designed it for herself. She pushed the thoughts away; she was meant to be the center of attention. The Twins were posing for each other, no doubt eager for the attention they'd be getting. Simmonne glanced down at herself for a moment, and it dawned on her why men's attire in the Dominion had so many pockets.

The Twins were quite excited about the trip, but Simmonne could sense Jenna's distaste for the upcoming venture. Despite being a native of the Dominion and the daughter of a baron, she was not eager to return. It was not hard to understand why—someone as strong-willed as her did not belong in a nation where women were property. The fact that her mother left the family title to her half-wit brother no doubt had something to do with it as well.

While Simmonne tugged gently at the outfit to ensure the adhesives held, she felt a chill run down her spine. At first she thought it merely the cool air of the transmission room, until realizing that the colonel's eyes were upon her. She glanced toward him, but where most men would avert their gaze he continued to look, undaunted. She knew that look, but few were so brazen with it. She realized she was blushing; there was no need to read his emotions to know what was on his mind.

"See something you like, Colonel?"

Not only did she fail to convey the confidence she had hoped, but realized her statement could be taken as a taunt. She winced slightly, waiting for his response. Why wasn't he answering?

She could not bring herself to make eye contact, so her eyes remained down toward the most honest part of the body. At times when 4CM made it difficult to casually read the feelings of others, she had trained extensively in understanding body language. She started with the legs—his were positioned with his feet pointing toward her. His weight was on the balls of his feet, one foot ahead of the other. As if he were about to spring forward.

She forced her eyes to rise as she continued scanning him. His fingers were spread, slightly curled as if about to grasp something. Even beneath his jacket she could see the swell in his chest, and beneath his sleeves his muscles bulged. She managed to bring her eyes up to his face. The black color of his irises made it difficult to tell the state of his pupils. But his brow was furled, his jaw protruding. She couldn't bring herself to look into his eyes but body language was clear—he was not merely leering at her. Whether consciously or subconsciously, he was ready to pounce on her.

Suddenly she felt completely naked rather than only mostly so, and wished for the robe she had just shed. Studying his body language had made her cognizant of her own. Her legs were together, her shoulder angled slightly toward him. Her right arm was crossed under her bust, and her left hand fingered the sapphire dangling from her collar. Her breathing was rapid and shallow. Whether or not he was consciously picking up on it, her posture was telling the predator she was submissive, vulnerable, and afraid. She chided herself. She might as well be throwing blood in the water.

She took a breath to calm herself. She could resolve this. All she had to do was drop her arms, spread her feet to expand her personal space, and straighten her posture. In fact, she did none of these things; even as her mind screamed for obedience, her body did not move.

"I was not expecting you to don the native garb," he finally answered.

Through great effort she managed to bring her eyes as high as his chin.

"I cannot have the Sylvanni think me a prude," she managed to articulate.

He took a step closer—too close, she wanted to retreat—but still she could not move. She felt herself shrinking, her shoulders rising toward her ears as he came close enough to lean down.

"I suppose perfection wants to be admired," he remarked and she shivered, feeling his breath against her ear. Why couldn't she step away, why couldn't she move?

"But a word of warning, Princess," he continued.

"Y-yes, Colonel?"

Her eyes remained affixed to his body.

"The High King has six wives, and probably more consorts than he can remember. But make no mistake, that man's mission in life is to put women in his bed. Give him a centimeter, and you will regret it."

She said the first thing that came to her mind.

"I deal with such attentions daily, Colonel. I would not tell you to keep your head down in a gunfight."

Almost immediately she regretted saying it, afraid it would come off insulting.

"Fair enough." He leaned slightly closer. "One more thing. The High King and I do not exactly get along. So you will not be seeing much of me, but I'll be around."

"Oh, all right." She nodded, taking a relaxing breath as he moved away. Good, this was good; once he was away, she could relax.

She jumped as he brought his left arm up, then he slid a finger over the device on his forearm and faded from her sight. Now that he was invisible, she bit her lip, certain he was leering even more intently. She took a step closer to Jenna, scanning the emptiness where he had once stood.

"Your Majesty?" the speakers above sounded. "Majesty? We are ready for the first transmission."

"We are ready," she answered.

Two of her guards joined the luggage on the platform, and with a flash of blue light they vanished.

"Next transmission in thirty seconds."

Two more were required to send her guards through, and then it was her turn. She led the way with the Twins at her sides and Jenna behind. Her remaining guards formed a perimeter. Where Panzer was now, she could not say. The machinery began to hum and the transmission chamber seemed to bend around them. The router room faded away, and for a moment she was weightless before everything turned black.

The only light came from the residual glow of metal pylons, and she shifted nervously in the darkness. Thousands of minds now surrounded her, most of them excited. As she took a step forward she felt Jenna's hand on her shoulder, stopping her. No, that hand was much too large to be Jenna's. Her knees began to tremble, until the hand moved and she was struck by a flood of lights.

"*Welcome!*"

Five thousand voices sounded together as metallic confetti sparkled through the air. The hand on her shoulder was gone. She glanced to the Twins and took a step forward to descend the stairs ahead. To her sides, lantai and women in pahri danced while throwing out more of the confetti to the beat of drum-heavy music. Aliens had meanwhile formed themselves into rows on both sides of a red carpet.

To her right stood the tahn'kodaz, large beings covered in fine snake-like scales. Their wedge-shaped bodies were masses of solid muscle atop hind legs that bent forward and back. A pair of humps lay between bulging shoulders. Broad, flat arms branched out to end in clawed hands that forced them to walk on their knuckles. Their angular heads were marked by colored crests of bone that extended from just above the eyes to follow the spine and turn jagged over the tails that made up half the length of their bodies.

Behind the kodaz stood the various makes of the techla, one of the few surviving machine-races of the Empire. Those delegated by their networked intelligence to deal with organic beings held a vaguely humanoid shape but were impossible to mistake for anything but a machine.

Behind the techla were the avarirs, semi-humanoid beings in tight-fitting suits they wore to contain their atmosphere. Finally on her right stood the thouse, arachnid-like beings somewhat resembling roliams, but far larger in addition to their extra legs.

To the opposite side, the kurai stood at the forefront, brandishing the bladed armor that marked them as members of their people's warrior caste. Behind the kurai were the buun, among the more alien races in terms of their appearance. Their heads showed six eyes in vertical rows toward the outer edges of their face, glaring down large snouts. Their broad bodies gave way into arms and legs that extended out as wispy tentacles. Additional lantai stood behind, all female. Simmonne had hoped she might see one of the males on this trip, but alas none were present.

Finally there stood the simians, named so by humanity who discovered their pre-industrial society. Until contact with the Combine, the simians were the tallest intelligent race ever discovered. Larger even than delta arens and taller than upright kodaz, they stood covered in thick fur that ranged across the spectrum of colors. The only parts of their bodies the fur did not cover were their ash-colored hands and feet, along with their mandrill-like faces.

Collectively, these races were known as the Rhinegrave Eight, so named for their oaths of fealty not to the emperor but to the sovereign of the Reichsylvannian Dominion. In parting to the sides of the carpet, they had opened the path to the Royal Family of the Dominion, who was surrounded by a ring of guards made up of kodaz, kurai, and simians in red power armor.

An extremely tall man known as the High King brandished long braids of blood-red hair bound in gold bands, with a similarly styled beard. He had no lack of vanity, sporting sheer sleeves to show off muscles that were impressive for a man old enough to be called an Elder. Six women stood with him—five blondes, and one with jet-black hair. The five were dressed in pahri fairly more conservative than hers, but wore golden garters with rubies and sapphires denoting their children. The most mature of the women wore a corisse, the High Queen.

Though appropriate to her smaller frame, she wore a crown identical in pattern to the High King's. Nine points rose overhead, bearing the engraved images of a human and the Rhinegrave Eight. Each of the miniature statues held up their arms beneath holograms denoting the Reichsylvannian Virtues.[12] Behind twelve lantai, the courtly thralls accompanied them, though they were little more than concubines in Simmonne's mind.

Simmonne led the way as she closed the distance to the High King. While his wife consorts each bowed, neither the High King nor his wife did so. The sovereigns of the Reichsylvannian Dominion bowed to no one. The High King, Jonas von Rhinegrave IV, raised his arms, signaling for silence.

"Princess Simmonne," he bellowed. "I welcome you to Reichsylvannia!"

Simmonne waited for the new cheers to die down.

"Thank you, Your Excellency," she returned, before turning to the aliens. "I thank all of you for such a warm greeting."

"Allow me some introductions," Rhinegrave continued. "My wife, High Queen Elena Alexander von Rhinegrave."

"A pleasure, Imperial Rose," she greeted, green eyes unblinking. She was the last scion of one of the Empire's founding families. With her union to the High King, now only Rhinegrave and Mandrake remained of the original twelve. Only Mandrake had avoided absorption by the Rhinegraves. While outwardly the High Queen always appeared poised, confident, and dutiful to her husband, the whispers told of different stories—that she and her husband shared not a kind word, let alone a bed, or even a common table at which to eat their meals.

"The pleasure is mine," Simmonne answered before the High King moved on.

All of these introductions were entirely unnecessary; everyone here know who everyone was. However, as they had never met in person, courtly

---

12 The Reichsylvannian Virtues for men are Valor, Honesty, Loyalty, Justice, Discipline, Thrift, Courtesy, and Creativity. The feminine virtues are Fidelity, Obedience, Honesty, Kindness, Friendliness, Courtesy, Abstinence (specifically from gluttony), Liveliness, and Subtlety.

protocol had to be observed. Simmonne greeted each of the wife-consorts and the thralls before taking her turn.

"May I present Vi-Baroness Jenna Prideaux of New Bengal"—she paused while Jenna bowed—"as well as my handmaidens Jennifer and Julie Katyusha."

"A delight." The High King smiled to each of them, and for a moment Simmonne was taken aback by the animal lust that he was hiding so well behind his courtly mannerisms. The colonel, wherever he was, had not exaggerated.

"Your Majesty," the High King continued. "If you would care to accompany me, I thought you might enjoy a brief tour of the *Rothburg*."

"I would love that, Your Excellency."

His wives parted to allow Simmonne to walk at his side while their respective guards formed rings around them. As she walked, it was a chore to keep the attentions of those around her at bay in her mind. She could sense the intense state of alertness in the minds of her guards. Among Reichsylvannians, a firearm was practically male jewelry. She could see that the presence of so many armed people made her guards nervous. Simmonne did not worry—woe to the poor fool who embarrassed the High King while she was under his protection. Simmonne made passing notice of the fact that the High Queen did not follow.

CHAPTER
3C

DESPITE TWILIGHT COLONY'S NEWNESS, it had already become host to several chains. Among them was Derf's, one of the largest restaurant chains in the Empire. By night it was an adults-only bar where couples could meet. By day the establishment transformed into a family-friendly fast food venue where parents would bring their children and those without jobs would spend their days in networked recreation. Clearwater passed through the doors not long after the changeover was made, and took a seat in a booth.

"What can I get you, Lieutenant?"

Shocked, he turned to the young redhead asking for his order, surprised a franchise would spring for an organic waitress. Quickly his eyes were drawn to the Consolidated Automatech logo over her eye, signifying that she was in fact a mimicking automatech. He sighed.

"Bring me some sugar with coffee in it."

"Right away." Biology was hard to fight, and as he watched her leave, he had to remind himself that she was a machine.

Now was a good time to review, and in his NOD he pulled up the personnel files of his section. Most of the hundred souls under his command were beta arens, and his attention focused on those who were not. As a boy he often fantasized about wearing medals on his chest, and there was no shortage of commendations in this section. One Solar Cross, ten silver and eleven bronze Stars of Valor, thirty-one War Merit Stars, and thirty Red Ribbons, among his sergeants alone. Why had he been assigned this unit? These legionnaires were heroes; they deserved better.

His eyes scanned the restaurant. Civilians now heavily outnumbered the legionnaires. Those with jobs stopping in for their breakfast, those without likely settling into their favorite spots before passing the day swimming in media. His eyes came to rest on a family across the establishment, and pondered what they were.

With four daughters and two sons, he first mistook them for Reichsylvannians. At 1.8 meters Clearwater was short for a Solar, much less a Reichsylvannian, and the husband was shorter still. The wife was dressed like a professional, most of her body clothed, obfuscating the possibility of her being Reichsylvannian either.

Staring into his NOD, Clearwater accessed the tactical menu added by his military upgrades, gradually increasing the sensitivity of his hearing so that he could gauge their accents. While the father scolded the boys for some misdeed, the mother was explaining a school lesson to a daughter. Both parents spoke quickly, ending their sentences on upward inflections as though every sentence were a question. They were Elysians.

Looking at the children, Clearwater realized they were likely why the couple was living on this colony. Most Elysian worlds had strict reproduction limits, and such a large family was unheard of. Reichsylvannians were encouraged to have large families, but the idea of giving up her rights to move there likely wasn't an option to the wife. The economies of most other nations did not have enough jobs for families to regularly grow so large. Stipends to those who did not work assumed a two-parent, two-child family.

Here in the colonies, there were jobs, and a much more loosely defined society. It could provide a special level of freedom to live on a frontier not found elsewhere. This colony was so far away that as it continued to grow, it would eventually blossom into its own nation. People like them would help to shape it for future generations. All the while, legionnaires like him stood guard. The thought made him smile. It gave the brown—the uniform and lifestyle of a legionnaire—meaning.

His eyes and ears moved on to others in the crowd. Accents were hard to pin down, varying by region, planet, or nation. Luckily, military cyberware was able to interpret it for him. In this restaurant alone there were people from sixty planets and thirty nations. Losing himself in the crowd, he waited patiently until rising to his feet and waving for Taula to join him.

"Sorry I'm late," she said in a rush to sit.

He glanced at the clock in his NOD, catching it as it suddenly sped forward by more than an hour. A large dilation wave had just passed through the planet. It made his head hurt to think about the fact that time had just frozen for an hour relative to everything beyond the galaxy, and shaking his head, he turned his attention back to Taula.

"What can I get you?" the server soon inquired.

"Happy muffin and a fruit bowl please. And a coffee. I'll mix it myself, just bring cream and honey please." She then looked to Clearwater, and a brief silence ensued. "So, tell me about yourself."

Caught off-guard, he stammered for a moment.

"Well, I was born on Weiss, joined the Legionnaires, and now I'm here." He stopped to laugh nervously. "I'm afraid there's not much to tell."

"Brothers, sisters, wives?"

"Two, two, and none."

"Bachelor, huh?" she asked, taking her order from the server. "How old are they? Your siblings, I mean."

"Melanie is thirteen, Stephanie nine, Ryan just turned ten, and David is six."

"Seems your brother-sister count is a bit out of bounds."

He nodded.

"My dad was a decorated legionnaire. That entitled him to break ratio and have more sons. He even went on to be a Solar Cross recipient before he died."

She perked up, her eyes widening.

"What did he do?"

Clearwater shook his head and shrugged.

"We don't know. It happened during the Tethren Incident, but it was so secret they couldn't tell us. All we know is he volunteered for a secret mission, and didn't come back."

Her expression changed as she set down her coffee.

"How old were you?"

"Twelve."

She continued to gaze at him while he avoided eye contact.

"That must have been hard."

"Yeah," he whispered with a nod, before shaking his head and forcing a smile. "But hey, enough about me. Tell me about yourself. What do you do?"

"I'm an expeditionary sciences verification agent." Pride beamed from her as she answered.

"And…what does that mean?"

He pretended to understand as she rattled off technical jargon, but from her reaction he failed to convince her.

"Basically it means I know a little bit about a lot of stuff," she said simply. "When scientists out here make a discovery, my job is to review their notes, and repeat any experiments they made."

"Why repeat the experiments?" he asked. "Seems like a real duplication of effort."

"That's the scientific method. Science is only valid if your conclusions can be supported through repeatable experiments. I repeat the experiments before our findings are passed along, hence verification agent."

"Oh. So you must be really smart."

She winked.

"Double doctorate from Olympus Mons, graduated at twenty-three. I'm actually working on my third now."

"Did I say smart? You must be a genius!"

She shook her head side to side and smiled before tearing open her meal.

"So what do you know about the Temple?"

"Yeah, I think someone forgot to brief me. First it was I'd be briefed the day after I received my assignment. Then it was when I got here, then it was my DC will tell me what I need to know."

"Oh. So you don't know anything about it?"

"Nope, blank slate."

"Well then, I won't spoil the surprise until we get there. Speaking of which…"

"I requisitioned a conveyor." He motioned out the nearby window.

"Oh good, I won't have to take the tram. Let's go."

His eyes moved down as she bent over to claim her briefcase.

"Want me to carry that for you?"

"Oh, a gentleman," she answered, then handed him the surprisingly weighty case.

Following her to the door, he admired the large floral bow in her hair that trailed down to the slits in her skirt. As she stopped at the door, he realized she was glaring at him.

"You weren't listening to a word I said, were you? You were checking me out."

"Well, I, uh, I…"

"And you're shy too," she said with a giggle. "This is going to be fun."

"Uh, this way." He led her out the doors to the hovering vehicle, where gull-wing doors opened to invite them inside.

"Destination?" the vehicle inquired.

"001 Temple Lane," she answered, leaning back as the conveyor moved.

Turning onto the main road, the conveyor carried them to the edge of town and beyond, over the grassy field to approach the ancient structures. Legionnaires stood guard, waving them through.

"So they didn't tell you anything about these?"

"Nothing."

"We haven't been able to date them." She led him toward the largest structure where a ramp carved from rock led to an opening with no visible door. "The analysis of the structures suggests they are constantly rebuilt over time, though we haven't found what's doing it. But the real thing is the lower levels. We've dated things down there that suggest this place and this planet are more than eighteen *billion* years old. That's older than the local star, older than this galaxy."

Clearwater whistled as she led him past the checkpoint, following the path of artificial lighting.

"Wait, older than the galaxy? How did it get here?"

"Good question," she answered. "Either our measurements are wrong, or someone put the planet here. We can move a planet if we really want to. The Combine could as well, but neither of us were around twenty billion years ago. And there are things here, well…I'll show you."

He followed her onto an elevator and waited quietly as they descended. The elevator stopped on an open, well lit floor filled with work cubicles. She led him to a crowded cubicle filled with cargo pods crammed around a desk and chair. His eyes were drawn to a clear cube, an animal habitat of some kind sitting next to a large upright copper cylinder. While she took her briefcase and fiddled with the contents, he leaned down to the habitat.

"What's in here?" he asked.

"That's what I wanted to show you." She tapped on the enclosure before cooing, "Gulliver."

A mouse-like squeak came from a tiny plastic house, and a small creature emerged. Walking on its knuckles like a kodaz, the black-furred animal stopped to rise up on its hind legs, naked tail visibly wagging.

"What is it?" he asked.

"A super mouse." She smiled before leaning against the nearby cylinder.

"We've opened more than a hundred floors of this place, with more below. On many of them we found these devices in various sizes."

"What do they do?"

"Watch this." She grabbed one of the cargo pods and tossed it away to reveal another enclosure filled with white mice. With a gloved hand she reached inside to take one of the animals, and held it up. "This is your standard lab mouse. Sterile albino used for lab research that we can print as we need them."

"Okay, I'm following so far."

"Now watch."

She rotated the cylinder with one hand until a small hole came into view. Holding the mouse to the hole, she ushered it inside before moving to a small control panel on her desk. A small switch powered the device and the hole sealed seamlessly. The desk began to hum while the cylinder visibly vibrated.

"Uh…" he began.

"Just watch."

The cylinder began to emit a high-pitched whine before a loud *pop*, and the hole appeared again to release a cloud of smoke.

"All that to cook a mouse?" He scoffed, fanning the smoke away.

She raised a finger then held her hand to the hole.

"Come on, little guy, you can do it."

His jaw dropped. The creature that emerged was not the mouse, but something like the lone creature in its private enclosure. She held it up for him to see.

"What did it do?"

"It remade the mouse," she said, wide eyed. "Not just genetically; chemically it's the same, but its biology has been altered. It's bigger, it's stronger. Its immune system is more comprehensive, it lives longer, and now it's fertile."

"So…what, it made the mouse better?"

She laughed.

"In a manner of speaking. But that's not the big thing. Watch this."

Opening one of the cargo pods, she gingerly laid the creature inside before turning to the private enclosure.

"Gulliver, come here."

The creature responded to her command, climbing up into her hand and chattering as she brought it to eye level.

"Gulliver, say hi to Lieutenant Clearwater."

As she held the mouse to him, the creature rose up on its hind legs, then extended a forelimb and waved.

"You taught it tricks?"

"With surprising ease. Now watch this." Setting Gulliver on the desk, she opened one of the drawers, thinking for a moment before removing a large nut and a clear cube. After holding them for him to see, she placed the nut in the cube before placing it on the desk.

Gulliver ran to it, wrapping his arms around the cube and trying to bite into it. After several attempts the animal backed off and began to whimper.

"That's mean."

In reply, she merely held up a small shard of metal before offering it to the animal. Grabbing the metal in its hands, the animal gnawed on it for a moment before turning to the cube. Grunting, it began slamming a sharp point of the metal into the cube. Silently, Clearwater and Taula watched until the cube broke and the animal tossed the metal away and happily claimed its prize.

"It...it used a tool," he said with a gasp. "It used a tool."

"Tools are the most basic proof of intelligence, using objects to overcome biological limitations."

Gulliver chattered happily as it began to devour the nut.

"It made the mouse smarter," he whispered.

"Yes." She drew his attention back to the sphere. "The deeper we go into this place, the more complicated these things are to get into. Whoever built this place...I think they made it to try to more rapidly evolve the creatures on this planet. As they get smarter, they get into better tubes and get pushed further. I kept Gulliver because he's friendly, but some of the ones we put through...we had to stop pushing them when they started showing signs of higher sapience."

"Wait." His eyes grew wide. "If this thing makes races evolve, the Combine..."

"Their races claim this planet is sacred. There may be a reason why."

He bit his tongue, contemplating the implications.

"What else is going on here?"

"Let me show you where I keep my records, then I'll show you."

CHAPTER
3D

"S TEVEN."

Crying out, Steven shot up with his hands on his temples, his breath coming in short gasps. To his right Jasmine stirred slightly, in too much of a drunken stupor to be roused. To his left Natalie rolled onto her back, opening an eye at him.

"What's wrong?"

"Bad dream," he answered, rubbing his eyes.

Climbing over her, he stumbled to the washroom before closing the door. His heart was still racing as he moved to the faucet and splashed some water onto his face. He looked into the mirror and let out a sigh—and saw red mist on his breath. He lurched away.

"What the hell?" he whispered, holding his hands to his mouth.

"Steven."

He whirled around to find the source of the voice, but stopped to compose himself. Maybe he was not fully awake. Turning back to the mirror, he relaxed. The mist was gone, and he laughed nervously, looking at his reflection.

Without a sound the mirror shattered, its pieces falling into the sink without so much as a clatter.

"I'm dreaming."

The fragments of the mirror lay in the sink, each reflecting on its own, the eyes in the glass watching him. Somehow he knew there were seventy-one pieces. Grasping a small piece, he held it up, looking at the eye in the glass staring back at him. Something drew his eyes down, and the piece left his fingers in a flash. It silently fell with such speed that it shattered one of the stone tiles of his floor. The tile had broken into nineteen pieces. He didn't have to count them, he simply knew.

"Steven."

"This isn't real. This is a dream."

"Steven."

"Who are you?" He tried to bring an authority to his tone, but only a panicked whisper escaped.

"You know who I am. As I have known you, since the first firing of your neurons in your mother's womb."

"Encephalon." The mist returned to his breath as he said the word.

"Yes."

"What do you want? How are you speaking to me?"

His eyes moved to the door. Should he run? What was the point in running from a voice in his head?

"A part of me has been here since long before you existed. Those who brought it thought to imprison me. Blinded by their own ignorance, not knowing what they did not know, they thought they could seal me here. But they cannot impede what they do not understand, what they do not know."

"What do you want?" His voice trembled.

"Only for you to have what is properly yours."

The room began to spin around him, and he winced as bile formed in his throat. The bathroom seemed to melt in his eyes, and the stone tiles turned to glass. He knew this glass—the floor of the Emperor's Hall. Five kilometers square, this floor was rebuilt regularly with soil from every world on which the Empire had planted its flag.

His head was heavy, and as he looked down at his reflection, he held his hand to his brow. Astride his head was the Solar Halo, the largest most ornamented crown worn by emperors for formal events. Ahead lay the Seventeen Steps. On the highest step lay the Star Dais, a 100-meter tower of gold and crystal against the high back of the throne. Above, a hologram of a galaxy cast its light across the room.

He was surrounded. Countless faces all looked to him—senators, ambassadors, those who could attend in person on the floor, and those who could not—as a seemingly endless forest of holograms. They were divided among the stadium, carved into the ivory walls. His feet seemed to move of their own volition, carrying him toward the throne.

Divided among the Seventeen Stairs were smaller thrones, the higher stairs reserved for the scions of the sovereign. The lower stairs were arrayed for the officers of the Solar Court. His feet found the first stair, and his hand came to rest on a shoulder. With the second step his hand moved to another. He tapped each in the same way emperors silently confirmed those who would serve as the officers of their court.

His chair waited on the second to last stair, but his feet did not take him to it. On the final stair he turned, and raised his arm. Through the eyes of the crowd he saw himself speaking the words of commemoration. He watched his own demeanor change as his posture shifted, and the crowd gave themselves to his oration.

"It belongs to you, Steven. Not by some happenstance so petty as right of birth, but by fitness of will."

The hall faded in a cloud of fire, and his mind was in deep space. Imperial and Combine warships traded fire from vast distances. Ships were dismantled; their hulls breached as fires burned the atmosphere within. His eyes moved down. Legionnaires fought tooth and nail, surrounded and overrun by Vaar. A woman wailed as she held the only parts of her child that she could find.

"War is coming. Your people deserve a leader who can guide them to their final destination. There is more at stake than victory, and you must lead them to it."

Air filled his empty lungs as his eyes shot open, reacting to the hand on his shoulder.

"Steven, are you all right?" Natalie whispered.

What the hell did one say to that question?

"I'm fine."

"Are you sure?"

"Yeah, I'm okay." His palms ground into his eyes.

"Then maybe sleep in bed rather than in the bathroom?"

Lowering his hands, he gave her a look. Unkempt, half asleep, concerned, and still she was beautiful.

His eyes moved to the sink. Why hadn't she asked about the mirror, or the floor?

"Come on." She took his hand, encouraging him to rise. As she led him back to bed he stopped a moment at the door, looking back. The floor and the mirror were whole again. Feeling her tug his hand, he followed, and climbed back into bed before she joined him. He closed his eyes, relaxing a heavy head on his pillow.

CHAPTER
3E

BENEATH A YELLOW SKY, Oul'sor stood overlooking fields of red grass. Katone was to some a second Prithone, a world altered from its natural state. As much of the home world's surface was converted into an ever-growing factory, planets such as this were transformed into sanctuaries for its native species. There were many planets like it, but to Oul'sor this one was special. On this planet he had taught Vil'sor how to hunt, to wield a rifle, and the secrets of wooing Viss. But Vil'sor was not here now, and he had not sought the presence of his other sons.

Across his new body a dozen Viss were at work, all counted among his daughters. Though none of those working were exceptional, they were competent enough. Females of the Vaar species were so small, seemingly even more so now. Less than half the height of the males and only a fraction as heavy. Only their heads were protected by carbon plates, leaving the rest of their orange flesh exposed, which necessitated clothing. Their digits numbered only four on each hand and foot.

By his feet, a particular Viss dressed in silver silks as a sign of mourning. With his new height, her head barely cleared his feet. She stood silently, one of her hands resting on the giant limb nearby. His Al'cra, his little flower, his grand daughter Vil'na. So brave, so young, to hide her grieving wheeze from the ears of those around.

"We are ready," one of his daughters spoke from his shoulder.

"Then take your feet to the shelter," he answered, and held still while they climbed down his body. One of his daughters, Oul'za, moved to grab Vil'na until he interposed one of his giant hands.

"She remains," he commanded, and with a nod Oul'za moved to join the others. "Climb on my foot, Vil'na."

The young Viss nodded, and climbed up.

"Begin the exercise," Oul'sor said with a growl.

His new body was now adorned with armaments: a weapon slung beneath each forearm and four cannons arrayed across his back. Much as they did in his old body, the fingers of his new hands flexed and unfurled in anticipation.

In the multitude of screens that formed his vision, triangular reticles lit up around the body of four tanks as they moved onto the banks from within a nearby river. Hovering over the water, they approached him, brandishing four guns in pairs mounted opposite of the turret's flanks. His right arm bent as the weapon slung beneath extended to its full size. A large pack bolted to his back fed a round into the weapon and he fired a single shot. A moment later, all four tanks erupted in flames before slamming into the ground.

"Relaying target coordinates," the simulation master announced as a new screen opened to show another tank. This one was far beyond the visible horizon, sitting in a mountain range. "Fire off-bore."

The tank was magnetic north, so he turned south before firing. His sensors traced the path, and his burst of missiles arced around him to streak off toward the target. A few seconds later the tank in his screen exploded.

"Activating jamming field, inputting coordinates."

Another distant target lit in his vision, and he fired again. While his shot did not make a direct hit, it came close enough to score the tank with its blast.

"Making counter-jamming adjustments. Fire again."

A new target was presented, and this one suffered a direct hit.

"Beginning soft-target engagement."

Oul'sor's feet thundered against the ground as he turned. Hidden doors opened in the ground as small, human-sized drones stepped up onto the landscape. Their simulated weapons lit his shields as he focused on the nearest group. Had he lungs, he would have scoffed. The weapon on his right contracted while the one on his left arm expanded. He felt the recoil as the cannon fired. Electromagnets hurtled a Vaar's weight in metallic spheres thirty-six times the local speed of sound. The expanding cloud of spheres ripped into the drones, capturing all twenty of them in a single shot. Though the inert slugs carried no charge, they created small explosions as the impacts imparted enough kinetic energy to vaporize the polymers through which they passed.

More targets began to rise and he toggled the weapon to full auto, shredding them as they emerged. When the test was finished, several hundred of the drones lay in smoking ruins.

"Beginning large target engagement."

His attention was drawn to a lonely mountain standing in the open fields. A targeting icon lit up near the mountain's center. The quad-array of cannons on his shoulders came to life as they telescoped out to their full length. The charge levels rose through four gauges in his vision, and when they reached optimal, he fired.

Particle cannons were regarded by many as an obsolete technology, readily defeated by many defense systems. But as the old Vaar proverb said: "Brute force fails only with insufficient application." Each of the four beams was binary in nature, with a column of gamma rays projected to encircle a neutron stream. The four beams created glowing shockwaves in the air as they heated the atmosphere to plasma and struck the mountain. The neutron stream readily vaporized the rock of the mountain's face while the gamma rays penetrated to heat those that were deeper. The result was a blast that split the mountain, creating a rain of glowing rocks falling like meteors across the open fields.

"Energy on target, 3,000 urst, large-target test complete."[13]

"Now you see, Vil'na," he spoke as the cannons, white hot and smoking, retracted over his shoulders, "the weapons that will punish your father's murderer."

"But"—she looked up from his foot—"will it be enough?"

He forced his metal mouth into a smile, as he reached down. Much as he had when she was a newborn, he scooped her up in his palm and brought her to his face.

"There is no plan that may survive when carried into the den of the foe," he explained. "But with this, and my knowledge of the enemy, I will have the means to add him to the Void."

"Yuja," she whispered, the diminutive word for grandfather, "what is the Void?"

His eyes moved to the horizon. This was a discussion that should have been with one who was now within it. Now he spoke the same words he had given to his own children.

"No one really knows, except that it is where we must all go when our time is done. Some believe it is simply oblivion, the most complete of all rests. To others, it is the falling of the barriers between space, time, and thought. Where we join with all those who have ever been, and will ever be. To learn what awaits in the Void is the great journey we are all promised."

"Yuja, what if...what if you don't win?"

"If my battle is lost and the Void recalls me, I will only return to this life once more. And I will do so until justice is served. No count of deaths will stop me, and if he should die from some other cause, I will carry our family's vengeance to those who reside in the tower of his family lineage. The stars will be dark before your father's death goes unpunished."

He flattened his hands as she rose to stand in his palm and gaze into his now alien eyes.

"Yuja, we all miss him as you do."

He shook his head slowly.

"No, Vil'na. It is not the same. The pain to lose your father when you count so few years is great. But I hope you never understand that to lose your child is not the same. As a parent, you know that it is your privilege to enter the Void first. That it will be those left in your memory who carry the

---

13   3,000 Urst is equivalent to 8.36×10^{17} joules.

burden of grief. As a child, you know that without the winds of ill fortune, your parents will die before you. You know it; you can prepare for it. When it happens, you will be wrought with grief. But you will accept it as part of life, and your own life will go on.

"But when your child dies, it is something you cannot prepare for," he went on. "On Yuros, as I lay dying, unable to even scream as my blood stained the sand, I tried to shout for your father to escape. My last thoughts were the relief of knowing he had. But then, I am returned, and the first thing placed upon my mind is the knowledge that he was hunted as an animal and killed."

His facsimile jaw flexed, and his articulators emitted a mournful sigh.

"When you lose a child, Vil'na, it opens a hole in you that will never be filled. They do not live within you as a parent who has gone. A part of you has been destroyed, and will never be mended. There is nothing between the stars I want more than to have your father back. But he is gone forever. He is not the first son I have lost; he will not be the last. But he was the greatest. If he had died in battle against a worthy foe, perhaps I could endure his death and cling tightly to the legacy of his life. But I cannot do this, knowing that his death came at the hands of a coward, a terrorist who does not fight with valor, but who murders from the shadows. I cannot bring my son back, but I can use this time to honor his memory by sending his killer to the Void before I return."

"Yuja," she whispered, "I don't want to lose you again, too."

He tried to hold a smile on his face.

"We all choose our deaths, Vil'na. Even when we do not know it. We may choose our death in a moment of despair, or heroism. Or we may choose it without knowing, in how we live our lives, and the death to which we are pointed by our choices. But we all choose. I chose and received my death. Do not fear the destruction of what I have become; I am not he who was your yuja. I am his ghost, and I am here to do what I must before I may rest."

She rose on her toes, now loudly wheezing as the immaturity of years broke free and grief took over. Brandishing her teeth, she nuzzled against his cheek. Within his metal skull he cursed his new body, unable to return the gesture of affection.

"Then find him, Yuja," she whispered. "Punish the human who hurt my father."

He wheezed quietly as he cradled her with both hands. The winds blew and the sun crawled across the sky. He said nothing; he would hold her until her wheezing was done. He was not aware of time's passage until he saw the distortion, and the hollow one appeared at his feet.

"Oul'sor, it is time."

He nodded, and held Vil'na away to look into her eyes.

"Remember, my Al'cra, all that made your father great is within you."

CHAPTER
4A

THERE WAS NO PLANET-BOUND structure in the known universe larger than the *Rothburg*. Reichsylvannia wore the immense structure like a crown on its northern continent. The planet itself had to be modified to wear it, in a feat of terraforming. Eight spires stretched up through the atmosphere around a ninth. The center spire climbed until it intersected with the Web, an interlocking array of orbiting platforms completely encircling the globe.

Panzer stood in one of the orbital platforms, a sacred one known as Honor's Rise. Here among the resting grounds of High Kings were interred honored dead. Panzer walked on a path paved in gemstones as he passed by ancient mausoleums. The farther he walked, the newer the tombs he passed. At each, his presence set off the activation of a hologram, displaying the deceased in the primes of their lives. At a particular lane he turned and walked to the end.

There he was met by the hologram of a lithe woman in a red pahri. From under his arms he presented a wreath of flowers and placed them in a receptacle at the hologram's feet. These holograms were known as echoes, and were designed to carry imprints of the deceased's memories. When identifying someone it knew, the hologram could be brought to life, providing a simulation of the loved and lost. But the tomb no longer recognized him. His new identity had wrought too many changes on his face. Perhaps it was for the best. He had never found it wise to feed the part of his mind that desperately wished to pretend they were still here. Quietly he sat on a small bench, and simply looked to the hologram and listened to the simulated breeze.

"I'm sorry it's been so long." His voice was little more than a whisper. "I shouldn't have spent so much time away. Kind of hard, when you're in exile."

The hologram's emerald-like eyes sparkled at him.

"The Corps has so many demands; there's nothing left of my old life. I wonder sometimes what you would think, if you saw me now."

He took a cigarette in hand, and puffed quietly.

"I don't think you'd be proud of me. But I think you'd understand."

The cigarette split as his hand clenched.

"I miss you…every day. I wonder where we could be now, if things had been different. It's probably not healthy for me to do that, is it?"

He fell silent as he stared at the hologram, losing himself to the memories. Another time, another life…young love. The broken cigarette fell from his hand as he sucked in a deep breath.

"I know Rhoxx misses you," he choked. "He still lights a candle on your birthday. Every now and then I catch him thinking about those meat pies you made. One of the few things I've seen him enjoy that wasn't still alive and kicking. I think even Kassar misses you. I think they still blame themselves."

He paused.

"I had a dream the other night…we were back on Nova Calais, on the beach. It was just us, and the wind. The sun was setting, and you were asleep in my arms."

He sniffed as he stopped to rub his eyes.

"I tried, Elsa. I tried to go to sleep with you. But they woke me up, just…just ripped us apart a second time. Now, if there is anything after this life, I wonder if you'll even recognize me when I get there."

Slowly he rose to his feet, and bent down to better arrange the flowers beneath the nameplate that read *Elsa Speer*. He brushed his hand through the reproduction of flaxen hair before forcing himself to smile at her gaze.

"I love you, Elsa. That will never die."

He turned back to the jeweled path, and began to walk before stopping. His chin dipped as he let out the telepathic equivalent of a shout.

"I know you're here, Henthis."

On a bench by the main walkway a kurai in the armor of the Red Guard sat up as he heard the words in his mind. Even beyond the Dominion, the style of his armor was well known. Khalak consisted of an inner coat composed of overlapping scales of metal. Thick plates covered the chest, legs, and arms. Most noticeable were the many blades that sprouted from the armor. On his back, chest, and thighs, upright serrated edges stood in banks. Longer blades extended beyond the hand from below the forearm, matched by others on the shins. Three curved up from each pauldron. A design from a long ago era, intended to allow devastating cuts from any direction married to modern technology. This armor was worn only by members of the kurai warrior caste. On the armor's right chest, alien characters read *Nuset ahn Kalonen*.

Though he carried a rifle as every guard did on his back, he also wore a long sword tucked into its sheath, wrapped with red fabric. Few would ever earn such an icon—it was the symbol of a Kah'lennka grand master. Rarely more than an ornament in a modern battle, it nonetheless commanded respect from all who knew its significance.

"I did not wish to intrude, Vulan," the kurai answered.[14]

Panzer walked to him, and bowed slowly.

"I assume I have you to thank for bringing her here." Panzer spoke low, glancing back to the tomb.

"It did not seem right to leave her on that rock." Nuset spoke with a soft voice as the two moved to walk together. "A person's final rest should be in the lands of their birth."

"I'm surprised the High King allowed it."

"What he does not know will do him no harm."

Panzer shot him a sideways glance, and the kurai smiled.

"I do not only protect his body. I protect his honor as well, even if he is not willing to do so."

"Well, in any case, thank you."

"It has been many years."

"Well over a hundred," Panzer said with a nod.

"Do you remember when we walked this road together?"

"The fallen are dishonored, if not remembered by the living."

The kurai nodded approvingly.

"I heard a single whisper at court that you are a commando now."

Panzer eyed him as the kurai looked back, all four of his pupils narrowing.

"If I were, I couldn't tell you."

"And if you were, I would know," he answered with a grin. "Are you here for long?"

"Only as long as the princess."

"Yes," the kurai mused, talking with the aid of his hands. "The High King has put much preparation into this visit. I hear he even had his servants spruce up his bedchamber just in case."

Panzer's feet stopped, and the kurai stopped a moment thereafter.

"This bothers you." Nuset turned to him with a look between inquisitive and mischievous. "You want the Imperial Rose for yourself?"

"I don't even know her," Panzer replied, avoiding the kurai's eyes as they continued.

"That was not my question."

Silent for a moment, he eyed a passing tomb.

"She is easy on the eyes."

Nuset nodded.

"That is answer enough. Your face betrays little, but I have a feeling that something bothers you."

Panzer stopped to lean on a guardrail, glancing down through the glass floor of the platform at the crystal oceans below.

---

14 In the kurai language of Errdir, *Henthis* roughly translates to "master" or "teacher." *Vulan* in turn is a term referring to a prized student.

"I can't talk about it."

The kurai eyed him suspiciously as he lit another cigarette.

"What can you talk about?"

Panzer said nothing, and instead gazed up to the *Rothburg*'s center spire, rising out of the atmosphere.

"You no longer trust your old teacher?"

Panzer shook his head. "It's not that."

"Then it is…?"

"Henthis, what if you knew something very bad was going to happen…and when you tried to warn people, no one believed you?"

The kurai was silent for a moment, silently contemplating while popping his iron knuckles.

"I suppose that would depend on what it was."

Panzer sighed.

"In a very short time, the Empire and the Combine will be at war. I don't know exactly how long, but I've seen it. But the com…my commander doesn't believe me. Neither does the emperor, they think I am making much of nothing."

"Then you must continue to work to convince them."

"Suppose you were ordered to stop trying to prove it?" Panzer turned to him. "Because they disbelieved so strongly. Even though you knew exactly how to do it."

The kurai nodded as he continued to contemplate.

"Blind obedience is never the best way to serve anything. I would wait for the opportunity, but…this is already what you plan to do?"

Panzer nodded.

"Then why ask the question. You desire affirmation?"

Again Panzer nodded, saying nothing.

"Come with me."

"Where are we going?"

"The road takes you where you need to go."

Nuset led the way to a router, and following the kurai, Panzer stepped through. Within moments he was in a cave where the only light was cast by the bio-luminescence of fruit from vine-woven trees. A sound not unlike that of woodwinds echoed through the dim cavern.

"What brings us here?" Panzer asked.

The kurai did not answer but instead walked to one of the trees before taking an object from the ground. After unfurling several layers of black cloth, the grand master tossed the object to him. A sword, not unlike that of the master, now rested in Panzer's hand. The first humans to make contact with the kurai had simply dubbed it the claypier. But to the kurai it was the *vesnith*, the noble one's blade. Its sophisticated handle was like that of a rapier, but its long thick blade was more akin to what humans would consider a two-handed sword. A heavy weapon, it was meant for members of a physically stronger race.

Intricate layers of golden strands formed the hilt above an ivory handle. This one was a practice blade—not sharpened, nor properly hardened for combat. Its point was capped by a spherical stopper. His eyes moved to the weapon's blade, where beneath a layer of oil proper Errdir read, *I belong to Victor, a bright candle.*

"Never thought I'd see this again," he commented, thumbing the excess oil from the blade.

"Then we shall see if you remember how to use it."

The old kurai removed his armor and stood in simple brown robes. He took a new blade from the ground before discarding its sheath. His blade read, I belong to *Nuset, Master of Nine Forms.*

Panzer chuckled.

"We haven't seen each other in over 150 years, and your first thought is to spar?"

"The sword is good for discipline…"

"…And discipline is good for the soul," Panzer finished. "I remember."

"Very good. And as your people say, you do not truly know someone until you fight them. We have not seen each other in many years. Let us become reacquainted."

A proper vesnith was equal in length to the distance from the wielder's feet to his shoulders. Depending on how one held the weapon, it could cut, parry, or stab. But this blade was too small. Only the handle was of appropriate size, as it was meant to stay with its wielder as blades were replaced over the years. Panzer would have to use the length of his arms to compensate.

"So how high are we going?"

"When it is time for peace to reign, we will know."

Panzer nodded and held the weapon ahead while positioning his feet. Nuset took his own stance with his blade held overhead. For a moment, each eyed the other from brow to ankle, judging stance, positioning, reach, and predicting scenarios in their mind.

At least that is what Panzer was doing, though he suspected the master was doing something very different. Kurai empathy was not metapsionic in nature, but it was nearly as effective. Through their various senses they could easily detect the feelings of those with whom they were familiar. It was a combination of sensing a person's magnetic field, their scent, their body language, and their demeanor. Kah'lennka placed great emphasis on using this ability to predict a foe's actions. Humans later took up the lessons and applied them to metapsionics.

Nuset was the first to move, raising his blade higher and dashing forward. Panzer stepped in to meet him, using the blunt edge of his weapon to deflect the kurai's swing. As he counterattacked, Nuset deflected him in turn. When their bodies came together Panzer charged forward, using the advantage of his size to overpower the kurai. When Nuset moved to gain distance, Panzer struck at his exposed waist.

"You let me do that." Panzer leveled an accusing finger as they separated.

"I wanted to see if you would take advantage. You are a true student. Though separated from your teacher, you have not ceased your practice."

As they measured each other again, Nuset was again the first to move. This time when their weapons came together, the kurai deflected Panzer's blade upward before ducking low. Panzer hissed as Nuset's blade smashed into his shin.

"You are distracted," Nuset admonished. "The weight of your mind slows your body."

Panzer took his stance again. This time he stayed on the defensive, parrying the flurry of alternating high and low strikes. When the kurai came in close, he charged forward. This time, Nuset twisted around him, striking his leg before hopping to complete the combo with a blow to the back of his neck. Panzer growled as he stumbled, before taking his place again.

As they took their stances, Panzer attempted to probe the old kurai's mind, looking for a glimpse of how he would execute his next action. Charging forward, Panzer deflected the swift counter-stroke and pushed ahead, forcing the kurai to retreat from his bulk. He made no attempt at attack, instead focusing on deflecting the strikes that answered his closing of the distance, all the while waiting to sense the intent before an attack was made. With a flash in his mind, he deflected the master's blade and then drove the pommel of his weapon forward to bounce off the kurai's iron forehead.

Stumbling, Nuset shook his head, letting the disorientation pass before resuming his stance. The master wasted little time before attacking again, furious strokes forcing Panzer into retreat to maintain the distance to parry. When he moved to counterattack, the kurai's blade struck his inner thigh.

Panzer was still grumbling when Nuset resumed his stance.

"Is it time for peace to reign?" the kurai questioned at Panzer's down-turned blade.

Panzer shook his head before raising the sword high.

"Do you remember the first time I gave you that sword?"

"I remember you beat me bloody." Panzer chuckled. "Until I got mad and blasted you with a psionic pulse. Then you got up and beat me bloodier, before not letting me have any medical attention."

"And what was the lesson?"

"On the first beating? Block the attack or get the hell out of the way. I think the second one had something to do with not starting what I couldn't finish."

The master nodded, before attacking anew. The echo of deflecting blades filled the cavern. Hoisting his foot, Panzer swept Nuset's leg, before driving the blade's stopper into the kurai's gut as he fell.

"Very good."

As the fight resumed, it became more aggressive. Pushes became hard shoves. Elbows struck at opportune moments, all to force an opening. In an hour, sweat-soaked shirts had been removed and tossed aside. An hour later, the sweat on their skin was joined by the blood of incidental wounds. For every two strikes landed by the master, Panzer landed one of his own. There were no breaks in a Kah'lennka duel, and no time to rest. A battle between masters was over immediately when one proved clearly superior. Or, it could last for days between those who were evenly matched. With no score set before the match, this duel would not end until both decided it was time, or one could no longer continue.

"You remain distracted," Nuset chided, "and it makes you slow."

Panzer charged forward to attack, and was caught off guard as the kurai dropped his weapon. Nuset's hands closed around his forearms, and Panzer felt himself leveraged into a hip drag. Though he managed to complete the flip and land on his feet, Nuset's leg soon struck his knees from behind. On the ground, Panzer brought his arm up to block the leg aimed for his head. The moment on defense allowed the master to slip the sword from his hand and strike him in the gut.

As both sat up, Nuset shot him a scowl.

"I have been planning to do this for an hour. And you did not know it. The student I knew was impossible to plan for, as he would take the thoughts from my mind. Your mind is not clear."

Panzer wiped the blood from a cut to his forehead and scowled. He said nothing as Nuset scanned him.

"I feared you would walk this path," Nuset lamented, "and that you would come to this moment. You fight like a wounded animal. There is no joy in the battle; you see it as a burden. Even in the moment, you cannot focus. Doubt dulls your reflexes, and regret slows your actions. The one thought that gives you joy you push away. And every action reminds you of something you have done, or seen."

As the kurai returned his sword, Panzer glanced down at the name on the blade.

"There are many things to remember," he whispered, wiping the blade on his pants.

Rising to his feet, Nuset drew in a deep breath of the dank air.

"The boy I knew loved the fight. But you are not the boy who left this place so long ago. Back then, I worried that you were a candle burning so bright, it would burn out before living. You had learned the lessons, and the teachings behind them. But you had not yet come to understand their meaning."

Panzer watched Nuset walk to one of the trees. There he plucked one of the fruits emitting a soft yellow glow, while its tree pulsed docile tones. With calloused fingers, the old kurai tore the skin off the fruit before taking a whiff and biting into it.

"I know some of the things you faced. I knew the boy you were, but not how the man you became would handle them."

Nuset returned to sit beside him, offering half of the fruit.

"How often do nightmares find your sleep?"

Panzer glanced at him for a moment before looking back to the fruit. Humans called it the fire apple, as it tasted like a mouth full of hot embers, like most of what kurai ate.

"I don't dream."

"Ever?"

"I have my neuroware set to prevent my dreams from writing to my memory."

Nuset nodded as he continued to pick at his half of the fruit.

"I have had this moment in my life—when sleep brought me no joy, for the dreams that came. When I looked at the things I had done, and took measure of the toll I paid for the road I walked. You have forgotten peace. Whether he knows it or not, the aim of every warrior is peace. The fight is only so that the peace will be to our liking."

Panzer thumbed the fruit before allowing a sad utterance to escape.

"I don't mean to insult you, Henthis, but I'm not like you. It's been a long time since I cared what came after the battle. When I left, I joined the Legionnaires to provide an income for Elsa. I wanted to give her a life more than mediocrity and stipend. When she died, I died. I joined the commandos because fighting was all I had left."

He realized the old kurai was staring at him, waiting for his eyes.

"To pit yourself against your foe," Nuset continued. "To conquer him through might or guile. With each moment you felt alive, and with every victory, proud. Yet the conquest of your foe no longer satisfies you. Is this not so?"

Panzer didn't answer, and took another bite of the fruit.

"Perhaps we are not as different as you believe." Nuset smiled. "When comes the moment that you have taken so many lives, won so many victories, that you have nothing left to prove. All that made you feel alive turns stale. You no longer care if you win the battle; it has become a burden. You only want the war to be over.

"From the moment we are born and set foot upon the road, we incur a debt to death as the price of our passage. With every step we make our payments; with every shot we fire, every blade we draw, and every life we end. But then comes a time that you no longer care if you step off the road. You may even hope it leads you to the warrior who will make your final payment."

Nuset returned to his feet and walked to touch the bloom of one of the trees.

"I have felt this before. Our war does not end when those who sent us to it declare peace. We carry our war within, and fight it on every step. Our greatest foes come as the memories of those we have killed, or those we have lost. Every doubt that comes from the ones we could not save. Until we realize that what we are truly wishing for, is that our body pays the price our soul already has."

His stern expression gave way to a gentle smile.

"I have felt this way. Then, I come here. The last bastion of a home world lost long before I was born. Here, where trees grow descended from those that stood on holy ground, where my forefathers were laid to rest. I listen to the lullaby of their eternal sleep. I eat the fruit of trees that nourished on their ashes, and they are one with me. All those feelings and doubts are calmed, as I am centered."

Nuset turned back toward him.

"The goal of every war is peace. Especially the one we carry with us. To find that peace, we must find what centers us. We must carry it with us. If battle no longer thrills you, if it no longer brings you to your center, you must find what does. Find what centers you, and what appeases those voices screaming within. And the war of your life will end in victory. You will walk in peace with every step."

Closing his eyes, Panzer rose to his feet and bowed low, before finding Nuset's gaze.

The old kurai walked silently back to his armor to encase himself within.

"I must return to the High King now. But first, your sword."

As Nuset held out his hand, Panzer laid the weapon in his grasp. The kurai took the blade in both armored hands and began to twist. The blade let out a mournful howl before breaking. Nuset then offered the hilt back to him.

Panzer's eyes lit up in shock as he took the hilt, and the air was driven from his lungs.

"I don't understand," he whispered. "You're rejecting me as your student?"

His jaw clenched at the wound in his chest, and he waited for the blade to turn.

"You will know when it should be mended," Nuset answered, laying a hand on his shoulder. He waited for Panzer to look up. "And when we come to know each other again, I do not wish to find a man who is old before his time. I expect the candle that once cast its light on all those around him."

Panzer held the broken weapon tight to his side, looking into his teacher's eyes. They said nothing more, and soon Nuset returned to the router, leaving Panzer to contemplate in the grove.

CHAPTER 4B

WITH THE TOUR OF the *Rothburg* complete, Simmonne followed the High King until a router deposited her in the grand banquet hall. On the apex of the *Rothburg*'s highest spire beneath a transparent rotunda was a large banquet hall. Here beer and wine flowed through spouting fountains to the tune of music hand-played by a lantai chorus, even when the hall was empty—all so that it could truthfully be called the place where drink and music flowed always. The Reichsylvannians' name for this spectacle that stretched into the heavens? The Beer Hall.

Simmonne smiled to herself, certain that Jenna was already having panicked visions of the Twins in the fountains. Hundreds were gathered below the view of the stars, the elites of Reichsylvannian society. Subordinate nobility of the High King, their families, and their staffs were in attendance. Also present were the boards of directors for many of the Empire's largest corporations. Galaxy Staryards Corporation, who constructed the bulk of the Empire's warships. Consolidated Automatech, Dominion Terraforming, Galaxy Bank and Trust, and more had all been invited. The High King led her to the center of the chamber to stand between the points of a crescent table before signaling for the orchestra to ebb their volume that he may speak.

"Your Majesty, before we dine, the people of the Dominion have gifts."

"No gifts are necessary, Your Excellency," she said with a smile. "But I will certainly not say no."

They took their time. A new shuttle from GSC's luxury line, Noble Motors. Rare vintages of wine that she would not drink yet have to hide from the Twins. Even a pistol from Reichsylvannian Armaments that in private she would pass off to Jenna. She made sure to fawn over all of them, convincing the giver that each was her favorite. When they were done and servants were ferrying the gifts away, the High King led her to her place at the table.

On the outer curve, the High King's throne stood atop a pyramid of stairs. Wide arm and footrests branched out into reclined seats with more behind his shoulders, chairs for each of his wives. Simmonne's seat was similar, with the Twins sitting at her arms. Jenna, meanwhile, in her refusal to be an ornament, did not sit, and instead chose to stand with Simmonne's guards. She would find herself a meal later, as she always did. Across from the High King, Simmonne sat within the crescent as the table rose up toward them.

Her meal was presented in the form of fruits and vegetables in ridiculous proportions. Reichsylvannians never did anything small, including dining. After taking their dishes from the center table, the Twins pulled small trays over their legs and quickly began to eat. The High King meanwhile sat puffing from a hookah while his wives and guests began to eat. Such was the local tradition, that the host did not eat until after every guest had been served their meal.

While she eyed her food she was keenly aware of the High King's eyes undressing her in his mind. The powerful metapsion made no effort to hide his feelings. Meanwhile she could sense the Twins enjoying the attention coming from so many parts of the room. Simmonne tried not to blush as she glanced at the High King, and the petite wife with legs dangling over his shoulder who appeared to be having similar thoughts.

Dinner conversation ensued, as those around the table discussed politics, business, the Combine. Though she took a polite interest in the conversation, she was far more interested in reading the feelings of the room. This was her first chance to really see the Reichsylvannians outside of rhetoric and stereotypes.

Reichsylvannians were a strange dichotomy, between warriors and hedonists. Food, drink, and drugs illegal elsewhere were largely allowed here, with the responsibility to sample them properly on the individual. She had always suspected this was due to the underlying warrior mentality brought on not only by humans with a militant history, but the inclusion of three warrior races in the simians, kurai, and kodaz. When the warriors were not busy fighting, they had to be kept satiated by feasting.

"So, Majesty," the High King began, "tell me about this mission of yours."

Simmonne took a drink of water to clear her throat before answering.

"It is my father's wish that I greet the refugees gathered on Avalon. When the time comes, I will help ensure they are brought safely to the Empire proper."

"Your father always was a gentle one," the High King answered. "Never could turn anyone away."

Simmonne turned her head slightly as she glanced at him.

"It is my understanding that you refused to allow any of the quants to settle in your territory."

He nodded while taking another puff of his hookah.

"I do not care how many refugees His Majesty invites to the Empire, so long as he does not attempt to resettle them here. The Dominion has never allowed refugee populations to be settled in its territory, nor do I foresee a situation where it will."

Simmonne suppressed a smile, sensing the Twins perking up. They cared so little for anything political, but the refugee situation was an exception. They would not be able to keep from speaking.

"But surely you do not think it is a good thing to turn suffering people away?" Jennifer said first.

He turned to her, and Simmonne remained silent.

"So many peoples come running to the Empire, begging or even demanding we help them. As if we owe it to them."

"We are the most powerful nation in the universe," Julie asserted, leaning forward with her hands on her knees. "It is our responsibility."

He turned to her.

"It is not." He spoke firmly. "So many aliens come running and begging to be let in. Then as soon as we permit it, half of them start complaining. They complain that they have to earn Imperial citizenship, or how the Empire isn't built to accommodate them. Meanwhile our people die to keep them safe, to feed them, to medicate them, all while they try to assimilate into our society, which is too advanced for most of them to try."

He paused to extend his arm.

"Look around this room. The owners and senior operators of sixty-one out of the one hundred largest corporations in the Empire are in this room. We have the highest standard of living; we are the beating heart of the Empire's technology and industry. What possible benefit is there for us in allowing billions of refugees into our home? People who have no skills relevant to our society, who will simply go on stipend, and become discontent when they learn that they do not have what it takes to rise off of the bottom rung of society."

"So we should just turn them all away?" Jennifer was incredulous. "They're suffering!"

Simmonne laid a hand on Jennifer's thigh, signaling her to bring her voice down.

"Well, the Elysians are inviting them in. No surprise, they will take anyone. Impoverished and unsophisticated people are easily exploited. Yes, I would turn them away. The proper thing to do here is to arm and train these people so they may fight to reclaim their home…not invite them into ours."

"But—"

SIMMONNE: *That's enough, girls.*

JULIE: *But he's wrong!*

JENNIFER: *But—*

SIMMONNE: *Girls, this is not the time or place.*

The Twins' loud speech had drawn several looks from the large table and beyond.

"And people wonder why the Dominion doesn't allow women to vote," the High King remarked, drawing a laugh from the crowd. Simmonne watched as his eyes came back to her, and she briefly squinted an eye to read him. He was trying to get a rise out of her. If he thought it would be that easy, he would be disappointed. No surprise, however, that Jenna hated it here, when even the women were laughing at the High King's remark.

"But enough of that," the High King spoke again. "This is a celebration. It has been too long since a member of the Imperial Family visited us. A toast to Princess Simmonne and her fine companions."

She spent most of the meal scanning the room, searching for jealousy, contentment, happiness, resentment, finding little that stood out from any large crowd aside from the disproportionately small number of men. Not that it was a surprise. Reichsylvannians made greater use of genetic engineering than any other population, with natural childbirth being held as irresponsible and burdensome. With this technology they enforced their preferred gender ratio. No one could legally have a son until having a minimum number of daughters.

As guests completed their meals, they began to flow onto the hall's dance floors. Before long, the High King descended from his chair and rounded the table to hold out a hand.

"If you would, Your Majesty?"

"Well…" Simmonne paused to dab her mouth with a napkin. "I cannot deny my host a dance."

She climbed down from her chair to take his hand, and on the dance floor they waited until a new tempo began. With one hand holding hers, his other moved to her hip, and she followed as the waltz began. She found herself blushing again as he stared down at her. He was attractive, but she was not going to begin a relationship with someone who would leave this universe thousands of years ahead of her. To say nothing of the political snarl that would arise from a relationship between a Mandrake and a Rhinegrave. Rivalry between the two was nearly as old as the Empire, and not likely to end anytime soon.

His glare was beginning to make her uncomfortable, and she closed her eyes as the dance continued. The colonel's eyes came to her mind and she shuddered. Was he nearby? Was he watching? She found herself wondering if he could dance. The High King was almost tall enough to work as a stand in for the colonel. She giggled to herself at the idea—someone that frightening dancing. Why couldn't she stop thinking of him? It could not be a crush. This was not natural. Had he done something to her mind?

She opened her eyes briefly to glance back to her chair, feeling a moment of sadness. Jenna had taken her seat, intent on ensuring the Twins were not able to accept any of the overtures awaiting them. She was not about to risk losing sight of them long enough for them to do something that could cause embarrassment. But would it really be so much of a risk to let them have some fun? She knew the answer. The moment they were no longer supervised, both would be drunk, and then who knows what. It was cruel to make them live this way; all they wanted was to have some fun.

"Your Excellency." She glanced up to the High King.

"Majesty?"

"Would you be so kind as to offer my handmaidens a dance?"

He cast an eye over.

"But of course, Majesty."

When their dance ended, Simmonne walked with him back to the chair. Jenna could not insult the High King by turning him away, and Simmonne smiled as he led the Twins to the dance floor for a more up-tempo song. Jenna had followed, and though she remained off the floor, her hawkish eyes watched every step. After she returned to her seat Simmonne took a drink, thinking about another dance partner. She shuddered, remembering his fingers on her wrist in contention for the cheese. Oh, the heart attack it would give Jenna if he were to dance with her now. Where was he? Why did he need to stay out of sight?

She shuddered before glancing down to realize that one of the directors of Galaxy Staryards Corporation had extended a hand. She smiled to herself. Time to give Jenna a real workout.

CHAPTER
4C

THE CORE WORLDS OF the Empire were protected by the forces of the Solar Army, but the projection of power and the defense of outlying colonies fell to the Legionnaires. All Legionnaire assets of platoon size and greater included their own transports among their logistics assets. Such units were expected to be capable of rapidly responding to a crisis, and redeploy themselves without the aid of the Armadas. Today's exercise was an extension of that doctrine. The legionnaires loved their war games, and spent huge volumes of their time between wars partaking in them. For this operation, Third Section would drop in with the intent of securing a simulated listening post against unknown resistance.

Slowing from FTL, the dropship emerged in the star system, angling itself to the nearest planet in orbit of a blue giant. This was the kind of operation used in recruiting advertisements, asking Billy Public if he was tough enough. On the planet below, an atmosphere of carbon dioxide hosted sustained winds of 400 km/h, pressures of over 100 atmospheres, and an average temperature of over 1,000 Kelvin.

"Pilot to Section Lead, we'll be in drop position in two minutes," the pilot's voice sounded in Clearwater's com.

"Understood. Section, let's get ready!"

He grimaced before switching his coms from RECEIVER to TRANSCEIVER and re-sending the message. From opposing benches sprouting from both sides of the cramped cargo bay, his AICES-clad troops rose to their feet. Less than a meter away stood Sarge in a Grenadier-class AICES, marked by bundling a quartet of launchers around grasping claws and spherical bulging shoulders.

Directly ahead, the cargo-bay doors parted, revealing the intense blue light of the star now eclipsing the view. When his NOD dimmed, he was able to see the planet while the dropship moved into orbit. His eyes were suddenly drawn to his clock, which fast-forwarded, accounting for a three-minute dilation. The pilot obviously wasn't taking this drill too seriously, or he would not have disengaged his MID until the wave passed.

"Ready for drop in thirty seconds," the pilot announced.

Clearwater's pulse quickened as the dropship began to rotate, orienting its belly toward the planet. In his short time as a legionnaire, he had already discovered the part of the job he hated most: hard dropping. That was a fancy way of saying dropping in from orbit…and never firing braking-thrusters before impact. The speed, range, and accuracy of modern weapons turned the sky into a massive no-man's-land. There was no advantage to being at altitude that was not outweighed by the massive disadvantage of giving the weapons of so many potential foes line of sight to oneself. Hard dropping was meant to minimize the time spent in the air getting to ground and potential cover as quickly as possible. While the AICES was made to survive such impacts, that knowledge did little to counteract the primordial terror that came with plummeting through the sky toward a rocky surface.

"Pilot to section lead, you are go for drop. Section lead? You're clear for drop."

"Roger," Clearwater answered. "Deploy bots."

From the dropship's underbelly, the automatech, folded up and packed into their racks, rocketed out like missiles descending on the planet. Protocol was for the bots to deploy, then the AICES with the section commander leaving midway through the jump. He had positioned himself at the front, intent on taking the lead and going in first. But now that the moment came, his feet did not want to step off the deck. He was almost certain that someone pushed him, but the relevance of that fact was soon lost as he found himself falling toward the amber clouds of the planet below.

The thick atmosphere completely obscured the ground below, and he was forced to rely on a waypoint in his NOD to adjust his thrusters toward the landing zone. The meat-locker, more formally known as the operator compartment of the AICES, was separated from the outer hull by a layer of stopping gels designed to cushion impacts and diffuse the energy of weapons that penetrated the armor. Despite this, he could feel the machine shake around him as he was battered by the planet's winds. A quiet whine sounded as the environmental cooling unit engaged, conducting the heat on the hull to his shield systems to be radiated through the projectors.

Optical visibility was non-existent, leaving Clearwater with only his sensors to know how far he was from the approaching ground. It took three minutes to descend from the shuttle to the surface below, but watching the altimeter descend made it feel so much longer. Angling his feet, he held his breath. A loud crash rang through his ears and he felt his body contract.

Bond-forged titanium cut through solid rock like soft mud as he struck like the meteors constantly bombarding this planet. An exhale escaped and he stood upright, his vision filled by the billowing winds. Adjusting his sensors, he was rewarded with a synthesized image of the terrain. Directly ahead, a large volcano belched smoke into the relentless winds. A few kilometers to the left, a silver sea sparkled in his view. At first he thought it pretty, until realizing that it was an enormous lake of boiling lead.

The bots had already taken position while his section came down, coming much closer to their specific drop points than the half a kilometer by which he had missed. When operating alone, armored infantry moved in a phalanx. At the forefront, the automatech marched in file, 100 meters separating each bot in the line from the next. The AICES units marched behind, separated from each other by an average of one kilometer.

Their target was embedded in the base of the volcano at the far end of a canyon, the entrance of which lay 20 kilometers ahead. Tapping his thrusters, he rose out of the crater formed by his impact, and looked to his section.

"Passive sensors won't be much use here unless they're broadcasting," he advised. "Let's use that to our advantage. Press forward, low-intensity scans only."

SGT. DOLPH: Sir, I advise against broadcasting. Recommend P2P routed through the bots.

LT. CLEARWATER: Good idea.

SGT. DOLPH: Are you sure you want passive only, sir?

LT. CLERWATER: I'm sure. I didn't detect any active scans, if they know we're here they don't know how many. Let's not advertise it.

It was a risk, but without active scanning they'd be hard-pressed to know if the sudden impact was due to a hard drop or just a few of the many meteors in the ongoing shower. Best to let them assume the latter.

Plotting a course in his NOD, Clearwater engaged the auto-walk, and his legs moved with those of the machine. His eyes traced the rock walls that formed the cliffs and canyon ahead. A canyon was a perfect place for an ambush from an elevated position, and he set waypoints for the automatech to rise up on the walls. Images danced through his sensors as his AICES scanned every square meter of territory ahead, looking for anyone or anything attempting to blend in with the environment.

At five kilometers to the canyon, his sensors rang. Twelve kilometers away, on one of the rocky outcroppings of the volcano, the AICES had detected something. The armored head and shoulders of a light-infantry trooper were just barely visible past the rocks he was hiding behind. The AICES had picked out the silhouette of the large anti-material rifle the trooper was aiming down into the canyon. Clearwater was not picking up any active sensors; without them, it was unlikely the trooper had spotted the approaching phalanx.

LT. CLEARWATER: All units, hostile spotted, mark coordinates.

The AICES spotted another silhouette two kilometers up the canyon, another light infantry with a suppression weapon hiding behind a large boulder. With the target designated, he could just make out the bloom of heat. The trooper's shields were diffusing the heat from his armor, barely visible amid the ambient temperature.

It was clear now: The opposing force intended on ambushing him as he led his troops through the canyon. The only question was how many was he facing? Was there a single squad out there for whom this would be an exercise in hit-and-run ambushes on a larger force? Or was there a full section waiting to lure him in? Active scans would reveal that information in moments, but would give away the presence of his own units.

LT. CLEARWATER: *All units halt advance. Get scouts on the cliffs; I want to know what I'm dealing with.*

The twin phalanxes came to a halt, save for two automatech that continued forward. When they came to the cliffs, the machines jumped, coming atop the rock walls on either side of the canyon.

On the wall the machines stayed low, passively scanning the environment ahead, and relaying the data. They had picked out more than a dozen light infantry up the cliffs, who, like the others, waited in ambush. The question came fast to his mind. *Where were their automatech?*

"Hostile contact!" The broadcast from one of his sergeants caused him to flinch in his harness. Pivoting the machine, he turned to the messenger and his jaw dropped. The canyon ahead wasn't the trap; those covering it were simply waiting if he sent his troops there for cover.

The light infantry automatech were attacking, rising out of the lake of molten lead. They were not alone. As Clearwater turned to elevate his guns, he saw the Brutus-class mech rising out of the lead to follow. Twin 90mm revolver cannons flashed, raking his troops with simulated disrupter shells. Icons were flashing in his NOD, marking those troops taken out by the surprise attack.

SGT DOLPH: *Orders, sir?*

"All units, re-deploy on my anchor, redress phalanx to face the enemy troops. Tactical retreat."

His troopers moved in near perfect unison, their phalanx turning to a diagonal to face the molten lake. The automatech had been powered down, waiting for seismic sensors to detect their approach. Now the small, almost skeletal machines were tearing into his men.

"Re-deploy bots bring them around, surround and engage."

SGT DOLPH: *Sir, watch your broadcasts.*

His eyes remained fixed on the warmech. Even in this environment he could see the flashes of its weapons as they strafed his troops with simulated fire.

"Squads two, three, and four, focus fire."

He designated the warmech for them and elevated his own weapons. The twin rotary guns howled to life, each spewing 10,000 rounds of armor-shredding disrupter pulses every minute. Simulated hits washed across his view of the warmech's legs, but the machine kept coming.

"Intensify fire, use Mk-23s."

But when he depressed the trigger, nothing happened. The AICES did not respond to his command, and his NOD had turned red. The AICES' actuators let out a groan as it began to lean, before falling prone on the rock. High up on the volcano, the very first trooper he saw had taken him out. The GAC-1111 anti-mech rifle had been designed to give light infantry a tool to bring down warmechs and puncture heavy defenses. Anything within its visible horizon was prey, and the weapon had been turned on him. Following his broadcasts, the trooper had identified him as the leader before putting a simulated shot through his meat-locker. He was dead.

Now he could only listen as Dolph took command of his section. The light infantry were attacking, emerging from holes and cracks in the cliffs like ants defending their hive. Two sections had been waiting for him. The biologics had hidden themselves in the cliffs. It had been a gamble. If he had detected the automatech hiding in the lead, he could have destroyed them with ease. Without them, the egregiously outgunned light infantry would have had nowhere to retreat against the superior force of armored infantry. Why? Why hadn't he scanned the lake?

His thoughts turned. Why hadn't his troops suggested doing that very thing? Surely, out of all of these veterans, someone must have had at least a thought about it. His eyes widened as he knew the answer. They *did* think of it. Dolph had even tried to warn him, about forgoing active scans. He would have listened. Why didn't Sarge speak up more firmly? Why didn't any of the others? He knew why—they wanted to see if he would think of it himself. They had given him the chance to screw up, and he dove in head first.

The battle went on and concluded without him, Sarge had led his section to victory, but at a heavy price. More than a third of all his AICES had suffered simulated kills as well as half of his automatech—amounts that were inexcusably high for a meeting between light and armored infantry. More than a third of his organics had been killed—more than a third dead, if this had not been an exercise. The simulation ended and his control over the AICES returned. Brower broadcast from his warmech, now rising back to its own feet.

"Brower to all units. Simulation concluded. 1st Section, 2nd Section, damn good effort for being so outgunned. 3rd Section, Lieutenant Clearwater, we will discuss your choice of tactics in the officer's meeting."

"Yes sir," he grumbled.

LT. BROWER: Don't take it too hard, Clearwater; you're supposed to screw up here, that's how you learn.

LT. CLEARWATER: Yes sir.

LT. BROWER: One other thing. Don't target a warmech's legs. To support its own weight, they're usually the toughest part of its body. If you're going to try cracking through the tough parts, aim for the operator compartment. Otherwise, weapons are volatile; aim for them.

LT. CLEARWATER: Understood, sir.

"Brower to pickup, let's head home."

The various legionnaires gathered by the molten lake that had spelled his shame until the dropships came down from above. The opening doors of the dropship almost reminded him of a mouth opened wide to laugh at him. As he re-boarded and took a seat, he was contacted by the pilot.

"Lieutenant Clearwater, I have a priority message for you, personal, came in during the exercise."

"Let's have it." He sighed as the message was relayed to his NOD. At first he smiled, seeing a young redhead staring back at him. His enthusiasm faded as the message began, and he heard the tone of her first words.

"Johnny...it's, it's Nana. She's gone." She was trying not to cry. "She...didn't suffer. They told me there's no astranet where you are; I hope you get this in time. The funeral is in three days. Ryan and Sarah aren't taking it well; they need their big brother. I hope you get this in time."

His eyes raced to the timestamp as the message ended. Between the time delay for the message to arrive and the Hourglass time dilation...he had missed the funeral.

CHAPTER
4D

STEVEN SAT QUIETLY IN his lounge, silence broken only by the sound of breathing. Jasmine had long since passed out on the floor, snoring like an old man in her stupor. Another woman lay asleep in his lap, Becky Skinner, runner-up in Miss Empire. Charming her out of her clothes had been easier than he anticipated. A few words about how she was robbed in the contest, and a few flashes of princely splendor and she became putty.

It was more than that; she had given in too easy. There was almost no chase, she went with every suggestion, liked every idea. As he watched her chest rise and fall with her breath, he laid a hand on her breast, smiling as her body coiled at the sudden pressure. As a prince and not terrible to look at, women had always been easy for him. But it was too easy this time; she had been almost servile as she went along with his suggestions.

Unconsciously her hand moved to his as he continued to squeeze, and no sooner did he wish it away than it returned to her side. Something was wrong here, he could feel it. Something unnatural had happened tonight.

"Steven."

His head lowered, he didn't answer. His eyes moved back to the beauty in his lap.

"Steven."

She moaned quietly as he squeezed more firmly, before her eyes fluttered open.

"That hurts," she whispered.

He said nothing, yet she nodded at his desire to be silent.

"Steven."

"What do you want?" he answered, his eyes moving to the windows and the field of stars beyond.

"For you to learn."

"What's happening to me?"

"Look at her, Steven."

His eyes moved back down to Miss Elysium, who lay quietly looking up at him.

"Send her back to her sleep."

"How?" he asked, almost vocalizing.

"Will it."

"Will it?"

There was no answer, and taking a breath he looked into her eyes. He drew in a deep breath, feeling pressure in his chest. He felt a hand on his forehead that did not move when he looked up, and looking down he saw his hand on her forehead. The realization made him gasp; he was sensing her—not simply her emotions like some humble empath. The very nerve endings of her flesh were feeding his mind.

"Send her to sleep."

The desire for her eyes to close was enough to make it real; despite her knowing something was wrong, despite the crushing pressure in her breast, her eyes rolled back and closed. In moments the gentle breathing had returned, and she was asleep.

"How?" he whispered, watching her slumber.

"Your people bear my gift. I have simply opened your eyes to some of its potential."

"I…I can control her? Did I—"

"Impose your will on her to satisfy your biologic urges? Yes. And you did it so easily, you did not realize it."

"That, this, this is wrong! I—"

"Right and wrong are simple constructs. Determined by those with the power to enforce their will. You have the will to power. Do not fear its use."

His eyes were drawn to Jasmine as she lay snoring louder than before.

"Test your power."

"How?"

"Your body has many biological urges. Satisfy one. Have her bring you a drink."

"But I can get that from the net," he answered. "Is that—"

"Servants only have meaning if a master gives them purpose."

He moved a hand toward her. As his fingers worked, her snoring abruptly ceased. Sitting up from the floor, she quickly rose to her feet, her eyes still closed. Through her mind, through *her* NOD he sent the request and her hand came up to take the glass of water. His fingers worked slowly and she shuffled toward him. He smiled, feeling the cool glass as if it were in his own hand.

Her unconscious form held the glass up, and he drank as easily as if it were from his own hand. The glass lowered and he grinned. She was unconscious and unaware she was on her feet, completely under his control.

"This…is incredible." He spoke low, his fingers waggling, causing her limbs to follow suit. Laughing, he made her twirl, watching her dance under his control.

"From the moment you met her, you wanted to control her. Why?"

"I…I don't know."

"Yes you do."

His laughter faded, giving way to a sneer as he stared at the sleepwalking woman.

"She was such a bitch," he whispered. "So smug, knew that she was better than everyone. Spent her entire life as a little daddy's girl who never had to work for anything. Always felt that everyone owed her something."

"You resented this?"

"She never shut up. She'd argue for no reason, undercut everyone's opinion, and try to debate with no facts or logic."

Pushing Miss Elysium aside, he rose to look at Jasmine, seizing her chin between his fingers.

"How did you break her?"

"She was greedy. She wanted everything without working for it. Money, respect…she didn't deserve any of it. I let her tag along, gave her what she wanted. Then, she tasted marvat."

He smiled.

"She never had any self-control. The first time I gave it to her, she smoked so much it gave her brain damage. But she couldn't stop herself from coming back."

"And you were only too happy to provide."

"Not at first. I didn't want her to harm herself."

"That is not true, Steven."

He sighed, flicking her hair from her eyes.

"No. I wanted her to beg. To finally show some goddamn humility, to admit she needed something."

"The wise master ensures his servants need him always."

"Not so smug are you now?" he spat as he glared at her closed eyes. "Look at you now, nothing but a whore who lives for drugs and wine."

"It is a poor master who insults his servants, Steven."

"What do you mean?"

"You give them purpose; they give you status. Remember the relationship."

Quietly he nodded, lowering his hand from her jaw.

"I have given you great power to exert your will. But your power means nothing without people to yield to it."

He guided her over to a couch, and watched her quietly for a time.

"So I can really control people?"

"You can imprint your will on their subconscious mind. Even take control of their actions. But be mindful of other metapsions; those with the gift can resist your control."

"So what else can I do?"

No answer came, and taking a breath, he turned to his bedchamber. He stood in the door, looking to the bed where Natalie was asleep. She never so much as protested when he brought Miss Elysium home for the evening.

She was not jealous, and that bothered him. But he knew why she was not jealous: She did not care. When he made love to her, she merely lay back and let her mind drift. How he wanted her to be jealous, to care, but he knew that would not happen.

He sat down by her, brushing the hair from her eyes to reveal the dream regulator on her brow. His pupils narrowed as his mind pierced her dreams, like looking through an aquarium to the oblivious fish within.

He was here…that same man who had tried to steal her from him. The poor artist who was never worthy of her, who never had the talent to give her more than a stipend's life. The thief who tried to steal his true love. They were together in an open field. She sat listening to him make music.

A smile played across Steven's lips. Nothing had given him so much joy as knowing that kodaz ripped that insolent piece of trash apart like a wet napkin. His grin widened, contemplating how his rival must have wailed as half-meter iron claws tore him apart. If only he could have been there to see it, and hear that bastard's screams as his fists flailed helplessly against a scaly hide.

"Even in death he thwarts you."

"He didn't deserve her," Steven growled. "Not then, not now. Why? Why can't I make her forget about him?"

"You've done so much for her."

"I gave her a home in the Cathedral. I gave her a life of luxury and dignity!"

"You've always loved her."

"From the day I met her." He held back a sob, gently tracing his thumb across her cheek.

"He tried to steal her from you."

"She was mine!" he growled. "I wouldn't let him have her."

"Yet beyond the grave, he continues to fight for what is rightfully yours."

He took a breath looking down at her, his eyes narrowing.

"Not for long."

"What will you do, Steven? Erase him from her mind?"

"No." He shook his head. "That is not enough."

"It is the best solution."

"It is not enough!" He quickly calmed himself, checking that no one had been awoken by his shout.

"It is one thing to erase memories. It is quite another to alter them. You may not like the results."

"I will," he assured himself. "I know I will."

Looking back into the dream, he found the artist now lying atop Natalie. The image caused his blood to boil. The clear sky of the dream began to darken as the artist's demeanor changed. A loud crack echoed over the plains as his hand struck her face. Another strike followed, and she tried to coil up to protect herself.

"I'm sorry," he whispered, "but this is for your own good."

Her dress tore as the first drops of rain fell, an open hand turning to a closed fist as she cried for him to stop. After three strikes the only sounds she made were sobs as the artist shredded her dress. The memory of making love in a sunny field turned to a bitter rape on a bleak day.

Natalie sobbed in her sleep, a tear streaming out of her eye. His hand withdrew, and for a moment the enormity of what he was doing spilled through his mind.

"She is yours to do with as you please, Steven. But you would be wise to heed my warning. By altering the memories, you will alter the person."

"She's going to love me," he whispered. "If I have to alter every memory in her head, she is going to love me. She'll be happier when she does. She'll love the man she's with; she'll be happy with her life. How can I not do it?"

"It is your decision, and it will be your consequences."

He glared back into her mind, seeing the artist on his knee with a pathetic ring. That memory was the next to twist. He went through them, one by one. If she would not appreciate him for saving her from a meaningless life of destitution, perhaps she would love the man who saved her from an abusive lover. There were more memories, and he did not stop until he had touched them all.

When he was done and rose from the bed, she was curled up beneath the sheets, crying softly. Part of him wanted to sit back down and comfort her, but he stopped himself. She had to face this, and perhaps when morning came, she would appreciate this life.

CHAPTER
4E

ONCE MORE OUL'SOR STOOD in the Hall of Warlords, but no longer did he stand alone. At his right foot his loyal friend Hahk'xess. By his left, the one wishing to use him. The council had been called to order, and the time to speak granted. Hahk'xess was the first to break the silence.

"We are a people of few traditions to shackle our future. We have become what we are by our ability to adapt to those challenges that face us. But we cannot allow this, to turn our minds away from those traditions we do hold dear. For they exist, each of them with cause and reason, and none are to be taken upon one's voice without due reverence. Of the few we count, perhaps no tradition is more important than the vek'thim. The right for those dishonored in their death, or beyond, to return and reclaim the honor stolen from them. It is a right we place upon only our greatest citizens.

"Beyond this hall, there stands no statue of any warrior in the company of whom Oul'sor should feel shame. There are none alive with ears to hear my words, who should call themselves his equal. Many who sit upon this council earned their place by following Oul'sor's example. The Combine owes to none, and recognizes no debt to any who do as their duty demands. But Oul'sor has done far more. He is worthy of all respect we can lay upon him. With truth in my words, he is worthy of more."

Hahk'xess fell silent, awaiting a rebuttal.

Dolum accepted the challenge.

"Is it not true to say, Hahk'xess, that when life first surged anew in his mind. That among Oul'sor's first words was a readiness to reject the vek'thim, carried in the arms of belief that his death was to a worthy foe?"

Son of a dishonored slave that one, using his own words against him. Had he not been stripped of his armaments before appearing, he may have employed them.

"That you are the master of the clandestine," Hahk'xess answered, "gives you no freedom to use such shameful tactics in this council, Dolum. The words of one freshly ripped from the Void, barely aware of where he is, are not valid to be used as witness for any cause."

"The principle of the matter is valid, Hahk'xess, even if the words are not," Dolum rebutted. "Vek'thim is reserved for those who are dishonored in their manner of death. Oul'sor set his feet upon Yuros with a force of superior numbers, the boon of surprise, and knowledge of his foe's approach. He was then slain in battle, despite these strengths. By what measure that remains objective was he not simply defeated by a superior enemy?"

Oul'sor turned to Hahk'xess, praying his friend would drive a sword through the heart of this argument.

"We have few laws pertaining to the prosecution of war," Hahk'xess answered, "but one of them is that a foe must make himself visible, to be seen clearly as a foe and not an uninvolved. By his use of personal cloaking, the Crykeeper stepped out of the disciplined file of soldiery, and into the bounds of terrorism. There is no honorable battle, and no triumph of a superior foe in the actions of a criminal. By that act, Oul'sor, his son, and the many others dead at this murderer's hand are sullied. To bring redress to this crime, vek'thim must be recognized."

Oul'sor scanned the chamber, piercing the darkness to see the faces of the other warlords. It would take a super majority for his challenge to triumph. He did not see that majority in their faces, even as Hahk'xess was closing his argument.

"I believe, then, we are ready for a vote," Dolum began, before his mouth moved without sound.

"You forget that I am here," Indorai bellowed. "Though I doubt by accident. You will excuse me if I do not hang ornaments on my language as you Vaar are so keen to do. But I prefer purity of clarity to quantity of vocabulary."

The hollow silhouette spun, giving the impression that he was eyeing all in the chamber.

"I expect the undivided attention of all here. No matter the rules of your halls, you owe me, and with your ears you now pay."

He raised an arm, and an image—perhaps a hologram—illuminated above him for all to see. Oul'sor could not help but growl at the sight of the figure in black armor.

"A Solar seems such a fragile creature. In truth they are, if you pierce their technology. Something I will add you can only attempt with my help. Each of your galaxies has felt the sting of the emperor's commandos. It has long been their policy, to assign credit for the works of many to a single one. All with the goal of creating a specter to haunt your minds. That is the case with the object of Oul'sor's vek'thim. He has not done everything you believe he has, but he has done much of it. He has done more to harm you than any, and emptied three seats of this council. All while seeking those who betrayed you, to count as his allies.

"Look upon the Crykeeper, warlords. Think now of how many murders have been wrought with his hands. Know this: When the Crossroads returns, the Empire will seek to take it from you. This is the image of the thief who will be tasked with ripping it from your grasp. So you see, the object of Oul'sor's hate is not merely one warrior's grudge; it is a threat to your very future."

"He is only one soldier," one of the other warlords called down. "No war is fought, nor victory won by a single warrior."

"Your words would be heard more loudly," Indorai said, "if he had not already sent a war's worth of your people to the Void. You just listened without protest to the claims of Oul'sor's glory. Are you so blinded by your pride that you think there are none among other races of equal might?"

A murmur filled the chamber until a gavel hammered for silence.

"But more importantly, I am here so you are not blind to opportunity. You know as well as I do that war with the Empire will not be over quickly. Entire generations of Vaar will be born, and live knowing only war with the Solars. When you hold Oul'sor as a symbol to drive your people to victory, what kind of symbol do you wish? Your people have many generals, and many will establish grand reputations for themselves. But think of the individuals who make up the whole. Of the grieving mothers, of the sons facing the enemy's fire…they cannot relate to what a general faces. But they can relate to one warrior and his struggle against the foe. One father, and his quest for justice.

"When the dilation storm comes and your attack begins, entire worlds will be paralyzed while ships move freely. It is an event like no other. Imagine what a dramatic story it will be. The warlord triumphs over the commando at the edge of the storm. So again I ask: What symbol do you wish? One more general? Or do you wish to see Oul'sor scribe his name on the Wall of Victors? To show that even the greatest of the Empire's warriors is no match for your champion! To show that this great warrior found justice for himself, and that your people's justice against the Empire is becoming fact. Which symbol shall it be?"

The rational part of his mind, the part that had never trusted Indorai, knew that the hollow one was playing the crowd. But he could not find anger with it, even as he disrespected the dignity of this chamber. It was what he needed, and it was working.

"What do you suggest, Indorai?" another warlord questioned. "It would be most strange for the foe to accept a challenge to a battle of champions."

The hollow one extended an arm toward the forward podiums.

"Warlord Dolum has already crafted the solution."

"I have?" he questioned.

"Yes. Your plan to kidnap the youngest of the emperor's daughters as she visits the Time-Lost Galaxy. To hold her for ransom, and negotiation should your assault fail."

Dolum rose to his feet as shouting filled the chamber.

"How do you know of that, hollow one?" Dolum demanded. "Who speaks our secrets to you?"

Indorai's four voices laughed, drowning the rest of those in the chamber until silence reigned.

"Spymaster, you can only see me when I allow it. Why would you, of all warriors, believe I do not eavesdrop on you? Particularly when I have given you so much. So many weapons, so many secrets. Did you think I would not see for myself how you put them to use?"

Some of the warlords tried to shout, others shook their fists, but the hollow one purged the sound .

"When a member of the Solar Family travels, a commando always travels with them. They search for threats, look for actions such as that which you plan. They stand sentry, waiting to bring their might to the aid of royalty's bodyguards. And I just happen to know which of them shall accompany the young princess. So you see, this is not a matter to argue, but an opportunity to *seize*. You can claim the tool of your ransom, and demand entire worlds be surrendered without a fight. With the same act, you can deprive the emperor of his favorite commando, and grant Oul'sor his vek'thim. Only a fool would cast this prize aside. My words are finished."

Oul'sor looked to Dolum, who now served to hold order while Hahk'xess spoke as advocate.

"Very well," Dolum began. "The reasons for the challenge have been heard. Bring the darkness to us, and allow those who take Oul'sor's part to grant him light."

The hall darkened, and Oul'sor scanned the rows as one by one the lights descended. When all who wished for the light had received it, Dolum lowered himself to his chair.

"It's clear that you have your answer, Oul'sor."

CHAPTER
5A

THE PRINCESS HAD BEEN accorded the Crystal Palace, a spherical segment of the orbiting Web. The outer sphere of the palace existed as a ball of crystal crafted with a one-way transparency. Hovering in the center was the habitation sphere, ringed by numerous balconies. One of the Web's larger segments, the Crystal Palace was intended not only to house visiting royalty but their staff as well. In servants' quarters on the lower levels, Panzer sat quietly on a balcony.

Cigarette alight, he held the broken sword in his lap, while gazing toward Honor's Rise as it moved to keep itself within the sun's light. Nuset was right—not even two hundred years old and already he was an old man watching sunsets. He glanced down at the broken blade, and at the inscription it bore. With a scoff he tossed the weapon aside. He wasn't a bright candle anymore; he wasn't sure he ever was. His eyes turned back to Honor's Rise as it slipped out of sight. With the star eclipsed, the lights in the central globe came to life, prompting him to signal those in his quarters to deactivate.

He shouldn't be here. Somewhere in the Hourglass, or in one of the other Vaar galaxies, the Sovari Soma was in hiding. Throughout their territory the Vaar were preparing for war. All while he played vanguard to some little girl who would never be brought anywhere close to danger. What did it matter? Nuset was right—the thrill of fighting had passed for him. Only the warlords had brought him some measure of satisfaction, and among them only Oul'sor had put up enough of a fight to be a real challenge.

At least the blood lust of the Encephalon's influence had passed; sparring with Nuset had helped to send it off early. But he had learned from experience that was not the end. If the past was any indicator, this was the most difficult time, when parts of himself that he kept so tightly controlled crept to the surface.

"New conquests." He mouthed the words, and set his eyes on the highest balcony. Nuset was right about all of it. Battle no longer centered him, and he pushed the thought from his mind. While the kurai certainly had his suspicions, he couldn't know exactly what that thought was. What a challenge it would be, to pit his skills of infiltration against the Imperial

Guard. Could he do it? Slip in, and abscond with the princess without being caught?

Here they felt safe; their guard was down. He could slip in under cloak, ensuring she remained asleep with a little pressure on her mind. By the time she awoke, she'd be on his ship. By the time the Imperial Guard realized she was gone, his transponder would be trashed, and his ship untraceable.

He smiled to himself. Why stop with her? It would be cruel to take her away from her friends. Once he was in, nothing would stop him from taking all three. His smile widened at the thought of all three of them in his arms as he carried them to his bedchambers. He'd even taunt the Imperial Guard by leaving their clothes behind. The Empire would never catch him. He knew who they would send, where they would look.

He hissed, drawing in a breath of air to break the trance. What would Elsa think if she knew this was on his mind? What would Nuset?

Who was he kidding? Elsa would probably encourage him if it made him happy. And he had spent enough time on kurai worlds to know that for warriors, kidnapping the female they desired was expected. It was even ritualized, with a warrior having to sneak past the father and brothers of the bride-to-be to prove his worth.

He hung his head. Why? Why did the emperor have to use him for his little Encephalon chat, and then send him on this assignment? The old man knew the process did things to him afterward. Then having the gall to ask him to take care of the Imperial Rose; it was as if he were mocking him. Panzer sighed as he looked back to the horizon. His Majesty trusted him, had faith in him, his discipline. Yet here he was, betraying that trust by plotting how to abduct the man's daughter.

He popped his knuckles one at a time. Were his thoughts really so wrong? After all he had given the Empire, what had it netted him? A life as a widower, an exile, and a vagabond living on his ship. Did the Empire owe him nothing in return? After more than a hundred years as the emperor's errand boy, was one of his daughters too much to ask? All he had to do was sneak in there. The princess, the Twins, and a new journey together. It couldn't be any worse than this life.

They would hound him until the end of his days; no port would be safe harbor. His fellow commandos would be sent to hunt him down. That would not stop him; it was a big universe, he could go anywhere. His ship could run for ten years without overhaul—plenty of time to find a quiet little place to live beyond the Empire's reach. As soon as he had his prizes, he'd navigate to the center of a random galaxy, shut off the MID, and take up orbit around the central black hole. Time dilation would become his greatest ally. For his captives, it would be a relatively short stay, but upon leaving they would return to a universe that had long since passed them by. The trail would have gone cold, the search given up long ago.

"You want the Imperial Rose for yourself?"

Nuset had no idea what he was really asking. To feel her trembling as his hands roamed her body, knowing she belonged to him now... Yes, Henthis, he wanted to own her more than anything he had laid his eyes on. From the first time he had seen her as a grown woman, raising charity funds on astranet broadcast, he wanted to make her his. While his mind had smothered hers to stop her efforts at empathic intrusion, his thoughts had been of her body beneath his. She probably would not be keen on the idea, well aware she could have most any man she wanted. But that hardly mattered—might was the only true authority. He had the might, if he had the will...

The vision in the emperor's office returned to his mind. He had her in his grasp, but why the lantai disguise? Here in the Dominion was the most appropriate place for such a disguise, but why would he bother? He could look into the past almost at will, but seeing the future was another matter entirely and often he did not like what he found. Too often he ended up with questions he could not answer. If at some point in the future he had her, did that mean he had already made his choice? Was this moment of doubt simply a prelude to taking what was his? Maybe the Encephalon had done him a favor, stripping away the self-imposed shackles of restraint, so his actions could be as honest as his desires.

"Are you all right, sir?" Andira questioned.

He smiled.

"I'm fine," he whispered. "Have Rhoxx and the brothers made it back yet?"

"Not yet, sir; they are still making stealth departure from Acheron before the wormhole jump. Should I tell them to report early?"

"No, don't rush them."

"Yes sir."

He would have to wait at least until they arrived with his ship. They were sworn to follow him until the end of their days. They would not be happy about it, but they would follow. He'd destroy their lives; they would never see their own kind again except as enemies. He couldn't do that to them. Unless he took some time for them to find their own companions. Together they could start their own community, somewhere out there.

He would have to wait for the right moment, and when it came, seize it without ever looking back.

CHAPTER 5B

THOUGH HER EYES WERE closed, Simmonne was wide awake. Below a vaulted ceiling, she lay in a bed large enough for ten people. Despite the space available, the Twins were sandwiched against her on both sides. So paranoid was Jenna about protecting them, that when away from the Cathedral she would not allow them separate beds, let alone separate rooms. The mother hen slept under her own blanket at the foot of the bed. On a nearby table lay her body armor and pistols, ready to be equipped at a moment's notice. As if there were not thirty-six heavily armed gammas spread throughout her quarters to deal with intruders.

Simmonne opened her eyes and grabbed an invading hand before gently pushing it aside. Julie moaned quietly in her sleep. Every night the Twins would program their dream regulators to bring them visions of slumber steeped in erotica. When they were in their own room, that was not a problem. But sandwiched against her so that she could feel everything they did, Simmonne doubted she would be getting any sleep tonight.

She felt a pang of guilt. The Twins lived the same life as her. She had long ago learned to bury her feelings, and suffer them quietly. For them it had never been so easy. She loved them both, but she was not blind to their faults. There was only the faintest inkling of impulse control between them, virtually no shame. Though they resented Jenna's authoritarian grip on their lives even more than did Simmonne, it was likely the only thing that kept them from destroying themselves.

She worried for them. The court had paired them with her as supplementary pretty faces. If she ever managed to find her own life, what would happen to them? When the Imperial Rose was no longer a public figure, the court might no longer consider them worth keeping around. She would not let them destroy themselves, and had spent many nights contemplating her solution. The simplest solution would be to acquire her own title. Every scion of the emperor was given a fund they could use to colonize a star of their own. For those who didn't ascend to the crown, it offered an alternative: trade down to a lesser title, and gain a fiefdom once succession was decided. Few took the deal—but it was there.

She could colonize her own star, gain her own title, and financially they would worry for nothing. But she knew she could never control them; they required someone far more assertive. Someone who did not mind laying down the law to them, even if they could sense the annoyance or disappointment. Nor was she going to keep Jenna around to continue running their lives like an overprotective mother afraid to let her children grow up. Who was she kidding—she did not have the leadership skills to build a district from scratch.

Her thoughts turned to Steven. Her big brother was always there for her, even when he was not trying to be. He had given her the idea for a possible solution one night as she fantasized about his two beautiful brides. Jasmine, who so loved life. Natalie, so beautiful, so sensual yet dignified. By marrying both he had broken a few rules, and annoyed their fathers to no end. But with women outnumbering men six to one, having more than one bride was the norm to Sylvanni. If she found the right one to marry all three, she could be certain that they all remained together and that they lived as well as her. Their husband could handle the burden of keeping them out of trouble. From the way they responded to the emperor, Simmonne suspected they'd have far less trouble being obedient to a husband than to Jenna. But choosing just any Reichsylvannian would not do.

To Reichsylvannians, a man's place in society was to accrue wealth and status, and to be a positive influence on his community. Women were expected to make themselves into trophies for accomplished men as the most visible of their status symbols. Simmonne always expected to end up as some nobleman's trophy wife; it seemed a perfect match. But among these people, a wife was property; a husband could do anything to his wives he pleased. If she chose the wrong one, she would not pay the price alone. Though she did have plenty to work with. As an Imperial Princess, the Imperial Rose no less, there would be no more prestigious a bride. She could effectively have her pick of the litter.

That just left two problems: her father, and Jenna. The latter managed to frighten many of them off, though perhaps that was a favor. If they were not man enough to pursue her despite Jenna, they were probably not good enough. But then her father came in, and what few Jenna did not run off he did. Any mother-in-law would be envious of his ability to find fault in a potential suitor. She needed someone who would not be frightened of Jenna, and someone her father respected. That created a very short list, and trying to sort that list in her mind kept bringing her back to the same person. The same man she could not stop thinking about, no matter how she tried.

She had never had a man stick in her mind like this. Nor had the Twins for that matter; it was like something had broken in their heads. She had little doubt that if she removed their dream regulators and checked the programming, he was in there somewhere. Could it really be that easy? Had the exact man she needed simply fallen into her life?

She shuddered despite herself. The moment he looked at her at the breakfast table, when he grabbed her hand over the cheese platter, when he saw her in the pahri. The man frightened her; she could admit it to herself even if she would not to anyone else. But if he could make the Twins happy, she could make the best of it.

She began the process of extricating herself from the bed, moving slowly so as not to wake anyone else. She climbed over Julie before sliding out from under the sheets. Her pahri hung on a small rack nearby and she approached it with intent of dressing.

"Is everything all right?"

She almost screamed at the shock. Jenna was standing behind her, looking over her shoulder. She covered her heart with her hand to slow her breathing.

"I'm fine," she whispered. "I just figured I'd go out to the balcony for a while."

Jenna seized the pahri from her hands before dressing her.

"I won't be far; you can go back to bed," she offered. Jenna nodded, but Simmonne knew that until she returned to bed herself, her handmaiden would not. Six of her guards lined the balcony, including Isis, who greeted her.

"Everything is fine," she assured her as she walked along the pool that dominated the 100-meter balcony. She walked to the far edge, and glared down toward the one-way transparency of the outer globe to see the lights of the city below.

"Hostess," she began, "is Colonel Panzer awake?"

The AI managing her suit answered, sending a message to her NOD.

HOSTESS: No such individual by that name is present on grounds.

She rolled her eyes.

"Is the individual in number 2000 servants' quarters asleep?"

HOSTESS: Suite 2,000 is unoccupied.

Her fingernails rapped lightly on the marble railing. If she was going to seriously consider this, she needed to know a lot more about him. Her stomach churned in apprehension, but she turned to Isis.

"Isis, please tell Colonel Panzer I would like to speak with him."

Isis shot a glance to Jenna, whom Simmonne realized had followed her out.

"Milady, I do not think that is a good idea," Jenna remarked.

Jenna really did not like him, but why?

"Is there a problem?" Simmonne looked to her.

"I do not think it is appropriate," Jenna answered.

"I want to talk to him." She tried not to show the anger. "If he is going to be my vanguard, I want to know more about him."

Jenna and Isis exchanged looks. Neither was happy about the idea.

"If he is to have a hand in being responsible for my safety, I do not think it is too much to ask to have a conversation with him."

Jenna clearly did not like it, but for once it seemed she chose not to fight Simmonne on the issue and simply gave a nod to Isis.

"A few minutes," Jenna whispered. "After that I must insist that you return to bed."

Simmonne nodded and watched Isis step into a nearby router on the balcony's edge. After a minute Isis returned, and Simmonne felt a chill as the colonel stepped onto the balcony behind her.

He seemed to swagger with every step as Isis motioned him on. No longer in his uniform, he was dressed in black pants, wearing no shirt within his red vest. Suddenly she felt very small as he joined her at the balcony's edge.

"You called?" he asked, his voice sending a tingle down her spine.

Simmonne glanced to Isis and Jenna, less than a meter away.

"Alone," Simmonne whispered.

"Milady—" Jenna began.

"I wish to speak to him alone."

Jenna was annoyed, Isis was hesitant, but both nodded and backed away, motioning other guards to join them. They moved about halfway down the balcony. That was as alone as she and Panzer were going to get.

Simmonne tried to turn back to the colonel; she glanced at his eyes for a moment. His black irises made it difficult to tell, but she was fairly sure his pupils were dilated. At least he did not have the angry look from before. She found it easier to breathe by looking away, facing back toward the lit city below. She tried to look at him without turning her head, gazing out of the corner of her eye.

So many of her friends preferred slender men, lean and lithe, but that had never caught her eye. A man was supposed to be a hunter, something that could catch and overpower its prey so that it could not escape. She had no doubt he could do so. Particularly tall men were often built like rails, but not him. She turned her head slightly to glance at his arms, and shuddered as she recalled his look in the astranet chamber. His arms had to be thicker than her torso, with shoulders so wide she and the Twins could lay on him with room to spare.

"It is customary, when summoning someone, to have something to say," he remarked.

Now that he was here, she was not sure what she wanted to tell him. A quick attempt to read him proved as fruitless as before, so she continued trying to look without looking. A sound drew her attention and she watched him take a metal wallet from his vest and remove a cigarette. For a moment she thought it funny that a hand so large could manipulate the cigarette without breaking it. That habit would have to go. She almost laughed at herself—as if she could tell him what to do.

"Very well, if you have nothing to say." He began to turn away.

"Wait," she whispered. "I wanted to talk to you."

"What about?" He turned back to her.

She asked the first thing that came to mind. "Commandos are supposed to have scary code names. What's yours?"

"Crykeeper."

"What does it mean?"

"You'd have to ask the commandant. He's the one who hangs them on us."

"Have you ever served as vanguard before?"

"For your father, and for Steven."

"I get the sense that you and my brother know each other."

"We do."

She huffed quietly. If he was going to hide his feelings, he could at least say enough for her to analyze his words.

"How do you know each other? Is it only from being his vanguard?"

"We served together in the Outlands War, and knew each other before."

"So you helped him fight the Pillagers?" Few men could resist a pretty girl asking about their work.

"That's one way of putting it."

What was that supposed to mean?

"What were they like?" she asked. "The Pillagers?"

"You called me up to ask about something you could find with a simple astranet search?"

It annoyed him? Or had he figured out what she was up to? Damn it, she needed her empathy right now. Men were usually all too happy to try to impress her with their exploits.

"How strong are you?" she asked next. "I am told commandos are the strongest metapsions."

Perhaps a chance to boast would get him talking.

"That's classified."

Now he was just trying not to answer.

"You do realize I am a princess, right? I think I have clearance."

She watched as he turned his back to the balcony, momentarily panicking that he was about to leave. She heard a gentle scrape, and gasped, realizing that the furniture of the balcony had began to levitate. She began to count them, twenty tables, four chairs per table. She caught an angry glare from Jenna, who now sat in a hovering chair, her arms crossed and her face un-amused. Seemingly without effort Panzer rearranged the positions of the furniture before setting everything back down.

"That..." she stammered. "I've never seen anyone move so many objects at once."

"Commando," he said flatly.

"Well yes I know, but that's over a hundred items. Annabelle Chriss couldn't move that many! Even with cybernetic help."

"I am not Annabelle Chriss," he replied, before blowing smoke from his nostrils.

"That has to help in a fight at least."

"It takes a lot less effort to just shoot someone." He gave a shrug. "So did you call me up here to test my abilities?"

She turned back to the rail.

"I just wanted to get to know you." She was certain the words did not come out the way she wanted. "After all, you have a hand in my safety."

"You have thirty-six gammas and a psionic guard dog. I'm just an extra layer."

Her eyes moved back down to the city below.

"Are you from here, Colonel?"

"Accent give me away, did it?"

She nodded.

"This is my first time in the Dominion," she thought aloud. "I wish I could actually see it. I mean *really* see it, not the clean version everyone always has waiting for me."

"I doubt your guards would like that very much."

"They never let me do anything fun," she huffed.

She turned, realizing he was glaring at her again, hungry eyes causing her to shudder.

"Do you really want to see it?" he asked while raising an eyebrow.

She tore her eyes away.

"They say commandos are the strongest metapsions in the Empire. And that the strongest metapsions can see the future." She hesitated. "Can you?"

"If I could, wouldn't I know you were going to ask me that?"

"Did you?"

"Yes, but that's not why," he answered with a chuckle. "Yes, I can see the future. No, I can't tell you your future. That's not how it works."

"How does it work?"

"I see…flashes of things, past and future. Sometimes it's a person, or a thing. I'll know I'm about to shoot an enemy as he comes around a corner, before he actually does. Or I'll pick up a gun, and see myself in a firefight I hadn't anticipated. Other times I'll see a person, and know something will happen. But it's not as useful as you might think."

"How can it not be?" she asked incredulously "That would seem like a huge advantage."

He was silent for a moment, his fingers tapping on the rail.

"I see things that *will* happen, not things that might. Nothing I've ever seen did not happen, and nothing I've seen has given me agency to change it. Sure, I've seen things that I could have changed, but when the time came, I was not willing to. The universe abhors a paradox. Some believe that we can only see things that cannot be changed because changing them would then create said paradox."

"What do you believe?"

"There's still a lot about metapsionics we don't understand. We don't understand why only the strongest can see the past or future. We don't know what actually causes a person to be a metapsion. We do know that a metapsion's mind"—he paused—"doesn't experience space-time like everyone else. It could just be that time for us is nothing more than perception, and all time is a moment. All things are always happening from the beginning of the universe to the end. When we see the future, perhaps we are just remembering it."

He smiled.

"I don't know. The only time it really helps is when I see something good, then I at least can look forward to it."

"If you ever see something that involves me, will you tell me?"

He didn't answer, but instead turned to look down at the city.

"Colonel?"

His failure to answer caused her to shift her weight between her feet.

"Do you want to see it?" His eyes moved from the skyline to her. "Truly, want to see it?"

Her heart trembled, as she tried and failed to find his eyes again.

"Yes Colonel, I do."

What was she saying? She watched him take a step back from the rail.

"Look at me," he directed.

She turned to him, but could not bring her eyes over his chest. His right hand danced over a device of some sort on his left arm.

"What is that?" she whispered.

"Mobile router," he said with a smile. "A little commando toy."

Suddenly he reached out with one of those enormous hands, two fingers curling under the ring holding her top together. With a firm grasp he pulled her close, the fabric of her outfit protesting as it was nearly torn.

"Take your hands off of her!" Jenna, Isis, and her guards had all shouted in unison.

Her heart raced as the world around her warped, the balcony faded away, and soon she found herself outdoors in the darkness. Night air bit at her skin, leaves rustled around her. They now stood on a public router amid a quiet park. The park itself stood atop a tower, surrounded by the spires of skyscrapers.

Panic charged through her heart; her arms and legs trembled. He had just warped her out. Her guards had set up equipment to prevent that. How, how did he do that? Oh God, what was happening?

"W-where are we?" she whispered. She could not even see the *Rothburg*, merely the Web in the night sky.

For a moment he said nothing.

"You said you wanted to see the place," he finally answered. "Here you are."

What had she done? What had he just done? She began to panic, but his grip on her top did not let her move away.

"Relax." For a moment his voice was calming to her mind. Until she realized how strong he really was to so casually push his voice through the 4CM of her tiara. A whole new level of panic rose when she realized that she was not even wearing it. Her mind was naked, and she was alone with a metapsion of enormous ability. What if he read her mind, and learned what she had been thinking?

"Relax," he repeated.

"C-can you take me back?"

He pulled her tighter against him, while the other hand slid under her chin to force her eyes up. His eye contact caused her to tremble, paralyzing her.

"Do you really want to go back?" he whispered into her thoughts. *"Or do you want to seize this moment?"*

She found no words. The only thing she knew about this man was that he frightened her. Now she had just put herself at his mercy. A hundred thoughts were racing through her mind, and she began to blubber before he laid a finger over her lips.

She calmed herself. If he wanted to hurt her, he could have done it already. She could be brave. An opportunity like this might not come again.

He retrieved something from his pocket, and in a moment was affixing a small disc to the ring of her top.

"What are you doing?" she whispered.

"You won't be incognito as yourself," he explained. "This is a bozeman's disc, quite useful if you want to look like someone or something else."

She felt a small tingle move over her body as the device came to life. He took a step back, and she shuddered feeling the weight of his mind against hers. Her entire being seemed to contract, as if he had just lain across her, smothering her beneath him. She had to force herself to breathe, and accept the vision he placed in her mind. He was projecting, feeding her eyes the information from his own.

"I'm…I'm a lantai," she stammered, seeing herself. She moved slowly, examining herself through his eyes. The colonel's disc had shrouded her in hologram images. Her hair and eyes had turned inhumanly orange, matching the brilliant new coloration of her slightly altered pahri. On her ears, she could see the change in shape and addition of three points.

"With a body like yours, you won't go unnoticed," he explained. "But no one will think much of a random man out with his favorite pet."

She smiled involuntarily at the compliment.

"So, where are we going?"

"A little club I know of," he answered, "on the southern continent."

"Is it a nice place?"

He nodded.

"Then…" She hesitated.

"Yes?"

"Can we go somewhere else?"

What was she saying?

"Looking to slum it, are we?"

She nodded.

"I think I know just the place," he said with a smile. "Andira, check availability. Three Fat Guys, Lonheim District."

"Current patronage is sparse," a computerized voice answered.

She held her breath as he reeled her back in against him.

"You know, we'll both get in a lot of trouble for this."

He looked down at her with a wiry grin.

"Then let's make it worthwhile. Bukhail!" His projection of the last word caused her to flinch.

He led her to the edge of the park, to a series of catwalks extending out around the perimeter of the large building. There a conveyor now waited as others whistled through the air beyond on the path of invisible roads. His hand moved to the back of her neck, his fingers encircling her with length to spare. As they approached the conveyor, she shivered at the cold wind biting at her excess of bare skin and moved against the warm body nearby. He guided her to the vehicle before sitting down inside.

With her hands on her knees, she began tapping her heels apprehensively.

"Destination?" the conveyor questioned.

"Three Fat Guys, Lonheim District."

The vehicle began moving. Crossing her legs, Simmonne tapped her fingers on her knee. Nervousness was now competing with excitement. No Jenna, no guards, just an evening out to do as she pleased. In the corner of her vision she saw the colonel reach for her, and flinched. His arm slid behind her before wrapping around. He pulled her across the seat to him as if she weighed nothing.

Where most men were apprehensive about her catching them looking, he had gone from shamelessly leering to touching. Should she say something? Was this the right way to act on a first date?

A first date? She questioned her inner monologue. Is that what this was? Only once had she ever been on anything even resembling a date, all properly supervised by Jenna and the Imperial Guard. Now she was alone, and she realized she had no idea what she was supposed to do. This would be so much easier if she could just sense what he was feeling.

"Relax," he whispered, prying her hands apart from one another to hold one in his.

She had to take a breath to do so, but one thing she did know for sure: It felt good to be touched. Leaning against him, she closed her hand on his.

CHAPTER
5C

B EYOND THE ASTRANET, INTERGALACTIC communication was not an instantaneous affair. Messages had to be sent on long-wave warp streams bouncing from one relay to the next. When one accounted for the time delays of message travel and that of this galaxy, too much time had passed. Clearwater had missed the funeral. He stood in a misting rain, waiting for his ride. A favor called in by Lieutenant Brower would get him close enough to link-in, where at least astranet communications were now up and running.

His ride descended through the clouds, a small warship known as a monitor.[15] A hundred meters separated the tips of its flying-wing body. Like all Armadas warships it was painted in a brilliant white with golden trim. As it touched down, the weight of its kilosteel body elicited a groan from the reinforced landing platform. Clearwater approached the forward landing skid where the pilot had descended to meet him. The more pilots he saw, the less distinct they seemed. A somewhat short, wiry man maneuvered toward him.

"Lieutenant Clearwater?"

"That's me." He shook the offered hand.

"Commander Ike Zang," the pilot answered. "I'll get you close enough to Avalon to link-in, and give you as much privacy as I can. I'll only be able to give you about an hour."

"An hour, sir?"

"Sorry, that's all we could swing, son."

He nodded.

"I understand."

---

15   That monitors are warships is a common misconception among those outside of the Solar Armadas. Monitors are in fact not warships and are not counted among their number. Instead, monitors, along with outriggers and sloops, are counted as "pickets"." This misconception stems from the fact that unlike outriggers and sloops, monitors are built for direct combat rather than scouting or support functions.

He followed the captain up the ladder and into the cockpit. A white-haired gamma nodded in greeting while the captain pulled out a chair from the wall and motioned Clearwater to sit. Soon after the ship was moving, rising out of the atmosphere to set a course for Avalon. Clearwater glared into his NOD, waiting for the signal. The Minotaur-class ship was known as a speed demon. The trip would not take long. A hard thump rattled through the deck as the transpatial drive engaged, generating the wormhole to take the ship to its destination.

QUERYING LOCAL ASTRANET…CONNECTION ESTABLISHED.

"Hour starts now," the commander said. "You're good to call."

Clearwater nodded before bringing up a map of the Empire. He focused on a small satellite of the Dominion Galaxy, a dwarf galaxy called Troy. He zoomed in to touch a small world called Thespis, a fairly young colony with its third generation of settlers. He dialed in the number before closing his eyes, leaning back and exhaling.

His vision was dark for all but his NOD.

PINGING DESTINATION…

In a flash he stood in a familiar room, observing his surroundings as a hologram projection. A single face greeted him, a young redhead barely old enough for a pahri, but wearing a black mourning dress. Her brow furled at him as she spoke.

"Hi Jonathan." Her use of his full name was not encouraging.

"Melanie," he said with a smile, walking to her and wrapping hologram arms around her. He did not feel her reciprocate. "How are you?"

"I'm fine," she whispered slowly, stepping away.

"Where is everyone?"

"Asleep, it's 2:00 in the morning here."

He swore under his breath.

"I'm sorry, this was the only time I could call."

She cut him off. "Will you be coming home?"

He shook his head.

"I can't; they've frozen leave for all units in the region. I've asked for dispensation for bereavement, but haven't gotten an answer. I hate to wake them up, but I don't know when I'll be able to make a live call again. Would you mind?"

She shook her head.

"No," she said firmly. "It took me all night to get them to sleep. I'm not waking them up."

"Melanie." He hesitated. "Please? I just want to see them."

"No, Jonathan," she answered. "You're just going to rile them up, and once again I'll have to deal with them when you're gone."

"Melanie, I want to see them. It could be weeks before I can call again. Wake them up please."

"Don't you even think about telling me what to do," she spat, leveling a finger at him. "You gave up that right when you ran away to the Legionnaires, and dumped them all on Nana and me."

He winced, cut by the words.

"Melanie, I wasn't—"

"Weren't what?" she barked. "Running away from this because you couldn't deal with it? You know how hard it was for Nana to keep an eye on all of them? You know how hard it is to explain to a bunch of children why they can't talk to you? You know Stephanie asks me every day if you're still alive? You know when you didn't show up for the funeral they all started crying because they figured you must be dead too?"

"I…" he stammered. "I didn't even receive word until after—"

"And whose fault is that?" Her voice rose to a shout. "You're the one who ran to the other side of the universe!"

His cheek twitched.

"Melanie, how many times are we going to have this argument?"

"We never finished this argument."

"Melanie, someone has to pay the goddamn bills!" he shouted, his entire body shaking as his fists clenched in anger. He drew in deep breaths, trying to calm himself. He forced the tears from his eyes, forced himself to speak calmly.

"You like having name brand clothes so you can stand out when boys look at you? You like going to live events so you can meet quality people? You want Stephanie to be able to do the same? You want Ryan and David to be able to afford an education, so that maybe when they're men, they can do more than live on stipend?"

She lowered her eyes as he slowly composed himself.

"Nana's gone. Dad and Zach are dead, and no one knows where Mother is. That just leaves me. Thanks to Dad, the Legionnaires had to let me into Hell's Gate—that was my only option. Do you think this is how I wanted things to be?"

She covered her mouth, gazing at the floor. But he realized the sound of crying he now heard was not coming from her. He turned, scanning the den, until he saw three little faces peering in from a doorway.

"Hey guys." His voice softened. "Come here."

Two boys and a girl approached slowly, pouting as he knelt to extend his arms.

"Why are you fighting?" his youngest sister Stephanie asked as he embraced her.

"Oh Froggy, don't you worry about that," he answered, kissing her forehead. "Big brothers and sisters fight sometimes, you know that."

"Welcome home." She sniffled as his brothers joined in the hug and he looked slowly to each pair of brown eyes.

"I'm not back," he lamented. "This is a hologram."

"You're not back?" she asked, threatening to turn the tears back on.

"Where are you?" David, his youngest brother, asked.

"Well, right now I'm on a monitor. It's a small ship used to shoot other ships. That flew me close enough to space-station Avalon so I could call and see you."

"You're in a Minotaur?" Ryan questioned, perking up.

Clearwater smiled. Only ten years old and Ryan already knew exactly what he wanted to do with his life.

"Yes I am. I'm sitting in the shotgun chair now."

"Can I see it?" he asked.

"Sure." He toggled switches in his NOD to send his brother the feed from his biologic eyes. "There's the pilot. Be polite, wave back at him. Then there's the Girl in Back, and you can see the cockpit."

"Neat," Ryan whispered, devouring the image with his eyes. "Can I talk to the pilot?"

"I don't think we should bother him. He's busy operating the ship."

Ryan opened his mouth before closing it and nodded.

"When are you coming home?" David spoke up, and Clearwater tried not to frown.

"I'm not sure. My deployment is at least six months. But after that I can request transfer to another station. If I can get a good one with on-base housing, you can come live with me."

"Let's not get their hopes up yet," Melanie said, collecting them in her arms.

"So, you're not coming back?" Stephanie began to sniffle.

"Honey, it's just going to take a while. But I'll be back—"

"No you won't!" she cried as the tears broke loose. "Daddy didn't come back. Mommy didn't come back. Zach didn't—"

He moved forward to take her back in his arms.

"I *will*," he whispered. "What did I tell you about making promises?"

She wiped her eyes.

"That you never break them."

"That's right," he whispered. "And I promise I'll come back. Understand?"

She nodded and returned his embrace.

CMDR ZANG: Sorry to cut into your conversation, Lieutenant, but I'm afraid you'll have to wrap it up.

LT CLEARWATER: Sir, you said I'd have an hour.

CMDR ZANG: Sorry LT, but I've just received a recall order. We just had another refugee skirmish incident at the border. All monitors have been put on alert.

He scowled at the message.

LT CLEARWATER: I understand.

He looked back to his siblings, anxiously awaiting him to speak again.

"I'm sorry guys, something's come up. I have to go now."

"No," Stephanie whimpered. "You just got here."

"I know." He forced a smile. "But orders are orders."

She nodded, hugging him tighter while he looked to Ryan.

"Ryan, you're the man of the house while I'm gone. Take care of your little brother, and your sisters. David, be good and help your brother."

His father had said the words to him, so he said them to Ryan. They tasted of bile on his tongue. What did he know of telling someone to act like a man?

His brothers nodded.

"You have my account number," Clearwater said to Melanie. "The garrison gives me everything I need. So don't hesitate to take what you need."

She said nothing, and simply pulled the others to her.

"They say the astranet will be fully online here in a couple weeks. I'll call again as soon as I can."

Both of his brothers raised their hands in salute, and he returned the gesture as his hologram faded away.

The image of the Minotaur's cockpit returned to his view, and he sighed while leaning back. Ryan and Sarah, they didn't understand, couldn't understand. But Melanie…it was worse; she hated him, he saw it in her eyes. He wanted to cry, but he held back, resting his face in his hands. They needed him, and he wasn't there. Through his fingers he glared at his pants. To wear the brown, it made him so proud. But on the way back, it did no such thing.

CHAPTER
6A

THE PRINCESS HAD SAID nothing since sitting in the conveyor. It did not take a telepath to tell why; poor girl was so nervous that with an arm around her he could feel her heart racing. So this was it, this was why he had seen her in disguise. She went with him more or less willingly, and was now sitting with his arm around her. What had he done?

There would be hell to pay for this. Without her tiara, her guards had no direct means to track her. By using his mobile router he left no log in the astranet for them to track him. The moment he warped, Andira had created dozens of false routing logs, showing them warping to planets across the Dominion. The panic attack they must be having, trying to figure out which one was real. At the moment, they did not even know who to alert to aid in the search.

His brow curled in an expression bordering on rage.

She was his now. It had been a sloppy improvisation, but he had gotten her out. Now that he had her, her fate was sealed. He would allow her this last night out with the illusion of freedom. Tomorrow, she'd be starting her new life as his favorite...*slave* was such a vulgar term. High Kings referred to lantai who served carnal functions as frilla. Yes, she would be his favorite frilla. It served her right for being stupid enough to come with him. He'd even given her the chance to go back. The only question now was did he want to bend her mind to his whims, or enjoy the process of her coming to accept her fate?

His eyes moved to her hand in his, and the feeling of her thumb gently rubbing against his skin. His expression softened; he needed to be gentle. She was so meek. Soft but authoritative would likely be enough for her to comply. When his auxiliaries arrived with his ship, he would make the good faith effort to grab her friends. If they were still in the Crystal Palace, the timing would have to be perfect. But he could jump in, grab them, and warp out. The Imperial Guard certainly would not expect such a bold move after having just taken the princess. He smiled at the thought of all three of them together, sharing a leash.

"You are so quiet," she whispered.

"Idle mouth, busy mind."

"What were you thinking about?" she pressed, quickly scanning him, likely hoping he would not notice. As if he were going to tell her what was really going on. He would ease her into it, wait until she was on his ship to let her new reality sink in. But in the meantime, he could titillate her.

"Dirty things," he whispered.

"Like what?" The shift in her feelings surprised him. She really wanted to know.

"I'm thinking of you wearing a lot less," he whispered.

She gave a nervous giggle.

"I can't wear much less than I already am," she answered.

"You say that as if I'd let you wear anything," he countered, and she squeezed his hand a little tighter. He brought his other hand up to jiggle the collar of her pahri. "Well, this you could keep."

"Just my collar?" she murmured.

"Well, you need something for me to attach a leash."

"Colonel, I…don't think we know each other well enough to be talking that way."

"Nonsense. It's only as titillating because we barely know each other," he answered. She would learn not to talk back another time. Assuming he even allowed her the means to do so.

He felt her take another swipe at his feelings. She was wasting her time; no one had ever been able to sense him. But he would let her try. Her feelings, on the other hand, were coming in quite clearly. Her nervousness was tapering away from fear, moving toward that common to new experiences. How cute—she wasn't sure he was serious. She'd know how serious he was when his ship arrived, and just before taking her aboard, he ripped her current attire apart.

"Now look who's quiet."

"Keep talking," she answered. "Please?"

Deprived of her empathy, she was almost certainly doing her best to analyze everything he said. He could work with that; all he had to do was choose words to push her mind in the right direction. He opened his mouth before a torrent of pain surged through his skull, biting at the back of his eyes. Why did it have to be now? He released her hand to find the cigarette wallet in his jacket and remove one of the sticks. She gave him an objectionable look as he pulled the lighting tab and took a puff. Her expression soon changed when she realized it was neither tobacco nor marvat.

"What is that?" she asked.

"It's…a painkiller," he admitted. "An old injury, I have to dose it once in a while."

"You're in pain?" She began to lean away. Where did she think she was going? On reflex he pulled her back against him. She didn't seem to mind.

"Not as long as I have these. It's the easiest way for me to take it. I turn off my lungs' toxin filters and inhale."

"Can your nanites not do it?"

He shook his head, circling his temple with the cigarette before taking another puff.

"Stuff is all jumbled up in the goo," he explained. "Things are cross-wired and jury-rigged. Nanites can't really uncoil it, and no doctor wants to touch it."

Though she did not say it, he could tell the smoke was bothering her. This was her last night of freedom; he'd indulge her. He took a final deep drag before cracking the window and tossing it outside.

"Do you mind if I ask what happened?" She glared up with those pretty blue eyes, expecting a story. He was not going to ruin a good evening with it.

"Ask me another time," he answered, reclaiming her hand. "I believe we are talking about you."

She shuddered, still deliciously nervous about the unknown.

"Please keep talking," she whispered.

The conveyor began to slow, moving onto a physical road wrapping around a cluster of skyscrapers.

"We're here," he announced as the vehicle came to a stop.

"Thank you for riding RBS; we have arrived at your destination."

He stepped out and offered his hand. For a moment she hesitated.

"You're not afraid, are you?" he said. Her expression changed, and she took his hand, allowing him to guide her out. They now stood on a catwalk branching from one of the towers, more than a kilometer above ground. With little to shield her from a strong breeze, she moved up against him, eliciting a grin.

"Three Fat Guys?" she questioned, reading the hologram where an obese human, kodaz, and buun were visible.

He simply nodded and guided her to the door, where an obese kodaz waited.

"Five troy entry fee," the kodaz said before looking at the lantai. "You pet goin' be eatin'?"

He nodded.

"D'en she be free."

He waved his hand over the payment terminal before leading her through the doors, and up a set of stairs. Loud music played from the hologram of a kurai band surrounded by a facsimile of lantai dancers. This place was far from seedy by his definition; he would not take the princess to such a place. But compared to which she was accustomed, it would do. He could already sense her apprehension. He waited for her to object, but even with the mixed odor of booze, tobacco, and marvat she said nothing. Instead she quietly scanned the bar with her eyes.

Only a handful of patrons were present at this late hour. Nine lantai were present with their patrons. Six sat on pillows at their masters' feet, while the other three dressed in more vivid colors sat in the laps of those they were with. He lead her to an empty table in one of the bar's nine corners and pulled out a chair. Her eyes remained on the lantai in the room as he sat with his back to the wall. Curious as to what she would do, he watched as she turned back to realize he was sitting. She spoke once before leaning closer to speak over the music.

"Am I supposed to…?" She pointed to the pillow by his chair.

He shook his head and motioned her closer. As she approached he reached out, wrapping his arm around her and pulling her down into his lap. The vision made sense now—her presence and her disguise—but the events had yet to come to pass.

"The ones on pillows are servitors. You're disguised as a pet."

She eyed the lantai again.

"What exactly is the difference?"

He was fairly certain she knew. She was giving him a reason to talk, trying to get him to say something, anything so she could examine his words. For now, he would indulge her.

"Look where they're sitting versus where you are," he explained. "Lantai may think of themselves as slaves, but they do have a sort of hierarchy. Servitors are at the bottom and do menial labor—supervise automatech, secretarial work, what have you. Above them are seniors who do the same work but are more experienced. Then you have pets, who are generally the prettiest and often kept as companions. Since they have their masters' favor, they are at the top."

She nodded before shifting to make herself more comfortable in his lap. He smiled to himself, wondering if she would connect the dots on her disguise.

A small automatech buzzed from the counter at the room's center, coming to hover over the table.

"What can I get you this evening?" the machine inquired.

"Large pizza," he ordered.

"Large pie, what on it?"

"Pork, pepperoni, bratwurst, three-cheese blend, breaded bacon, and a side tray of crushed peppers."

The princess began to speak before covering her mouth. She turned to him and flashed a grin.

"Master, may I have only vegetables on mine?"

His heart skipped a beat.

"Of course. Bot, amend order. Previous toppings on one half, vegetarian special on the other."

"Order amended. Nutritional antimatter on one half, the food that food eats on the other. Would you like anything to drink?"

"Nuke me, and NegCal cola for her."

"Your estimated wait time is ten minutes," the drone remarked before buzzing away.

"Getting into character?" he asked.

Her grin widened and she giggled.

"Why not?"

He laid a hand on her shoulder and pulled her closer to whisper in her ear.

"Give it time, and that will be your only word for me."

Half a smile played on his face as she shuddered in his lap, before leaning back against him.

CHAPTER
6B

S IMMONNE'S HEART HAD NOT slowed since the colonel took her from the *Rothburg*. A thousand thoughts were racing through her mind, yet she couldn't find the means to speak them. She turned, shifting her legs around to sit across his lap and lean into him. She smiled, enjoying the feeling of his body against hers. She took a moment to glance around the bar. While a few had noticed when she entered, and she was attracting the occasional look, she was mostly being ignored. Out in a public place, people were acting as if she was not there. No one was pointing, none were asking to take a picture or requesting an autograph. In the emotions of the room she sensed no shock or surprise. No one knew who she was.

The automatech brought their drinks, and taking hers, she took a sip before setting it on the table. She wanted to talk to him, but what was she supposed to say? What did people talk about on a date? Should she ask him about his work? Or would he not want to talk about it? As a commando he had no family for her to ask about. Why did she have to find herself speechless? The most powerful metapsions were brilliant people. What if she said the wrong thing and made herself look stupid?

She closed her eyes and focused on getting back into character. So long as she played the part, she knew something to do besides sit quietly. For a moment she pondered if he had chosen her disguise as an excuse to get her in his lap. With the feel of his body against hers, she did not care. She reached up, hesitating before slipping a hand under his vest and rubbing his chest. She tried to remember how she had seen lantai pets behave, and mimic accordingly. So she gently traced her fingers over his chest, pressing against the hard muscle.

He glanced down at her to make eye contact from which she retreated, and the arm around her shifted. She gasped, feeling his hand slip under the waist-chain of her pahri, and his palm came to rest on her bare hip. His other hand moved to her thigh, where he began to trace his fingertips up and down.

Her breath came so rapidly she was becoming lightheaded. Should she ask him to stop? She knew she should, that was not a question. Did she want him to? Maybe, if he did not take it too far…but how far was that? She tried to read him, to sense something, but still she could not. But if his expression was any indicator, he was enjoying himself.

"Colonel," she whispered, prompting him to offer an ear, "you won't tell anyone about this, will you?"

"Not a soul."

He smiled and she relaxed slightly. No matter how much she wanted otherwise, tomorrow she would be the Imperial Rose again, and she had a reputation to protect. With her full attention on his hands she closed her eyes, enjoying the music and the sensation of being touched. When she felt his hand leave her thigh, her hand shot out, grabbing on to his forearm. She could not get the words out, but found herself hoping that he was reading her mind.

When his hand did not return she opened her eyes and he motioned toward the table. The automatech had brought their pizza. She scowled at the dish. Food was so far from what she wanted right now. Reluctantly she released his arm and watched him take a piece before doing the same. With a small bite she found that it was better than she had expected from such a place.

"How is it?" he asked, taking another bite.

"It's good," she answered with a nod. She held her piece with one hand and moved the other to the hand still on her hip, hoping that the presence of her hand would ensure his remained.

While nibbling on the pizza she looked around the bar, surveying the other patrons. One man at a far end sat with two women. She could not see their garters to determine if they were wives or girlfriends, but the man had an arm around each. They were putting on a show for him, kissing and pawing at each other. At another table a pet was sitting in her patron's lap, firmly gyrating on him. She realized that the lantai was giving her master a lap dance. Simmonne giggled at the thought of doing the same for the colonel. Even if she had no idea what she was doing. Whatever anyone said about Reichsylvannians, at least they spent time in the real world. Where others across the Empire spent so much of their free time stupefied in the astranet's virtual reality, Reichsylvannians spent their time in actual reality and with each other.

The colonel noticed none of this, or did not care. Of course he didn't—he was Reichsylvannian, nothing happening here was abnormal behavior. Instead he was continuing to eat. Her eyes narrowed on the pizza in his hand, annoyed that it was receiving more of his attention than her. Not about to take second place to a pizza, she grabbed his attention by moving. He held her steady as she moved to straddle his thighs, facing him.

Her heart was racing again, and unable to look him in the eyes, she nibbled away the last of her slice. Slowly she leaned back to place her hands on his thighs, and forced herself to make eye contact briefly. She knew then she had recaptured his focus.

Perhaps he took her meaning, perhaps he read her mind; either way, he tossed his slice to the side. After deliberately cleaning his hands with a napkin, he reached past her to close his hands around her forearms. When he leaned down, she realized he was about to kiss her. She turned her head away. She'd never kissed anyone to whom she was not related. One potential suitor had tried, before Jenna had separated them. She tried to slow her breath, becoming lightheaded once more.

"Look at me," he whispered.

She hesitated, but he remained close, his breath on her cheek. This was why she had seized the moment, why she came with him. As he leaned closer she closed her eyes, before feeling his lips against hers. She kept her lips together against the contact, and tried to move her hands but he held them firmly in place. Hesitantly she surrendered her lips. She felt his tongue against hers and relaxed, and unsure of what exactly to do, she remained still.

When he broke away she sat quietly for a moment, still tasting his lips on hers. She barely knew this man—didn't know him at all really—and he was doing as he pleased with her. He had just given her first kiss, what would he do next? She was not going to wait to find out. She leaned toward him, and he tilted his head back. She tried to follow, but his hold on her arms kept her in place. She realized he was toying with her; all she could do was follow his movements until he let her in.

She tried to control her thoughts. If she allowed them to become too racy and he was reading her mind, it might come off as an invitation. Reichsylvannian women were well known for being chaste until marriage. Would he lose interest if she made things too easy for him? Why was she debating this? She wanted more. She could not rationalize it, and did not care to. She moved for his lips again, and this time he allowed her to close the distance.

When he broke contact she sat quietly, staring at his chest while his eyes moved over her. What was he feeling? Was he happy? Aroused? She could not sense it, but looking up at his expression told her enough. He had the Imperial Rose wrapped around his finger and was quite pleased with himself.

He shifted to hold both of her wrists in one hand and reached past her to take a drink of his beer. She peeked back through the dim light at the dancing lantai, studying her movements, and the expression on her master's face. He was certainly enjoying himself, so she watched the movements carefully, memorizing the patterns.

"See something you like?"

Something about his voice commanded her head to whip around, as surely as if he had taken her chin in his hand. When she did not answer he took another sip of his beer, which drew her eye. Realizing she was looking at the beverage, he tilted it toward her.

"Care to try?"

She did, but she couldn't. She had never had alcohol before, and her judgment was already in shambles. She simply shook her head, quietly looking at him. She gave another glance back to the dancing lantai. A lap dance was certainly not first-date behavior, but she did not care. The alternative was to continue sitting in silence. She was not the Imperial Rose tonight; she was simply a pet in her master's lap. It was time to live a little, for it would likely be a very long time before an opportunity like this came again. She sat up straight and slowly pulled against his grip. He allowed her arms to slip free.

He had quietly watched her the entire time. The thousand questions she wanted to ask were gone. Her body tensed as she grabbed hold of his vest and closed her eyes, readying herself for what she was about to do. No sooner had she reached her focus than it was shattered by his hand on her hip, and suddenly she was lost once more.

"Relax," he whispered, his voice soothing her mind. His other hand was back to tracing patterns on her thigh.

She let out a nervous exhale. *Sit quietly or do something*. She chose to begin sliding her hips back and forth in his lap.

What was she doing? She did not behave like this. She felt his hand leave her thigh and a moment later he slipped a finger through the loop of her collar, giving a firm tug. Pulled forward, she quickly latched on to his arm to stabilize herself, but did not stop.

She bit her lip, feeling him respond to her. She knew her face was red, but the half-smile on his face could not hide what was going on behind his eyes. She had him captivated, and wherever they truly were, they were in their own world now.

Was he reading her mind? Was he doing this to her?

Her body came to an abrupt halt. He could have been manipulating her mind this entire time. He could have even put the impulse in her head to sneak out with him. He could be putting all this confusion into her mind. Her heart raced as she began to panic. If only she could sense him, she could know what was happening here.

"I didn't say you could stop," he whispered.

His words went in one ear and out the other; they were not what spoke to her mind. For an instant she felt something…something from him. When he said it, for just a moment, she felt…desire, and aggression. She was moving again before she realized it, holding tighter to his arm. She had to sense him again, she would. She bore down harder on him, while her mind pushed at his.

Simmonne giggled when the hand on her collar pulled her down tighter, and held firm. He was keeping her exactly where he wanted her.

"Would you like anything else?"

She shot an irate glare at the automatech.

"Go away!" she barked, swatting at the machine. Though she missed, she threw so much into the strike that she would have fallen out of the colonel's lap were it not for the hand on her collar.

The machine fluttered away and she turned back to the colonel, and the wiry grin on his face. She was not sure how long a lap dance was supposed to last, but she was not stopping until she tasted his feelings again. She used his arm for leverage, her own excitement rising each time he tugged on her collar. But she sensed nothing. Just as before, he was a total blank. She was going to get to him, one way or another—she had to.

His grip on her collar slackened; the firmness beneath her receded. Her eyes flew open and she realized he had his face covered…he was in pain again. That was not going to stop her! Her hands fiddled with the pockets of his vest until she found the cigarette wallet. Her hands were trembling as she pried it open to seize one of the sticks and press it to his lips. He lowered his hands and glanced at her before taking the cigarette and pulling the lighting tab.

While he took a puff she leaned away from the smoke, tapping her fingers anxiously on his knees. He sat with his eyes closed, taking deep drags and exhaling through his nose. While he did she glanced around, to realize the other patrons were on their way out, leaving them alone in the bar. She wanted to urge him to smoke faster, but held her tongue.

The break allowed her mind to wander. They only had so much time before they'd have to go back to face the music. Every minute he spent puffing was one she was not feasting on those emotions he was keeping so deeply buried. This was taking too long. She bit her lip as an idea crossed her mind, and she scanned the bar once more to be sure they were now alone.

Her hands moved to the ring holding her top together, and she watched his eyes as she turned it slowly. She hesitated, blushing at the hungry eyes glaring at her. She knew she shouldn't, but the need to sense him again was too strong to let reason interfere. She twisted the ring fully, covering her breasts with her arm as the top came open, hoping to tease him into lowering his guard.

He took a final breath from the cigarette before snuffing it out. She jumped as his hands clamped down on her forearms, and slowly brought them over her head until he held both of her wrists in one hand. For a moment she tried to free her wrists, trying to bring her hands down to cover herself. She realized then she may have started something she wasn't ready to finish.

"Nervous?" he whispered.

"N-no." She tried to sound resolute but was well aware of her failure.

"I think you are," he taunted.

He was right, and this was going too far. Now very aware of the vulnerable position she had put herself in, she tugged harder against him.

That was not going to get her anywhere; his grip was far too strong. His fist tightened, not enough to truly hurt, but enough for her to know that she was not going to slip free. Panic set in, but she was paralyzed by it. What was she going to do? What was he going to do?

Her body went stiff as his other arm moved, and reached past her. With an arm still holding her firmly in place, he took his drink from the table and sipped slowly, still eyeing her. He could at least say something, anything, anytime now.

He finished the drink before setting the glass on his armrest. His fingers dipped into it to seize a piece of ice. What was he doing? Her eyes flew open wide and she let out a gasp, feeling the chill of the ice against her breast.

"Colonel…" she hissed, while her back arched. Then she felt it: the desire, the satisfaction. That was it! The man had his emotions muted to her, but the predator inside was not so easily caged. Exposed and at his mercy, she had lured it out.

"Something wrong?" he teased her, tracing circles around her nipple with the ice.

She shook her head while he alternated between her breasts.

She knew she shouldn't have let it go this far, how low an opinion he had to have of her right now. But she couldn't bring herself to care with the taste of his feelings on her tongue. She began moving her hips again, feeling his body come back to life. Her teeth nibbled, as if trying to sink them into the tiny trace of emotion that was slipping through. For a moment she pondered if he had baited her, feeding her tiny bits of his feelings to lure her in.

"No, I didn't."

His voice *was* in her head—he was reading her mind!

"Only a little."

He shouldn't be doing that uninvited.

"And taking your top off wasn't an invitation?"

How was she supposed to argue with that?

"You're not. Just keep doing what you're doing."

She nodded, and concentrated on rubbing harder against him.

"That's right."

"How," she whispered. "How do you hide your feelings?"

"Hush, no more questions."

She concentrated on her movement, trying to feel as much of him as possible. If he just let her have his feelings, she could enjoy the moment. Such primal aggression caused her to shudder as it overpowered her senses. Her breath came more rapidly, and she moved faster before letting out a tiny squeak as his hand closed on her breast. She held still, averting her eyes from his gaze on her red cheeks. Slowly she relaxed, and calmed her breathing.

He held her in place for some time, his hand on her breast, thumb tracing circles around the nipple to warm the chill left by the ice. When he released her wrists, her arms moved to close her top, but his hands quickly seized her arms again.

"I didn't say you could cover up," his thoughts admonished her.

She was certain she should find the comment objectionable. But the emotion, the sweet emotion on her palette, she lowered her arms with an obedient nod. One part of her mind was screaming that this was all wrong; the other part was fixated on the intoxication. She leaned into him, wanting to feel his body against hers and in his arms she closed her eyes. She sensed contentment, self-satisfaction, so powerful they washed any feeling she might have had away. With one arm he returned to eating while she sat quietly. He could do whatever he pleased, so long as she could sense him.

She had no idea how much time had passed when she felt him suddenly suck in a deep gasp. She barely noticed, until he took hold of her arms and tilted her away.

"You may cover up now," he instructed. With a silent nod she closed her top. Her attention was turned to the side by a distorted series of digital noises and she saw the automatech jerking in midair.

"My companion is erasing its memory of our visit," he explained. "We have to go. My ship will be here soon."

Her heart sank at the words. His feelings were beginning to fade, and she grabbed at him, now terrified that they would slip away completely.

"Relax," he whispered.

She whimpered when they vanished, before drawing in a sharp breath. What the hell just happened to her? She glanced at the automatech. She had not even considered that the establishment had security sensors.

"Don't worry; she'll get them all. Yes, I'm sure."

She covered her mouth, sliding out of his lap as he rose to his feet. What had she done? How did she let herself do that? Oh no, why did she let it go so far? Acting like that on a first date, how low an opinion he had to have of her now.

"Stop that." The admonishment caused her to shudder.

She looked to him as he waved a hand to pay the bill, and his companion, Andira he called her, zapped the machine's memory again. His hand moved to the back of her neck once more, and he began to lead her toward the door. Silently she cursed herself. He was going to think her a whore.

"Stop that," he repeated.

She wanted to cry, she wanted to get to know him, and all she had done was ruin his opinion of her.

"Keep that up, and I'll take you over my knee."

His words caused her eyes to light up.

"Yes, I would."

"You should really stop reading my mind," she whispered.

"Stop liking it and I will."

"Colonel, I'm not a—"

He stopped abruptly, his hand around her neck causing her to do the same. She felt his breath on her shoulder as he leaned down.

"Such worries have no place with me." Every word was punctuated in her mind, throwing off the rhythm of her heart. His other hand closed around her arm. *"Never regret a good evening."*

She lowered her head, regaining control of her rational mind. She took stock of the situation. He was behind her, a hand on her neck. Men who walked with their women this way were using body language to mark their territory, silently signaling to others that this female was his by blocking their potential avenues of approach. The gesture calmed her; maybe she was overthinking it. But if some part of him cared enough to behave that way, then perhaps she hadn't ruined his opinion of her.

He guided her out the door before releasing her neck, his arm reaching around her to manipulate the device on his arm. Why did the night have to be over so soon? Part of her hoped he was still reading her mind, that he knew she did not want to. Take her somewhere, anywhere but back to her life.

"Hold still."

The world warped around them, and soon they were back in the park where the evening had begun. She glanced up at the Web, before beginning to pout.

"Under the circumstances," he began, "I am sure you will understand if I don't take you back myself."

She nodded before he turned her around, and lifted her chin with one hand.

"Look at me," he whispered, his other hand sliding under the ring of her top until he held it tightly to pull her up against him once more.

"Look at me," he repeated.

She couldn't bring her eyes up, and his hand on her chin tilted her head until she looked into his eyes. His thumb traced her lips, her legs trembled, and she gasped, feeling herself drawn inward, becoming lost in his glare.

Everything was dark, her mind was clouded, she did not know where she was. She forced her heavy eyelids open, as if awakening in the dead of night. Letting out a yawn, she realized that something was in her mouth. She brought her hands up toward her lips, finding them heavy. Blinking the sleep from her eyes, she saw the gold and fur of manacles on her wrists, connected by a thin fiber. Touching her fingers to her lips, she realized she was gagged, and she shook her head.

A large muscular arm was wrapped around her, looking down at it she realized she was completely naked. Why wouldn't she be? That was how it was supposed to be. She shook her head. Why was it supposed to be that way? Because those were the rules. What rules? What was going on?

She began to sit up straight, and the arm around her tightened. Her wrists came together as the fiber between them contracted, creating a metal clink in the silence. Her ankles had been drawn together as well, and the chain she only now realized was attached to her collar pulled her back to the chest against which she had been sleeping.

"Where do you think you're going?" she heard him whisper, sending a chill down her spine.

She gazed up to the outline of his face in the darkness. She tried to apologize; he hadn't given her permission to leave his lap. But as she tried to form the words the narrow bit between her lips vibrated. The gag canceled out the sounds before they could leave her mouth, rendering her silent as his hand tightened on her breast. With a silent nod she relaxed, nuzzling against his chest and closing her eyes.

Night air filled her lungs as the reverie passed. Her entire being was quivering. She let her eyes fall away from his gaze, moving to his hands. The one beneath her chin descended until both were gripping her top. Her body went as taut as the fabric, and she was certain it was about to tear. She flinched hearing a metallic click, and he stepped away having reclaimed the disc he had attached earlier.

For a moment she could only stand trembling, the feeling of being drawn into such a powerful mind still nipping at her nerves. Her eyes slowly moved up. He was smiling, an almost smug look on his face. She began to raise her arm…until the world around her twisted and the park faded away. She was back in the Crystal Palace, standing on the router in her quarters.

She was not sure how long she simply stood on the router before her mind reclaimed control of itself. What was that? Was that what he wanted from her? She shook involuntarily as a chill arced through her spine. If that was what he was expecting, the two of them would need to have a talk—

"Simmonne!"

The Twins sprinted toward her, both throwing their arms around her.

"Are you okay?"

"Did he hurt you?"

She wrapped her arms around them.

"I'm fine." She smiled against the overwhelming sensations of their fright. "Really, I'm fine."

Several of her guards came running as well, while another summoned Isis and Jenna.

She paused, her NOD flooded with the backlog of messages from Jenna, Isis, the Twins, and her guards from the moment of her disappearance. He, or his companion, had blocked her messages, kept them from distracting her. She quickly cleared them away, returning the worried faces of the Twins.

"Well?" Julie began.

"What happened?" Jennifer finished.

She shook her head, clearing the image from her mind before looking to them and smiling. If that was what he was expecting, they would need to have a talk. But for now, the Twins were going to be so jealous.

"I'll tell you all about it."

CHAPTER
6C

TWO DAYS INTO BEREAVEMENT and Clearwater had not left his quarters. Sitting on a small couch he read from a list of reports detailing the outcomes of the platoon's various war games. One would be waiting for him when he went back on duty, and he was not going to embarrass himself again. But even as he tried to focus his thoughts turned back to his family, and their eyes when he had to leave.

He jumped at the sound of a noise, looking around his empty quarters. When the sound came again he realized someone was at his door.

"Who is it?"

"Taula."

What was she doing here? Civilians weren't allowed on the Legionnaire compound. Stupid—she was his DC; she was permitted to come see him. He rose but stopped himself from inviting her in. His eyes moved down to the stained T-shirt and faded pants. It wasn't proper, but he quickly pulled on his uniform jacket.

"What do you need?" he asked, buying time to fetch a clean pair of pants.

"Well, not talking to the door would be a start."

"Uh yeah, one second."

Tripping over his boots, he moved to the door and waved it open.

"Can I come in?"

"Oh, sure." He stepped aside.

"I thought legionnaires were supposed to be organized," she commented at the disarray.

"Yeah, I…"

"I know," she answered. "Brower told me when you missed our meeting."

"Oh, sorry about that."

"So, are you okay?"

"Yeah." He nodded. "I've just been…well actually just been sitting in the dark reading reports."

"That's not fun." She scoffed. "That will just make you more depressed, not cheer you up."

"Well, I…yeah you're right."

"How about this." She clapped her hands together. "You go take a shower, so they won't smell us coming, and we'll go do something."

"Uh, sure. Yeah, I'll just, go do that. Make yourself at home."

Tripping over his boots a second time, he moved to the washroom. He paused, looking at himself in the mirror and the patchy stubble on his face. He was quick into the shower and quick out, clearing his face of the stubble with a Lazer-Razer while still under the water. As he exited the shower, he realized he hadn't brought any fresh clothes into the bathroom with him.

Cursing he calmed himself.

"Taula?"

"Yes?"

"Uh, would you mind to wait outside a moment?"

"Sure."

When he heard the door close he rushed out of the bathroom and opened his closet.

"Where did you want to go?" he called as he contemplated his attire.

"Fred's."

"Fred's," he whispered to himself. At least it was informal.

Finding a nice shirt and slacks, he checked himself in the mirror before joining her in the corridor.

"You look nice," she commented.

"Thanks." He smiled, looking at her.

Her expression soured for a moment before she began walking.

"So Fred's?"

"Well there's not a lot else around here."

"I suppose not."

After leaving the barracks, they walked the short distance where loud music was now blaring from the establishment. Together they stepped into the smell of smoke and booze. How they got that smell out every morning upon returning to Derf's was a minor mystery.

Four humans and a buun made music for the establishment ahead of a dance stage in the center. The place was unusually empty, and he had to remind himself that most people had to work the next day, the colony's population having few on stipend. He followed Taula to a booth and sat, feet nervously tapping on the floor. When Taula's eyes turned to the server he eyed her intently, focusing on the bare shoulders exposed by her top.

"For you?" An automatech turned to him.

"Uh." He looked down at the menu, only now realizing how hungry he was.

"Bring me the porterhouse."

"How would you like that cooked?"

"Mooing. Sides, give me the cheese fries, and the cabbage." He paused, realizing he had not eaten today. "Actually bring me four orders."

"All the same?"

"Same for all."

"Four steaks?" Taula asked as the server walked away.

"I haven't eaten today."

"Yeah, but *four* steaks? And sides?"

Sitting up straight, he curled his arm to drive up the muscle beneath the cloth of his shirt.

"Have to feed the muscles."

"I suppose so," she answered with a shrug. A moment later the server returned with an appetizer.

"I love the pickles here," she remarked, quickly scooping the deep-fried food onto her plate. He merely watched as she greedily inhaled the appetizer.

"Aren't you going to have some?"

"I'm good." He held up a hand before she insistently held the plate to his face.

"You have to have some."

Huffing quietly, he took a taste of the pickles, careful to disguise his revulsion.

"So, how were your brothers and sisters?"

"Not…great," he said with a groan. "Most of them are too young to understand why I can't just pick up and run home. And Melanie, she thinks I just ran away."

"How old is she again?"

"Thirteen."

"That's a difficult age," she said. "Only a year away from being an adult, but people still treat her like a child."

He nodded.

"If she was a little older…." He shook his head. "I don't know. I just…."

He paused, a tear forming in his eye.

"Jonathan, I'm sorry, I didn't mean to—"

"Its all right." He waved his hand. "After mom left, she didn't know how to handle it. I think she wanted someone to blame. With Dad and Zach gone, that just leaves me."

She glared at him for a moment, clearly mortified.

"Your mother abandoned you?"

He glanced at her before looking away.

"Yeah." He nodded.

"Did your dad have only the one wife?"

"Yeah, said if you loved the one, you didn't need a harem. Looking back, I think Dad was so in love with her, he didn't realize she was just using him for a military paycheck. I don't think she ever wanted children either, just had them because Dad wanted us. I remember Zach and I feeding the others, tucking them in. Took me a while to realize it wasn't normal for the older siblings to be doing all that work.

"Mom just didn't care. She never did. My dad left reviewing our genetic profiles in her hands. She didn't even care enough to look over them before we were born. My brothers and sisters were lucky. Me, it's why I'm dumber and shorter than everyone else."

"Oh Jonathan, you're not dumb."

"Yeah, yeah I am." He nodded. "A man has to know what he is and isn't good at. I'm not very smart. If Dad didn't earn a Solar Cross, they wouldn't have accepted me into Hell's Gate."

"You made it through," she pressed. "Most people can't say that."

He looked into her eyes, and forced a smile before flexing his free arm.

"I'm not very smart, but I'm really good at moving heavy stuff."

She gave a sad smile, before trying to shift the conversation.

"I'm guessing Zach is your older brother?"

He nodded.

"When Mom left, she cleaned out Dad's bank accounts and just disappeared. Zach joined the Legionnaires to support the rest of us."

"That was good of him." Taula smiled. "Is he still a legionnaire?"

He shook his head.

"Zach was killed in a training accident. I went to Hell's Gate a few months later."

He glanced over as she took his hand.

"I'm sorry, Jonathan," she whispered.

"He did what he had to do. So did I. Don't get me wrong, I always wanted to be a legionnaire. Just…not quite under these circumstances."

"Were you close to your grandmother?"

He nodded.

"She did her best to take care of us, but she wasn't expecting to have to handle a horde of kids in the last years of her life. My brothers, they're smart, they have real talent. Dad's benefits feed us all, gave us a nice house. But it's not enough, and those benefits end when they turn fourteen. If my brothers are going to have a good education, it takes more. If my sisters are going to find their ways into good social circles so they can meet good men…someone has to pay for it."

She squeezed his hand firmly until he made eye contact.

"You're a good man."

He smiled back, feeling her squeeze tighter before pulling away. Freshly printed steaks were laid before him as the server returned.

"Well, happier thoughts now," she commented, taking her utensils.

"And you give me grief about four steaks?" He gave a scoff as he looked at her food.

"Busy day."

"Well done?" He eyed her steak.

"At least mine is dead."

"So's mine," he answered, stabbing one of the rare cuts of meat with his fork.

"Moo. Don't eat me, please!"

He lowered the piece of steak for a moment before making a face and biting into it. Few things could be as satisfying as a rare steak. While they ate, his eyes moved to her ears, and the gemstone studs that decorated them. Lantai tended to prefer vegetables, and above all, sweet fruits. That part of her heritage must not have made it through…and there it was. After taking the first bite, she reached over to the side of the table, taking the sugar meant for coffee and pouring it on her steak.

"What?" she asked, seeing his face.

"Nothing." He tried not to laugh. "Bad enough you destroy the steak by having them cook the flavor out of it. Now you're just defiling the corpse."

With an annoyed look, she poured more of the sugar before setting it aside.

"So, anything new in the temple?" he asked between bites.

"Every day." She paused. "Lots of rumors going around."

"What about?"

"Ghosts."

He perked up.

"Ghosts?"

"Yeah, sounds crazy of course. But several people have reported seeing someone who wasn't there. Some of the technicians have complained about tools appearing in strange places, or even disappearing. Things like that."

"Think there's anything to it?"

She paused to dab her lips with a napkin.

"Well, I don't think the place is haunted. But there's enough people reporting strange things that there might be something to it."

He leaned forward.

"Like what?"

"Well, if apparitions are appearing, there's probably a hologram network we haven't detected yet. Who knows. If I'm right about that place's function, they may have even intentionally created illusions of ghosts to frighten off races that hadn't outgrown superstition Or if there is a hologram network, it could simply be malfunctioning."

"What about the missing tools?"

"I think the explanation there is much more mundane. Techs are overworked; they borrow without asking, or forget where they put things. One suspicious thing happens, then everything starts to look suspicious."

"Yeah, maybe."

He only half-listened as she continued talking, spouting various theories about what could be the cause. While she went on he spent the time eyeing her bare shoulders. When he was sure that her eyes were away from his, he allowed his gaze to move down to her chest in the tightly fitted top.

How she could spring so quickly from such a large meal shocked him, but the moment she was finished her hands were on his, pulling him from the booth. With only a handful of people this late at night, they had the place almost to themselves. She stopped at the far corner of the restaurant where several tables waited.

"What did you have in mind?"

"Billiards." She smiled.

"Terran or Hyperian?"

"Hyperian, of course."

He took the cue she offered before following her to the table and smiled to himself. Hyperian billiards was played on an anti-grav table, with the balls suspended in the field. Holograms serving as walls would move through the field at intervals, providing surfaces off which to bounce the balls. To sink a ball into one of the holes on the upper or lower surfaces required the cue ball to first be bounced from one of these walls. He didn't say anything, but was supremely confident of his chances. The military cyberization vastly enhanced his spatial reasoning; this was not going to be a fair contest.

After stacking eighteen balls in a cube, she released it to the field where they hovered, waiting for the break.

"You break." She tossed him the cue ball.

"Ladies first." He tossed it back.

She took the ball before moving it gently into the field. After lining up with her cue, she struck hard, sending the balls scattering through the field. His eyes lit up when she quickly followed the cue ball, deflecting it off one of the walls to sink her first ball. Perhaps this wasn't going to be so easy.

She had sunk six of her nine before missing one. His palms were moist as he stalked the slowing cue ball, lining up his shot in his mind. He winced as he struck the ball, letting out a breath as his target found its hole. He tried to focus as she eyed him across the table, as one by one he sent the balls home.

"You're good at this," she remarked before setting up a new game.

"So are you."

"I used to play with my dad." She tossed him the cue ball.

"He play a lot?" he asked, initiating the break.

"When he's home. Says it helps him strategize."

"What's he do?" Clearwater asked as he sank another ball.

"He's an admiral in the Armadas."

She giggled as he struck the cue ball too hard, sending it out of the field.

"Oh" was all he managed to get out.

She retrieved the cue ball.

"Last I talked to him he said he'd be here in the Hourglass soon."

"That's...good."

She managed to make all but her last ball in before missing the moving wall and scratching. Reclaiming the initiative, he sent his balls home to win the second round.

"Three out of five?" She smiled.

"Sure."

After she set the rack he broke again, and was on ball 7 when a jab to his butt from a cue caused him to miss.

"Hey!" he protested as she slid past him.

"I didn't do anything," she proclaimed with a grin.

Watching her contort to strike the moving ball, he debated jabbing her back, but the courage to do so never came. When she scratched on the final ball, he became suspicious. Was she the kind to throw the game so he wouldn't feel he had been shown up? Thinking on this, he lined up for his shot, but he missed as she blew gently in his ear.

"Oh come on." He groaned, watching his ball sail out of the field. She giggled and reclaimed the ball before sinking her last.

"Go again?" he asked as she smiled.

"Sure. Can you get us some drinks?"

"Yeah, be right back." He hesitated; something about her tone was off. He walked to the service counter where a single man was waiting for an order.

"Clearwater."

"Lieutenant Brower." He had to stop himself from saluting on reflex. "What brings you here?"

"Officer's poker. My turn to pick up snacks."[16]

"Uh, isn't that against regs, sir?"

"Oh, look who's an expert after a month on duty," Brower snarked. "No, officers can't gamble with enlisted, nothing stopping us from doing so with each other so long as the CoC isn't undermined."

"I see."

"Fraternizing with your DC?" Brower's eyes moved to Taula.

"There's no regulation against it, sir."

"Not specifically, but it does fall under Article 11 if it interferes with your duties," Brower commented, taking the food as it came. "Of course being oblivious is a wonderful defense."

"Sir?" He was not sure how to take the comment save to be confident it was an insult.

"Oh, nothing." He smiled, paying for his food. "I just know if a girl like that was giggling and poking me, I'd probably be doing something other than billiards."

---

16   While food printers are capable of preparing most any dish, many restaurants have proprietary recipes that are considered the intellectual property of their owners.

Clearwater's expression changed as he glanced back to Taula.

"Or not." Brower shrugged. "Have a good evening."

"You too, sir," he whispered, still eyeing Taula.

With drinks in hand, he walked back to her.

"Thanks." She took the mug before drinking quickly.

"So…" The rest of the sentence did not seem to want to find his lips.

"Yes?"

"You uh…"

"Yes?"

His stomach churned as he tried to find the words.

"I'm waiting," she said impatiently.

"You want to get out of here?" He ground his teeth as she looked back at him, sipping from the mug. His heart began to race as she sipped longer, and longer.

"Sure."

The weight lifted from his heart before returning as she took his hand. As he led her to the door, his heart began racing.

"Where are we going?" Taula asked as they approached the door, bringing him to a stop. That was a damn good question. He couldn't take her back to the barracks—that would invite the other officers into his business. Sheepishly he turned back to her.

"Uh, your place?"

When she smiled, he led her out the door. The expedition dorms were a few blocks away and as they turned that way she stopped suddenly, removing her heels.

"I hate these shoes," she whispered, resolving to carry them.

"Then why wear them?"

"They're cute." She held them up. "Don't you think so?"

A shoe was a shoe.

"Absolutely."

The expedition dorms were little more than a collection of small, cube-shaped pre-fabs arrayed in rows. A delta sentry shot a glance at Clearwater as they walked past the gate, and she led him to the cube bearing her name.

"Home sweet home," she said, opening the door. The smell of air freshener was almost overpowering, a sensation lost as she tugged his hand. Inside the small living room she led him over to a couch covered in pillows. After clearing them away she sat, prompting him to do the same.

"So," she began when he said nothing. "What do we do now?"

He bit his lip, trying to muster his arm to move around her.

"You know, the shy thing is only cute to a point," she whispered in his ear.

Taking a breath he turned, wrapping both arms around her.

"Gentle," she gasped, prompting him to loosen his grip. "Don't want to squish me."

"Sorry," he whispered, looking into her eyes. His mouth was dry as he leaned in and pushed his lips against hers before moving away.

"What was that?" She laughed.

"A kiss?" He hesitated.

"That's not a kiss." Reaching up, she grabbed his hair in her hands before pushing her face into his, her tongue pushing into his mouth. After several seconds she broke away. "That's a kiss, silly boy."

Her hands move to his shoulders and his arms dropped as she pushed him back against the couch before moving into his lap.

"Its okay to touch me," she whispered. "I won't scream."

As he laid his hands on her hips, his eyes were drawn to her hands as she withdrew her arms into her top. Already in overdrive, his heart beat even faster as she slipped the top off and tossed it aside. Leaning down, she kissed him again before her hands moved back, and his hands slid up her side as she unclasped her bra. As the garment fell her mouth opened, and his ears were assaulted by a shrill wail.

"You said you wouldn't scream!" He panicked as her hands came down on his wrists.

"Your grip!" she cried. "Loosen your grip!"

As she jerked away he let go, leading her to fall out of his lap, hitting the floor with a thud.

"Oh God!" He sprang to his feet, finding her coiled up in a ball holding her sides.

"I think you broke my ribs!" she wailed, curling up tighter.

"I'm sorry!" he shouted. "Uh, do you have a first aid kit?"

"Bathroom," she moaned, gritting her teeth.

Running in circles he stopped to compose himself, finding her bathroom nearby.

"Damn it!" He swore as his haste to open the medicine cabinet resulted in the mirror being torn from the wall. With kit in hand he ran back to her, dumping its contents on the floor. He seized the mediron inside and brought it to her leg, jabbing her with the needle. As the healing nanites moved through her blood she slowly relaxed, and drew in a deep breath.

"Are you okay?" he whispered.

Still breathing heavily she sat up, grabbing her top and slowly sliding back into it.

"I…think you should go," she whispered, her eyes to the floor.

"Uh, okay. I'm…I'm sorry."

He stumbled through the door and out of the domicile. Outside he balled his fists as he began cursing.

"Stupid, stupid!" he growled, moving away from the door. On the ground nearby a large rock caught his attention and was soon assailed by his foot. An instant later the loud cursing of one of the sentries prompted him to duck low and scurry away.

CHAPTER
7A

AFTER PARTING WAYS WITH the princess, Panzer had used his router to leave Reichsylvannia, transporting himself to the world of New Bengal. The home world of the princess' most zealous guard dog was one of the last places they would look for him. Though it had forced his auxiliaries to reroute their trip to pick him up, perhaps for the last time.

He sat on a bench in the darkness, overlooking a white sandy beach and a crystal lagoon. The cool breeze relaxed his muscles as it carried away the smoke of his cigar. What had he done? How had he let his discipline collapse so completely? From his earliest memories, his desires had always been to dominate others and bend them to his will. Nuset had spent years teaching him the discipline to contain that impulse, to use it to become a warrior and a leader, rather than a monster. For a moment, he became that monster. He had spit in the very eye of the man who raised him.

The princess, she had no idea how close she came to having her life destroyed. It was so easy when a person wore a coat of fame, to forget that there was a real human being within. Poor girl was so starved for affection that she let him have his way with her. It was the only thing that saved her. Whether she knew it or not, by being so compliant she had disarmed the trap into which she had stumbled. No need to force her to do anything when she was so eager to please.

How had she sensed him? In nearly two hundred years, no one, not even his biological parents, had ever been able to touch his mind. People could only sense him, read his thoughts, or even communicate by telepathy if he made the conscious effort to enable them. He had done no such thing with her. Something was going on here, something unnatural. He had spent every ounce of control ensuring that it really was her last night free, ensuring he did nothing to her mind. He did not even read her thoughts until she began disrobing. But when she sensed him...for a moment as she danced for him, it was as if time itself had stopped. As if the universe itself had paused in place, just to give him more time.

Shame knotted his stomach. A little more pressure and he would have vomited. That poor girl was so desperate for intimacy that she pounced on his feelings like an addict ravaged by withdrawal. His head turned, his jaw clenching until he had bitten through his cigar. Spitting out the butt, he took the cigar from the ground, and drew in a puff as his NOD flashed.

The commandant was calling. This was it—time to face the consequences of his actions. He would be drummed out of the Corps, likely imprisoned for what he had done. And he would have to look the emperor in the eye and explain himself. He drew in a breath and answered the call.

"Colonel." The commandant's eyes glared at him, voice gripped in an annoyed tone.

"Commandant," he returned.

"Would you care to explain to me, why on one of the few nights I chose to sleep, I was awakened by the executor of the Imperial Guard?"

He was not in the mood for the commandant's drawn-out lectures. *Just get it over with and be done.*

"I would think it rather rude of him to call you and not explain why."

The old man's eyes squinted at him in reply.

"You want to play this game with me, Colonel?"

"No," Panzer answered. "I think we'd both be happier if we got to the point."

"Remember who you're talking to, Colonel." The commandant pointed an accusing finger. "Explain yourself. *Now.*"

He had crafted an excuse. Time to see how well it worked.

"I was just testing the Imperial Guard," he answered. "I must have neglected to have my companion send the notice."

The commandant's expression did not change. Beady eyes glared at him.

"Do you take me for a fool, Colonel?"

"Do you think I would be dumb enough to say yes if I did?" Panzer retorted. "I don't know why you're angry with me. You should be having a conversation with the executor about why his halfwits allowed someone with a mobile router to come within arms' reach of Her Majesty."

"Probably because they assumed on the good name of the Corps that the person carrying it was not a threat. Just as they do not force you to disarm when you approach a member of the Imperial Family."

"Which makes them incompetent in my book. If I am going to be responsible in part or in whole for her safety, I have to know what kind of people I am working with. I can tell you for certain that Prince Steven's bodyguards would not allow me to approach him with such a device, even despite the two of us having a personal relationship. Even if they do not perceive me as a threat, they wouldn't take the risk that he and I might try to give them the slip and go out drinking."

"I've heard enough of your shit," the commandant barked. "I don't know what really happened. I do know if it were up to me, you'd be on your way back to Acheron to spend some time in one of our interrogation cells."

The old man paused to compose himself while Panzer glared silently.

"As it stands, I have been given concise orders from His Majesty to let the matter go."

Panzer cocked an eyebrow.

"Yes." The commandant noted his expression. "It seems that once again being the emperor's pet is going to save your ass, Colonel. Now I am going to try to salvage this situation. Even though I know you're full of shit, I'm going to use your lie and have a talk with the executor about the Imperial Guard's protocols. And you are going to make a religion of that lie. I don't care if you have a hundred telepaths baking your brain into a vegetable. You are also going to issue an apology to the Imperial Guard. I would have you issue one to the High King for creating a disturbance, but since I do not want another incident—"

"I will draft a formal apology to the executor of the Imperial Guard. The High King, however, can kiss the most poorly washed portion of my ass."

The commandant huffed.

"Don't presume on his Majesty's good favor, Colonel. I am quite sick of your attitude. Now, you will carry on with this assignment, you will do it by the book, and you will do it with a good attitude. Then, once this assignment is over, you and I are going to have a very long talk about the behavior expected of a commando, and whether or not you are still a good fit for this organization."

"Understood," Panzer hissed as the call ended, his hand morphing to display a middle finger.

Leaning back, he took a deep breath, forcing himself to relax. The emperor had just saved his ass. Why? The old man was so protective of his children. Why was he being given a pass? He knew something, but what?

It did not matter. Something like this would not happen again. He would not be the monster Nuset had worked so hard to slay; he would not bring darkness. He would be the candle his teacher had lit. He wanted to hate the Encephalon, to curse him for doing that to his mind. But he couldn't. If not for him, he would have carried out this operation by the book; he would have barely gotten to know the princess at all. Despite what had happened, it had worked out. In some strange way, the Encephalon had done him a favor.

The moment he regained control of himself, he ended their date, but by that point he had already gotten a glimpse of the person inside. The one waiting to come out. He smiled to himself. Simmonne did not seem thrilled by the vision he had placed in her mind. But that would come in time. He knew now what kind of girl she was. She was going to be his, but this time, she would come to him. Now that he had planted the seed…he would be the candle, and she would be the moth drawn to his light.

He glanced up as he felt a gust of wind, and his NOD chimed. His ship had arrived. He rose from the bench and paused before extending a foot to come down on the invisible ramp. He ascended to pass into the ship, and familiar corridors became visible. Someone was waiting for him.

"Bossss," a guttural voice greeted him. A tahn'kodaz stood on all four limbs, taller than Panzer despite his hunched posture. Fine scales like those of a snake covered his body in colors reminiscent of swamp water. Like most kodaz, he walked on the knuckles of his hands to avoid dulling the half-meter skeletal projections that formed iron claws from his fingertips. A mouth-full of freshly polished iron teeth gleamed in a maw like that of a crocodile.

"Rhoxx." Panzer eyed him. "You look good for a dead guy."

"Me da alwayss sssayin' my head bein' too t'ick for anyt'in get t'rough," the kodaz answered.

"Any dain bramage?"

"Blasst takin' part o' my quartah-lobe. Sssome memory losss. Not remembrin' my oldesst child's mo'der. Never really likin' her anyway. Been ressetin' sssome o' my passswordss, and not rememberin' dat joke I wantin' tell. Not'in' goin' be keepin' me from my dutiesss."

"Well...." Panzer chuckled. "I suppose if you can walk, you can march into battle."

"Ssso," the kodaz began, "perhap you be tellin' me, why 'em commandant be holdin' us up from our departure?"

"Oh." Panzer waved his hand. "Just a miscommunication."

"D'at misssscommunication be havin' do anyt'in wit' Imperial Rossse?"

"It might have," he answered, waving for the kodaz to follow.

"Sssshame we not doin' be ssee much o' her. I wasss hopin' ogle her awhile."

Panzer paused to shoot him a glance.

"I really don't understand why aliens like her so much. She looks nothing like a kodaz. I'd think she'd be repulsive to you."

"Bah, get hun-up on looksss bein' a human t'in'. Knowin' how much work goin' into somet'in', give it value. Like a piece o' art, or a really well-made gun."

"Uh huh," Panzer answered as he rounded the corner to his armory. There he stopped, seeing two crates waiting for him. He exchanged glances with Rhoxx before opening the first crate.

"Jorri," he whispered, reaching down into the crate. He removed the large weapon within, marked by a triangular hand guard, fluted barrel, cylindrical hypercoil capping the muzzle, and pods flanking the hand guard beneath a small scope. No longer in production, she was an example of the Jormungandr 25mm assault cannon, among the most powerful man-portable disrupter weapons ever made.

"Halcyon be workin' days wit'out sleep, get her back to you," Rhoxx explained while Panzer fondled the weapon.

"Did you miss daddy?" he whispered, stroking the metal of the hand guard.

"I t'inkin' you havin' an uneahlt'y attachment, 'tat rifle."

"Don't listen to him," Panzer whispered. "He's just jealous."

Rhoxx scoffed in return, blowing a gust of hot air to whistle between his teeth.

Panzer inspected the weapon briefly, breaking it down and reassembling it.

"I wasn't sure she'd ever shoot again. I swear that old lontil can fix anything."

With several magazines and a drum, he returned the weapon to its place, filling the conspicuously empty gap in his wall of weapons. He then returned to the second crate to find it full of spare parts for his armor. One of the downsides to using so much equipment that was not standard-issue was having to carry all the spares he might need with him before every mission.

"How are the brothers?" Panzer asked as he stowed the armor.

"Be sparrin' in da cargo bay."

With a nod Panzer exited the armory with Rhoxx behind, and made his way through the ship. At the cargo bay he could hear the clanking metal as the two kurai sparred with one another. In the doorway he watched as the two resumed their positions, ready for another bout.

Kassar ahn Onylon and Novin ahn Rennandin, not truly brothers but called such as did all who were members of the kurai warrior caste. Both stood in the bladed khalak armor, but instead of claypiers they wielded verris, long single-edge blades.

"Morning, Colonel," Novin spoke as both stopped to turn to him and bow before turning back to each other.

"Colonel," Kassar acknowledged him in a voice that rarely rose above a whisper.

"I see you two are feeling better," Panzer said, watching them.

"I have two new arms," Novin answered. "This seems a good way to test them."

"You should hope they are faster than the old ones," Kassar taunted.

The two moved toward each other, deflecting blades echoing off the walls before Kassar pushed Novin away to strike him in the forehead with the pommel of his weapon.

"Half-point for me," Kassar said. "One more score and I win."

"Carry on," Panzer excused himself and stepped outside. A moment later he heard the ruckus again, followed by Novin swearing.

"I think the new arms are even slower than the old ones."

Kassar's taunt only served to amplify the stream of profanity.

"Sir," Andira called. "The fleet will arrive in one minute."

"Understood; once they've jumped in, take us to the *Hurricane*."

"Yes sir."

CHAPTER
7B

SIMMONNE HELD HER BREATH as Jenna placed the call. The Twins stood just behind her, with her guards forming a circle around a floor-mounted projector. The machine came to life, illuminating a hologram of her father. The enormous image loomed over her, and his eyes found her quickly. For a moment she was certain he was suppressing a smile before his gaze moved on.

"So, shall we discuss the past night's mischief?"

Unable to sense him through a hologram, she awaited the worst.

"Your Majesty," Jenna spoke up. "I've submitted my full report. I—"

She was silenced as the emperor held up a hand, and his eyes returned to Simmonne.

"Simmonne." His words made her knees weak. "Where did you go last night?"

"I, I…" She lowered her eyes. "I went out with Colonel Panzer."

"Did you now?" His tone—it wasn't angry, maybe amused? "Where did you go?"

"To a bar," she whispered.

"Speak up."

"To a bar," she answered louder. "We went to a bar."

"What was its name?"

She glanced up at him before returning her eyes to the floor.

"Three Fat Guys."

For a moment he said nothing, no doubt looking up the location in his NOD.

"Not what I would have expected," he mused. "I would imagine the colonel would take you somewhere nicer."

"It…" She hesitated. "It was my idea, to go someplace normal."

"I see. I am sure they were surprised to have an Imperial Princess in their establishment."

She shook her head.

"They didn't know. He, Colonel Panzer, he put a device on me; it disguised me as a lantai."

"Mmhmm, and what did you do?"

"We ate pizza, then he brought me back."

"So just to make sure I understand this," he began, and she winced, ready for the assault, "you slipped out, started a panic, ate pizza, and came back. Did I miss anything?"

She shook her head.

"Very well. You will draft an apology to the High King for the disturbance. Don't let it happen again."

Her eyes dilated. Was that it? She slowly glanced up to his hologram, finding a gentle smile on his face.

"I...I won't."

"Well," he clapped his hands together. "Enjoy your trip, and I—"

"Majesty," Jenna spoke again. "I...I think we need to talk about this. Colonel Panzer—"

Jenna fell silent as the image turned toward her.

"You would do well not to attract my attention, Miss Prideaux." His expression turned to a scowl. "I hold you responsible for this incident—and you, Isis."

The gamma came to attention as he turned to her.

"Us?" Jenna stammered. "Majesty, we—"

"Are responsible for keeping an eye on her," he interrupted, "for preventing incidents like this, among others from happening. A job you failed to do, leading to a panic."

Simmonne eyed him. Something was wrong. His face and his tone said he was angry, but his posture said otherwise. He was...faking? Pretending to be angry with them?

"Sir, we couldn't expect her vanguard would do something like that," Jenna protested. "He—"

"Brought her back safe and sound after snatching her right out from under your noses?" he interrupted her again. "Are you upset with the colonel for what he did, or because he made you look incompetent?"

"Majesty," Jenna stammered, and Simmonne had to force herself not to giggle. So rarely did anyone put Jenna in her place, make her feel like the child. She knew she shouldn't, but Simmonne could not help but enjoy it.

"Majesty," Isis spoke up, "how could we be expected to be suspicious of her vanguard?"

The emperor turned back to her.

"My guards keep an eye on my own children, in case one of them should try to retire me early. Just because they are on a trusted list does not mean you give them absolute freedom to be above all suspicion."

"But Majesty." Jenna pointed to Simmonne. "She—"

"She what? Gave in to the temptation that every single member of the family feels at one time or another to slip away for a while? Its part of your job to be sure that doesn't happen. And it had better not happen again. Am I understood?"

"But Majesty, he could've done anything to her. He could've even taken it from her mind so she wouldn't know he did it."

"Did you scan her?"

"Yes, we—"

"Was there any sign of foul play?"

"No, but—"

"Then why are you still trying to argue with me, Vi-Baroness?"[17]

Simmonne fought the urge to smile as she watched Jenna's face. If her handmaiden grit her teeth any harder, they would break.

"I…apologize, Majesty," Jenna answered, bowing her head.

"Good. And as to your recommendation that Colonel Panzer be reassigned, the answer is no. He will continue as vanguard, and you will extend him every professional courtesy. Am I clear?"

"Yes, Majesty."

Simmonne's smile finally broke through when her father turned back to her.

"Be safe."

She nodded as the image faded away. She was not sure what, but something was going on. She knew her father to be a provident but he so rarely shared what he saw. Did he know something she didn't? She had little time to contemplate it, feeling the radiating anger as Jenna turned toward her.

"You may be off the hook with him…" she began, fuming. From her anger it was a wonder she was not screaming. "But not with me. You sent us all into a panic."

Blanking her face, Simmonne nodded.

"I am sorry, Jenna."

"Don't apologize to me," Jenna spat before roughly grabbing her arm and spinning her to face Isis. "Apologize to Isis, since now the emperor thinks she's incompetent."

She wanted to pull away and scream for Jenna to shut up. But that would get her nowhere, so she held it in. There was no way she would even pretend that she regretted what happened, but she supposed she did owe Isis an apology.

"I'm sorry, Isis."

The aren shook her head, silver eyes blinking.

"No apologies necessary, Majesty."

---

17   The "Vi" prefix in the Solar peerage is synonymous with junior. It is applied to the children of nobility who, barring ascension to full title, carry it for the duration of their lives. Exceptions are made for the titles of count and viscount, where the junior titles are vinacount and viracount respectively.

Simmonne grinned. To an aren, the closest thing to God was the emperor. From the supreme authority she had been told, she was in the wrong, and there was no more to discuss.

"Apologize to them." Jenna turned her to the Twins. "While you were eating pizza rather than letting us know where you were, they were in tears worried about you."

She eyed the Twins, both of whom looked away. In the time between her being sent back and Jenna's return from orchestrating a search, they had feasted on every detail she would share. Now they turned away, unwilling to accept what they believed to be an unwarranted apology.

"I'm sorry," she said flatly, and both pretended they had heard nothing. Simmonne hissed as she was turned back to face Jenna.

"This will not happen again, Simmonne," she warned.

Simmonne bit her tongue and merely nodded.

"Now," Jenna began, composing herself, "the *Hurricane* is waiting."

For most people, transport to the ship would simply mean stepping on a router. But that did not make for the show expected of royalty. Royals had to be seen, and with that need in mind Simmonne soon found herself on a landing platform. *Mandrake-27*, her personal shuttle, approached the Crystal Palace with an escort of eight monitors. The relatively small vessel was a dropship, originally designed to land an entire Legionnaire platoon on a planet until converted for her use. On board she sat in a small chair by a window, and looked out as the ship took flight. It was rejoined by the monitors that flew in close formation to escort her out of the star system. A short MID dash later, and Aetius' fleet came into view.

More than 30,000 ships, from frigates to a single supercruiser, were now in formation. To most nations, the small fleet was an incomparable force. To an Empire with the resources of an entire galaxy cluster, it was a drop in the bucket. Simmonne glared out of a small viewport as her shuttle approached the largest ship, nestled at the formation's center. Even she knew that it was rare for warships to hold such a close formation that more than one could be seen with the naked eye. But this was a special case, as they prepared to use the nearby Dominion Gate to reach the distant Hourglass Galaxy.

Her pilot plotted a scenic course, ensuring that her ship was seen on the approach. Simmonne's eyes remained affixed to the largest ship at the center of the formation. The flagship of the Solar Armadas, namesake of her family, the *Hurricane*-class supercruiser. In all the known universe, there were no warships but her siblings that compared to her sheer size.

Like most Solar warships, she was shaped like a flying wing with a teardrop body flanked by sprawling wings. Thee hundred and forty one kilometers of kilosteel separated her nose from her exhaust baffles, with more than double that distance between the tips of her wings. Simmonne had seen this ship many times in news reports and in holo-fiction, but never in person. Only now as it eclipsed her view did she appreciate its enormity.

Her shuttle approached a segmented tower rising from the ship's spine, often mistaken as a command structure. In truth it was simply a large weapons platform, but behind it lay the VIP hangar into which her ship descended.

"Everyone ready?" Jenna asked as the ship touched down, revealing a hangar full of soldiers. Simmonne took a breath and found herself hoping for a familiar face in the waiting crowd.

"Ready." She stood between the Twins within the perimeter of her guards and made her way down the boarding ramp to the ship's rear.

A thousand boots sounded together as crew and legionnaires stomped their feet and came to attention. At the bottom of the ramp, four individuals awaited her. One she knew as one of the most respected officers in the entire Solar Armed Forces. Four galaxies arrayed around a fifth on his shoulders marked him as a fleet admiral. His red admiral's uniform was obscured by decorations on his chest and arms, and his red eyes lowered as he bowed in greeting.

"Princess Simmonne," the alpha aren said, "welcome to His Majesty's ship, *Hurricane*."

"Thank you, Admiral Aetius."

He raised upright as she introduced her entourage, before turning to his own. Another admiral, a human sporting a single galaxy on his shoulders, a kodaz in the uniform of a legionnaire, and an Armadas crewmen in a blue uniform and kurai body. She was not as familiar with the ranks of enlisted men, but surmised that the chevrons on his arms indicated a non-commissioned officer.

"Majesty, allow me to introduce Rear Admiral Terrance Gilyard, the skipper of this fine ship. Brigadier-Marshal Skaal, commander of the fleet's Legionnaire contingent."

She smiled to each of the two officers as they bowed.

"And this is Sorel ahn Ultet, our ship's boatswain."

"A pleasure." Simmonne smiled.

"The pleasure is mine, Imperial Rose."

"Your Majesty," Aetius continued, "I am happy to welcome you to the *Hurricane*. However, I have much to which I must attend for the upcoming trip. I hope you will not be offended if I hand you off to Admiral Gilyard, and our Boatswain who are eager to give you a tour of the ship."

"Not at all, Admiral; please do not let me get in your way."

He bowed once again and with the kodaz Marshal dismissed himself, allowing Admiral Gilyard to step forward.

"If you are ready, your Majesty, we will begin the tour in engineering."

CHAPTER
7C

APPROACHING THE EXPEDITION DORMS, Clearwater walked with his hands full. Under one arm was tucked a box of Heartfire Chocolates, the sickliest sweet orbs of sugar known to man. A bundle of flowers dominated the other hand as he spoke to himself, growing more nervous with each step.

"Taula I'm sorry." He shook his head. "I wanted to apologize."

What to say beyond that point was not coming to his mind, and he was running out of steps. Soon he was in front of her dorm, and stepping up the small flight of stairs, he rang the bell.

"Who is it?" she called from inside.

"It's...Jonathan. Uh, can I talk to you?"

"Just a minute."

One minute became five, which became ten. He was thinking of leaving when the door opened and he turned. Taula stood before him, brushing still wet hair before his eyes were drawn to Gulliver on her shoulder. The mouse rose up to wave at him. Reflexively he waved back to the creature before his eyes moved to hers.

"Taula, listen, I—"

"Come in," she interrupted, stepping aside.

Taking a breath, he entered and followed as she led him to a small table where they both sat.

"Listen, I—"

"Are those for me?" she asked, pointing to the flowers.

"Yeah." He offered them to her, before following with the chocolates.

"Heartfire?" She read the box. "These must have been expensive, I didn't even know they were selling them here."

"Yeah, Taula, I—"

"Thought you could apologize for breaking my ribs by bringing flowers and chocolate?"

"Uh, yes?"

Wordlessly she opened the box and took one of the candies from within. Still saying nothing she placed one in her mouth, crushing it between her teeth while watching him.

"You're cute when you're terrified," she said after swallowing.

He breathed a sigh of relief, watching her take another chocolate. Tearing a small piece off, she handed it to Gulliver, who sniffed it before chirping loudly and eating.

"Bringing him home with you now?" he asked, pointing to the animal.

"The company is always harping on us to find ways to make things more profitable. I'm testing Gulliver to see if he'd make a good pet. And don't change the subject, you're not getting off that easy."

"Okay." He nodded.

"My mother warned me about soldiers and their hands. You should have used your nerve-heighteners."

"Yes." He nodded. "I'm sorry, I just…didn't think about it. I've never had to use them before."

"And you won't need to for a while." She gave him a stare to accentuate her point. "Now, seeing as how you broke my ribs, I think you need to be punished."

He sat back slightly.

"Punished?" At a loss for words, he said the first thing that came to mind. "Uh, you don't mean in like some kind of kinky way…do you?"

"Oh no." She shook her head. "I have something truly terrible in mind for you. Something women have been using to punish men for thousands of years."

His pulse quickened.

"And…what's that?"

She smiled.

"A chick flick. And I don't mean sitting here watching it on our NODs. You're taking me to the theater, and you are going to sit through the sweetest, sappiest, most cringe-worthy thing I could find."

He breathed a sigh of relief.

"I suppose I can endure that."

"Oh, I'm not done," she said. "I'm going to buy the biggest drink, the biggest popcorn, and the biggest box of candies I can find, only eat a handful of them, and you are going to pay for them."

"Okay." He nodded. "Is…that all?"

"No. I want a nice meal too. And I don't mean Fred's. There's a new place open—you're going to take me there too. But I don't want to fight a crowd so we'll go after the movie."

"Sure." He grit his teeth slightly, troy signs dancing through his mind.

"Good, since you are here, I will go get ready. Gulliver can keep you company. Try not to crush him."

"Of course." He brought his hands up as she turned her shoulder, and the creature came to his palms, sniffing his hands intently.

"Ow!" he exclaimed.

"Yeah, he likes to chew on fingernails. Better watch out."

While she went to her bedroom he tried to move the creature to his shoulder, but found it clinging to his hands.

"Come on, little guy," he urged, but the creature did not obey, still hanging on to his hand and chewing on his thumbnail. Using his other hand, Clearwater brushed the creature off, which gave an annoyed growl from his shoulder. The moment he sat his hand down, the creature jumped from his shoulder to the table, ready to attack his hand again.

"Come on guy, give me a break," he whispered raising his hand. Looking around, he spied a glass sitting on the nearby counter. After a check that Taula's door was closed, he grabbed it. Gulliver chirped curiously for a moment before he brought the glass down, trapping the creature inside.

"Ha." He smiled at the animal. "You smart enough to get out of that?"

Tempting fate did not pay off, as Gulliver rose onto his hind legs and threw himself into the glass, knocking it over.

"Damn it," he grumbled as the creature returned to his hand. "Outsmarted by a mouse."

He winced as his nail was chewed to the quick.

"At least alternate," he hissed. He was not sure if it understood, or simply took the next closest nail and moved on to his index finger. Looking back to the counter, he saw a possible solution, and quickly poured a small amount of sugar on the table. Thankfully Gulliver found the sugar more appetizing than a fingernail and proceeded to lick it up. He soon found that to keep his hands safe, the sugar had to flow, and every few minutes he would pour a little more.

"You know"—he turned to the sound of Taula's voice—"he learns quickly. If you give him sugar not to chew on you, he'll figure out that's all he needs to do to get it."

He stood looking at her, wearing a black dress with open sides.

"Wow" was the only word that came. "You look…good."

"Thank you." She smiled.

"Did I say good? You look amazing."

"Are you ready?" she asked, walking to him.

"I kind of feel under-dressed now." He glanced down at his utility uniform.

"You're fine. I like uniforms."

She fed the sugar dish into the cage, where Gulliver began squeaking.

"That will keep him busy for a while," she remarked, offering her hand. "Shall we go?"

Gently taking her hand, he led her out the door.

"So what are we going to see?"

"Well, you got off easy. The only chick flick they have is *Fall's Pendulum*."

"Yeah I've heard that name a few times, what's it about?"

"I read the book. It's actually based on a true story. About a girl who's abducted from her colony by the Pillagers, and falls in love with her captor.

But there'll probably be some action at the end when the Legionnaires come to get her, so you won't be completely miserable."

"Oh, well that's good."

The theater stood near the town's edge. This early, there were only a few customers at the entry terminals. As they approached the door, Taula broke from his hand to move to the customer terminal.

"Taula Gilyard," she spoke. "I reserved a private theater."

"Welcome Doctor Gilyard," the AI greeted. "What feature would you like to see?"

"*Fall's Pendulum*."

"That title is a new release. Would you like to incur bonus points by writing a review after the showing?"

"Not this time."

"Will this be an interactive showing?"

"No thank you."

"Would you like any refreshments?"

"Yes, extra large Vanilla Stripes for me." She turned to him.

"I'll have the same."

"Also extra large popcorn with butter, that's real butter not synthetic. And a large box of Sappers."

His face twisted at the thought of the candy—deep-fried chocolate balls with a breading held on by boiled syrup.

"That's two XL Vanilla Stripes, XL Popcorn with real butter, and a box of Sappers. Your total is fifty-two troys."

Gritting his teeth, Clearwater waved his hand over the payment terminal. If they were going to rob him, they could at least show the basic courtesy of pointing a gun.

"Thank you…unregistered user. Would you like to register and join our rewards club?"

"No," he groaned.

"Enjoy the session."

Beyond the door, two chairs stood overlooking a recess in the floor of the dimly lit room. As they sat, their refreshments rose with a small table from the floor. Taking the box of candies, Taula fiddled with it for a moment, trying to slip her nail under the wrapper. Growing annoyed, she sighed before slapping the box against his chest.

He pinched the top of the box carefully, images of the box coming apart and the candies scattering flooding through his mind. Delicately he tore the container open before handing it back to her.

"Have you ever had these?" she asked. "You have to try one."

Even as he shook his head, one was quickly placed in his hand.

"Try it." She jabbed with an elbow.

Hesitantly he placed the candy in his mouth and bit down. Gagging on the overpowering taste, he swallowed before reaching for his drink, now sour in comparison.

"I think I just OD'd on sugar." He coughed while she giggled. "I don't understand how anyone can eat that stuff."

"It's starting," she whispered as the overhead projectors came to life, and holograms filled the floor below. Settling in for the drudgery he took the popcorn from the table and sat it in his lap. His heart skipped a beat as she reached for it, and as she took a handful he laid his arm across the back of her chair. While she watched the show he gazed at her in the corner of his eye, trying to find the guts to move his arm down to her shoulder. As the time passed and he saw her shed a tear he bit his lip, debating if he should lower his arm. He took a breath to relax, an instant before an image flashed in his NOD.

ALL UNITS, EMERGENCY CONDITION.
FROM: LT. BROWER
ALL OFFICERS TO BARRACKS IMMEDIATELY!

"Not now," he whispered, prompting Taula to look up at him.

"What's wrong?"

"It's an alert," he groaned. "I…I have to go."

Leaning away, she nodded.

"Go."

"I'm sorry." He rose from the chairs. "I really am."

"It's okay." She smiled. "Go."

He turned to race out of the theater. The Combine better be invading. Why? Why did this have to happen now?

CHAPTER
7D

THE HOUR WAS LATE in the Cathedral, Natalie and Jasmine were already in bed, both passed-out drunk. Steven was wide awake and well-dressed. His company had arrived. Four men, one woman, and a kodaz had all answered his summons. They sat at a round table, waiting for him to sit and begin the meeting.

Senator Edgar Moore, believed by many to best the next prime speaker, head of one of the senate's three houses. Yazeed Alhi, Lieutenant Justice of the senate's Justiciar branch, Baron/Admiral Yun Bak, once Steven's commanding officer. Lieutenant Administrator Axle Hoff, of the Solar Department of Justice. Duchess Helga Falk, of the Elysian Commonwealth. Finally Daul Virantel, a marshal of the Legionnaires. They grew quiet when he entered.

"I thank each of you for coming on such short notice," Steven began. "I'm sorry I could not tell you why. But you never know who might be listening."

He turned to his guards.

"If you will excuse us."

Reluctantly the deltas filed out of the room, before he closed the door.

"So let's get on with it," Duchess Helga scoffed. "I have pressing matters."

"Patience, milady." He forced a smile. "None of them are more important than this."

He took his chair and popped his knuckles, silent for a moment to allow them just a little bit longer to stew over why they were here.

"I will go straight to the point. As some of you have no doubt expected, very soon I will be emperor."

He gave them some time for the words to sink in.

"So, the old man finally made a choice?" Senator Moore questioned.

Steven smiled in return.

"For now, it is a secret matter. That is part of why I called you here. What I have to tell you cannot leave this room."

He waited as one by one they nodded.

"I have it on good authority that some will not take it well. They may even challenge my fitness to rule in the senate. That is why you are here. Now, we've all known each other for a while. I am sure I can count on each of you for support."

He eyed them one at a time, carefully scanning their surface thoughts.

"We followin' whoever the senate confirms." Marshal Virantel broke the silence, pausing for a moment to adjust his speech regulator. "Nothin' will change that."

The taste of alien thoughts was always so vile, but the kodaz spoke truthfully.

"Of course, and I would expect no less. But I am concerned about morale issues if there is a leadership dispute. That is why I invited you and the admiral. To make sure you are aware of the possibility."

"You know you have my support." Admiral Yun turned to him. "But I must concur with the Marshal. My loyalty must reside with whomever the senate confirms."

There was no lie in the admiral's mind. That was disappointing. Perhaps there was not as much loyalty there as he had hoped.

"Certainly. I simply do not want our soldiers worried about who is leading the Empire, should something transpire with the Combine. Such a succession dispute could be seen as an opportunity."

Both officers nodded in unison at the implication.

"Yes, well," Duchess Helga spoke up, "what I'm hearing is that you want favors."

He grinned, pointing a finger at her.

"Well, you all know me. You know I like to do favors, particularly for those who have done them for me."

He turned to Senator Moore.

"As Prime Speaker, any vote of No Confidence will require your approval to proceed. If one of my dear siblings disputes my leadership, I would be most appreciative if you looked unfavorably on their application."

"I feel compelled to mention," Administrator Hoff said, "this conversation is quite illegal."

"Laws are meant to punish wicked people for the evil they do." Steven turned to him. "But good people cannot allow the letter of the law to triumph over justice and necessity. I should think the next administrator general would know this truth."

Steven smiled, and after quietly contemplating, Hoff smiled back.

"So what's in it for me?" The duchess brought his eyes back to her. "Why am I here?"

He pointed to her again, waggling his finger.

"You have been a very naughty girl." He stopped to chuckle. "Aurora Technologies is about to be indicted on charges of corporate espionage against Consolidated Automatech. As a major shareholder of that company, that could be very bad for you. Nobles have been forced to abdicate over that kind of thing."

Her face paled, and he had to suppress a smile at the panicked thoughts racing through her mind.

"That's classified," Hoff protested. "You can't just let that slip."

"Relax," he said to both, holding up a hand to silence them. "We're at this table to make solutions. Now, Duchess…may I call you Helga?"

Still pale, she nodded.

"Helga, we both know if that indictment comes, bad things will happen."

This was the part he loved, nailing such a haughty bitch to the wall. The delicious fear, the desperate mental gymnastics to try to find an escape. Before the Encephalon's boon, he'd have been unable to taste it through the 4CM systems in her dress. Now, it was like pouring sugar on his tongue.

"Now, let us suppose for a few moments. Let us suppose that there is no real way to stop that indictment from coming. Let us further suppose that when this happens, Aurora stock prices will plunge to the point that they become ripe for hostile takeover. In that situation, I would not hesitate to think that the High King of the Dominion would eagerly buy up majority control of the company. Since Aurora is an internationally traded company, the Elysians will not be able to stop him. That would in turn allow him to dismantle Aurora, destroying Consolidated Automatech's biggest competitor. He'd also get to kick the Commonwealth in the shins as payback for all those attempts to create and fund feminist groups in their nation that your queen claims never happened.

"Let us further suppose that the Elysian economy was already in such bad shape as a result of the economic warfare that you provoked. That the loss of Aurora would drag the whole nation down. Queen Mae would be forced to abdicate her position. That would leave the new emperor responsible for choosing her replacement.

"So we go on to suppose that a particular duchess of the Commonwealth, a major shareholder in Aurora, escapes the indictment. That the Justice Department finds that the actions were taken without her knowledge or consent. That would allow her to buy out her competition in the company while the Commerce Department keeps the Reichsylvannians bogged-down in anti-trust proceedings. That would leave this hypothetical duchess as majority owner of Aurora. More importantly, it would make her the savior of the Elysian economy, and a shoe-in to take the recently abdicated title of queen."

Her expression was a mix of terror and apprehension. But behind her eyes he listened as she contemplated his words, following the progression as he led her by the nose. Finally she nodded.

"It…would be good to be that duchess."

They all turned as Justice Alhi rose to his feet.

"I don't think I can partake in this conversation any longer." He cleared his throat. "If you will excuse me."

"I think you will want to hear the rest of this."

"Respectfully, I've heard as much as I care to."

Steven's eyes narrowed as he glared down his nose at the short man.

"Put your ass in that chair, Justice." The change in his tone shocked those around him. "I am not finished with you."

Hesitantly the justice sat back down, placing his elbows on the table. Though his expression was calm, his thoughts were flooded by worries of what was waiting for him if he did leave. Steven had to stop himself from smiling. Not that long ago he had to focus intently to read the thoughts in another's mind. Now he barely had to do more than look at them.

"All right, what do you wish to say?"

"You are here for the same reason as Senator Moore. You are one of three votes needed for a motion of No Confidence to go forward."

"And you think after what I've heard here, I won't consider it?"

"No, you won't." Steven's smile returned. "You're not, because you lost all your savings the first time Aurora's stock crashed. You've been struggling for six years now to keep your assets. Your retirement—not to mention your standard of living—is looking pretty shaky. Especially when that indictment hits."

The justice was silent as his eyes were cast down.

"That big house of yours on that tropical paradise, in danger of being seized. Those universities you're paying for your grandchildren to attend? Their parents can't afford that alone. That pretty little wife you just married who's a quarter your age? Well, I don't know if she'll continue to think you're so charming when you're no longer a wealthy man."

Steven grinned again.

"You've had a very long and distinguished career in the senate. You've done a lot of good things there. I don't think its right that someone who has done so much good ends up on stipend in his final years. Just imagine what you could do for your family, and the life you'd have, if a grateful emperor appointed you a baron. Think of that. A whole planet to call your retirement home, with the money and resources to terraform it into whatever you wanted. You could give it to your children to administer, and ensure a very comfortable living for them and their progeny. Now that sounds like a hell of a retirement to me."

Steven's fingers tapped lightly on the table.

"I like to do favors, Justice, especially for those who do them for me."

"All right," he whispered, unable to bring his eyes up. "You have my vote."

"As always you are a wise man." He rose from his chair. "Well, that concludes our business. You're welcome to stay and enjoy my hospitality as long as you like. And thank you for coming."

All but Admiral Yun rose from the table and made their way out.

"Something more, Admiral?" Steven asked.

"This is a dangerous game you're playing, son," the admiral remarked. "This could come back to bite you."

Laughing, Steven sat on the table, looking down at his old commander.

"I was born to play this game."

"Look, I've been an admiral long enough to know how politics work. Just be careful—when you've got people by the balls, they start to get desperate. And desperate people are prone to doing stupid things."

"You just let me worry about that. Can't make an omelet without breaking some eggs."

"I just hope you know what you're doing." The admiral rose to his feet. "But I want you to know, I'm not looking for any favors. As soon as things calm down with the Combine, I plan to retire. That said, you have my support."

"I knew I could count on you," Steven answered, shaking his hand before the admiral departed.

When the door closed he let out a sigh, reflecting on the events that had just transpired.

"Do you think they'll do their jobs?"

"You did well. They will do what they must, all except the justice."

"Do you think he will be a problem?"

"He will support you when the time comes. But his conscience will eventually win out. Around the time his grandchildren have graduated, he will come forward. He will have to be disposed of before then."

"If that's what it takes." He shrugged. "Then that's what it takes."

"No trace can be left to you. My agents will handle the matter, when the time comes. Go now, lay with your wives. There is much to be done, and you will need your rest."

CHAPTER
7E

WITHIN THE CARGO BAY of a great ship, Oul'sor stood in the company of seventy-seven Vaar warriors. Armored in all but their helmets, they sat on stools by large cargo pods, grumbling at the food in their hands. Each held a plastic bag of brown gel that they poured into their gullets. They were the 4th Echelon of the Urutagh Mel'tanni, who their foes would call the Deniable Operations Service.

Chosen from the ranks of the infantry, every warrior was a veteran of at least two hundred years of service. Each chosen for his intelligence, ability to control aggression, and reason. More warlords were elevated from the ranks of the Urutagh than any other branch of Vaar society. There was a time when a naive version of himself believed that nothing in the universe could stand against them. That innocence was shattered the first time the Urutagh encountered a Solar Commando.

Oul'sor's eyes moved down to the shrouded alien who even now stood at his feet, silently watching the others eating. The Vaar capacity to regenerate was one of the many advantages for which the lesser races feared them. Under stress, their body temperature would more than double as they metabolized fat to heal wounds suffered by their soft tissue. This same ability formed the basis of the Vaar immune system, where infected tissue was simply destroyed by the body and regenerated anew.

The warriors were eating from bags of fat and metabolic steroids. But this was a new mixture. Indorai had provided it, claiming it would vastly enhance their regeneration. Though reluctant to take the offering without assurance, they followed orders, complaining only about the taste.

The upcoming mission would be one of the most dangerous they had ever embarked upon. Even if they achieved complete surprise, they would be facing elite warriors behind the lines of a technologically superior enemy. At least one Solar Commando was sure to make an appearance, hopefully the right one. If they were delayed too long, they would be caught in the coming dilation storm. They could be fighting in one instant, and deep in the midst of an enemy fleet the next.

"You are sure this will happen as you say?" Oul'sor turned down to the shrouded alien, who seemed to turn to look up at him.

"Certain," Indorai answered.

"How do you know it will be the Crykeeper?"

In reply Indorai reached out, placing his hand on Oul'sor's foot. He shook briefly as imagery flooded through his mind.

"Do not fight it. Watch, and listen."

His vision was replaced by the image of two beings, humans, standing on a balcony. One was shorter than the other, with far longer hair and a protruding chest—a female. The image drew nearer, so that he could see their faces. He recognized the female, the one the Solars called the Imperial Rose. He did not know the face of the other, but somehow he did and he growled.

"Crykeeper," he whispered, continuing to watch.

The image shifted and he saw them seated together at a table, the female in the male's lap while she moved on him. Mating, he could only assume. He could hear their words as they spoke to one another, but with the vision bypassing his translators he could only guess at what they said, not that he cared to do so.

"A connection has already formed between them." Indorai's thoughts were clearer than ever in his mind. *"Follow your mission. When she is in danger, the object of your hate will appear. When that happens, I expect you will know what to do."*

"I care nothing for the female," he growled. "But if she is the key to the Crykeeper—"

"Satisfy your revenge, Oul'sor, but do not forget your mission. There is more at stake here than your personal grudge."

"She is their responsibility," Oul'sor returned. "If the Crykeeper shows himself, nothing will stand in my way."

The vision faded as Indorai withdrew his hand.

"Do not forget who gave you this opportunity, Oul'sor."

Saying nothing, he looked back to the Urutagh. As they finished gorging themselves on the fat, each took a large pill before climbing into the nearest cargo pod.

"You are sure they will not be detected?" Oul'sor questioned. "Solar sensors are much more advanced than our own."

"Diplomatic crates receive only cursory examinations to ensure there are not undeclared weapons," Indorai explained. "Since they will arm themselves at their destination, no weapons will be detected. Those pills will render them to chemical stasis; the scanners will mistake them for a shipment of food."

"That will work for them." Oul'sor turned to a collection of larger crates behind himself. "I will not be hidden so easily in this body."

"You will have to fabricate your weapons and acquire ammunition when you arrive. But your crates will simply allow them to determine the presence of machinery."

Oul'sor eyed the markings on the crates, listing their contents as components for atmosphere regulators.

"I hope you are correct, Indorai."

"Let us be sure of that," the hollow one answered as a pair of guards escorted a small group of aliens toward them.

Four violet-skinned humanoids walked with their heads cowed, afraid to make eye contact with those they passed. The quants were such wretched creatures. The largest males were smaller than even a human female. Too weak to fight, too stupid to build a society worth saving, too cowardly to stand their ground and do battle. Oul'sor could not decide if he hated them for being wastes of perfectly good organs, or pity them for their miserable existence.

When the four came to Oul'sor and Indorai, he could see their bodies trembling. Red, featureless, lifeless eyes glared down at the deck. They had so little pride, they would not even look up. No Vaar would ever show such shame, no matter how dire their circumstance.

"Captain Mukesh." Indorai turned to the quant standing in the center. "Thank you for coming."

The quants remained silent, but their trembling grew more intense as the hollow one walked a circle around them.

"You have done as you were instructed?" Indorai questioned.

"Y-yes," Mukesh answered, turning to one of his comrades who quickly laid a chest on the ground. Without so much as touching it Indorai opened the chest, and emitted a scoff.

"How precious," he taunted. "Gems, jewelry, your people's constitution? As if creatures like you could ever form a strong nation. You can't even defend your own homes."

"We did as you asked," Mukesh began. "What—"

Indorai cut him off. "I ask you for nothing. You continue to exist only through my goodwill. When I speak, you obey."

Mukesh shifted nervously.

"We did as you commanded." He bowed lower. "What do you wish now?"

"You will take these." His four voices gave a short laugh. "Treasures, to Avalon. Once there, you will seek out the Imperial Rose, and you will beg her to take custody of these artifacts for safekeeping in the Empire."

"Of course," Mukesh answered, bowing yet again.

Oul'sor watched in silence, growing uncomfortable. The quants were indeed pathetic creatures, but was there a need to constantly remind them?

Indorai ceased his orbit to loom over Mukesh.

"Hold out your hand."

The quant's eyes narrowed, his entire body wincing as he obeyed. The hollow one moved, and a small medallion became visible in his palm.

"This transponder will allow the noble warriors you see here to find Her Majesty when the time comes. You will thank her for safeguarding your people's treasures, by offering it as a gift."

"Certainly, happily, empty one." Mukesh quickly pocketed the trinket. Even Oul'sor jumped as Indorai's voice suddenly grew louder.

"Do you think I do not see your duplicitous thoughts?" Indorai's voices echoed off the metal walls. "You deign to reveal this plot to her, and beg sanctuary."

"No." Mukesh suddenly glared up to Indorai, expression locked in what Oul'sor could only assume was fear. "I—"

"Do not lie to me." Indorai's voice suddenly lowered to almost a whisper. "If you succeed in this mission, you and your families will be well taken care of. But if you should give in to temptations of treachery…"

Indorai's silhouette shifted; both Oul'sor and the quants took a step back as a long tendril, seemingly forged from silver light, emerged from his hollow form. Soon a second branched out, and the quants visibly shook at the display. Oul'sor's head darted from side to side as suddenly more hollow images appeared, brandishing their own glowing tendrils. The quants cried out as the tendrils seized their arms, plucking them from the ground. The appendages seemed to lengthen, encircling his victims until their bodies were cocooned.

"As you can see"—sixteen voices now spoke in unison—*"I can be in more than one place, at one time. All you care about, and all the places they go. I will be there. I will not destroy them with speed and mercy. I will prolong their natural existence, that they may endure 1,000 years of suffering. And you will be there to see it all. Your own torment will only come after. Contemplate this as the wages of treachery, and the cost of failure."*

The quants cried out as the glowing tendrils vanished, leaving them to fall to the ground. The seeming copies of Indorai were gone as well. As Mukesh began to speak, Indorai raised a hand, silencing him.

"My ears do not seek your platitudes. Do as you are told. Now be gone."

The quants rose quickly to their feet, then bowed their heads and scampered away.

"Was that necessary?" Oul'sor questioned.

Indorai turned to him.

"To threaten their families," he pressed, "would equal profit not be gained from assuring them that you were watching?"

"I saw his thoughts, Oul'sor, and did as I needed."

"A problem remains," Oul'sor continued. "It is understood that those who approach the feet of royalty consent to a scan of their minds and grasping of their intent. How do you know this will not be discovered?"

Indorai laughed.

"Because I will be there," he answered, "and any who attempt to probe their minds will read only worry that she may refuse their request."

Oul'sor's posture hunched as he brought his eyes lower.

"If you can do that, why not apprehend the princess yourself? Or at least place the device upon her?"

"Surely as many years as you have been warlord you need not ask," Indorai returned. "This dirties the hands of the quants, and links them to this act. Your people can then use that against those quants impelled to assist you. The threat of revealing their aid in this, and compromising the Empire's mercy, I think you will find an excellent fulcrum to leverage their obedience."

"And creating illusions, menacing their families with a thousand years of suffering?"

"I think your personal tragedy has affected your judgment, Oul'sor. I created no illusions, and did what I needed to motivate them. Worry about your tasks, Oul'sor, and leave me to mine."

Oul'sor wanted to shout at the hollow one, to demand that he explain himself. To justify such an evil act, such a terrible threat. But he could not. He might need Indorai's help if this mission failed.

"Now Oul'sor, it is your turn."

Indorai motioned to a scaffolding where several techs awaited.

Oul'sor stood upright as the scaffolding came to surround him. Quickly the techs went to work. First they separated his arms and placed them into one of the pods. His head came next, rising off his body and remaining on the scaffold as his torso and his legs were sent to their own pods.

"She will be in possession of the transponder shortly after you arrive," Indorai explained as Oul'sor's head was lowered into the final crate. *"I have no doubt about our assets now. Focus on the Imperial Rose; she is the key to what you want."*

A small short ran through his mind as Oul'sor's head was powered down. As his vision dimmed, the image in his mind was of the princess. He would find her. If the Crykeeper came, he would destroy him. If not, he would flay the very flesh from her bones, until the coward showed himself.

CHAPTER
8A

STEPPING OFF HIS SHIP, Panzer checked the uniform of the day for a final time. He wore the white of an Armada's line officer. On his collar was the image of a three-masted sailing ship to mark himself as a captain. A badge on his right chest presented him as a member of fleet intelligence. Some would notice him, but the only people who might question him were those who already knew who he was.

At the edge of the hangar, a router waited to send him the bridge. The 100-meter chamber was arrayed in two decks, with tactical personnel on the lower deck and command staff overlooking them. All walls were lined by gamma arens at their terminals, working as networked minds to coordinate the fleet.

He stepped off the router and briefly eyed the central display that dominated the floor of the lower chamber. There was shown the full formation of the fleet as it prepared to make the long trip. The fleet was at FTL, now approaching the Hourglass Gateway. The enormous metal ring in space was tied to a twin in the target galaxy. Through the gateway they would make the voyage to cross the vast expanse separating the Solar Galaxy Cluster from the distant Virgo Cluster. With the aid of the ring, the trip would take only a few days. Without this permanent instillation, the trip was one that could be made over the course of weeks and only by the largest ships.

On the upper deck Panzer scanned the overhangs, finding the ship's executive officer sitting in the command chair. Panzer approached and the alpha aren rose to greet him.

"Reporting in," Panzer said.

"Welcome aboard, Captain...Hightower was it?"

"Correct, Captain," Panzer answered, shaking his hand. "I'm here to speak to Aetius."

The aren nodded.

"Admiral Aetius is in his office."

Through a hatch at the rear, Panzer exited the main bridge to enter the admiral's bridge. The separate command center served as a workplace for the admiral and his staff to manage the fleet without the two bridge crews getting in each other's way. At the rear of this bridge was the office he sought. Panzer entered silently, to find Aetius surrounded by several officers. He waited patiently until Aetius noticed him.

"Staff, please excuse us." The admiral interrupted the conversation. The other officers quickly filed out, some shooting glances at the badge Panzer wore. They said nothing; a couple knew who he was. The rest would simply assume that Fleet Intelligence needed to convey something to the admiral in private.

When they were alone, Panzer was the first to speak.

"Got your message, you wanted to see me?"

"Yes, thank you for coming," Aetius answered. "I had a few things to discuss."

Panzer's eyes lit up as a file was sent to his NOD, and his jaw dropped when he opened it.

"He's alive?"

"One of our bugs intercepted it last night. Intelligence suggests he's resumed working with DOS. We don't know what they are doing yet."

"I can't believe he's alive," Panzer stammered. "I shoved a grenade down his throat. Literally, I shoved a Vaar shrapnel grenade into his gullet. Even for a Vaar to survive that—"

"Obviously enough of his brains survived," Aetius finished the thought. "I thought you'd like to know."

"Yeah. Damn, killing him was an accomplishment. Oul'sor was one of the oldest warlords. Probably going to end up seeing him again at some point."

"You should also know," Aetius continued, "one of the DOS you killed recently was named Vil'sor."

Panzer eyed him.

"Lovely, so he'll have an ax to grind. Did you confirm the relationship?"

"Tried to," Aetius answered, eyes moving through his own NOD. "Going through Vaar records suggests he has some six hundred children. I'm guessing that's probably not the case."

"I wouldn't be so sure. Vaar warlords have reproductive rights to anyone they wish. Even if they aren't flattered by the honor."

"Seeing as how the Vaar aren't very big on genetic engineering, it's a wonder he had any time to go off to war."

Both chuckled.

"Well, thanks for the info. Was that it?"

"No. Come with me."

Panzer followed the admiral back into his bridge. They traveled to a router, and were transported to a new room. Three decks of terminals were each filled with gamma arens, save for the occasional alpha supervising them.

"This is new," Panzer remarked. "I...think."

"It is. Using the PACKET you took from the *Polarized Aggression*, we've broken the Vaar's primary, secondary, and tertiary encryption ciphers. Once we get to the Hourglass, every bug in the galaxy will feed into these terminals. Thanks to this, we'll know the location of every Vaar ship, the deployments of every shore battery, and the strength of every infantry force. And it's all thanks to you."

"I didn't do it alone, Admiral," he answered. "We lost six commandos and thirty auxiliaries, taking that thing off of the *Polarized Aggression*."

"But, it was your idea to do so. Wasn't it?"

He nodded.

"I figured, since we were there. At least some good has come from it."

"So long as the Vaar continue to use the same ciphers, they won't be able to break wind without us knowing. When they do switch, which we estimate will be in about three months, our knowledge of the encryption protocols will allow this facility to break their new codes within a few days."

"Very impressive."

Another file dropped into Panzer's NOD.

"I've set up a direct link to this terminal for all commandos operating in the region. Give that to your AI, and you'll have full access to this facility's files."

"That's…outstanding, Admiral."

"Seemed the least I could do."

Panzer began to speak but stopped himself, as there were too many ears present.

???: So, 30,000 ships?

ADM AETIUS: I asked for 200,000. But his Majesty worried that it would provoke the Combine. I don't know what else to do, Colonel. They just don't want to believe it."

???: Well, for what it's worth. I'll feel better knowing you're in the Hourglass.

ADM AETIUS: Between this flotilla and the ships already there, I'll have about 50,000 under my command. If the Vaar come over that border, at least it might slow them down.

"At least we'll have some warning," Aetius said, returning the conversation to verbal. "Every life this intelligence allows us to save is thanks to you. I thought you should know that."

"Thanks, Admiral, I appreciate it. You haven't by chance caught any chatter about the Sovari Soma?

Aetius shook his head.

"I'll let you know if we do."

CHAPTER
8B

S IMMONNE WALKED AND LISTENED while Admiral Gilyard spoke. The man had so much pride in his ship one would have thought it was his child. They had just come from engineering, where banks of reactors larger than most ships each bottled power greater than the output of main sequence stars. Their next stop was the ship's foundries. While the admiral rattled off every little detail, her mind was focused elsewhere. Now that some time had passed and the events of the night had really sunk in, her brow was slightly furrowed.

Who did he think he was? Believing that she'd let him tie her up, even put her on a leash like a pet? She was an Imperial Princess, not just any but the Imperial Rose! If either of them was going to be a plaything for the others amusement it would be *him*. He would be the one tied up and helpless for her amusement, rather than sit there with that smug look on his face like some kind of, of…something!

"Your Majesty?" The admiral's voice drew her attention. "Is something wrong?"

"My apologies, Admiral, I was just thinking. Please continue."

He did not miss a beat.

"As I was saying, Armadas ships aren't just big, they're massive. Part of what distinguishes our ships is how they are built. Most civilizations, they build ships out of hulls and frameworks. Some use other methods. Take the Combine, for example: They can match the density of kilosteel but not its other properties.[18] Their ships are mostly hollow; their construction is rather like a giant aerogel. Instead of rooms they have bubbles, and corridors make up the primary support structure.

"An Armadas ship, by contrast, whether it is a monitor or supercruiser, begins its life as a solid block of kilosteel. The shape is then carved out of that block, while rooms and corridors like this are bored into it. As a result,

---

18 Kilosteel refers to a variety of building materials, all of which have a density of approximately 1 kilogram per cubic centimeter. Type-41 Kilosteel used in constructing warships has a melting point of 11.21 GK, tensile strength of 77.1 PPa, and compressive strength of 84.4 PPa.

even the *Hurricane*, which has a lot more open volume than most, is better than fifty percent solid kilosteel. That's part of what makes us so tough. Not only do we have several stars worth of energy in our shields, but if you get through that, you'll have to break many kilometers of one of the strongest materials known to science. Why if we were to ram a Combine ship, they'd shatter like antique glass."

"Very impressive," Simmonne remarked, doing her best to feign an interest as her mind wandered. She tried to imagine the colonel in the position he had sought to place her, but the image would not materialize in her mind. Who was she kidding? She could not even look him in the eye, even stop herself from trembling when he was near. She shuddered, remembering those enormous hands closed on her wrists.

"We build all of our assets under the assumption that they will be put to use against enemies of similar or greater capabilities," Gilyard continued. "The dense hull makes it highly resistant to hostile fire. More importantly, density is one of the only defenses against warp weapons. As a warp weapon penetrates, the warp pulse begins to fill with matter faster than it can dispose of it. The more it fills up, the quicker it dilates and loses its effectiveness. So your only defenses are warp shielding, super-dense materials, or exotic materials that exist in their own warped state. But building a ship out of astranium or Reichsylvannian steel would take so long, and be so expensive, the resulting vessel would be too valuable to send into combat. So we use kilosteel, and anyone shooting at it has to puncture several kilometers from any angle to try to hit something vital."

"I see," she answered automatically. "Very impressive."

He led her through a router to a catwalk overlooking a noisy chamber. Below, machinery hummed and sparks flew while automatech worked.

"The *Hurricane*'s tactical abilities are impressive. But this, this is what makes her a marvel. An old soldier's saying is that amateurs talk tactics, but professionals talk logistics. Armadas warships are far more than gunboats. Within these hulls are factories, foundries, automatech printers, aren breeding centers, and more.

"When we go into battle, we don't just shoot the enemy. We can go into orbit around a star, and tap it for fuel. By using its hydrogen to fuel our printers, we can manufacture almost anything we need. We can flood the enemy in disposable automatech, replace casualties with new arens, repair and refit other ships, manufacture other supplies. Or we can become hell's version of an artillery platform, refilling our own ammunition as we send a constant stream of missiles at the enemy. In peacetime, we can use all these same resources to provide aid to disaster-stricken worlds."

She was not even paying enough attention to be certain she had offered an impressed platitude. She shuddered as she thought of the colonel's vision, her body trussed up and helpless. Her breath quickened. Being bound might not be so bad, but he was not going to gag her. Why would he want to? No, that was going too far.

"During the Outlands War, I was in command of the battle cruiser *Yamato*. When we learned of the situation on Miner-9, we singlehandedly broke the siege of the planet. We destroyed or drove into retreat over three hundred Outlands ships. But we were banged up pretty bad. Whereas most navies would scuttle the ship, we tapped the local star and repaired ourselves until we could get underway again. Then we linked up with the *Hurricane*, who refitted us, and we were back in action less than a week later."

"You took on three hundred ships with just one?" Jennifer questioned. The admiral turned to her.

"I think you will better appreciate how on our next stop. But yes. We could have simply hung back and attacked them from standoff distance. However, I felt it was important to induce panic and send them into full retreat. So I ordered the ship to jump directly into the center of their formation."

"That must have surprised them." Julie tried not to laugh.

"To their credit, they tried to fight us off, but we had them outgunned. By positioning ourselves where we did, we ensured that so long as we were operational, they could not threaten the planet. Now if you will all follow me, we'll take a look at what most people really want to see…armament!"

Simmonne followed him through another router, and they came to a long corridor filled with doors marked by numbers.

"Due to the level of automation involved, even the *Hurricane* requires a crew of only about 120,000 across all four watches. That's not counting the Legionnaire complement, of course. The largest share of the organic crew is gunnery staff. All of the ship's weapons are divided into banks. At every bank are weapons systems supervisors. No target is fired upon unless the WSSs confirm it as hostile and grant the AIs permission to engage."

"Wouldn't controlling it from the bridge be more efficient?" Jennifer inquired.

"In some ways yes, others no," the admiral answered. "The problem with that…a ship like the *Hurricane* can annihilate every world in a system in short order. That's simply too much power to place in the grasp of a handful of people."

The admiral led them through one of the doors to a small office where a single crewman leapt from his chair and snapped to attention. Simmonne did not immediately recognize his species. Blue skin, six eyes in two columns, and a circular mouth full of needle-like teeth. Her NOD scanned him, providing a diplomatic cheat sheet. He was an ingridi, a race of oxygen-breathing carnivores admitted to the Empire nine hundred years ago.

"This is Crewman." The admiral hesitated. "Forgive me if I butcher this, crewman. Adszi Mrrrilstishtiki."

The alien answered with several grunts translated into communicable speech by an implant.

"Close enough, sir."

"Crewman Adszi here is a distinguished individual. The first member of his race to qualify for posting to an Armadas ship."

"You must be very proud." Simmonne turned to him.

"Yes, Majesty," he answered while bowing.

"The crewman will help us demonstrate the weapons array." The admiral directed with a wave of his hand.

"Of course, sir. Your Majesty, if you would take the seat."

She nodded and slid down into the chair.

"Now just scan the optical port."

She glanced to the port on the computer terminal, allowing her NOD to interface with the ship.

The alien moved his hands, adjusting the view they now shared until Simmonne saw a new ship. The long vessel was marked by a hammerhead nose, short wings sprouted from a bulbous nose ahead of a tail that extended back to where several pylons formed an X. Large blisters sprouted across its hull—internal chambers. She recognized the design from the news, a Combine frigate.

"The Commando Corps acquired this ship for us," the admiral explained. "GSC spent the last year taking her apart and putting her back together to study its design. Now that they've learned all they can from it, we're going to dispose of it. The ship is online, with a drone crew to operate her. Crewman, take it away."

"Yes sir. Majesty, do you see the yellow indicator in the corner of your screen?"

"I do," Simmonne answered with a nod.

"Focus on that. Now in the new screen it should ask if the target is hostile."

"It does."

"Tell it yes."

She did as he instructed and was rewarded with a new image.

HOSTILE TARGET CONFIRMED – COMBINE TYPE-II FRIGATE

RTT: 1631 LY

TOT: 3.11 Minutes

HKP: 99%

"At your pleasure, Majesty."

Her eyes moved to yes, and once she selected the option, everything else was automatic. Another smaller screen opened showing an image of the *Hurricane*'s hull. A hatch flew open and a large turret rose from the new opening. The turret angled out toward space then adjusted itself before missiles streamed out.

Her image shifted to a map. One icon displayed the *Hurricane*; a second was red, the target ship. Between them five icons in yellow represented the missiles as they raced toward their target. The weapons climbed out of the Dominion galactic disc, allowing them to navigate a straight path to the other side of the galaxy.

"The theater missiles will cruise to the target at six million *c*." the admiral explained. "They can cross 100,000 light years to hit their target if we have the targeting data."

"They can travel that far?" Simmonne turned to him.

"They're only making the trip one way," he answered. "Combine missiles have barely a third of the range."

As the minutes counted down, her mind began to wander again. She closed her hand around her wrist, thinking about how manacles around them would feel. If she were tied up, she would not have to worry about what she was supposed to do. She brought her hand to her mouth to suppress a giggle. But being gagged… She curled two fingers before gently biting her knuckles. That might not be so bad, if it wasn't too big. At least she wouldn't have to worry about trying to think of something to say. Wait, why was she trying to rationalize this? He was *not* doing that to her.

"The missiles are now deploying submunitions," the crewman explained, drawing her attention back to the moment. "To circumvent point defenses."

The counter in her NOD approached zero, and now twenty-five icons descended on the Combine frigate. For a moment the icon was obscured by bright flashes. The image shifted to a visual, revealing that the frigate was now a field of debris.

"Were its shields up?" Julie whispered.

"Yes," the admiral spoke over the crewman to answer her. "Her point-defenses took out four of the submunitions. But she just couldn't stand up to what was left. The *Hurricane* can put 50,000 missiles per second into space. Anything without a strong point defense system is helpless. Ships with point defenses are forced into formations to overlap their fire, or they are just as helpless."

"That's…terrifying," Simmonne said, closing her NOD.

"Peace through superior firepower," the admiral answered. "And that's not even her strongest weaponry. She has torpedo launchers for anything foolish enough to get close, and large cannons for fixed targets."

"Maybe you can explain something to me," Jennifer began. "Why do some disrupters fire warp pulses and others fire shells?"

"Firepower would be the short answer. With an ordinance gun, the shell it fires produces the warp field. Unlike a gun barrel, a shell is only meant to be used once, so it can be much more heavily charged and create a much stronger warp field. That makes shells better at penetrating warp shielding, and the more intense field more rapidly disperses accumulating matter so it can penetrate a lot more before the field collapses. The downside is that you have to carry all those shells as ammunition. A normal disrupter cannon on a ship you simply hook up to generators and it can fire as long as the generators are running. A soldier with a rifle can carry power cores that can give him dozens or even hundreds of shots. With shells, each one is single use. So they're really only for situations where immediate firepower is more important than sustained fire."

"So how are they different from missiles?" Simmonne asked.

"The line can get very blurry. But missiles are always guided, have longer ranges, and rather than constantly maintain a destructive warp field they save most of their energy for a single burst. The big difference between a missile and torpedo is that they often use the same hulls but one trades fuel and speed for even more firepower. Well, if you will follow me we will finish the tour on the bridge."

She rose to follow before turning back to the crewman, who had begun to speak but stopped.

"What is it, crewman?"

"Majesty, if I may?" He held up a small device. It took her a moment to realize it was a holo-recorder.

"Of course."

She took the device before handing it to the admiral.

"Do you mind?"

"Not at all, Majesty," the admiral answered. Simmonne smiled. She could see he minded, but went along.

"Stand with me," Simmonne directed. She took the nervous alien's arm and curled it around herself before smiling.

"Got it," the admiral said, handing the device back to the crewman.

She followed the admiral to the nearest router, and then to the bridge. There the crew quickly came to attention.

"As you were," Gilyard ordered, sending them back two work as he led her to the upper deck. "And here we have the nerve center for the entire ship. We should be arriving at the Hourglass Gate now."

A rattle moved through the ship as it slowed from warp travel, and the floor display lit to show a metal ring in space, glowing as it built power.

"Once the fleet hits that ring, we're on our way." Gilyard turned to her with a smile. "Would you care to give the order?"

"Me?" Simmonne smiled as he nodded. Stepping to the edge of the command deck, she looked down, finding the pilot, an alpha aren looking up to her expectantly.

"Take us in," she ordered.

"Aye, Majesty," the crew answered together.

The *Hurricane* led the way toward the ring as the glow became brighter. A shell of light expanded out from the ring, forming into a globe as the wormhole was opened. As the *Hurricane* moved into the sphere, the hull bucked, and the image faded to a field of blue.

"And we're on our way." Gilyard clapped his hands together. "In one week, you'll be in the Hourglass Galaxy. Now if you'll come with me, I'll show you around the bridge."

"Lead the way."

CHAPTER
8C

I N A DARK CHAMBER far beneath the surface, Clearwater stood behind Taula. Ahead of them, roliam techs operated a plasma drill while attempting to cut through a closed door. Other scientists and their escorts packed the corridor, all waiting to see what lay beyond. Clearwater's eyes focused on Taula as he thought back to the theater. Stupid readiness drill, why did they have to have one just when he was working up his courage?

The scientists were sure this chamber would be one of the most important in the temple. Now Taula would be so busy; who knew when they would have time to try for another evening together?

"It's not working," one of the roliams announced. "The door's temperature is unchanged. Something is funneling the heat away faster than we can inject it."

"So why not blow the door?" a kodaz scientist asked.

"Without knowing what's on the other side?" Taula turned to him, before looking back to the techs. "Any more luck scanning?"

"Nothing," the roliam answered. "Something is causing our sensors to reflect. We can estimate the size of the room, but that's it."

Taula glanced back at Clearwater.

"What about a disrupter?"

The roliam glanced at the door, before looking back to her.

"We don't detect any warp resistance in the door. It should work, but with a disrupter's penetration, we don't know what we'll damage on the other side."

Taula turned to an old man in a lab coat, who simply nodded.

"Do it," she directed.

She urged Clearwater forward, and he approached the two roliams.

"Shoot where I mark, please," she commented, using her multiple arms to chalk spots on the door.

With his pistol in hand, Clearwater adjusted the settings in his NOD, raising the frequency as far as he could to minimize the penetration. The roliam had drawn seven X's, three down the door's center and one in each corner.

"Fire in the hole," he said, motioning them to get behind him. He took aim before stepping back and doing so again. The first shot lit the chamber. As the warp field displaced the matter, electrons were freed from their molecular bonds around the new hole in a blast of static. He took a step farther away and fired again, creating a hole for each place marked.

"Now what?" he questioned, holstering the weapon.

"Now we use low-intensity charges to shatter the door, rather than blow it in," the roliam explained. "Everyone back, please."

When he turned back to the group, something caught Clearwater's eye. Farther up the corridor, someone stood alone. Squeezing past Taula, he maneuvered through the packed crowd, hoping to see who it was. Yet when he made to the back of the crowd, they were gone.

"Fire in the hole!"

He flinched at the blast of air when the roliams set off the charges, but kept his eyes ahead. Someone had been standing there, he was sure of it. He touched his cheek, pausing his NOD and rewinding through the last several seconds.

Someone had been there. His biologic eyes had not seen it, but his optical nanites had. Something humanoid was standing in the corridor, watching them. He froze the image. The specter was there. Its body had no features; it was merely a faint outline in the darkness.

"Ghost?" he whispered.

With his pistol in hand again he flipped a small flap up, and glared through the transparency. The pistol's sensors scanned the corridor, but revealed nothing.

"Something wrong?" Brower spoke over his shoulder.

"I..." He glanced back at him before looking down the corridor. "I think I saw the ghost."

"Getting jumpy on me, Lieutenant?"

"No sir." He shook his head. He eyed Brower, sending the image still frozen in the corner of his NOD.

Brower's posture shifted as his eyes widened.

"The hell is that?" he asked.

Clearwater shook his head, scanning again with his pistol.

"Brower to topside, send a couple of bots down here with emissions pods."

"Problem?" One of the scientists joined them.

"Just being cautious," Brower assured her. "Nothing to worry about."

While the scientist rejoined the others, the two of them now swept the corridor with their weapons.

"There's nothing there now," Brower announced. "Come on. We'll let the bots deal with it. But keep sharp."

"Yes sir."

Together they rejoined the rest beyond the newly opened door. The new room was filled with the same pods Taula had shown him, but these were larger. Enough so that they could fit a grown man, even a delta aren.

Clearwater moved to rejoin Taula, his eyes racing through the chamber as she examined one of the pods with a small device.

"I think I was right," she whispered to him. "These pods are covered in calculus problems."

"Neat," he answered, not really listening as he continued to pan the pistol across the room.

"What's with the gun?" She was looking at him now.

"Just scanning the room," he assured her.

After several minutes, clanking sounds announced the arrival of two automatech that joined them in the chamber. A circular pod spun on the head of each as they analyzed the chamber with their sensor packages. He linked his NOD to the bots and watched their scans as they went over every square millimeter of the chamber. His focus was then interrupted by a scream…Taula!

He turned toward her. One of the pods had opened, bathing her in a blue light. Her hands were on its sides, her legs were spread. It was trying to pull her in. His mind flooded with images of what kind of monstrosity might emerge if she became trapped inside.

"Help me!"

He threw his arms around her, tried to pull her away. But the pod had a hold of her; the blue light did not allow her to move. Planting his foot, he prepared to wrench her out of its grip, but stopped. Images of her screaming in his lap filled his mind. He tried to push her to the side, out of the light.

"Get over here!" Brower shouted as several more legionnaires joined them. Taking her arms and her legs they pulled, but still the light did not let go.

"Toward me, on three!" Brower shouted. "One, two, three!"

Taula cried out as five legionnaires worked together, applying steady force to try to push her aside. The light turned green, and Clearwater lurched forward as the pull intensified.

"Warp it!" Brower yelled. "Clearwater, warp it!"

With one arm still around her, his other went down to his thigh and, taking the pistol, he aimed for the pod. The first shot caused the light to shimmer, on the second it faded back to blue. With the third shot the light faded, and the group was thrown to the side.

He landed on his back with Taula on top of him.

"Are you all right?" he asked, placing a hand on her cheek.

"I'm fine," she gasped. "I'm all right."

"Everyone get back!" Brower shouted. "Out of this chamber now."

ANOMALY DETECTED

Clearwater squinted at the words, a report from the bots.

LT BROWER: Warp grenade, oh-one percent power.

One of the bots turned, and from its shoulder fired a projectile toward the corner of the room. The grenade burst creating a shimmer in the air, illuminating the phantom that stood there. Clearwater held up a hand, squinting against the glow.

"Identify yourself!" Brower shouted, drawing his weapon.

Clearwater turned. The ghost, it was real. In the corner of the chamber. Or was it? From the source of the mist, all he could see was what appeared like rippling air.

"Get the civilians out of here!"

Pushing Taula toward the door, Clearwater aimed his own weapon toward the distortion. The ripples moved, contracting in on themselves, until he saw the same hollow image as before.

"Identify yourself!" Brower repeated. "Identify yourself or we will open fire."

Clearwater gasped as the words flooded into his mind.

"I mean you no harm." The voice was soft, distinctly feminine, yet something about it caused his knees to shake.

"Who are you?" Brower demanded.

"I mean you no harm," she...*it* repeated. *"But you do not belong here. This planet is not for you."*

"What do you mean?" Clearwater questioned.

"I cannot stay to explain it to you. They will know I am here. Please, leave while you can."

The silhouette spread out, reforming into the ripples before it and the mist faded away.

"Warp grenades," Brower directed. The two automatech created more of the low-power detonations, but this time nothing was revealed.

"Brower to topside, starting now no civilian is to enter the temple unescorted. I want rifles and grenades on all legionnaires. Officer's meeting in five minutes."

Clearwater looked to the lieutenant, who glared back at him.

"I don't think we're dealing with ghost stories anymore."

CHAPTER 9A

THE HAVEN-CLASS SPACE STATION had two primary functions, first to provide the space of a planet where one did not exist. Second was to awe the people, in particular the scientists and engineers of foreign powers with its simple existence. Four arms extended out from a central globe, each to a length of 400 kilometers beyond the 100-kilometer center sphere. In defiance of gravity that would love nothing more than to crush the entire station into a ball, Avalon beckoned to the denizens of the Hourglass Galaxy.

The station's kilosteel construction gave it enough mass that with a little technological aid, the station held its own atmosphere around its arms. Cityscape dominated the upper and lower surface, providing the facilities expected of any planetary metropolis. To date, most of the station was empty, waiting to be filled by future colonists.

Panzer's nameless ship dropped out of warp and descended toward the station. He stood in the ship's nose, looking out through the transparency while Andira guided them in. The Corps' secret hangar resided in the station's central sphere. Even when its doors opened, it was hidden by hologram projections.

On approach, his eyes glared out over the swarm of refugee ships docked with the station. How many were here now? Two million? Three million? Ten? More arrived every day, thousands crammed into ships that were only meant for a few hundred. For many of these ships they would stop only to drop off their passengers, repair, and refuel. Then, the crew would try to slip across the neutral zone to do it again. The refugees were searched, tagged, and crammed into shelters. Until the local astranet was fully operational, there was nothing else to do.

He shook his head. None of that was his problem, and his opinions about it did not matter. His job was simple—meet up with local security and investigate impossible threats. At least, that was what things were supposed to be.

"Colonel," Andira said. "Admiral Aetius for you."

"Patch him through."

The admiral appeared in his NOD. "We have a situation."

"Hit me."

"We've intercepted orders from Combine high command. The Vaar are moving their units into an attack posture. Their shore batteries are being put on standby, and new cipher codes are being issued to all units ahead of schedule. It could just be an exercise, a show of force with the princess here. It wouldn't be the first time they did something like this. Or…"

"Or it could be a prelude to an attack," Panzer finished. "And if you redeploy based on the information, they'll know we've broken their code."

"Exactly." Aetius nodded. "It's the change in base cipher that bothers me. Three months ahead of schedule. Our projections show they won't be in position until after the changeover. Normally I'd take a secondary defensive posture and try to break the code—"

"But with the princess here, it'd be best if we know something sooner."

"That's how I figured you'd see it, Colonel. Anything you can do?"

Panzer pondered for a moment as his ship slipped into the hangar.

"I'll look into it and be in touch ASAP."

"Thank you, Colonel."

"You not goin' do what I be t'inkin'?" Rhoxx questioned from behind.

Panzer turned to him.

"Is there a choice?"

He walked past the kodaz, headed for his armory.

"I want you to check in with Avalon security."

"I t'inkin' I goin wit'."

"No, one of us has to do the job."

"It bein' my resssponsssibility, goin' wit' you."

"No, you check in with security. It'll be your responsibility to get me out of there if I get caught."

Once saddled with his armor, he walked to the wall, and laid his hands on the large weapon.

"Welcome back, Jorri," he whispered, loading the drum magazine and jamming it in place. Box mags soon formed a bandolier over his chest as Jorri was placed on his back. His knife and pistol were next, but he did not stop there. Where he was going, more might be required. A pair of autopistols was mounted to each thigh, and a collection of grenades on his hip.

"You wantin' I fetch a lantai, carry a few more for you?"

"Very funny," He answered. "Andira, keep the engines in pre-heat, just in case."

"Yes sir, downloading now."

He was cloaked before he left the ship; he had a long way to go and little time.

CHAPTER
9B

IN ONE OF THE *Hurricane*'s hangars, Simmonne approached her private ship. *Mandrake-27* She had wanted to use the new ship gifted to her on Reichsylvannia. But Jenna and Isis both had insisted she wait until the Imperial Guard had torn it apart, looking for boogeymen.

The ship's hull was a teardrop between two large wings, and an open boarding ramp awaited her. With the Twins in tow, she waved to the techs throughout the bay before boarding. There was so much showmanship in being royalty. It was not enough to simply fly down to her destination. She would spend at least an hour making low-altitude flyovers in formation with a squadron of Minotaurs. Only after everyone had a chance to see her arrival did her ship actually maneuver for a landing. As she stared out at the crowd, she bit gently on her knuckles, her thoughts far away.

On a small couch by a window Simmonne looked down on the crowds awaiting her. Curiosity and excitement mixed with a cloud of alien emotions, and she turned her mind away. It was too easy to become lost in the feelings of a crowd. The ship made its final pass, flying just above the cityscape. Skyscrapers climbed from the hull of the station as one would expect of any major city. But the tallest feature was the skyway. The elevated highway was reserved for VIPs to quickly cross the station, using electromagnets to propel conveyors faster than they could fly. As the pilot descended for landing, she even managed to make out the occasional sign welcoming her to the station. Finally the pilot brought the ship to rest on a landing platform, where a blue carpet waited.

"How do I look?" Simmonne asked, rising to her feet.

"They'll be falling all over you," Jenna said with a smile before turning to the Twins. "Remember—all smiles, we've never been happier to be anywhere, in the history of ever."

Both nodded and together they made their way off the ship. A concussion wave of sound struck her skin as the crowd cheered. With a hand high, she waved to them while her guards boxed her in. She could have cut the apprehension in the air. To them, every person beyond the fence surrounding the platform was a threat. Every person inside, only a slightly smaller threat.

As on the *Hurricane*, three officers waited to greet her. Two legionnaires, and something in a red Armadas uniform.

"Your Majesty, welcome to Avalon," the Armadas officer greeted her. "I am station commander Commodore Elizabeth Garren."

Simmonne's eyes moved from the commodore's feet to her hair. Less than ten percent of military officers were human. Less than one percent of men in the Empire could meet the standards for military service. Less than one percent of the one percent were women. Had Simmonne not familiarized herself with the station's command staff during the trip, she would not have guessed.

JULIE: That's a woman?

JENNIFER: I think it used to be.

SIMMONNE: Girls, be nice.

"Thank you," Simmonne had to shout over the crowd, before waiting patiently as the commodore introduced the legionnaires.

"A pleasure, gentlemen."

"If you please, your Majesty," the commodore shouted back. "We'd like to get you inside."

"Certainly, Commodore."

The entourage moved to the side as Simmonne's conveyor was unloaded from the shuttle. There were few places she could be safer than in the seven-meter armored monolith. Three more conveyors unloaded to carry her guards, and she moved to her car as Isis motioned the door to open. The Twins took one of the couches on the side, while the officers sat at Jenna's direction before Isis joined them.

"I want to say it is an honor to have you here, Majesty," the commodore commented.

"Thank you, Commodore."

The conveyor began to move, leading the convoy out of the gate and onto the street.

"We've prepared a tour of the station for you," the commodore began. "I figured—"

Simmonne brought her hand up.

"I appreciate that, Commodore, but between the *Hurricane* and the *Rothburg* I believe I need some respite from touring. I would prefer to get started with my mission here, and see the refugees."

Jenna and Isis both looked to her as the commodore nodded.

"Very well, Majesty, we will set up a tour of the facilities for you."

"I think you misunderstand me, Commodore. I would like to see the facilities now; I need to gauge the actual situation these people are in."

"Majesty," Isis spoke up. "The station's security staff needs time to secure the area."

"Are they not searched for weapons when they arrive?" Simmonne looked to the commodore.

"Of course, Majesty, but—"

"I hardly think people who are here to beg us for protection are going to hurt me." She smiled.

"Majesty, there is still a risk." Isis spoke low. "Perhaps—"

"Isis, do you really think there's a quant huddling in his shelter with a knife, just in case I show up for a look?" She smiled to her overprotective bodyguard.

"There could be," Isis answered deadpan.

"So," Simmonne said, turning to the commodore, "to the refugee areas?"

JENNA: Respectfully, this is not a good idea.

SIMMONNE: I have thirty-six armed guards, Isis, and yourself. I am confident I will be fine. Please do not undermine me in front of the commodore.

Making a face, Jenna nodded quietly.

"Very well, Majesty." The commodore was hesitant.

The cityscape turned to a blur beyond the windows as the conveyor accelerated, leaving the docking ring to reach one of the station's arms. Once clear of the docking rings, the vehicle rose from the ground, climbing over the skyscrapers to bring itself to rest on the skyway. The conveyor shook briefly as it was grasped by the skyway's electromagnets, and propelled to higher speeds.

While the commodore spoke at length about the station, Simmonne's mind was elsewhere. Looking at the skyscrapers, she thought back to the arcologies on Reichsylvannia, and a smoke-laden room. She tried to push it from her mind; this was her big opportunity she had to keep her focus. But the memory did not fade.

CHAPTER
9D

I N THE LATE NIGHT Steven sat on his bed, looking down at Natalie as she slept. His racing pulse caused his hands to tremble as he brushed the hair from her face. The die was not yet cast; he could still stop the future that was barreling toward him. Deep inside, a small voice whispered that was exactly what he needed to do. But another, louder voice insisted otherwise.

"You've waited your entire life for this, Steven."

"I know," he whispered.

"You fought the Outlands War. You destroyed the Pillagers, and brought justice to millions. How many atrocities never happened because of you?"

He said nothing, continuing to stroke her hair.

"I…" He paused, taking a deep breath as tears tried to form in his eyes. "What will she think of me?"

"Why did she marry you, Steven? You knew she did not love you. Why did she accept?"

He wanted nothing more than for those words to be a lie, but they were the truth. She did not love him when she said yes. She did not love him in their years together. Only now, with altered memories, might she learn to. There was only one reason she could have said yes. In him, she saw a future emperor, and at his side a crown for herself. How could there be a better life than that of an empress? Unlimited wealth, every available luxury, enormous power, and no real responsibility.

"The promise of your marriage was unspoken, but it was still a promise. What will she think of you, should you not deliver?"

Sighing, Steven touched her face gently, trying to smile as she mumbled in her sleep. For the first time he had ever seen, far off in her dreams, she was thinking of him. If he concentrated, he could see it—the cloudy image of them together on the throne.

"Do you think she will stay if the crown of empress passes to another?"

"I…don't think I can do it. I don't want to do it."

"It is the cruelty of your existence. For all things, there is a price in suffering. Yours and others. Is there a thing you will not suffer for her?"

"No," he whispered, as a tear streamed down his cheek. "Nothing."

"Then you know what you must do."

"I—"

"Do not hesitate. Do not let your resolve slip now, to have what you deserve, what she deserves. You must take what is rightfully yours."

He nodded quietly, before turning back to Natalie.

"I loved you since I first saw you. I did everything I could to make you love me. I've given you everything I can. All but the one thing you really want. I promise, Natalie, I promise you, you will be empress. Whatever it takes."

He rose from the bed and pulled the sheets up to her shoulders before leaning down and closing his arms around her.

"You'll be sitting on that throne beside me. At the top of every social ladder, it'll all be ours. I promise."

He rose slowly after kissing her cheek. She would make a better empress than any of his sisters, better than the wives of any of his brothers. As much as the Empire needed him on the throne, it needed her on the one beside it. His eyes moved over to Jasmine, who lay snoring.

"And *you*." He shook his head. "You'll be lucky to know anything has changed."

His eyes moved back to Natalie as he stood upright.

"You know what you have to do."

"I know, and I will."

He approached the door, that small moment of doubt gnawing at him once more. But when he looked back toward the bed, that voice was silenced forever.

CHAPTER
10A

DESPITE RARELY MAKING USE of it, the Combine had accepted the Empire's invitation to establish an embassy on Avalon. The Embassy Block stood on Avalon's northern arm, near the station's center. A normal visitor could simply walk or take a conveyor, but Panzer was no ordinary visitor. His trip would be far more complex and time-consuming. The streets were bright as the artificial sky simulated midday. With luck he would be done before it had turned to night. Under cloak, he walked Avalon's streets to find a particular alley. There he knelt to open a hatch labeled *COM-DUCT ACCESS*.

Every building was wired into the station's central network by ducts like these. Unfortunately they were constructed with automatech and roliams in mind, not the unusually large man now wedging himself in. With little room to move, he was forced to slither through the duct, using his forearms and shins to crawl deeper into the station. For 10 kilometers he did this, with only the sound of metal scraping and his own breathing. The occasional dilation wave passed by, turning his vision red and forcing him to wait until he could progress. The worst part were the right-angle turns that he was forced to funnel himself through. Eventually his path was halted by a metal plate, welded into the duct.

"Well this is new," he muttered.

The Vaar had obviously viewed a schematic of the station, and identified this route of possible entry. Tiny sensors had been embedded into the plate, no doubt to warn security of any attempt to remove it. By doing so they had cut the com-links, isolating themselves from the rest of the station. That was their right; embassy grounds were sovereign territory, but that would not stop him.

Pushing himself up with what little space was available, he used his mind to bring a pair of devices from his belt. The first was a small cylinder, which he used to spray a black film onto the plate. The nanites within the film worked to confuse the sensors, convincing them that nothing of what was about to happen truly was. He guided the second device with his mind, cutting into the edge of the plate. Severing the plate from the duct, he let it fall before crawling over it. If all went to plan, he would return later to put it back, hiding the fact he was ever here.

A hundred meters past the plate, he contended with more sensors as the com-duct merged with an air vent. There he was forced to compress himself even further. Once he was in the vent, he slithered the remaining distance until coming to a grate. His sensors showed no threats on the other side, and closing an eye he concentrated on the bolts holding the grate in place. He worked them loose and held the grate away with his mind, then crawled out of the duct.

The shroud of his cloak allowed no sound to escape as he struck the floor, and he returned the grate to its position as he called up the embassy floor plan in his NOD. He had emerged in one of the basement levels, in a small corridor connecting maintenance rooms. Following his map, he sought one room in particular, finding it labeled in Vaar characters. After waving a hand to open the door, he stepped inside, then quickly closed it.

Contact with the Empire had made the Vaar very protective of their facilities' networks. New standards required all hardware carry a unique identification that had to be programmed into the central mainframe before it was allowed network access. The Empire called such a code NACI, the network access control identification. He would need to acquire one. The small room he entered contained controls for the water filtration and sewage systems. Among the devices on the wall he found a small panel and slid it open, finding the communications up-link he sought. Opening smaller hatches, he found what he needed, a line of Vaar characters yielding this terminal's NACI. Once it was scanned, Andira was ready to spoof the embassy's computers with a false identity.

"Ready, Colonel."

He took another device from his waist, grabbed a small wire and pulled it free before plugging it into the device. The repeater would allow Andira to connect without raising suspicion by connecting wirelessly via a NACI assigned to a wired device. When he left, he would recover the repeater and return the wire to its home, the Vaar being none the wiser to his ever having intruded on their network.

"Accessing network," Andira said. "Attempting to circumvent AIIC. Access failure."

"Reason for failure?"

"Network security has been upgraded; there are too many AIs for me to risk fooling them all. I will require more hardware than your armor provides."

"Damn. All right, we'll have to proceed without it." He paused as icons lit in his NOD. Someone was coming. His foot pressed to the wall and as he adhered, he climbed until he hung from the ceiling.

Moments later, two Vaar came around the corner ahead, each followed by a silver drone buzzing in the air behind their heads. They scanned the corridor with their rifles.

"They send a security team over a network glitch?" he whispered to himself as the pair approached. He was forced to draw himself up closer to the ceiling, the crest of their helmets passing mere centimeters beneath him. The first warrior opened the door to the room Panzer had just left, and the other glared inside with his weapon ready. Panzer's hand moved to his knife. He hated to leave evidence that he had been here, but if they found the repeater…

One of the silver drones hovering behind the Vaar suddenly spun, spherical body rotating to bring a red sensor toward him. Panzer froze, even holding his breath as the drone's sensor pings registered in his NOD. If the drone detected him, Andira would have mere nanoseconds to hack it and jam its transmission. Meanwhile he would have to drop and neutralize both warriors before they could cause an alert.

"This is getting ridiculous," one of the Vaar growled. "Each glitch should not be a condition of emergency."

The other Vaar said nothing, noticing the actions of his drone and positioning his eyes to the seemingly empty ceiling where it pointed. Panzer's grip tightened on the knife.

"Team seven to central," the Vaar finally spoke. "Nothing here."

Panzer's eyes narrowed on the Vaar. If they thought they were being watched, that is exactly what they would say. Their 4CM systems were hot; he could not scan their minds to be sure.

"Let's go," the second Vaar remarked.

The two warriors moved away from the room, beckoning their drones to follow. As they reached the intersection one turned, hurtling a knife toward the point on which his drone had been focused. The blade struck the ceiling, creating a cloud of sparks before falling to the floor.

"What was that?" the first Vaar inquired as his partner moved to recover his knife.

"Establishing certainty," the warrior answered, as he passed by Panzer who was now pressed tightly against the wall.

Panzer let out an exhale as they departed, and returned to the ceiling as he began walking to follow the floor plan on a path to the embassy's lower levels. The most direct route to his destination was also the one most likely to result in detection. He took a more roundabout approach, passing through the embassy's cargo holds.

In one of the bays his attention was drawn to a collection of large crates. Curiosity demanded he look, but that was not why he was here. He proceeded through the bay, on his way to the communications shack. When he approached the shack's door, he could hear the Vaar at work inside.

"I want the PACKET re-synchronized to Prithone at every interval," one Vaar spoke to a pair of Viss seated at a computer terminal. "I want no errors due to time distortion."

Now came the delicate part—working right under their noses without their knowing. He inched toward the wall until he was standing with his body parallel to the floor, then he slowly worked his way down. He had to move slow enough that he did not cause any air distortion that they would detect in such close proximity. Between each step he counted to a hundred, forcing himself to be patient, to make the painfully slow trip. To move any faster might attract attention. He was not even a fly on the wall; as far as the Vaar had to be concerned, he was paint.

His legs burned as he finally brought his feet to the floor beside the terminal. In his NOD he loosened a plate on his forearm and began counting again. Every ninety seconds his right hand could move another inch toward his left. From there he spent several more minutes drawing a cable from his arm. Finally he was in position to plug the cable into the terminal. Once inserted he slowly crouched while Andira set about working. He did not so much as breathe without adhering to his schedule, so long as the Vaar were within arm's reach.

"Accessing," Andira said. "Local AIIC is stronger than anticipated."

???: Can you bypass?

"Yes, but I will have to work very slowly so as not to be noticed by the operators."

???: No kidding. How long?

"I estimate three hours."

???: Then don't waste time talking to me.

CHAPTER
10B

S IMMONNE'S CONVEYOR CAME TO a halt outside of a large building as clouds overtook the afternoon sky. Intended as a parking garage for conveyors, the building had been converted to house some of the refugees pouring onto the station. Her guards filed out first to form a perimeter before Simmonne joined them.

"Princess, Princess!" Pedestrians shouted and waved from beyond a picket line set up by the station's legionnaires. Waving to those calling her name, Simmonne proceeded toward the ramp leading into the makeshift shelter. The first thing that caught her attention was the stench, causing her to cough and briefly cover her mouth and nose with her sleeve. Audibly gagging, the Twins did the same as their eyes surveyed the garage.

Makeshift beds were strewn across the first layer of the garage, with the aliens packed in so tight that families practically slept atop one another. Garbage, decaying flesh, and bodily waste created a perfect storm of odor that made her eyes water. Many of the small aliens were drawing close to the outer perimeter formed by the legionnaires that preceded her guards. Others tried to rise but could only look her way, hindered by visible injuries.

Worse than the smell were the feelings she was forced to shut out. Anger, misery, hatred, despair, all enhanced by feelings of hunger and sickness. All remarkably easy to sense as alien emotions went.

JULIE: I'm going to be sick.

JENNIFER: I already am.

Simmonne felt her stomach churning, and had to stop herself from turning and running to escape. She forced herself to lower her arm and continued to scan the first floor.

"There's so many of them," she whispered.

"So far, close to thirteen million have come to the station, with more every day," Commodore Garren explained. "We're having to pack them in like roliams just to make room."

Simmonne turned to the commodore.

"Not even a quarter of this station's buildings are occupied," Simmonne retorted. "And you are forcing them together like this?"

"Unfortunately we've had to segregate them out so we can keep an eye on them. Not only are many carriers of potentially communicable diseases that could affect Imperial races; many of these people have taken to theft and mugging. We almost had an incident a month ago when six of them tried to rob a kodaz merchant who beat three of them to death in retaliation."

Simmonne's blood began to boil.

"Commodore, I do not see a single food printer on this entire floor, and perhaps one lavatory. What do you expect them to do?"

The commodore was visibly taken aback.

"Majesty, I understand how this looks, but I do not have the resources to install those facilities in every shelter."

"You don't have the people to install food printers?" She had to stop herself from shouting.

"M-Majesty," the commodore stammered, and Simmonne could sense her surprise. "We bring in food four times a day."

Simmonne turned back to the quants, scanning until she saw a pair of what were obviously children.

SIMMONNE: Isis, bring those two to me.

ISIS: Yes, Majesty.

She remained wordless, allowing the commodore to stew while Isis fetched the pair of children and led them over. A female judging by her upright posture stood with what Simmonne presumed was her older brother.

In her NOD Simmonne rifled through her language files, finding the most common of quant dialects. Activating the auto-speak she relaxed, allowing her nanites to operate her mouth and vocal chords.[19]

"What are your names?" she asked in their language.

"I'm Mai'ta," the boy answered. "This is my sister Eila."

She smiled, taking a knee to bring her eyes closer to the boy's while trying to ignore their filth-born stench.

"Mai'ta, have you bathed since you've been here?"

"No."

"How often are you being fed?"

"They bring us food three times a day," the boy answered.

"The adults take it," the girl spoke up, hiding behind her brother.

"What do you mean?" Simmonne asked.

"They bring the food and leave it," the boy explained. "And then everyone goes for it."

"Brother hasn't eaten in three days," the girl piped up again.

Simmonne smiled to them before rising and turning to the commodore.

---

19 The ability of nanotech to cross language barriers is often known as the "human advantage," and is historically seen as vital in the ability to establish and maintain the Empire along with humans" place within it.

"So you bring food to a shelter full of hungry people, and you don't have your legionnaires pass it out?" Simmonne admonished, reaching for the children and pulling them to her. "Perhaps you would like to explain to them why they haven't eaten?"

"M-Majesty…" The commodore searched for the words as Simmonne glared.

"Commodore, I want food printers, water recycles, and proper lavatory facilities installed in each of these shelters. And I want it done *now*."

"Majesty, I…I don't have the people for that." The commodore bowed her head. "Every technician I have is busy trying to meet the emperor's deadline for full astranet connectivity."

"Then hire contractors," Simmonne hissed, trying not to lose her temper while people were watching.

"Majesty, please try to understand." The commodore lowered her head farther. "We are already overworked, and over budget. I don't have the money or people to spare."

Simmonne looked down to the children while the girl pinched her dress, curious about the material. Her grimy fingers left tiny prints on the immaculate cloth.

"I will pay for it." She looked back to the commodore. "Bill it to my office on the Cathedral."

"It will be difficult to find more technicians out here—"

"Then see to it personally," Simmonne interrupted before scanning the legionnaires. "You there, Captain."

Hearing her call, an alpha aren ran to her and quickly bowed.

"Yes, Majesty?"

"You have mobile food printers for when you are in the field, yes?"

"Yes, Majesty."

"I want a squad to bring a printer to each shelter, and supervise food handouts once every four hours until the printers are installed. I also want medics brought in to treat some of these wounded."

The aren eyed the commodore before bowing.

"Yes, Majesty."

"Majesty." The commodore stepped closer, speaking low as the aren left to carry out the command. "Respectfully, I don't appreciate being berated in front of my subordinates. Nor—"

"Would you prefer we spoke with the emperor about this?" Simmonne cut her off. "This situation is inexcusable, and if you will not fix it, I will."

Visibly biting back a response, the commodore bowed.

"Yes, Majesty."

Simmonne knelt back down to the children at her feet.

"Are you really a princess?" the little girl asked.

"Yes I am." Simmonne smiled, fighting back the urge to grab both children and take them back to her quarters for a hot meal. Instead she turned to the brother. "Where are your parents?"

"Dead," he answered. "Father died fighting the monsters in the streets. Mother died when they blew up her ship. Is…" He trailed off.

"Go on," she urged, holding back a tear.

"The adults say the monsters are afraid of the Empire, that you will protect us. Is that true?"

"I cannot speak for the Vaar," Simmonne answered. "But the Empire will protect you."

He nodded, pulling his sister close.

"You're a good boy, looking after your sister."

"Your Majesty," the commodore began, "message from control. The Vaar ambassador has requested an emergency summit at 1900 hours."

"What about?" Simmonne asked, rising.

"They did not say; they are requesting all ambassadors convene. Do you wish to attend?"

"Yes." She nodded. "We should prepare."

She turned back to the children.

"Be good, food is coming."

They nodded silently as she moved to leave, waving as she turned to look back. As she returned to her conveyor, two of her guards stood with three quants in white uniforms. One of them held a metal box in his hands while the other two bowed their heads.

"Majesty," Isis began, "these two have requested to speak with you, officers from the quant Navy."

"Your Majesty." One of them stepped closer. "Please forgive the impudence of this meeting, but I have had to act covertly. I am Captain Mu'kesh. I came to Avalon on the *Hopeful Venture* under orders from my government."

"Welcome, Captain. How can I help you?"

"As I explained to your guards…" He motioned to the one with the box, who slowly opened it, revealing a container full of gems and parchment. "This box contains a number of my people's cultural treasures, those we managed to smuggle out of our capital when the Vaar came. I have been instructed by my people's provisional government to ask you to take custody of them, for safekeeping in the Empire."

She looked to the box, and back to him. He was apprehensive. Likely nervous she may refuse, and embarrassed at having to ask.

"Of course, Captain." She nodded. "I will send them to the Cathedral, and we will keep them safe until your people request they be returned."

"Thank you, Majesty." He bowed before reaching into the pocket of his uniform. "I was also asked to give you this, a gesture of appreciation from my people."

He held up a gold chain, suspending a gem-studded medallion in the image of a sun.

"Will you accept this?"

"Of course." She smiled, taking the medallion from him, and slipping it on. "I will wear it, and think of your people."

Doing his best to mimic a human smile, he bowed, and she could sense his relief.

"Thank you, Majesty, with your leave I must return to my ship."

"Of course, Captain."

Two of her guards took the chest of treasures and the quants hastily took their leave.

CHAPTER
10C

CLEARWATER FELL OUT OF bed as a massive thunderclap rocked the barracks. Scrambling to his feet, he looked around the dark room before running to the nearby window. He activated the transparency and glared out. He gasped.

In what normally appeared as an empty lot, a new feature was visible. A missile turret had risen out of the ground and angled itself toward the sky. The colony's orbital defenses had engaged; they had fired on something. The thunderclap was the air displaced by the missile's warp field as it raced out of the atmosphere. Was it an attack?

LT. BROWER: All officers and squad sergeants to briefing room immediately.

He scrambled for the door but stopped short, thinking better of running to the briefing naked. He emerged from his quarters hopping on one foot as he secured his boots before joining the others on their way down to the ground floor.

In the briefing room, Brower stood before a hologram of the planet, his eyes focused on a red icon in orbit.

"What's going on?" Clearwater asked, moving beside him.

Brower held up a finger, waiting for the rest to file in.

"Listen up," the senior lieutenant began, "a Vaar ship just wormholed into the system. Automated defenses have responded. The ship has sustained critical damage and is plummeting through the atmosphere as we speak."

Brower waved his hand to adjust the hologram.

"She'll impact on the northern polar cap in less than a minute." He paused to scan the gathered lieutenants and sergeants. "That ship is over a kilometer long. I don't know why she came so close, but we're about to have an environmental catastrophe on our hands. I want all units to begin emergency procedures. We're far enough inland that we don't have to worry about tsunami. But we're looking at massive quakes, possible tectonic shift, a lot of bad shit. I want civilians in the emergency shelters until we know exactly what we're looking at. We may have to call in an environ-team to try to save the local ecosystem."

Brower's eyes moved back to the hologram as the small icon vanished.

"We're going to have big quakes in a few minutes. Sections five, six, and seven, deal with the civilians. Section eight, take your guns out to this mountain range. If we have more Vaar coming I want our artillery ready to greet them. Some of the Vaar may have made it to escape pods before the crash so I want a team to go look for them. Lieutenant Greene, take Section Two."

Brower's eyes moved to Clearwater.

"Clearwater, I want you to go with Greene. It's time to cut your teeth a little. Search the polar cap for any signs of survivors. I don't expect any, but go look anyway. When you don't find any, get your asses back here."

"Yes sir." Clearwater nodded.

"Dismissed."

From the briefing room to the armory he ran with Sarge at his side, manning his AICES and waiting for his section to assemble outside of the barracks. This was it, a real mission. Not an exercise, not a training drill, an actual mission, and maybe, contact with the enemy. He shook his head as his clock suddenly sped forward in response to a dilation wave.

He left it to Sarge to inform the section while he brought up a map of the polar cap. By now that area was a cloud of steam and supersonic shockwaves. The odds of finding survivors were almost nil, but just maybe, Vaar were there. His clock sped forward again—another wave had passed through the planet.

He glanced upward to the sound of whining engines. A flying wing descended toward them. The Longrunner-class dropship was the fastest in the Legionnaire arsenal. On touching down, its boarding ramps beckoned to them. His feet hesitated, but he moved with his section toward the ship and into its cargo hold. With almost every step, his clock lurched forward again. A veritable dilation storm was erupting out of the galaxy's center. He did not have time to think about that now.

"Welcome aboard," the pilot greeted. "We have aerial bots on the way to scout the region. We'll have you there in ten minutes."

Clearwater sighed as his NOD's clock suddenly raced forward by more than an hour. With all crew and bots loaded, the Longrunner began to climb. She would break twenty times the speed of sound before she had left the atmosphere, and would then carry them halfway across the planet in a matter of minutes. Clearwater's clock lurched forward twice more before the ship reached its orbital trajectory. Maybe the Vaar had been trying to mask their arrival with those waves, and simply miscalculated?

CHAPTER
11A

ANZER'S LEGS BURNED FROM holding his squat position. Between
Andira's work and the sudden burst of dilation waves, he had spent
nearly six relative hours squatting. At least a dozen waves had passed,
tinting his sight red. The Vaar had undergone a shift change, but a trio
remained in the communications shack with him.

"Security circumvented," Andira announced. "Reading positron rotors.
Downloading new cipher code."

???: Can you download their communication logs as well?

"I am already doing so."

???: Alert me as soon as you are finished.

"Sir, I have downloaded the receiving order for the cargo pods we
passed on our way. It seems the embassy commander was required to
personally receive them. All other personnel were ordered to evacuate the
deck. I recommend we investigate."

???: I concur. Finish up.

"Completing download. I will decode and cross-reference the
information when we return to the ship."

He removed the plug from the terminal, drawing the cable back into his
armor as he slowly stepped away. After an hour spent removing himself
from the communications shack, he made for the cargo bay. As he
approached the cargo bay he paused, his eyes turning toward a long corridor.

When one spent so much of their life trying to avoid detection, every
little shadow on the outskirts of peripheral vision seemed an imminent
threat. Something had moved, and his eyes now scanned for it. When they
found nothing his mind was added, yet he sensed only the 4CM fields of the
Vaar in surrounding rooms. Shaking his head, he proceeded on to the filled
cargo bay. The crates had been arrayed in files. He approached one and
climbed to the top, before sliding the lid open and peering inside.

The crate was empty.

He moved on to another and opened the lid, finding it empty as well.
Picking crates at random, he opened a dozen before something caught his
eye. He dropped into the crate and plucked a small piece of plastic from the
floor, stained by a brown film.

"Andira, can you identify what was in this bag?"

"Scanning. It appears to have contained an iron-rich lipid compound."

"So, it's iron and fat?"

"Correct."

"Would the Vaar metabolize this?"

"With great efficiency."

He turned the bag over in his hand, watching the remnants within dripping.

"Andira, full scan. I want to know what was in these crates."

"Sir, that risks giving away our presence."

"I'm aware. Do it."

"Scanning. Reading carbon sheddings, traces of water, salt, and traces of biologic acids. I believe an adult Vaar was lying in this crate for an extended period."

"Vaar gorge on fat before they go into battle," he commented, before climbing out of the crate. Near the center of the room he turned a full circle, before holding out his hand. He had to see it, and cast his eyes into the past.

A single Vaar, the equivalent of a colonel, walked between the crates. At each one he pressed a small button, and soon after another Vaar climbed out. Once out, the newly freed warriors moved to the walls, grabbing weapons and armor from mobile racks. Panzer's vision followed the colonel, the embassy commander. At one of the crates a lieutenant climbed out, and the colonel bowed to him.

"Oh no," Panzer whispered. A bow of the head was the Vaar equivalent of a salute. Yet in this case the respect was shown to the junior officer. Among the Vaar there was only one thing, one billet that placed one in such high esteem that they were shown deference by senior officers. Their presence, the changeover in the encryption cipher, all of the activity over the border. All this time he was convinced that the war he saw was years away. But with all three factors, he realized it was about to begin.

He had to alert someone, but what was their mission? When the embassy commander inquired about their presence, they refused to answer. Could it be sabotage? They could try to weaken Avalon, perhaps knock out some of it shields, or a few of its weapons. That couldn't be it; with the first facility hit, they'd be up to their asses in legionnaires long before they'd done any real harm. There were too many to simply be gathering intelligence, or serving as forward observers for missile attacks.

His heart beat faster, as Simmonne flashed through his mind.

"Andira, I need Rhoxx on the line, now."

"There is a greater than fifty percent chance—"

"Do it, Andira."

"I readin' you," Rhoxx's voice came.

"Rhoxx, listen to me very carefully. I want you and the brothers to collect the princess, her entourage, all her stuff. Take them to my ship, get them off the station, and do it quietly. Her guards will have a challenge question. 'What color is the wind?' Your answer will be, 'Pale as death.' Once you have her on board, alert Avalon security. But not before; I don't want to start a panic. Confirm."

No answer came.

"Rhoxx, confirm!"

"Sir," Andira interrupted. "The Vaar have erected a reciprocating warp field around this cargo bay. Our communications are blocked. We've been discovered."

The sound of thundering footsteps approached, and glancing up he tapped his thrusters. He hung from the ceiling as doors at both ends opened, and Vaar flooded into the cargo bay.

CHAPTER
11B

AVALON'S EMBASSY HALL WAS a great coliseum-style arena made up of five layers of seating, allowing delegates to look down to the podium where a speaker would address them. Simmonne could sense the apprehension in the room as she took her seat on the highest balcony, behind a banner that had been laid out with her sigil. Her eyes focused on an empty station in the balconies, where none of the Combine staff were yet present. Diplomats filed in quickly and soon the hall was filled with chatter among those contemplating what the Combine wished to say.

When all were gathered the lights dimmed, signaling for quiet as new light was cast on the speaker's podium. A lone Vaar ascended the stairs toward the podium, stepping four at a time with his long legs. Ambassador Tul'veth, according to her briefing on the station, a Vaar warlord too old to serve as a soldier, but well respected among his people. The lull in the chamber faded as the Vaar prepared himself, and for a moment he gazed up, directly at Simmonne. As he began to speak she leaned in, listening to the translation.

"I will begin by thanking all ambassadors, and her Majesty of the Solar Family for attending on such short notice. I will not waste time but come to the matter at hand. To present this address, I yield my time to the grand warlord, Hahk'xess."

The ambassador stepped back, and the hologram of a new Vaar illuminated behind the podium. Hahk'xess, the supreme commander of the Vaar and the most powerful being in the Combine. Simmonne's stomach turned, knowing this was not a good development. Hahk'xess began speaking, the depth of his voice causing reverberation throughout the hall.

"Six of our years ago, the Solar Empire arrived in the Time-Lost Galaxy. Not long after its arrival, the Empire began to colonize worlds in this galaxy, including those placed under protective quarantine by the Interstellar Combine. We are all aware of how things have developed since that time, and I feel no need to revisit them here."

The Vaar stopped, casting a glance up to Simmonne.

"I would be remiss, however, if I did not mention those grievances that the Empire has refused to redress. Before the Empire's arrival, the Combine was successfully prosecuting a war against the quant nation, the Evul'ta, and the Nakori. Following a skirmish wherein Combine warships seeking the Empire's withdrawal from the quarantined worlds, the Empire imposed what it calls a Neutral Zone in this galaxy. How an Empire that had been in this galaxy for only a few weeks thought it could impose its will on a nation like the Combine that has resided here for centuries, is a mystery.

"By establishing its Neutral Zone, the Empire created protectorates of nations with whom the Combine was at war. In doing so, the Empire denied us the successful conclusion of these wars for which many of our warriors gave their lives. Were this not enough, the Empire then began a systematic campaign to undermine the Combine's power in this galaxy and others."

Hahk'xess paused as a map of the Hourglass Galaxy illuminated above him.

"Since the creation of the Neutral Zone, the Empire has violated the very spirit of neutrality by providing a steady stream of arms, equipment, food, and medicine to resistance forces carrying out acts of terrorism in Combine territory."

JENNIFER: Is he really going to stand there and complain that we've armed people whose homes he stole?

Simmonne held up a hand, signaling for quiet.

"Due to Solar efforts, many Combine warriors and civilians have lost their lives to terrorists armed with Imperial weaponry. The emperor further stated that he would not recognize the legitimacy of territories obtained via conquest, and continued to recognize the ambassadors of nations that no longer existed. He even went so far as to declare these ambassadors governments in exile and to form treaties with them. Nations that sought peace with the Combine were encouraged to continue their futile efforts through the promises of additional armaments and technology exchange.

"Not satisfied to merely arm our opposition, the emperor then ordered his Commando Corps to begin clandestine operations intent on undermining the Combine's military. Unlawful, despicable attacks have been carried out by these agents in all five of the Combine's galaxies. But nowhere has their presence been felt more strongly than the Time-Lost Galaxy. Perhaps the most well known of these incidents was the destruction of the warship *Polarized Aggression*—an act the agents of the emperor attempted to hide by remote guiding the ship into a singularity, sending to the Void the whole of the ship's crew."

He paused, his jaw flexing in anger. Simmonne wrung her hands as she watched him. This could not be what she thought it was. It had to be posturing; he couldn't really be doing this.

"Six Vaar warlords have died fighting these state-sponsored terrorists, paragons of our society lost forever. The Commando Corps' crimes do not end there, as many Combine citizens and warriors have been abducted, or killed by Solar Commandos. No less than two assassination attempts have been targeted toward me, no doubt due to my vocal opposition of the Empire's presence in this galaxy.

"While the emperor sent his minions against us, he also engaged in an effort of economic warfare against the Combine. The emperor sought potential allies anywhere he could, convincing any nation he could to embargo the Combine, deny us safe passage through their territory, and to terminate efforts of peaceful cooperation. Any nation that would not agree was then threatened with the destruction of their economies by being flooded with cheap Imperial goods. To avoid such economic damage to our own nation, the Combine declared an embargo against the Empire. In complete disregard for the authority of our government, the Empire has readily sold its goods to Combine citizens, even going so far as to construct black markets within our borders. All in the hope of bringing the Combine to eventual economic capitulation.

"Two years ago, the emperor pushed our nations a step closer to war by ordering his Armadas to render military assistance to ships and crews hostile to the Combine. This aid included providing sensor and communications data from Imperial ships, resupply and repair in Imperial ports, and direct military intervention to aid ships, many carrying fleeing terrorists in crossing the Neutral Zone to the Empire. The resulting confrontations have resulted in the deaths of yet more Combine citizens.

"Nine months ago, Vaar warriors captured by terrorist forces managed to escape into Imperial territory. These warriors were quickly apprehended and returned to the custody of the terrorists, who later executed them. Seven months ago, Imperial military forces were sighted in the territory of nations hostile to the Combine, helping to install armaments and build military facilities."

He paused to take a breath. Simmonne's feet tapped nervously, her own apprehension fueled by that filling the room with his words.

"Since that time the emperor has reinforced his military presence in this galaxy, outright refusing to hear the Combine's overtures to draw down military forces in the region, and with it, the likelihood of war. Despite Combine protests, the Empire has continued building up its astranet with the goal of eventually allowing it to bring in an unlimited supply of arms and soldiers that could be used against us.

"Perhaps the greatest wound to our people, however, has been the emperor's repeated refusal to entertain our requests to pull his colonies from that territory our people have protected in quarantine for centuries. Our protests have fallen on deaf ears, even when we have tried to explain the significance of these worlds. This sacrilege is something we have been forced to endure in silence until now.

"Not all nations exist as equals. Great nations can only coexist peacefully when they recognize the sovereignty and hegemony of one another. The emperor has not chosen to walk this path, but has instead incited a program of hegemonic warfare against the Combine. The history of all peoples is rife with examples of great tragedy, that could have been avoided if those with the power to do so had found the courage to take action sooner."

Simmonne shuddered as the Vaar's eyes moved back to her. He was really doing it. Didn't he realize what he was doing? Did he know what he was starting? How, how could any government leader be so foolish? She wanted to be angry with him, the panic in the room was rising, and only by focusing on her own anger did she avoid being overwhelmed by it.

"A short time ago I convened the Council of Warlords, and asked for their votes on how to handle the matter of the Empire going forward. With an overwhelming majority, the warlords have voted to find that courage, and undertake those actions the Empire has made unavoidable. The Combine requires neither the aid, trade, or friendship of the Empire, but it demands that its hegemony and its sovereign rights be respected. Thus the Council of Warlords has voted...to declare war on the Solar Empire."

A quiet filled the chamber as his words were taken in, and Simmonne cried out at the sudden rush of fear she sensed ripping through the chamber.

"We have done all in our power to avoid this conflict, but recognizing it as likely, we have prepared ourselves. As I speak, Combine forces are crossing the illegally mandated Neutral Zone. We shall dismantle the Imperial presence in this galaxy, and drive you back to the reaches from whence you came. Once the Empire has been expelled from our dominion, we will entertain talks of peace. If the Empire should refuse, we will follow you, and bring to your home the war you have forced on us all."

"Let's go." Simmonne winced as Jenna seized her arm, and pulled her out of the chair moments before alarms began to sound and the hologram of Hahk'xess faded away.

CHAPTER
11C

ND-31'S NORTHERN CONTINENT EXISTED as a titanic mass of ice extending all the way down to the ocean bedrock. The Vaar ship was so damaged that it had begun breaking up before it even entered the atmosphere. Wreckage was now scattered over thousands of square kilometers of the polar continent. When the ship hit, it drove through the ice, all the way down to the bedrock. Now the surface of the entire continent resembled a large pane of glass with spider web cracks.

Clearwater scanned the continent through the Longrunner's sensors. He was no expert on impact events, but he knew enough to know something was wrong. Imperial ships larger than monitors stayed well away from planets. Not only could the mass and gravity of their kilosteel hulls cause quakes, storms, and tidal waves, but an impact event would be catastrophic. Vaar ships were made of illstas, roughly a third the density of kilosteel. Their hulls were mostly empty space. Yet even accounting for that, for a ship of this size, that left billions of tons falling through the atmosphere.

"This doesn't make a damn bit of sense," Lieutenant Greene remarked. "Not reading any planetary defenses that could have absorbed the blast. That impact should have vaporized half the continent. Not even reading any orbital ejecta, only minor signs of seismic disturbance. Temperature at the impact zone is below freezing. Just doesn't make sense."

"That's good for us," Clearwater offered. "Might be survivors down there."

"Life scans show negative," Sarge interjected. "But depending on how they're equipped, only way to be certain is to go down there."

Greene was silent for a moment.

"I'm going to take my section to the main crash site and see what we can recover. Clearwater, this region."

A map opened in his NOD, highlighting a region between the continent's new fissures.

"These look like escape pods," Greene continued. "Take your section, start in that area and work your way out. I want all units scanning...everything. We've been seeing weird shit on this planet since we arrived. Something nullified most of the impact; I want to know what it was. Prepare for drop."

"Yes sir."

Sarge readied the troops and soon they were descending in the wake of the falling automatech. Taking no chances with the broken ice, Clearwater fired the AICES thrusters, allowing himself a gentle landing. At Sarge's guidance, his squads dropped in concentric rings around him within a perimeter formed by the bots.

"Full sweep," Clearwater directed. "Full on active scans. Report anything you find."

He turned to Sarge, who used the arm of his AICES to pry open the hatch on an escape pod that lay within a crater.

"Lieutenant." Sarge motioned him over.

A dead Vaar lay inside the small pod, barely large enough to hold the warrior within. Sarge nudged the body, garnering no response.

"Pod must have been damaged," Sarge commented. "Hit the ground so hard it shattered his plates."

"Guess even a Vaar can't survive falling from orbit. Clearwater to all units: Collect all corpses, we'll take them back with us. Check 'em for intel."

He turned back to Sarge.

"What do you think, Sarge? Scout team? Saboteurs? Skirmishers?"

"I don't think so sir," the aren answered. "That's some pretty ornate armor he's wearing."

Clearwater glanced back to the Vaar. Sarge was right—this warrior's armor was a brilliant silver, covered from head to toe in gold and gemstone engravings. His helmet was particularly elaborate, sporting a three-pronged fan with each cast in layers like overlapping petals of a flower.

"You're right," he answered, scanning the armor. "That is fancy. What do you think it means?"

"Looks like an honor guard to me."

"That doesn't make any sense. What the hell is an honor guard doing out here? And why were they so determined to get here?"

"At the moment, I couldn't even speculate."

"Sir! We've got a live one!" one of his kurai sergeants shouted.

Clearwater and Dolph exchanged glances.

"On my way."

With Dolph close behind, he raced toward their transponder to find where his men and several bots had surrounded their find. A single Vaar lay prone beneath a piece of the ship's wreckage. Luminescent blood stained the ice, and the warrior audibly gasped for breath.

"Medic!" Clearwater shouted, before approaching the warrior more closely leading his troops to part from his path. "Has he said anything?"

"Just gibberish," one of the betas answered.

The Vaar turned to Clearwater. Blood flowed from between his teeth as he tried to speak.

"*Gurgazz, nast, solstai, zetz…sols.*"

Clearwater's NOD flashed.

VAAR LANGAUGE DETECTED – UNCATALOGUED DIALECT. ANALYZING…

"Crap," he whispered as they were joined by the medic who quickly knelt by the Vaar. "Doc, can you save him?"

"I'm not an expert on Vaar anatomy," the beta answered. "But I will try. It's a minor miracle he is alive at all."

"Shit," Sarge muttered. "All units, remember bind all corpses. We don't want any of them springing back to life and taking us by surprise."

Clearwater guided his AICES to kneel by the Vaar while the medic scanned.

"Sir," Dolph spoke up, "Sergeant ahn Culan has been studying their language extensively."

"Call him. Then inform Lieutenant Greene of our situation."

The Vaar drew in a breath before speaking again. Clearwater in turn routed a video feed to his approaching sergeant.

"*Dru lok, Sovari Soma, naat bit, gargggs'vi, ad dul!*"

The Vaar reached out for him, grabbing the arm of his AICES as he repeated the phrase.

"Sergeant, did you get any of that?"

"Only pieces, sir," ahn Culan answered. "I think he's speaking the Voltim dialect; we only have a partial dictionary for that one. It's pretty rare."

"Can you make out any of what he's saying?"

"Something about finding his memories. Keep him talking, sir, and maybe the computer can help. Ask him his name: '*Vadda kess.*'"

Clearwater looked back to the Vaar.

"*Vadda kess?*"

The Vaar blinked several times, wheezing as he gathered the strength to speak again.

"*Ullenk.*"

"*Ullenk,*" Culan repeated. "Okay, no contraction. He's either an orphan, or it's an assumed name. Ask him if he knows his parents: '*Oghal vadda kess.*'"

"*Oghal vadda kess?*"

The Vaar shook his head.

"*Uhr'kep.*" He paused, coughing blood from the nasal slits in his facial plates. "*Got…gott'a…*"

"I'm losing him," the medic remarked, before jamming a mediron into a patch of flesh exposed by broken plates.

"*Uhr* means war," Culan explained, now joining them. "But the '*kep*' suffix, I think that means 'anti' or 'non.' *Gott'ama* means 'came' or 'coming here.' I think he's trying to say he's here with peaceful intentions."

"They came in peace?" Clearwater questioned.

"I don't think that's what he's driving at sir," Culan continued. "More that they just weren't looking for a fight."

The kurai listened as the Vaar continued to sputter, repeating the same two words: Sovari Soma.

"Now he's back to babbling about his memories," the kurai said, moving his AICES to shrug.

"Attention all units." Brower's voice broke over the com, muting every other voice. "Priority alert. All units return to base immediately. We're raising the planetary shield, remain in-atmosphere."

"Sir, what's going on?" Clearwater asked.

"Vaar ships have just wormholed into the system. All units return to base immediately."

His pulse quickened. How many ships? Why were they here? Was it an attack?

"Sir?" Sarge turned to him.

"You all heard him," Clearwater called. "All units gather for pickup."

He glanced back down at the wounded Vaar.

"Bring him with us."

He began to turn and stopped, his eyes moving out toward the ice. For a moment, something was there. He dialed the AICES' sensors up to full, but it was gone.

"Ghost?" he whispered.

"Sir, we have to go," Sarge said from his side.

"You're right, move out."

CHAPTER
11D

THE EMPEROR AND THE empress both were metapsion Elders. Each morning, before breakfast, before work, they began the day in meditation. In a private chamber within their abode, they would sit together. Some days their minds would spar; other days they would simply sit together and touch the minds of the Cathedral. For this they preferred their privacy, only the company of one another. It was the one place Steven could be sure their bodyguards would not interfere.

His parents' guards had let him pass—why wouldn't they? He was their son, their beloved son. At the door to their meditation chamber he waved his hand to signal them, and waited for them to bid him entry. The door opened and he was greeted by the serene sounds of nature in a distinctly empty, spherical room. Still in their robes, his parents sat in the center, facing each other.

"Steven?" His father turned to him. "What brings you by?"

"Dad, I need to talk to you."

His parents exchanged glances, and he nodded.

"Certainly."

His mother excused herself to the side of the room, calling a glass of water to her hand.

"What's on your mind?" his father asked, walking to him as the door closed.

He took a breath, steadying himself.

"I need to know, Dad. I think you've already decided who will succeed you. I can't put my life on hold any longer. I need to know—who will it be?"

His father smiled.

"Steven, if I'd made up my mind I would have told you."

That was a lie, he knew it was. He did not need to read his mind to know.

"Dad." He strained to seek his father's eyes. "Please don't lie to me. Just tell me. Who is it?"

His father glanced to his mother, who silently nodded.

"All right Steven," he whispered with a frown. "What would you think if I left it to Raymond?"

Not when a plasma conduit had burst in his hand, not when his best friend split his scalp in a childhood fight over a girl, not even when a deranged man's bullet had struck him—no wound had ever hurt more than that question.

"I…" He hesitated. "I don't think Raymond has the personality to be emperor. He's smart, he's charming. But he doesn't know how to…I hate to say it. He doesn't know how to manipulate people. How to guide their emotions, or how to guide them to draw the conclusions he wants. He's a great military tactician, I'll admit that he's better than me. But he is not a shepherd of men."

His father nodded, walking a circle around him.

"Which occurred to me as well."

For a moment, hope filled his heart.

"What would you think if I left it to David?"

Steven eyed the old man.

"David's an even worse choice. He has more temper than reason; he'd start a war just because someone insulted him. He…he disgraced the family by being suspended from RAAMS; he can't keep his face out of the news. Would you really consider him?"

The emperor glanced back to his mother.

"What would you think…if I left it to Simmonne?"

Steven snorted as he tried to quell the forming laugh.

"Simmonne? She'd be the worst choice. She is my baby sister and I love her. But Dad, she can't even dress herself without Jenna's help. She doesn't even know where reality is, let alone is she in touch with it. She would bankrupt the Empire trying to give everything to everyone. Do you think she could lead us in a war? The Outlands, the Maxnin, the Vaar, they'd see her rise to empress as a sign of weakness."

His father sighed, glancing at the floor before looking to him.

"You know, I sought each of their opinions about making you emperor. Would you believe every single one of them endorsed you? Raymond said he thought you were the best he knew at leading people where they needed to go. David called you the most methodical man he knew. Simmonne, she was your biggest cheerleader. You know what she said to me, Steven? She said you were the only one who she always knew would be there for everyone."

He sighed.

"I think it'd break her heart to know you have so little faith in her."

In all the lectures, all the childhood scoldings, in all those times he had disappointed them…he had never felt so small, and shame drew his eyes to the floor.

"I had hoped you would prove me wrong, and find something good to say about at least one of them. I think you have your answer."

His face twisted in a mix of pain and anger; his vision blurred at he glared up at his father.

"It's never been enough, has it?" His voice cracked. "Nothing I've done. I've fought two wars, and negotiated the end to a dozen more. I've colonized entire star systems, and created thriving economies. I've done everything you ever asked of me. I fixed the treasury; I purged corruption from the senate. I sabotaged the Rhinegrave-Allison merger to protect our family. But it wasn't enough. Why, why hasn't any of it been enough?"

He gritted his teeth. He would not cry, no matter how much it hurt, not a single tear.

His father turned, showing his back as he gazed upward.

"Steven, the Mandrakes have ruled the Empire for 100,000 years. In all that time, there has never been a popular uprising to overthrow us. Do you know why that is? It is because every emperor before me chose a successor who understood a simple truth: We are not rulers, Steven. We are hereditary governors. We serve the people of the Empire. In compensation for our service, they give us wealth, they give us power, they give us privilege. You never learned, Steven, that a Solar Emperor lives his life for the good of his people."

"But—"

His father turned back to him.

"Do you think I am blind, Steven?" His eyes were angry. "Do you think I don't know what happens under my roof? Do you think I don't know what you did to Jasmine? You took a beautiful, strong-willed woman, and you broke her with drugs. And for what? Because she made you feel insecure? Because you resented her? Or because you simply wanted an obedient toy?"

He searched for words; they did not come. The emperor continued.

"But that wasn't enough for you. I know, Steven. I know you loved Natalie. I know her engagement broke your heart. Look at me."

Sucking in a breath, Steven gazed up.

"I know you murdered her fiancé."

"I…I—"

"You paid an insane kodaz to kill him. A crazy man who would never be anything but a burden to society. But a man who had a family that loved him. You paid him to murder the man she loved, and then you bribed law enforcement to murder him. I know this because the prosecutor-general came to me with the evidence. He wanted to warn me before he went public."

The old man paused, shaking his head.

"There is nothing a father would not do for his son. So I…I ruined him. I bribed him with a title of count to keep quiet. Then, after a few years, to be sure he'd never be a threat to you, I fabricated evidence that allowed me to force his abdication, and destroy his credibility. I ordered your best friend to destroy all of the files under the lie that they were fabrications. To this day, he believes he saved you from someone who was trying to destroy you over a personal grudge against me.

"I have spent my entire life trying to be a good leader, to put my people and the Empire before myself. In 2,400 years as emperor, it is the only thing I've done for which I've been ashamed. I destroyed a good man, and used my most trusted servant as part of a lie. But I told myself that once you had Natalie, that would be enough. You'd finally be happy, and you could move forward. But you did not let me hide from the truth.

"Your friend, your only friend, destroyed the Pillagers. He didn't even complain when you took all the credit. And you did nothing for him in return. You had Natalie, but even that was not enough. You use women, you use your friends."

The emperor sighed, holding up a hand to silence Steven as he tried to speak.

"There is nothing a father would not do for his son. But I never had the luxury of allowing my status as a father to be the most important thing in my life. I failed you, Steven. I failed to teach you to respect people, to love them. And I failed to teach you that sometimes, no matter how much you want something, it's not yours to have. I cannot make you emperor."

Steven drew in a gasp. He closed his eyes. His entire body tensed as if waiting for a sudden strike to land. Though clenching teeth and trembling body he forced the whisper past his lips.

"Who?"

"I offered it to Raymond, and he declined. He said he did not want the responsibility, that he did not want that life. He wants to spend his days in the Armadas, and I respect his choice."

He asked again, barely audible.

"Who?"

His father waited for him to look up.

"Simmonne."

The despondence drained from his face, displaced by rising anger. Simmonne, the one sibling he trusted. The one he never saw as a threat, now stealing the crown from his brow.

"You think so little of me, that you would choose her over me?"

"You're right, she is a poor choice. She's happier to be obedient than to lead, and she's the least intelligent of all my children. She feels when she should think, and she knows absolutely nothing about the realities of the world. Her only ambition in life is to find a husband, and have a horde of children to smother with her affection. But of all my children, she is the one I know would never abuse her power. I sent her to Avalon for a taste of the cruelties of the world. I believe she can be coached, that she can learn. And if she can't, well…with the exception of you, she's always been a good judge of character. She will marry well."

His entire body quaked, no longer with grief, but with the rage building within. Yet his father continued.

"You can return to the Armadas, and the career you began there. Or you can return to the systems you colonized, and live quite comfortably as a count. But as emperor, the crown is something I cannot give you."

"You know what you have to do."

"I'm sorry, Dad," he whispered. "I'm sorry I was never good enough."

The words cut deep, and as his father moved to hug him Steven stepped forward. Two hundred years of anger flew in a psionic punch. His fist met his father's jaw, and the emperor's head exploded in a mist of blood.

"No!"

His mother's scream drew his eyes a second before a psionic wave launched him against the wall. Like a frightened child caught in some misdeed, he glared up at her. The psionic powerhouse of the Mandrake family was still alive, and very angry.

"Get up, Steven. Remember your promise. Don't fail her now."

CHAPTER
12A

MORE THAN A HUNDRED Vaar had flooded into the cargo bay. The majority was arranged in file on opposite sides of the chamber, blocking all exits. The rest moved in pairs, one with a weapon, the other with a handheld sensor. They knew someone was here, and were determined that there would be no escape. Given enough time, Panzer was sure he could wait them out, remain motionless until they were convinced he had somehow snuck past them. But time was a luxury he did not have.

His only choice would be to fight his way out. But there were more than a hundred sensors here, all running at full power. His first priority had to be getting out of the room as quickly as possible. His hands moved to the machine pistols on his thighs. The timing had to be perfect. With so many sensors even through his cloak, they would detect the power spike when he switched the weapons off of safe. With his mind he plucked two of the grenades from his belt. The hammer-shaped heads of each were twisted a half turn, setting them for an impact detonation.

"Andira," he whispered, "the moment I fire, dump everything you can into jamming."

"Ready, sir."

He forced his breath to come in deep inhales, calming his mind. His focus turned to the grenades in his psionic grasp, and each whistled on a path to opposite sides of the room. Vortex weapons, upon detonation, created a whirlpool warp. The vortex's edges cut like blades of near infinite sharpness, slicing through the Vaar, the walls and the floor as matter was displaced by the whirlpool amid a thunderous bellow.

Free electrons filled the chamber with the flash of lightning pulses as they arced through the warped debris. While startled warriors turned toward the detonations he dropped from the ceiling, arming his weapons. He landed on one of the cargo crates and capped off a burst from each weapon on the nearest pair before dropping to the floor. In an instant the chamber was filled with bullets and warp pulses, panic fire as young warriors sprayed with their weapons.

Turning, Panzer focused on one of the cargo crates, an eye closing as he pressed against it with his mind. The crate groaned, scraping on the floor before slamming into another. A pair of Vaar was trapped as those crates smashed into another pair. With a step forward, Panzer sent the entire line of crates toward a section of the wall scored by his grenades. The crates bowled through the Vaar and he followed, using the cleared path to follow the crates. When they struck the wall the crates came to a halt, and he offered them another thrust, pushing them through. More than half of the Vaar were still hosing the cargo bay with fire but he was now beyond its confines. Alarms blared through the corridors as he dashed for an exit.

"Initiating communications break-in," Andira announced.

"Lock down that deck, all exits," a Vaar ordered.

Panzer fell into a slide as a bulkhead began to lower ahead of him. He cleared the first, and the second. His feet stopped when he made contact with a third bulkhead.

"Damn," he whispered, rising upright. "No time to wait."

Raising a hand he took a step forward, throwing his mind against the bulkhead. The metal let out a howl of protest as it contorted. As he closed in on the bulkhead he offered his shoulder, and fired his thrusters. Weakened by the psionic blow, the bulkhead shattered on the super-hard surface of his armor, allowing him to plow through.

"Cordon breach 2-7-1," the Embassy commander relayed to his troops. "Hostile located; all units converge. Lock down all lifts, begin encryption rotation…now."

Panzer winced as a loud wave of static washed through his helmet.

"They've changed systems," Andira said. "Reacquiring."

His feet came to a stop, and he threw himself into the wall as his vision turned red and the corridor was filled with explosive blasts. As quickly as it had come, the storm of explosives was halted. He lowered the arm shielding his head and glanced around—no holes in the walls, no showers of sparks. There were no shells coming in, only the passage of a provident moment that ended with the fading of the red haze.

"Team seven in position, growler deployed." A Vaar voice brought him back to the moment.

Panzer moved slowly, and as he approached the corner ahead he held up one of the autopistols, using the built-in sensor to glare around the turn. Fourteen Vaar blocked the path, all with weapons ready. At their center was a large tripod-mounted gun, a 52mm autocannon, the infamous growler.

He plucked another grenade from his belt, twisting the head before stopping himself. Behind he could hear the approaching Vaar as the cordons meant to trap him near the cargo bay were raised. Peeking around the corner again, he smiled to himself, and returned one of the machine pistols to his hip to free his hand.

Reaching into the corridor, he clamped his fist down and drew his arm back. The Vaar operating the growler let out a cry of shock as he was drawn with the cannon toward the corridor's end. With the gun approaching Panzer stepped out, taking aim with the weapon he still held. A short burst to the helmet and the growler's operator fell away from the weapon. Soon after, the others flooded the hall with fire.

Panzer in turn ducked back behind the wall as the growler moved to join him. With his open palm he took the grenade back in hand, and offered it to them. One more problem was solved by the application of explosives. His attention turned toward the growler as he angled it toward the Vaar approaching from the rear. With the weapon in position he pulled the trigger before bending the metal to loop it around the handle.

The growler did exactly as its name implied, filling the corridor with its trademark noise as it launched hypersonic shells into the approaching Vaar. That would buy him time; the Vaar would likely wait for it to run out of ammo rather than advanced into the hail of 52mm shells now ripping the corridor apart in a storm of anti-tank rounds.

The question now was where to go.

"Andira, how we doing on their coms?"

"They've unified their encryption rotation on a random number generator. I won't be able to pick up more than a few syllables before the code changes again."

"What about our coms?"

"Unable to ping local systems."

"So much for that. What's my quickest way out of here?"

"Refuse disposal."

"Yes, but I have this odd feeling they're expecting that. Any other suggestions?"

"The facility's conveyor garage is on the level directly above us."

"Nearest lift?"

"Proceed down the corridor 105 meters, on your right."

Perhaps the Vaar were feeling more aggressive than he anticipated. As his feet moved, the hall was suddenly filled with a gout of flame as the growler along with its ammo were destroyed by the impact of several grenades. Pushed forward by the concussive blast he dashed for the lift, and quickly pried the doors open. The moment the doors were open the shaft was filled with disrupter fire. On the level above, Vaar fired down through open doors, attacking the movement.

"I really need to start carrying more of these," he groaned, grabbing his last grenade. After arming the weapon he stepped into the shaft, and his shields flared as disrupter pulses slammed into him. With a grunt he hurtled the grenade, clearing the Vaar at the door. On his thrusters he climbed to the next level before turning back. The lift was one more level up and, focusing on it, he pulled with his mind. The lift groaned; sparks flew until he overpowered the magnetic field and allowed it to fall. A most unwelcome surprise for a lone Vaar who had stepped into the shaft to gaze upward.

"Andira, which way?"

"To your left, fifty meters."

Breaking into a full run he followed her directions, until rounding a corner where more than a dozen Vaar waited for him.

"That is the only way to the garage," Andira advised.

"Then only one way to go."

Sprinting, he filled both hands, and disrupter pulses lanced around him as he dashed into the field of overlapping sensors. The machine pistols fired, weak pulses but emerging at a rate of 5,000 per minute from each weapon. He did not fire for effect, merely to send them scrambling for cover while he angled toward the door. With a psionic blast the metal door was blown off of its hinges, and he emerged in the garage.

Armored conveyors were arranged in a line and he dropped into the nearest one. His hands raced across the controls as the machine came to life, and hefted itself from the ground.

"I am unable to access the door controls," Andira cautioned as the canopy sealed. "Vaar on your right."

Those he had just bull-rushed were now flowing into the garage. Immediately their fire lit the shields of the conveyor.

"Andira, can this thing break through those doors?"

"Uncertain."

"Good enough for me," he answered, pushing the throttle. The conveyor's engine howled, the doors grew closer, and held firm. The forward half of the vehicle collapsed in on itself and Panzer was slammed into the console as the vehicle came to a sudden halt.

"Not what I had in mind," he groaned. He lifted a pistol and used its fire to carve a way out of the bent canopy. While the Vaar continued firing on the disabled vehicle, he ducked low and scurried back to the still parked vehicles.

"Sir, they have reinforced the door with a level nine force field."

"Not making anything easy are they?"

After taking cover behind one of the other conveyors, he aimed toward the Vaar still firing on the broken machine.

"Sir, massive reinforcements inbound."

The machine pistols howled as he swept the surprised Vaar. Several were on the ground before the others retreated to the corridor. But he had what he needed. His eyes moved across the bodies of the dead and the wounded. His face twisted as he pushed his mind through their 4CM fields, and plucked the grenades affixed to their armor. He gagged as the grenades came to him, suppressing the urge to vomit as the 4CM fields protecting their owner's corpses protested his mind's actions. With a dozen grenades orbiting his body, he opened the canopy of the next conveyor and boarded.

"Let's hope this works," he whispered, arming the weapons and propelling them toward the wrecked vehicle. Closing the canopy he hit the throttle, aiming for the wreck as the grenades detonated. The nose of his new vehicle met the blast wave, plowing into the wreck even as it was blown askew and slamming into the door. The metal bent, pieces were ejected from the force field, and the conveyor stopped.

The vehicle's nose had penetrated the door, but now he was stuck halfway through.

"Damn it," he growled, leaning on the throttle. The Vaar chose this moment to return to the garage and disrupter pulses slammed into his vehicle from behind.

Raising his hands, he focused on the door. Pain sparked behind his eyes. An incredible weight seemed to bear down on his brow. Held in place by the force field, the door refused to move. He winced as Andira pumped chemicals into his bloodstream. Needles in his armor jammed through the flesh of his arms and legs into the straining muscles. The veins pulsed in his forehead, his arms, and capillaries burst in his cheeks. There was a loud groan, and he was thrown back as the door raised just enough for the conveyor to power through.

Shaking his head, he grabbed for the control sticks, and straightened himself on the road.

"Andira, lock in on the princess' transponder, give me a waypoint. We're making sure she gets off the station."

CHAPTER
12B

H ER SHOES HAD BEEN left behind, and rushed on by her guards, Simmonne felt her feet make only occasional contact with the floor. Charging through the crowds, her guards bowled through those too slow to move. Together they stampeded more like a pack of deltas than petite gammas. Before she knew where she was, she was dropped into her conveyor, with the Twins crammed against her. By the time Jenna and Isis had climbed into the vehicle, it was already accelerating. The bulk of her personal guard followed in their own conveyors, smashing through those in the way to escape the lot.

"Avalon Control, this is *Mandrake-27* Security," Isis barked. "Avalon Control, do you read?"

"What's wrong?" Jenna asked, with a calm that belied the nervousness Simmonne could sense within her.

"I can't get through," Isis answered. "The network is down. I can't reach Avalon control, I can't reach the *Hurricane*. I'm trying the shuttle; they can pick us up on the skyway."

"What about the missiles?" Jenna barked.

"We have to get off the station," Isis returned. "The skyway is the quickest way. We need to get out before the shields fail."

"Do it."

The air around her rippled as the conveyor's concussion field flared, canceling out the otherwise jarring collision as her driver rammed through a truck blocking their way.

"The shuttle has acknowledged; they're on the way," Isis shouted up to the driver.

Lights flashed overhead. Combine missiles having made the long journey from shore batteries rained down on the station's shields. Simmonne began to look up, before Jenna covered her eyes.

"Don't look," she warned. "The flashes could blind you."

Subconsciously Simmonne wrung her hands as the surreal events unfolded. This morning everything was peaceful, everyone was calm. Now she could sense panic from every person she passed, and from every conveyor on the road. What happened? What was going on? How did everything change so quickly?

The conveyor rammed into another, pushing it aside to gain access to the skyway's on-ramp. She glanced back at the now mangled car behind, hoping its occupants were all right. To her sides the Twins were deathly silent, no more able than her to grasp the reality of what was happening.

Her eyes moved to Isis as the aren reached into her dress and produced a metal box. With the push of a button it extended into a small rifle. Simmonne's eyes were drawn to the weapon, which represented a clear reinforcement of the situation.

"Time to intercept, two minutes!" the driver called back to them.

The car continued to ascend, following the highest of the roads until it leveled out. Over the rooftops the missile impacts tore the sky like a lighting storm. The flashes grew so bright Simmonne was forced to cover her eyes.

"Shuttle ahead!"

"Bogey behind us!"

She looked to the rear, where a ship climbed above the skyway, following them. The ship's round belly extended out to four wings housing engines on each terminus. Its hull was painted in green, the markings of the quants. A refugee ship?

"Pick us up now!" Isis screamed.

Her shuttle approached, quickly reversing course as it turned tail to face the conveyor and its cargo doors slid open. The shuttle dipped, descending until its belly sparked on the road.

"Get us in!"

The car lurched ahead as the driver accelerated. Simmonne's eyes remained fixed to the ship behind, her hands shielding from the flashes above. She saw plates moving across the ship's body, and cannons gleamed in the light as they were pushed out of the hull.

The car rocked as it entered the cargo bay, and her convoy followed in single file. The doors began to close, the shuttle began to rise, and the guns of their pursuer came to life.

"Get us out of here!" Jenna screamed.

"Mayday, mayday, this is *Mandrake-27*, we are under attack. Repeat, we are under attack!"

The conveyor's concussion field could not cancel out the larger body as the shuttle quaked, and they were cast in darkness.

"We have to circle, and exit away from the missiles!"

Simmonne was not sure who spoke as she wrapped her arms around the Twins. Seconds later, a blast tore through the shuttle and the light returned as the cargo bay was torn open.

"We're going down!" the shuttle's pilot shouted. "Get out, get out, get out!"

"Go, go, go!" Isis screeched to the driver as the cargo doors opened again. The driver threw the conveyor into reverse, crashing into the next car in the convoy and pushing them all out of the ship's cargo hold. The Twins' screams echoed in shrill stereo as the conveyor moved into free fall.

From the conveyor's belly a pair of delta wings unfurled as the vehicle shifted to flight mode. Simmonne turned back, watching the other conveyors follow the morph. Behind, the quant ship followed, its own body scarred and pitted from the firefight with her shuttle.

"Avalon Control, we need support. Fleet, someone! This is *Mandrake-27*, we are under attack!" Isis was becoming desperate, adding to Simmonne's own fear. She averted her eyes as guns sprouted from her conveyor and opened fire on the ship. Her eyes moved down, glaring at her trembling hands.

Though their accuracy was perfection, the guns of the conveyors were meant to protect against angry crowds and other small vehicles, not dropships. Their combined fire did little more than illuminate the shields of her pursuer in a red glow.

"I can't outrun a shuttle!" the driver shouted back against Isis' demands. "I'm taking us down!"

The conveyors broke the sound barrier as they dived below the layers of the skyway, and the driver began weaving through the support struts. The dropship followed, staying out of the rows of obstructions.

"Get us back into the station," Jenna shouted. "They can't follow us into the hull!"

Movement in the dropship's belly caught Simmonne's eye before something fell away. It was not alone—a long line of somethings dropped out behind. Black wings expanded from the shoulders of armored figures. With horror struck the realization—they were Vaar.

Her conveyor crashed through a barricade, taking one of the in-ramps into the station's internal roads. The Vaar followed, thrusters on their wings guiding their pursuit. They passed over bewildered civilians to follow the convoy into the station.

"What the hell?" Jenna's whisper was barely audible.

The conveyor's guns zeroed in on the Vaar, spraying them with fire. The Vaar in turn moved into formation, overlapping their shields against the firestorm. The conveyor shook as one of its guns was blasted free. Simmonne glanced back in time to see one of the Vaar lose his shielding. A disrupter clipped his wing, and sent him slamming into the wall of the tunnel.

The nearest of their formations drew closer, breaking up to divide themselves among the cars. Behind, her guards juked and swerved, trying to block their advance. One of the warriors slipped below them in a dive, and advanced toward her.

"On our right!" Isis shouted while readying her rifle.

As the warrior closed in, the driver abruptly braked, bringing the Vaar forward before she cut into a turn. Metal howled as the two bodies collided, and the Vaar became pinned between the conveyor and the wall. Sparks flew as the warrior was ground against the hull, and a series of loud bangs rang through the conveyor. The warrior was hammering his free arm furiously against the vehicle, trying to deform its hull enough to free himself. When his shields gave out, one of his wings flew away, and her driver turned, allowing him to fly into an uncontrolled spin.

"I need a straight shot to outrun them!" the driver screamed. "I have to take us outside!"

"Do it!"

The conveyor bucked at the sudden turn as the driver moved to an out-ramp, scraping against the walls of the tunnel through the station's hull. Her guards followed, and their formation separated just enough for two of the Vaar to slip past. While the pair drew closer, the car picked up speed, ready to leave them behind. The vehicle shook at the sudden addition of mass as an armored claw clamped down on the hull. The world became a cacophony of spinning lights and screams. Her driver moved in a corkscrew, attempting to sling the warrior off.

A sensation to Simmonne's side caused her to turn, and she let out a low gasp as a chill ran down her spine. The red visors of the warrior's helmet glared through the transparency, right at her. She realized he was reporting in, telling the others he had confirmed which car was hers. A moment later, a small disc was in his hand, which he slapped against the hull before he let go. The conveyor's hull flexed around her as the disc exploded.

"I've lost engines!" the driver yelled while the conveyor began to fishtail. "Activating crash procedures. Brace for impact!"

Losing altitude, the vehicle approached a field of large cylinders beneath the skyway, water towers.

A green light filled the cab as the concussion field spooled up to full power. Everything was frozen, she could not move. Even her hair tossed by the event hung still in front of her eyes. Crashing through the towers, the car upended before breaking through another. The transparent canopy shattered, but the shards remained in place, trapped in the concussion field.

Finally the car stopped as it broke through a third tower and fell into the water within. With the presence of the water the concussion field remained intact, but holes torn in the vehicle's body allowed the water to begin flooding in. With the field still active, Simmonne could not move.

"Cut the field!" Isis shouted. "Cut the damn field!"

No answer came, and the cab was flooded with red water flowing in from the cockpit.

"Conveyor, voice recognize Isis. Override and terminate concussion field!"

Simmonne sat trembling as Isis used her rifle to force the broken canopy open.

"Come on, hold on to me."

In shock she did not move, and Jenna guided her arms around her. On her handmaiden's back she was lifted out of the conveyor, glancing behind to watch Isis doing the same with the Twins. One of the other conveyors pulled up to the hole torn in the tank, and gently guided itself inside. The door opened and the gammas within filed out. One held tight to the conveyor, and extended her arm down. The next dangled from the first, until several were extending down to them.

"Hold tight," Jenna directed, taking the arm of the nearest gamma. Isis followed as they climbed the rope of arens. The driver guided the car out of the tank. Simmonne winced as she felt a blast of heat. The dropship had found them, and had put several shots into the conveyor. The vehicle shook, and began to fall.

Simmonne felt something give—the collar of Jenna's dress—and screamed as she felt herself in free fall. Just as she became certain the fall would kill her, the air fled her lungs and she landed on her side. The pain and the awful sound of the conveyor crashing caused her to curl up in a ball, her hand pressing at her wounded ribs.

"Are you all right?" Jenna was on her in a moment.

She gasped as she forced an eye open, seeing the flesh torn from the side of her handmaiden's face.

"Come on!"

She was being dragged, and in a moment was surrounded by the Twins again. Now knowing exactly where their targets were, the Vaar attacked in force. Jenna threw her body over the three of them as one of the remaining conveyors exploded. The Twins were in tears as tiny shrapnel rained down on them. An instant later Jenna was dragging all three of them until they were wedged between one of the towers and the pipes branching down from its sides.

"We have to get out of here!" Jenna shouted.

"No!" Isis waved her hand. "Stay put, this is a defensible position!"

"But the Vaar—"

"This isn't an assassination," Isis interrupted. "If they wanted us dead, we would be. This is an abduction."

"Abduction?" Simmonne whispered.

"All units on my position," Isis continued. "Defensive position."

Simmonne watched as the dropship circled the water towers, dispersing additional troops. Finally it dropped something else, something larger than the others. It sent a tremor through the deck as it landed, before uncoiling into the stature of a warmech with four giant cannons sprouting from it shoulders. The enormous machine's knees stood higher than the crests of the warriors around it, looming over the battlefield.

"Simmonne, look at me." Jenna's hands were on her face. "Whatever happens, stay down. You hear me? Stay down!"

She nodded, watching her handmaiden reach into her dress. She produced a small metal band, a psionic booster, and placed it on her own brow.

"Princess Simmonne Mandrake!" A voice bellowed so loud she was forced to cover her ears. "You are surrounded and hopelessly outnumbered. Come out and surrender!"

Isis directed the remaining gammas into position as the Vaar who had been in flight shed their wings to take position beyond the water tanks.

"Princess, I promise you and your people will not be harmed if you surrender now. Come out! Or we will come in."

Her eyes darted between Jenna and Isis as both took their positions.

"Princess Mandrake, this is your last chance. Surrender now!"

"Warp 'em!"

At Isis' command, the air was split by thunder, the Twins cried out at her sides, holding tighter to her. The Vaar quickly ducked behind the cover of the tanks, while the mech made no effort to move. Each of the Vaar held out his left arm where a metal framework unfolded, and was soon covered by a glow. Power shields, auxiliary shields meant to supplement their personal defense screens.

Simmonne glanced around the tank. Ahead of the mech two columns of Vaar were approaching. In the front column the Vaar held their power shields ahead, while those behind returned fire. When the power shield broke, the warrior ahead interposed himself with the one behind, allowing their march to continue unabated.

"Grenades!" Isis shouted.

Hot wind washed through the field of tanks as electricity thundered through the air.

"On our flanks!"

"Coming up behind!"

The approaching phalanx of Vaar answered with their own grenades, and Jenna acted. With her arms outstretched, she halted the devices midway through their flight, and followed with a return to sender.

"They're getting closer!"

"Fix bayonets!"

Each gamma moved in unison, drawing long blades from their dresses to mount them on their guns before resuming fire. Jenna moved as if she was locked in a dance, picking up shrapnel, debris, ripping pipes from the tanks, and hurtling them at the Vaar.

Simmonne turned to the sound of a mutual scream. A few meters away one of her guards had impaled a Vaar in the knee; his bayonet had drawn down from her shoulder to her waist.

"No," she whispered, watching her protector's body open up in a mist of blood.

"*Mandrake-27* to anyone, we need help now! Crykeeper, where are you?"

Her eyes moved. Her guards were dropping like flies, either to fire from all sides, or Vaar bayonets. There were just too many of them; they couldn't hold.

She turned to see a Vaar sprint around one of the tanks, charging Isis.

"Isis!"

The gamma turned, her disrupter tore into the Vaar's head, and the warrior fell.

"Grenade!"

"More on the right!"

Isis cried out in pain as the air was filled with the odor of searing flesh. The gamma's body convulsed as it was ravaged by static discharge, and she fell to clutch her now severed arm. Moving quickly, Jenna grabbed her, dragging her back toward Simmonne.

"I'm all right," the gamma said. "My rifle? I need a pistol."

"Inner thigh!" Jenna shouted back as she continued to pummel the Vaar with scrap.

The mech was the next to move, throwing its arms out to carve a path through the water towers as it approached. Each footstep created a terrible quake in the metal ground.

"We have to get out of here!" Jenna shouted while Isis reached under her dress to take one of the pistols.

Ground trembling, the mech drew closer, still breaking the towers out of its way.

Isis rose to her feet, firing now with the pistol.

"Come on."

Simmonne looked up as Jenna grabbed her.

Water flooded down as the mech's arm tore into the tower above, drenching them.

Simmonne was on her feet in time to turn as another Vaar came charging around. Before Simmonne could scream he pounced on Isis from behind, bayonet gleaming a second before it met her back. The gamma's cry of pain was cut short by the flow of blood from her mouth as she was hoisted from the ground.

"Isis!"

Jenna spun on her heel, throwing her arms forward. The Vaar cried out in shock as he was hurtled backward, and Isis fell as the bayonet was drawn out of her. Jenna meanwhile stumbled, as if a strong blow had landed on her head. She fell. She was down for only a moment, before clawing her way back to her feet.

Simmonne ran to Isis, and was stopped by a hand on her chest. Only gurgles escaped the gamma's lips as Isis pushed her away, mouthing the words to run.

"Come on!"

Jenna grabbed her arm, pulling her away, but stopped.

They were surrounded.

Vaar warriors stood on all sides, guns ready.

"Drop the weapon!" one of the warriors shouted.

Simmonne's eyes raced, and she found the pistol in Jenna's hand.

"Drop the weapon!"

Jenna's head swiveled, and her arm began to rise. Simmonne reached out, grabbing Jenna with both hands to stop her.

"No," she whispered. "Not you too."

"Drop the weapon, now!"

Jenna glared at her before turning back to the Vaar, and with a sigh she dropped the pistol.

Simmonne's eyes moved over the battlefield, her guards. No, they couldn't be dead. They…they were just wounded. Certainly they were. But why weren't they crying out in pain, why weren't they clutching their wounds? Why weren't they moving? They were just wounded, just wounded…

Two of the Vaar came forward, and dropped a set of manacles in front of Jenna.

"Restrain them," the warrior directed. "No tricks, or you will all pay."

Tears welled in Simmonne's eyes as Jenna bent to take the restraints.

"Just do what they tell you," Jenna whispered in her ear as the metal closed around her wrists.

"Behind their back!"

"You're valuable; just do what they say, and they won't hurt you."

Simmonne nodded as the Twins were cuffed.

"Now yourself."

While Jenna cuffed herself, the mech came forward, coming down on a knee to bring its eyes level with Simmonne.

"Pleased to meet you, Imperial Rose," the pilot spoke. She sensed something, something strange. There was no pilot; somehow, the pilot and the machine were a single entity.

She turned her head away as the great Vaar bore down on her. Its enormous hand opened, and in a second all four were drawn together in its grasp.

"Collect the wounded," the great Vaar directed. "Meet us on the skyway."

CHAPTER
12C

THROUGH THE *LONGRUNNER*'S SENSORS Clearwater could see the glow of the planetary shield's layers now coursing through the planet's exosphere. The repulsion field could block landing ships and most weapons, but was useless against naval disrupters. Without warp shielding, a warship could peel a planet like an onion, its disrupters piercing through conventional shielding with terrific ease. The warp shield had not yet been raised; it couldn't be until the moment of certainty that it was needed. Such a strong warp field would interfere with the gravity between the planet and its host star, with more severe repercussions the longer the shield was raised.

If the Vaar were here to fight, one of two things would determine the outcome. Should the Vaar move in or attack, the warp shield would go online. If the Armadas did not arrive in time, the decision would be made to allow the planet to drift farther and farther from its natural orbit, or the shield would be lowered, allowing the Vaar to bombard and destroy the conventional shield before landing their troops.

The *Longrunner* dipped, descending toward Twilight. Civilians filled the streets as legionnaires scrambled to lead them to the shelters. Clearwater's thoughts turned to Taula, and the hopes that she was already safe in the scientists' reserved shelter. His eyes moved to the Vaar that lay on the shuttle's floor, still clinging to life as three medics attended to him. What did he know?

"Raise the warp shield!"

Clearwater's heart skipped a beat as he heard Brower's voice.

"What the hell?"

The pilot's voice brought his attention back to the sensors. A yellow glow lit the night-cast landscape, stretching through the valley to the distant mountains beyond.

"Raise the warp shield!" Brower shouted louder.

"Sir, the shield is up," an artillery officer answered.

The light began to condense into shapes, thousands of them, maybe more. Somehow, someone was wormholing directly to the surface, despite the warp shield.

"All units to the security cordon immediately!"

The *Longrunner* touched down, and the doors flew open. Clearwater was caught up in a stampede as both sections stormed out. Daylight on this world was a dim candle in comparison to the light now filling the sky. Around the city the security cordon began to rise, a wall twenty-five meters tall and nearly as many thick.

Something caught his eye, and he turned, letting out a gasp. The ghost—it was here, kneeling over the wounded Vaar. The three medics attending him were motionless, as if frozen in time. He took a step, watching as the spectral image laid a hand on the Vaar. A bright flash caused him to wince, and when he opened his eyes, both the ghost and the Vaar were gone. Where, where did they go? His eyes moved to the medics who now turned their heads side to side, bewildered at the sudden disappearance of their patient.

"This way, sir." Sarge urged him to follow while his section moved to take their position on the rising wall. Whatever had just happened, he had no time to worry about it now. Automatech flooded the wall's upper levels, joining batteries of automated guns. Through an entrance in the floor Clearwater followed Sarge up to the midlevels as the glow across the landscape faded.

"Oh no," Clearwater said with a gasp, looking out of a gunnery window to the no longer empty fields. Where there was once nothing but grass an army had materialized. Vaar, tanks, warmechs, and artillery now stretched from a point just over a kilometer away out beyond the horizon.

"Holy shit, there's got to be a million of them," someone said.

"Raise the theater shield!"

A thunderclap ripped through the ground as a new shield system came online, casting its glow into a globe extended just beyond the reach of the security cordon. Clearwater was paralyzed, as if his body had left his mind behind. His eyes moved over the Vaar, but they were not alone.

Between the Vaar and the colony, another group of aliens were arranged into formation. Serpentine bodies stood on six legs, while they brandished a pair of mantis-like claws. Bifurcated jaws hung open, allowing twin tongues to dangle amid the fog of their breath. Fellow natives of the Vaar home world, their masters used them as expendable attack dogs. Their masters' name for them was the enspa.

His heart beat so rapidly that his entire body shook. This was not training, no exercise. The Vaar were here, and they had come to fight.

Reports came in from around the platoon. The Vaar had filled the valley, surrounding the town with an army more than a million strong.

"Listen up!" Brower's voice broke the trance as he glared out at the Vaar. "I see the same thing you do. I know exactly what you're feeling. Steel yourselves; we're the only thing between what you see out there and the civilians at our backs. You are Solar Legionnaires; you are the pride of the Empire. This is why we are here. Stand together. The fleet is out of contact but they must know what is happening. We must hold our lines until reinforcements arrive. Watch each other's backs, keep your eyes on your com-monitors, prioritize their officers."

A series of shrill tones filled the air, echoing through the valley. Each Vaar stood with his jaw clenched, grinding his metal teeth. The sound, the metal dragging on metal, from more than a million mouths. The tactic was meant to elicit fear in their foes, and it for Clearwater it was working. When the sound of sharpening steel faded, the attack would begin. It took so long, knowing that the moment was coming.

"Oh God," he whispered. "We're screwed."

The sound faded, and a new aria filled the valley. The thunderous footfalls and high-pitched shrieks as the enspa spilled forward. The Battle of ND-31 had begun. Like water from a collapsing dam they flooded into the valley, sprinting over 100 kilometers an hour. Together they howled and shrieked, eager to find something to fit between their teeth.

Behind the enspa, the Vaar opened fire on the colony. Rifles, tanks, warmechs, artillery, all sounded together. So much fire broke against the colony shield that Clearwater lost sight of the army from which it originated. So many weapons fired together, the wet grass around the town caught fire. Undeterred by the flame, the enspa continued to close the distance.

"Perimeter defense," Brower said calmly. "Arm anti-personnel mines, ready on perimeter turrets."

New explosions scattered the smoke as the enspa met the minefield. Though smaller than an acorn, the mines exploded with such force that those triggering them were reduced to clouds of bloody mist. This offered no trepidation to those behind, who continued to charge. Minefields were arrayed to funnel an enemy into specific avenues of approach where he could be dispatched by artillery and automatic weapons. For this notion the enspa gave no thought. Those that found the empty approaches happily raced through them. Those that found minefields did not hesitate. Perhaps they were too stupid, or maybe they were simply unwilling to take any path but the one most direct to what they believed to be waiting meat. When they were within 1,300 meters, Brower spoke again.

"Even perimeter turrets, engage."

Gun turrets between the cordon and the shield perimeter sprang out of the ground, turning out toward the enspa. Wave turrets were designed for just such an assault, firing not in pulses but in constant streams to cut down infantry wave attacks. Enspa were trisected by the twin gun turrets sweeping through their approach, which cut them down in overlapping fields of fire. So many were cut down that their blood soaking the ground soon extinguished the grass fires.

"They're still coming," Brower shouted. "All units fire at will!"

Legionnaires and automatech opened up on the tsunami of claws and teeth. Clearwater's eyes remained affixed; his body did not move. Something hard struck him from behind, and shaking his head, he stepped forward to the window and fired. He did not aim for anything in particular, merely pointing his guns into the flood.

The AICES' twin 40mm disrupters emitted a loud whine as they fired together at 10,000 rounds per minute. The hail of disrupter fire blanketed the terrain, adding to the alien bloodbath occurring below. Clearwater drew his sight over a cluster of the creatures, and under his fire they came apart in a cloud of blood and static. With the pack before him shredded, he moved on to another, firing as he swept the machine's arms.

SGT DOLPH: Might want to consider burst-firing there, LT.

Clearwater forced himself to take a breath, and let off of the triggers so that the disrupters' temperature could fall out of redline. He cast his eyes to the cannons, red-hot from the sustained burst. His body trembled so hard that his AICES believed the movement to be intentional and its arms likewise shook.

"They're still closing!" Brower sounded again. "Triple-heads, full dispersal, fire!"

Toggling to the new weapon, Clearwater forced hatches in the AICES' shoulders to open. Small missiles streamed out of the racks this revealed, toward the charging aliens. The triple-head was named for its three warheads. A soft-target weapon, the first shell burst in a magnetic charge hurtling hypersonic shrapnel. A millisecond later, the second warhead detonated, scattering more of the micro-mines the enspa were already contending with. Finally, the third and largest charge was set off, spraying the landscape with UG-2.

UG-2 was developed less than a year ago for this exact situation. To most races of the Empire, it was harmless. But to the enspa, with their non-hermetic armor, a concentrated nerve gas. Nearly 1,000 legionnaires on the cordon, and the automatech above them blanketed the area. And soon the Enspa were screaming in a green fog of deadly vapors. Clearwater's eyes zeroed in on one of the creatures. Its body twisted, fluids poured from its mouth, and the creature fell. Like a poisoned insect, it rolled onto its back, curling up to die.

"They're falling back. Cease fire, cease fire!"

Clearwater let off of the triggers, and closed the hatches. He allowed a sigh of relief, before feeling a tremor in the ground.

"What is that?" he murmured with a gasp, and zoomed in on the horizon. Something big was coming, shaking the ground with its footsteps, and it was not alone. The machines approaching from the horizon towered over even the warmechs scattered through the Vaar ranks.

A long body was carried by eight legs, each branching up and out from the sides of the body to a weapons platform on high knees before descending to the ground. A large spherical head terminated in a pair of forks housing a single, massive cannon. His sensors read that the cannon was more than fifty meters from the ground. With each step, one leg would elevate before sliding forward on a hip track and then descending with a thunderclap. Once all eight had moved forward, that same track was used to pull the body forward, so that the process could repeat.

"What the hell are those?" Clearwater whispered.

Sixteen of the machines approached from the north, while more came from the other directions. Yet more were visible coming over the horizon. As the machines drew closer, their heads began to glow. The cannons around which they were built came to life, and gigantic disrupters fired in continuous beams.

The beams struck the ground before coming to the perimeter of the shield, tunneling through the soil until reaching the protective field. Even the theater shields were unable to stop the beams completely. Clearwater stumbled as the security cordon shuddered.

"Focus fire, target their main guns!" Brower shouted.

Clearwater fired with his disrupters, while engaging the launcher on his right shoulder. Anti-armor warheads howled from the weapon, joining the hail of fire lashing out at the machines from the colony. The shielding of the colossal mechs shined bright enough to obscure the machines within. Yet their shields held, even against the fire of the Imperial's armored units.

"Targeting crews designate, we need arty now!"

Several legionnaires painted the machines with targeting beams, illuminating them for the distant artillery.

"Battery Two, fire!"

Wherever they were, the hidden artillery engaged the colossi, and seconds later plasma trails lit the night sky as missiles skimmed below the planetary shield before plunging back into the atmosphere. Clearwater's eyes narrowed on the machine he had targeted as the artillery found its mark. The waste heat of massive disrupter charges bathed the forest of infantry beneath the machine in fire and electricity. The colossus' defenses held against the first salvo, and the machine soldiered on. The two salvos that followed were not to be stopped. The first round of the second salvo erupted against the machine's spine. The blast completely perforated its body, with excess energy continuing down to open a crater in the ground. The subsequent impacts sheared away three of its eight legs. The machine wobbled for a moment, spreading its remaining legs to balance itself. It did not move from there. While still somewhat intact, it was out of the fight.

Others were hit by the salvo, with one losing enough of its legs that it plummeted to the ground, creating a shock wave of rock and dirt as it impacted. The rest of the colossi continued to advance, and more appeared on the horizon.

"Battery Two, relocate and prepare to fire again!"

Having given away their position by firing, the crews of the artillery now had to hastily displace. Missiles were already rising from the Vaar ranks to follow the path of the attack and seek out the source. The remaining colossi along with those coming over the horizon fired anew with their main guns, once more tunneling to the foundations of the security cordon. The beams followed the same tracks as before, and the wall began to buckle.

Holding tight to the nearby shutter, Clearwater groaned as cracks formed in the wall and the deck shifted. One of his betas lost his balance and crashed into him, causing him to lose his grip. Moving against the quaking floor, he struggled to return to his position.

"Battery One, fire!"

Able to fire with impunity from within the colony shield, the direct-fire artillery attacked, pounding the machines with their cannons. The colossi targeted by the cannons saw their shields penetrated and large sections of their armor obliterated, yet they continued forward.

"Battery Two, we need fire now. Setting markers."

The targeting beams painted the machines again, and Clearwater held his breath as he waited for the missiles to fall. This time the Vaar were ready and the gun batteries astride the knees of each machine fired into the sky. As they descended, the missiles moved in violent, weaving corkscrews, making themselves more difficult to intercept. Some found their targets while others were destroyed before reaching their mark.

"Pour it on, pour it on!" Brower shouted. "More firepower!"

Clearwater flinched at the blast of flame as one of the machines was decapitated. Uncontrolled, it fell forward, collapsing on a sea of retreating enspa as it buried itself in the bloody mud of the valley. Despite their ponderous movements, the sheer size of each step was rapidly bringing the colossi to the colony.

"Battery Two, scoot, scoot, fire again in thirty seconds. All other units, pour it on!"

Aiming at the nearest machine, Clearwater zoomed in on its cannon before firing. Even with his full section and several others focusing fire, the target was simply too big. While many of their attacks managed to pierce the shields, those that did were left too diminished to contend with the massive armor.

"Battery Two, painting targets. Fire!"

The colossi continued to approach, but no fire came.

"Battery Two, fire! Fire damn it, fire!"

Still no missiles came. Wherever the second battery was, the Vaar had located them, and now they were gone.

"Perimeter defenses, activate AV mines!"

The ground quaked as one of the machines found a mine, and its foot vanished in a cloud of electric arcs. The colossus lurched as the remnants of its leg burrowed into the ground, bringing it to a halt. For a moment the machine did not move, until a small explosion jettisoned the wounded limb. Moving the rest to compensate for the loss, the machine righted itself.

It proceeded forward.

"They're right on top of us!"

"All units hold fire, Brower to shield control. Reconfigure, maximum opacity!"

The theater shield darkened. The landscape beyond vanished. At maximum opacity, the shield would allow nothing through, not even visible light.

A deafening sizzle filled the air, drawing all eyes upward. The colossi had come to the shield perimeter. Clearwater watched as the nose of one machine pushed through the barrier. Incandescent as layers of its armor were boiled away. Below the machines, the soil began to morph into glass as the heat was channeled through their bodies to the ground. As more of the machines moved through the barrier, Clearwater watched as the rear legs of the closest colossi slowly crouched. His mouth hung open as he realized what it was about to do.

"Get out, get out!" Clearwater shouted, urging his men to abandon their post.

The colossus' forward legs came down atop the wall, and the cordon groaned at the massive weight added to the already damaged structure. Stumbling down the stairs and out of the cordon, Clearwater turned back. The wall trembled under the machine's weight. Pieces of shrapnel ejected from the concussion field to cut through civilian buildings like a scythe. The air filled with a loud snap, and as if it was in slow motion, the machine descended. The impact of hundreds of thousands of tons coming down knocked him off his feet, and the air was filled by the sound of the collapsing wall.

"All units, fall back to secondary defense points, now!"

On his feet, Clearwater turned back.

"Oh no," he said with a whimper.

The colossus was now standing in the shield, and between its legs, a path had opened through the colony shield to the army beyond.

CHAPTER
12D

HIS MOTHER'S PSIONIC PUNCH had sent Steven careening face-first into the wall. Blood ran to his right eye on its way down to mix with that coming from his nose. Struggling to his feet, he glared back to her, now crouched over her husband's body.

"Do what you must, Steven."

With a nod he took a step forward, and enraged eyes turned toward him.

"How could you?" she shouted. "Steven, what have you done?"

"I'm sorry, Mother," he whispered. "Don't fight it. I want this to be as painless as possible."

Her eyes lit up in shock at the speed he covered the ground toward her. His hand closed around her neck as he drew her up, and her face turned red as he began to squeeze. Her nails clawed at his wrist as her cheeks flushed and her pupils dilated.

"Get off of me!"

The psionic wave blew him back with such force that he felt his ribs break. But he did not let go, and she was carried with him as he slammed into the wall. He winced as her nails clawed at his face, gouging into his bleeding eye.

"Don't fight it," he urged. *"It will be over soon."*

His pupils dilated as he added the force of his mind to that of his hand, while she attempted to pry him from her neck. Her eyes closed; he could feel her mind fading. Half of a smile played across his face. It was quickly wiped away as her eyes flew open, and she drove the heel of her hand into his chest. The combined physical and psionic strike sent him reeling, and her neck slipped from his grasp.

Landing on his back, he clamored to his feet to find her on her knees, holding a hand to her throat.

"Guards!" she tried to scream, but only a wheeze escaped.

"They cannot help you now, little empress."

Her expression filled with terror, hearing the strange voice for the first time.

She turned her sight back toward Steven.

Where so many women would plead, beg him to stop, to not hurt them…she did not. There was not an ounce of fear in the woman. Only anger filled her eyes as she returned to her feet and set her gaze on him.

The room began to quake, and Steven struggled to remain on his feet. He had hoped to kill her quickly—not only so she would not suffer, but to avoid fighting the true psionic power of the family.

Glassware flew from the nearby bar, paneling ripped from the walls, lights were torn from the ceiling. Steven elevated his hand, trying to deflect the incoming storm of projectiles zeroing in on him. A piece of the wall stopped inches from his fingertips; he used it to deflect an incoming chair. A light struck the ground beside his foot. He held out his other hand as a drinking glass emitted a sonic boom on its path toward his face. But he only deflected it enough that it tore his left ear away on its path to shatter against the wall.

Recoiling in pain, the lapse in concentration left him vulnerable. The empress stepped toward him, moving her hands in a wave. The floor between them wrinkled as she created an explosive blast of air. In desperation Steven brought his hand up, and threw the full force of his mind into the wave. His fingers were blown from his hand like leaves in the wind. The bones of his left arm shattered, before the whole of the arm was torn away and the flesh was ripped from his face and neck. His eyes were gone; he barely felt himself hit the wall with no legs to catch him as he fell. Blood pooled in his lungs around the ribs that had punctured them.

"I…I failed." His thoughts turned to Natalie, still asleep in their bed. *"I'm…sorry, Natalie."*

"Your work is not finished, Steven."

An irresistible urge filled his lungs, and his throat. The air billowed, and his chest expanded as an otherworldly warmth filled him.

"Become more than what you are."

Within his body, molecules of oxygen and nitrogen were transmuted. Pressure filled his eye sockets until the light returned and he could see once more. His mother stood but a few meters from him, her arm up to shield her eyes from the light flooding the chamber. His eyes turned to his destroyed arm, surrounded in the red mist. So too were his legs; in fact, the whole of his body was so encased. The mist faded, and his body was whole again.

His mother lowered her arm, and glared at him in shock.

"What are you?" she whispered. "You're not my son."

With a renewed strength he rose to his feet, while his mother stepped away.

As the shock drained from her face, it was replaced by new resolution. Her fists clenched as she turned toward him, ready to finish what she started. His own mind turned inward, toward an old memory.

He was a child, no more than three. He sat in his mother's lap, all the while her hands were tickling him to the sound of mutual laughter.

"I have to destroy you," she stammered, balling her fist as he drew toward her.

"Do it, Mother. Kill your little boy."

He sent the image, the memory into her mind. The anger drained from her face, her head canted back, and she gasped. The momentary reverie, the sweet memory of her first child was all the opening he needed. Just one memory, a rare memory, of time when they were not an empress and a prince, but a mother and son.

His arms wrapped around her, and slowly she returned the embrace.

"Steven?" she whispered, still lost in the memory. "I love you."

He smiled.

"I love you too, Mommy."

His hands crept upward, one cradling her head as the other returned to her neck. Her body convulsed. Lost in her own mind, she believed he was tickling her. He stared down into her dumbstruck eyes as her mouth fought for air. Her arms began to fall from his shoulders, and her eyes rolled back. With a final shudder she was stilled, and he released her body to the floor.

His breath came in short gasps as he glared down at her. Her eyes now closed, the last vestiges of thought flickering in her mind as the memory faded. They were gone, both gone. It was over.

"Your throne is not yet secure, Steven. You know what you must do."

Still panting he nodded, and turned for the exit. He closed his eyes, his mind showing the way. Every consciousness in the abode was a string upon which he would make music. He drew the servitors in to collect their bodies, in their minds gathering garbage. On his way out of the royal abode his parents' guards followed him, now locked into the same trance as the servitors he left behind. One more challenge to what was rightfully his remained.

CHAPTER
13A

AVALON'S SHIELDS WERE WEAKENING under the nonstop barrage of missiles, lighting the sky that was now attempting to simulate twilight. Some of the warheads were slipping through, creating mushroom clouds as they impacted in the distance. The armored conveyor's engine roared as Panzer accelerated across the skyway. He did not have long. In his NOD he followed the waypoint to the princess' transponder. The alien dropship came into view, hovering over the skyway as it prepared to land.

"Reading seventy contacts," Andira announced. "And one armored unit."

He cocked an eyebrow, focusing on the large warmech at the front of their formation. Within one hand the machine grasped the Imperial Rose and her clique. Rage burned behind his eyes; his blood boiled at the sight. He shook his head. Now was a time to be calm. Scanning the markings on their armor, he knew better than to believe them. They were not the grunt infantry their markings suggested; these Vaar could only have come from one place: the Deniable Operations Service.

"Andira, any luck reaching Rhoxx or the others?"

"Negative."

"Too late now. Focus on jamming, shields, and concussion field. It's going to be a long night."

"Yes, sir."

His eyes moved to the dropship as he pushed the conveyor to accelerate further. To avoid ripping their prisoners apart with a ship-grade warp shield, the dropship would lower its defenses to bring them aboard. That was his one opening. With all the speed the skyway could offer, he flipped the switch to take the vehicle airborne, aligning the nose with the ship's cockpit.

Whether the pilots of the ship believed the approaching conveyor was an ally in need or simply expected him to turn away did not matter. They reacted too late to his approach to save themselves. He drove his fist upward, forcing the conveyor's canopy open to a blast of supersonic air. His thrusters fired, and he launched himself from the vehicle. One hand moved to his back to seize the weapon there, and bring it forward.

"Sing, Jorri."

The collision between vehicles saw the conveyor's shields flash, scorching the dropship's armor as it busted through the canopy. As he passed over the dropship, Jorri extended to full size in his grasp. When Panzer slipped between the ship's canting tails, he fired. The 25mm assault cannon came to life, growling as she let loose a torrent of disrupter shells. Savage overkill. Jorri's fire ripped through a line of the Vaar and the skyway below as he drew the fire through their formation. Those parts of their body not dragged along with them were turned inside out by the penetrating warp shells. His feet met the skyway, and for an instant the impact left him visible before his cloak reformed.

Some in his line of fire had suffered only horrific wounds rather than immediate death. He strafed them again to finish the job. The remaining able-bodied Vaar rose into the air, scattering like flies. As each climbed they summoned power shields, quickly moving to cover their heads. Panzer's eyes turned briefly to those injured prior by the Imperial Guard. It felt craven to attack those wounded already, but he strafed them all the same. With the Imperial Rose at stake, he could not risk their regenerating enough to join in on the fight. Ahead, the out-of-control dropship clipped the skyway before tumbling down to smash into the towers below. With a chirp, Andira cracked the Vaar communications. The first words to reach his ears were a frightened exclamation.

"It's Crykeeper!"

"Andira, tactical analysis of that mech."

Jogging ahead, he dove over the side to follow them down.

"Analysis," she spoke as an image appeared in his NOD. "Unknown model, belt-fed missile device, right arm. Unknown model, flak cannon, left arm. Unknown model, particle cannons, shoulders. Four-channel 4CM projection, multi-faceted primary, secondary, tertiary, and quaternary shield systems. Astranium armor."

"Astranium? How thick?"

"My scans cannot penetrate the plating, but based on the machine's architecture I estimate between 0.3 and 0.4 meters."

"What is this thing?"

More than half of the Vaar on the skyway were barely clinging to life when he arrived. His surprise attack had eliminated nearly half of the remaining, leaving seventeen immediate threats, plus the mech. The Vaar had broken into pairs as they descended, and he took aim at one. Jorri cut through them, leaving headless corpses to fall toward the streets below. Detecting the attack, the still-falling Vaar returned fire. Their shots were close, even with Andira's jamming foiling their targeting.

Barking orders, the warmech's pilot extended an arm in his direction. The fourteen warriors now moved in unison, loading spherical grenades into under-barrel launchers. Panzer angled his feet to the ground and thrust toward the sky as they fired. The grenades burst through the air, throwing out the glowing filaments they hoped would reveal his position.

He had to keep moving. If a filament gave him away, or they were allowed to overlap their sensors long enough to isolate his position, he'd be dead in short order with this many enemies. But he could not stay in the air for long. Every atom of displaced atmosphere was more data for their sensors to track him. The fight needed to go to ground.

He cut thrust beyond the umbrella of falling filaments, and turned toward another pair of warriors as they came down on one of the skyscrapers. With a flick of his thumb Jorri switched to burst fire as he took aim. His first shot struck at an oblique angle, annihilating the warrior's power shield and the arm that held it. A second shot ripped the warrior's body in two. Panzer's aim followed as the second warrior leapt from the building, and he fired again.

Spread across the towering structures, the Vaar took cover behind whatever they could, anything that might blunt Jorri's attack. The warmech continued down to street level, firing its own thrusters only to spare its prisoners immediate death from the impact.

"We've lost too many. We have to call for backup!" one of the Vaar shouted.

"Show some courage," the mech's pilot answered with a snarl. "We have him outnumbered. Engage and destroy."

"The warmech's sensors are building power," Andira warned. "I estimate only a few minutes before he detects us."

"We'll see about that," Panzer answered. His feet came down on the balcony of a small eatery. He aimed down the ten stories to the machine, focusing on its sensors. Toggled back to autofire, Jorri roared, spewing warp shells. The mech's shields flashed and turned an angry red, but they did not give.

"Oh, that's not good."

The platform exploded an instant after he leapt clear, and his feet came down to crush the roof of a cheap conveyor. The streets were mostly clear, and what few civilians remained scrambled to get indoors. After firing off another burst at the mech, he hit the ground and slid beneath another conveyor.

"Filament grenades fire!" the pilot shouted while Panzer scanned the machine.

"Andira, any damage?"

"Negative; its shields are holding."

"Might have bit off more than I can chew here. I need Rhoxx and the brothers, now."

"Colonel, the Vaar are putting out a massive counter-jamming overlay. I cannot break through their jamming while keeping us undetected."

"Damn. Focus on stealth."

"Colonel, Avalon's shields have collapsed."

"Noted."

Two warriors touched down on the street behind him less than a kilometer away. Their heads moved in time, overlapping their sensors as they scanned for him. A gift. With only two sources close together, they were perfect for a feature known as home-on-jam. Despite facing away from them he extended Jorri's muzzle out from under the conveyor, and let off a burst. The shells made a hard turn out of muzzle and met the Vaar at their faces.

More than a kilometer ahead, the mech took a step to adjust its posture.

The quad array of cannons on its shoulder began to glow with radiant power as they expanded to their full length. In time with the movement of the machine's head, the cannons angled down the street, and fired. The yellow beams filled the streets with flame as the accelerated particles superheated the air to plasma. In a single smooth motion, the pilot drew the beams up the street.

Panzer dashed into an alley, grasping the corner of a nearby wall as a cataclysm of fire washed through the streets. The four beams vaporized the plastic of the road, continuing down into the metal before reaching the station's armor. Solar architecture incorporated bond-forged metals and concussion fields throughout. Buildings were made to stand up to modern weaponry, endure the implements of mass destruction favored by terrorists, and endure the worst nature could throw at them. While the buildings swayed like trees in a strong gale, sucking the heat down into heatsinks in the station's body, they created a perfect funnel for the approaching blast.

The bellows of flame spread into the streets and alleys, hefting parked conveyors up into a shockwave of fire and debris. Panzer pressed himself against the wall to his back, groaning as the blast wave struck. Holding tight to the wall, he set his thrusters alight, trying to avoid being blown away. His eyes focused on the gauge in his NOD indicating the strength of his shields, and their steady decline. When the beams reached his alley, the pressure was at its apex and he lost his grip on the wall. His feet skidded on the plastic road as he tried to crouch, minimizing his profile to the overpowering winds. The beams disengaged, and the sudden drop in pressure caused his thrusters to hurtle him forward into the street. He landed in a river of slag, left behind by what had once been a main road.

Warning icons flashed in his NOD, while Andira's own warnings filled his ears. He was alive, but now, for kilometers in every direction anyone caught outdoors and unprotected was now no more than ash and memory. A long channel six meters deep had been carved into the street, providing a bed for the river of molten mass. Ash and smoke created a shroud that hid all but the glow as the buildings radiated from the heat.

"Colonel, cloaking system has failed!" Andira shouted.

Pushing himself up from the slag, Panzer kept low and navigated the billowing smoke with his sensors. He advanced slowly, scanning for the mech, holding Jorri ready. Andira found the mech and guided his eyes toward it and the life signs of the four women in its grasp. They were alive, protected by the machine's defense screens. So long as the Vaar planned to employ weapons that destroyed so indiscriminately, they would have to remain there.

He glanced upward for a moment, looking into the umbrella of vaporized debris rising through the atmosphere. The Vaar were extricating themselves from hastily sought shelter to resume their scans.

"No visual on target," one of the Vaar called. "We're still reading jamming. It's not dead yet."

"Keep looking," the pilot growled in reply. There was something familiar in that voice.

"Radiant field capacitance has been degraded," Andira continued. "I can restore the stealth screen but effectiveness will be diminished."

"Do what you can," Panzer answered.

Fires burned through the streets from destroyed conveyors, street signs, and buildings with open doors or windows. Panels in the street and sidewalks slid open, belching clouds of white vapor. Made up of millions of lighter-than-air nanites, these fire suppressants sought out the fires to smother them, adding even more smoke.

"We have the objective; we should withdraw," another of the Vaar said.

"No!" the pilot railed. "We are staying and killing that abomination. Teams six and nine, deploy and sweep. Now!"

This made no tactical sense. The Vaar had what they wanted. Why wouldn't their leader let them withdraw?

He glanced up to the Vaar on the rooftops, designated by glowing outlines in the soot. Two pair dropped to the road on opposite sides of the new channel the mech had carved. Hesitantly they advanced toward him, each constricting themselves behind their power shield. Every few steps one of the warriors from each pair would turn to scan the area behind.

He began to aim Jorri but stopped. Her shells were designed to be as hard to detect as himself, but against so many sensors looking for him and with his cloak weakened, it was a gamble. Slinging the rifle, he instead took the knife from his thigh. He had one good option now. Rat war, the tactic of fighting in such close proximity to the enemy that he risked hitting his own if he tried to lend aid from afar. If nothing else, it would hopefully discourage the mech from letting off another full-power blast from its cannons.

Rather than use his thrusters, Panzer climbed out of the channel and crouched behind a burning wreck. Several overturned conveyors were stacked atop each other, the cloth of their interiors burning. Andira created a visual effect to outline the cones of the Vaar sensors in his NOD. In the regions where their cones converged, they were most likely to see through her jamming. He timed his movements to stay out of the overlap and moved to meet them.

His eyes were affixed to the pair that shared his side of the channel. He edged a little closer, ducking behind a cargo conveyor and tightening his grip on the knife. When they stepped closer he dashed around the wreck to meet them, his blade moving in an arc. The blade cleaved a path through the warrior's left arm, eliciting a cry of pain and shock. Sidestepping, Panzer dodged the blind swing of the warrior's power shield while circling behind. The Vaar fell as the knife cut through the back of his knees. Panzer stepped away as the Vaar collapsed against the nearby wreck, before shuffling forward and driving the blade into the warrior's skull.

Unable to see the assailant carving up its partner, the other Vaar planted his feet before dashing forward in a shield charge. With the bayonet of his rifle howling to life, the warrior thrust wildly, trying to strike the invisible foe.

Panzer retreated behind the burning conveyor, circling around to strike from behind. The Vaar pivoted, spotting the whipping smoke of his movement and sweeping with the power shield. The swing caught Panzer mid-pounce, and both were rocked as their respective shield systems rebuffed each other.

Thrown back by the impact, Panzer landed on his feet, and quickly spun on his heel to avoid the thrust of the warrior's bayonet. He was illuminated by the sensors of the pair of Vaar across the channel, who both took aim.

Panzer moved in toward the Vaar in melee, placing it between himself and the warrior's ally to block their line of fire. The warrior in melee moved rapidly, swinging its shield before thrusting with its bayonet in a trained series of attacks.

Though he dodged each blow, Panzer had to remain close to keep the warrior as cover. Holding out an arm, he closed his hand as he focused on the nearby conveyor pile. His arm curled and the burning wreck lurched toward them. Acting on reflex, the Vaar raised his shield and stepped into the impact, vaporizing a path through the burning hulk. With the Vaar's attention divided, Panzer charged forward, applying mind and body in a kick to the warrior's knee. As the Vaar fell, Panzer followed it down, driving his blade through its visor.

His hands moved to the Vaar's arm, and he hefted it to raise the power shield as the pair across the street opened fire. The power shield began to dim, and he focused on the pair, sending out a psionic wave. When they staggered, he dashed away, grabbing the fallen warrior's power shield in his mind. As he slipped out of the Vaar's sensor cones, he drove the power shield toward them, baiting the pair with the illusion that he was behind the shield and leaping across the channel toward them.

The two warriors bat the shield away, knifing the empty air with their bayonets several times over before realizing he was not there. By the time they did, he had crossed the channel, approaching from behind. A sweep of his blade cut through the knees of the warrior to his left. The warrior to his right spun and thrust toward him with his bayonet. When he missed, the warrior recoiled behind his power shield, expecting a counterattack and was not disappointed. Panzer brought his leg up in a roundhouse kick. As his leg drew toward the shield, his mind drove it harder, and while he was rendered visible by the contact, the warrior was unable to capitalize. The blow sent him reeling and Panzer pursued.

When his foot met the ground Panzer continued forward, following with a psionic punch. Bile welled in his throat as he forced his mind to puncture the Vaar's 4CM field. But he pressed on, striking the warrior's shield as he skipped forward into a sidekick. Through cybernetic strength and psionic might, he overpowered the immense alien, but the latter remained on his feet, taking the hits on his shield.

As he transitioned into another strike, Panzer intentionally slowed himself, inviting the warrior to counterattack.

The reciprocal strike came with a stab of the bayonet, providing an opening as Panzer shuffled around the weapon. His blade skimmed the warrior's rifle until severing the hand that held it.

Panzer stepped in, twisting to bring the blade down through the warrior's legs. The Vaar fell to its knees and Panzer completed his circuit, coming face to face with the warrior and driving the blade through the alien's gorget. The two glared toward each other's helmets as the Vaar gargled, blood in his throat, and Panzer silenced him with a stab through the forehead. His cloak reformed and Panzer turned toward the wounded warrior trying to climb to his feet, his wounds already regenerating.

The mech interrupted the execution by lighting its particle cannons. Each fired in short, scattered bursts into the trench and the surrounding buildings. His goal was not to destroy, but to reveal the cloaked foe by kicking up debris. Disrupter pulses rained down as the Vaar above tried to lay a protective screen around their comrade.

The warmech moved again, elevating its right arm, revealing the weapon slung beneath and firing off a three-round burst. Each projectile shattered into a bundle of four missiles that raced toward Panzer. Acting on cybernetic reflexes, Panzer dropped to a knee before rolling under the missiles. The missiles smashed through storefronts, showering him and the wounded warrior with fragments.

With disrupter fire drawing closer, two bolts struck his shields, revealing an exact location and allowing them to focus their fire. Scrambling to his feet, Panzer ran from the constricting cloud of fire before diving through a shattered window. On the ground he raced to find concealment in a corner. The walls soon became porous as disrupter pulses followed, and he drew himself tight into the corner while grabbing Jorri. The ammo counter was nearly empty, and jettisoning the drum magazine, he plucked one of the box replacements from his chest.

"Where are our reinforcements?" one of the Vaar shouted over the com.

"Keep firing!" the pilot yelled back just as the machine touched off another burst of missiles. The armor-piercing warheads bored effortlessly through the walls before detonating inside. Each erupted to throw off a field of green gel. In the Solar language, the formula was called apollium, and while it did not truly burn or undergo a nuclear reaction, once detonated it would radiate thermonuclear levels of heat. The gel dispersed rapidly, but not so quickly as to be impeded by the protective screen of his shields, which allowed it to cling to his armor. The final missile through the walls was the detonator, setting off the reaction of the apollium scattered through the clothing store.

The massive plume of heat pushed him through the wall, and he crashed into the guardrails of a router terminal. For the moment his shields had protected him from suffering the ignition of the appollium on his armor. It did not last. Seeing the guardrail bend, the Vaar fired on it, driving disrupter pulses into his shields. As he stood against the rain of gunfire, Panzer moved to run, and a lone bolt pierced his shields. As a small plate on his right shoulder was obliterated, the ambient heat set off the apollium reaction.

He gasped as he made it to his feet, his armor shifting in color as it tried in vain to radiate the heat away through its very source. Warning indicators obstructed his vision as the temperatures soared, and his feet began to melt through the road beneath him. An electric tingle filled his nerves. His nanotech was drawing power from his armor, forcibly holding the cells of his body together even as they tried to vaporize amid the growing heat. His groan was cut short, and his helmet filled with the steam rising from his throat.

Now with a lit beacon, the Vaar fired at will. Their attacks drew together, ripping into his armor while he tried to move for cover. He stumbled as his shields gave out, and a single pulse tore through his hip. He could not run; his limbs moved only stiffly as his nanites strained to hold him together.

"Cease fire!" the pilot bellowed. "Let him burn!"

Panzer clawed at his faceplate, forcing it open as steam leaked from his mouth, his nose, even his tear ducts. The apollium began to smolder and a measure of control returned to his limbs, allowing him to crawl to the cover of a narrow alley.

"An'ila." He gasped, closing his faceplate. "An'ila, way cal I zeek?"

"Ambient temperature has exceeded your cranial diffusion," she answered. "You have nerve damage, motor control is impaired."

"...ou hink?"

"I will attempt to off-load motor control to your nanites. This...will hurt."

He could not even vocalize the pain, as Andira temporarily cut the neurons controlling his mouth. Every pain receptor fired, as if every trauma he could suffer came to him at once. He could only writhe on the ground as she seized control of his nanotech. Within seared flesh the nanites cut and bypassed neurons, and frayed nerved endings, jury-rigging his nervous system and each other to restore control to his body. His eyes had not survived the apollium burn; the input of his armor's sensors was now routed directly to his visual cortex. As she finished, he lay curled up in a ball, his limbs trembling.

"That should manage until you can receive proper treatment. Try to say something, Colonel."

"Ouch," he wheezed, willing himself to sit up and lean against the nearest wall. He reached for Jorri and panic shot through him as he realized the weapon was gone. The apollium had melted the sling and detached the weapon from his body. He scanned the streets, finding the rifle lying in a pool of molten plastic. Holding out a hand, he called it to him. The weapon was slow to answer. The bypass job on his brain had affected his psionics. He sighed in relief when it finally arrived, and his expression quickly soured. The apollium burn had left the weapon much too hot to fire. Until it cooled, trying to fire off a shot would likely cause catastrophic failure.

"His cloak is down. Does anyone see him?"

"Too much interference, can't read him."

"Go down there and finish him!" the pilot screamed.

"Andira, I really need my cloak and my shields back," he whispered, straining to rise. While his limbs now followed his command, they were slow to respond to his will.

"The cloaking system is fried. I'm sorry; there's nothing I can do. Primary shield projectors have fused. Engaging secondary systems."

To save his life, Andira had been forced to use the shield system to forcibly expel the heat, but in doing so she had allowed the projectors to melt. The secondary projectors were weaker, slower to recharge. He would not survive that level of punishment again.

His attention moved toward the center of the station in response to a loud boom. The missile attacks on the station had thus far avoided this area, where the DOS team was operating. But a single missile had erred, striking several kilometers up the road. A shockwave rippled through the streets as a mushroom cloud rose in the distance. Conveyors and building fragments were thrown into the air by the blast. Arcing through the sky, the debris traveled up and out, before gravity drew them back down to rain from above.

He stumbled into a run, moving away from the cargo conveyor that wedged itself into his alley from above. The ground began to quake. Avalon's structural integrity had been compromised.

The tremors quickly became more violent, tripping him as he tried to run. He touched his thrusters, which strained to carry him off the ground as cracks formed in the street. The skyscrapers swayed as levels of superstructure collapsed one atop another and roads began to cave in. Entire buildings were swallowed by the collapse, including the one still burning from the apollium.

Finding a relatively stable building, Panzer touched down on it. A quick scan revealed that the mech had climbed back up to the skyway, now broken in several places.

"What does it take to kill this thing?" one of the Vaar yelled. "Warlord, we have to retreat!"

"I know you're listening, Crykeeper." The pilot's smile was evident in his voice. "I see you."

"Our jamming has been compromised." Andira warned a moment before a pair of beams came down from above. Their source—a small device on the head of the warmech...a targeting designator.

"Oh no," he wheezed. "Andira, find me a manhole."

He turned and dove off the building, angling down toward the street with his arm and rolling on impact.

"Up ahead, take the first right."

The targeting beams followed as he raced to follow her directions.

"Turn left."

He rounded a corner and found a metal hatch where raised print read COM-DUCT ACCESS. He quickly pried up the hatch using the strength of his armor to rip its lock open. A Vaar monitor had detected the request for a missile and obliged, the weapon coming down as Panzer dropped into the manhole. His feet were already making the motion to propel him into a run before meeting the floor of the duct.

The disrupter charge of the falling missile detonated, destroying the walls that formed the alley where he had sheltered, the walls and rooftops of the surrounding buildings, and levels of the foundation below. His forward motion was slowed as air was sucked from the duct into the expanding column of fire above. The duct began to collapse and, dodging wreckage, he chose one of the forking paths and fell into a slide as his vision turned black.

For a time the only proof in his mind that he survived was the muted noises in his ears. Slowly, light returned and his NOD cleared.

"Colonel, are you all right?"

He gasped for air several times before answering.

"Now what the hell do you think? How are you?"

"Operational."

He rose amid a cloud of steam as a broken line poured water on his still glowing armor. Looking up, he saw the sky, exposed by the destruction of the street above. He quickly found his bearings, realizing he was now on the opposite side of the skyway, just below an elevated highway running below and parallel to the skyway itself.

"We got him," one of the Vaar exclaimed. "We killed the Crykeeper!"

"Don't assume, keep scanning!" the pilot barked.

"I've stepped down jamming so that they will not detect direct interference," Andira explained. "I will elevate levels as necessary but it will give your survival away. I recommend a withdraw."

"Andira, highlight his aerospace designator. We're not doing that again."

"Yes sir."

An icon appeared on the mech, marking the device on the crest of its head. Only two of his thrusters were still functioning as he climbed back to the street level. He deftly pulled the magazine from Jorri and sighed in relief to find that the red box still remained on his left shoulder. Devastator cores, much more powerful than the standard ammunition but far more stressful on the weapon. In most situations, he carried them for breaching security doors. Perhaps they would do here. He only hoped Jorri had cooled enough to fire.

He rose slowly toward the skyway, careful to keep it between himself and the machine while remaining outside of the Vaar sensor cones.

CHAPTER
13B

BELOW THE SKYWAY SIMMONNE could make out little beyond the clouds of smoke. Her heart raced as she strained to look for signs of her would-be rescuer. Much of the battle between cyborgs had occurred so quickly she saw the fighters only in motion blurs. The fire suppression gas was finally winning its fight and things were becoming quiet.

"No," she whispered. "You can't be dead. Please, please be alive."

Her body was moved as the great Vaar turned, and she could sense an air of cautious satisfaction. Hanging her head, she closed her eyes. Their last hope of rescue was gone.

The light of the great Vaar's shields penetrated her eyelids, and she glared up as something atop the machine's head was obliterated. The great Vaar let out a roar as it turned, and the heavy guns on its shoulders split the skyway. She winced as a gout of flame approached, before breaking against the machine's defense screens. Her pulse raced as hope was renewed. Panzer was alive.

The great Vaar moved around her, turning and straining to find his attacker before it glanced down toward her. The Twins cried out and she held deathly still as the metal hands fumbled. Two fingers of the free hand closed around her legs, and she screamed as she was suddenly held upside down. She whimpered, realizing that she was now dangling over the edge of the skyway.

"Crykeeper!" the great Vaar shouted with such volume that she wailed at the pain in her ears. "Catch!"

She turned to Jenna and the Twins, their mouths opened into a scream as gravity took hold.

"No!" Her heart and mind raced together as she descended into the smoke. She could not even scream. No, this couldn't happen, please, she didn't want to die. She couldn't die here, not like this. Her eyes sought him as the world streaked past. Where was he? He couldn't, he wouldn't just let her die.

As the street raced toward her she clamped her eyes shut, before feeling something metal snake around her from above and draw her in.

"I've got you."

Her eyes flew open to glare down at the arm around her waist, and she sucked in a gasp as she felt her body slowing. Was it real? Her bound hands groped at the metal body behind her. It was real, he saved her. Her breath came in short pants as she felt him shift to hold her in both arms. Her eyes closed as she tried to bring her breathing under control, feeling their bodies slowing. She knew the voice in her mind; he'd come for her. Surely everything would be okay now.

She winced as they came to a stop, and she fought the restraints holding her arms in a vain attempt to throw them around him. Her breath came in deep gasps as she pressed her body into his, still shaking. She glanced over her shoulder. He had slowed to a stop on an elevated highway below the skyway.

"Are you all right?"

Before she could answer, the great Vaar's voice echoed through the streets.

"Now die!"

Her eyes flew up as the machine's arms angled down toward them, extending the weapons slung beneath. A moment later she was set on her feet so roughly she fell on her side, hissing at the surge of pain in her ribs. Her eyes moved to the armored figure looming over her, moving so fast she could barely make out his motions. Throwing his arms to the side he let out a pained growl, before pieces of the highway flew upward between them and the monster above. An instant later she was scooped up in his arms and he bent over her, and the world erupted around them.

Explosions tore through the thrown fragments of the highway before descending on them both. Her eyes clenched shut against the blinding flash of his shields, her scream drowned out by the blasts tearing the world around them asunder. Her body shook at a sudden tremor, and she cried out as she once more felt herself falling. The highway began to collapse, and he drew her tight against him as he began to slide downward. Everything turned dark as they passed through a pall of smoke, and she was forced to close her eyes.

"Damn it!"

She opened one eye, seeing the glint of metal as the large rifle was knocked from his back. His thrusters whined and sputtered; his feet sparked as they attempted to dig into the road to slow their fall. Her mouth flew open into a scream as she felt herself thrown into the air, and he slid away into the smoke. What had he done? Falling once more, she wailed in fright before the air around her slowed. Feeling as though she had struck a cushion, she descended slowly until returning to his arms.

An instant later he was moving, charging through the fire still following them from above until he looped around the corner into an alley.

"Are you all right?" he questioned, glaring around the corner.

She tried to answer. But panic and adrenaline interfered. Why? Why would someone try to kill her? What had she ever done? Why was someone shooting at her? Why was any of this happening? All that escaped her lips was a frantic blubbering, until the sensors of his helmet turned back to face her. She was silenced as his hand curled upward, covering her mouth and most of her face.

"Are you all right?"

She drew in deep breaths through her nose, trying to calm herself.

"Are you all right?" he repeated.

She had never been less all right—people were shooting at her! But it was okay, he was here now, he could make them stop. She nodded her head, even as she was forced to close her eyes again against the veil of smoke. With her eyes closed her thoughts turned to Jenna and the Twins, still held in that monster's grasp.

"Colonel," she wheezed as his hand lifted from her mouth, "you have to save them! You have to get the others!"

She forced her eyes open to see him peer around the corner again.

"I don't think I can."

Her chest tightened at the words. Did he really just say that?

"Please." She coughed. "You can't just leave them!"

"If I leave you, you're going to suffocate in this smoke, or die if that mech goes hot on those particle guns again."

"Please, you can't leave them!"

She fought her restraints again, trying to grab his face and force him to look her in the eyes.

"Are you willing to risk your life on it?" He turned back to her. "If they want you alive they probably won't do that again. But he did just drop you off the skyway and then shoot at you. So I don't get the impression their leader is concerned for your safety."

"I'll risk it!" She stared into the visors of his helmet, trying to plead with the eyes behind them. "Please! You can save them!"

"If I can get to my rifle, maybe."

As he sat her down she stood trembling, before jumping as he brandished an enormous blade.

"Don't move." His arm curled around her, and she felt a tug against her wrists followed by the loud shearing of metal. Hesitantly she brought her hands forward, glaring down at the now separated manacles on her wrists. A moment later she threw herself forward, wrapping her arms around him. Had he been a blanket she would have surrounded herself, her arms squeezing until her ribs burned.

She slowly turned her head as she felt him lean down, and his hand closed on a drainage grate by her feet. With a hard pull he tore the grate free, before stepping forward and kneeling to lower her into the channel below. Dangling from him, she pressed her face into his chest, unable to let go.

"Princess, you have to let go."

The words made sense, but her body would not comply.

"If you want me to save your friends, you have to let go."

Still she could not command her arms, until she cried out in feeling his hands close on her forearms.

"Simmonne, I know you're scared but I can't feel anything. If I have to pry you off, I could crush you. Let go."

She wanted to, but she couldn't. His hands moved down to her hips.

"Relax."

Her breath seemed to echo through her head as her eyes rolled back, and her muscles went limp. For a moment even her heart did not beat, as he set her down in the channel. The chill of the shallow water in the channel nipped at her nerves; her head sunk forward as he sat her down. Her heart began to beat again, and her head rolled around her shoulders as control returned to her muscles. She glanced up in time to see him wedge the grate back in place before pointing down at her with a single finger.

"Stay."

She tried to watch him leave, rising up to peer through the grate. Her hands pushed up on it, but it did not move. The same weight added to keep children from prying them up to play in the tunnels made this grate far too heavy for her to lift.

Unable to watch, she lowered herself back down. She slipped off one of her stockings before soaking it in the water. She held it to her mouth to serve as a filter. All she could do now was wait. Her thoughts remained on her friends, and that horrible creature as her body coiled up into a ball.

Panzer had to save them, he had to.

CHAPTER
13C

NO LESS THAN TWENTY of the giant mechs had succeeded in braving the artillery and the mines to breach Twilight's theater shield. Their first targets upon doing so were the local artillery batteries that claimed two of the machines before they were destroyed. Now with gaps opened in the shield, Vaar and enspa were flooding into the colony.

Keeping pace with Sarge, Clearwater followed the aren around a corner. The streets were quaking with the fury of armored units trading fire. Legionnaire tanks were pounding the giant mechs, trying to close the gaps they had opened. The Vaar pouring in would seek to disable the theater shield. If they succeeded they could simply withdraw, and pound the colony with artillery.

Disabling the shield would be no simple task. The shield generator lay in a hardened bunker several kilometers beneath the colony. The projector array consisted of thousands of devices scattered across rooftops, street corners, and other locations. More than half would need to be destroyed before the shield fell. To hinder this task, shield control was putting out so much jamming that identifying the projectors would be difficult. But now so much jamming was laid upon the colony that it was affecting the legionnaires' sensors.

"Brower to Clearwater, move to grid nine and cover the heavy mortar teams."

"Roger, moving now." He motioned to his troops, and together they moved toward a four-way intersection. There, two squads of light infantry operated a large mortar out of a corner cafe. From there they lobbed explosives over the buildings to the feet of the colossi, forcing the Vaar to cross a forming sea of apollium to gain entry.

Sarge directed the individual squads of the section into position, with some rising to rooftops and others sheltering in the buildings. Nearly half of their automatech had been destroyed when the colossi brought down the wall. Those that remained dispersed among his troops. This would not be one of those battles where the organics could simply hang back while the machines fought.

"Vaar to the north!" The voice of one of his troops was garbled by heavy jamming.

A pair of Vaar tanks turned onto the street, followed by columns of infantry. As Clearwater raised his weapon, another arm from Sarge's AICES came down on them.

"Not yet, sir," the aren cautioned. "They haven't detected us. Let them stick their necks out."

"Good thinking," he spoke over the sound of mortar shells, and followed Sarge into an alley. With so much jamming Clearwater risked an active scan for a better look. The tanks were shaped as spheres, rolling along firing guns mounted to their sides. The Vaar moved behind in a crouched posture, expecting an ambush.

"First squad knock out the tanks," Sarge directed. "All others, target the infantry. Range?"

"Target bearing 450 meters," one of the bots answered the query. It continued to speak, counting down the range as the Vaar closed. "Three hundred meters. Two five zero meters."

SGT DOLPH: Anytime, sir.

"Open fire!"

Leaning around the building, he let disrupter pulses fly. Troops on the rooftops sent missiles into the tanks, while the rest focused their aggression on the infantry. Most of the Vaar lay bleeding before knowing they were under attack. The rest made a scramble for cover. Wincing, Clearwater backed away as disrupter pulses tore into the building nearby. Taking a breath, he stepped back out, zooming in on the offending warrior. He held down the trigger and watched as the Vaar's body was torn to pieces.

"Grenades, intercept!"

His automatech filled the sky with disrupter pulses, becoming point defenses as the Vaar attempted to hurtle grenades toward them. But something else caught Clearwater's eye. A single Vaar had taken cover in an empty building, and held a strange device out toward them. A gun? No, a targeting marker. Clearwater took aim, but was too late.

One of the colossi had turned toward them, open hatches on its body exposing missile racks.

The flimsy pre-fab buildings were never built to stand up to such punishment, and the world became a cloud of fire and wind as five-kiloton charges detonated above. His shield levels spiked, his feet skidded in the over-pressure, building fragments slammed into him from one side as he fought to avoid being bowled over. He let out a scream as his feet slipped, and the roof above descended toward him.

"Sir, are you all right?"

Clearwater strained to rise, climbing out of the rubble to return to his feet.

"Mortar six, why aren't you firing?" Brower's voice ripped through the com while the cannons of his mech ripped through the belly of one of the colossi.

"Come on." Sarge threw an elbow at him before leading him to one of the collapsed buildings. In the rubble he spotted the disembodied forearm of one of the light infantry troops. More lightly armored and shielded, meant to go places an AICES could not, they were not equipped to survive the attack that had just flattened the city block.

"We have to get that mortar back in the fight!"

Sarge's AICES opened and the delta climbed out before grabbing a large piece of rubble and chucking it away.

"All units maintain defensive position! Lieutenant, I need your help, sir."

He froze. Leave his AICES? His impenetrable armored housing in the middle of a fight?

"Sir?"

He swore before toggling the switch and climbing out of the machine. Slipping on the rubble, he climbed upright as Sarge jerked the long metal tube out of the ruins.

"Auto-loader's damaged!" Sarge shouted, raising the tube before slamming it back down into the rubble to set it in place. "We'll have to go manual. Ammo, there!"

Clearwater followed the pointing finger, and used both hands to drag the brown box out of the rubble. Briefly his eyes moved over the lettering labeled *75mm ADI*. He threw open the crate before clutching one of the heavy bombs in his hand and turning to Sarge.

"Hang!"

"Hung!" he shouted back as he held the mortar over the tube's muzzle.

"Drop!"

He released the weapon and quickly curled away from it. The mortar screamed. Clearwater was knocked prone by the sudden displacement of air and looked up in time to see the eruption as the mortar landed at one of the colossi's feet.

"Hang!" Sarge bellowed as he climbed back to his feet.

"Hung!"

"Drop!"

He braced himself against the blast, remaining upright as the mortar fired.

"Hang!"

"Hung!"

"Drop!"

His muscles ached, his mind raced, he fired round after round, moving too fast to know where he was.

"Greene to Clearwater, Greene to Clearwater."

He held his hands up to cover his ears, hoping to more clearly hear the voice in his head.

"Clearwater."

"Brower's mech is down in your grid. Can you assist?"

He dropped his arms, scanning the town. The mech was no longer standing.

"Roger. We'll move in."

He glanced to Sarge before both quickly retreated to their machines.

"Sir, we can't abandon this position. I'll take two squads to help."

He began to nod, but he stopped and shook his head. Maintaining the defensive perimeter was more important.

"No, I'll go. You stay here and hold this position."

"Sir..." The aren hesitated. "Yes, sir."

"Calm," he whispered to himself, gasping as he tried to steady himself. "Squads two and two with me!"

Comprehending the intent of his message, squads two and three followed as he approached the waypoint to Brower's position. With the troops behind, he dashed through ruined structures before turning toward the main street. Brower's mech lay in smoldering pieces half a kilometer ahead. In his NOD he saw the icons of Vaar advancing on his position.

"Move in, secure the wreck! Suppressing fire on these coordinates."

Missiles streamed up from his troops arcing over the mech before plunging down in the streets beyond. The approaching Vaar did not let the attack go unanswered, and Clearwater winced as he sprinted through an explosion.

Nearing the mech, he could see the smoke filling the cockpit, barely able to make out the fists flailing against it.

"Squad two covering fire, squad three, let's go."

He dashed ahead, stomping over the scrap metal to climb up onto the mech's disembodied torso. As he approached the nose the cockpit flew open in a cloud of smoke, and a sickening scream filled his ears. Brower fell out of the machine, flailing his arms as he tried to smother the flames devouring his flesh. For a moment Clearwater was still. Could that mass of scorched meat really be his commander? He willed himself to step forward, a moment before Brower's head exploded.

"No!" he screamed, his eyes scanning for the murderer, who was across the street, prone atop a pile of rubble. To the Vaar who had fired the shot, it had been an act of mercy, putting a wounded warrior out of his misery. None of this occurred to Clearwater as he continued to scream, holding down the triggers and shredding the Vaar. His shields flared as the other Vaar joined in on the cycle of retaliation. Half stumbling and half running, he withdrew behind the cover of the mech.

"Greene to Clearwater, what is Brower's status?"

His jaw quivered as he stared at the now headless corpse.

"Dead. Vaar bastards killed him!"

"Damn it. We're crumbling on all sides. All units withdraw. Prepare to buzzsaw at the town's center."

A new waypoint flared in his NOD, but his eyes remained on Brower's body.

"Sir?" A heavy arm clanked against his AICES' back. "Sir?"

Sergeant ahn Culan tore his attention away.

"Your orders, sir?"

"Withdraw," he whispered. "Move to the waypoint."

He moved upright to usher his men on, retreating from the fire as more Vaar moved in on the downed mech. So much jamming, he could only make out the route. They could be running headlong—

His feet skidded to a halt as a tank plowed into the street ahead of him. As the machine rotated toward him he fell prone, and opened his disrupters. The tank fired several shots into his troops, before retreating to escape the imminent failure of its shields. Clearwater was not yet on his feet when a torrent of Vaar spilled around the nearby corner.

His disrupters followed those at the front of the oncoming rush, until he began to turn, realizing that one of the Vaar was barreling directly toward him. Before he could pull the Vaar into his field of fire, the warrior threw his weight into the impact, and the AICES was sent reeling. Trying to keep the machine upright, Clearwater left himself open to the follow up. The warrior slammed into him again, sending both through the window of a vacant storefront.

Landing prone, Clearwater began to rise before the Vaar's foot came down on him from above. A second later the AICES shook as the warrior attempted to drive his bayonet through the seams of the machine's armor. In a panic Clearwater swung his arm, sweeping the warrior's leg and causing the Vaar to fall on him. For a moment alien and machine struggled against each other as Clearwater rolled over atop the Vaar and rose onto a knee.

Roaring from within his helmet, the Vaar drove the bayonet of his weapon into the AICES and pulled the trigger. Clearwater winced as disrupter pulses ripped into his armor, and he retreated to his feet. The Vaar rose with him, stopping dead in his tracks as Clearwater jerked the triggers in full panic. The warrior was cut in half by the twin streams of warp pulses, leaving both halves of his body to fall in a pool of smoke, blood, and electricity. Still in full panic, Clearwater continued to hold the triggers, shredding the alien's remains into smaller and smaller pieces.

His disrupter pulses carved through the floor and the ground beneath as he continued to fire. What had once been a Vaar warrior was reduced to a crackling trench in the ground when Clearwater finally let off the triggers. Still drawing panicked breaths, he continued glaring down, looking for more of the hostile creature's body to target. There was nothing left of the warrior to threaten him now, and his thoughts turned to his men.

Dashing back out of the store, Clearwater quickly scanned the street. Why was he worried? His men had handled themselves, leaving a field of dead Vaar ahead of them.

"All units fall back and sawtooth!" Greene's voice shouted. "Move, move!"

Clearwater motioned his men on, racing for the center of town.

He rendezvoused with the rest of his section, as they set up at Derf's.

"Everyone in position!" Sarge shouted, breaking a window with the arm of his AICES to aim outside.

"Jugs!" one of his troops shouted. "We've got juggernauts incoming from the north!"

"Oh no," Clearwater whispered, afraid to turn, as if not seeing it would ensure it was not real. Juggernauts were the shock troops of Vaar infantry standing nearly four meters tall without their armor. They were combed from the ranks of the criminally violent, the brutal sociopathic. More miniature mechs than aliens, their loss of personhood saw them heavily cyberized. No longer warriors, they were living weapons that would pay their debts to society by dying for it, or by carving a path through the most heavily entrenched foes.

Blood-red armor obscured their bodies, with green sensors glowing from beneath a cobra-like hood extending from their helmets. Large twin antennas on their shoulders added to the already asphyxiating levels of jamming. Each carried a rotary cannon with each hand, while their pauldrons were formed by missile racks. They formed ranks less than a kilometer away, line abreast to branch through the street.

"Sawtooth!" Sarge shouted. "Sawtooth now!"

The legionnaires arrayed themselves across Derf's and the nearby buildings, in groups of three to form the jagged formation Sarge had ordered.

Realizing they had been spotted, the juggernauts moved to action. Those in the streets trained their guns, shaking the ground as each filled the air with disrupter fire. With weapons ablaze they hunched down, before breaking into a run. Loud crashes of metal on metal joined the sound of their guns. Those without line of sight to fire did not allow the buildings to funnel their formation. Instead they ran as well, barreling through the walls of any buildings in their path to keep pace.

"Concentrate fire on my target. Fire!" Sarge yelled. In lieu of conventional shield and armor defenses, the juggernauts were protected by the merger of the two systems into warp plating. While it yielded less long-term endurance, it brought a much greater initial resistance to incoming fire.

With his sensors now useless, Clearwater was forced to sight using only his eyes, and he held down the triggers. His section concentrated their fire on Sarge's target, and Clearwater's jaw dropped as the disrupter pulses only chipped away at the juggernaut's plating.

"Switch to missiles. Fire!"

With the jamming forcing the missiles to be dumb-fired, many missed their targets. Compensating for their aim, his troops continued to fire, and the targeted warrior was rocked by several direct hits. But the juggernaut did not fall; losing his left arm did nothing to stop him. Staggered for only a moment, the beast quickly rushed to catch up to his comrades, refusing to be left behind.

"They're closing. Intensify fire!"

Clearwater held the triggers of his disrupters so tight his hand quaked, and the juggernauts drew in. How could something so large run so fast? One moment they were across the street, and the next moment his feet left the ground as one of the jugs swept its arm, knocking him from its path. He landed on a billiards table that shattered under the weight of his AICES. The walls trembled, and the ceiling above cracked before falling inward as the juggernauts powered through the building.

Forced to climb out of rubble once more, Clearwater quickly rose firing at the jugs from behind as their charge now carried them away.

"Lieutenant Greene, you have juggernauts approaching from your six!" Sarge shouted. "Repeat, jugs approaching from behind!"

"Incoming!" another of his men shouted.

Now standing on the roof of what had been Derf's, he gazed into the channel carved through the town by the juggernaut's charge. It was in that moment, when he saw a sea of Vaar and enspa rushing forward, that he knew he would die here. Their ranks stretched through the juggernaut channel, all the way back to the gaps in the theater shield and the legs of the colossi.

"Open fire!" Sarge screamed.

Clearwater hung his head, even as he raised his arms and pulled the triggers. Hundreds, maybe thousands of guns answered. Icons began to flash in his NOD as the lives of his troops were snuffed out. He cringed as explosions tore through the rubble around him, pelting his AICES from all sides.

Clearwater's head whipped between his shoulders as one of the rolling tanks zeroed in on him and slammed a volley of anti-armor rounds into his side.

He heard nothing over the ringing of his ears as his AICES fell, and emergency protocols engaged to open the hatches and eject him from the smoking machine. His eyes were closed, his hands moved to his head. He could no longer hear, but he could feel the reverberation of the weapons still firing all around him. The sheer agony in his skull—it shut out the world as he lay in the rubble. Every thump of his pulse stroked the pain in his skull as though someone were bashing a rock into his head.

He forced his eyes open, squinting against the pain the light carried into his eyes. He struggled to make out the image of a kurai. Sergeant ahn Culan, bereft of his own AICES, brandished a long blade as he cut through the incoming stream of enspa with one hand and fired his pistol with the other. Behind the kurai another legionnaire in a smoking AICES was firing with the one arm he had left, until a burst from one of the Vaar tanks put him down.

Clearwater jumped as a hand closed on his collar, and he was dragged behind a pile of rubble. A hand cradled his head, and he glanced up into Sarge's face. The aren's lips were moving, but he could not make out the sound. A message flashed in his NOD. Why couldn't he read it? Why didn't the letters make sense?

His head shook as the sound slowly returned, the unwelcome wail of battle as guns thundered and enspa roared. His nanites were finally overcoming the trauma, restoring his senses. It would have been more merciful if they had left him in a stupor. Now able to comprehend what he saw, he scanned the area. Only a few of his troops were still standing, fighting with rifles and side arms behind the cover of wreckage. Most had not survived the destruction of their AICES. Such a proud, distinguished unit—surely this was not how they were meant to end.

He turned back to Sergeant ahn Culan, intent on shouting at him to find cover. He was too late: the kurai was on the ground, his sword still flailing, cutting into the enspa even as their scythe-like arms were ripping him apart.

"Sir, you need to fight!" Sarge shouted down at him, while firing over their small piece of cover with his pistol.

Fight? What was the point? They were dead. Didn't he understand? They were all dead men.

"Damn it sir, fight!"

Sarge shouted as he drew back, and launched his fist forward to intercept a pouncing enspa and send it hurtling away. Clearwater tried to shake the confusion out of his head, and reached for the pistol on his thigh. Looking down at the weapon, he gripped it more intently. He was going to die, but he was not going to die a coward.

Crying out, he leaned around the cover, capping off rounds into the charging aliens. The sea of Vaar had split; a few hung back in cover while they rest flowed around his section's position. They would let the enspa overrun them. Clearwater fired quickly, picking off enspa at random. He would run out of ammo before he ran out of enemies.

His eardrums were shattered for the second time as a grenade landed nearby, ripping through the cover he and Sarge shared and sending them sprawling. Clearwater sputtered as he glanced down at his side, at the new wound where shrapnel had perforated his arm on its way into his ribcage. His NOD flashed an angry red, and new characters lit.

CRITICAL INJURIES DETECTED – LUNG TRAUMA. INITIATING EMERGENCY REPAIRS.

He gargled on his own blood as his nanites sutured the wounds, and sewed the halves of his lungs back together. Quivering in pain, he sat up looking for Sarge, even as he was blinded by smoke. Still panning through the din, he crawled toward a broken wall and leaned into it. His eyes watered as he tried to call out. He saw a tall figure in the smoke and waved his arm toward it.

"Hey!" What was meant to be a shout came as a strained whisper. "Sarge!"

As the smoke cleared he realized the figure was a Vaar, standing over the body of his sergeant. Clearwater raised his pistol, taking aim as Sarge moved. As the Vaar brought its bayonet down, Sarge rolled over, grabbing the weapon with both hands. Roaring to his feet, the delta stood toe to toe with the Vaar as both wrestled for control of the rifle. Clearwater's muzzle danced as he tried to get a clear shot. Sarge abruptly turned, leveraging the Vaar over his hip and tearing the rifle free of the alien's grasp. Before he could capitalize, the delta staggered; his eyes briefly looked to Clearwater before glancing down to the fresh wounds in his body.

Sarge turned, bringing the alien weapon up before he was shot again. The aren lowered a hand, collecting the intestines spilling out of his side, before a final shot through his chest brought him to his knees. The Vaar he had disarmed quickly reclaimed his weapon and placed the muzzle to Sarge's head before pulling the trigger.

"Sarge," Clearwater gasped, glaring down at him as the blood spilled out over the rubble.

Clearwater's eyes squinted; his mouth flew open in a rage as he worked the trigger. The Vaar in his sights shuffled away as his shields flared before spinning and returning fire.

His entire body convulsed, the stench of burning flesh flooded into his nostrils, and his body went limp.

FATAL INJURIES DETECTED – INITIATING PRIMARY PRESERVATION PROTOCOL.

The words in his NOD—what did they mean? He glared past them as he stared down at himself. A burst of warp pulses had ripped through his torso. He was not certain how to handle the sight of his liver as it lay smoking on his thigh. All he could surmise was that he was dead.

PRESERVATION ERROR – MEMORY BACKUP FAILURE, NO CARRIER.

He was outside the astranet, his nanites could not establish the wireless uplink to backup his memories. Without a memory backup, even if he was recovered there might not be enough left of his personality to warrant reanimation. The platoon had its own backup system. Why wasn't it working?

PRESERVATION ERROR – MEMORY BACKUP FAILURE, SECONDARY SYSTEM, NO CARRIER.

He could only hold one eye open as he glanced to the direction of the Legionnaire barracks, now a flaming ruin.

PRESERVATION ERROR – NO CARRIERS, MEMORY BACKUP FAILURE. INITIALIZING LOCALIZED DATABASE.

PRESERVATION ERROR – BLOOD LOSS CRITICAL, NANITE COUNT INSUFFICIENT FOR STATIC PRESERVATION.

On the day of their death, how many people awoke knowing it was their last? He could not back up his memories. His nanites would preserve him until they ran out of power, and then he would be lost forever. His vision began to darken, and he opened a small file, a video memory. His siblings sat across from him, eating cake as they celebrated his graduation from Hell's Gate. He looked at each of their faces, and with no lungs left he merely mouthed the words.

"Melanie, I'm sorry. Stephanie, Ryan, David, I love you."

He glanced up as a Vaar now loomed over him. His attention moved back to his siblings one last time. His eyes closed, and his heart stopped.

In other parts of the town the battle continued, but it was already decided. Twilight had fallen.

CHAPTER
13D

A S EMPEROR, MASON MANDRAKE had always insisted that all members of the family dine together so long as they were in the Cathedral. Perhaps it was his way of reminding his children that for all their privilege, they still answered to someone. Perhaps it was simply so that in some way, they could pretend to be an ordinary family. For Steven's purposes it did not matter, for breakfast in the Cathedral was the one time anyone could be sure that most of the Family would be gathered in one place.

From the Imperial Suite he marched at the head of two forces of arens. Every member of the family was guarded by their own brood of aren bodyguards. Each brood was loyal only to their designated scion, and would protect them even if it meant doing so from other members of the family. Steven now marched at the head of those that had protected him since his birth, in addition to those that had safeguarded his parents. Had they been seen, a familiar eye may have spotted the problem.

When multiple formations of the guard marched together, there was a priority for every combination. The Imperial Guard did not consider an emperor a threat to his children, so his guards would march at the center to surround the traveling royalty. The guardians of the Emperor's children would then march on the outside. They would never march together, interspersed as they were now.

Of course, they did not march on their own volition. At this moment, it was debatable if any of them even existed as individuals. Their minds belonged to Steven, the sight of each of their eyes, the sound of their ears— all of their senses were at his notice. Their feet moved in perfect sync with his own, even their pulses following the rhythm set by his heart. Of all the aren breeds, deltas were the most resistant to telepathy. The construction of their brain, their psychology, only the best telepaths could read their minds and none could perform remote viewing. With the benefits of even moderately operational 4CM, they were effectively immune to anything more complex than empathic reading. But not to Steven. To him they were puppets, and the Encephalon had handed him their strings.

A lantai servitor caught his eye as she stepped into the hallway. She wore the dress of a maid; her only function in life was to create the prestige that came from having a sapient, organic being who did work normally reserved for an automatech. Her silver eyes darted to those moving through the hall, she scurried to get out of the way…and stopped. She had noticed the emperor's guards, but also the absence of the man who should be walking with them.

"Forget what you see."

Steven had meant only to send her along and back to her duties, for her to pay no mind to what she witnessed. But his mind struck too hard, her hair whipped around as her pupils dilated and a short gasp escaped her throat. The sound of her body hitting the floor was drowned out by the march of the arens, and she did not move. Every memory that had ever been within her mind was gone. No matter—what memories could a slave have that were worth keeping?

"I can sense the questions in your mind."

"There will be questions asked," Steven answered. "Many will be suspicious. But I know you will not lead me astray."

"How do you know this?"

Every aren stopped as he did, turning to look at the destroyed lantai crumpled on the deck.

"Who would give such power without purpose?"

"Very good, Steven. A hundred thousand years of labor begins to bear fruit. My most loyal servant journeys to you now, to aid you in your time of need. From beyond the bounds of your time and space he comes to you. Help him on his way, Steven. Across all the universe from beginning to end, help him see your moment. Know him as I have known you, call his name, and he will be there."

Steven's eyes rolled back as he unconsciously moistened his lips. From his mouth came only a whisper, but as he felt the word in his mind, the walls rumbled with his telepathic shout.

"Indorai!"

A strange hum filled the corridor; the lights darkened before a stifled glow forced him to raise a hand and shield his eyes. An intense heat sent ripples through the air. No, it was not heat, it was the mist. The scarlet haze now filled the hall, flowing out from a single being. Crouched, it stood wrapped in glowing tendrils the color of empty space, but between two of those tendrils stared the glow of yellow eyes.

Steven squinted his eyes as he tried to focus, but the brilliant image faded away. The mist thinned, and the imposing figure seemed to melt along with it. Moments later Steven saw only the hollow silhouette and flowing strands behind it.

"Your call is strong," four voices spoke warmly to his mind. *"It is so good to meet you."*

Steven opened his mouth, but Indorai continued.

"Do now what you must do; I will handle the rest."

Perhaps he should have had questions, but he had only confidence and so continued to lead the arens on their course. He was the first to enter the dining hall, and while the deltas assumed their positions, he took what was now his chair. He waited patiently. Soon they would all be here.

His mind began to drift. By now there should have been an alert. The Cathedral should have detected that both the emperor and empress were dead. With the situation unknown, the personal guards of each of his siblings should have been ushering them off to their own panic spaces. Yet one by one they came, as if nothing was wrong. Was this the Encephalon's doing? Steven smiled to himself. He was not sure how he knew, but he did. This was Indorai's doing, somehow. As powerful as Steven felt now, inwardly he knew this was only the beginning.

One by one his brothers and sisters came. None said anything about him having taken the head seat of the table. In a few of their minds he sensed the apprehension that perhaps this was how they were meant to learn of his succession. Others simply wrote it off, assuming their father would order his chair be vacated when he arrived. It did not matter, for soon they had all come. Raymond, Joseph, Alexis, Brendan, Lila, Michael, Stefan, David, Shane, Emily, Jessica, Bethany, Charlotte, Katherine, Liza, Deborah, Sophia, Nora, Anthony, Christian, Adam, Julia, Elaine, Parker, and Jason. Only Simmonne was absent on this day's gathering.

He wanted to gloat; he wanted to jump to his feet and loudly proclaim that victory was his. The games were over, the competition was settled. Every sister who had tried to pout their way to their father's heart as only a daughter could do. Every brother who had broken his back to outperform the others. Every sibling who had tried to take what was his. They had failed. He had won, and so much did he want to grind their egos against his victory. But that was not the behavior of an emperor, for every task now had to be carried out with dignity. He rose to his feet and raised a hand as he prepared to speak, and was interrupted.

"Steven." His brother Raymond drew the irate glare. "Where are Mom and Dad?"

"They won't be coming," Steven answered. "It was best that I had the privilege of delivering the news."

He watched their eyes as they all glanced to each other, eavesdropped on their minds as all inquired what the others knew. But not Raymond. His mind was racing as he tried to reach their parents in his NOD, and received no answer.

"Steven," Raymond whispered, "what have you done?"

"Dear brother," Steven said with a smirk. "I've won."

As Steven raised one hand, his guards and those of his parents brought their rifles to the ready. As he raised his other hand, the remaining guards were frozen, their reflexive actions halted midway. Several of his sisters screamed together before their voices were drowned out by the drone of disrupter fire.

Steven took a glass of water from the table, hoisting it just before the table shattered. He sipped quietly as he watched them, their bodies tearing open to be drained of their vital fluids. It occurred to him that there was a time this sight would have bothered him—had an earlier, weaker version of himself been watching. The version of himself who had naively tried to plan ahead, to be sure he could be generous to each of them. The weaker Steven who had wanted all of his siblings to be happy even if they did not have the crown. That man had even spent time contemplating the happiness of Raymond, the grasping, covetous second-born that had spent all their years trying to take what was his.

Today a better version of himself watched his parents' lesser seed in their vain struggles to survive. With all the psionic power gathered here, they may have had a chance against such an ambush. But under the weight of Steven's mind, they had no power. Like the helpless children they were, soon the blue floor had turned red.

His eyes scanned the tapestry of carnage. Julia and Bethany were embracing, hanging tight to each other as they wailed in agony. Stefan and Adam lay convulsing, their brains and bodies coming to terms with the fact of their death. There was not enough left of Raymond for Steven to concern himself with. His thumb traced the rim of his glass before he took a sip, looking through their eyes. Error messages filled their NODs, and together all were unified in fear as they realized that these were their final moments.

Only a few seconds had passed when the gunfire ended, and the chamber was soon silent save for a handful of death gasps and quiet moans of suffering.

The red mist flooded into the room as the hollow one, Indorai, joined them.

"What now?" Steven asked.

Indorai turned toward him, and Steven could sense the smile.

"I told you, I would handle it," the quadraphonic voice answered. "And I shall." His glowing tendrils seemed to reach into the mist, and as they drew inward, each pulled something with it. Indorai's posture straightened as his tendrils rose higher, each suspending the body of a Vaar.

"Your sister and your friend were kind enough to provide these bodies," Indorai explained. "Or at least, they are doing so even now. Who better to blame for the death of a ruler, than the elite hands of his enemy?"

"Very wise." Steven nodded. "But the Vaar cannot reach the Cathedral. How—"

"You worry too much, brother." Indorai paused to laugh. "They could get here, not only across the distance, but past all of the security. If they had the transit code of an Imperial scion, they would need only the reach a router within the main footprint of the astranet."

"Of course." Steven smiled as he glanced down at his sister Nora, spouting blood from the open wound in her neck. "They would come in through the back door. But they would face less security, not an absence of it. And those codes are secret, unique to each of us."

"Hence, bodies," Indorai answered, expanding his tentacles to pose the corpses throughout the chamber. "The rest has been handled."

Steven could sense the hollow one's psionic grasp on them as his tendrils reached into the mist to pull yet more bodies forth.

"You know, the illusion will fail if you are unharmed."

"Yes." Steven took a drink. "I figured as much."

"Temporary, of course," Indorai answered, now walking toward him. "Come. We must finish the job."

Setting his glass on the arm of the throne, Steven walked to him as the final corpses, those of his mother and father, were posed.

"Be at peace," Indorai's thoughts whispered even as Steven felt himself embraced by the creature's arms. *"You will be harmed, but you will not die. Resist the urge to regrow your wounds. For a time you will sleep, but you will awaken. And when they fear that all is lost, you will be the miracle they need."*

With a slow nod Steven bowed his head, releasing the arens to Indorai's control—a very different form of control; the hollow one did not overpower their thoughts. Instead he simply seized each of them, smothering their bodies in his mind until he overpowered their muscles. A nervous tremor moved through his arms as he saw muzzles raised and grenades deployed. Indorai's tendrils closed around him, and his eyes were forced shut.

The sound was muted—not blasts, merely gentle vibrations. The pain was distant; even the loss of a limb barely something to notice. His legs were gone, but he did not fall; he was gently lowered to the ground. His jaw hung from only one side of his head; it was a funny sensation feeling the blood in his throat.

"All has been handled. You will endure, and have what is yours. Sleep now, for there is much work ahead."

CHAPTER
14A

PANZER PEERED OUT OF the alley, pistol in hand. While carrying the princess, a round had struck his back, knocking Jorri loose somewhere along his path. His search for the weapon was momentarily distracted by the argument between the Vaar.

"We're supposed to take her alive!" one of the warriors shouted to the pilot. "You're jeopardizing our mission!"

The mech reached out, grabbing the warrior hovering in front of him by the legs and slamming him to the skyway. A second later the mech stepped on the hapless warrior to pin him in place.

"That—is not—my mission!" the pilot roared, shaking the women in hand. "I care nothing for these over-refined pieces of breeding stock! The Crykeeper is down there, and I mean to slay him."

"Give us the prisoners," one of the other Vaar demanded as they all trained their weapons on the warmech. "We're not waiting around to be killed by the Crykeeper. Do as you please, warlord, but we will come back with reinforcements."

"Warlord," Panzer mumbled to himself as he eavesdropped. "Could it be? Andira, what's left?"

A wave of red washed through his vision, silencing the Vaar and halting him in place. To his perception, it lasted only a few seconds before moving on.

"Nice warning there, partner," he said with a scoff.

"Apologies sir, damage to your sensor system has left me unable to detect the approaching—"

The world froze again.

"Waves. I will attempt to reconfigure."

He let out an annoyed growl.

"So about that damage report?"

"All shield generators have burned out from overburden. Primary shield projectors destroyed, secondary projectors offline due to power loss, potential operation at seventeen percent. Concussion field, jamming, 4CM, and cloaking power cells have been exhausted. Your armor integrity is down to forty percent, you have sustained heavy trauma, and your body is becoming quite insistent on dying."

"So…not much then?"

"Protecting an unarmored organic from that mech's attack forced me to dump power from all systems."

"You did the right thing, but we're not done yet."

"Colonel, you have the Imperial Rose and have sustained heavy trauma. I recommend retreat."

"Somehow I don't think they will all just watch as I run away, and I don't think I'm going to be able to evade them in this condition while carrying her with me."

"Fine!" the pilot shouted, drawing Panzer's attention back as the former roughly set the women on the skyway. "Take your secondary objectives and flee, cowards. I will deal with the Crykeeper, and show you why none of you will ever be called warlord!"

The mech leapt from the skyway, and never decelerated. Like a meteor, it struck the road below, sending tremors through the deck.

Panzer's eyes affixed themselves to the machine's particle cannons. He could not afford to let them fire again. Above them, the remaining Vaar had secured the other women, and carrying them in their arms, they began to vacate the battlefield. Rage twisted through his stomach as he watched them leave. He had to end this confrontation quickly.

"Its just us now, Crykeeper!" the pilot bellowed. "At least have enough dignity to come out and face me!"

Even in his current condition he could sense the fury, and he realized what he was facing. Not a machine pilot by a warlord, but a cyborg in the form of a warmech.

"You seem familiar," Panzer shouted back. "Have I killed you before?"

"Don't you recognize me, Crykeeper?" it growled back. "After all, you're the one who put me in this body."

"It's almost as ugly as your last one, Oul'sor."

"So you do recognize me," Oul'sor answered. "Good. I want to be sure you know who killed you. They told me you would appear to save your princess. You killed my son, Crykeeper. The only one that ever amounted to anything. For my death I've no ill will, but my soul can find no rest in the Void while my child's killer still lives.

"I'm going to kill you Crykeeper, and bury that rifle of yours with my son. But I want you to know, I'm going to kill your princess. I'm going to rip each of her limbs off, one by one. They will be my pen when I use royal blood to write my name over yours on the Wall of Victors."

Panzer's teeth ground together and his hands balled into fists. He let out a breath, forcing his nerves to calm. Rage needed to be his ally, not a fifth column in his defenses. This was personal, and personal fights had a tendency to become sloppy. It would be foolish to waste the advantage.

"I've had dinners that put up more of a fight than your son. I would think I did you a favor, Oul'sor."

The insult had the desired effect, and Oul'sor let out an enraged roar before charging toward him. Panzer dashed across the street to the opposing alley, narrowly avoiding the blast that tore through a nearby wall as Oul'sor fired with his flak cannon. Each shot threw out a cloud of thirty explosive spheres, each detonating on contact to hurl a cloud of hypersonic flechettes.

Panzer fell to slide beneath a wrecked conveyor as Oul'sor reached the alley. As he returned to his feet, the conveyor was shredded behind him and he turned onto another street.

Oul'sor howled as he wedged himself into the ally, tearing at the walls as he forced himself through. Panzer breathed a sigh of relief. As long as the Vaar was too irate to think tactically, he might be able to get out of this situation.

Emerging, Oul'sor fired a snapshot with his flak cannon while Panzer turned to another alley. If he could lead the Vaar far enough away, he could circle back for Jorri, and try…something.

"What's wrong, Crykeeper?" Oul'sor bellowed. "Is cowardice the only way you know how to fight?"

"You know, if my son had died begging and pleading for his life, I wouldn't be trying to talk to someone else about courage!"

When Oul'sor broke out onto the next street Panzer turned, using his pistol to blast through the transparent doors of an office building and dash inside.

"Coward!" Oul'sor screamed, and in a blind fury the sprinting Vaar turned and threw his bulk into the building. The structure yielded to his force, shattering on impact with the astranium plates. While Panzer exited the building's rear onto a main street, Oul'sor clawed his way out of the tower collapsing around him.

This wasn't getting him anywhere; he had to slow him down. Moving to another alley, Panzer rounded the corner and waited for Oul'sor to plow through. When the irate Vaar complied, Panzer met him, leaping forward onto one of the giant armored feet. With his pistol in hand, he shoved the muzzle into a small gap in the joint and worked the trigger as fast as he could. Fire and sparks shot out of the armor as the pistol cycled, and Oul'sor's foot drew back. Kicking forward, the Vaar drove his foot into a nearby wall, and Panzer was dislodged from the smooth metal. On the ground he quickly rolled away from the foot that moved to crush him, and scrambled to his feet. While Panzer tried to transition into a run, Oul'sor's foot came forward, accelerated by its own thrusters into a collision.

The impact sent Panzer into the air, tumbling head over heels. Shattered sensor systems turned the world into a psychedelic storm as his brain tried to make sense of the corrupted data. Without his thrusters he could not stop himself and the momentum carried him higher. A small dilation wave no more than a few seconds delayed him before he continued airborne. His flight ended when he smashed through the window of a skyscraper, and tumbled to a halt after breaking through the wall of what had once been a lavish office.

Prone, he let out a cough, spraying blood onto his faceplate. With his concussion field offline he had only his already severely damaged armor to absorb the heavy blow. Even cybernetic bones had yielded to the hit, contorting his spine and sending jagged fragments into his lungs. At least the apollium burn and Andira's bypass job on his nerves had mostly destroyed his sense of pain. Perhaps making Oul'sor angry wasn't such a good plan.

He retched into his helmet as he forced himself to sit up, and found that his head could not properly right itself. The contortion of his spinal column forced his head to cant to the left. The kalediscope of colors settled into a red shroud as he climbed to his feet. The building was on fire; on the street level below, Oul'sor was sending apollium warheads into the tower. With no choice but to evacuate, Panzer staggered through the nearby hall to the tower's opposite end, and went out a window. The conveyor on which he landed did little to cushion his fall.

He ignored Andira's question about if he were all right, *after having been kicked through a building.* But at least now he was on the same street as Jorri. His arms flexed unnaturally as he forced himself to rise and slide off the conveyor.

"Colonel, dilation wave approaching. ETA unknown."

As Panzer climbed to his feet, Oul'sor came around the corner.

"Got you!" the Vaar growled as the armored claws clamped down on him.

Panzer was hefted from the ground and brought level with Oul'sor's sensors as the claws began to squeeze.

He strained to free his pinned arms as his body contracted, but there was no strength left. Too many bones were broken. The nanites in his muscles were all that were keeping them working, and the actuators of his armor were barely functional. He tried to focus on the claws with his mind, but even there, too little strength remained. He could only prolong the inevitable. What little remained in his stomach joined blood from his lungs as they were forced into his throat.

Panic alarms flared in his NOD as a loud crunch rang through his armor. Blood began to flow out as lesions formed in his flesh. He barely heard Andira's words.

"Inverting shield polarity."

With the polarity reversed, what little remained of his backup shielding began to draw power from Oul'sor's defense screens.

"Discharging matrix."

The energy was jammed through both his armor and his nanites. For a brief instant his arms managed to spread out, and the claws around him whined as he dropped free. He landed prone, and half running, half crawling, he dashed for Jorri, passing between Oul'sor's feet.

When he tried to follow, Oul'sor turned too quickly, and the damaged joint of his ankle hit a bind, causing him to plummet to the street.

"Damn you!" Oul'sor railed, raising up on his forearm and taking aim with the flak cannon. The hypersonic rounds struck from behind, exploding against Panzer's back. The rounds that hit did not penetrate his trauma plates, but they did send him rocketing forward before leaving him to tumble through the street. A handful of flechettes had missed the trauma plates to pierce the armor and embed in his flesh, but now he was close enough to see Jorri. He cried out at the pain when he extended a hand, but managed to call the weapon home.

With the rifle as a crutch, he returned to his feet and turned to face Oul'sor as he cycled the action. The Vaar's body may have been in an astranium housing, but his weapons were not.

While Oul'sor rose, Panzer glared down Jorri's scope, engaging the jamming pod on the right rail. The first of Oul'sor's missiles veered wildly off course in the jamming field, taking any path but the one to their target. While Oul'sor took a moment to deactivate their guidance systems, Panzer fired. The devastator shells smashed into Oul'sor's shields. For a moment the protective screens held, before Jorri powered through. The shells tore a channel through the Vaar's weapon.

The shot detonated one of the missile canisters as it was loaded, splitting the weapon and setting off a chain reaction. Oul'sor struggled to detach the magazine from his back before it could be set off and cast it aside. Bringing his left arm up, the Vaar took aim before Jorri tore into the second weapon.

Vocalizing his rage, Oul'sor discarded the second weapon, and the particle cannons on his back came to life. Panzer took aim at the unfurling weapons but stopped—they had already built up too much power. If they were destroyed, they'd release their energy no different than if they were to fire.

Oul'sor wasn't moving—the dilation wave had struck. Or was it a provident moment? He didn't have time for this, there was no time; he had to do something—now.

"Simmonne," he whispered, and the image of her body flaking apart in the flame coursed through his mind. Consumed by the expanding fire, her body vanished; not even ash remained in her place. His limbs quaked with fury.

"No," he spat, the blood in his throat gurgling. This would not happen, he would not allow it. Oul'sor would not take her from him.

"Dilation wave, imminent."

"Die!" Oul'sor's scream sounded, his cannons flared, and the world stopped.

The smoke on the air did not move; dropships in the distance hung motionless in the sky. All was still, except for the four golden rays expelled from the barrels of Oul'sor's weapons. Moving close to the speed of light, they were the only thing not brought to relative stop in the wave. Oul'sor had already fired.

No!

He couldn't move, he couldn't act, but it did not matter. Oul'sor had fired; he was already dead. Simmonne was dead, her fate sealed the instant the cannons fired. Panzer could only watch as the four beams stretched through the reddened simulacrum of his vision. The beams were gold, and the red field shifted around them. He drew in a gasp as the wave passed, the beams converged, and the world melted away. Even the red haze was gone, save for a tiny point of light in distant darkness.

The point exploded.

A tidal wave of color washed through his vision as he felt himself flying. His body crashed through some kind of barrier before he tumbled to a stop. Prone, he let out a cough, spraying blood on his faceplate. The battling colors drained away as his sight returned to normal and he looked around to find himself in what had once been a lavish office.

Blood gargled in his throat as he tried to speak the words. His vision hadn't turned red as a result of cranial trauma, or sensory interference.

It was a provident moment.

What good did that do him now? He had failed, he was going to die, Simmonne was going to die.

No.

He would not allow it.

The walls began to glow; on the street level below, Oul'sor was sending apollium warheads into the structure. With no choice but to evacuate, Panzer staggered to a nearby window. As he shattered the window he stopped, glaring down at the conveyor waiting to receive him, and the nearby street corner. In a few moments, Oul'sor was coming around that corner. Could he change it? Could he finally make things happen in a different way? The conveyor did little to cushion his fall, but his limbs were already flailing, drawing him out of the cratered vehicle and onto his feet.

"Colonel, a dilation wave is approaching."

He said nothing. As his toes meet the road he crouched forward, eyes on the street corner. He felt the heavy footfalls, and at the first glint of the Vaar's armored body, Panzer shot forward. Lurching around the Vaar's foot, Panzer darted between his legs.

Oul'sor caught sight of him, and turned to follow. He turned too quickly; the damaged joint of his ankle hit a bind, causing him to plummet to the street.

"Damn you!" Oul'sor railed, but failed to draw a bead as Panzer rounded the corner of the tower.

The contortion of his spine caused him to over correct with each step, but he pressed forward. He made a full circle of the building, returning to the street and his path to Jorri as Oul'sor returned to his feet. The burst of the flak cannon slammed into him from behind, rocketing him ahead. The flechettes chewed at his flesh; he cried out as he extended a hand and called Jorri home.

Rolling onto his back, Panzer sat up, glaring down Jorri's scope as he engaged the jamming pod on the right rail. Oul'sor's missiles slammed into the surrounding structures, but this time, Panzer's aim turned to the four cannons. The devastator shells smashed through Oul'sor's shields, clipping the cannons as Panzer strafed the muzzle over the Vaar's shoulders.

With the guidance system of his missiles deactivated, Oul'sor drew down on him again. What remained of Panzer's face turned to a grimace as his left hand released Jorri, and he held his hand ahead. He focused on the muzzle of the missile launcher, pushing with all of his mind that remained. The missiles began to tumble out of the muzzle, with some arcing into the sky, and others nose-diving into the road.

Jorri's next burst tore into the missile launcher as a new canister was loaded, splitting the weapon and setting off a chain reaction. While Oul'sor struggled to detach the magazine from his back, Panzer returned to his feet and took aim. Oul'sor shed the magazine as Jorri tore into his flak cannon.

"Dilation wave, imminent."

"No!" Oul'sor's cry dragged out over his ears. "I...will... not...lose...here!"

The Vaar moved in slow motion as plates across his metal body slid apart and exposed a gap in his side. He withdrew a large rod as it expanded into a spiked hammer. With a head larger than the conveyors littering the battlefield, the barbed weapon belched a single gout of plasma before the red haze returned, and the world stopped.

Were he able to move, were there still a face beneath his helmet, Panzer would have been smiling. He had done it, he had changed it. In all the provident moments, in all the premonitions, he had finally changed what he saw. The surge of aggression in his mind was sweet ecstasy. Victory was near. He had pruned the branches; all that was left was to burn the Vaar down.

He readied himself, his gaze on the sensors lining Oul'sor's face. His finger felt the pressure of the trigger; they began to move as time restarted and the Vaar barreled toward him.

Jorri did not fire.

Panzer titled the weapon and glared into the action, finding the problem. The apollium burn had caused the shells to swell in the magazine. One of their number had expanded to full size before entering the firing chamber, creating a jam. Backpedaling on his feet, he gripped the magazine and ripped it from the well while angling Jorri's muzzle into the sky. He shook the weapon, using the other hand to strike it with the magazine. The stretched core came loose, and he jammed the magazine back into the well as Oul'sor loomed over him.

Jorri howled; the concentrated fire shattered the sensors across Oul'sor's face as the hammer descended. Panzer leapt away as the hammer struck the road. Plates across Oul'sor's body slid apart and disharmonious sound waves began emanating from the new gaps.

"He's using echo location," Andira advised.

"Yes, I noticed," Panzer barked.

"I cannot hide us without the cloak."

"Too late for that now."

Favoring his damaged ankle, Oul'sor turned, sweeping down with the hammer. Panzer leapt to the side as the hammer carved a path through the wall of a nearby tower.

Aiming for Oul'sor's head, Panzer dumped the last of the devastator shells, trying to carve a path to where he hoped the Vaar's brains were encased. It did not work. Even with the devastators, he could not penetrate the astranium plate after four layers of active shielding. Jorri fell silent, and with no devastators remaining, conventional shells would have to suffice.

Oul'sor faked a swing with his hammer before bringing his foot forward. Unable to avoid the blow in time, Panzer turned, bringing up his left arm. He was sent careening away before deflecting off the corner of a building and rolling through the street to wedge under a conveyor.

"Damn it," he groaned, using Jorri to push himself up. "I think I've had about enough of this shit."

His left arm hung at his side, his shoulder and every bone below now in pieces. Only a moment later did he realize that his left hand had broken completely free of his arm. The disembodied appendage was nowhere to be found. Blood leaked from the cracks in the armor and the cinched metal around the remains of his wrist. He looked back to Oul'sor, who readied himself before charging again. Moving to intercept, Panzer jogged forward while transferring Jorri to his back. As he closed in, Oul'sor turned, moving to slide on his feet while raising the hammer behind him. When the distance closed, the Vaar swept the hammer down to meet him.

Panzer saw it—not where the hammer was, but the crimson image of where it would be. Falling to a knee, he lay back, sliding under the head of the weapon as one of its spikes scraped his faceplate.

He rolled as the Vaar passed, and grabbed hold of the metal foot to reel himself in. With his one useful arm he scaled the foot and up the massive leg while Oul'sor ground to a halt. His feet adhered to the metal and he climbed while Oul'sor tried to strike him with the haft of the hammer. He reached Oul'sor's back and continued to climb up between the shoulders.

His hand went for his knife as he found a seam in the armor and drove the blade home into the base of Oul'sor's neck with whatever strength remained. Even astranium yielded to the bite of fifty-eight centimeters of Reichsylvannian steel and he forced the blade between the armored plates.

Oul'sor turned and contorted, trying to throw him off. Even as the Vaar threw himself into a building and his feet were knocked loose, Panzer held tight to the blade. When Oul'sor fell to the ground and rolled he did not let go, even as bones broke under the giant body passing over him. He continued to hold firm and draw the blade down, hearing the muscle fibers snapping in his arm. The blade began to move through the seam and slid under the astranium plate.

Both were sent airborne as Oul'sor fired his thrusters, then cut the flow and slammed back into the deck. Panzer's helmet smacked against the armor and for a moment he was left dangling from the knife. But he held firm, and pulled himself back up. Oul'sor dropped his hammer and tried to reach back to grab him. He was impeded—mounts on which his particle cannons once stood denied him the flexibility to bring his arms back. While the Vaar slammed into another building, the armored plate moved, and a gap formed as Panzer pulled.

Releasing the knife, he reached back to grab Jorri, and jammed the muzzle into the gap. He jerked the trigger, sending the shells into the internal structures of Oul'sor's body.

Oul'sor skidded to a stop and began convulsing, his voice sorting through pitches as his body's internal components were annihilated.

After a final, vain thrust into the air, Oul'sor's body gave out.

As they descended, Panzer dropped free and both crashed to the deck.

Silence finally settled over the streets with neither of the two moving. Slowly Panzer rolled onto his back and glared up at the skyway. The other women were long gone, by now in the midst of innumerable Vaar. He made several attempts to rise before he succeeded, with Jorri working as a third leg.

"This isn't over…Crykeeper." Oul'sor seemed to wheeze as his body twitched.

"It is for you."

Panzer fell to a knee and held the rifle out, dumping the last of his magazine into the destroyed sensor panels. The lights across his body went out as Oul'sor's movement stopped, and the machinery went silent.

"Colonel, Vaar reinforcements approaching."

He tried to turn, intent on finding the princess, before collapsing.

CHAPTER
14B

ONLY THE SOUND OF still smoldering fires now filled the streets above. Sitting in the drainage channel, Simmonne glared up. Her eyes ached, nearly blinded by some incredible flash of light. Who won? Was he still alive? Her heart raced and she tried once more to push the grate up to no avail.

She flinched as an armored hand grabbed on to the grate, and tossed it away. For a moment she began to panic, her blurry eyes unable to make out who or what was glaring down at her. As her vision cleared she exhaled, seeing the faceless helmet glaring down at her. He was alive—he won! He was alive. Had he saved them? Her arms grouped for him, latching on to his arm as he reached for her.

"Come on." Even the digitized voice seemed to wheeze as he extended a hand to her. She held tight as he raised her up, and she climbed out. He lay prone on the ground, and with great effort forced himself upright. Immediately she fell to her knees, throwing her arms around him, squeezing until her wounded ribs ached. He was alive, and now everything had to be all right.

"Come on," he repeated, wrapping an arm around her. "We have to go."

"What about Jenna and the Twins?"

Her head turned side to side, certain they were somewhere nearby. Of course they were—he could do anything, he had to have saved them.

"There's nothing we can do for them," he gasped. "We have to go now."

He didn't just say that; she must have misheard him. She clung tighter to him as he returned to his feet.

"No." She tried to fight as he pushed her on. "No, you saved them. Where are they?"

Her eyes were drawn to the glint of a ship as it descended toward them. The colonel turned, and quickly guided her behind.

"Simmonne, you're going to have to run," he said. "Run, find somewhere to hide."

"But, but—"

"I can't keep up, I'll be dead in a few minutes anyway," he wheezed. "Run; I'll hold them as long as I can."

The ship's sides opened, and more Vaar began to drop out onto the streets.

"Run." He turned toward her. "Go!"

He gave her a push, but she did not move. Where was she supposed to go?

"Colonel—"

His arms quickly encircled her as she felt the heat of an explosion. As she opened her eyes she saw the new shuttle disintegrate as the bewildered Vaar ran for cover. What was happening?

"About time," Panzer gasped. She followed his gaze to look up as something fell from the sky. For all but the clawed hands, it appeared like a giant lobster descending from above until slamming into the street ahead of them. From cannons on its shoulders, it sprayed the Vaar with munitions, and fired with additional weapons held in its smaller limbs.

Her head swiveled as two objects fell at her sides, two warriors who rose upright in armor brandishing gleaming blades.

She held tighter to the colonel as she felt a gust of wind, and he guided her back.

"Let's go, let's go!" one of the bladed men shouted, using a long rifle to snipe a Vaar as it peered over a rooftop. "We've got a typhoon of dilation waves incoming, we have to go now!"

She stumbled as her foot met a ramp, and the colonel guided her up. Behind him the three armored figures followed, and suddenly she was in a metal corridor.

"We're in. Andira, get us out of here," Panzer barked. The ramp rose, and the ship began to climb.

"Nice of you guys to show up," Panzer quipped, before falling to his knees.

The armored lobster moved to his side, helmet splitting open to reveal the face of a kodaz.

"Hangar be takin' a direct hit," the kodaz replied. "We gettin' here, sssoon we be diggin' our way out."

The bladed men reached down to help the colonel back to his feet, and began to guide him through the corridor.

"Wait, what about the others?"

They ignored her, and she raced to follow them into the med bay.

"Colonel?"

The kurai grabbed for his armor and began stripping it away. Simmonne heard what sounded like ripping fabric, before her nose was assailed by the odor of charred flesh. Turning, she fell on her hands and retched on the deck. The sound of flesh fused to the armor and tearing loose continued to fill her ears as the colonel's armor was removed.

"Wait," she heard him gasp.

"Sir," one of the kurai said, "you're dying. We have to get your armor off and get you into the deep fryer."

Simmonne turned as his finger pointed toward her.

"Tend to her."

"Sir."

"Her first!" he barked.

Suddenly a pair of arms captured her, lifting her off the deck like a doll and carrying her toward one of the tables. It was not the colonel, nor one of the other warriors. A woman, young despite her silver hair and dressed in a corisse, sat her down on a med table.

"Who, who are you?" Simmonne asked, looking into the woman's cyan eyes.

"I am Andira, Majesty," the woman answered. "This unit is one of my peripherals."

She nodded slowly as the cyan eyes scanned her.

"Rib fractures, deep tissue bruising," Andira announced. "Partial hip dislocation."

She watched Andira reach under the table, before flinching as a mediron was driven into her thigh. The pain of the stab quickly faded, along with the rest that ravaged her body. She tried to turn back to the colonel, embroiled in a coughing fit while the kurai struggled with him.

"Get her out of here," he managed to choke out. "She doesn't need to see this."

"Be comin' wit' me Majessty." The kodaz turned to her. "Pleassse."

"But…Jenna and the Twins."

"They're…gone, Princess," Panzer strained to say. "We have to get out of here."

The kurai wrestled with his limbs, and one turned to the kodaz.

"Get her out of here damn it."

The kodaz turned back to her.

"Pleassse, Majessty, thissss way."

The huge alien guided her with one arm, out of the med bay and back to the corridor.

"Mister, we can't leave them," she pleaded with the kodaz. "Please, you have to do something."

"Andira." The kodaz glanced up. "What bein' t'a ssstate o her friendss?"

"Jenna Prideaux and the Katyusha Twins were abducted by Vaar DOS agents. Current location unknown." The AI's voice now came from the walls.

The kodaz glanced back to her.

"Not bein' anyt'in' we able doin' now." He shook his head. "When 'em colonel back on him feet, we ssseein'."

Tears welled in her eyes as he continued to guide her through the halls, until stopping at a particular room.

"Bein' t'a colonel'sss quartersss," he explained. "Pleassse, be remainin' here."

He opened the door, and motioned her toward it.

"No," she whispered. "We can't."

Her feet moved slowly, taking her inside.

"My name bein' Rhoxx. Be callin' if you needin', or tellin' Andira. I bein' on t'a bridge."

The kodaz stepped away, the door closed, and Simmonne collapsed in a heap. Her arms and legs drew together in a fetal position as she began to cry.

Her guards, the sight of their broken bodies flashed over in her mind. They were…dead. They were really dead. The image of Jenna and the Twin's in that awful machine's hand. This isn't how it was supposed to be, this wasn't supposed to happen. Where was the colonel? Why didn't he arrive sooner? Why didn't he save them? Why? Why did this have to happen?

CHAPTER 14E

THE FIGHTING BETWEEN AVALON'S legionnaires and the Vaar invaders was still ongoing, but the battle was over. Against the unending tide of Vaar reinforcements landing across the station, it was only a matter of time. The civilian population would be herded, and transferred to prison worlds. The vast caches of Solar technology would soon become madness-inducing subjects of largely futile Vaar efforts to reverse engineer.

None of these things mattered to Indorai, unseen, and intangible as he walked carelessly through ongoing firefights. Most of the Vaar would never know his role in assisting them, from disrupting the station's communications to sabotaging its defenses. It did not matter; they did not need to know. They were happier not knowing, believing that this was their victory. They had no concept that every victory would bring their doom closer.

With every victory, the Solars would see them as an ever-increasing danger. With every battle won, they would be viewed as a more credible menace. They would become bolder, fooling themselves into believing they could actually defeat the Empire. In the end, they would succeed only in provoking their own destruction. Their ignorance, their pride…like twin poisons, both would ultimately destroy them. Eventually the Empire would abandon their high-minded principles of restraint and judicious force. The more dangerous the Vaar became, the sooner it would become a war for survival. A war that was never going to be a fair fight.

The Vaar were doomed, and in a handful of years they would be a broken people. Those that remained would spend their final days trying to survive the vengeance wrought by all those they had wronged in ages past. Their fate was sealed long before they dared to dream of the stars. He sought now one of the few who could earn his people's place, somewhere beyond this immutable future. Finding a perch atop one of the towers, he glared down to the street below, to the fight he had come to see. To him they moved at a crawl, as such limited beings always did. All the better for him to enjoy their fight.

The commando and the warlord, giving it their all to destroy each other. An invisible mouth smiled as Indorai watched them fight. But as the battle drew toward its end, Indorai stepped off the high tower and descended to the streets below. The commando tore into the warlord's guns, but now the final four were ready to fire. Oul'sor was so stubborn, stuck in his ways, married to old weapons such as particle cannons and missile launchers. He had not even taken the disrupters that had been offered. Indorai drew closer, moving toward the commando as he sprayed the warlord with his weapon.

"Now is the moment of truth, brother," Indorai whispered. "Now, you must show us that our efforts have not been wasted."

He craned his neck, enjoying the gentle sensation as the wave struck, and the lesser beings were frozen.

"Oh no," Indorai laughed. "You see it, don't you? You will die, but you will not die alone. Your princess will die with you. She'll be ripped from your grasp, and all those fantasies of conquering her will be for naught. What will you do?

"There is no place among us for the weak. Either you die here, or you change your time. Can you do it? Can you be more than the moment? Can you save her? None of your kind have ever been able. Mute witnesses, they merely watch time's march. But if you can do it, it will be here, in this galaxy, where time is already broken. Here, providence ends and action must begin. Can you become more than what you are?"

The dilation of the wave hit its apex, the distortion moved on, and the commando was swept away.

"Yes!" Indorai raised his fists in jubilation and turning his eyes to the commando now passing out of the wave and sailing through the sky. "I knew you would not disappoint us."

He brought an arm up, shifting through the streets as their battle concluded. He now stood over the commando, as he crawled toward a broken drainage channel.

He took a knee as he watched the Imperial Rose climb out and embrace him.

"Yes, now claim your prize. We worked very hard to make sure you had something you would truly appreciate."

He extended a hand, catching the commando's shoulder so that he did not fall on the woman embracing him. Gently he helped them to their feet.

"You are truly everything we hoped for, the strongest your people have produced. I shudder to think of what you will become. For an instant, you even sensed me in the embassy as I followed you. I wonder, if you weren't so near death, would you sense me here, now? How many voices would you hear?"

He stepped away, and watched until their friends came and they sailed away into the sky.

"And now you understand, Oul'sor."

He turned to the broken wreck lying in the street.

"The futility of it all. In a single battle, all you were was destroyed once again. Such is the fate of everyone in this accursed place. To be born, grow old, grow weak, and die. Your existence begins, only to end. To see all you were and all you created lost sooner or later in the march of time. Even with a second chance, you could not change anything. But I knew, you could push our friend to his limit, and carry him beyond."

His hands came to rest on the mech's head, his fingertips indenting the metal before piercing through. With a single pull he tore the head of the mech in half, with no more difficulty than opening a book. By doing so he revealed the broken capsule within, housing the warlord's brains. He bent to take the capsule, and shattered it to hold the soft tissue in his grasp.

"You are weak, but your will is strong. We will spare you the wretched fate of your kind, Oul'sor. You have earned your place, and have been chosen to become more than what you were. It is a rare privilege to be adopted as one of the master's children, when the rest of your kind are unworthy. I hope you will appreciate what is conferred upon you."

His mouth opened and a vortex of air formed with the atmosphere flowing into his body. Red mist formed around his hands, and a new skull took shape around the brains in his grasp. Not iron like the bones of other Vaar, but something else. Something the limited minds of this universe could not fully grasp. A new spinal column materialized beneath the skull, expanding into a new skeleton. Indorai took a step, and ushered the bones to stand on their own. They became the new focus of the air-consuming vortex and crimson mist.

"Where you were mortal, you are now eternal. You will see the universe from beginning to end, and when the last of its stars burn out, you will move on. Where you were weak, you shall be powerful. Where you were doomed to failure in battle against gifts you lacked, you shall now wield that power yourself. Rise, Oul'sor! Become more than what you were."

Amid the Vaar's howl, a collective breath was held across space. Every provident moved together, sensing something. To some déjà vu, to others a passing moment of worry or illness. But of the few that existed, all felt it. The change in the past, present, and future. To the sound of a titanic scream, a new provident had been born.

To Be Continued…
Solar Winds – Crossroads

Meet author Bryan G. Shewmaker
and get updates for forthcoming books
in the Solar Winds series!

www.TheEncephalon.com
www.Facebook.com/SolarWindsSeries

APPENDICES

APPENDIX 1

HISTORY OF THE SOLAR EMPIRE

PREFACE

AT THE START OF the Hourglass War, the Solar Empire had existed for 100,016 years. To detail every major event that has transpired in that amount of time would require an encyclopedia spanning hundreds of volumes. As a result, this entry is meant only to skim the history of the Empire. It only covers events that were the most critical in shaping the nature of the Empire or were most relevant to the issues it faces in the modern age.

Astute readers may notice that the history presented here is not always consistent with history as understood by major players in the modern era. This is not a coincidence. Light shines only on the present, and the past is forever in shadow. The more distant the past becomes, the less clear it is. History is also subject to revisionism, both well-meaning and politically motivated. That which is presented here is the true history of the Empire, how it came to be, and the challenges it faced to become the superstate that it is.

1A
PRE-HISTORY

IN A BIT OF cultural chauvinism, the humans of the Empire generally regard its formation as the beginning of true civilization. All that came before it, from the discovery of fire to the first trips into space, were merely the steps of infancy. This attitude is not helped by the fact that most of humanity's history was lost in the Therican War. With so many worlds scourged, museums, databases, and antiques were all destroyed. When it was an open question whether there would be a tomorrow, preserving yesterday became a very low priority.

The only thing about which Imperial scholars are certain when it comes to history before the Empire is how little they know. So much has been lost or corrupted by the forgetfulness of centuries. Were it not the result of such great tragedy, the Empire's picture of the past might even be comical. The Empire knows, for example, that the United States of America, British Empire, Soviet Union, Spanish Empire, Roman Empire, and more all existed. But it has serious debates about which came first, which coexisted with the other, and which led to the other.

Neil Armstrong and Buzz Aldrin are still remembered as the first men to set foot on Earth's moon, but myth has largely replaced history. A common belief in the Empire is that the two men were wealthy industrialists who self-funded the venture. Every Imperial scientist knows Newton's Laws, but historians do not agree whether Newton was a man, an institution, or even the mascot of an institution. Albert Einstein is remembered, but the name Einstein is falsely believed to have been a title given to great thinkers. Into the modern era, Imperial academics bestow the Einstein title ("Ynsteen" in the Solar language) in the same way Earth once awarded the Nobel Prize. Many other great scientists and inventors such as Volta, Faraday, and more have been forgotten completely.

In the end it matters little—just as those living in the industrial age had no name for the man who first discovered how to make fire. These baby steps in civilization occurred long ago, and society has moved forward.

1B
THE INTERSTELLAR CONFEDERACY

Founding Date Unknown

TO UNDERSTAND THE SOLAR Empire, it is helpful to understand what came before it. Within the Empire, the Confederacy is often thought of as the first, and ultimately unsuccessful, attempt to build an interstellar civilization. The invention of the first massless impulse drives allowed humanity to begin expanding away from Earth to other star systems. Humanity soon inhabited more than five thousand worlds, though humans are no exception to the laws of evolutionary pressure. In new environments, human diversity increased dramatically. Those who lived on worlds with new gravity, new climate, and new pathogens began to show changes over time. In some cases, the differences grew large enough that there existed scientific debate whether the colonists in question should still be considered human.

In those days, there was no true interstellar government. Though Earth tried to maintain control over its colonies, the faster-than-light travel technologies of the day were simply too slow. As colonies grew and new cultures developed, they began to pull away from each other. But massless impulse drive technology would and did gradually improve. As the colonies began to interact with each other more regularly, problems arose. The result was the Colony Wars. Fought over reasons ranging from ethnic hatred to income inequality, the Colony Wars cost around thirty-one billion lives. Much of humanity's new diversity was lost, and worlds that had been colonized into thriving hubs were left in ruins.

The Interstellar Confederacy was founded to prevent such a conflict from occurring again. Though it was more of a federation than a true confederacy, every planet maintained a high degree of sovereignty. But matters that affected multiple planets were to be the responsibility of the Confederate government. For a time, it worked.

The Confederacy lasted for approximately 1,800 years. It began as a society built with a heavy emphasis on personal freedom, a highly limited central government, and the inclusion of all peoples. Irrespective of race, religion, gender, creed, or planet of origin, all were welcome. The golden age of the Confederacy saw a period of unprecedented wealth, technological development, and a rising quality of life. It oversaw mankind's first contact with a sapient intelligent species and united humanity in a way unmatched by anything before. But to all things there is an end.

By its 1,500th year, the Confederacy was a society in decline plagued by social ills. The nuclear family had almost vanished, with more than 75 percent of children being born to or living with single mothers. Marriage was at one of the lowest rates in human history, due largely to divorce and family courts so heavily biased that the average man would not so much as consider it. A general celebration of ignorance had grown in the culture. Higher education had morphed into a vehicle for political indoctrination, leading the fields of science and engineering to decline. The middle class of society had effectively ceased to exist, with only the super rich and the desperately poor remaining. Criminality was rampant with more than 35 percent of adult males having a criminal history.

The general population had become so polarized in their politics that they could no longer agree on basic precepts of morality, let alone civic duty or government policy. Much of the central government's power grabs were attempts to keep the population from turning on itself. Though it managed to hold on for another three hundred years, the Confederacy became an increasingly totalitarian state. As with many totalitarian states, it ended with the blood of many of its own citizens on its hands. The Confederacy was doomed and would not have survived much longer even had the Thericans never arrived.

1C
THE THERICAN WAR

-13–0 Anno Nostri (AN)

NO EVENT IN HISTORY has had a more profound impact on the collective psyche of humanity than the Therican War. The war would see previously unimagined levels of death and suffering. For generations, the war left humanity with a bitter hatred for all things alien. The war would see the fall of the Interstellar Confederacy and the rise of the Solar Empire. And it would shape the unending mission of the Empire—to unite all intelligent species under one rule so such a travesty could never occur again.

Intelligent life is a rare thing in the universe. Even rarer are species of sufficient intellect and bearing to warp the fabric of space-time and achieve interstellar travel. Time scales of the universe are measured in millions and billions of years. Two species can evolve in the same galaxy, at adjacent stars. They can come into being, grow, develop, expand, and eventually succumb to extinction. All with eons separating them from any opportunity to meet.

From whence the Thericans originated has never been determined. When they arrived in the Solar Galaxy (then known as the Milky Way) from Andromeda, there were only six species capable of interstellar travel. Humanity was one of these species. But much to the disappointment of many humans, the other five had no interest in interaction. With the travel times involved, interaction itself was a purely voluntary affair. Two of the alien species, the M'gah and the Elrua, would survive the war to be later integrated into the Empire. Almost nothing is known about the other three. They were exterminated by the Thericans, and the only proof they once existed lies in a handful of ancient Confederate maps. They are recounted in history simply as the Lost Races.

It is not true to say that humanity had allies during the war. With the distances and travel times involved, no meaningful cooperation could have been possible. The myth that several races fought together is a deliberate revision of history by the Empire done on political grounds.

The Thericans first arrived in the Scutum-Crux arm of the galaxy, on its opposite side relative to Earth. The Thericans immediately began attacking the Lost Races. Word of this would eventually reach the Interstellar

Confederacy, as some of the battles were observed by Confederate cartographer probes mapping the galaxy. The Confederacy chose to ignore the situation. As far as the leadership was concerned, it was a far-off conflict fought by xenophobic aliens with no bearing on humanity. Thus the Confederacy dithered and squandered thirty years' worth of warning about their impending doom.

Only one man took the threats of the Thericans seriously—Manfred Wagner. The son of wealthy parents, and a career military officer, Manfred was an admiral in the Confederate star fleet. In prior generations, it was his family's wealth that funded the research and development of the first massless impulse drives. But Manfred was exactly the wrong man to sound the alarm, as he was a man with many enemies. He was a true soldier in a military used primarily by its government as a massive jobs program for otherwise unemployed citizens. He was also a political pariah. Manfred lived in an ostensibly egalitarian society and had a reputation for both racism and sexism.

While allegations of racism levied against him were largely unfounded, those of sexism were not. Manfred openly blamed most of the Confederacy's social problems on the voting habits of women. He despised women's presence in the military, likening them to child soldiers. When he began approaching the press about what his superiors called a "vague and unfounded alien threat," he was accused of inciting panic. This was all his enemies needed to finally force his resignation. Manfred left the military and, despite his controversial views, was able to win election as governor of Mars. His considerable wealth, good looks, and personal magnetism soon won him the epithet "Prince of Mars."

In the past, Mars had been the industrial capital of the Confederacy, but the planet had been reduced to an impoverished slum due to generations of corrupt politics and suicidal economic policy. As governor, Manfred went to work breathing new life into long-abandoned factories, readying them for a war he felt was inevitable.

But even Manfred did not realize how soon the attack was coming. While the Thericans were busy with the Lost Races, they sent a wave of stealth probes toward the Confederacy. In orbit of every inhabited world, these probes dispensed the deadly pathogen that came to be known as EVE-V. Further information about this virus can be found in its own entry. The pandemic that resulted from EVE-V soon brought the Confederacy to a grinding halt as billions of people, all women, fell deathly ill. While the Confederacy mobilized to deal with the pandemic, the Thericans attacked in force.

The first region to fall was the Phaeton Expanse. Located in the Sagittarius arm of the galaxy, this region was remote to the rest of the Confederacy. But Phaeton contained about two hundred inhabited worlds and more than twenty-one billion inhabitants. The Thericans effortlessly swept aside the regional defenses and bombarded these worlds from orbit. These bombardments were so comprehensive that not even single-celled organisms survived. All of this was done so quickly that no warning was sent to the rest of the Confederacy. Only when scout ships were sent to the region to determine why all communication had stopped did humanity realize it was at war.

The Confederate military badly misjudged the Thericans' plan of attack. It was expected that the invaders would make a direct approach to Earth, and defenses were arrayed accordingly. The Thericans did not oblige. They moved in a broad curve, gradually spiraling inward as they wiped out outlying colonies before working their way in. The Confederate armada and the Thericans finally met in the Battle for Siddhartha Abyss. The Siddhartha Abyss was one of the most densely populated regions in the Confederacy, and nearly the entire Confederate navy was committed to the battle.

The Therican ships were far more advanced than anything humanity had seen. No less than a dozen Confederate ships working together were needed to destroy even the smallest Therican vessels. The Thericans were not only stronger but were far more numerous. The Confederacy committed more than 1,500 ships to the battle, most of them carriers for AI-controlled drones. Of these, the Thericans allowed only three to escape to spread news of the crushing defeat.

Social order in the Confederacy soon began to break down. Humanity was not only in the grips of a catastrophic pandemic but was now facing a far more advanced species that had effortlessly crushed the military. To have any hope of defending itself, the Confederacy now had to hastily assemble a new fleet, and faced enormous shortages. EVE-V had effectively removed the female half of the species's ability to contribute. Men were reluctant to go fight what seemed like a hopeless war and leave female relatives to die painful deaths as a result of the virus.

The conflict dragged on for thirteen years, far longer than was necessary. After scourging a system, the Thericans would take their time. Often they would wait weeks or months before moving on to the next target. But each time they launched a new attack, they made a mockery of those deployed to stop them. Even as nearly every man or boy with a pulse was put to work fighting or building weapons, nothing could stop the assault.

As the situation grew increasingly desperate, Confederate President Shinzo Ito called Manfred Wagner back to military service. Many at the time objected. Manfred was a polarizing figure at a time when humanity needed unity more than ever. But to the president, what humanity needed most was a soldier, not another socialite with a rank insignia. None who had come before him had found any success. Manfred was thus appointed supreme commander for all Confederate forces.

Manfred's first challenge as SC was to force the rest of the leadership to accept the grim reality. Many held out hopes that some way could be found to turn the tide of battle. Others hoped that the Thericans might stop short and eventually demand surrender. But to Manfred, the situation was clear. The combination of the war and EVE-V could not be a coincidence. This was a war of extermination. While the virus was killing the female half of the population, the Thericans were giving the Confederacy plenty of time between battles to rebuild. All so the male half could be fed to them on the battlefield. Humanity had one choice left: to escape.

In the early days of the EVE-V pandemic, Manfred had successfully quarantined a large population of uninfected women on colony ships from Mars. This would be the foundation of Project Safe Seed. Men and women free of the virus would be placed on these colony ships, and they would ride out into space. Somewhere beyond the Thericans' reach, they could then begin rebuilding human society. Manfred ordered war production to shift from expensive carrier ships to cheap planetary defense vessels. He would give the impression that humanity was fighting a war of attrition, while readying Safe Seed.

But before humanity could think of fleeing, it had to know just how far the Thericans' reach extended. To answer this question, Manfred instituted Project Commando. A handpicked team of marines was chosen. These men would be given the task to board and capture a Therican ship. A tall order, considering that the entire war had been fought ship-to-ship. None knew so much as what a Therican looked like, or even if humans had the requisite anatomy to operate one of their ships. But if the mission was successful, the commandos would bring the captured ship to Mars. There a team of scientists, engineers, and linguists waited to examine it.

By the time Project Commando was ready to embark on its mission, most of the Confederacy was gone. It was now only a matter of time until the Thericans moved on Earth and Mars. But with the operation's launch, the commandos were able to capture a small Therican scout as it approached the Solar system. With the success of this mission, the path to salvation had been opened.

Project Safe Seed was impossible. From the scout, the scientists learned that the Thericans had come from Andromeda. If the Thericans had the ability to travel between galaxies, there was nowhere humanity could flee that was beyond their reach. But this was not the only discovery. The Thericans had a disturbing amount of information on humanity. This included a translation of all human languages to their own. Linguists and engineers were able to use this database to learn more about the Thericans.

The Thericans were not a hive-mind; every Therican was an individual with its own character and personality. But all Thericans were linked by some means to a central entity they called the One Mind. This One Mind served to coordinate the entire species, keeping them unified on common goals. This led scientists to dub it the Common Control Organism. More importantly, the Common Control Organism had come to the Milky Way, taking up residence on a barren planet in the galactic core.

The Confederacy now had a meaningful target, but one that was out of reach. The galactic core was both distant and difficult to navigate. The only ship the Confederacy possessed even capable of reaching it in time was the captured scout ship. So with the Thericans now approaching Earth, Manfred asked the commandos who captured the ship to accept a suicide mission. They would take the captured scout, travel to the galactic core, find the CCO, and destroy it.

While the commandos were in transit to the galactic core, the Thericans arrived in the Solar system. They bypassed the colonies of Jupiter, Saturn, and Mars as they made straight for Earth. The Confederacy poured every ship it had left into its last stand. The Battle of Earth was the largest battle that had been fought up to that point. Despite the most determined resistance they could muster, the defenders could not save humanity's home world. Earth was bombarded until it was a molten rock that would eventually cool to resemble its moon. The cradle of civilization was gone.

The commandos struck as the Thericans turned back for Mars. Because they were forced to maintain a communications blackout, the details of their journey will never be known. What is known is that they reached the One Mind's planet and crashed their ship into it at FTL. While they were too late to save Earth, they succeeded in preserving humanity.

Without the One Mind, the effects on the Thericans were immediate and profound. Many of their ships turned on each other. Others were set adrift, crashing into planets and stars as their crews slipped into inescapable lethargy. Others simply drifted into space as their crews quit eating, drinking, or caring about matters like a pressurized hull. More than a thousand years later, explorers in Andromeda would find the ruins of Therican outposts, all of them long empty, their crews having died of starvation and exposure. The war was over.

Though the Thericans had been defeated, humanity's future was anything but certain. Prior to the war, the Confederacy counted about 5,011 planets and eight trillion people. By the war's end, that number would be reduced to less than one hundred planets, most of these being small start-up colonies with little to no infrastructure of their own. Of the population, only a handful survived to face the effects of EVE-V, crippling resource shortages, the onset of a technological dark age, and an uncertain future.

1D
EVE-V

EVE-V IS AN ACRONYM for the Estrogen Vector Entropy Virus, a biological weapon developed by the Thericans for use against humanity. EVE-V is the most deadly and resilient plague humanity has ever faced. Its death toll was orders of magnitude higher than all other major plagues in humanity's history combined.

Most academics believe that EVE-V was a direct attack on mankind's ability to procreate. If a man is given a hundred wives, he is likely to father an army of children. But a woman with a hundred husbands is unlikely to see a meaningful difference in her lifetime fertility. This means the most efficient way to exterminate the human population is to kill as many women as possible. Years before they attacked humanity overtly, the Thericans hurtled thousands of probes across the Solar Galaxy. Undetectable by the Confederate sensors of the era, these probes quickly took up orbit around every inhabited planet. There, they began dispensing their deadly payload into the atmosphere.

EVE-V was designed to ensure maximum spread throughout the population. The virus is often described as feeding on estrogen; however, this is a simplified explanation given to laypersons. Estrogen served as a chemical catalyst, supercharging the virus's reproductive rate upon entering the host's body. Early generations of the virus were largely inert. They multiplied rapidly through cell division but did not attack the host directly. This left the infected as contagious carriers, who could and did unknowingly spread the virus to others. But each generation grew more rapidly and became more invasive. By the time the first patients began showing symptoms, nearly everyone who had been infected fell ill at once.

Once EVE-V came out of its dormancy stage, it would begin penetrating the cells of the host's body. After infiltration, EVE-V attacked the host cell's DNA, mutating it into a new EVE-V cell or worse. This led to a cascade of health failures as the subject's body quickly became overwhelmed. The infection and destruction of white blood cells soon gave rise to immunodeficiency and opportunistic infection. Some cells subject to EVE-V attack and DNA corruption would be mutated into causing highly aggressive cancers. Those who survived through these maladies generally perished to massive systemic failure as organs died.

Across the Confederacy, hospitals were flooded as millions and soon billions, all women, fell ill. With outbreaks on every planet, the Confederacy was hard-pressed to respond in force to any of them. The burden to act largely fell on the planetary governments. These efforts would range from qualified successes to abject failures. The most successful containment effort was on Mars. There, Governor Manfred Wagner ordered the mandatory testing of all women and girls for signs of the virus. Those who were found to be uninfected were relocated, by force if necessary, to controlled environments, and eventually quarantine camps. Unknown to the general public, these camps were surplus colony ships. These ships kept constantly on the move to protect their passengers.

It is a sign of the moral decay gripping the Confederacy that Manfred was forced to purchase these ships out of his own fortune. His efforts to seize the ships under his emergency powers were halted in court by the New Horizons Corporation, which refused to surrender them without compensation. Manfred bought the ships outright, and in doing so he saved twenty-one million women and girls from infection.

Most other efforts were met with far less success. As humanity's home world, Earth had been the most heavily targeted for infection. Sweeps conducted by the Earth government failed to find any women or girls who had not contracted the virus. On many other planets, those who were uninfected were left with no choice but to quarantine themselves, as overtaxed government resources failed to provide meaningful assistance. As the outbreak was reaching its apex, the Thericans attacked in force.

Humanity simply had too many crises to face at once. Resources that would have been stretched to the breaking point by either event now had to be divided among both. On many worlds that had imposed some form of effective quarantine, these eventually broke down, leading to little more than delayed infection for the women who had been spared.

EVE-V resisted all attempts at a cure and was frighteningly difficult to eradicate. The virus demonstrated an ability to survive extremes of pressure and temperature that no living thing should have been able to endure. Engineers were forced to build large reactors with pressurized plumbing where water could be heated to many times its boiling point, simply to purify it of EVE-V contamination. For those infected, no treatment proved effective.

The human body is host to trillions of cells, any one of which could serve as a host for the virus. Even when radical and experimental treatments managed to reduce the virus to undetectable levels, it would always rebound. The only treatments to meaningfully affect the virus were themselves fatal if continued long-term. Some promise had been shown in nanotechnology, but this hope soon evaporated as the infrastructure to create nanites was annihilated by Therican bombardment. Nanites, like many other technologies, were becoming extinct as the factories and personnel responsible for creating them were exterminated.

In the end, little could be done for the infected beyond trying to make them comfortable. With the sheer number of sick, even these efforts were unavailable for most. From the onset of symptoms, life expectancy was generally no more than six weeks. In several instances, the Thericans bombarded planets where only men and boys remained, toiling away in the hopes that production of war matériel would provide some small measure of revenge.

But women were not the only victims of EVE-V. Estrogen is hardly unique to humans. Entire ecosystems were thrown into chaos as infected animal populations died. Dogs and house cats would have gone extinct if not for the fact that Manfred Wagner was an animal lover and made room for them in the quarantine camps. Many more animal species were not so fortunate.

The effects of EVE-V on the male population are often glossed over in history. It was incorrectly determined early in the war that men were immune to the virus. As a result, the Confederacy made no effort to prevent men from contaminating each other. The combination of testosterone and low estrogen was enough to retard the virus's growth and prevent the development of symptoms. But it did nothing to stop men from becoming communicable carriers. By the time the Confederacy realized this, it was both too late and irrelevant.

The crippling of the female population had massive implications for the work force and the war effort. Virtually every man and boy were pressed into service by whatever means he might be useful. Whether this was being crammed into warships to go fight, crammed into factories to build matériel, or crammed into hospitals to help tend the sick and wounded. Even if it had made it a priority, though, the Confederacy could not have prevented men from turning each other into carriers.

By the war's end, every woman who contracted EVE-V had died. Young girls who suffered infection did not survive the onset of puberty. The virus destroyed nearly the entire female population. Even with the massive deaths inflicted on men as a result of the conflict, by war's end, men outnumbered women by around 144 to 1. This would have dramatic ramifications in the days and years ahead.

Violence had broken out before the war's end as the dearth of women had led many men to violence in the hopes of claiming one of those who survived. As this risked infecting the survivors, such efforts were dealt with harshly. Death by firing squad became the only, and often swift, punishment for any man accused of kidnapping, rape, or assault in regard to these women. With the war's end, one of the Confederacy's last acts before its dissolution was to place all uninfected women under direct military supervision.

Efforts during the war toward finding a cure had focused heavily on testing the uninfected for any signs of resistance to the virus. While these studies failed to find a cure, they did find that all the uninfected women did have a resistance to the virus, though not an outright immunity. This resistance came from an unexpected place, a legacy left behind by mankind's ancestors. Neanderthal DNA. All the uninfected women carried a specific gene pairing that had been inherited from Neanderthal ancestors. This gene pairing interfered with EVE-V's ability to alter their DNA and to make copies of itself. While short of a true immunity, it delayed the progress of the virus enough that these women's immune systems were able to fight it off. Less than 2 percent of the men of the Confederacy had escaped infection, and they too all bore the specific Neanderthal gene pair. These men were even more resistant to the disease. It had been identified early that testosterone retarded EVE-V's growth. This likely had been an intentional design as a live man was likely to infect more women than a dead one. But in any case for those men with the appropriate gene pair, it left anything short of an intentionally massive dose incapable of infecting them.

The women who had escaped infection long enough to be placed in quarantine were the ones lucky enough to survive. The men who had proven resistant were the only ones who would be fortunate enough to have families in the future. For most of the men who survived, a family would never be possible. They would spend the rest of their days working and fighting to secure resources for the uninfected. All so that something of the human race could survive.

For the women who survived EVE-V, the nightmare was not yet over. These women had become an extremely precious commodity. In the Summit at Olympus, their fate was decided. They would be apportioned among the kings to serve as the mothers of the new population each was expected to grow and cultivate. Some would go on to be treated like queen bees in their new homes, afforded the few remaining luxuries and having their pick of men. Others would become little more than property, doled out by their new liege to men he sought to bring to fealty. Yet others became state assets, subject to reproductive schedules and birth quotas with approved men. In any case, the message to them was clear.

Humanity had been left holding a ticking depopulation bomb. The current population would soon grow old and die. There was no automation left to care for them in their old age, and too few youths lived to replace them. Humanity needed children—as many as possible by whatever means. The very concept of women's rights was destroyed. For the next several generations, a woman was deemed too valuable to be permitted to do anything but raise children. Those who could not produce babies would serve as helpers to those who could. Generations later, women in most of the Empire slowly regained rights equivalent to the men of their home nations, varied though they were. But in some, women's rights of self-determination have never returned.

Yet even this was not the whole of EVE-V's legacy. It would rear its head again six hundred years later in the form of the Scythian Plaque and herald the arrival of the nanosingularity.

1E
THE SUMMIT AT OLYMPUS

Year Zero
Our year (AN)

There was a time that I was blind. I believed that our worst enemy was each other. And then I watched as all I knew and loved was destroyed. I was forced to look little girls in the eye and tell them they had to die because we could not cure them. Forced to watch boys as young as six go and die fighting in a hopeless war. Forced to tell grieving husbands that we were helpless to avenge the deaths of their wives and daughters. I had no choice as our species was murdered. A crime perpetrated by a power whom we knew nothing of, whom we could not possibly have slighted or provoked.

I am naive no more. I am blind no more. I know now that we have worse enemies than each other. I live today only by the grace of those who gave their lives for us all. So I offer this vow.

Never again will I be blind. Never again will I allow humanity to be so weak that it cannot defend itself. Never again will I look a human child in the eye and tell them that they must die. I will defend humanity from all threats, both from within and without. To this end and for all time, I commit my life, my fortune, my destiny, and my progeny.

But I cannot do it alone. You have all seen what I have seen. You have experienced the horror as we were made a sacrifice upon the pyre of evil. Hard times are behind with many more ahead. We must gather now to face them. Let us forge a new destiny for humanity here, so that every life that has ever been lived, was not in vain.

Manfred Wagner, opening address

THOUGH HUMANITY HAD SURVIVED the Therican War, its future was anything but secure. Most of humanity's planets had been destroyed. More than 90 percent of the population of the Confederacy was killed either by the Thericans or by EVE-V. But numbers are inherently relative, and there were still billions of survivors for whom there was now too little infrastructure to meet their basic needs. Mars and the other surviving worlds had been transformed into massive refugee camps, ravaged by hunger and disease. Many of the remaining planets were not self-sufficient before the war, and certainly not capable of supporting the survivors. If drastic action was not taken, the survivors would simply be the last to die.

Manfred Wagner was seen by many as the man who saved humanity. Through Project Safe Seed, he had secured what was by far the largest population of uninfected women. As supreme commander, he had instituted Project Commando, which ultimately brought an end to the war. With Mars as the only surviving major colony, he was in control of the largest and most resourced population that remained. To plot the path forward, Manfred convened a summit of some of the most influential men who still lived. This summit was held in his personal mansion in the shadow of Mars's tallest mountain, Olympus Mons.

All the men summoned to attend were leaders in matters of politics, economics, technology, and resource acquisition. Together they would form the royal dynasties that would shape the future to come.

Christopher Mandrake. For most of the war, Christopher Mandrake had served as the vice president of the Interstellar Confederacy. He was regarded by most as a quiet and well-mannered man but also one of considerable intellect. He did not speak often, but he never failed to find listeners when he did. He would be the Confederacy's last and shortest-serving president when his predecessor, Shinzo Ito, refused to evacuate and was killed in the Battle of Earth.

Jacques Moreau. Moreau was the majority owner of New Horizons Corporation, the largest firm dedicated to planetary colonization prior to the war.

Nicolas de la Nieve. Owner of Miracles Incorporated, a firm that had led the way in many medical sciences, particularly life extension.

Akeno Sato. Both a scientist and an engineer, Sato had owned Micro-Tek, a company that had specialized in computer technologies prior to its destruction with the scourging of the planet Silicon Anima.

Yuan Di. Prior to the war, Yuan had been known as "The Money Man" to the Confederate population. He was the nation's leading mind on financial matters, and he was considered humanity's foremost expert on economics.

Ajeet Khatri. Owner of Dead Metal Inc., a large corporation that had specialized in providing raw materials, be it from strip-mining uninhabited worlds or through salvage of existing assets.

George Smith. Owner of several corporations that had specialized in cultivating food to feed the once massive population.

Richard Alexander. A brigadier general in the Confederate Marine Force. Alexander and Manfred rarely agreed on much, and Alexander was not nearly as outspoken. But like Manfred, General Alexander had long objected to the military's use as little more than a welfare program masquerading as soldiery.

Anton Zhukov. A scientist and engineer, Anton Zhukov was generally regarded as the smartest man alive after the war. He was the Confederacy's leading expert on faster-than-light technologies and their practical applications.

Donald Moore. Prior to the war, Moore was the wealthiest man in the Confederacy, having built many extremely successful corporations. Though the war had largely destroyed his fortune, he remained an expert on personnel management.

Angelo Castelletti. A career doctor, Castelletti had served as the Confederate government's chief adviser to the president on matters of public health. He had also personally overseen efforts to combat EVE-V.

Manfred Wagner himself rounded out the gathering. As governor of Mars, he was effectively the most powerful man alive, and with most of his personal wealth on the planet, he was also the richest.

As Manfred addressed the council, he put to them the premise that for the difficult times ahead, the Confederate form of government was insufficient. There would be many hard choices to make, and they would have to be made both quickly and decisively. One of these choices would be for humanity to take what it needed in order to survive. Thus, he submitted that a new government was necessary, and that since one of that government's first acts would be one of conquest, an empire was only appropriate.

With Earth gone, Manfred proposed that this new imperial government be known as the Solar Empire. All of those gathered at the summit would become kings in the new empire. They would take charge of leading the population, growing them into a new civilization, and reap the rewards for their efforts. But Manfred was fully aware that many on the council had vastly different views from his on how to run a society. He also proposed the concept that came to be known as sovereign dominion. So long as he met his obligations to the larger empire, each king would be free to govern his territory as he saw fit.

Initially the other members of the summit were less than enthusiastic about his idea. Most favored trying to reform the Confederacy. But the urgency of the problems facing them, and the promise of sovereign dominion was enough to sway the leaders to Manfred's position. But a new argument arose over who should be the emperor for this new empire.

Roughly half of the council favored Manfred. He had proven his leadership through the war and was regarded as a hero by most of the surviving population. But others staunchly opposed the idea. Sovereign dominion or not, they opposed placing someone of Manfred's politics in charge. Manfred surprised them both when he refused to stand for the office.

To the council, Manfred said that his deep ties to the military were sure to result in the creation of little more than a military dictatorship. But without Manfred, the council could not agree who would be a better candidate, so Manfred himself put forward the nomination of Christopher Mandrake.

Christopher was an intellectual man capable of understanding the challenges ahead. He had the strength of conviction to push humanity through the hard decisions but the strength of character to restrain it when necessary.

Why Manfred gave up a position of such power and prestige is unknown; it is almost a certainty that he could have forced the issue in his favor. Scholars have long debated the matter with some taking his reasons at face value. Others believe he wanted to more narrowly focus his efforts, building his "perfect" society without having to worry about the rest of humanity. Whatever his reasons, his refusal to assume the office meant that his nomination stood.

Christopher Mandrake rose to become Emperor Christopher I, and the founder of the Mandrake Dynasty. But some of Manfred's supporters were not completely sold on the idea. While they respected Christopher, many felt he lacked the charisma and personal magnetism necessary to hold the office. They pushed for the creation of a higher order of king. If the emperor proved too weak, the Empire would have a high king instead. In the end, Christopher, with the help of the rest, proved himself. The Mandrakes have held the office of emperor ever since.

After the summit, Manfred Wagner took on a new name. Though Swiss by heritage, he had been born in the Neo-Rhine region of Mars. Thus, he took on the name Manfred von Rhinegrave. His dynasty and his title of high king live on to this day in the Reichsylvannian Dominion. Together the Mandrakes and the Rhinegraves did more than any other to build the Empire into what it would become. They remain the only dynasties founded at the summit that would continue into the modern Empire.

1F
THE LONG MORNING

0 AN–1,000 AN

THE COMBINATION OF EVE-V and the Therican War would bring about a new dark age for humanity. Entire industries had been eradicated, the equipment and the people destroyed by the war. Entire disciplines of science and engineering were lost as few to none survived with the applicable knowledge. The planet of Silicon Anima had effectively monopolized the development of AI, and its destruction left only the simplest replacements available. The planet Titan had nearly monopolized the sciences of genetic engineering, also lost. Earth had long remained the leading producer of massless impulse drives, also lost. Across the board, technology fell, but perhaps no loss was more devastating than that of the Teller-type thermal converter.

The invention of the Teller-type thermoelectric converter had revolutionized the energy industry by drastically simplifying the process of generating electrical power. While not the first system designed to use the thermoelectric effect, none that predated were nearly so capable.

Prior to the Teller-converter's invention, most forms of electrical generation came down to inventive ways of boiling large quantities of water to spin turbines. But the converter allowed the direct conversion of kinetic energy in the form of heat to electricity. No spinning magnets, no huge turbines, and no massive quantities of water. While the technology to produce the thermal converter had not itself been lost, the means to miniaturize the technology had been all but obliterated. The surviving factories of Mars had specialized in huge, high-demand units for applications like starships and cities. The planet had imported smaller converters from Earth. The loss of many planets that had provided components had greatly limited the ability of Mars to mass-produce those converters it still had means to manufacture.

The loss of small thermal converters impacted hundreds of technologies ranging from consumer goods to weapons. A small device like a smartphone with a thermal converter could actively recharge its batteries by using the owner's body heat to generate electricity, or by being set in a sunny window. The cybernetic implants of the day had similarly been designed to tap the host's heat for power and recharge their batteries. Even many personal vehicles were built around thermal converters, burning hydrogen to power electric motors. Thermal converters, which by virtue of their operation cooled their local environment, had also obsoleted many refrigeration technologies. It is not a stretch to say that nearly every piece of technology reliant on electricity had to be modified or redesigned to account for the converters' loss.

The invasions of the M'gah and the Elrua did not help. The Teller-converter was a human invention, which neither species had managed to duplicate. Both relied on more primitive means. Power by any means necessary soon became the mantra. It was here that the invasion of other species had proved useful. Among humanity the thermal converter had so effectively obsoleted other means of power generation that other technologies had been largely abandoned and forgotten. Humanity would reverse-engineer the power systems of the M'gah. Human homes and even cities were soon relying on any means of generation they could, be it nuclear, solar, hydroelectric, or even the burning of hydrocarbon fuels.

The thermal converter was far from the only loss. The field of medicine suffered many extreme setbacks. In the Confederacy's final days, human lifespans had grown to a median expectancy of three hundred years. In the years after the war, this would shrink to as low as fifty for the general population. Weapons technologies were subject to numerous setbacks, with ballistic weapons returning to vogue among infantry and armored vehicles.

Most scholars place the end of the Long Morning as the year 1,000 with the invention of the transpatial drive. But a more accurate presentation of the history would put this date sooner in 600 AN. This time corresponds to the nanosingularity, and shortly thereafter the rediscovery of how to miniaturize the thermal converter. But for the six hundred years prior, much of the Empire's technological efforts had been to prevent a fast descent into darkness, and Confederate-era artifacts had been priceless treasures.

1G
THE FIRST CONQUEST WAR

11 AN–57 AN

THE FIRST CONQUEST WAR was fought between the newly-formed Solar Empire and the M'gah Estate between the years 11 and 57. The devastation of the Therican War left humanity with many critical shortages. Both the M'gah and the Elrua had similar needs to humans in terms of atmosphere composition, gravity, and temperature. The M'gah had chemical needs similar enough to humans that it made their food at least edible. Through all its troubles, the one resource humanity had a lot of was men capable of fighting. This led Manfred von Rhinegrave to press for war against the M'gah.

Emperor Christopher Mandrake and other leaders were initially opposed. This led the new emperor to make several increasingly desperate pleas to the M'gah for help. But even when requesting nothing more than food for starving people, the Empire was refused. The M'gah seemed content to let humanity go extinct and lay claim to its few remaining worlds. The Elrua were no more helpful. Their food was inedible, but their planets were otherwise somewhat livable. The Elrua, however, refused to admit any refugees that might "damage their spiritual purity." After several years and with food shortages taking a toll, Emperor Christopher relented and gave Manfred von Rhinegrave the go-ahead for war.

Even more so than his contributions in the Therican War, the First Conquest War secured Manfred's reputation as the greatest general in human history. This may or may not be conclusively true, and such things are difficult to measure objectively. But no general before or since has accomplished so much while facing so many handicaps. Most of the Empire's leadership saw the best-case scenario as forcing the M'gah to provide aid simply to make human raids stop. Others felt that Manfred's war was little more than a chance for humanity to go down fighting.

Warships had become largely irreplaceable assets. While Mars had been the location where most were built, in truth they were assembled there with parts made on other planets, primarily Earth. The industry no longer existed to manufacture many of the critical components. The technology for producing AI had mostly concentrated on the now-destroyed world of Silicon Anima. For a time, the lives of AIs were considerably more valuable than most of the troops they fought alongside. A lost AI simply could not be replaced. Even in terms of weaponry, humanity faced a large handicap. Confederate marines had relied on binary plasma weapons. Imperial troops were forced to fall back on chemically-propelled ballistic weapons.

The M'gah had no such limitations. They had spent the Therican War building up their own military in case they were the next target. Their industry was operating at capacity. Their war-oriented technology had not been as sophisticated as the Confederacy's but was now well ahead of what the Empire was capable of producing. As the war dragged on, humanity would grow weaker while the industry of the M'gah made them stronger. Victory seemed out of reach to most.

Once again named supreme commander for humanity as lord-marshal, Manfred confronted these challenges in a number of ways. One way was to place an enormous emphasis on training soldiers of all stripes to utilize captured tools and technology. This is espoused in a famous quote:

> If you have no gun, pick up a knife or even a rock, and sneak up on the enemy. Now you have a gun.

Humanity opened the conflict with the M'gah by attacking the planet of Gishal, which the Empire would later rename Starfall. A student of military history, Manfred drew inspiration for his operation from the Japanese attack on Pearl Harbor and the British raid on Taranto in the Second World War. Fleet combat at the time was very different from the modern Empire. Fighting at FTL was effectively impossible as there were no FTL weapons to speak of, nor sensor systems capable of efficiently guiding them had they existed. Warships were tiny in comparison, often made of relatively lightweight materials. Both the Confederacy, also the early Empire, and the M'gah designed their warships to readily enter the atmosphere and come to rest in a planet's oceans. This obviated the need for preparing large landing fields and allowed the ships to readily use electrolytic systems to draw hydrogen from ocean water for use in producing fuel.

Gishal had served as a staging ground for the M'gah. They had positioned a large portion of their fleet there to await a possible Therican attack. With war's end, they had stood down from their state of readiness. None among the M'gah's leadership took the prospect of an attack from humanity seriously. The large concentration of military force was unprepared to respond to a sudden attack.

When Manfred's fleet arrived at Gishal, his ships came out of warp towing asteroids, which were then hurtled into the planet's oceans. The impacts devastated the floating ships, either through direct hits or the ensuing tidal waves. The few that managed to get into space were too few to save the planet. In less than an hour, the new Solar Armadas had struck a devastating blow, and the first campaign by the Solar Legionnaires began soon after.

While the assault on Gishal did not cripple the M'gah fleet, it did destroy the only force capable of timely intervention in the region. It would take the M'gah months to bring in a new force from across their empire. Manfred used this time to land legionnaires on more than a hundred worlds and secure a foothold in M'gah territory.

The ground war was a very different situation. The combination of the Therican War and Manfred's reforms to the military had turned the new Solar Armed Forces into the most disciplined military in the galaxy. But the M'gah were quite capable in their own right and had a massive advantage in matériel. There really is no other way to frame it, save to say that humanity simply outfought the M'gah. The Solar Legionnaires won several major conflicts when outnumbered, out-teched, and out-resourced. For the humans, there were only two options: press the attack and maybe die or go home and wait to die of famine.

The war against the M'gah lasted for about forty-seven years as Manfred and his forces systematically carved up and conquered the nation. If the M'gah had a glaring weakness that contributed to their downfall, it was their lack of competency in guerrilla warfare. The M'gah had not fought a war among themselves since reaching space and had little experience in asymmetric conflicts. While resistance cells often formed, they rarely proved anything more than an irritant to occupying forces. This allowed the Empire to garrison captured worlds with relatively few troops and continue to press the attack in force. The military expertly followed Manfred's directive to employ any captured equipment.

By the time of the Battle of Comal, the M'gah home world, Manfred's fleet had more captured M'gah ships than his own. The Solar Legionnaires were using more captured tanks and other armored vehicles than domestic and fed entirely on food plundered from M'gah worlds. The Battle of Comal was the last major battle of the war. As he had many times before, Manfred won the battle with the use of deception.

Humanity had captured so many M'gah assets that it was now well aware of the latter's capabilities, including the range of their sensor systems. Imperial intelligence had learned that the M'gah had recently begun producing newly upgraded sensors, and they learned what their effective range was. Once again, Manfred made use of asteroids, but this time as decoys. He ordered his ships to tow large numbers of asteroids toward Comal before stopping on the very edge of the M'gah's new detection range. The M'gah, unaware of the Imperials' new information, thought the faint contacts were Manfred's forces massing for the attack, unaware that they were visible. The deception was aided by the installation of communication repeaters on the asteroids to broadcast fake messages.

The trick worked better than Manfred had hoped. Rather than position their fleet to meet the incoming attack, the M'gah saw an opportunity to lay a trap of their own. They quickly dispersed their ships away from the home world, ready to surround and trap Manfred's "fleet." By the time M'gah scout ships identified the ruse, Manfred's real fleet was on approach. Having dispersed to carry out their plan, the M'gah were too spread out in the wrong places to meet the sudden thrust of the Armadas.

The M'gah army had been gutted already in prior battles. Desperate to prevent Imperial troops from landing, the M'gah fleet raced back to their home world. But this panicked approach resulted in their ships arriving in small waves, easily eliminated by the Armadas's concentrated forces. Most of the invasion force arrived intact, and the planet was pacified in less than a year. The remainder of the war became little more than a formality as the few worlds that did not join Comal's surrender were taken and resistance cells were destroyed.

Perhaps the most interesting part of the war was not in the battles but in the events that came after. These events and the players involved would shape the very identity of the Empire for future generations. It would also see the end of a royal dynasty before it could truly begin.

The Therican War and the events afterward had left much of humanity with a hatred for all things alien. To keep the hatred in check proved a difficult challenge for much of the Empire's early leadership. Nowhere was this clearer than with King George Smith. Smith had been the Confederacy's leading expert on all matters related to farming and the mass distribution of food. So quite naturally he was given jurisdiction over a large portion of M'gah territory. His mandate from the Imperial Court was simple. People were starving. Feed them.

But the court had not fully realized the implications of such a broad directive. King George rapidly set about constructing massive work camps on M'gah worlds. These camps were soon producing food, clothing, and medicine at a blistering pace. But word reached the Imperial Court of the deplorable conditions in these camps. Worse were stories that King George was actively enslaving the M'gah, selling young members of the species to powerful persons as domestic servants. Displeased with this development, Emperor Christopher sent a message to King George that this was to stop. Though George acknowledged the message, it soon became apparent that he had not heeded it. Thus, the emperor sent High King Manfred to personally deal with the situation.

At Manfred's direction, the young M'gah sold into slavery were soon returned to their families. Manfred further ordered that all M'gah impressed into service in the work camps be paid for their labor, involuntary though it might have been. But no sooner had Manfred left, than King George went back to his old policies. This time he was even more heavy-handed, actively forming death squads to confiscate the monies that had been paid and terminate any among the aliens who dared to complain about their conditions.

When news of George's actions reached Emperor Christopher, he was irate. The emperor ordered that King George be arrested for his defiance to the throne, but the emperor never got the chance to bring George to trial. Word had already reached Manfred of what had transpired. The high king returned to Comal to meet with King George personally. Their conversation lasted for about five minutes. It began with King George claiming that sovereign dominion gave him the right to run the occupation as he pleased. It ended with Manfred shooting King George in the face on the bridge of his own flagship.

Manfred's execution of King George caused a degree of discord among the other kings. When called to account for his actions, Manfred maintained that he was justified in doing so. King George had been given jurisdiction over the area but had not officially been granted those territories as part of his dominion. Therefore, sovereign dominion did not apply, and George's actions had been no less than defiance to the will of the throne. The other kings did not like this answer but chose to accept it.

In his personal memoirs, Manfred would later recount that George's execution had been about sending a message to the other kings. The wars of conquest were not about raping and pillaging the galaxy for personal enrichment, but to ensure humanity's survival and future prosperity. Both Manfred and Christopher had a dream for the Empire. That one day when the troubles of their time were past, it could become a beacon of order and prosperity in the universe. That human and alien could one day join in this future. But for that to happen, it was necessary that those aliens integrated by force understand that it was a matter of necessity, not malice. Such an understanding might never be achieved if the conquered aliens were enslaved, degraded, and abused.

In any case the message was received, and the kings took as gentle a hand as was reasonably possible in administering conquered territories. M'gah movements to break free of the Empire would eventually die down over time. In later generations, they would take advantage of Emperor John II's reforms to live in isolation but would remain a part of the Empire itself. Though much of the history of the Conquest Wars has been rewritten over the years, Manfred von Rhinegrave maintains a sort of folk hero status among the M'gah. There he is held up as a lesson that desperate times may push a person to desperate measures. But in the end, one still has the choice to act for the greater good or for ill. From Manfred's memoirs on the subject came what has long since become the motto of the Empire itself.

In order, prosperity.

1H
THE SECOND CONQUEST WAR

64 AN–100 AN

AFTER ITS SUCCESSFUL CONQUEST of the M'gah nation, the Solar Empire began to set its sights on securing complete control of its home galaxy. The only major power remaining was the Elrua. The Empire was aware of other intelligent species that were years or even generations away from any prospect of space travel. It had been the policy of the Interstellar Confederacy to ignore these primitive societies, but the Empire's ambition was to unite the whole galaxy under a single rule.

The Second Conquest War was not so much a single conflict but one large and many smaller fought in conjunction with one another. The Elrua Estate occupied a large portion of the home galaxy's Cygnus arm. With the limited FTL systems of the day, it would be an extremely distant conquest. Those dispatched to subdue the Elrua would have only what they took with them. The supply lines were simply too long and slow to be counted on.

By this time, control of the Empire was passing to the first generation to be born beneath its flag. John Mandrake I now held the throne as emperor. Opposite him Wolfgang von Rhinegrave, high king and lord-marshal of the Solar Armed Forces. The decision to conquer the rest of the galaxy began as a bit of a contentious one. Emperor John I was no pacifist, but the bulk of his time and energy was directed toward consolidating the Empire's new holdings. High King Wolfgang was more aggressive, intent on pushing to expand the Empire's reach. Eventually it was the other kings, intent on expanding their territory, who forced the emperor's hand. If the Empire did not conquer, the kings were prepared to do so on their own.

The Imperial fleet led by High King Wolfgang arrived in the Elrua Estate on Day 211 of the year 121. The war against the Elrua had few major battles, and almost as soon as the Empire arrived, the outcome was clear. The Elrua were a deeply pacifist and spiritual people. They had little history of conflict among themselves prior to space travel, and none afterward. Their weapons were primitive in comparison to the rest of their society. High King Wolfgang would describe their tactics by saying:

The Elrua fight like an army of teenage girls. They shriek and scream loudly but throw few punches. At most they slap at you and immediately retreat whenever one falls. Their leadership is paralyzed by indecision, too concerned with acknowledging every point of view. Their weapons are so poor that I would not insult my ass by using them to wipe it. Their ineptitude has stolen the thrill of victory and replaced it only with the relief that comes with completing an obligation.

The sheer size of the Elrua's empire meant that it took several years to fully conquer. Many among the Elrua took the Imperial invasion as divine punishment. All in all, the war was one of the least bloody in history given relative numbers. The Imperial military so easily outmaneuvered and outfought the Elrua that casualties were few. Entire Elrua armies were captured as Imperial forces trapped and isolated them. The majority of the Elrua submitted to Imperial control after a handful of crushing defeats.

The conquests of the more primitive species throughout the galaxy were rarely more eventful. Most species and their territory were simply annexed into the Empire. Some of the more primitive species openly welcomed the humans as gods. Others held enough of a command of science to understand that humanity was simply too far beyond them for resistance to be naught but futile. Only a handful resisted and were generally cowed by Imperial displays of power.

Not every species had to be conquered or annexed. On a planet now called Rollin, the Empire encountered a species of insect-like aliens. Rollin itself was woefully unsuitable for human colonization. The planet's gravity was more than double what it had been on Earth. Temperatures shifted by day and night to deadly extremes. The atmosphere was filled with plenty of oxygen and with a cocktail of other chemicals that would poison any human dumb enough to breathe it.

While Rollin was not a place to live, the planet was exceptionally rich in relatively rare metals. Rollin housed enormous reserves of gold, palladium, iridium, chromium, uranium, and titanium. A treasure chest floating in space at a time before alchemic printing had been perfected. The roliams, as they came to be known, were approximately bronze-age people. Despite their primitive society, they had no delusions about the humans who landed on their planet. They quickly figured out exactly what the strange creatures in sealed armor were: visitors from a place far away.

Very soon what would emerge was one of the most successful interspecies relationships in history. The roliams made no effort to resist the humans who landed, and immediately retreated from any show of force. Soon they began to bring offerings. When food was rejected, they brought metals instead. As soon as they gained a handle on human language, the roliams requested a meeting between leaders.

Roliams breed in truly astounding numbers and had already reached a threshold where their planet simply could not support a larger population. The roliams had no means with which to go to other worlds, but the humans did. Roliams evolved from ancestors who lived in hives, and while their social structure was much more complex, many similarities remained. Roliams do not work for wages or personal gain; a roliam exists to better the hive. Roliams do not have much in the way of personal ambition. An individual is but one unit of a highly renewable resource. The humans quickly saw the value in the offer the roliams made. If they would be taken to the stars, the roliams would make themselves useful to the "human hive."

The roliams became the first species to voluntarily join the Empire. For many, it was a match made in heaven. The roliams could exist in the same environments as humans but could also live in those far more toxic. There was no need to compete over territory. Though it was difficult for roliams to learn new skills after their first year of life, their ability to learn during that first year was prolific. This made them simple to train for low- to mid-skill labor. Roliam workers did not demand wages, vacation, or special accommodations They lacked human ego, never seeing a job as beneath them or trivial if it was necessary. All roliam workers required were food and a place to sleep. With AI research set back hundreds of years by the Therican War, they were a perfect match to address the shortfalls left by the loss of automation.

The relationship between the two species was purely exploitative. The humans exploited the roliams' willingness to work without strange things like payment. The roliams exploited the humans' ability to take their population to new worlds. But it was a relationship that worked very well for both parties. The roliams swore fealty to the Mandrake Dynasty and were welcomed into the Empire. Today they are the most reproductively successful species in the known universe. The labor provided by the roliams catapulted an industrial, and with it, scientific revolution that would eventually propel the Empire out of the Long Morning.

An often-overlooked aspect of the roliams was the change they brought to humanity. The Therican War and events after had left most humans with a deep mistrust, if not outright hatred of aliens. Though some found it difficult at first, the presence of the roliams was perhaps the greatest factor in changing this attitude. Roliams soon became ubiquitous in society, doing everything from mining ore to caring for the elderly. As a species that worked tirelessly for the greater good of society, they soon carved a niche for themselves. In the process, they gave humanity a leg up on life's difficulties that had not been experienced since the golden age of the Confederacy so long ago.

Even into the modern Empire, the roliams remain one of its most visible species. They are one of the few that did not take the offer to live in isolation, and remain a part of the greater Imperial community into modernity. Though the return of automation would eventually obsolete them from many forms of mundane labor, they remain ever present in the workforce. Roliams specialize as youth in fields of science and technology, ready to assist those with greater longevity and longer learning spans. In many nations, they remain almost inseparable from industry, with many a scientist, engineer, and manager having a staff composed at least partially of roliams.

1I
THE SCYTHIAN PLAQUE, AND THE NANOSINGULARITY

600 AN

BY THE YEAR 600, the Empire was in a steady state of growth. Technologically, it remained a heavily anachronistic mix as many industries were still rebuilding to their former status. Great emphasis had been placed on terraforming technology. In the year 550, terraforming had recovered enough that the Empire looked to begin resettling many of the worlds that had been lost in the Therican War. One of these planets was Scythia.

Scythia was a barren, rocky planet but was host to a massive supply of fresh water in vast subterranean lakes and rivers. Prior to the Therican War, the Confederacy had begun the process of terraforming this planet. One of the steps had been exposing the buried water to the surface and introducing aquatic life to create the foundation of a new ecosystem. But the war abruptly brought these efforts to an end as the resources were needed elsewhere.

Unknown to the Empire, Scythia had been contaminated with EVE-V. Refugees fleeing the destruction of the planet Titan had crashed on this world. Though the survivors of the crash eventually died, they had brought the plague with them. EVE-V found new hosts in the form of a trout that had been introduced to the planet's water. The virus found these fish difficult hosts, and to survive, it had mutated into a new strain. The fish became carriers and kept the virus like a waiting trap.

The Empire had foreseen the possibility of encountering EVE-V in the reclamation efforts and had generated a number of contingency plans. These plans were immediately put into action when EVE-V was detected in the planet's fish population. The Solar Armadas moved in, and Scythia was quarantined. But the quarantine did not hold.

While examining the contaminated fish, a laboratory accident led to several members of the terraforming expedition being exposed to the new mutant strain of the virus. Unfortunately this included a woman named Maiere Childers, daughter of Franco Childers, one of the wealthiest private citizens in the Empire. Terrified of losing his daughter and unable to secure her removal from the planet, Franco Childers went rogue. He hired a team of mercenaries to run the Imperial quarantine and rescue his daughter.

The mercenaries were successful and managed to take Maiere off the planet over her own protests. They were unaware that the first-aid scanners they used to check her for EVE-V were defective. She had been infected by the new virus, and now the mercenaries had been as well. By the time the Empire realized what had happened, these mercenaries had disappeared.

On Day 3 of the year 600, hospitals across the Empire became flooded with sick patients. But this new strain of EVE-V was very different from its ancestor. The new virus did not rely on estrogen to catalyze its reproduction and was not hampered by the presence of testosterone. It did not discriminate between genders, readily pushing men to symptoms just as quickly as women. It was also boasted a *far* shorter dormancy stage in the bodies of human patients. It was soon renamed for its telltale signs. The buildup of plaque on the organs and in the blood vessels of the infected, made up from masses of dead cells, became the virus's unmistakable calling card.

It is unclear how the virus managed to spread so rapidly across the Empire. This was a time before the astranet of the modern age. Interstellar travel was still a very difficult and expensive affair for private citizens. It seemed impossible that the mercenaries could have visited so many worlds in such a short time. But regardless of how it happened, the virus soon began showing up wherever humans resided.

The science of nanotechnology had been almost completely destroyed in the Therican War. Nearly all practical production had been located on Earth, and on Silicon Anima. By the year 600, nanotechnology was beginning to make a return but was in its infancy. It was in no position to provide a medical solution to the problem of the Plaque. This changed when the leaders of the companies developing the technology were approached by members of the Solar Commando Corps.

The Corps gave the corporations design schematics not only for a new generation of nanites but their programming language and specs for the tools to make them. When questioned about the origin of this technology, the commandos answered that it was alien in origin. Further questions would lead to the replacement of the questioner with someone less inquisitive.

Those who had been given the specs for these new nanites quickly realized they were far more than a cure for disease—that humanity itself would be changed by their use. But the moral and ethical questions were forced to yield to necessity. There was a crisis ongoing, and without the nanites billions were going to die. Production began, and those infected with the Scythian Plaque were the first to make the transition from homo sapiens to homo solaris.

Much like the virus they destroyed, the nanites would enter the cells of the body and take up residence before replicating themselves. The nanites could then easily destroy any viral cell attempting to gain access to host cells. But they were capable of far more.

The nanites had memory, capacity, processing power, and capability to spare. It quickly became apparent that they could be retasked with little more than an update in programming and could reconfigure themselves to thousands of new uses. They could even replace themselves with more specialized versions to meet the needs set out for them. In short order, the Scythian Plaque was defeated. When the benefits of these nanites became apparent, many flocked to adopt them. This would be a permanent change. The nanites took up residence in all the body's cells. Even sperm and egg cells. Those born from "nanized" parents would start with their benefit from the moment of conception. In less than two generations, the nanites had spread to the entire population.

The effects of cellular nanites were almost countless. They did not simply stop the Plaque, they were practically panacea. They could identify any virus or bacterium in the body and destroy it. They could repair DNA damage resulting from exposure to ionizing radiation, correct errors in the genetic code, and more. The nanites were so effective at caring for the host body, that medical science soon underwent a dramatic shift to be based around helping the machines perform their medical functions.

In addition to wiping out nearly all forms of sickness, the nanites had a way of standardizing the human template. Prior to their introduction, one's planet of origin could make an enormous difference. Those who grew up on high-gravity worlds were often shorter than those who did not. Those raised on low-gravity worlds were often taller but with weaker bones and many other limitations that made a transition to other environments difficult. The nanites intervened in these situations, helping gravity-children grow to normal heights or reinforcing the bone structure of those from low-grav worlds. Their presence in embryonic development spelled the end of most birth defects.

The nanites' effects on society were equally numerous. Their presence in the body caused the human lifespan to explode. The primary limiter on human life-expectancy came to be tied to the eventual breakdown between the brain and the nanites it hosted, a process that took thousands of years. They brought with them new intellectual capabilities, such as the power to index one's memories, so people could remember all events of their life. They also brought a slight change in dietary habits, as Solars now needed to ingest material to provide the nanites with fuel and resources for replenishment. But in the end, it was perhaps the most transformative change humanity has ever experienced.

As the technologies, programming language, and other elements of the technology improved, it would significantly narrow the gap in abilities between man and machine. Soldiers, athletes, and gamers would soon be able to boast reaction times exponentially faster than any who had come before them. Scientists would be able to conduct research by directly integrating into the computers with which they worked. Artists were able to expand their minds in new directions, and audiences could perceive new things such as paintings including colors in UV light. After the nanosingularity, humanity had truly entered a new frontier of existence.

1J
THE WAR OF KINGS

1,219 AN–1,317 AN

THE LONG MORNING OF the Empire came to its end with the invention of the transpatial drive. This new drive system was a step beyond anything that had been developed by the Interstellar Confederacy. The drive's development heralded an age where mankind was no longer restoring but progressing. But this development would also open the door to a conflict that would test the unity of the early Empire.

By the year 1,000, the Empire's royal families had become quite powerful. They each ruled large swaths of the Solar Galaxy, granting them vast territories from which to draw people and matériel. The transpatial drive did not simply hasten the process of traveling across the galaxy, it made travel to other galaxies a practical venture. Almost as soon as the first scientific expedition returned from the neighboring Andromeda Galaxy, the race was on among the royal families to claim a piece of the new pie.

One would think that an entire galaxy would mean there was plenty for everyone. But the royal families did not see it this way. To them, Andromeda was the future, and whoever claimed the largest part would be the author of that future. The race was on, and it did not remain peaceful for long. A reality of the times was that the royal dynasties had grown too powerful for the throne to rein in.

All transpatial drives operate by locking in on distant warps in space-time, generally a massive object's gravity. For the primitive drives of the era, only the supermassive black holes at the center of most galaxies were suitable navigation points for intergalactic travel. Thus, the galactic core of Andromeda became the doorway through which the Empire flowed into this new galaxy.

As they had in the Solar Galaxy, the Rhinegrave family was given the task of integrating the alien powers of the region into the Empire. Prior to their campaign in the Solar Galaxy, the Thericans had purged Andromeda of its most advanced species. In the interim millennia, a handful of new species had risen to take to the stars, but these species were no match for the expansionist Empire that flowed into their galaxy. Most of these species were simply annexed, knowing they did not have the strength to resist. Others resisted and were defeated, sometimes with contemptible ease.

While the Rhinegraves were conquering the aliens, the other families began sending their own expeditions through to claim territory. The early conflicts between the houses began with subterfuge. Unmanned cargo ships would go missing or meet with mysterious accidents. Ships carrying crops to be sown on new worlds would arrive to find that their cargo had been poisoned. This quickly became an escalating cycle of retaliation. The families began deploying their private armies to the region to protect their interests. Only the Moore family, who would eventually create the Orion Estate, would stay out of Andromeda completely.

As accusations flew and tensions rose in the Solar Galaxy, the emperor spread his forces throughout the realm to maintain order. But the Empire of the time simply did not have sufficient resources to do the same in Andromeda. The presence of the Empire exacerbated tensions in Andromeda. With Imperial ships around to prevent any local fighting, the kings were free to send more resources to the neighboring galaxy. Legends maintain that Emperor Michael I sat down with the families and told them that if they wished to fight, they could do so, so long as the fighting remained in Andromeda. While this story is generally held to be no more than a myth, the families soon realized that if the bloodshed stayed on the frontier, the throne would not interfere.

It was the Sato Dynasty that was the most directly responsible for the transition from clandestine campaigns to open warfare. Long considered a cursed family, the Satos had suffered numerous and serious setbacks over the years. Most of these setbacks came through no fault of the family. At the time of the Andromeda expansion, they were the weakest of the families, barely clinging to power. For the Satos, securing a piece of Andromeda was their last, best hope to secure a future for themselves and their people. The family committed nearly all its resources to Andromeda, hoping that they would go largely unnoticed by more powerful players. But they were not so fortunate. Many of the larger families had already concluded that it would be best to knock out the bit players before contending with each other.

The Satos saw numerous acts of sabotage, most of them perpetrated by the Alexander family. Growing desperate, the Satos planned an act of mass sabotage to be pinned on the Moreau family. It was at that point that everything went wrong. Agents of the Satos family planted explosive devices on a number of Alexander colony ships. These devices destroyed the ships, along with their colonists. When the Alexanders examined the wreckage, faulty analysis failed to implicate the Moreaus and implicated the Yuans instead. Demanding to see the evidence, the Yuans' even more faulty analysis concluded that it had been the de la Nieves attempting to frame the Moreaus.

Believing the Yuans with whom they had long been allied, the Moreaus launched an attack on the de la Nieve family's assets in Andromeda. The Nieves were soon joined by their own allies in defending their territory. Battle lines formed as the families began to ally with each other, each determined to kick out the opposition to carve up Andromeda for themselves.

The first alliance to form was the Coalition for Future Prosperity (CFP), which would see the union of the Alexander, Moreau, and Yuan families. The second to form was the Andromeda Accord between the de la Nieve and Zhukov families. The final alliance was between the smaller Sato, Castelletti, and Khatri families.

Though the situation between these families eventually became outright warfare, a few rules were observed for the conflict. To avoid forcing the throne into the dispute, the Solar Galaxy was deemed neutral ground. So too was the galactic core of Andromeda, which was under the direct purview of the Rhinegraves. Any interference in the Rhinegrave mission to integrate the native species was sure to force both the Rhinegraves and Mandrakes to come down hard on the infighting families.

Transpatial gateways were soon built at the center of both galaxies, and a strange form of ritual began. Ships heading to Andromeda found themselves under escort by the Solar Armadas. On the opposite end, they would be escorted out of Andromeda's galactic core by the Rhinegraves.

While alliances had formed between the families, these were nothing more than alliances of convenience. The level of backstabbing that went on between them can only be farcical in retrospect. Eventually this led to the Khatri family abandoning both the Iron Alliance and its campaign in Andromeda. This would also see the splitting of the CFP after the Battle of AG-HP-10,016. In that battle, the Yuan family suffered heavy losses to the Andromeda Accord. Losses it would not have sustained had its allies not been intentionally holding off on bringing reinforcements.

It has been said by some that the true winner of the War of Kings was the Rhinegrave family. By this point in the Empire's history, the Rhinegraves already dominated the arms market and had become a powerful banking empire. Though it did not involve itself directly in the conflict, the family happily sold arms and extended credit to all parties involved. The Sato family, who had kickstarted the conflict, eventually accumulated exponentially more debt than they could repay. This resulted in the head of the dynasty, Iso Sato, offering his daughters to the Rhinegraves in marriage. Many historians believe that this was a calculated move, and that having seen the writing on the wall, the Satos chose to merge with the Rhinegraves before their family could be destroyed by the conflict.

Other dynasties were less fortunate. By the time that they withdrew from the Iron Alliance, the Khatri family had already bankrupted the economy of their home territories. This led to a minor revolt at home, which eventually grew into a full-fledged rebellion. It would end with the Khatris joining the Lost Dynasties when the ruling family was dragged from their palace and murdered in the street by an angry mob. The throne responded by occupying their territory with Imperial troops, and the Khatri's assets were later divided.

The Zhukov family was the next to fall. After several crushing defeats to the CFP, the Zhukovs withdrew from Andromeda completely. But by this point, like the Satos, they had incurred so much debt to the Rhinegraves that their entire nation became insolvent. The family was forced to sell more of its territory and assets until becoming a shadow of its former self. It soon chose to merge with the Rhinegraves when it became clear that they would never be able to regain the status they had lost.

The de la Nieve family would survive the conflict, but only barely. While it had wisely chosen to avoid incurring massive debt, this left it unable to continue financing its campaign. The family was eventually bought out of their Andromeda claims by the Alexanders, and returned to the Solar Galaxy.

Many have speculated that the throne intentionally allowed the war to happen so that the families would bloody each other enough for the Empire to once more rein them in. Whether by design or not, this is eventually what happened. After ninety-eight years of continuous fighting, the order finally came down from the throne to the Rhinegraves. They were to cease all flow of arms and monies to the belligerent parties. This alone did not end the conflict. Both the Moreau and Yuan families had managed to transplant a significant industrial base to Andromeda. Eventually, the Rhinegraves were forced to move in and bring an end to the fighting with the threat of their fleets.

After the war and with the families too weakened to protest, Emperor Michael I imposed what became known as the Great Reformation. The families that had claimed the largest shares of Andromeda were given a choice. They could relocate to Andromeda completely on an Imperial timetable and cede their holdings in the Solar Galaxy, or they could retain their holdings in the old galaxy while seeing their territory in Andromeda split. The Moreau, Alexander, and Yuan families would all opt for the former option. Over the following years, they would gradually relocate to Andromeda and form the pillar nations of the Elysian Commonwealth, Republic of Andromeda, and Yuangi respectively. Following this, the territory of all families was set, and they would no longer be permitted to expand beyond their newfound borders.

This would lead to the rise of the sovereign duchies, as the Empire would continue to expand and new families were appointed to rule smaller territories. By breaking the Empire up into numerous smaller powers, it was hoped that a repeat of the War of Kings would be avoided in the future.

The territories left behind by the transplanted families were themselves broken up into new duchies. Though the de la Nieve family would make it through the war, the dynasty did not last long after. The family was never able to recover from the confidence lost with its people over the war's outcome. As the family increasingly lost control over its subjects, it was eventually removed from power by the Mandrakes and replaced with the Andretti Dynasty, who rule the nation of Del Tierr to this day. The last living members of the de la Nieve family eventually married into the Rhinegraves.

The Castelletti Dynasty was the last to be destroyed by the conflict. The family had successfully transferred most of its limited industrial base to Andromeda, only to see it destroyed by the Yuans. Despite the family's best efforts to rebuild in the Solar Galaxy, they could never overcome their crushing debt. Eventually they followed the lead of the Satos and de la Nieves by marrying into the Rhinegraves.

1K
THE CONQUEST OF TRIANGULUM AND THE GREAT MIGRATION

1,321 AN–1,409 AN

AFTER THE WAR OF Kings, the Rhinegrave family found itself in an excellent position. It had made it through the war unscathed. It had effectively sucked most of the wealth out of the other families, who would be in debt to them for generations. However, the Rhinegraves had garnered only a small portion of Andromeda in the form of those alien nations they had conquered. They had already seen growing cultural animosities between their people and the rest of the Empire. This led High King William von Rhinegrave to conclude that his people needed a galaxy of their own. Andromeda may have been claimed, but Triangulum was just next door, relatively speaking.

William's plan caused some consternation in the rest of the Empire. The other families were upset at the prospect of Rhinegraves being allowed to claim new territories for themselves, while *they* were forbidden to do so. The throne was uncomfortable with the idea of any family having an entire galaxy at its disposal. But there was little any of them could do. The Rhinegraves had missed out on their opportunity to claim a portion of Andromeda, while annexing that galaxy's natives and ensuring that the galaxy's galactic core remained neutral territory. As far as they were concerned, it was their turn.

While measures had been taken to change the situation, the Rhinegraves remained the true leaders of the Imperial military. Unlike the other families, the Rhinegraves had not been de-fanged by the war but were now stronger than ever before. To try to stop them outright carried with it the risk of a whole new conflict. So Emperor Michael I set the condition. The Rhinegraves could have Triangulum, if and only if they conquered the galaxy themselves. If they were to use any of the Empire's assets or have help from the other families, the galaxy would be apportioned.

William had little difficulty with this condition. The War of Kings had left his dynasty utterly buried in cash. With this funding, William rose an invasion force that was arguably more powerful than the Solar Armed Forces of the era and set out into Triangulum. But this new galaxy would prove a very different challenge. Unlike Andromeda and the Solar Galaxy, Triangulum had never been subject to a Therican purge. Likely it had been next on their list had they completed their prior campaign.

Initially the Rhinegrave expeditions found Triangulum barren in terms of star-faring species. But the galaxy did host far more naturally habitable planets than initially expected. For several years the Rhinegraves expanded in a form of planet-hopping from one sector to the next. During this campaign, the Rhinegraves came across a primitive species known as the tahn'kodaz. At the time of their discovery, the kodaz were in the middle of a great crisis. The eruption of a super volcano on their home world was rapidly destroying the planet's biosphere, threatening to render the species extinct. High King William made the decision to save the kodaz and ordered his ships to rescue as many of the aliens as possible.

Initially, William had planned to move the kodaz to a new planet before continuing on his way. But he soon found that the kodaz had other ideas. The species was much more intelligent than their low technology had led the Rhinegraves to expect. Their lack of technology was as much a function of anatomy as anything else. While large and powerful, their limbs were poorly designed for the task of performing activities such as making tools. The inability to make simple tools made it impossible to make more advanced tools.

The kodaz were perfectly capable of understanding the concept of space travel, and having learned that it was indeed possible gave them no desire to once more be confined to a single planet. The survivors pledged their eternal loyalty to the Rhinegrave Dynasty if they would be taken to the stars. Many of these early kodaz eagerly pushed to serve the high king's military to prove their loyalty. Much in the same way the roliams had once pledged themselves to the Mandrakes. As a result, the kodaz became the first species admitted to the Empire while swearing fealty to someone other than the Mandrake family.

The fact that the Rhinegraves could claim the loyalty of an entire species further angered the other dynasties. They had been expressly forbidden from doing so by the throne. In this instance, the throne allowed it. Michael I stated that it was a privilege extended to the Rhinegraves in exchange for not engaging in fighting that had threatened the stability of the Empire. It came after a conversation between High King William and Emperor Michael, wherein the former reminded his emperor that the Rhinegraves had *allowed* the Mandrakes to take the throne. It was only appropriate that the Mandrakes be deferential in their treatment. Privately, the emperor had been infuriated by this exchange. But Michael ultimately decided that he had enough on his plate trying to sever the disturbing amount of influence the Rhinegraves held over the Solar Armed Forces.

As the Rhinegraves continued to expand through Triangulum, they eventually found that the galaxy was already host to an interstellar empire of its own. It has been common throughout the ages for the victors in conflicts to vilify the vanquished. In the case of the Nasei Empire, such intentional vilification was never necessary. The Nasei controlled just under a fifth of the galaxy and, aside from the Thericans, were the most ruthless enemy humanity has ever faced.

When the Nasei encountered another intelligent species, their default response was eradication. In many ways, this was a gift for High King William. He had come to conquer, and the only foe capable of challenging him was one for whom no one was likely to show any sympathy. Unfortunately for William, it was the Nasei who learned of his presence first. The Nasei launched a surprise raid on six Rhinegrave colonies, completely eradicating the population of each. The resulting war was one of the bloodiest and most ruthless affairs in which humanity has been involved. It has always been the policy of the Rhinegraves to meet force with force and show that any acts of cruelty to their people will be returned in kind. The Nasei showed an eagerness to slaughter prisoners of war (POWs), and any civilian population that came under their guns. The Rhinegraves did not hesitate to respond, executing Nasei POWs and readily using weapons of mass destruction to bring planets to heel. Particularly when Nasei soldiers and civilians chose to commit suicide rather than be captured or conquered.

The primary advantage in the Rhinegraves' arsenal was the same one that got them to Triangulum—the transpatial drive. The use of this drive system allowed Rhinegrave ships to launch devastating surprise attacks without warning and then withdraw before they could be engaged by reinforcements. This was an ability the Nasei lacked and had few means to defend against. This allowed the Rhinegraves to gradually break their empire down, often landing heavy blows with relatively few casualties in return.

The ground campaign was different, and the Nasei fought bitterly to defend every planet. Often, they went so far as to employ scorched earth policies that would starve their own people if it meant denying resources to the enemy. When they ran out of troops, the Nasei would force civilians, even children, into militias to serve as the last line of defense. Initially when the Nasei were reduced to fighting with these civilian militias, William would order his troops to destroy any remaining local infrastructure and withdraw. In doing so, he hoped that the civilians could be starved into submission, obviating the need to kill them. But it soon became apparent that the Nasei would rather poison themselves and their children than submit.

William soon realized that if the Nasei would rather murder their own children than accept defeat, he had no obligation to try to spare their lives. But William was aware of the historic parallels at work. In this galaxy, he was the invader. His own memoirs show a determination to try to spare the Nasei if he could. But the Nasei were determined not to cooperate. Those that did show a willingness to surrender were labeled traitors and executed by their own.

By the time William's forces were ready to move on the Nasei home world, the latter had already killed more of their own people to prevent surrender than had William's troops on the battlefield. In a final act of suicidal defiance, the Nasei waited until Rhinegrave troops were landing on their home world before sending a message to William's fleet. The Nasei promised that though the humans would win the war, they would find no spoils. The Nasei detonated antimatter bombs buried throughout the planet. While this act destroyed an army and killed many of William's troops, it also wiped out the last major Nasei population. Since that time, the word *nasei* has come to be synonymous with an act of self-sacrifice executed purely out of spite.

The war was over, and the whole of Triangulum now belonged to the Rhinegraves. Though a handful of Nasei would survive the war, the tiny population would never rebound. Official records indicate that the Nasei are either in hiding or, far more likely, are extinct. But the Rhinegraves had won more than a galaxy in the war, and soon after, a second species joined the kodaz in swearing their loyalty.

The kurai had been a space-faring species for more than a century before first contact with the Nasei. First contact ended with a generational war that saw the kurai on the losing side. By the time of the Rhinegraves' arrival in the galaxy, the Nasei had already destroyed the kurai home world. Their population had been reduced to less than ten million, waiting on holdout colonies for the day that the enemy showed up to finish the job. It was the warrior caste that approached the Rhinegraves. Since the Rhinegraves had won the war for the galaxy and saved the kurai in the process, it was only fitting that the victor gain the allegiance of those that remained. Whether the other castes shared this sentiment or simply decided it was best to fall in line is largely immaterial. The kurai joined, becoming the second species to cast their lot with the Rhinegraves.

The Rhinegraves had one last obstacle to claiming the galaxy for their own—the Alexander Dynasty. Still irate at the Rhinegraves having been permitted to lay claim to an entire galaxy for themselves, the family fabricated evidence suggesting that they had been secretly supplying matériel to aid in the conquest. The family then presented this "evidence" to the throne, demanding that they be apportioned a piece of Triangulum.

This put the Rhinegraves in the dubious position of trying to prove a negative. All parties involved knew the claim was a farce. The Rhinegraves had more than enough matériel of their own to have needed help from the Alexanders, but the accusation would give the throne leverage to demand the splitting of the Rhinegraves' new territory if the Mandrakes chose to pursue it. William chose to forgive the Alexanders' debt incurred during the

War of Kings as an inducement to withdraw their claim. But this shameless attempt to steal a piece of the Rhinegraves' conquest would create a bitter enmity between the two houses. This would eventually blossom into the longest blood feud in human history. Though the feud would go through hot and cold phases, it would exist through most of the Empire's long history. The feud came to an end only with the marriage of Elena Alexander to Jonas von Rhinegrave IV and the eventual dissolution of the Alexander Dynasty. This union finally ended a feud that lasted longer than most civilizations.

With the matter resolved, William chose an idyllic planet near the center of the galaxy to serve as his new capital. He named this planet Reichsylvannia and began his final plan of transplanting the entirety of his people to the new galaxy. Though William did not live to see the end of this work, in the following years, all his people were ferried to a new home. The resulting nation became known as the Reichsylvannian Dominion. In eras prior, the followers of the Rhinegraves had been known as the Rhinevolk, but in their new home came to be known as the Reichsylvannians. The family's old assets were eventually sold off or gifted to other families, and the relocation was complete.

That this event is known as the Great Migration is not due solely to its size, as there was a larger overall migration from the Solar Galaxy to Andromeda. Rather, it is the sheer rapidity with which it was accomplished. The entire mass relocation took place in under one hundred years, far faster than the migrations between the Solar and Andromeda galaxies.

1L
THE EXPANSION

1,600 AN–4,000 AN

IT WAS DURING THE Expansion Era that the Solar Empire would gradually lay claim to the Solar Galaxy Cluster. This period involved a great deal of exploration, more than a few wars, and a gradual population explosion. However, its formative effect on the Empire does not extend far beyond its acquisition of territory. None of the alien species the Empire encountered could challenge its expansion, and the few who resisted were overcome with considerable ease.

While there were few civilization-shaping events from the Expansion itself, it would lay the foundation for the formation of more than half of the duchy-nations that exist in the Empire today. The Expansion and the formation of these duchies happened rather organically. Early colonies were set by those wishing to live on the frontier, and more arrived until the frontier gave way to civilization.

This period would see the creation of the Unified Exchange Network, which over time would grow into the astranet that today binds the main territories of the Empire together. The Expansion era would also see an unprecedented increase in the Empire's alien population. The majority of these aliens were primitive, however, and most chose to live under the option of isolation. The actual impact this had on the Empire's culture was minimal.

The era of relatively easy expansion would come to an end with the Kaurken War.

1M
THE KAURKEN WAR

4,007 AN–4,641 AN

WHEN TWO CAPABLE, HIGHLY-MOTIVATED, and mutually expansionist powers collide, there are only a few possible outcomes. Either one gives up its expansionist ambition, they form an accord to expand in different directions, or they fight. The Kaurken War was a major test for the Empire and its leadership. In the years before, the Mandrake Dynasty had worked very hard to delicately sever the bonds between the Solar Armed Forces and the Rhinegrave Dynasty. This war would be the former dynasty's first test of its ability to command the military directly. For the Empire as a whole, the war was a test of the will to expand at a time when its own existence was not threatened by a failure to do so.

The word *kaurken* in the Solar language is an evolution of the earlier word *krauken* in Titan English, itself an evolved form of *kraken*. The name was given to the species of large aquatic aliens who would be the Empire's nemesis for over six hundred years. These octopus-like aliens were relatively few, but fiendishly intelligent. The Kaurken are the first recorded species to have made the long and difficult trek not simply between galaxies, but galaxy clusters. A venture they undertook over the course of many centuries. The Kaurken had been driven far out of their home stars by another power that the Empire would eventually discover thousands of years later in the Praetheen Unity.

While the Kaurken were relatively few, they were extremely adept at building what humans would consider military automatech. Their ships were utterly massive and, in many ways, superior to those of the Solar Armadas. As to the Kaurken themselves, very little was ever learned about them save for their biology. They not only refused to share information about themselves and their culture but were extremely adept at keeping secrets. Their language was utterly incomprehensible to humans or indeed any species in the Empire. Even telepaths proved little help. The function of their minds was simply too different. All that is known about the Kaurken comes from members of the species captured by the Empire. A summary of the species can be found in a quote from Miles Leison, an admiral in the Solar Armadas.

> I know not what to make of these Kaurken. We can't even figure out how to communicate. Those we have captured have all died. Not because we killed them or they themselves, but because they needed something we could not provide. Yet we could not understand what it was, and they could not or would not communicate it to us. They reject all we offer them in food, and even computer modeling of their biology to create proper water for them results in death within a few days. The telepaths cannot find thoughts in their minds, only the emotions one might expect of an animal held against its will. But no animal could build the weapons at their disposal. Whatever their powers of reason may be, it is beyond our ken.

The two powers met in the Andromeda-V galaxy where the Kaurken were already in the process of pacifying native species. Once a planet was conquered, the Kaurken would reshape the local biosphere to fit their own preferences, rendering extinct most native life. Emperor Justin Mandrake saw the presence of a hostile species in the galaxy as an opportunity to integrate several civilizations without a fight. He was correct. The only two star-faring species quickly jumped at offers of Imperial protection. The primitive species, meanwhile, were not only in no position to challenge the Empire, but far less likely to resist when they learned that their choice was either the Empire or the Kaurken.

Most of the Kaurken War was a cold war that lasted over six hundred years. The two powers did meet in combat early in the Battle of Andromeda Sekanda. A. Sekanda had become the center of Imperial power in the galaxy. The planet was home to the l'rell species, which had been only too happy to join the Empire. As the center of Imperial power, A. Sekanda became the Kaurken's target for pushing the Empire out of the galaxy.

The battle counted as an Imperial victory but was largely indecisive. The Kaurken assaulted the planet in four waves of increasing intensity. After the battle, military planners would conclude that the Kaurken were testing the rapidity with which the Empire could mobilize reinforcements. The attacks were rebuffed, but attacker and defender suffered heavy casualties. The two sides were simply too evenly matched.

The Empire responded to the attack by greatly reinforcing its military presence in the region. But Emperor Justin chose not to launch a counterattack. Disturbed by the performance of his forces, he ordered a stiffening of defenses and quickly looked to research and development to provide an edge over the Kaurken. The Kaurken launched no further attacks of their own and seemed to adopt a similar position.

At home, the Imperial military had several problems that greatly affected its ability to meet the emperor's desire to upgrade his forces. The Rhinegrave Dynasty effectively *is* the military-industrial complex of the Empire. While other families and nations have defense industry of their own, it has always lagged far behind in terms of both industrial output and technological sophistication. As part of efforts to sever the Rhinegrave's influence over the military, the Empire had shifted procurement for the Solar Armed Forces to the Elysian Commonwealth and the Republic of Andromeda.

"Golden garbage" became the soldiers' moniker for arms and equipment manufactured by the Elysians. Matériel made in that nation was often extremely expensive and quite aesthetic. But it was prone to malfunctions and many shortfalls resulting from designers with poorly prioritized concerns. Republican equipment was mired with problems of the throne's own making. In order to cut costs for the sake of quantity, Emperor Justin often ordered equipment that fell into what is known as the "multi-tool paradox." All engineering efforts are a compromise between factors such as cost, complexity, and utility. The more jobs a tool is designed to perform, the worse it will be at performing all of them. Emperor Justin's insistence on multi-mission equipment created design demands that Republican engineers simply could not meet. As a result, Imperial troops were often left with only a single inadequate tool to perform dozens of different tasks.

Emperor Justin further hampered the Empire by directly intervening in military matters for which he lacked the experience to fully understand. This went as far as personally ordering troop deployments, and in several cases personally outlining the defense strategy in the event of Kaurken attack. But Emperor Justin was a narcissist by any standard and refused any counsel or to admit that he was out of his depth. In several instances, the Empire was so poorly organized and deployed that a sudden Kaurken attack could have forced it out of the galaxy.

Over the ensuing cold war, the Andromeda-V galaxy was effectively split down the center. Unlike the Empire, the Kaurken did not have the resources or strategic depth to engage in costly research and development programs. Instead they focused their efforts on making their forces as numerous as possible. That the Kaurken did not attack at many of the several golden opportunities handed to them by Emperor Justin's incompetence suggests they may have had internal political issues of their own.

The cold war finally turned hot on Day 300 of 4,612 AN. Day 300 of every year is Founding Day in the Empire. The day commemorates the Summit at Olympus and the founding of the Solar Empire. But it is more than a patriotic holiday. It is a time of gift-giving and of family, rooted in the celebration of the second chance at survival given by the Empire's founding. As one might expect, the Empire was not as vigilant as it might have been on this day, and the Kaurken finally launched their assault. Once more, their target was Andromeda Sekanda.

The war against the Kaurken was the first "modern" war, particularly in fleet battles. Sensor technology had finally progressed to the point that FTL weaponry was truly feasible.

Costs to produce massless impulse drives had fallen to the point that they could be manufactured in quantity for disposable items such as missiles. The Kaurken could not produce MIDs cheaply enough to use in missiles and were forced to rely on long-range disrupter cannons. This would have given the Empire an insurmountable advantage of range in fleet combat. If its leadership had the vision to exploit it.

Unfortunately, Emperor Justin had become very distrustful of the capabilities of the equipment at his disposal, due largely to impossible design demands for which he was responsible. He threw out this advantage, which he assumed to be overstated, while designing the defense strategies his admirals were compelled to follow. This combined with the sheer incompetence of his plans led to several sweeping victories for the Kaurken as they pushed through disorganized Imperial resistance. Andromeda Sekanda was lost, and the l'rell species was nearly rendered extinct when the majority were killed by the biosphere reshaping of their planet.

The fate of the l'rell is considered one of the great sins of the Mandrake Dynasty. Not simply because of the losses they suffered, but the complete indifference shown to them by the throne. Efforts to aid the surviving l'rell who had been off-world at the time were few. Emperor Justin considered them "useless" and faulted their poor performance in contributing to the defense of their world as the reason for its fall. The surviving l'rell felt so abandoned by the throne that they renounced their loyalty to the Mandrakes. They would eventually be welcomed by another family. In the modern Empire, the l'rell are known as the buun, a word that in their language meant "survivor," and they now stand as one of the Rhinegrave Eight.

The hot war with the Kaurken would last for twenty-nine years and be fought in over six hundred star systems. This war would also see the first use of a new weapon. The arens had been created by the Imperial military as part of efforts to ensure its superiority over the royal houses. However, as with its advantages in FTL weaponry, the Empire largely squandered the arens. Emperor Justin saw them as inherently expendable and had often unrealistic expectations of their capabilities. This combined with the myriad of other errors would see the Empire nearly pushed from the Andromeda-V galaxy as the war dragged on.

By the year 4,620, the Empire had yet to launch a major offensive and was barely clinging to the galaxy. Most of the native species who had flocked to the Empire's banner had since abandoned it. Most tried to make pleas to the Kaurken to spare their worlds. Meanwhile, the expense of the war and the mounting number of deaths were beginning to cause serious political unrest at home. Across the Empire's nations, the people were becoming weary of the war. Monies spent on the war and additional taxes levied on the nations resulted in mounting economic hardships.

On Day 50 of 4,620 AN, Emperor Justin Mandrake was assassinated. Who exactly was responsible for his death has never been determined. Speculation runs from his sister, to the military, to possibly even the Commando Corps. With none of his children old enough to assume the throne, it passed to his wife Lana I. She became the first reigning empress in the Empire's history and proved to be exactly what was needed at the time.

Empress Lana knew nothing about grand strategy, military tactics, logistics, or much of anything else about war. Most of the court considered her an empty skull. She had spent most of her youth as a party girl disinterested in study or career. Most of her marriage to Emperor Justin had been spent enjoying the countless luxuries that went along with the position of empress. But Lana had one critically important quality that her late husband did not. Humility. Aware of her own limitations, Lana removed what had been the primary obstacle to the Empire's success up to that point. Rather than try to manage the war directly, she turned major decisions over to her commanders and military advisers. Those who failed were replaced, and those who succeeded were sent to their next assignment. She also made the decision of returning the bulk of military procurement to the Dominion. They had both the technological edge and the industry to churn out matériel at a pace the rest could not.

Within a year, the tide of the war turned sharply. Imperial troops were soon armed with a steady influx of the best weaponry the Empire could give them. Commanders immediately began to make use of their advantages in fleet combat. Rather than disposable fodder, the arens were put to work as the highly capable and valuable soldiers they were.

The war was effectively won at the Battle of Sector Three. In this battle, the Solar Armadas took full advantage of its superior weaponry to decimate the main body of the Kaurken fleet. In ground campaigns, the Empire abandoned the late emperor's policy of mobbing the enemy with arens and automatech. Instead, it pursued far more effective strategies of maneuver warfare. This proved extremely effective as the Kaurken had adapted their defenses to the prior tactics and found the shift difficult. The Battle of Sector Three destroyed the Kaurken's ability to go on the offensive, and the rest of the war would be the Empire dismantling their territory.

No living Kaurken ever voluntarily surrendered to the Empire. The few who were captured were incapable of attempting escape or fighting back. All eventually died in Imperial custody despite the best efforts to keep them alive. The Kaurken themselves never formally surrendered. On Day 55 of 4,641 AN, the few remaining Kaurken ships fled the Andromeda-V galaxy, taking their population with them.

What became of the Kaurken afterward is unclear. While they had an extremely primitive form of transpatial technology, it was exactly that—primitive. It had taken them centuries to reach the Solar Galaxy Cluster. As the Empire consumed the rest of the cluster, it never again encountered them. Some believe that they made the even longer trek to a different galaxy cluster, an effort which would have taken thousands of years if it could have even been done with their technology. Others believe that they may have gone extinct. There exists evidence that after the Battle of Sector Three, the Kaurken suffered an internal power struggle, which may have spelled doom for them later. With the defeat of the Kaurken, the last force capable of stopping the Empire from claiming complete control of its home galaxy cluster was gone.

Empress Lana would hold the throne for another thousand years before eventually passing the title down to her son, Charles. In the hopes of preventing a repeat of her husband's failure, she instituted changes to the Imperial line of succession. She redrafted them to include the provision that all males of the family be required to give a term of military service in order to be eligible to assume the throne. Through the rest of her reign, she was often known as the "great delegator" to the Imperial aristocracy. She rarely took a direct role in managing government affairs. Her preferred approach was to put experienced people with relevant expertise into positions of power and use the weight of her office to support them. Despite or perhaps as a result of her hands-off approach to running the Empire, she helped to usher in the Pax Solaris. Even into the modern Empire, she is often used as a lesson—namely on the importance of delegation to competent people, and that sometimes the best thing a leader can do is to get out of the way.

1N
THE PAX SOLARIS

5,000 AN–50,000 AN

THE PAX SOLARIS WAS the first golden age of the Solar Empire and the greatest period of economic expansion in known history. This period would last for about 45,000 years of unprecedented societal growth. This is not to say it was a period without trials, wars, or difficulties, but none of the wars fought during this era were ever a threat to the Empire's existence, nor were the wars of this era even significant enough to affect the daily lives of Imperial citizens. Social difficulties came and went. Entire nations grew, blossomed, decayed to internal conflict, and fell. But they always rebuilt, for the Empire of which they were a part was strong. It was there in the present, and there was no doubt it would be there in the future.

The Pax Solaris would see many primitive alien civilizations rise out of the stone ages and strike into space where they were given the choice to join the Imperial whole, or to isolate themselves. It would see cultural revolutions and backlashes. The period would also see reforms throughout the government but few that affected the average person.

The Pax Solaris was also a period of great technological development. Many of the technologies now ubiquitous in the modern Empire were either invented during this period or driven to states of development beyond anything seen before. Among these was the development of the alchemic printer, capable of transmuting abundant hydrogen en masse into heavier elements. Over time these systems would become increasingly advanced, replacing most forms of manufacturing. This would turn the Empire into a post-essentials society, particularly when combined with advances in power generation technology. It became a simple matter to provide every resident in the Empire with more than enough food, water, shelter, and energy to survive in reasonable comfort. Wealth soon came to be measured largely by possession of what assets the printers could not create in arbitrary quantities.

It was during the Pax Solaris that the Solar Cathedral was built as the new Imperial capital, located at a midpoint between the Solar and Andromeda galaxies. In a largely symbolic move, much of the cathedral was built with material taken from worlds across the Empire rather than produced through alchemic printing. The Cathedral has served as the capital and home of the Mandrake Dynasty ever since.

Perhaps most importantly, it was during this era that the modern astranet began to take shape. Interstellar, even intergalactic communication could be accomplished instantaneously in ways that were far more stable and reliable than attempts made before. It would eventually lead to the development of the astranet router, making inter-planetary teleportation anywhere within the astranet footprint a practical reality. Interstellar travel was now in the hands of even the poorest and least affluent people.

But all these factors did have far-reaching ramifications that would ultimately spell the end of the golden age and the coming of the Great Collapse.

10
THE PRAETHEEN WAR

51,306 AN–51,320 AN

BY THE YEAR 50,000, the Empire had already expanded to every galaxy in the Local Group. But it was not until Millennium 51 that there was a serious political will to attempt expansion into another galaxy cluster. To do so was no simple matter. While a transpatial drive makes intergalactic travel possible, as with any other form of travel, difficulty increases with distance.

The Empire was in a state of steady decline. Many of its nations had gone down the same paths of social failure that had plagued the Interstellar Confederacy ages before. A further complication was the rise of numerous pro-democracy movements' often violent protests sowing discord throughout the Empire.

Emperor Nathaniel Mandrake had concluded that the cultural decline had progressed too far to stop. His attention turned to what should be done after the collapse that was sure to come. The technology was becoming available to send ships to the Near Galaxy Cluster (known to antiquity as M81) in a reasonable amount of time. Nathaniel chose to make use of that. He would begin colonizing at least one galaxy in the region. In these colonies, he would transplant the most productive and pro-Empire citizens he could find in the hopes of creating what would become the last vestige of Imperial glory.

But Nathaniel found few who shared his interest, and volunteers to go to these new colonies proved extremely rare. He was forced to break with over 40,000 years of Imperial policy and offer the royal dynasties the opportunity to once more expand their territory. Even then, he found few takers and was forced to motivate them with a financial incentive.

Unknown to the Empire at the time, the Near Galaxy Cluster hosted an intergalactic species of its own in the form of the Praetheen Unity. While technically an empire unto themselves, the Praetheen have a very different take on the concept. The Praetheen had no interest in trying to create communities of any aliens found in their space. But the Praetheen's own sense of ethics did not allow them to simply exterminate alien species.

The Praetheen practiced a policy of containment. So long as aliens remained on their planets, they would not be bothered. If a species grew large enough to need a new planet, the Praetheen might transplant some of the population to another. But they would not abide any species developing FTL travel that might enable them to challenge for dominance of space. The Praetheen themselves had abandoned the use of planets in favor of structures that the Empire would consider star hives.

The Empire first placed its colonies in what came to be known as Hayes' Galaxy (known to antiquity as Bode's Galaxy). The Praetheen had no presence here but soon took notice of the Empire. The Praetheen politely but firmly refused any opening of trade or formal relations. But what the Empire did not know was that their arrival had left the Praetheen utterly terrified. The Praetheen had just encountered a species they could not possibly hope to contain. Worse, the newly arrived humans integrated aliens into their society. The Praetheen feared the Empire might eventually desire to do the same with those they had kept in containment. Or even the Praetheen themselves.

The Praetheen have an ability to simply *care* about the future that is beyond the ken of most. They think thousands, even hundreds of thousands, of years ahead, down to the rate at which they will grow their population and expand to new homes. In their estimation, it was only a matter of time until there was a conflict with the Empire. They determined it would be best to fight that war while the Empire's presence in the region was still small.

Each party would go on to find that their opponent was far more powerful than anticipated. The war would hasten the coming of the Great Collapse in the Empire, and it would cost the Praetheen more of their citizens than any civilization has lost in a war before or since.

(i)
The Battle of Hayes

THE ENTIRETY OF THE Praetheen War would be marked by costly mistakes in judgment on both sides. The Empire took the isolationist bent of the Praetheen to mean that they were no threat. Limited analysis of their ships created the false conclusion that the Empire had an enormous technological edge, so it placed only a token presence of the Solar Armadas in the region to defend its colonies.

The Praetheen made several mistakes with regard to the Empire. While small by today's standards, the Imperial ships of the era still measured in dozens of kilometers. Not comprehending that the Empire did not take them for a threat, the Praetheen believed the small number of ships was indicative. They believed that the Empire's fleet was very small, made up only of a few large ships meant to intimidate potential foes. They had no idea what kind of power they were about to provoke.

The Praetheen are a species of total-conversion cyborgs, little more than organic brains in bodies the Empire would consider automatech made from programmable matter. All Praetheen are joined by an astranet-like network that allows them to share thoughts, memories, sensations, even skills and personalities. There is no such thing as a specialist in Praetheen society. Each citizen does what is needed. If necessary, they will download the skills required, and a personality competent in their use to perform their duties. This includes soldiery.

Praetheen ships were quite small by Imperial standards but were almost completely automated with even the largest having crews in the single digits. With little space dedicated to organic needs, they were often capable of punching far above their weight class. Their small crew requirements allowed them to maintain a standing force of millions of ships for minimal investment in personnel.

The Praetheen hoped that they could drive the Empire out with a single overwhelming show of force. To that end they gathered four million of their ships, and on Day 55 of 51,306 AN, set them loose on the one hundred colonies the Empire had placed in the Hayes Galaxy. As the battle took shape, the faulty assumptions held by both sides would cost them.

The Praetheen believed that aside from superior transpatial technology, the Empire was otherwise behind them in most areas. The Empire in turn believed the Praetheen were behind in practically every area. In truth they were evenly matched. Imperial weapons were generally more powerful and had longer ranges. Praetheen weapons were more accurate, making the effective range of each almost equal. Imperial armor and shield systems were superior, but the lack of need to dedicate equipment to sustaining an organic crew with things such as atmosphere and gravity allowed the Praetheen to pack much more armor and equipment into their ships of any given size. Praetheen sensors had a much longer range than Imperial sensors. What the Praetheen did not know was that the Empire had already used and abandoned similar sensor technologies for being too easy to spoof and jam.

When the Praetheen fleet poured into the galactic core of the Hayes Galaxy, there were only 150 Armadas ships to greet them. Imperial misinformation on the Praetheen's capabilities led their commanders to believe that the engagement would be an exercise in swatting gnats. Neither force showed much hesitation to throw themselves headfirst at the other.

The resulting melee saw 104 of the Empire's 150 ships destroyed, along with an unknown number of Praetheen estimated in the thousands. Overwhelmed, the surviving Imperial ships had no choice but to retreat through the Hera Gate that had been arrayed to expedite travel between the galaxy clusters. The gateway itself was destroyed by the last Armadas ships to retreat. While they had suffered far more casualties than anticipated, the Praetheen hoped this would convince the Empire not to return. Luckily for the colonists who had been abandoned by the withdraw, the Praetheen showed no interest. They too would be contained to their planets and ignored so long as they did not attempt to build any starships.

While shocked by the attack, Emperor Nathaniel had no intention of letting go of the galaxy cluster so easily. But his ability to respond to the attack was greatly limited. Though the Empire would not admit it, it was in the grip of a depression as economies across its nations continued to shrink with no end in sight. Barely a third of the Solar Armadas was functional. Most of its ships were in mothballs, as falling tax revenue left them without crews. These economic woes along with many others would prevent the Empire from ever answering the Praetheen in full force.

The destruction of Hera Gate had also complicated matters considerably. The Near Galaxy Cluster had been reached by sending automated ships to lay a series of navigation beacons between the two galaxy clusters. Ships could then use these to make smaller transpatial jumps on a progressive path to the cluster. This network was woefully unprepared to support a significant fleet.

The Republic of Andromeda, Reichsylvannian Dominion, and Yuangi were responsible for most of the colonies that had been planted in the Near Galaxy Cluster. All three were livid that after Imperial assurances of safety, the colonies had been left so defenseless. The kings of all three nations chose to mobilize their royal guard to deploy to the region.

(ii)
Operation Winter

IT WOULD TAKE SIX years for the Empire to return to the Near Galaxy Cluster. By this time, the Empire had amassed a relatively underwhelming force: 265,000 ships of the Solar Armadas and approximately 11 billion legionnaires. They were soon joined by 61,000 ships from Yuangi, 8 carrier strike forces numbering 1,200 ships from the Republic of Andromeda, and 32,000 ships from the Reichsylvannian Dominion. On Day 176 of 51,312 AN, they returned to the Hayes Galaxy.

With the enemy's long absence, the Praetheen believed that the Empire had abandoned the cluster, so they left only a token force to watch for any return. That force was horrified to find that far more ships arrived than they had believed the Empire was capable of building. The royal guard forces were left to defend the colonies and the newly established Saturn Gate. The Empire went on the offensive.

Long-range observation before the war had led the Empire to conclude that the Sans Galaxy (formerly Holmberg II) was the center of Praetheen civilization. Indeed it was, and the Empire quickly jumped in to press the attack.

(iii)
The Battle of Sans

IN THE ANNALS OF military history, the Battle of Sans is often known as the "Sans Debacle." The fight for the Praetheen Galaxy was nothing more than two wholly incompetent forces bludgeoning each other to death. The Praetheen at least have the excuse that they had never fought a war against a peer adversary. When they had fought the Kaurken thousands of years before, they had done so with an overwhelming technological edge. For the Empire, the entire campaign showed just how far the standards had fallen for both membership and command throughout the military.

Perhaps the worst debacle to come out of Operation Winter would be the Battle of Hive 41. The Empire sought to demoralize the Praetheen by conquering one of their star hives. While such an operation had been contemplated, it had never actually been attempted. A star hive is made up of swarms of habitation satellites arrayed around a star. It is a megastructure capable of housing truly astronomical numbers of organic beings. Even more with a species like the Praetheen.

The Empire determined that the hive it designed, No. 41, was the most susceptible to attack. Very quickly, the Empire learned two things. The first was that the technological parity between the two sides vanished on the ground. The Praetheen were woefully behind in technologies such as orbital support, armored fighting vehicles, and artillery. The second lesson was that the first did not count for much when every Praetheen could be converted into a foot soldier at a moment's notice. Their programmable-matter bodies were even capable of manifesting passable weapons. The legionnaires that attempted to land on the hive soon found themselves on the defensive, huddled desperately behind the umbrella of their artillery.

What was supposed to be a demoralizing blow to the Praetheen quickly devolved into a frantic attempt to extract the legionnaires before they were overwhelmed. The attempt was met with a massive counterattack from the Praetheen fleet. Such events would be typical for the next five years, as both sides continued to underestimate the strategic depth and capabilities of the other.

But the fight for Hive 41 led to a decision on Emperor Nathaniel's part. If every Praetheen could be militarized as easily as flipping a switch, then there were no Praetheen civilians. Commanders were authorized to treat all Praetheen as military combatants and destroy any population center as needed.

(iv)
The Battle of Point Zero

BY THE SECOND QUARTER of 51,319 AN, the Empire had made significant strides against the Praetheen by tearing down their Unified Protocol Network. The UPN was the species's equivalent to the astranet and vital for the transfer of skills and personalities from one Praetheen to the next. The damage sustained was having a disastrous effect on the Praetheen. Large numbers of Praetheen found themselves cut off and no longer able to adapt to the various tasks. Militarily, the Praetheen were being forced to fall back as new network scramblers provided by House Yao were significantly disrupting the foe's ability to coordinate their fleets. Some unsung heroes of these successes were the members of Operation Lockjack. At the direction of the Commando Corps, millions of cyber-criminals were rounded up and made to study the Praetheen network. The more damage they did to the UPN, the more their sentences were reduced. With operations like Lockjack and many more, the Commando Corps is the only branch of the Solar Armed Forces that did not cause disappointment throughout the war.

Unfortunately, these successes led to a growing sense of overconfidence among Imperial command. The Praetheen were being driven further into their own territory, but they were not defeated. They still possessed a colossal population and industrial base from which to continue raising forces to fight the war. The Praetheen began concentrating their ships on what was known as Navigation Point Zero, the star hive that was their analogue to a capital.

There have been many instances in history where the side losing a war has attempted to draw its opponent into a decisive showdown. Often the winning side will do its best to avoid such a confrontation. When one is winning the war, there is little incentive to take any unnecessary risk. Unfortunately for the Empire, growing overconfidence and mounting political pressure to bring the war to a quick end won out over military prudence.

Admiral Becksei, who commanded the Armadas's forces, had grown arrogant after several sweeping victories. His plan to attack Point Zero left the local royal guard forces out completely. With fifty thousand ships of the first and second armadas, he planned to approach Point Zero in a four-pronged pincer, tearing down the UPN as he went. With the damage already inflicted upon the network, the loss of Point Zero would almost certainly lead to its complete collapse.

The Praetheen were ready for him. Point Zero was a well-developed star hive housing inordinate numbers of Praetheen, all of which had been put to work to convert the hive into a massive star fortress. In the months leading up to the battle, the Praetheen installed millions of new weapon and shield systems. The Praetheen fleet gathered from across their territory to prepare themselves for the decisive battle. Yet again, the Empire underestimated the total forces the Praetheen would be able to bring to the fight. This Praetheen fleet was the most massive in their people's history. Nine million ships included a new class of battlecruiser rapidly designed as a counter to the often-decisive presence of the Armadas's large warships.

The Battle of Point Zero began on Day 109 of 51,320 AN, as Imperial ships encountered Praetheen defenders on their approach to the star hive. These Praetheen were quickly overwhelmed and retreated, luring Admiral Becksei into a false sense of confidence that the enemy was gasping its last breaths. As the pincers of his formation prepared to come together and surround Point Zero, the Praetheen unleashed the massive fleet bottled up there. Each pincer of 12,500 ships ran headlong into a massive wall of more than 2.2 million Praetheen vessels.

Much of the battle played out over the course of three days. The new Praetheen battlecruisers proved an utter failure, being dominated in engagements with Imperial ships. But this failure of their new design proved only a minor facet of the war. By the third day, Admiral Becksei had lost most of his own large ships, and losses among his smaller ships were devastating.

Determined to win their decisive battle, the Praetheen surrounded the Imperial fleet, hoping to prevent any withdraw or escape. They were almost successful. By the time he realized there was no hope to win the battle, Admiral Becksei was forced to order his ships to scatter.

Until the Solar Eclipse some thirty thousand years later, the Battle of Point Zero was the largest military disaster in the Empire's history. Three quarters of the Imperial fleet sent to battle was destroyed, either during the fight or shortly after as crews scuttled their ships to prevent their capture. When combined with the loss of legionnaires aboard, this totaled more than four hundred million organic lives. Of those ships that escaped, nearly all needed extensive repairs and many would instead be scrapped upon their return to port.

The Praetheen suffered immensely in the battle as well. All their new battlecruisers were destroyed, along with between 6.5 and 7 million of their standard ships. The Praetheen themselves had been pushed to their limits. While they had saved Point Zero, the damage already done by the Empire to the UPN was proving catastrophic. System glitches and cascade failures were periodically leaving large populations cut off from the network. Productivity among their citizens was falling across the board. The Praetheen people were coming to understand the concept of a morale crisis. It would already take years to repair the damage, and if that work did not begin soon, the results threatened to prove apocalyptic. The need to end the war quickly saw the Praetheen organize their remaining ships for one last offensive in the hopes of driving the Empire out for good.

For the Empire, the loss caused many problems. In comparison to its population, the loss of hundreds of millions in a single battle is insignificant. But the losses at Point Zero further inflamed anti-war sentiment in the general population. The anti-war sentiments fueled the democracy movements that were already sowing chaos across the Empire.

(v)
The Battle of Saturn Gate

THE BATTLE OF SATURN Gate would be the last major battle of the war. With his fleet broken, Admiral Becksei retreated to the Empire to see to the repair of his ships and replenishment with new forces. This left only a small Armadas presence in the region. The defense fell to the royal guard forces of the Republic of Andromeda, Reichsylvannian Dominion, and Yuangi.

In command of the Republican force was Admiral Yanci Hale. Hale was a veteran of Armadas service before retiring to take a position in his king's royal guard. Though an able fleet commander, he had little experience in actual combat. The Dominion fleet was commanded by High King William von Rhinegrave III. William had little battlefield experience, but as is expected of every high king, he was extremely well-schooled on the subject. While still high king, William had effectively gone into retirement. He had come to lead the fleets so that his son Richard could gain experience leading the nation back home.

The largest of the royal guard fleets in the region was the Yuan fleet led by Admiral Fan Yao. Fan was the niece of Yuangi's then-King Banqi Yao. While still quite young, she demonstrated an aptitude for fleet tactics. This combined with her royal bloodline saw her make a lightning dash through the ranks of the nation's royal guard. Eventually her uncle personally appointed her admiral over the ships in the colony zone. A feat she accomplished at the age of twenty-six.

Though required to work together, the three commanders had little liking for each other. Both High King William and Admiral Hale were deeply concerned about Admiral Yao, a fact spelled out in their war logs well before the Battle of Saturn Gate.

Of her, High King William wrote:

> No doubt she has a mind for tactics and is certainly capable. But that child is a bomb waiting to go off in the hands of whoever holds her. She has been told her entire life that she is special, and I fear she has come to believe it.
>
> She is good, but not so good as she thinks. I have found that it is practically a law of physics. When any person's ego grows so far beyond their capacity, the universe will conspire to humble them. This is why we do not give posts of high responsibility to children. That when the universe decides the time for humility has come, the pain is felt by few. Fan Yao has been promoted to the admiralty. When she is humbled, she will not be alone. But when a bomb explodes, it is not the fault of the bomb. But rather, the one who set it upon those destroyed by it.

Admiral's Hale's opinion of her was much more concise:

> Better to have an incompetent peer at my side than one hungering for an opportunity to prove herself.

The concerns of both William and Hale would prove prophetic in the battle ahead.

Hot on the momentum of their victory at Point Zero, the Praetheen quickly swept forward with a fleet of four million ships. The local commanders almost lost the battle before it could begin. Admiral Becksei had left the Near Cluster to oversee the assembly of a new fleet. In his place he left his aide, Admiral Greg Petrov. Petrov was a man who commanded zero respect from any of the three commanders. Separately and privately, both High King William and Admiral Hale approached Petrov and asked him to relinquish command. When Petrov refused, he was killed by the explosion of his personal shuttle. Though never proven, it is generally accepted that William had him killed. But even among his own troops, little mourning was shown for Petrov. Admiral Hale wrote of him:

> How such an ill-tempered, incompetent, and thoroughly unlikable man can come to admiralty I will never know. If he is typical of fleet commanders now, it is small wonder we are losing this war.

With Petrov gone, the three royal guard leaders could not agree on a chain of command. Admiral Hale claimed authority as the most experienced in fleet operations. High King William claimed command as the senior Imperial official in the sector. Admiral Yao refused to follow either without the orders of her king, the emperor, or Admiral Becksei.

This left the three unable to agree on a plan of action. As Rhinegraves often do when on the defensive, William favored laying a well-planned trap in the hopes of forcing the enemy into a vulnerable position. Admiral Hale favored a layered defense that would attempt to peel off sections of the Praetheen fleet to be destroyed piecemeal. Admiral Yao favored a direct counteroffensive.

With time running short and the three unable to agree, Admiral Yao broke ranks and decided to go it alone. House Yao has tried several times to whitewash history, claiming that her charge was an attempt to buy time for the other commanders. But in the end, it was the exact kind of glory-seeking venture the others had feared, as revealed in her logs. It would also mark the Yao Dynasty with a stereotype of recklessly aggressive behavior that took centuries to break.

> Where the Armadas failed, I will succeed. And the Empire will know it was while the beady-eyed old man trembled and the 'glorious' high king hid behind a woman.

Admiral Yao did have some reason for her confidence. Her fleet was the largest of the three and had many of the heavy ships that had so often proved decisive against the Praetheen. But generations of economic woes in Yuangi showed. Most of her ships were heavily dated designs, crewed by men with too few training hours. In the span of three hours, the Praetheen surrounded Yao's fleet before systematically annihilating it.

Admiral Yao would survive and be repatriated to the Empire after the war. Public outcry in Yuangi over the event came to be known as "Fan's Folly." It was so great that her uncle, the king, declared her actions sedition to the throne. Fan Yao was executed on Day 77 of 51,321 AN. High King William would later speak on her fate.

> She was a clever and ambitious girl but given to the hot temper of youth. Nepotism saw her promoted to a station above her maturity and competence. When she inevitably became the author of disaster, she was scapegoated by the same people who had written her doom. No doubt she deserved punishment for such a costly error, but Fan Yao was as much a victim of poor leadership as those she led to their deaths.

The loss of the Yuani fleet left both William and Hale in the lurch. Without the Yuani fleet, neither of their original plans had a hope of working. But neither was willing to abandon the sector unfought. With little time to bicker, Admiral Hale yielded to the high king so that they could face the Praetheen together. As a pair they devised a plan still used by the Armadas to this day, known alternatively as the "Hale Storm" or "The Rhinegrave Shuffle."

The two commanders were badly outnumbered, but not without advantages. It has been said by some that the Reichsylvannians would rather eat rocks than cut funding to their royal guard. There is a grain of truth in this. High King William commanded the most technologically advanced fleet in the region, with the most heavily trained crew. Republican fleet doctrine has always been highly defensive in nature. Carriers packing many thousands of fighters serve as mobile bases that can evade attackers while harrying them with constant attack waves. While these fighters struggled against large warships, they proved extremely effective against smaller vessels like those used by the Praetheen.

A common tactic when facing an enemy fleet with FTL weaponry is known as the wall-up. In this formation, all ships in the fleet form a wall perpendicular to the approaching enemy. While this formation leaves ships on the perimeter vulnerable, it provides a high degree of overlap for interceptor-systems to ships in the center. More importantly, it helps to equalize the distance between all ships in the fleet and targets on which they focus fire. This helps to ensure that ordnance (such as missiles) arrive as close to each other as possible, increasing their chances of overwhelming enemy defenses.

Admiral Hale's carriers along with their escorts would serve as bait. The Saturn Gate was the obvious target for the Praetheen. Admiral Hale's carriers would take up a position far enough from the gate to be out of Praetheen sensor range but close enough that they were almost certain to be spotted by enemy scouts. Hale would send ten thousand of his fighters with a small detachment of Dominion ships. They would take up a position opposite him, far enough away that they were unlikely to be seen by sensors or scouts.

The bulk of the Dominion fleet would take up a position much farther out, in an extremely dense star cluster with each ship hugging the stars. There they would be indistinguishable on long-range sensors from the stars they orbited.

The problem with laying a trap is that sometimes the enemy doesn't take the bait. Even when his reasons for not doing so are a mistake on his part. Despite Admiral Hale's position, the Praetheen scouts blundered and failed to pick up his carriers. Hale's own fighter-scouts had detected the Praetheen on approach. Unable to believe that the Praetheen had failed to see him,

Hale concluded that they had decided to ignore his fleet and go straight for the Saturn Gate.

The Praetheen meanwhile had become very cautious. Their failure to detect any waiting defenders led them to two possibilities. Either the royal guard had withdrawn without a fight and abandoned the sector, or a trap was waiting. They continued their approach to the Saturn Gate but quickly fixed themselves into a highly defensive sphere formation. For the plan to work required the Praetheen to pass very near to one of the larger stars in the area. If kept in their spherical formation, their fleet would be well positioned to blunt the attack waiting for them.

Admiral Hale made the bold decision to attack with his fleet. Rather than throw his fighters at the enemy, he deployed them around his fleet to serve as external interceptor batteries. He then launched his fleet at the Praetheen. Hale's fleet was far too small to win a confrontation, and the Praetheen took his actions as a defiant last stand. They split their fleet with a portion moving to engage Hale and the rest continuing toward the Saturn Gate.

With the Praetheen splitting, Hale sent the command to the mixed fighter-ship force to begin their run. The Republican fighters and Dominion ships made a dash for the Praetheen, running their sensor scramblers to the point of burnout. The deception worked, leaving the muddled Praetheen sensors unable to distinguish tightly packed fighter formations from warships. The Praetheen believed the royal guard had attempted to snooker them into a trap but sprung it too quickly. Indeed a trap was coming but from a different direction.

The Praetheen quickly reformed and walled-up to face what they believed was an incoming fleet. Admiral Hale then sent the message to High King William. The main force of Dominion ships engaged in a simultaneous transpatial jump to the star NG-BS-144 just as the Praetheen passed by. In a maneuver that few crews could have pulled off with the finicky transpatial systems of the day, the Dominion ships arrived together positioned into their own wall-up. They arrived above the Praetheen formation. The Dominion ships were then able to focus their firepower from an angle at which the Praetheen's defenses were least able to respond. Soon Dominion ships were tearing into the Praetheen.

Despite having managed to close the trap, the defenders were not able to fully overcome the enormous disparity of numbers between the forces. Admiral Hale's force was destroyed. The Praetheen quickly reformed and surrounded William's fleet. The result was nine hours of protracted combat that continued well after the point that the outcome was clear to both. The battle ended with the annihilation of the Praetheen fleet, but they took with them nearly the entire royal guard force, including William's flagship *H.K.S. Slepnir.*

Admiral Hale survived the destruction of his ship and was later recovered. Together with several members of his crew, he was awarded both the Solar Cross and the Dominion's Star of Kings. But in the end, the victory at Saturn Gate counted for little. With the Imperial economy collapsing around him, Emperor Nathaniel Mandrake chose to open peace talks with the Praetheen. This outraged High King William. He was convinced that the Praetheen determination to fight to the last ship at Saturn Gate indicated that for them, it had been a death-or-glory mission. In his estimation, the royal guard had finally broken the Praetheen. The terms of peace only served to enrage him further.

The Praetheen War was ended by the Treaty of Gan. That treaty left the Praetheen as the only power to face an Imperial invasion and survive. But that survival came at an incredible cost that has never been fully tallied by the Empire. The treaty declared that the entirety of the Near Galaxy Cluster would be recognized as a zone of Praetheen interest, mandating the removal of all Imperial colonies. While Yuangi was in no position to protest, both the Republic of Andromeda and the Dominion were livid. After fighting so hard to keep the colonies, the Empire was now forcing them to be abandoned. Initially both refused to withdraw their colonies and prepared to reinforce the region with their own assets. But both sides eventually backed down, seeing that enough trouble was coming at home that they could not afford to overextend themselves trying to hold territory so far away.

Neither nation allowed the outcome of the war to be forgotten. For generations after, Nathaniel Mandrake would be known as the "Coward's Emperor" in the Republic of Andromeda. Never ones for subtlety, the Dominion went a step further. Into the modern era, the Praetheen War Memorial stands on the southern continent of Reichsylvannia. The scrolling text of this wall lists the name of every soldier of the Empire who died in the war, all beneath a marquis that reads:

> For all time, may this monument stand. May the squandering of so much valor and sacrifice temper us. That we never begin what we will not finish.

In military officer academies, the story of Fan's Folly is taught. It is offered up as a cautionary tale about valuing talent too heavily over experience. A warning against pushing gifted young people into positions they do not yet have the maturity to handle.

Who the "loser" of the Praetheen War was is somewhat relative. The Empire considers itself to have lost the war due to its failure to secure the Near Galaxy Cluster. Precious little contact has been had with the Praetheen since that war. But it is known that they considered themselves the losers in the conflict. This has led to conjecture that at some point the Unity's motivation became the Empire's dissolution. It could also be that to the Praetheen, the cost of the war was simply too high for whatever success they found to be regarded as an authentic victory. In terms of kill-to-death ratio, the Praetheen War may be the most lopsided conflict in history. By war's end, more than sixty Praetheen star hives had been destroyed, with many more heavily damaged. Exactly how many Praetheen were killed, the Empire may never know.

1P
THE GREAT COLLAPSE

52,276 AN

THOUGH THE SOLAR EMPIRE has never disbanded, there existed a period of some six thousand years where it existed as little more than a name. This period, often known as the Great Intermission, began with the Great Collapse. What separated this collapse from those of past civilizations was not simply the scale but the rapidity with which it occurred. Two nations, the Reichsylvannian Dominion and Yuangi, are often blamed for initiating this event. While it is true that they may have thrown the grenade, they did not pull the pin.

By Millennium 50, nearly all the nations of the Empire were in a state of cultural decay. For most of the Empire's history, the prevalence of automation has meant that holding a job is a privilege. Most citizens live on a government-issued stipend through which they purchase their needs and entertainment. Those capable of producing goods on which others are willing to spend the discretionary part of their stipend are the monied working class. Many jobs exist simply to fill positions where organic beings would prefer to interact with other organics than machines. But there are other jobs where the limitations of AI simply do not allow it to fill the position. While these jobs are few, they are vital to society.

By this point in history, the average resident of the Empire had lived in such abundance that they had grown slothful. The general population was so lazy, so unambitious, that even critical jobs were often going unfilled. Residents found it easier to simply live on their stipend and idle away their days in the virtual reality servers of the astranet. Meanwhile, many social issues were reaching a point of critical mass.

Perhaps the most dire of these was political polarization, which pitted the citizens of Imperial nations against those in others. People with no jobs have a lot of free time, and with no work to take pride in, they are easily drawn to political causes. Animosity between incompatible cultures was hardly new to the Empire. Indeed one of its primary jobs has always been keeping the peace between these cultures, but the years leading up to the collapse illustrated a time when the Empire was clearly failing in these duties.

In the Elysian Commonwealth, literal terrorist cells had blossomed, carrying out attacks against the corporations of the Reichsylvannian Dominion. Their reasons ranged from wealth inequality to that nation's treatment of women. In Del Tierr, a similar phenomenon was occurring with many Tirrish citizens committing terrorist acts in protest of the police state in Yuangi. The problems continued up through the government, with many nations imposing effective embargos against others in violation of Imperial law. Imperial duchies found themselves routinely feuding with each other over personal issues in the aristocracy with the contempt filtering down to their citizens. In many instances, the presence of the Imperial military is all that kept some of these feuds from escalating to war.

While some of the population was motivated to find some meaning in their life by taking up causes, the majority were too lazy to be bothered. The moral decay that had taken place during this time is itself the stuff of legends. A study conducted by the Imperial government in the Elysian Commonwealth found that less than one in ten adults under the age of forty had not engaged in at least one public orgy. Less than one in three sons had a relationship with their fathers. More than 75 percent of those surveyed did not believe it was morally wrong to steal if the victim was someone of greater personal wealth. About 80 percent found it at least acceptable to imprison a person based solely on their political beliefs.

The situation was little better in most other nations. While many had other problems, nearly all had serious issues that ranged from family structure to civic duty, to a respect for the rights of others. Society was crumbling, and there was little that seemed poised to stop it. The only exempt nations were the Dominion and Yuangi. For better or worse, the Dominion has always been highly resistant to cultural changes.

Yuangi, in efforts to combat its own internal discord, had become the most massive police state humanity has ever known. Personal freedoms for the citizenry became almost nonexistent. If critical jobs were going unfilled, someone capable would be appointed to them. Failure to carry out the appointed duty meant incarceration in a "hole camp." There the offender would spend their days using hand tools to bore holes through solid rock, and their nights filling the holes with dirt. Discipline in these camps was harsh, and many citizens sent to them never returned.

The larger Imperial government was having many problems of its own. The Imperial troy is an unholy union of fiat money and cryptocurrency. The money is produced according to an algorithm in order to create a steady but stable growth in the money supply. The currency is then distributed to citizens on stipend who purchase goods and services from producers. The income of the producers is then taxed by their national governments who are in turn taxed by the Empire. The only thing that gives the troy any value is the willingness of the productive members of society to accept it for their services. With jobs drying up and the economy tanking, tax revenues for both national governments and the Empire plummeted. This led the Empire to impose ever-increasing taxes on the only nations that were remaining solvent, namely the Dominion, Yuangi, and the Republic of Andromeda. This targeted taxation only increased the sense of discord among these nations.

Perhaps the greatest problem was the rise of several pro-democracy political parties throughout the Empire. While none of these groups ever put forward dissolution of the Imperial monarchy or separation from the Empire, they did advocate for the abolition of the national monarchies and the noble aristocracy. The nobility had become a convenient target for blame in the ailing nations, and these groups soon gained traction. In the Republic of Andromeda, long considered the most democratic of all the Empire's nations, one of these groups succeeded in overthrowing the national government.

This placed enormous strain on the Solar Armed Forces. The Empire has traditionally been reluctant to interfere in purely internal matters within any nation, but the Empire requires the presence of the royal and noble families. The spread of these groups to many nations meant that it was no longer a matter of internal politics for any single nation. Soon the military was spread throughout the realm. This would directly contribute to the Empire's failure in the Praetheen War by ensuring that it could never bring more than a small fraction of its power to bear in that conflict.

The SAF meanwhile was suffering enormous difficulties. Service in the military previously seen as a privilege had become a burden that few wished to take on. The general population had adopted an attitude that crossed the line from pacifism to cowardice, with few wishing to take any job involving personal risk. Recruitment routinely fell short of needs, and all branches were forced to downsize drastically. The Solar Armadas alone was forced to put more than two-thirds of its fleet in mothballs. Falling tax revenue had made the ships too expensive to operate, and lack of recruits left them with no crew. The difference in personnel could have been compensated for via the use of arens. The arens were themselves a target of the democracy movements, and it was feared that increasing their numbers further would only fan the flames of discord.

The Praetheen War would only accelerate the inevitable. To fund the war, Emperor Nathaniel Mandrake was forced to break with the policy of his predecessors. He ordered the Imperial Treasury to modify the algorithm for the issuance of new troys and increase the money supply's rate of growth. As one might expect, this resulted in massive inflation, and it came at the worst possible time.

Nathaniel's choice to end the war over the objections of the Dominion and Yuangi, combined with the crushing taxes both were paying, proved the final straw. Irate at this outcome and tired of carrying the other nations on their backs, both acted. Since taking the crown of Yuangi, the Yao Dynasty has always been known for being incredibly miserly. The nation's government held enormous stockpiles of cash. The Dominion, meanwhile, was an economic superpower among the other nations.

On Day 1 of 52,276 AN, Yuangi opened its treasury and began making massive payouts to residents across the Empire. People awoke and were at first overjoyed to find that a mysterious benefactor had gifted them with a fortune. The Empire's serious inflation problem soon ballooned into hyperinflation. On Day 30, the Reichsylvannian Dominion announced that its companies would no longer accept Imperial troys in exchange for goods and services. Nor would they continue to export to a collection of blacklisted nations. In place of the troy, the Dominion brought out what came to be known as the Dominion ducat, which Yuangi agreed to accept.

The two nations had broken so many Imperial laws that some expected civil war to be inevitable. But it never came. The value of the Imperial troy crashed, and people found themselves awash in worthless cash. Riots broke out across the Empire. Those who could, soon rushed to trade their worthless troys for ducats, leaving the Empire largely unable to do anything about it.

Now having left the Empire with a colossal mess to clean up, both the Dominion and Yuangi largely withdrew. Though they stopped short of declaring independence for themselves, they did everything but. Imperial military bases in both territories were soon forced to evacuate under veiled threats. In other nations a modicum of order was kept only by the presence of Imperial troops. To militarily confront either nation would have meant redeploying troops from regions that could not spare them. Other nations soon followed suit, realizing that the Empire had too many problems to help them. All blatantly disregarded any edict by the throne or law of the Senate to cease their actions.

What little military equipment the Empire did not buy from the Dominion came from the Republic of Andromeda and Yuangi. The Solar Armed Forces largely imploded as a result. The Dominion and Yuangi were no longer selling. The Republic was in a state of anarchy and could not have picked up the slack in time to make a difference.

Within five years, the collapse was complete. Though all its nations still gave lip service, the central power of the Empire had been broken. It was reduced from being the government of governments to little more than a neutral mediator in disputes between the nations. One that could effectively do very little if they did not choose to voluntarily comply. The Empire did not regain its status as the true central authority until the time of the Unification Wars several thousand years later. In more nations than not, society collapsed completely. Though some nations avoided this fate, it largely came as a result of increasingly brutal and ruthless methods by the national governments to re-establish order.

In many ways, the collapse did bring about some improvements for the other nations in later years. Prior to the collapse, the Dominion, Republic of Andromeda, and Yuangi had gained a stranglehold on nearly all sectors of industry. Cut off from free markets with these nations, many were forced to once again develop their own. Throughout the aristocracy, the weakest and least capable members were often forced out of power, and eventually replaced by those more capable. Despite all the suffering it caused, the collapse became a desperately needed reset on society.

1Q
THE REUNIFICATION WARS

58,403 AN–58,511 AN

THE GREAT COLLAPSE SAW the nations of the Empire break away into autonomous states that only turned to the throne as a source of neutral ground. In the intervening years, the power of the Empire shrank drastically. Though the Empire did its best to keep the peace, without the lost might of the Solar Armed Forces, it did not manage to do so for long. While the Reichsylvannian Dominion and Yuangi turned to isolationism, many of the other nations did not have the self-sufficiency to do so.

Ironically the only thing that allowed the Imperial government to continue functioning was the multitude of isolationist nations made up of xenophobic aliens. These nations continued to pay their taxes and host military bases, completely disinterested in anything occurring outside of their territory. As a result, these nations were the ones to benefit from the military protection the Empire could still offer.

A number of relatively small wars soon erupted between the nations as the SAF grew increasingly impotent. Though they were forced to cooperate, the nations soon came to blows over their relative positions. These conflicts revolved around matters ranging from border disputes to attempts by others to secure dominance in the new industries they'd been forced to develop. Because the Empire did not have the strength to unilaterally force an end to these conflicts, it was forced to remain neutral to avoid alienating any of the nations. Some of the warring nations would cease to exist, while others would break away from their parents. While all these wars were relatively small, the sheer number of them turned the Empire into an extremely chaotic place.

The long period of chaos was prolonged largely by the stubbornness of the throne. Nathaniel Mandrake carried no small measure of blame for the collapse. He refused to accept blame, and he spent the rest of his days blaming both the Dominion and Yuangi. He would pass this attitude on to his son and successor, Damien, who refused to make any overtures to either nation. The truth that the throne refused to accept was that it needed all the pillar nations to hold the Empire together, including the Dominion and

Yuangi. The Elysian Commonwealth, Del Tierr, and Orion Estate had never contributed as much to the Empire as either of the other two. The Republic of Andromeda was in no position to contribute to anything. For the Empire to be made whole again, the Dominion and Yuangi would have to come back to the table. But neither nation showed an interest in doing so, and the throne made no overtures.

Emperor Damien was eventually succeeded by Nathaniel II, but his reign was short-lived. Nathaniel II was dangerously insane and fantasized about launching a great campaign to conquer the Dominion and Yuangi to force reunification. Though his generals impressed upon him several times how dangerous this idea was, he refused to give up the ambition. The Solar Armadas was in tatters, operating antiquated ships that had been forced to remain on active duty long beyond their service life. The Dominion continued to update and produce new designs, which it shared with Yuangi. Fleet conflicts between them would have been disastrous. The Solar Legionnaires' numbers had fallen to levels woefully insufficient for such a conquest. The Solar Army barely existed at all. To attack either nation would do no more than provoke them into formalizing their independence. It could even lead to a nightmare scenario with the two shattering the Empire's tenuous grip on life.

Fortunately for everyone involved, Nathaniel II was also an extremely enthusiastic drug abuser. He killed himself and his wife, Mary, one night when both overdosed on the extremely powerful and very illegal narcotic known as C2C. This left a bit of a leadership crisis in the Empire because at the time there were no eligible heirs to the throne. Under the guidelines established by the Summit at Olympus thousands of years before, authority over the Empire should have passed to the high king of the Dominion. At least until such time as one of Nathaniel II's children were old enough to assume the throne. However, as the Dominion had checked out, the court was forced to pass the title to Christopher III.

Christopher III ascended the throne at the tender age of eleven. He would later come to be known as the boy who saved the Empire. Though still very young and impressionable, Christopher had been well-known beforehand for his keen intellect. He had grown up hearing much from his father about the "greedy, warmongering pigs" of the Dominion and the "greedy totalitarians" in Yuangi. He reasoned that both were greedy, and one liked to fight. The Empire was full of small wars that needed to be stopped. The answer seemed obvious. Christopher personally traveled to Reichsylvannia to meet with High King Gavin von Rhinegrave, himself an old man at the time. Christopher simply asked what it would take for the Dominion to come back.

The Dominion had remained relatively strong but was still suffering many hardships of its own. Much of the nation's wealth has always come from its exports. It had much to gain by helping to make the Empire whole again. It did not hurt that High King Gavin took a liking to the boy, once recounting, "Would that every emperor were as wise as that boy, the Empire would outlive the universe itself."

The two negotiated for several days, with Christopher ultimately convincing the high king to help restore the Empire. With the high king's support, Christopher traveled to Rongxing, then-capital of Yuangi. Since the collapse, Yuangi had gone through a bitter succession dispute between two sides of the Yao Dynasty. Christopher arrived to find the nation amid a civil war between two potential heirs, Ganxi Yao and his cousin Ying-Yu Tso.

With the high king's help, Christopher was able to negotiate an agreement between the two. The young emperor had no doubt that there would be some nations that refused to go along with his plans of reformation. He proposed to give Yuangi over to Ganxi Yao. Meanwhile, to Ying-Yu, he promised that if she withdrew her claim to Yuangi, he would allow her to carve out a new territory of her own from nations that refused to peacefully submit to reunification. Both eventually agreed.

With the Dominion and Yuangi behind him, Christopher was able to begin rebuilding the Solar Armed Forces into a power to be feared. This alone was enough to coerce the Elysian Commonwealth, Del Tierr, the Orion Estate, and many of the smaller nations once again to begin fulfilling their commitments. However, that left many who did not.

Among the pillar nations, the Republic of Andromeda remained defiant. The Alexander Dynasty still clung to the title of king, but it had been reduced to mere figurehead status. The noble aristocracy below them had been almost completely eliminated. The nation was now run by an elected parliament and its prime minister. All these politicians had been pushing for some time to formalize their independence. While Christopher found King Liam Alexander more than willing to return, he was completely unable to convince the elected leadership to do the same.

On Day 60 of 58,403 AN, the revitalized Solar Armadas and Legionnaires swept into the Republic of Andromeda. The Republic had long been well respected for its military prowess, but it was not on display in this conflict. Much of the Republic's martial strength came as a direct result of the Alexander Dynasty's influence. The Alexanders and those loyal to them quickly fell in with the Empire.

The Republican Star Forces had been gutted in the years since the collapse, mostly as a result of being dismantled by the elected leaders to fund social welfare programs. The only major battle of this conflict was the Battle of Atlantis, to seize the nation's capital. The term *Atlantean Victory* is still used in the SAF's parlance to describe a major battle that quickly fizzles into a rout. The Republican fleet quickly collapsed in the face of a determined Armadas push. Troops on the ground were soon tripping over themselves to affirm loyalty to the king rather than fight a brutal street-to-street war across the surface of their planet. The will to keep the politicians in power simply did not exist among the troops. The Alexander family soon regained control over the nation and began appointing a new nobility to replace those that had been murdered by pro-democracy mobs.

With the last of the pillar nations once more in the fold, the Empire then turned its attention toward the duchies. Not all of them came back to the table so easily. Many had no eagerness to resume paying taxes to the Empire. Others were unwilling to lay down arms in the feuds over which they were currently engaged. Over the next hundred years, the Empire was forced to occupy more than thirty of these duchies and install new leadership. Unfortunately Christopher III's promise to Ying-Yu Tso was never fulfilled, as she was assassinated by her sister as order began to return. Rather than reward a murderer, Christopher chose to have the villainous sister executed. Those who had followed Ying-Yu eventually went their own way, scattering to new homes across the Empire.

When all was said and done, the boy-emperor had made the Empire whole again. Christopher III remained on the throne for the rest of his life until dying of old age. He did more than simply reunify the Empire. He would lay the foundation for its second golden age, the Pax Imperica. He supervised the reopening of markets, the restoration of the troy as a controlled and valuable currency, and worked extensively to calm tensions between the nations. The Pax Imperica would last some twenty thousand years until the Solar Eclipse. For that, Christopher III is considered by many to be the greatest emperor in history.

1R
THE SOLAR ECLIPSE

80,192 AN–80,216 AN

ON THE 131ST DAY of the year 80,192, thirty-one nations of the Solar Empire formally declared independence as the Solar Dominion. The Empire's second golden age, the Pax Imperica, had come to an end. The rebellion included three of the Empire's pillar nations: the Reichsylvannian Dominion, Republic of Andromeda, and Yuangi. Catalysts for the war were found in both Imperial tax policy and the throne's violation of the ancient principle of sovereign dominion.

The Solar Dominion's rebellion would kickstart more than twenty years of continuous warfare and was the most costly war the Empire had fought to that point. The war saw the end of one royal dynasty and led directly to the fall of another, generations later. By several orders of magnitude, more Imperial citizens and residents were killed in this conflict than all other wars the Empire had yet fought, combined. The war would end only with the exposure of conspiracies, the abdications of many rulers, and a negotiated peace.

Twenty thousand years is a long time, though not quite so long to a civilization with members who themselves routinely live for thousands of years. Effects of the war are still felt into the modern Empire, with friendships and hatreds born in the conflict still alive and well. But the full details of the Solar Eclipse, numerous as they are, should perhaps be shared in their own volumes.

1S
THE VIRGO EXPANSION

99,600 AN–Present

ON DAY 1 OF THE year 99,600, Emperor Mason Mandrake gave his "New Horizons" speech to inaugurate the new year. He lamented the Empire's lack of expansion since the time of the Solar Eclipse. He concluded his speech by challenging Imperial industry to establish trade routes and colonization in the distant Virgo Galaxy Cluster. Not since the Praetheen War had the Empire attempted to make inroads to another galaxy cluster, and for good reason. Even the distance between galaxies is easily dwarfed by such a massive void. Though the Empire had sent probes to Virgo in prior eras, the prospect of colonizing it seemed as vain as the hopes of interstellar travel before the invention of the massless impulse drive.

But after 150 years of intense research and development, the Empire's industry answered. Countless sums of money led to a revolution in the design of transpatial drives and a new class of explorer ships to make the long journey. Upon their arrival, these ships set up permanent gates in four galaxies, and the floodgates were opened.

The Empire found the galaxies of the Virgo Cluster unusually rich in life, finding hundreds of intelligent species with which to interact. The Empire's desire to expand into the region was bolstered by the sheer eagerness many civilizations showed to voluntarily take their place in the Empire. It soon learned that this was due to the influence of a regional superpower known as the Interstellar Combine.

Initially the Empire had very little contact with the Combine and would not until it first placed colonies in the Hourglass Galaxy in the year 100,000. In the interim years, it found itself more heavily occupied with the Outlands Star League.

1T
THE OUTLANDS WAR

99,853 AN–99,857 AN

THOUGH MANY CIVILIZATIONS IN the Virgo Cluster welcomed the arrival of the Solar Empire, there was a coalition that did not. Thirty-three civilizations led by a nation dubbed the Maxnin Regime all found themselves in a state of panic as a new superpower began to swell in their region of the universe. The Empire would later dub the coalition formed by these civilizations the Outlands Star League.

Well before the Empire's arrival, many of the civilizations in the region had been victimized by an entity calling itself the Fleet of No Nation. The translations of the more polite terms used by the general population saw them dubbed the Pillagers by the Empire. The Pillagers were a pirate armada unlike any other. They had all the discipline of a professional military, a uniform chain of command, their own regulations, and recruiting standards. In many ways, they were a civilization unto themselves, but one built purely on raiding as a purpose unto itself.

When the Empire first arrived, the Pillagers avoided Imperial assets like a plague. Their first look at the Solar Armadas was enough to keep the raiders at bay. This changed after a secret conclave between the leaders of the Fleet and the Outlands Star League. Both saw a growing threat from the Empire. To the OSL, the Empire seemed poised to surround and eventually consume them. To the Pillagers, the increasing might of the Empire in the region meant that their own days were numbered. Thus the two groups chose to work together. The OSL would provide the Pillagers with safe passage through their territory, and the finest equipment available, if they would turn their efforts toward the Empire.

For more than a decade, the Pillagers raided Imperial colonies, unprotected civilian shipping, and attacked small Armadas ships when they could muster enough force to do so. With the OSL providing safe passage, the Empire found these raiders difficult to track and exterminate. Eventually, Emperor Mason Mandrake had enough. He dispatched his son Steven Mandrake, with elements of the first armada, with one mission. Hunt down the Fleet of No Nation and destroy it.

While Steven Mandrake led the Armadas in pursuit of the Pillagers, the plight of those victimized by them was brought to the mainstream consciousness by the publication of the novel *Fall's Pendulum*. Though only loosely based on actual events, it detailed the story of Elysian-born colonist Rachael Fall. Fall was abducted by the Pillagers and held by her captors until she was rescued in one of the first operations performed under Prince Steven's direction.

After seven years, Prince Steven's fleet eventually cornered the bulk of the Pillager armada and destroyed it in the Battle of CG-BS-760. Shortly after the battle, the Empire found proof that the Pillagers had been receiving aid from the Outlands Star League. They had been exposed, which threw the members of the OSL into panic. This panic was exacerbated by the fact that the story of Rachael Fall had elicited a significant response from the Imperial public.

The OSL felt that it had no choice but to launch an attack on the Empire before an invasion could be marshaled against them. The OSL had no false confidence in being able to beat the Empire in an all-out war, but it had hoped that a decisive show of force might convince the Empire that settlement in the region was not worth the cost. It failed, spectacularly.

With far more limited FTL capabilities, the OSL was forced to adopt a strategy centered around securing supply lines and transit routes. One of the most important targets was an Imperial colony world dubbed Miner-9. The OSL spent the next six months amassing their forces while Prince Steven's task force mopped up the last of the Pillagers. On Day 277 of 99,853 AN, the OSL launched its invasion of the Imperial colonies. The Empire had not suspected such a stupid action and was caught off guard. The momentum of the OSL's surprise was soon lost when they came to Miner-9.

Miner-9 had been host to a Legionnaire company, well armed with planetary defense weapons. Over a six-week siege, the OSL made six separate attempts to land troops on the planet, intending to capture the Imperial resources that had been stationed there. All six of their attempts were rebuffed by determined legionnaires. Eventually, the OSL grew desperate, and managing to open a breach in the planet's defenses, they commenced general bombardment. The bombardment killed more than half of the planet's colonists, but still the legionnaires rebuffed further assaults.

The siege of Miner-9 would later be broken by the battlecruiser *H.M.S. Yamato*, under the command of then-Captain Terrance Gilyard. Over the next six weeks, warships and legionnaires would begin pouring into the region. Over the next four years, the Empire would systematically dismantle the Outlands Star League and its member states. Most of its nations would eventually be conquered and integrated as Imperial territories. The few nations not conquered were deliberately allowed to maintain their sovereignty, reducing the territory the Empire needed to defend directly as it continued to expand into and explore the region. The war ended on Day 61 of 99,857 AN when the last remaining Maxnin forces formally surrendered to ships of the Solar Armadas.

APPENDIX 2

THE
SOLAR EMPIRE

THE MORE THINGS CHANGE, the more they stay the same. Humanity has spread to multiple galaxies. It has discovered sciences and invented technologies that have changed the nature of the human condition. Alchemic printers and advanced power generation have brought on an era where even the poorest citizens live comfortably without shortages of essentials. The nanosingularity has vastly stretched the human lifespan and granted potential to merge man and machine that allows scientists to contemplate with more computing power than an entire species's worth of conceptual power. Humanity has developed the means to warp space-time and travel millions of light-years in a casual span of time.

The reality of day-to-day life is far different for denizens of the Solar Empire than it was for its ancestors. But in the end, the adage remains true: Though humanity finds itself in different circumstances, humans remain human. There are still rich and poor, smart and stupid, criminal and law-abiding. Humans still eat, sleep, breathe, and seek out pleasures to fill their time. There are still times of war and peace. The human being is the product of an evolutionary process that lasted billions of years from the first single-celled organisms. While evolution may one day turn humanity into something beyond what it is today, the humans of the Solar Empire are differentiated from their ancestors more by circumstance than anything else.

2A
BREADTH

THE INVENTION OF THE transpatial drive brought with it a means of such expedient travel that the intergalactic voyage became a practical venture. If there is one truth that is born out of human history, it is that if man has the ability to go somewhere, he will. Humanity has used the power of the transpatial drive to travel to every galaxy in the Local Group. It has not simply visited other galaxies, but other galaxy clusters. Humanity has seen the light of galaxies so far away, that they would have never been visible had the species not left Earth.

The Solar Empire maintains undisputed control over the Local Group of galaxies and has placed colonies in all of them. It has continued to expand and explore beyond these borders and into neighboring galaxy clusters. The Empire has colonies in over one hundred galaxies ranging from single-owner private planets to massive star hives hosting many septillions of residents.

The heart of the Empire is found in the Solar, Andromeda, Dominion, and Magellanic galaxies which dominate the Local Group. These are the regions that are most heavily developed and populated, somewhat akin to major cities surrounded by metropolitan sprawl.

2B
TECHNOLOGY

TO ONE LOOKING AT a timeline of the Empire's inventions, it could easily give the impression that its technology is stagnant. This is an illusion created by a number of factors. It is often assumed that any given technology will eventually be rendered obsolete and replaced by something else, but this assumption is inherently false. The laws of physics set a defining limit on what is and is not possible within the reality of the universe. While indeed some technologies eventually become obsolete, others do not.

Very often, technology is simply added to the ever-expanding catalog of capabilities humanity has at its disposal to address problems. The humble hammer was invented early in the history of mankind's technological development. It remained in service for thousands of years, as it reflected one of the best and most simple means to accomplish the task for which it had been designed. In daily life, simplicity is almost always valued over complexity, and often the best engineering solutions are those which require the *least* technology. It is inescapable that the more technology required to perform a task, the more complex it becomes. The more complex any given thing becomes, the greater the room for error.

The Empire has reached a point of maturity for many technologies that have existed for so long that those major improvements that can be made, have largely been made. This has led to reaching a point of diminishing returns where the research and development necessary to yield further improvements require enormous sums of time and resources for modest gains. Major improvements can require the discovery of new physics.

With the breadth of knowledge it already has, the discovery of new physics can often require studying the universe at such tiny scales that it can take many years of constant observation before recording data that can confirm or dispute a hypothesis. Often, scientists are forced to brute-force their research with hyper-computing, simulation, and observation to make any kind of progress. Some estimates suggest that it could take millions of years before science could make the discoveries needed to affect meaningful change in the technologies the Empire already has. In effect, all of physics' low-hanging fruit have already been claimed.

2C
SAPIENCE, RIGHT OF BIRTH, AND THE CHAIN OF LIFE

IT HAS LONG BEEN an unfulfilled ambition of the Mandrake Dynasty to install a uniform code of rights to be enjoyed by *all* sapient beings. Efforts to make this a reality, however, have failed in the face of sovereign dominion, which grants national sovereigns the authority to determine the rights of their residents. In the end, the throne has been able only to define the rights of those who earn Solar citizenship. In order to do this, it is necessary to define what constitutes a sapient being. The Mandrake Dynasty has long predicated this judgment on two interlinked philosophies known as the "Chain of Life" and the "Right of Birth."

Christopher I, the first emperor, was the man who coined both terms. In his writing, he spelled out that it was irrelevant if the universe was created by the laws of physics, or a creator deity. What mattered was that the universe begat life. The Chain of Life is the bridge from past to present, spanning all generations back to the very first single-celled organisms. The Chain of Life theory stipulates that the universe brought such beings into existence, and that said existence is a natural phenomenon. Through the generations, by enduring the ruthless calculus that is survival of the fittest, those who are part of the Chain of Life have earned certain rights. One of which is to exist. This right of existence flowing from the Chain of Life is Right of Birth.

These concepts apply only to those whose existence is seen as a continuation of the Chain of Life itself. This includes those who are born or exist as a direct result of the desire to procreate. Clones, arens, and AI, no matter how self-aware or intelligent they may be, do not have rights. They do not exist as part of the Chain of Life, and hence have no Right of Birth. They exist only as the result of intelligence manipulating the natural universe, rather than as a product of the natural universe itself. These beings exist as intelligent tools, not people. By contrast, a child created through genetic engineering and the mixing of parental genes outside of sexual procreation is considered part of the Chain of Life. They were created specifically to continue the chain as offspring of their parents.

For most people, these concepts have minimal impact, for unless they earn Solar citizenship, their rights are determined by their national sovereign. But the doctrines herein do limit who can attempt to earn Solar citizenship, and influence many laws such as those pertaining to the creation of self-aware AI. Most of these laws place prohibitions on designing an AI's behavior to seek independence rather than servitude. Further, the doctrine *does* limit who the national sovereigns can recognize as sapient beings. The throne may not be able to define the rights of a resident within a nation, but it can define who can be recognized as being eligible to have rights.

These doctrines are not without criticism or countertheories. In the Reichsylvannian Dominion, the nation recognizes the techla as a "machine race." Granted, they are a bit of a special case, as they were created by a now-extinct species as part of a failed attempt to transfer their sapience into machines and sustain their existence through an extinction event. Nonetheless, the techla are considered sapient beings within the Dominion. Forcing the issue is something the Mandrake and Rhinegrave dynasties have decided not to do as the techla live exclusively in the latter's territory. Because the techla are not considered sapient beings by the throne, no member of the species can earn Solar citizenship if it desires to do so. While the techla are the most prolific, they are not the only example of national sovereigns failing to embrace these doctrines. A sort of understanding has been reached in these matters, with no party willing to disrupt the status quo by challenging the issue directly.

2D
POPULATION

THE POPULATION OF THE Solar Empire is so vast that it can be easy for one to become lost in the numbers. With the technology at its disposal, the Empire does not require a large population, and its civilization could exist with less than a million living people. However, a founding goal of the Empire was to ensure the continued survival of humanity. This goal would later include all sapient races beneath its banner. The more prolific a species is, the more difficult it would be for any agency, be it natural or malicious, to exterminate. The Empire has consistently pursued the growth of its population through its one hundred thousand–year existence.

Before delving into the numbers, it is important to understand where all these people live. Star hives are the ultimate realization of a concept first envisaged in prehistory by a man named Freeman Dyson. Star hives are collections of self-replicating habitation satellites in orbit of a star. A hive typically begins small, often with fewer than a dozen satellites, but exponential growth allows this number to expand rapidly. The primary limitation on a hive's early growth is how much power it can liberate from its host star before supplemental power must be added from other sources.

The standard hive satellite is a metal sail measuring 200 kilometers wide, 400 kilometers long, and 10 kilometers thick. The concave inner surface, which faces the star, is dedicated to collecting stellar radiation, while the outer broadside, facing away from the star, and roughly forty percent of the satellite's internal volume are available for habitation, with infrastructure dominating the rest. All told, each satellite provides 320,000 cubic kilometers of internal livable space and 80,000 square kilometers of livable surface. In the densest configurations—where the interior volume is subdivided into stacked residential layers—a single hive satellite can offer more than 80 million square kilometers of total habitable area. For comparison, before it was scourged by the Thericans, Earth's landmass was around 148 million square kilometers.

The Empire has long favored building around blue stars due to their high luminosity. Especially large blue stars—such as blue hypergiants—are often known as *crown stars*. These stars are jealously guarded by kings and archdukes and are rarely apportioned to their nobility. Hives constructed around them can support trillions of satellites with ease. With such vast amounts of free power, individual satellites can each sustain trillions of residents, resulting in human populations reaching into the septillions.

The matter and energy drawn by a hive during initial construction often help to stabilize the host star and extend its lifespan. Such immense stars— and the hives that accompany them—are rare. More common are hives built around main-sequence blue stars. These lesser blue stars can still support populations in the low septillions.

Once a hive is fully integrated into the astranet and its supplemental power infrastructure, orbital mechanics become the primary limiting factor for satellite capacity. Specifically, the limit becomes the ratio of the swarm's combined mass versus that of the star. Blue stars are relatively rare in the cosmos, and not all of the type are suitable for use. Other star types, such as white and yellow, are also used as hive sources, but being significantly smaller host commensurately smaller populations.

The exact number of people a satellite or hive can support varies significantly. The most densely populated centers are known as denements, and a denement satellite can accommodate 3.5 trillion human residents using only internal habitation space. By contrast, more affluent individuals live with vastly greater personal volume. Wealthy citizens may own entire satellites, or more. As of the year 100,000, the Solar Empire counted some half a billion sanctioned hives around stars of various types. This number excludes hives not used primarily as habitation centers. All of this is in addition to the countless planets colonized and deep-space habitats constructed throughout the Empire's history.

By far the most populous species in the Empire are the roliams. Individually, roliams require only a fraction of the resources needed by most species to survive. Their numbers are so vast that they are practically the substrate of the Solar Galaxy Group. In places no other species will—or can—inhabit, the roliams readily take up residence. They are found in abundance on worlds with toxic atmospheres, snowbound ice worlds, volcanic death worlds, and radiation-blasted surfaces. Lifeless moons, rogue planets, and large asteroids are all fair game, as tunnels are dug, pressurized, and then inhabited.

Yet even with the multitude of such celestial bodies available, it is within their own form of hive that most roliams are found. A jova hive is similar to a star hive but utilizes a specialized spherical satellite designed to orbit a gas giant. Rather than drawing power from starlight, these hives generate energy by tapping and fusing hydrogen from the host world. Jova hives can easily support hundreds of sextillions of roliams for tens of millions of years before their hydrogen supply is exhausted. When the same concept is scaled up to a brown dwarf, it becomes a swarm hive. Under similar principles, the largest swarm hives can comfortably support septillions of roliams.

The Empire can only estimate the true number of roliams, based primarily on the number of hive seeds they have been issued. As of the Year 100,000 census, that number stood at four undecillion—most of which are concentrated in the Solar, Andromeda and Magellanic galaxies. This astronomically high number requires some perspective: if each Roliam weighed only one gram, their combined mass would be approximately six hundred seventy million times that of pre-Imperial Earth.

Despite being the Empire's most numerous species, roliams have almost no direct effect on Imperial policy or government. Roliams do not understand the concept of representative government, do not run for office, nor do they vote in elections. They don't conceptualize why the "drones of society" should be permitted a say in how it is run. Roliams are barred from politics to *protect* representative government. Otherwise they would simply vote for whomever they were told to vote for, and bury every other species under an avalanche of numbers. Roliams will default to human authority in most cases, be it the emperor, a local noble, or an employer. Because roliams do not demand wages, have no personal ambition, and do not covet luxury, many population estimates omit them entirely.

Humanity clocks in as the Empire's second most numerous species, and it is for humanity that the Empire has the best numbers. Thanks to the nanosingularity, every human is born with an on-demand astranet connection. The Empire has robust privacy laws to prevent people from being monitored and tracked at all times. However, all persons are required to answer the census conducted every one hundred years. Anyone within the astranet can accomplish this by wirelessly uplinking and answering a five-minute questionnaire, so the numbers are as accurate as can be expected. Over the years, humans have benefited from the longevity of millennia-long lifespans. To keep the population from exploding beyond the ability to house it, most humans wait until their second millennium to have children. Some jurisdictions even require that a breeding license be obtained. As of the year 100,000, the human population stood at 341 nonillion.

The total population of the Empire—counting all non-roliam beings recognized as legally sapient—is approximately 375 nonillion. This number can be deceptive and is highly concentrated geographically. The majority of the Empire's total population lives in the Solar, Andromeda, Dominion, and Magellanic galaxies. To compare the population of the Empire to other civilizations is, in most cases, a pointless exercise. The total population of most non-Imperial species is a rounding error or less in comparison. The two most notable exceptions are the Praetheen Unity and the Interstellar Combine. However, due to poor relations with both, their total populations were unknown at the start of the Hourglass War.

Of course, all of this raises a very valid question. What do all these people *do*? A poignant question since automation long ago replaced most of the workforce. The answer is that it depends. The average person's biggest decision each day will be how to entertain themselves. Roliams think nothing of forgoing automation and performing tasks like farming in order to have something to fill the time. The question of what to do with one's free time is as old as free time itself. Imperial society simply means there is more time to fill, and more to do with it.

2E
GOVERNMENT

THE EMPIRE DESCRIBES ITS form of government as an "oversight monarchy." But before one can truly understand the Imperial system, one must understand sovereign dominion. Sovereign dominion is a sacred covenant between the emperor and the rulers of each nation. Sovereign dominion spells out a list of obligations that each sovereign and their nation must meet to the Empire. If these obligations are not met, the emperor has both the right and authority to address the situation. The obligations of sovereign dominion can and have been expanded over the years. To add obligations requires the consent of no less than three quarters of the reigning sovereigns at the time a new obligation is proposed. To remove an obligation requires the emperor's consent.

The obligations of sovereign dominion are as follows:

1. The nation must pay taxes levied upon it by the throne, or by the Solar Senate with the emperor's consent.
2. A nation must host bases of the Imperial military upon the request of the throne.
3. Each nation must maintain a self-defense force that can contribute to its own defense in times of war and peace. These forces must answer the call of the emperor to assist in war if the throne deems it necessary. Further, a nation must share all military technology with the Imperial government and cannot refuse to sell arms or matériel to the Solar Armed Forces.
4. Each nation must respect all rights extended by the throne to any individual granted Solar citizenship.
5. Each national sovereign must adopt Solar as the official language of his court, his government, and teach that language to all residents.
6. Each national sovereign must provide for the welfare of his or her residents through basic education, law enforcement, and emergency services.
7. Each national sovereign must maintain the peace and tranquility of his realm.
8. Each nation must follow the foreign policy of the throne.

9. Each nation must adopt the Imperial troy as its national currency. All government and commercial transactions must be made with troys as legal tender.

If a nation and its leader are in compliance with all obligations of sovereign dominion, then the national sovereigns have full autonomy to govern the internal affairs of their nation. A nation in compliance cannot be obliged to follow any law or edict that impinges on its internal sovereignty.

It is important to understand that the Imperial government is not a nation by, of, or for the people. The Empire is a government of governments. Its job is to set laws and policies for how the nations interact with each other and affect the Empire as a whole. In many ways, the Empire is everything the Interstellar Confederacy tried and failed to be. It is a national superstate that regulates the activity of the member nations while having little contact with the common citizenry.

No common person in the Empire is born with Imperial citizenship, and are instead classified as residents of their nation of birth. Solar citizenship is earned, and the rights and privileges of Solar citizens are defined and extended to them by the throne. The rights and privileges of residents are defined solely by the national sovereign where they reside. Kings and archdukes are absolute rulers and could not give up that distinction even if they wished to. The throne holds every sovereign personally accountable for the peace and stability of their nation. They must have the necessary authority to meet that responsibility.

The emperor is the head of state and has complete authority in all areas that do not tread upon sovereign dominion. The emperor is fully empowered to make law via edict. Historically, however, the Mandrake Dynasty has delegated most of the obligation of legislation to the Solar Senate. The throne has made it clear that the Solar Armed Forces and the Imperial Treasury are off limits. Only the emperor has authority over these institutions.

The Solar Senate is a three-chamber body made up of the House of Nobles, Citizens' Congress, and Council of Justiciars. Every individual in the Empire with a noble or royal title has a seat in the House of Lords. Their voting power in that body is proportional to their position in the peerage. The leader of the House of Lords is the first lord, who sets the agenda for the chamber. While technically an elected position, in practice it is a hereditary position held by the high king of the Reichsylvannian Dominion, being second only to the emperor in peerage.

The Citizens' Congress is led by the prime speaker. The Congress is made up of individuals who have earned Solar citizenship and have been elected to their offices. The number of seats any nation is entitled to in the Congress is directly tied to the number of Solar citizens residing in that nation. The Citizens' Congress is led by the prime speaker, who is elected to the position by fellow senators.

The third and final body is the Council of Justiciars, led by the chief justice. Justiciars are appointed to the position by the emperor from a pool of candidates who are experts in Imperial law. The Council is by far the smallest of the three chambers and, unlike the other two, cannot propose legislation. The sole purpose of the Council is to review measures passed by the others and judge them on two criteria. The first is that a measure does not violate sovereign dominion. The second is that a new measure does not contradict or overlap with an existing law without addressing that previous law. Once a measure is approved by all three chambers, it can then pass into law.

It is after this that the oversight in "oversight monarchy" comes into play. It is both the right and duty of the emperor to use his power of edict to nullify any law passed by the Senate that he feels is against the good of the Empire. It has also at times fallen to the emperor to use his power of edict to act when partisan bickering has left the Senate in gridlock.

While emperors typically name their successors, every candidate must be confirmed by the Solar Senate. The Senate must confirm that an heir is legally competent to discharge the duties of the office. If the Senate finds a chosen heir is not competent, it will pass to another in the line of succession. It is also within the power of the Senate to remove a sitting emperor if they should prove mentally incompetent, or treasonous. This is extremely difficult to accomplish and requires a three-quarters majority from each chamber. If an emperor is removed in this manner, succession is followed as if he had died.

Both the power of the Senate and the emperor remain limited by sovereign dominion. This has been a contentious issue at some points in the Empire's history. One of the primary examples was the Solar Eclipse. Conflicts arise when "ripple effects" of a nation's internal activities affect those in other nations. Ever since the Solar Eclipse, the throne has adopted the position that ripples alone are not sufficient grounds to justify impinging on a nation's internal sovereignty. In modern history, more than half of all nullification of Senate laws by the throne has been a result of national blocs ganging up on each other in attempts to use the Senate to violate sovereign dominion.

2F
ECONOMY AND TREASURY

THE IMPERIAL TREASURY IS the only entity authorized to produce legal tender. The individual nations, even those that are isolationist, are forbidden from producing their own currencies. The currency of the Empire is the Imperial troy, symbolized by the character Ŧ. The name of the troy comes from the root "troy ounce" because in its earliest days, the Empire operated on a precious metal standard. Each troy was then subdivided into thirty-one grams symbolized by the character ĝ. When the Empire abandoned the precious metal standard, the exchange ratio was changed to one hundred grams per troy to simplify accounting.

The troy exists as a union of fiat money and cryptocurrency. It is produced by the treasury according to an algorithm tied to many factors such as population growth. The Empire has long preferred to work toward a state of steady economic growth rather than waves of boom and bust, leading it to carefully control the money supply. This has had the effect of keeping the value of an individual troy quite high. The average stipend-receiving family of four can live on less than a troy a day. That is a consideration in the money-supply calculations as attempts are made to keep this status quo.

The vast majority of troys and grams in circulation exist as digital currency circulated via the astranet. The Empire does produce physical currency, and it is used both in foreign trade and in areas of the Empire where astranet coverage is spotty or absent. Physical troys are produced from a substance known as troy gold. This is gold that has undergone an extremely difficult process, which arranges the individual atoms in a highly complex and repeating pattern as a defense against counterfeiting. This makes genuine notes easy to detect with a variety of scanning devices but exceptionally difficult to forge given the extreme precision involved. Under careful supervision, this troy gold is sometimes provided to jewelers and others who specialize in making things meant to serve as obvious displays of wealth.

Physical troys are forged from gold leaf, which is then encased in a hard but transparent lamination. These troys come in denominations of 1,000, 500, 250, 100, 50, 20, 10, 5, and 1. Physical grams are manufactured in troy gold coins in denominations of 50, 25, 10, 5, and 1. Troy notes measure

8.731 by 20.605 centimeters. As the first emperor, Christopher Mandrake is depicted on the Ŧ1 note. Manfred von Rhinegrave, the only non-emperor on currency, is depicted on the Ŧ1,000.

In addition to physical troys, the Imperial Treasury also produces its own form of bearer bond. Like ancient notes of the same name, they pay interest and are unregistered. They are a favorite means of the aristocracy to hoard wealth but are also purchased for large exchanges by private citizens. Their large denominations and freely liquid nature make them popular in criminal enterprises. The Empire accepts this because it makes it easier to disguise its use of these bonds for its own clandestine activity. Like physical notes, they are manufactured from troy gold. The fact that Imperial currency is produced from gold helps to instill value even if it is traded with primitive societies. Meanwhile gold itself maintains its historic association with wealth due almost entirely to its use in minting physical troys.

As with all advanced societies, the gap between the wealthiest and poorest people is quite large. On a primitive pre-industrial world, there is little difference between the wealthiest and poorest dirt farmers in terms of the absolute value of their property. In the Empire, the gap between the rich and poor is truly astronomical. With such abundant energy and the technology of alchemic printers, however, the Empire's poor often live better than the wealthy of many civilizations.

Those on stipend make up the lower class of society. Those with actual jobs make up the monied middle class. Those with the wealth to pay wages and create jobs make up the upper class. The nobility and royalty with their vast fortunes are often considered economic classes unto themselves.

2G
NATIONS, SOVEREIGN DUCHIES, AND TERRITORIES

THE SOLAR EMPIRE IS made up of six nations and 154 sovereign duchies. The term *nation* is properly applied only to those with their own royal dynasties and can trace the history of their rulers back to the Summit at Olympus. In common parlance, however, the term *nation* is generally applied both to nations and sovereign duchies. This leads to the true nations being referred to as "pillar nations."

The sovereign duchies came into being, following the War of Kings. Their creation was intended to prevent a repeat of that conflict by enabling the Empire to continue to expand, but ensuring that a small group of nations could not become too powerful for the Empire to keep them from making war on each other.

As iterated prior, every true nation has its own royal dynasty headed by a king. The sovereign duchies in turn have noble dynasties headed by an archduke. While there are no alien kings, there are numerous alien archdukes. Many of the Empire's more isolationist species live in their own sovereign duchies with archdukes of their own species, and limit their contact with the rest of the Empire.

Imperial law requires that a population center of one million people or more have at least a noble overseer. There must be someone that the throne can hold personally accountable for the well-being of that territory and the people who reside within it. If a noble or even a king should allow their territory to fall into chaos, fail to provide for the common defense, or fail to establish and maintain basic civic services, they can and will be replaced. Whether it is by a higher-ranking noble to whom they answer, or by the emperor himself.

If there is no royal or noble dynasty to govern a region it gains the distinction of territory. Territories are made up of the poorly developed and often sparsely populated regions that are not part of any nation or sovereign duchy. Territories fall under the direct jurisdiction of the throne via the power of the Solar Armed Forces. This technically places all territories under martial law. Territories can range from small to vast, and in some cases include entire galaxies. The Mandrake Dynasty has long recognized that territories are often populated by those who prefer living on the fringes of society. If a territory becomes sufficiently populous, the emperor may appoint a noble to rule it or incorporate it into his own thronespace. In most cases, however, the desire of these people to live on the frontier is respected, and the SAF is instructed to ignore them unless they create a problem or another power attempts to exert a foothold in the territory. If the SAF is forced to intervene, military commanders have broad discretion in dealing with the situation.

The term *territory* may sometimes be conflated with, but does not include, regions considered *thronespace*. The regions known as thronespace are well-developed areas belonging directly to the emperor and administered by his civil authorities. The Mandrake Dynasty maintains some thronespace holdings in both the Solar and Andromeda galaxies. Perhaps a better example of thronespace can be found in the Large and Small Magellanic Clouds. These galaxies are wealthy, well developed, and governed by civil authorities rather than being subject to the SAF's martial law. Similarly, a king's or archduke's territory not apportioned to subordinate nobility is referred to as that king's or archduke's *crownspace*.

It must also be noted that some territories are extremely heavily populated as a significant portion of the Empire's roliam population lives within them. Roliams on these worlds are largely known for keeping to themselves and eschewing a great deal of technology as a means of filling their time.

2H
THE PILLAR NATIONS

WHILE THE EMPIRE HAS many nations, the pillar nations deserve special distinction from the rest, for they form the true heart of the Empire. The pillar nations represent the largest, most developed nations in the Empire. While there are some duchies that can rival the total size and influence, there are none that can completely match the pillars. The pillars dominate Imperial politics, field most of the taxes, and often contribute the most residents who will go on to earn Solar citizenship.

(i)
Del Tierr

Galaxy:	Solar
Demonym:	Tirrish
Capital:	Mundo Marvia
Founding Dynasty:	de la Nieve
Ruling Dynasty:	Andretti
Population Rank:	fifth

DEL TIERR COVERS APPROXIMATELY a third of the Solar Galaxy, lying in the galactic "north" relative to the star system Solar. Since the Solar Eclipse, Del Tierr has emerged as a cultural leader in the Empire. The nation is famed for cultural exports such as cuisine, literature, and music. Del Tierr is a heavily industrialized nation and one of the Big 4 in terms of output. It stands fourth behind the Reichsylvannian Dominion, Yuangi, and the Republic of Andromeda in furnishing the Solar Armed Forces with men and matériel.

Del Tierr was founded by the de la Nieve Dynasty, which ruled the nation until the War of Kings. The many costly setbacks of the war heavily degraded the esteem of the de la Nieve family. This would eventually lead the Mandrakes to remove them from power before their nation could implode into civil war. In the de la Nieves' place, the Andretti Dynasty rose to power and has ruled the nation since.

While the general public primarily thinks of the nation's cultural exports, Del Tierr is also a major exporter of ships. While the astranet renders ships obsolete for many aspects of interstellar shipping, in some areas they remain vital. Some goods cannot be transmitted via the astranet, and there remain areas of the Empire with poor to absent astranet coverage. Tirrish galleons primarily allow commerce to flow in these regions.

In addition to its civilian shipping, the nation has a significant presence in the arms market. Del Tierr is the only other nation that has consistently proven an ability to compete with the Reichsylvannian Dominion in the field of warships. While warships are built across the Empire, in most nations they are simply licensed copies of Dominion designs. Del Tierr has managed to field several of its own successful designs and bring home contracts for the Solar Armed Forces. The Armadas's current monitor, frigate, and light cruiser classes are all Tirrish designs. The nation also rivals the Republic of Andromeda as the leading exporter of star fighters, both manned and unmanned.

The nation's royal guard is known as the Tirrish Star Guard, and opinions of this force are mixed. The Tirrish naval arm, known simply as the King's Navy, has a less-than-stellar reputation. While the nation has proven masterful at building ships, its experience using them in battle is less praise-worthy. The King's Fleet was poisoned long ago by an inundation of political influence. Nearly all the service's officers are nobility, and promotions often depend more on connections than merit. The Tirrish marines by contrast are some of the most respected infantry in the Empire. These troops are famed for their discipline and ability to conduct difficult operations while often short on matériel. Unfortunately, the King's Marines are seen as the "poor man's force" in the nation. With the overwhelming clout of the King's Navy, it is often overfunded while the marines do without.

(ii)
The Elysian Commonwealth

Galaxy: Andromeda
Demonym: Elysian
Capital: Elysium
Founding Dynasty: Moreau
Ruling Dynasty: —
Population Rank: first

THE ELYSIAN COMMONWEALTH WAS once one of the wealthiest, most industrious, and most technologically advanced nations in the Empire. In the modern era, it is effectively a failed state. The nation's decline may pause from time to time but it never reverses. The Commonwealth was founded after the War of Kings, when the Moreau Dynasty released its holdings in the Solar Galaxy to take up new residence in Andromeda.

The Commonwealth was once the Empire's cultural leader. On countless worlds abroad, the latest fiction that had entered the public consciousness was almost invariably Elysian. When those in other nations decided to vacation abroad, their destination was almost always the Commonwealth. Perhaps most importantly, the nation was a leader in providing higher education to the public. It should be noted that the nation was also known for having possibly the laziest, most immoral, and most politically partisan population in the Empire. More than any other nation, the leadership of the Commonwealth had a despised reputation for meddling in the internal affairs of other nations.

All of this changed with the Solar Eclipse. That conflict saw the nation's industrial capacity ravaged, the toppling of its founding dynasty, and an economic cataclysm that has never ended. In the war's aftermath, most of the nation's best and most productive citizens left, never to return. An economic depression eventually became the new normal. The only megacorporation to remain was Aurora Technologies, a leading manufacturer of automatech and consumer electronics. Had it not been for the fact that the corporation is owned almost entirely by Elysian nobility, it too likely would have moved on.

In modernity, the Commonwealth has more dukes and counts than every other pillar nation combined. This was a direct result of what was known as "the Great Selloff," during which the succeeding royal family was forced to carve up and sell large portions of their domain to satisfy post-Eclipse obligations. For much of this post-Selloff nobility, Aurora Technologies underpins their fortunes. Were Aurora not the glue for so many mutual owners, the Commonwealth might have broken into sovereign duchies. Yet the obligation to pay so much to so many leaves Aurora largely unable to compete with foreign rivals in research and development. Aurora is forced to make its living by selling "economy" products, furthering the Commonwealth's reputation for producing cheap but low-quality goods.

The nation's royal guard is the Commonwealth Defense Force. At one time, the CDF was considered one of the best collections of combat personnel in the Empire. Today the CDF is the laughingstock of uniformed services. With the Commonwealth's decline, the nation has followed the same folly as the Interstellar Confederacy. The Commonwealth now uses the CDF as a tool to promote social mobility and give jobs to the jobless rather than as an actual military. Modern CDF soldiers are notorious for poor training, lack of discipline, and wielding equipment that has been obsolete for generations.

No ruling dynasty is listed because there isn't one. After the fall of the Moreaus, no family has managed to hold power long enough to really establish itself as a dynasty. Instead, the nation has been subject to a revolving door of leaders, each more interested in enriching themselves than in uplifting their people.

(iii)
The Orion Estate

Galaxy:	Solar
Demonym:	Ori
Capital:	New Titan
Founding Dynasty:	Moore
Ruling Dynasty:	Novak
Population Rank:	fourth

THE ORION ESTATE HOLDS the distinction of being the pillar nation that is home to the Solar star system, even if it has been largely forgotten. Earth was destroyed in the Therican War, and when the Rhinegraves left Mars in the Great Migration, they stripped down everything on the planet to transplant to their new home. None after them found the idea of recolonizing the planet from scratch appealing. All that truly stands on Mars today is Olympus Mons University, the tenements for its students, and faculty housing.

The Orion Estate is best known among the other nations as the Empire's classroom. The estate is home to many of the Empire's top centers for higher education. Among them, Olympus Mons University, the Kim Academy of Economics, and more. The classrooms of these schools and others are open to everyone. Countless numbers of people travel to the nation every year to partake in the education it offers.

Despite its prominent role in educating the public, the estate itself is largely an absent voice in Imperial politics. Very few of its residents volunteer for service in the Solar Armed Forces, leading to a relative lack of representation in the Solar Senate. The nation's nobility has historically been disinterested in outside affairs and often vote in whichever direction the political winds may be blowing. It is the only pillar nation that remained completely neutral in the Solar Eclipse, and in nearly all other major political shifts in the Empire's history.

While it is not practical for a pillar nation to be isolationist, since coming to power, the Novak Dynasty has sought to avoid outside entanglements wherever possible. The family has gone so far as to install brutal tariffs on many foreign-made products for the sole purpose of preventing economic ties from becoming too strong.

The nation's royal guard, known as the Orion Guard, is generally considered a second-rate force. Its soldiers are well trained and educated but equipped poorly. The nation largely refuses to treat its royal guard as anything but a burden. The force is often armed with surplus, or more likely retired SAF equipment acquired secondhand.

(iv)
The Reichsylvannian Dominion

Galaxy:	Dominion
Demonym:	Reichsylvannian (to outsiders) and Sylvanni (to residents)
Capital:	Reichsylvannia
Founding Dynasty:	Rhinegrave
Ruling Dynasty:	Rhinegrave
Population Rank:	sixth

THE REICHSYLVANNIAN DOMINION HOLDS the distinction of being the wealthiest, most industrialized, and most technologically advanced nation in the Empire. The Dominion also holds the distinction of being the nation least popular among its peers and of being the only nation that is still ruled in modernity by its founding dynasty.

The Dominion was founded after the Conquest of Triangulum. Over time, the Dominion grew from having the smallest human population in the Empire to the largest. This would make it the most populous nation in the Empire, but only by discounting the roliam populations of other nations. Roliams have never fully trusted the Rhinegrave Dynasty and thus have rarely settled in its territory. Additionally, the nation's population figures often include the techla, who, being considered AI by the Empire, are not recognized as legal sapients outside the Dominion. At the same time, the Dominion often excludes the lantai from its counts, for the same reasons many estimates omit roliams. When these factors are considered, the Dominion comes in last place among the pillar nations.

Perhaps the most important facet of the Dominion is its extreme wealth. The Dominion's gross domestic product is not simply the largest, it is larger than the next five combined. GDP per-capita and standards of living are second only to a handful of extremely small duchies with high-wealth populations. Of the Empire's top ten thousand corporations, the Dominion is home to 7,500 of them. This includes nine of the top ten, and more than half of the top hundred. For those eligible to do so, the nation is generally regarded as the best place in the Empire to own a business. The Dominion's wealth means that even those who hate it are often swayed by the money it can throw around.

The Dominion is the technological capital of the Empire, due partly to its aforementioned wealth. There are few endeavors more costly than research and development. The Dominion can spend vast fortunes on research and development that other nations can't. This keeps the nation in a state of technological superiority in both military and civilian applications. The profits from selling its technologies bring in additional wealth and the cycle continues. The Dominion government also uses more of its tax revenue to stimulate research than the next forty-four nations combined.

The Dominion is tied with the Orion Estate for the distinction of being the Empire's classroom. The Dominion is home to many of the most prestigious universities. These include the Reichsylvannia Academy of Advanced Military Sciences, which is the top military academy in the Empire. Other schools include the Woglinde College of Engineering, the Cohen School of Enterprise—"where billionaires are made"—and the Hevis Academy of Physics. These schools are highly discriminatory as to who they admit. They do not offer classes to many alien species, nor are classes offered to women, as Dominion culture considers doing so both wasteful and harmful to society. These schools are renowned for their disdain toward "soft" subjects such as art or philosophy. While many of the best and brightest men in the Empire find education in the Dominion, women and disallowed aliens typically seek education in the Orion Estate.

The role of genetic engineering in Dominion society cannot be overstated. Most experts in that field who survived the Therican War ended up in the service of the Rhinegrave Dynasty. Over many generations, the Reichsylvannians have used genetic engineering to improve the population. Improvement, in this case, is alignment with the values of their culture. While never officially recognized as such, genetic engineering is a de facto human right in the Dominion. For parents not to ensure their son is tall, handsome, intelligent, and strong is to throw him to the wolves in a society that plays for keeps. To fail to ensure that a daughter is beautiful, fair-tempered, and graceful is to doom her to a life of loneliness as more desirable women monopolize the attentions of good men. It was in fact the prevalence of genetic engineering in the Dominion that led it to become commonplace in the rest of the Empire. As the results became more and more pronounced, parents across the Empire realized their own children risked being left behind.

For better or worse, the Dominion is generally regarded as the most stable society in the Empire. While the nation has had its own ups and downs, it is the only nation in the Empire that has never collapsed and been forced to rebuild. The Dominion places the stability of its society above all else and has proven incredibly resistant to social change over the millennia. The nation has no qualms about exiling those who try to change social norms. It has no tolerance at all for foreigners attempting to affect change. Those who have visited the Dominion from foreign lands to stage public protests have been met with lethal force. The outcries from their homelands be damned. The Dominion is a very closed society despite its export-heavy economy. The nation allows precious few migrants, and it is closed to the endless hordes of adventurer sightseers. Those who enter illegally are deported the first time, imprisoned the second, and executed the third. Even those allowed in are often subject to heavy culture shock. In the Dominion, there is a right way and a wrong way for nearly every social interaction.

Dominion residents have fewer rights extended to them by their sovereign than most. The rights they have are often far more expansive. The Rhinegrave Dynasty considers property rights the only true right. Property rights in the Dominion are a near absolute. Only the high king can summarily strip a person of property without cause. For all subordinate authorities, the burden to do so is extremely high. Nobility can and have been executed on the high king's order for violating residents' property rights.

Dominion residents are one of only two pillar populations with a recognized right to own weaponry. The ability to defend one's life and property are considered an outgrowth of the right to have property. This right, like the rest, is subject to species and gender demarcations.

The Dominion is also unique in that it is the only pillar nation that does not mirror the Imperial government by having a national legislature of elected officials. The high king is the absolute ruler of his realm but is assisted by the high chancellery. Chancellors are appointed by the high king based on recommendations from experts in appropriate fields. After appointment, chancellors are empowered to make regulations as the high king's proxy. While the high king does not have an elected body, most of his nobility does.

Reichsylvannian men are often stereotyped as wife-beating bullies who fancy themselves supermen. The women are stereotyped as hyper-submissive beauty queens who could not begin to think for themselves. While both stereotypes held by foreigners are not completely fair, they are not completely wrong either.

The average Reichsylvannian man stands two meters tall, with an applied intelligence score of 275, placing them seventy-five points higher than the human median in other nations. While Dominion men do not generally flaunt their higher intellect, neither do they show any false humility if it is brought up. As to the latter part of the stereotype, what is considered wife-beating in other lands is considered being a good husband in the Dominion. Just as a parent must discipline their children, a man must discipline a wife who misbehaves. Failing to do so is spousal neglect.

The stereotype around Dominion women is somewhat accurate. Dominion women are generally regarded as beautiful. It is telling that 80 percent of fashion models who are human women are Reichsylvannian. A woman's intellectual prowess is considered unimportant beyond providing good genes to her offspring. While it takes a lower priority in genetic engineering, the average Dominion woman has an AIS of 220, meaning she is above the human median by twenty points. It is not that Reichsylvannian women cannot think for themselves. In the end, it is not her opinion but her senior male authority's (SMA) that matters, and that is simply a fact of life. While it is said often that women cannot vote in the Dominion, this needs some clarification. In Dominion vernacular, "to vote" does not refer solely to the act of voting itself. Instead it is used broadly to any exercise of political franchise.

The stereotype that Reichsylvannians are hedonists is quite simply false and is rooted in propaganda that was rife during the Solar Eclipse. It is true that many things such as narcotics and other pleasures regulated or illegal elsewhere are generally allowed. However the Dominion places a premium on personal responsibility. There is nothing to stop a person for using narcotics, but similarly is there no social safety net to catch them if they should have a problem. Both genders are known for being chaste before marriage, albeit for differing reasons. In terms of having morals and practicing them, the Reichsylvannians have few rivals. Dominion society takes an extremely negative view of what it considers immoral behavior.

The Dominion's royal guard is perhaps the best trained and the most technologically advanced military force in the Empire. Even the Solar Armed Forces often lag by at least a generation. In general, a military does not replace a piece of equipment simply because something better comes along. It is after all quite expensive to outfit and re-train an entire army. But the Dominion has money to spare and considers its royal guard a point of national pride. This has led to a popular joke among Dominion troops. "Don't like it? Don't worry, we'll get a new one next week."

While a bit hyperbolic, the Dominion has no reservations about dumping money down the wormhole to ensure its soldiers have the best technology. This works out rather well for the Solar Armed Forces. The SAF will often gauge how well a piece of equipment has performed in Dominion service before acquiring it for itself. This allows the SAF to outsource much of its research and development costs to the Dominion.

The reputation of Dominion troops for being the best trained is well earned. The Dominion has long used the Solar Armed Forces as a training tool. Eager youngsters wishing to serve are directed to join the SAF. If they distinguish themselves in the emperor's service, they will be invited home for the privilege of serving their high king's royal guard. As a result, the Dominion Star Forces are a service heavy in military veterans. The nation's royal guard has been called upon to assist the SAF in more foreign wars than any other national service, though the greatest source of esteem must come from the Solar Eclipse. In that conflict, the DSF proved it could face the larger Solar Armed Forces and win. Ever since, the intelligence services of every SAF branch have kept a watchful eye on the DSF.

The Dominion Star Forces are made up of four branches. These are the Grand Fleet, Grand Army, Könskreeger, and Vorhan Tohl. The Grand Fleet holds the distinction of being the only royal or noble guard force to operate its own supercruisers. This is illegal under Imperial law, but the Dominion does not care. It is the nation that builds the supercruisers. To play nice, the Dominion calls them "heavy battleships" in official paperwork, and the Solar Armadas pretends not to notice.

The Grand Army is a first-rate force known for having the highest training hours of any "regular" troops in the Empire. The Grand Army is a distinct force from the infamous Könskreeger, (from ancient German, *königskrieger* or "king's warriors") These feared shock troops are some of the most elite in the Empire, renowned for the lengths to which they will go to conquer enemy territory. During the Solar Eclipse, it was sometimes enough to force a planet or star hive to surrender simply by deploying the Könskreeger.

The Vorhan Tohl, also known as the Redguard, are known for a level of fanatical loyalty that is often underestimated by foreigners. Only kodaz, kurai, and simians are permitted to join the Vorhan Tohl. For these species, membership in the Vorhan Tohl is one of the highest offices in their culture. Candidates are selected in infancy and put through constant training throughout their lives. For many it is a family business, and there are Vorhan Tohl families that have served the Rhinegraves for over a hundred generations. Only members of the ultra-elite Special Assignments Contingent protect members of the dynasty. The rest are responsible for protecting the family's assets both public and private.

Cultural mores in the Dominion have often forced men of the family to prove themselves as warrior kings or princes when a war allows them to do so. Rhinegraves have fought in both fleet and ground conflicts throughout the Empire's history. Since their inception, the Vorhan Tohl have always been at their side. The Rhinegrave-Alexander feud saw many Rhinegraves assassinated by their foes. This number dropped to zero once the Vorhan Tohl became the family's sole protectors.

No discussion of the Dominion would be complete without directly addressing the nation's treatment of women. The Empire is a relatively equal place. Even in nations like Yuangi, where citizens effectively have no rights, the lack of rights is shared by all. This is not so in the Dominion.

Dominion society considers women intellectually and morally inferior to men. Regardless of their actual intelligence, women are considered too irresponsible to make good decisions for themselves. Further, women are considered too selfish to be permitted a decision-making role in society. All women in the Dominion are literal property and have no rights under the law. Even the high queen is naught but a figurehead meant to set the example for the women of the nation. Every girl is born the property of her SMA or senior male authority. By default, this status is held by her father and will pass to her husband upon marriage. If a woman's SMA dies, that status will pass to the latter's nearest male relative. If a woman immigrates to the Dominion, she must officially renounce residence in her old nation and must have an SMA ready to take ownership of her. This system has filtered down to several of the Rhinegrave Eight with a dominant gender recognized in five of them. The exceptions are the lantai, tahn'kodaz, and techla. The point is rather moot with the lantai, the kodaz have extremely low sexual dimorphism, and the techla are neuter.

The Dominion is not without its own sense of fairness. Because women are property, they are not considered entities under the law but rather extensions of their SMA's person. Because of this, women cannot be held accountable under the law for the majority of criminal wrongdoings. If a woman commits a crime, it falls on her SMA to discipline her while he faces the consequences of the law. Nothing, however, stops a man imprisoned for the crimes of a woman he owns from requesting that she be lodged with him during his incarceration.

There does exist a doctrine in Dominion law known as "auctor se." In most cases, auctor se is reserved for instances where a woman has committed numerous and or serious crimes (such as murder) despite the best efforts of her SMA. In these cases, a court can declare her auctor se, wherein her relationship with her SMA is dissolved and she can now be held accountable. This is extremely rare. Women have always had a lower propensity for crime than men, and Reichsylvannians have one of the lowest propensities for crime in the Empire. There has been more than one man who chose punishment rather than see a woman under his care declared auctor se, leaving him with the shame of having to admit he failed to keep her in line.

The status of auctor se can also be sought voluntarily. Even the sexism of the Dominion has some limits and acknowledges that there are women who are exceptions. Even if it considers them to be astonishingly rare. With her SMA's approval, a woman can petition a court to grant her this status if she can demonstrate competency to manage her own affairs, financial matters in particular. If she can demonstrate this, auctor se will be granted, and she will be recognized as her own person. But this comes at a high cost. The Dominion does not wish to encourage this behavior. A woman who obtains auctor se in this way must leave the Dominion and can never take up permanent residence there again. She will invariably find herself shunned by those she once called her friends, other women in particular.

The nation's capital is pronounced Ryess-sil-vin-eye-ah. The name is rooted in Martian German, which remained the official language of the high king's court for many centuries. Martian German had undergone significant lingual drift from its early roots even before the Empire. As a result, the name does not translate very well into either Ancient English or Solar. The most common translation is "realm of prosperous company." Reichsylvannian Dominion could then be understood to mean "realm of the prosperous, and their holdings." Even into modernity, the high king is generally referred to as such only by outsiders. The majority of Reichsylvannians recite the title as Grosskönyg, (Groz-cone-ig) which translates much more simply to "grand king."

(v)
Republic of Andromeda

Galaxy: Andromeda
Demonym: Republican
Capital: Atlantis
Founding Dynasty: Alexander
Ruling Dynasty: Stofferson
Population Rank: third

THE REPUBLIC OF ANDROMEDA is generally regarded as the freest society in the modern Empire. Its residents have more rights extended by their royal family than any other population. It is one of only thirty-six nations where residents have freedom of speech, and one of only two pillar nations (three nations overall) where residents are recognized as having the right to own weaponry for self-defense. In this case, they are forbidden from any weapon deemed "military grade." Among the pillar nations, it is second only to the Elysian Commonwealth in terms of how easy it is to travel or immigrate. Unlike the Commonwealth, there are large numbers of people who want to settle there.

Republic residents are well-known for their patriotism, sometimes nauseatingly so to the populations of other nations. The leadership of the nation is positively masterful in the art of propaganda, and Republicans have plenty of reason to take pride in their nation.

The Republic was founded after the War of Kings and the migration of the Alexander Dynasty with all its followers to Andromeda. That conflict had been particularly brutal on the Alexanders and their people. They had barely managed to cling to Andromeda, and after the war had a much weaker presence in the galaxy than either the Yuan or Moreau families. Despite the many handicaps it faced, the leadership of the Alexander Dynasty and grit of the population allowed the Republic to rapidly flourish.

For much of the Empire's history, the Republic would be locked in a three-way battle with the Reichsylvannian Dominion and the Elysian Commonwealth for the distinction of being the Empire's wealthiest nation. All while its leaders, the Alexanders, took part in the longest blood feud in history against the Rhinegraves.

The nation's fortunes would take a sour turn during the Solar Eclipse, and the Republic arguably suffered more than any other nation in that conflict, with nearly half of all casualties sustained by both sides inflicted within their borders. The war left the nation bankrupt and with many devastated worlds. Over time, the residents of the nation rebuilt and within two generations had surged back to the position of the Empire's second-largest economy.

The nation's royal guard is known as the Republic Star Forces, made up of the Republican National Defense Force and the Republic Armada. The RSF is considered a first-rate force and is second only to the Dominion in the number of times it has been called upon to assist the Solar Armed Forces in foreign wars. The Republic Armada is a professional force but unique in defense doctrine built primarily around the use of star fighters and carrier ships. The fighter pilot as the knight of space is a national icon to the people of the Republic and well represented in domestic fiction. The Republican National Defense Force is made up mostly of part-time citizen-soldiers who train periodically throughout the year. The Republic is third behind the Dominion and Yuangi in material, and second only to the Dominion in the number of residents that give service to the SAF.

In recent years, the Republic has been undergoing a slow decline. The Stofferson Dynasty has not proven the equal of the Alexanders they replaced. The Republic has long been the most democratic pillar nation, as the Alexanders often deferred to the elected national Senate. With the Alexanders gone, the Senate has exercised increasing amounts of control and exacerbated issues of political polarization in the general population.

(vi)
Yuangi

Galaxy: Andromeda
Demonym: Yuani
Capital: Jinsegi
Founding Dynasty: Yuan
Ruling Dynasty: Yao
Population Rank: second

YUANGI IS WELL-KNOWN THROUGHOUT the Empire as a totalitarian police state that does not hesitate to use force against its own citizens. It is also a nation mired in a history of sectarian violence, aristocratic infighting, interspecies hatred, and more. Many believe that the totalitarian policies of the nation are the only thing to keep it from tearing itself apart. More than 65 percent of all anti-terrorism efforts in the Empire are focused on Yuangi. For several thousand years, the Mandrake Dynasty has maintained contingency plans to break the nation into sovereign duchies. At times, chaos in the nation brought that plan close to necessity.

In the early years of the Pax Solaris, Yuangi became ground zero for the Coolite Movement.

Often forgotten in the rest of the Empire, the Coolites had a profound effect on Yuangi. Samel Coolidge came to public prominence as a cult leader-turned-politician. Coolidge borrowed from ancient Earth religions, proclaimed himself a messiah, and preached a new society that tore down all distinctions of social class. This movement became problematic when his followers began bombing corporations and openly attacking members of the nobility. Eventually the reach of this movement became so great that it was able to assassinate the Yuan Dynasty's leadership.

While the rest of the Empire was in a state of feast, Yuangi descended into famine. A bitter succession war erupted. With no direct heir left to the nation, all the higher nobility made a bid for the crown. The civil war in Yuangi lasted for 684 years and devastated much of the nation's infrastructure. A noble house would rise to take the throne and hold it only a few years before it was deposed by another. With no clear successor to support, the Empire chose to let the Yuani people sort the matter out themselves. Eventually the Yao Dynasty seized power and secured the crown. The Yaos slaughtered any member of the nation's nobility who would not pledge fealty. All elected officials were similarly executed along with any Coolite that could be found. Coolidge himself would eventually be captured, and his remains were encased in the nation's capital, Jinsegi.

The Yaos invented the punishment of encasement for Coolidge and his followers. The condemned is immersed in a nanite-rich fluid that gradually hardens into a solid block. The condemned is kept alive by the nanites, which deliver oxygen and nutrients to their bloodstream. The condemned thus lives the rest of their life in a state of complete sensory deprivation. This process can extend the lifespan considerably, leaving ten thousand years or more for the punishment to run its course.

The Coolites who had followed their messiah proved extremely difficult to eradicate. Their movement went to ground and would continue to cause problems in the nation for generations after. Much of the police state was established in the pursuit of purging the movement from society. It eventually succeeded, and the last of the Coolites fled to other nations. There they would lay the seeds for the pro-democracy movements that helped bring about the Great Collapse. But by this time, the police state had become the norm.

Modern Yuangi is a less-industrialized and less-automated nation than the other pillars. This is by choice and directive of the Yao Dynasty, which actively seeks to create jobs to keep its people busy. This had some economic benefit, as there are those willing to pay for the novelty of fruit and vegetables grown by hand, or meat from real cattle nourished on those products. Many other products that are routinely made via automation are handmade in Yuangi, and thus sometimes command a novelty price on the export market.

Yuangi is behind only the Dominion in matériel, and third only to the Dominion and Republic in personnel provided to the Solar Armed Forces. The nation has never managed a strong presence in the market for ships, personal armor, or guns, but builds many other forms of matériel. Yuangi is the leading developer of armored vehicles such as tanks and warmechs. While it got its start in this field as a result of efforts by the Empire to reduce its dependence on the Dominion, the Yuani have since proven quite adept.

Yuani tanks have perhaps the best combination of economy, ease of use, ease of production, and acceptable performance, which makes them ideal weapons of war. Their warmechs carry a similar reputation, being rugged, easy to repair, and far more simple to fabricate than those made in other nations. The controls of Yuani warmechs are so user-friendly that official training software has little difference from astranet games meant to allow players to simulate operating such a machine.

Yuangi is the only human-led nation in the Empire with a secret police force. The Internal Security Agency is well-known and feared by the population. After the chaos wrought by the Coolites, Yuangi formally banned organized religion within its borders. The ISA was established first to stamp out religious movements, and eventually grew in scope to the all-seeing eyes in the nation today. Somewhat disturbingly, other nations have, from time to time, sought the ISA's assistance in monitoring their own residents. The one time the ISA agreed to help a foreign nation, it was nearly destroyed by the Solar Commandos. The Corps killed more than half the agency's personnel in a single night. Since then, the ISA has refused to aid outside authorities, and it has kept its eyes inward. While those in other nations are safe from its influence, it is a reality of life for those in Yuangi. It is simply accepted that there are no secrets from the ISA. It hears every conversation, watches every transaction, and monitors every gathering.

Yuangi's royal guard is made up of the Shenga Armada and the Commons Regiments. As with some other royal guards, opinions on these forces are highly mixed. The Yao Dynasty is legendary among its people for its complete unwillingness to spend money until it is necessary. This shows in the royal guards' dated equipment. Most of the Shenga Armada is made up of ships purchased from the Solar Armadas upon being retired. Even the

Commons Regiments's tanks and warmechs are secondhand, often traded back to the nation for discounts on future procurement by the Solar Army and Legionnaires.

Yuani soldiers are famed for their dedication and their professional work ethic. Due to the Yao Dynasty's unwillingness to fully fund its military, many of its soldiers lag well behind the number of training hours recommended by the Solar Armed Forces. Yuani soldiers are known for making up the shortfalls on their own time and at their own expense. Often they travel abroad to cross-train with troops of other nations.

The nation's name is rooted in Siddharthan Mandri, an evolution of Mandarin that had been commonly spoken in the time of the Interstellar Confederacy. Its meaning translates rather simply into "Yuan's Place."

21
CITIZENS, RESIDENTS, AND TERRITORIALS

THE EMPIRE HAS FIVE distinct levels of citizenship, each with its own rights and privileges. These are royalty, nobility, Solar citizen, resident, and territorial. Royalty are the rulers of the pillar nations and have full authority to govern their territory as they see fit. Royals are also empowered to subdivide their territory and appoint nobles to help in the administration of their vast holdings. Though the archdukes who rule the sovereign duchies are considered nobility rather than royalty, this is mostly semantics. It only really affects matters of courtly protocol—and the line of succession if the entirety of the emperor's dynasty were to be wiped out. A line of succession exists wherein the title of emperor could pass on to a royal dynasty but not to the nobility.

No person is born a citizen of the Empire itself; this distinction must be earned. Solar citizens have a number of enumerated rights that are extended to them directly by the throne and must be respected by even the national sovereigns. These rights include the ability to run and vote in elections to the Solar Senate, protections of due process in criminal proceedings, the ability to own armaments for self-defense, the right to face an accuser against an accusation of criminal behavior, and immunity from execution or encasement for any crime but treason. While a nation does not have to permit any a Solar citizen from settling in their territory, they cannot deny these rights to any they admit. The Mandrakes take the rights of Solar citizens very seriously.

The most common means to earn this citizenship is to give a term of service to the Solar Armed Forces. The minimum number of years required varies from species to species as it is weighted on median lifespan. For most species, this corresponds to no less than 10 percent of average life-expectancy. An exception exists for soldiers who are wounded in combat as a result of enemy action. Such soldiers gain their citizenship immediately, as they are citizens by right of blood.

Military service is not the only means to obtain this citizenship. It can be conferred directly by the emperor as is the case with the Miss Empire pageant. It can also be earned through non-military civil service that benefits the Empire at large.

Those who are not born with royal or noble distinction but reside in a recognized nation gain the status of resident. The rights and privileges of the residents are defined entirely by the sovereign of their nation. In some nations, these rights are extensive, while in others, less so. Rights in this context are defined as restrictions the sovereigns place on their nobility and subordinate authorities. National sovereigns are absolute rulers and could not give up this distinction even if they wished to. With the sovereigns having this power, this leads to considerable differences in the rights residents hold from one nation to the next. In any case, rights are jurisdictional, and travelers must be aware that rights they have at home may not be the same in a land they visit.

Those born in the Empire's territories gain the distinction of territorial. The primary difference between territorials and residents is that so long as they remain in the territories, they are subject to the martial law of the Solar Armed Forces.

2J
THE SOLAR PEERAGE

THE SOLAR EMPIRE REQUIRES that all population centers have a noble or royal dynasty that the throne can hold personally accountable for its well-being. Any region that lacks a ruling dynasty is recognized as a territory and falls directly under martial law. The peerage includes all persons of royal title, noble title, and Solar citizenship. Most people, residents, and territorials do not have a recognized place in the peerage at all.

Dons and higher members of the peerage are considered the legal owners of any territory within their purview. This status grants them the right to sell land, levy taxes, enact laws, and assume ownership of any property left without a legal heir. While nobles have the authority to make laws within their territories, these laws must conform to the investiture outlined by the king or higher-ranking noble who originally granted the territory. As with the relationship between the emperor and the Solar Senate, most nobles have a noble assembly to which they delegate the majority of lawmaking.

In order to be eligible to inherit their parent's title, all sons of human nobility are required to give a term of service in the Solar Armed Forces. Daughters are exempt from this requirement. Alien species that hold a noble title have similar requirements, but they can vary greatly depending on sexual dimorphism and other factors. Most of these aliens give their service to the Solar Army, as both the Armadas and Legionnaires are highly selective on which species are permitted to serve in their ranks.

It is indeed very possible, though costly, for any citizen or even resident to ascend to the peerage of the Empire. Corporations and other entities are not permitted under Imperial law to own planets or other habitation sites. The most common method by which a person joins the peerage is to pay the cost of establishing a colony and attracting people to live there. A person who can do so is then eligible to apply for recognition by the throne as a noble of rank appropriate to the size of their territory. This venture requires the permission of an already-existing noble if it is conducted within their territory.

The full peerage is listed below in the following format.

Title
Child Title
Formal Address
Territory

Solar Emperor/Solar Empress
Solar Prince/Solar Princess
"Your Majesty" or "Your Solar Majesty"
The Solar Empire

High King/High Queen
High Prince/High Princess
"Your Excellency" or "Your High Excellency"
The Reichsylvannian Dominion

King / Queen
Prince/Princess
"Your Highness" or "Your Royal Highness"
A pillar nation

Archduke/Archduchess
V'archduke/V'archduchess
"Your Eminence"
A sovereign duchy

Duke/Duchess
Vi-Duke/Vi-Duchess
"Your Grace"
A duchy (typically around 1/40th of a pillar nation)

Marquess/Marchioness
Vi-Marquess/Vi-Marchioness
"Your Honor"
A march (typically between 1/30th and 1/25th of a sovereign duchy)

Count/Countess
Vinacount/Vinacountess
"Your Brilliance"
A county (typically 1/100th of a duchy, or a share of similar size when ennobled by another rank)

Viscount/Viscountess
Viracount/Viracountess
"Your Influence"
A district (typically at least one star hive)

Baron/Baroness
Vi-Baron/Vi-Baroness
"Your Lordship"
A barony (typically one planet, or a portion of a star hive)

Don/Donna
Vi-Don/Vi-Donna
"Your Worth"
A hearth (typically a moon, large continent, or segment of a star hive satellite)

Solar Citizen
N/A
"Citizen (Name)"
N/A

A special note goes to the position of Don/Donna. As the lowest rung of actual nobility, they are considered to hold a special place in regard to the general population. Only those directly in their employ are expected to use their honorific address of "Your Worth." They are generally referred to by their given names rather than surnames in the same way one might refer to a family member such as an uncle. A duke named John Smith would be addressed as "Your Grace" and referred to as "Duke Smith" or even "His Grace, Duke Smith" depending on the formality of the situation. A don named John Smith would be referred to simply as "Don John." When members of the peerage address each other, dispensing with the formalities is done purely at the pleasure of the more senior member.

While those who hold Solar citizenship are properly addressed and referred to as "Citizen" before their name, for the sake of brevity this is rarely done outside of formal proceedings.

2K
THE SOLAR LANGUAGE

THE MODERN SOLAR LANGUAGE came into being as a result of an edict passed by Emperor Charles Mandrake I during the Pax Solaris. Prior to Charles, the official language of the Empire was known as Titan English. This dialect of English came into being during the time of the Interstellar Confederacy on the planet Titan. Though Titan's original colonists include a slight majority of English-speakers, it also included sizable minorities who spoke German, Spanish, Mandarin, and Japanese. Over time as human colonies expanded, Titan found itself as an almost perfect middle point between all the Confederacy's colonies. The planet blossomed into a trade hub, and its local dialect became the unofficial trade language of the Confederacy.

Emperor Christopher Mandrake made Titan English the official language of the Solar Empire shortly after its formation, where it remained until the time of Emperor Charles I. As emperor, Charles had grown concerned that the difficulty for a non-native speaker to learn Titan English was hampering efforts to integrate alien species as long-term members of the Empire. He ordered the creation of a council of linguistic experts whom he directed to simplify the language.

The Solar language has no silent letters; every letter in a word is pronounced. Solar also minimizes the instances of any two letters making the same sound, such as *c* and *k*, *c* and *s*, or *g* and *j*. This was in an effort to simplify the phonetics of the language before making strides to ensure that most words were spelled phonetically. For a speaker of Ancient English trying to learn Solar, the matter is complicated somewhat by the fact that there had been several shifts in Titan English from that language's earlier roots. Solar itself has existed for thousands of years, and as a result, a considerable amount of drift has taken place in wording, spelling, and pronunciation.

As with most things done by a government task force, the results were decidedly mixed. While in many ways the language was made more simple, it failed to address the primary complaint levied by non-humans, which was the number of homographs and homophones.

Emperor Charles I's reforms would see Solar instituted as the new official language of the Empire. It remains mandatory learning for all residents of the Empire, even those who live in isolationist nations. It is the only language used in official records and documentation by the Imperial government. The Empire has made great efforts to preserve the language and minimize its mutation over the ages. Despite this, it has not obliterated other languages. Many are spoken throughout the Empire, and despite the Empire's efforts, there remain distinct dialects of the language spoken in various regions. While the differences in these dialects rarely are significant enough to present a language barrier, they often serve as an immediate flag to mark outsiders.

The following guide will give an overview of proper Solar beginning with its alphabet.

Aa, Bb, Çç, Dd, Ee, Ff, Gg, Ĝĝ, Hh, Jj, Kk, Ll, Mm, Nn, Oo, Őő, Pp, Qq, Rr, Ss, ßß, Tt, Ŧŧ, Uu, Vv, Ww, Xx, Yy

Binaries: Solar includes letters known as "binaries," which were created to replace a number of two- and three-letter combinations that were common in English. The binaries are as follows:

Çç   Known as the "chi," this letter is used to replace the English *ch*

Ĝĝ   Known as the "ing," this letter is used to replace the *ing* suffix

Őő   Known as the "oo," this letter is used to in place of the *oo* sound. Over the course of years, lingual drift has caused Ő to replace O in both spelling and pronunciation in many words

ßß   Known as the "shi," this letter is used in place of the English *sh*

Ŧŧ   Known as "thee," this letter is used in place of English *th*

Double vowel: Whenever the same vowel is written twice in sequence, such as "aa," it is indicative of a dominant pronunciation.

Name vowels: Name vowels are quite simply vowels written with an umlaut. To differentiate names in print, Solar requires that the first vowel in the name of a person be written with an umlaut. If both the given and surname of a person are written, the first letter of each is written with an umlaut. This does not apply to the names of things or places, only people.

(i)
Letters: English vs. Solar

E   In addition to replacing *I* as noted below, many words ending in *Y* are written instead with *E*, as phonetically appropriate.

C   The letter *C* no longer exists, replaced by *K* or *S* as phonetically appropriate.

F   *F* replaces the "ph" combination whenever the two would have made the same sound.

I   The letter *I* had already begun to disappear from the language by the time of Titan English, and hung on only in its use of names. In Solar it is replaced in both spelling and pronunciation by *E* in most cases, and *Y* in others.

G   *G* is no longer used in any case where *J* would be phonetically appropriate.

W, V   Due partly to the German influence on Titan English, these two letters trade places in both spelling and pronunciation from the perspective of an English-speaker.

Z   The letter *Z* no longer exists, replaced in most instances by *X*, but occasionally by *S*.

(ii)
Name Examples

Ancient
  English: Robert Panzer
Solar: Röbert Pänser

Note: The word "Panzer" is ancient German and means "armor." English-speakers would pronounce the word by the Z-sound, whereas in its father language the word is pronounced with an *S*. In Solar, the word uses an *S* to be phonetically correct.

English: Simmonne Mandrake
Solar: Sÿmmonne Mändraak

Note: English speakers would likely assume the English spelling of her name is simply a fancy variation on "Simone" and would pronounce her name appropriately. They would not be wrong per se, as her name is an evolution of the earlier name. However to the people of the Solar Empire, her name is pronounced "Si-moh-né." Another way for English-speakers to understand the pronunciation of her name is to replace the second syllable of her name with the name of the famous artist Monet.

English: Jonathan Clearwater
Solar: Jönatan Klëarvater

Note: While the spelling is different, speakers of both English and Solar would pronounce this name identically.

English: Manfred Wagner/ von Rhinegrave
Solar: Mänfreed Vägner/ won Rhyngraaw

Note: Despite the difference in spelling, the pronunciation of this historic figure's name is largely unchanged.

English: Christopher Mandrake
Solar: Krÿstofer Mändraak

Note: Despite the difference in spelling, the pronunciation of this historic figure's name is unchanged.

(iii)
Sample Sentences

English:	Robert Panzer smokes cigarettes for pain, and cigars for pleasure.
Solar:	Röbert Pänser smokes çegaretts fõr paan, õnd çegars fõr plessur.
English Phonetic:	Robert Panser smokes chigar-eets foor pain, oond chi-gars foor pless-ure.

English:	Simmonne Mandrake was too affluent to realize that only well-off people could afford a Ŧ5 cover charge.
Solar:	Sÿmmonne Mändraak vas tu eefflõant to realyse tat õnle vell-õff peepl kõuld eefford a Ŧ5 kower-çarj.
English Phonetic:	Sim-Monet Mandrake was too E-floo-ant to real-ice that oon-lee well-oof pee-ple coo-uld E-ford a five-troy cover charge.

English:	Jonathan Clearwater was too shy and inexperienced to know how to handle a sexually aggressive woman.
Solar:	Jönatan Klëarvater vas tu ßy őnd enexperensed to nov hov to handl a sexuually aggresewe voman.
English Phonetic:	Jonathan Clearwater was too shy oond een-experienced to know how to handle a sex-U-ally aggress-eve woman.

English:	There is no room in Steven's heart for anyone but Steven.
Solar:	Ŧere est ne rőm en Stëwen's hart főr evan bőt Stëwen.
English Phonetic:	There est nee room een Steven's heart foor ee-wan boot Steven.

English:	Can you please pass the sugar? No, get your own damn sugar.
Solar:	Kan yő pleas pass ŧe sőgar? Ne, get yőr őn dam sőgar.
English Phonetic:	Can yoo plea-as pass the soogar? Nee, get yoor oon dam soogar.

English:	The quick brown fox jumps over the lazy dog.
Solar:	Ŧe quek brovn fox jumps őwer ŧe laxy dog.
English Phonetic:	The qeu-eck brown fox jumps oover thee lazy dog.

(iv)

Sample Sentences Continued

English:	AICES: Armored Infantry Combat Exo-Suite
Solar:	AEKES: Armored Enfantre Kombat Exo-Sőete

English:	"In order, prosperity."
Solar:	"En őder, prősperety."

English:	Nuke-brand beer combines dangerously powerful stimulants with an extremely high alcohol content. Additionally, it is mildly radioactive. Solars with all the benefits of their nanites are one of the few species that can safely drink it.

Solar: Nuke-brand beer kombeens danjerősly poverful stemulants vet an extremele hae alkohol kontent. Addetenalle et es melde radeoakteve. Solars vet all te benefets ov tere nanets ar őn ov te fev spesees tat kan safele drenk et.

English: I, do solemnly swear my allegiance to His Majesty the Solar Emperor. As a member of the Solar Legionnaires, I will maintain the safety of the Empire and all of its subjects. As an officer of this service, I will set the example for those below me. I will never act in a manner that brings shame to my uniform. I will obey the orders of those appointed over me. And I will expect no more from my subordinates than I will give of myself.

Solar: E, dő solemele sware my allejeans to Hes Majeste te Solar Emperor. As a member ov te Solar Legeonnaeres, E vell maentaen te safete ov te Empyre őnd all ov ets subjekts. As an offeser ov tes servys, E vell set te exampl főr thős below me. E vell never akt en a manner tat brĝs ßam to my unefőrm. E vell őbey te őders ov tos appooned őver me. Őnd E vell expekt ne mor from my subőrdenates ten E vell gev ov myself.

2L
THE SOLAR ARMED FORCES

THE SOLAR ARMED FORCES were established as the military of the Solar Empire shortly after the Summit at Olympus. The SAF originally consisted of four branches: the Solar Armadas, Solar Army, Solar Legionnaires, and Solar Commando Corps. A fifth branch, the Imperial Guard, would be formed at the behest of the Commando Corps in the years after the Kaurken War.

In the modern Empire enlistment, commissioning and service in any branch of service are extremely competitive. Automation replaced the bulk of the workforce many thousands of years in the past. The ability to have a job and an income rather than a government-issued stipend is a privilege. Jobs that entail personal risk and mandate travel are often the highest paying. It should therefore be no surprise that military jobs are some of the highest paying in society. All three of the main services take full advantage to be extremely picky and select only high-quality candidates. Even the army, which is well-known for being far more lax than the Armadas or Legionnaires, exercises rather stringent standards.

To earn a commission in the Armadas or Army requires that a candidate graduate from an approved military academy. This is a bit of a high-risk and high-reward prospect for potential officers. The services are under no obligation to hire an academy graduate and will only reimburse the costs to those who are selected for service. As a result, most officer hopefuls seek sponsorship from a specific branch before attending. Such sponsorships do guarantee both selection and reimbursement, so competition for them is even more intense. The Legionnaires are the only main service that allows officer commissions outside of academy graduation, via its Hell's Gate program. That said, most officers in that service (around 84 percent) that are not alpha arens are academy graduates.

Humans are only permitted into the Solar Armed Forces as officers. The reasons for this are twofold. First it helps to maintain the image of humans as the controlling force of the military. This is important for multiple reasons, not the least of which is that the Empire has a number of species that do not get along. These same species have come to trust humanity to keep the peace and provide security. The mere perception that humans are not solidly in control of the military could itself cause enormous unrest or even violence. Especially given the unfortunate reality that some species in the Empire are only peaceful because military strength encourages them to remain so. The services prefer that humans within the military be seen primarily in leadership roles.

The second reason is entirely more practical. Humans are the dominant species in the Empire for a reason. Humans are intellectually superior to the majority of alien species. While the difference can range from extreme to marginal, it holds true for many comparisons. Many alien species simply cannot field large numbers of members who can meet the cerebral standards for an officer position. There are of course exceptions, and officer positions are not denied to any person based solely on their species. While humans won the intellectual prize of the evolutionary lottery, there are many species who fared far better in the physical categories. Many species are stronger, faster, less fragile, and less subject to psychological trauma from violent experiences. While humans are granted many advantages from cellular nanites, with a modicum of cybernetic enhancement many aliens can make up the difference. When such aliens exist and wish to serve to obtain Solar citizenship, there is little reason to have human-enlisted personnel. This is especially true when automatech and arens can be mass-produced to perform a wide host of duties.

The armed services make heavy use of automatech, though control over it is deliberately decentralized. The Empire could, in theory, field a fully automated military. But few are comfortable with placing vast armies of autonomous killing machines under the control of a small elite. Meanwhile, military service instills a sense of duty, identity, and loyalty in those who serve—qualities essential to a stable society.

The Solar emperor is the commander-in-chief of the Solar Armed Forces. Only the emperor may declare war or deploy the military. The highest military rank is that of Lord-Marshal of the Solar Armed Forces. This rank was created specifically for Manfred von Rhinegrave. In the modern era, it is mostly a defunct title. The rank was abolished prior to the Kaurken War. It would later be reinstated during the Reunification Wars solely so the boy-emperor Christopher Mandrake III could appoint a supreme commander to be his proxy. Since that time, the rank has existed only as a contingency if such an event should again arise.

Table 1 — Solar Armed Forces — Rank Structure

Solar Armed Forces – Rank Structure		
Solar Armadas	Solar Army	Solar Legionnaires
Flag Officers		
Lord-Marshal of the Solar Armed Forces		
Solar Admiral*	Solar General*	Solar Marshal*
Grand Admiral	Grand General	Grand Marshal
Armada Admiral	General of the Armies	Marshal of the Legion
Fleet Admiral	Staff General	Field Marshal
Admiral	General	Marshal
Vice Admiral First Class	Corps General	Vice Marshal 1st Class
Vice Admiral Second Class	Lieutenant General	Vice Marshal 2nd Class
Rear Admiral	Brigadier General	Lance Marshal
—		
Commodore *Note*		
Field Officers		
Fleet Captain *Note*		
—		
Captain	Colonel	Colonel
Commander	Lieutenant Colonel	Lieutenant Colonel
Lieutenant Commander	Major	Major
Prime Lieutenant	Captain	Captain
Lieutenant	1st Lieutenant	1st Lieutenant
Junior Lieutenant	2nd Lieutenant	2nd Lieutenant
Ensign	3rd Lieutenant	3rd Lieutenant
		4th Lieutenant *Note*
Non-Commissioned Officers		
Solar Boatswain*	Solar Sergeant*	Solar Sergeant*
Boatswain of the Solar Armadas**	Sergeant-Major of the Solar Army**	Sergeant-Major of the Solar Legionnaires
Prime Boatswain	Sergeant-Major	Sergeant-Major
Master Boatswain	Master Sergeant	Master Sergeant

Boatswain	Sergeant First Class	Senior Sergeant
Vice Boatswain	Staff Sergeant	Staff Sergeant
Junior Boatswain	Sergeant	Sergeant
Supervisor	Corporal	Corporal
Enlisted		
Crewman-Senior	Private 1st Class	Lance Corporal
Crewman	Senior Private	Infantryman 1st Class
Crewman-Junior	Private	Infantryman 2nd Class
Crewman-Probationary	Enlistee	Infantryman 3rd Class

* Indicates a rank that is held only by a single individual at any time. Flag officers in this category are appointed only in time of war to serve as the senior official of that service. The enlisted ranks represent individuals chosen from senior NCOs to serve as advisers directly to the emperor on matters of training, discipline, morale, and treatment of officers. The enlisted ranks are temporary with terms of five years to ensure His Majesty hears more than one perspective.

** Indicates a rank that is held only by a single individual at any time. These individuals serve as the senior enlisted adviser to the chief of staff of their respective service on all issues pertaining to enlisted personnel.

Note 1: The rank of commodore is senior to all line officers but junior to all other flag officers. Armadas personnel of this rank are typically tasked with localized commands such as star bases.

Note 2: The rank of fleet captain is inferior to all flag officer ranks but superior to all others.

Note 3: The rank of fourth lieutenant is typically conferred only on alpha arens produced within the theater of battle to lead hastily raised aren forces that replace battlefield casualties.

Note 4: Astute readers may notice that the rank of "brigadier marshal" is missing from this list, and that "first sergeant" does not appear in the Legionnaires' portfolio. "Brigadier marshal" is a term of interservice rivalry, often used by Armadas flag officers as a barb at Army and Legionnaires personnel to conflate the two services. Obviously such a joke would go over the head of someone not versed in military affairs. "First sergeant" is a title, not a rank or grade in the Solar Legionnaires. It is held by individuals (usually senior and staff sergeants) who have attended the New Officer Induction Program. NOIP graduates have received special training to help newly commissioned officers assume their first commands. If for any reason the new lieutenant is unable to fulfill his duties, the first sergeant is authorized to take command of the unit.

(i)
The Solar Armadas

THE SOLAR ARMADAS IS the emperor's arms, extending his reach across the traversable universe. The Armadas is responsible for the defense of space, not only in engaging hostile forces but in performing duties such as anti-piracy, anti-smuggling, the rescue of imperiled civilian ships, and more. The Armadas also carries out deep-space exploration, even though a great deal is also performed by private interests.

The Solar Armadas is divided into five individual armadas, each with its own specific duties. The First Armada is referred to as the "flag force." In times of peace the First Armada shows the flag throughout space, and in the event of war will likely be the first to go into action against the enemy. The Second Armada is the "guard force." Ships of the Second Armada are generally scattered across the Empire, ready to meet any attempt by a foreign power to encroach on Imperial territory. The Third Armada is the "training or reserve force." Most who join the Armadas will receive their first assignments in the Third Armada gaining actual experience in their duties before eventually being transferred to the first or second.

In times of war, the Third Armada serves as a sort of ready-reserve for the first and second. If a ship from one of the other Armadas is destroyed, it will be immediately replaced by a ship from the Third Armada. The Third Armada will then receive its replacement once built. If a ship is not destroyed but so heavily damaged it cannot partake in missions, it will be transferred to the jurisdiction of the Third Armada while it is repaired. The Fourth and Fifth armadas are the "mothball forces." While each has a full complement of ships, these are kept in protective storage during times of peace. If a major war breaks out, these ships will be brought out to join the war.

The Solar Armadas is perhaps the single most important element of the military. When the Armadas moves into a region of space, it is effectively impossible to dislodge the Empire until they are dealt with. While likely being the most boring, logistics is perhaps the most important part of war. It matters not how well trained or equipped soldiers are if they lack food, ammunition, and other essentials. The Solar Empire has no supply lines to cut—the warships of the Armadas *are* the supply lines. Their massive factories can provide an effectively unlimited flow of new matériel both for themselves and to troops on the ground. They can replace casualties with new arens and automatech constructed within, giving the upper hand in almost any war of attrition. They can even create a "mininet," bringing the astranet with them to ensure this flow is not easily disrupted.

In short, the only way to win is to go toe-to-toe with the Armadas and remove it from the battlefield. For most civilizations, this is simply impossible. Most lack both the weaponry and the number of ships that would be required to meet the Armadas in battle. Many civilizations would be hard-pressed to destroy an Armadas warship even if it powered down all its weapons and shields and simply allowed itself to be attacked. Armadas warships are protected by warp-shielding that would enable such a vessel to endure a supernova. Their titanic hulls are made of materials such as kilosteel, which could be hurtled into a star and still exist billions of years later when that star goes supernova, neither melted by the heat nor misshaped by the pressure. It is not a stretch to say that it is often easier to destroy an inhabited planet than to destroy an Armadas warship.

Armadas warships are built larger than they have to be in order to accomplish their mission. This is not done without reason. A warship is an inherently expendable asset, something its government may send to war and not get back. The size of these ships helps to demonstrate the Empire's engineering and matériel superiority. It forces a potential foe to ask if they wish to provoke a power than can spend so much matériel on a single, disposable asset.

(ii)
Ship Types

ALL SHIPS IN THE Solar Armadas recognized as warships fit into the categories of either capital ships or line ships predicated largely by their size and mission.

Capital Ships

Supercruiser: The supercruiser is the largest and most impressive ship in the Solar Armadas. Only five exist at any given time to serve as the flagship of their respective armada. The supercruisers are not meant to serve as front-line combatants; they are command ships. In actual use, a supercruiser is essentially a mobile fortress. It will take a position behind the lines serving as the command and control ship and providing constant replenishment of matériel to all Imperial forces in the region. In that capacity, it will often serve as the core of the local mininet. Supercruisers are anything but vulnerable. They equip more firepower than a battleship with the strongest defense systems put to space. They are more than capable of defending themselves against an enemy that manages to slip behind the lines for an attack.

The current class of supercruiser is the *Hurricane*-class. These ships have remained in service for so long that they have become the unofficial icons of the service itself. All active-duty supercruisers have at least a few second- and third-generation crews, with some having ninth and tenth generation from shorter-lived species. These ships are kept competitive through constant upgrades and overhauls. The five ships of the class are the *H.M.S. Hurricane*, *H.M.S. Typhoon*, *H.M.S. Blizzard*, *H.M.S. Tsunami*, and *H.M.S. Cataclysm*.

These immense ships have a length of 341 kilometers, a wingspan of 971 kilometers, height of 94 kilometers, and hull mass of approximately 5.71×10^{21} kg or over five quintillion metric tons.

Battleship: Battleships are semi-unique in Armadas service as they are one of only two capital ship types that do not devote a significant portion of its internal volume to logistics facilities. While these ships do have such facilities, they are aimed only at providing for the battleship itself. Battleships are built for the sole purpose of sharing firepower with the enemy. They are outside the service's general organizational structure and are assigned based on need. Battleships may be used to supplement a fleet's firepower or be sent out alone as hunters where they prowl for targets of opportunity. Given their relative autonomy, command and posting to a battleship often carries a certain prestige. They are magnets for drawing the best commanders and crew. Invariably, those who crew supercruisers will almost always be drawn from those who have served on battleships.

The current class of battleship is the *Scarborough*-class. All ships of this class are named for famous Armadas personnel from admirals to distinguished crewmen. The lead ship of the class is *H.M.S. Scarborough*, named for Admiral Leslie M. Scarborough, who is considered the father of modern fleet doctrine. The *Scarborough*-class measures 238 kilometers long, 679 kilometers wide, and 65 kilometers tall with hull mass of approximately 2.14×10^{21} kg.

Battlecruiser: The battlecruiser is the core of the fleet and generally its flagship. Though not as capable as the larger supercruisers, they often fill a similar role. Battlecruisers are second only to supercruiser in total volume dedicated to logistics functions. Unlike supercruisers, battlecruisers are fully expected to join the battle proper with their substantial firepower. A battlecruiser is considered a match for anything of its own size.

The current class of battlecruiser is the *Legacy*-class. All ships of this class (including the lead ship, *H.M.S. Yamato*) are named for famous or even mythical warships throughout the history of humanity, and all species permitted to join the Armadas. These ships have a length of 238 kilometers long, wingspan of 679 kilometers, height of 65 kilometers, and hull mass of approximately 1.96×10^{21} kg.

Heavy Cruiser: The heavy cruiser is like the battleship in that it is meant primarily to provide firepower rather than other forms of support. The heavy cruiser and the cruiser are often built on the same hull. Heavy cruisers trade the bulk of the logistic capacity for greater firepower, armor, and shielding. Like battleships, their primary purpose is to destroy other ships, but unlike battleships, they are part of the general fleet structure. On average, a heavy cruiser has roughly 2.4 times the firepower of a cruiser.

The current class of heavy cruiser is the *Loredai*-class. All ships of this class are named for aliens who have given exemplary service to the Solar Armadas. The *Loredai*-class measures 204 kilometers long, wingspan of 582 kilometers, height of 56 kilometers and hull mass of approximately 1.34×10^{21} kg.

Line Ships

Cruiser: The cruiser is the workhorse of the fleet and a near-ideal balance between firepower, protection, mobility, and support capacity. Though the cruiser may be a jack of all trades, able to effectively perform any job reasonably asked of it.

The current cruiser design is the *Indefatigable*-class. Though most of the older ships of the class have been scrapped or sold off to noble guard forces, it remains in production despite being the oldest design in Armadas's service. No design yet produced to replace it has managed to meet its reputation as the "jack of all trades that is terrible at none." The *Indefatigable*-class has a length of 204 kilometers, wingspan of 582 kilometers, height of 56 kilometers, and mass of approximately 1.34×10^{21} kg. As they are built on the same basic hull, the *Indefatigable*- and *Loredai*-classes have near-identical dimensions.

Light Cruiser: The light cruiser serves as the fleet's shield, its primary job being to protect itself and other ships from attack. Light cruisers dedicate more of their volume to interceptor, sensor, and jamming systems than any other warship type. They are typically deployed on the edges of the fleet formation, screening the larger vessels. Light cruisers are the bane of long-range attackers, fighters, and more. While they do equip large anti-ship weapons, their primary duty remains the defense of other ships.

The current light cruiser class is the *Karuga*-class. Karuga is a kurai word, roughly translating to "night sentry." It measures 177x504x49 kilometers with a mass of approximately 8.74×10^{20} kg.

Destroyer: In any fleet, much of its total firepower will be provided by destroyers. While their own firepower is only a fraction of that of larger ships like battleships and battlecruisers, destroyers are much more numerous. The destroyer is a no-frills vessel, often lacking in things such as guest quarters, VIP accommodations, and other nonessentials. While it maintains more logistics facilities than it needs to support itself, the excess is much more limited than in other vessels.

The current destroyer design is the *Deimos*-class, named for the Tirrish planet Deimos, not the Martian moon of the same name. It measures 85x242x23 kilometers with a mass of 4.21x10^20kg.

Frigate: Frigates are the smallest vessels to be considered warships and serve a variety of functions. They are used as screening vessels, scout ships, harassers to large ships, and more. Like the destroyer, it lacks many of the "extras" that are found on larger ships. The current frigate design is the *Rogue*-class and is one of the newer designs in the Armadas. As of the outbreak of the Hourglass War, the Rogue was still in the process of replacing the earlier *Beneo*-class. The Rogue measures 34x98x9 kilometers with an approximate mass of 6.26x10^18kg.

More than any other ship class, Frigates are significantly larger than what is necessary to accomplish their mission. This is completely intentional as it often makes a noted impression on a potential foe who sees that the Armadas's smallest warship has a wingspan of nearly one hundred kilometers.

Picket Ships

Any ship that is not purely a support vessel (such as a transport) and too small to be considered a warship falls into the category of pickets.

Monitor: The Solar Armadas do not use manned starfighters. Against the warships of a peer adversary, fighters are often worse than useless. A ship small enough to be considered a fighter is hard-pressed to carry sufficient armament to engage enemy warships. It is impossible for them to mount defenses strong enough to survive the anti-fighter weapons that will be deployed against them. Fighter attacks on Armadas warships or those of a peer adversary generally entail massive swarm attacks, which sustain murderous casualties for minimal results.

Fighters in the modern era also lack one of the key advantages of fighters in ages past, that of range. When fighters can extend beyond the range of a warship's weapons, they have a niche to fill. Armadas warships carry MID-driven weapons that can usually attack from farther away than either party of a conflict can see. Meanwhile, any ships they might be used against have ample volume to carry weapons larger than the very fighters they will be used to engage. This virtually ensures that fighters deployed against a warship will sustain long periods of enemy fire before they can even retaliate.

A further complication is that locomotive systems such as a transpatial drive can only be made so small. Most fighters cannot accommodate a device of sufficient capability to make its installation worthwhile. This makes fighters dependent either on a carrier ship or the astranet for intergalactic travel. The former imposes numerous design demands on the carrier ship. The latter makes the fighters useless when they are needed beyond the astranet's reach.

The monitor is the tool designed to blend the economy of a fighter while addressing its limitations. Monitors remain small enough that hundreds can be built for the price of even the smallest true warships, yet they are large enough that they can mount worthwhile armaments, defenses, and a capable transpatial drive. Like their larger cousins, these ships include the logistics facilities that allow them to operate independently without reliance on a carrier ship. Monitor crews can and do pull deployments weeks or months long. In wartime, monitors have carried out deployments lasting for more than a year.

Perhaps a bit ironically, monitors are themselves carrier vessels for unmanned fighters. Unmanned fighters are used to perform scout duties, and they protect the monitor from harassment by any enemy fighters they encounter. While a monitor is not a match for a true warship, wolf packs of four to twelve monitors can pose a credible threat to small warships such as destroyers and frigates. Though monitors are hard-pressed to destroy such targets, they can still achieve mission and mobility kills. Warships invariably pack systems such as weapons, shield protectors, and sensors that must exist outside of the ship's protective bulk. All these systems can be vulnerable to monitor attack. In major fleet battles, monitors often target ships on the outer fringes of the enemy formation, helping to degrade the protective screen they provide around larger and more valuable targets.

The current Armadas monitor is the *Minotaur*-class, which measures a wingspan of 109.6 meters and a length of 84 meters. As with battleships, there is a certain prestige attached to the position of monitor pilot. Such individuals have a great deal of independence at the helm of an extremely powerful weapon. A single monitor has more than the firepower necessary to destroy the livability of an inhabited planet. It is for this reason that every monitor has a two-person crew, with the second being a gamma aren. This leads to the term *GIB* or Gamma (or girl) In Back. It is also why monitors always utilize tandem seating that puts the GIB behind her pilot. In battle, the GIB not only handles communication and sensor functions but controls the ship's automatech fighters.

Sloop: The sloop is essentially a heavy scout reconnaissance craft employed by the Armadas. Sloops are built for speed and are some of the only ships in the Armadas to utilize rotary masless impulse drives. The current sloop is the *Rook*-class and is generally considered the fastest MID-driven ship ever built. The Rook is so fast and the technology used to obtain those speeds so great, it is the Rook, not any of the great warships, that serves as the flagship product in Galaxy Staryards Corporation's marketing. The Rook has defeated more than two dozen attempts by technology demonstrators to take its records for absolute speed. Each time one of its records is broken, the Armadas takes on a new test and opens the throttle a bit more. The Rook is so fast that the standard evasive procedure when the ship is attacked is simply to accelerate.

Rooks were used extensively to probe the territory of the Interstellar Combine prior to the Hourglass War. More than eight thousand missiles were fired by the Combine at intruding Rooks. None scored a hit. The Rook is one of the few ships that will routinely operate outside of a galactic plane simply because it can outrun any attack directed at it.

The official specifications of the Rook are that it is 393 meters long with a span of 203 meters. Nearly all other details about the ship are classified. In addition to its speed, it carries the most advanced sensor and jamming equipment ever devised, and technicians must carry the same security clearance as those who operate the ship.

Outrigger: There is perhaps nothing more important than a commander's ability to see the battle. Outriggers are large sensor platforms designed to gather data for the fleet. They are fitted with powerful active and passive sensors, counter-jamming equipment, and heavy communications systems. Why these ships are called outriggers is a matter of some historical dispute that may never be solved. Outriggers work heavily in tandem with light cruisers to help provide a protective screen for the fleet.

Outriggers have been gradually phased out in the Solar Armadas and remain only in mothball forces. Others continue in operation within the noble guard forces of the Imperial nations. In the service of the Armadas, the outrigger's duty has largely been subsumed by sloops.

Star fighter: While the Solar Armadas does not use manned fighters, many of the noble guard forces do. The noble guard uses star fighters for a variety of reasons. A nation can easily acquire thousands or even millions of fighters for the cost of one warship. These fighters can be in many places at once, doing many things at once. Noble guard fleets are often more concerned with matters such as anti-piracy and suppressing insurrection than they are contending with a foe comparable to the Armadas. If they were faced with such a foe, they need only keep pressure on the enemy until the Armadas arrives.

The Armadas utilizes unmanned fighters, and all warships have the facilities to produce them as needed. These can be used not only to deal with harassing enemy fighters, but they can serve as expendable drones. They can scout distant areas and work as artillery spotters that allow warships to put fire on targets beyond the resolution of their sensors. They can serve as an extra layer of defense by becoming remote point defenses and helping to engage long-range attacks.

Del Tierr, the Elysian Commonwealth, and the Republic of Andromeda all make extensive use of manned fighters in their national fleets. Together with fast carriers meant to elude and retaliate against invaders, they form the core of the Republic's anti-ship doctrine. They are used by Del Tierr largely as "offensive scouts," attacking vulnerable targets while simultaneously serving as spotters for warships. The Commonwealth uses both manned and unmanned fighters because its economy cannot support the cost of a warship fleet large enough to secure its vast territory. The Dominion builds fighters mostly out of jingoism, lest someone insinuate one of the other nations could build a better fighter than them.

(iii)
Solar Armadas Organizational Structure

AS WITH THE OTHER services, the Solar Armadas operates on a fairly rigid organizational hierarchy with a base-10 structure.

Table 2 — Solar Armadas Organizational Structure

The Solar Armadas	First, Second, Third, Fourth, and Fifth Armada
Armada	10 galaxy fleets led by an armada admiral with a supercruiser as the flagship
Galaxy Fleet	10 quadrant fleets led by a fleet admiral with a battlecruiser as the flagship
Quadrant Fleet	10 zone fleets led by an admiral with a battlecruiser as the flagship
Zone Fleet	10 sector fleets lead by a first vice admiral with a battlecruiser as the flagship
Sector Fleet	10 fleets led by a second vice admiral with a battlecruiser as the flagship

Fleet	10 task forces led by a rear admiral with a battlecruiser as the flagship
Task Force	10 squadrons led by a fleet captain with a heavy cruiser as the flagship
Squadron	10 points led by a captain with a cruiser as the flagship
Point	1 cruiser, 2 light cruisers, 5 destroyers, 2 frigates, led by a commander with the cruiser as the flagship

Note: Flotilla is a relatively loose term and is generally applied to a fleet of between 30,000 and 100,000 ships. Flotillas are almost always mixed units made up of ships and personnel from multiple armadas. Flotillas are typically deployed near potential conflict areas. In the event of a conflict, this allows the crews of the flotilla to gain early experience that they can then take back to their home forces.

(iv)
The Solar Army

THE MISSION OF THE Solar Army is to defend the Empire's worlds and population. If an enemy were to invade the Empire, it is the Army that bears primary responsibility for defending its worlds. Additionally, the Army bears primary responsibility for preventing insurrection before it begins. It is often the presence of the Army, its regiments and its star-fortresses, that ensures no nobleman too ambitious for his own good considers rebellion against the throne. While its mission is primarily defensive, the Army can and will be used offensively in major wars.

The Army is the most diverse force in the Solar Armed Forces. Both the Solar Armadas and the Solar Legionnaires allow only certain species to join their ranks. This is entirely a practical measure. Both of those forces focus heavily on minimizing their logistical footprint and maintaining uniformity across the breadth of their organization. This policy does not allow them to make special accommodations for alien species. These branches accept only species that can survive comfortably in a human-typical environment.

This policy creates a bit of a social and political problem. One of the few paths to Solar citizenship is through military service. Service must be made as widely available to the general public as is reasonable. It is here that the Army steps in to take up the slack. The Army does not discriminate against any species that is loyal to the Empire. In many cases, it will use those with differing needs based upon those needs. If, for example, the Army has a group of enlistees that breathe methane, they will be placed into a regiment with other methane-breathers and used to garrison an appropriate planet.

Unlike the Legionnaires' organic force structure, the Army utilizes a regimental structure. Regiments are highly specialized and are grouped into brigades with differing specialties to support each other. Every regiment has its own history, its own traditions, and its own uniform. Regiments generally perform their own recruitment and may perform their own equipment acquisition. Regiments are invariably tied to planets and other population centers from which they historically draw personnel. Often, the civilians of these worlds will follow the progress of the regiment closely in war, somewhat like avid fans of a sports team.

Despite its critical role in the Empire's defense, the Army sometimes suffers from the stigma of being the lesser service. Its training and enlistment standards are lower than those of the Legionnaires, and they are sometimes viewed as second-rate troops in offensive campaigns. This characterization is entirely unfair. While the standards to join the organization are indeed lower than that of the Legionnaires, Army personnel are professional soldiers who, like those in the other branches, can and have given their lives in the line of duty.

(v)
Solar Army Organizational Structure

DUE TO THE ARMY'S regimental structure, its organization is somewhat more loosely defined than those of the other services. Regiments are highly specialized in specific fields such as infantry, armor, artillery, etc. Because a highly mobile armor regiment will require a different amount of infantry in support than a static artillery unit dedicated to planetary defense, this leads to some variation in the numbers.

Table 3 — Solar Army Organizational Structure

The Solar Army	25 grand armies as of 100,016
Grand Army	100 army groups commanded by a grand general
Army Group	100 galaxy armies commanded by a general of the armies
Galaxy Army	100 field armies commanded by a staff general
Field Army	100 corps commanded by a general
Corps	10 divisions commanded by a corps general
Division	10 brigades commanded by a lieutenant general
Brigade	10 to 25 regiments commanded by a brigadier general
Regiment	10 battalions commanded by a colonel, with a lieutenant colonel as executive officer
Battalion	10 companies commanded by a major
Company	10 platoons commanded by a captain
Platoon	10 to 25 sections commanded by a first or second lieutenant
Section	10 squads commanded by a third lieutenant
Squad	10 soldiers commanded by a sergeant

(vi)
The Solar Legionnaires

THE PRIMARY RESPONSIBILITY OF the Solar Legionnaires is the capture of enemy territory. Whether it is an enemy planet, space station, star hive, or any other form of real estate, it is the duty of the Legionnaires to secure it.

In addition to these duties, legionnaires serve as marines on Armadas ships and handle the task of protecting outlying colonies.

The name Solar Legionnaires was chosen deliberately (as opposed to Solar Legion) by Manfred von Rhinegrave to highlight the importance of the soldier versus the organization of which he was a part. A student of military history, Manfred drew heavily upon the marine forces of the ancient United States of America and the British Empire, as well as the French Foreign Legion, when creating the service. In particular, the mantra of the US Marines that "every marine is a rifleman" and the assumed identity clause of the Foreign Legion. A hundred thousand years later, the tradition-minded organization has kept many of the policies that were originally put in place.

Every recruit to the organization must begin their career as either light or armored infantry. Armored infantry must cross-train as light infantry. Only after a minimum of five (and more likely ten) years in service can members apply to fulfill another position. Even if they move on to other roles, legionnaires will continue to drill and train as infantry in addition to their new duties. Whatever position he holds, a legionnaire is expected to be capable of serving as an effective infantryman should the need to deploy him as one arise. The Legionnaires are also the only service with an assumed identity clause. In lieu of Solar citizenship, those who have committed non-capital crimes may choose to join the organization under a new identity. While serving, they are immune from prosecution and will be pardoned of their crimes should they fulfill their term of service. If they should continue in service afterward, they may then begin working toward the requisite number of years required for Solar citizenship.

The Legionnaires are also the only organization that offers a path to join as a commissioned officer outside of formal education at a military academy. The infamous Hell's Gate and the New Officer Training Program were created to do exactly that. While Hell's Gate includes some training, it is primarily a selection program rather than a training program. It does not help that even graduates tend to conflate it with the NOTP that follows immediately after. Hell's Gate exists to find those who have the motivation, if not the education, and selects only those who pass a grueling program designed at every stage to make them quit. On average, less than three in one hundred candidates will pass Hell's Gate on their first try. Roughly ten in one hundred who return will make it through on a second attempt.

Whether by Hell's Gate, an academy, or general enlistment, the standards to join the Legionnaires are the highest of any of the three main services. On average, less than one in 100,000 who apply are even admitted to Hell's Gate. Even for those who graduate from the academies, only about 30 percent pass the New Graduate Officer's Exam to be allowed into service. Those who fail will often either join one of the other services or return home to serve in the noble or royal guard of their home nation.

In battle, the Legionnaires are considered the masters of maneuver warfare and combined-arms tactics. They are an armor-centric force relying on tanks, warmechs, and armored infantry to provide their main offensive punch with support from artillery. Light infantry are masters of both urban warfare and marine operations, seizing population centers and boarding enemy ships.

(vii)
Solar Legionnaires Organizational Structure

THE SOLAR LEGIONNAIRES UTILIZE an organic force structure where every unit of platoon size or larger is a mixed unit. Out of respect to their brother service, the Legionnaires never use the term "regiment" to refer to any of their organizational groups, just as the Army never uses the term "legion." This organizational structure is rigidly defined on a base-10 grouping.

Table 4 — Solar Legionnaires Organizational Structure

The Solar Legionnaires	5 active-duty grand legions as of 100,016
Grand Legion	100 galaxy legions commanded by a grand marshal
Galaxy Legion	100 field legions commanded by a marshal of the legion
Field Legion	100 legions commanded by a field marshal
Legion	100 Corps commanded by a marshal
Corps	10 divisions commanded by a first vice marshal
Division	10 brigades commanded by a second vice marshal
Brigade	10 cohorts commanded by a lance marshal
Cohort	10 battalions commanded by a colonel, with a lieutenant colonel as executive officer
Battalion	10 companies commanded by a major

Company	10 platoons commanded by a captain
Platoon	10 sections commanded by a first lieutenant 2 light infantry, 3 armored infantry, 2 armored, 2 artillery, 1 transport
Section	10 squads commanded by a second or third lieutenant
Squad	10 soldiers, 100 automatech commanded by a sergeant

(viii)
The Noble Guard

THE EMPIRE CAN AND will defend any of its nations that come under threat, but every nation is expected to maintain its own defense force, if for no other purpose than to hold the line against an aggressor until the Solar Armed Forces can arrive to take over. But so too can these forces be called upon by the emperor to join the SAF in waging major offensives. Though there are both royal guard forces held by the pillar nations and noble guards held by the duchies, collectively they are referred to as noble guard.

The quality of noble guard forces depends largely on how seriously any given nation takes the duties of self-defense. It has been so long since an outside force threatened any nation that the nations tend to treat their noble guards as Imperial reserve forces that they are forced to finance. Nations tend to use these forces primarily for disaster relief and suppression of insurrection should it become necessary. Every national sovereign is required to maintain such a force, and this duty is generally apportioned down through the ranks of the nobility to share the cost.

The noble guard forces have at times been problematic to the Empire, namely in the War of Kings, Great Collapse, and Solar Eclipse. Several of them have proven valuable as reserve forces—namely the Republic of Andromeda, Reichsylvannian Dominion, and Yuangi. It is an open question if an attempt by the throne to abolish these forces would itself provoke insurrection by national sovereigns, but in the end the most valuable contribution of the noble guard remains in that it allows the Solar Armed Forces to project the bulk of its power into foreign space without leaving the homelands undefended.

(ix)
The Imperial Guard

THE IMPERIAL GUARD WAS formed after the Kaurken War to take over the duty of protecting the Solar Family. This role had originally been handled by the Solar Commando Corps, which had for years pressed to take a less-visible role in military affairs. All members of the Imperial Guard are arens, with the modern force made up primarily of deltas. Deltas cannot be bribed, coerced, blackmailed, or intimidated. There is virtually nothing one could do that would convince them to betray the emperor. The same is true of all arens, which makes them natural choices to serve as bodyguards.

In addition to protecting the Solar Family directly, the Imperial Guard is also responsible for the defense of the Solar Cathedral. In this capacity, they serve as both its garrison and its police force. The actual number of Imperial Guard in service at any given time is a closely guarded secret. Unlike similar services that protect kings and nobility, the Mandrake Dynasty has long preferred the Imperial Guard keep its ornamentation to a minimum. They maintain equipment commonality with the Solar Legionnaires and rarely decorate their armor any more elaborately than gold-tinted visors on their helmets. The gold visors are reserved only to those guarding members of the royal family.

Special mention must go to the "Rose Thorns," as they were dubbed by the media of antiquity. The Rose Thorns (known officially as Unit 3) are those responsible for the personal defense of each generation's Imperial Rose. Given the fact that the sheer size of delta arens can make them menacing to many species, the Imperial Rose has been guarded by a specially designed variant of gamma arens since that breed was invented.

The Imperial Guard is not designed to project force; its only job is to protect the Solar Family and their home in the cathedral. The organization operates infantry, tanks, artillery, and orbital defense assets. The Imperial Guard does not operate any of its own ships, as defense of the space around the cathedral falls to a special unit of the Second Armada.

(x)
The Solar Commando Corps

THE FIRST MEMBERS OF the Commando Corps were drawn from men who had been selected for Project Commando but did not partake in the mission to destroy the Common Control Organism.

The Commando Corps is generally considered the oldest of all the armed services. Due to the heavy amount of secrecy involved in the organization, few understand exactly what its members do. Commandos may be used to gather intelligence, but they are not spies. They may be used to perform assassinations, but they are not specifically assassins. The mission of the Corps is to handle clandestine matters that require the use of force to resolve, and to do so in secret.

All Corps missions are deemed "absolute secret," the highest level of secrecy in the Imperial military. These missions are never declassified. The Corps has no qualms about making disappear anyone who digs too deeply into their affairs. Whether this is a potential spy or an overly ambitious journalist is immaterial. While they primarily handle clandestine affairs, commandos are often the special forces of last resort, taking on those missions deemed too high risk for other services. Another unspoken duty of the Corps is its role as a secret police force. Civilians are beneath the organization's notice, but those in power know they risk drawing the Corps's eyes if they should entertain thoughts of rebellion against the throne. The Corps refers to this duty as "housekeeping." Its most notable action in this field is known as the Silent Night. In one night, the Corps killed 7,019 senators and noblemen, all of whom were conspiring to deny the rightful confirmation of a new emperor.

Commandos are not restricted by the laws and customs of war. A commando is entitled to use any weapon or method to accomplish his mission how he deems fit. By that same token, they are not protected by these same laws and customs. If a commando is captured, there is nothing to stop an enemy from treating him as a spy or even a terrorist. Given the extreme sensitivity of the information a commando is privy to, they are expected to protect what they know at any cost. If that means committing suicide to prevent capture, so be it, though it is highly preferred that, if possible, they instead disguise themselves as members of another military branch and escape at the first possible opportunity. To maintain their clandestine status, commandos do not wear their uniform or insignia in the field. When operating near forces of the other services, commandos will generally wear the uniform of those nearby to blend in. Only those with a need to know will be apprised of the commandos' true nature. Commandos only wear their own uniforms in formal functions, primarily within the organization itself. Most officers will go years at a time without ever wearing the service's uniform.

The standards to join the Corps are the most stringent in the Solar Armed Forces. Only humans can be officers. Commandos are fanatics. With the enormous power and freedom they are given, a fanatical dedication to the Empire is seen as necessary to be entrusted with the position. Beyond this fanatical loyalty, and being human, candidates for officer positions in the organization must meet the following criteria:

1. Must be a combat veteran

2. Must possess a telepathy score no less than T-11; higher is preferred

3. Must possess a psionics score no less than P-9

4. Must have no living family or other personal connections who will miss them during long absences

5. Must be in the top 3 percent of physical conditioning across the armed services at the time of admittance

6. Must demonstrate a psychological willingness to kill based on the needs of the mission rather than standards of morality or ethics. They must possess the good judgment to know when it is necessary. The organization wants those who will easily make hard decisions; they do not want bloodthirsty mass murderers

7. Must be able and willing to take on a new identity, including facial reconstruction, and specialized nanites that will give false readings to any attempt to examine their genetic material

8. Must either undergo or have undergone evade, resist, escape training programs

9. Must have no record of major disciplinary action in military service

10. Must carry at least a seventh-degree expertise ranking in numerous small arms utilized by the Solar Armed Forces

11. Must carry at least a fifth-degree expertise ranking in no less than three vehicles, one of which must include basic stellar piloting and navigation

12. Must qualify for absolute secret security clearance and be judged willing to do whatever is necessary to defend the information to which they have access

The Corps rarely makes exceptions to requirements on this list but will occasionally exempt one or two for a candidate that demonstrates provident ability. Only those requirements that can be addressed via training after joining are considered to be waived. Only the emperor himself can grant further waivers.

All officers carry the rank of colonel and the distinction of being an agent of the emperor. They are considered senior to all military personnel, barring flag officers. Flag officers also carry the distinction of being agents of the emperor. While a commando cannot issue an order to a flag officer, every flag officer knows it behooves him to cooperate with a commando's request. Conversely, a commando has no obligation to follow an order from a flag officer but is encouraged to foster cooperation when it does not interfere with their mission.

Every officer is permitted to assemble an auxiliary force of additional soldiers to assist him in his duties. The requirements to become a commando auxiliary are much more relaxed and largely boil down to whatever that commando considers a necessary qualification. Like the commando themselves, these auxiliaries must be able to disappear and be entrusted with the highest levels of security clearance.

The commandant of the Commando Corps is considered a flag officer equal to the Solar ranks of the other services. Technically, this makes him the most senior military officer in the SAF during times of peace. However, the commandant, like the rest of his organization, is outside the regular chain of command. The commandant is responsible for assigning missions, identifying potential candidates, arranging the recruitment of those candidates, and testing them for admission into the service. While he is the leader of the organization, commandos are the kind of people who can and should operate with a high degree of independence. Though rare, the most important job of the commandant is that of internal security for the organization. While there have been very few instances, if a commando should become a renegade, it falls on the commandant to hunt down and terminate him. Only the commandant and the emperor may issue direct orders to any commando officer. Only a commando officer may issue orders to his auxiliaries.

2M
THE ARENS

THE ARENS WERE FIRST produced roughly fifty years prior to the Kaurken War. The original intent of the arens was to enable the Imperial government to pull a sort of sleight-of-hand. The Imperial public—the human portion in particular—has long been suspicious of AI-controlled weaponry. Many atrocities were committed in both pre-history and during the time of the Interstellar Confederacy when lone individuals or small groups had control over massive and completely obedient AI armies. The Empire has long kept organic, particularly human, soldiers as an important and visible part of the military. To have organic troops in the field provides some advantages. The more distant a control center is from the units in controls, the more of which can interfere. By having troops local to the battlefield, command and control over AI weaponry is easier to maintain.

The reliance on organic troops is not without downsides. Matériel can be produced on-demand, but it takes years to raise a live soldier so that he may replace a dead one. This impedes the Empire's ability to achieve its goal of having infinitely replenishable forces.

Casualties can inflame public opinion. What the Empire desired was a soldier that it could infinitely produce, yet one that was "human enough" that people would not protest their being placed in command of automated forces.

The first arens were created through a process known as "spin-cloning." In this process, a living being is synthesized from base chemicals spun into nucleic acids, cells, functional organs, and eventually a complete organism. Along the way, the anatomy of the arens is redesigned and relied heavily on cybernetics. Arens are cybernetic organisms made of both flesh and machine while requiring both to survive. Compared to a human, these early arens had a more simple and more effective anatomy. These arens were then raised purely as soldiers.

The first battles in which the arens were involved generally ended in costly defeat. This was not due to any deficiency in the arens but as a result of Emperor Justin's insistence on using them like automatech. The arens were routinely sent in to overwhelm enemy forces, and if necessary, to bury them in bodies. While the fighting prowess of these early arens was superb, it could not overcome poor doctrine. It was only after Justin's death that the arens began to shine. Soon the arens proved themselves as adept field personnel serving in the same role as organic troops, exactly as they were meant to.

Modern arens have very little in common with their ancient ancestors beyond the name. Numerous distinct breeds have risen to specialize in particular roles. Modern arens are born with not only the benefits of cellular nanites, but by default have all those benefits conveyed in Military Cybernetics except when unnecessary.

All arens are bound in behavior by the Twelve Directives. The general public often has a misguided view of the effects of these directives. They are *not* unbreakable compulsions on an aren's behavior; an aren technically can act against these directives. Instead these directives are baked into an aren's psychology and ultimately form the cornerstone of their conscience. While an aren can violate the directives, they would need a compelling reason to do so.

Directive 1: Obey the will of His Majesty, the Solar Emperor.

Directive 2: Protect the security and interests of the human race.

Directive 3: Protect the security and interests of those aliens loyal to the Empire.

Directive 4: Do not attack civilians except in self-defense.

Directive 5: Obey the Solar Code of Military Law.

Directive 6: Respect the laws of friendly civilian authorities.

Directive 7: Obey all orders from superior officers pursuant to Directive 5.

Directive 8: Refuse all orders that conflict with Directive 5.

Directive 9: Never bring shame to the Empire or its military.

Directive 10: Preserve aren life over automatech. Preserve human life over aren life.

Directive 11: Do not speak to civilian media without authorization; refer them to public relations.

Directive 12: Never surrender unless ordered to do so by a superior officer.

It must be noted that the Empire considers the arens to be machines, not wholly sapient beings. This is a view the arens themselves share. The use of arens has been a controversial topic at some points, and they have been likened to slave soldiers. To add somewhat to the controversy of their status, arens are fully eligible to hold rank and receive military commendations. This is a distinction that automatech do not share. To an aren, however, there is no need to search for purpose in life. They were built with a purpose, and life has little meaning if they are not working to fulfill it. While most refer to the various subtypes of arens as "breeds," the official term is "series." Subtypes within a series are models.

Arens do not feel fear, do not experience pain in the same way as humans, and are not subject to the many emotional traumas combat can inflict. They cannot be bribed, blackmailed, or intimidated. The loyalty of the arens to the Empire is absolute. Arens do not lack a sense of self-preservation but know they exist to fight for the Empire. For an aren, there is never a choice between self and the mission. The answer is always the mission.

(i)
Alphas

OF ALL THE AREN series, alphas are the closest to being human in terms of temperament, mentality, and behavior. Alphas can be said to have the most free will of any aren breed and are the series most capable of acting against their directives if they find a need. Alphas are produced specifically to fill positions as officers in the Solar Armed Forces. Alphas can be created to lead hastily assembled and manufactured armies, or to help the Empire reach its minimum-accepted force compliment. However, as most officer positions in the SAF are filled by people working to earn Solar citizenship, alphas are the rarest series. Many alphas in service were originally created when the Empire produced armies on-site for a battle so as not to have to wait to bring in additional forces.

There are a total of seventy-two variants of alpha produced for specific fields—those who work in the intelligence services are a different model than those staffing warships. Alphas generally receive extremely high marks from both commanders and subordinates. Some soldiers even prefer alpha commanders as they are more even-tempered than most organic officers. No alpha has ever been convicted of a war crime, and they are seen to have an almost perfect balance between the needs of the mission and the lives of their subordinates. Alphas will send men to their death if it is necessary, but they will never throw away their forces carelessly.

Alphas have a capacity for nonlinear and abstract thought that is superior to the other series. Arens are capable of improvising in ways that the other series generally are not. Alphas have fully sapient personalities, personal preferences, and individual senses of ambition. Other arens will not generally concern themselves with something like earning a promotion. If the higher-ups choose to grant one, so be it. Alphas by contrast will actively work toward advancing themselves and proving they deserve such a position.

Anatomically, arens are very similar to human men who have undergone military cyberization. However, their basic organic anatomy is much more simple and effective. An alpha's circulatory system is far less complex and has fewer points where injury could lead to lethal blood loss. The similarities diminish in the brain. The brain of an alpha is completely redesigned to remove unneeded portions while maximizing capabilities such as analytical ability and reflex processing.

All models of alpha stand two meters tall and have an average mass of three hundred kilograms. Their size is deliberately chosen to make them larger than most organic troops, making them more imposing as authority figures. While all models of alpha have a similar appearance, they are built using a randomization algorithm. This serves to give each alpha a sufficiently unique appearance to be easily identified and personified. Aside from the Solar flag officer ranks, which are reserved for human personnel, there are no other barriers to an alpha's ability to advance in the chain of command.

(ii)
Betas

ON THE ORGANIC-MACHINE spectrum, betas are the farthest to the machine side. Betas are often and not incorrectly considered automatech with organic components. Beta arens are made to fill the billets of enlisted soldiers, and quite frankly to be expendable. To this end, betas are deliberately made less human. Betas do not have fully sapient personalities, do not have individual preferences, do not have individual ambition, and do not form personal relationships. Many steps have been taken from attenuating their psychology to modifying their word choice to prevent organic soldiers from forming emotional attachments to them. Betas are meant to be sent to their death at any time, with no one mourning their loss.

Beta arens have very little in terms of personality. A beta with nothing to do will default to a task such as sentry duty, janitorial duty, or some other monotonous but necessary task. While they can effectively communicate with others, few betas will speak unless spoken to. Betas are rigidly logical in their decision-making, and are effectively incapable of operating outside of accepted standards of conduct. Betas are the only series that do not have the benefit of court-martial if accused of wrong-doing. While such a situation is practically unheard of, a beta who would merit such a court-martial is labeled defective and is replaced.

Other arens require far less sleep than humans, but betas do not require sleep at all.

By weight, betas are approximately 90 percent cybernetics and share very little with humans beyond their external appearance. All variations of beta are 1.67 meters tall with a mass of one hundred kilograms. They are designed to minimize physical size so that they take up less space and impose a minimal logistics footprint. Despite their uniformity of personality, they are the most varied of all arens in term of models produced. There are 214 models of beta, specialized for various roles. Betas benefit from an algorithm to give them a unique appearance, but its effects are minimal. Many soldiers will comment that all betas look alike. Beta arens do not have names and are nominated by serial numbers.

(iii)
Gammas

GAMMAS ARE THE MOST recent addition to the series of arens, though in the modern era even they have been a staple of the military for thousands of years. Gammas are designed as living computer interfaces. The primary function of the series is to interact directly with computerized systems and with each other to form a unified network of minds. Most gammas serve in the Solar Armadas, specializing in sensor and communications equipment. When gammas are linked together on a network, what one gamma knows, all know. When one gamma receives a piece of information, the combined processing power of all gammas on the network is put to work analyzing it.

Gammas have sapient personalities, of a sort. Soldiers sometimes comment that if you have met one gamma, you have met them all. The networks formed by gamma arens share information so freely that it is not uncommon for an individual gamma to have memories belonging to another. It generally falls on the senior gammas in a network to monitor memory, sharing among other tasks, and ensure that no member on the network retains information that they should not. As with betas, most gammas do not have individual names and rely on serial numbers. Some gammas are assigned names or perhaps even "earn" them. Most gammas with individual names are senior members of the series whose duties involve regular person-to-person interaction directly with organic personnel.

Gamma arens are the only "female" arens, though the term is somewhat of a misnomer. Gammas, like all other arens, are neuter as they lack reproductive anatomy. The decision to design gammas with a female appearance was an arbitrary and opinionated choice made by the lead designer. Modern gamma arens have non-human hair colors such as blue and green. Supposedly this came about at the request of Imperial soldiers who wished to more easily identify a gamma from a woman. Most gamma arens are enlisted, while the most senior may be junior commissioned officers. As with betas and deltas, gammas have no real sense of personal ambition and do not actively seek career advancement.

Rose Thorns are the gamma arens created for the Imperial Guard to protect each generation's Imperial Rose. As the official last daughter of the emperor, the Imperial Rose is said to have a special place in regard to the people. She is the royal scion least likely to inherit the throne. One can approach the Imperial Rose with less worry that they risk misspeaking or embarrassing themselves in front of a future sovereign. The Mandrake Dynasty has actively worked to cultivate this image and has often taken steps to make the Imperial Rose seem more approachable. One such decision was to have the Imperial Rose protected by gamma arens. While the Rose Thorns are listed as gammas in the Imperial Guard's inventory, anatomically they have more in common with deltas aside from their feminine appearance.

(iv)
Deltas

DELTAS SERVE IN THE Solar Armed Forces in the roles of non-commissioned officers, military police, and in certain special forces units. Deltas are the largest series of aren with most models standing 2.25 meters tall with a mass of 420 kilograms. A common joke among soldiers is that deltas do not have discipline; deltas *are* discipline. As non-commissioned officers and military police, they are the most visible sign of military discipline within the force structure. Deltas themselves have sapient personalities, many of which are the regulations of their respective service given flesh. If a military regulation exists, a delta will follow it. Of all aren breeds, deltas are the least likely to act against their directives. If a delta acts against directives, it is a certainty that he was under orders to do so. Betas *could* be said to be even less likely, but it is a non-issue as they lack the measure of free will shared by other arens.

Deltas were first created when the Empire began admitting aliens into the Solar Armed Forces in large numbers. Part of the rationale behind the deltas' development was for them to play the "bad guys." Human doctrines of military discipline were extremely strict in comparison to that of most aliens. By making deltas the disciplinarians for enlisted soldiers, human officers were spared direct association with the unpleasantness that came with being punished for infractions of military discipline.

While deltas will live and die by regulations, they are not incapable of independent thinking and action. Their physical resilience is the highest among all arens, even more than betas, which are more machine than living. This has made them popular among certain branches of the special forces. This is typified by the "Emperor's Angels," the deltas that form the Search and Rescue Contingents. SARC is a multi-service organization with the duty to penetrate enemy lines and rescue soldiers trapped behind them. SARC has proven so effective at its duty that early on, they fed the tendency of some of the more primitive alien species to deify the emperor. Their knack for pulling troops out of hopeless situations led to the belief that the emperor had performed a miracle by sending SARC. As a percentage of their numbers, SARC is the most decorated service in the Solar Armed Forces.

Delta arens are also the chosen breed to fill the ranks of the Imperial Guard, which protects the Solar Cathedral and the members of the Mandrake Dynasty. The Imperial Guard has two versions for this task, the DS-CG-1 and -2. CG-2 models share some attributes with alphas and form the Imperial Guard's officers.

APPENDIX 3

TECHNOLOGY

3A
THE HYAMS EFFECT

ONE OF THE FEW great scientific minds of pre-history to be remembered into the modern Empire is Walther Hyams. It is his work and the scientific discoveries made under his supervision that made the modern technology of the Empire possible. Hyams had a particular fascination with wave/particle duality. Since de Brogile's proposition that electrons behave as waves, humanity has known that matter had wave-like properties. For many years, this was an interesting bit of knowledge but one with little practical value. It fell to Dr. Hyams to accept, and finally prove, what physicists beforehand had only suspected. Namely that if matter had wave-like properties, then it could be manipulated via waveform and not simply by other matter. But even Hyams did not foresee just how far his work would take him. In the end, the creation of the field of warp-physics would be the most significant development since man learned to harness electricity. Much like electricity, it would come to touch nearly every aspect of life in one form or another.

Hyams coupled his work in wave manipulation with that of cosmologist's search for a universal wave function, and the well-known mathematics of wave interference patterns. In doing so, Hyams discovered that there was no wave/particle duality, but rather that matter *was* a waveform.

Prior to Hyams's work, humanity had understood the universe as mostly empty space with distributions of matter here and there. According to Hyams, space was the most fundamental building block of existence. Rather than being empty volume in which matter sat, space was more akin to the leftover materials after one has erected a building. At the most basic level, matter existed as strings. These strings, as he defined them, were ultra-localized self-repeating waves or distortions in space-time.

Albert Einstein in explaining his work had once likened space-time to a sheet, with gravity being akin to a massive object pressing down on that sheet. Hyams would later co-opt this analogy in order to explain his own theory. If one had a sheet, it would inevitably have wrinkles. As the sheet grew larger, those wrinkles would range in size from small to large. With an even larger sheet, so many wrinkles would exist that they would eventually take on patterns. As the sheet continued to grow, these patterns would range from simple to complex and eventually repeat. If one had a sheet the size of the entire universe, these patterns would be repeated many times over. Meanwhile, the more wrinkles that were present in one part of the sheet, the greater the effect their presence would have on the surrounding portions.

But Hyams's work was initially met with a great deal of resistance. To quiet his doubters and bring on more scientific minds for continued work, he conducted his Proton Teleportation Experiment. Waves can interact with, merge, and manipulate one another. Through his work in studying this phenomenon, Hyams had learned that gravity was not the only force that could alter the geometry of space-time. Under the right circumstances, he could do the same with the electromagnetic force. In a laboratory the size of a football stadium and drawing more power than a major city, Hyams managed to teleport a proton approximately one one-millionth of a centimeter. His method of using electromagnetism to reshape space-time was heavily researched and refined. Over the years, it came to be known as the Hyams Effect. It is this effect that would later be harnessed to develop much of the technology that drives the Empire.

Hyams's theories would dramatically alter physicists' understanding of the universe—from the nature of matter and energy as changes in localized wave functions, to alternate theories on the origin of the universe. The Hyams Effect has had the most profound impact on human civilization. Financed by the wealthy Wagner family, two men named Albert Müller and Zhang Tsu would use Hyams's work to create the first massless impulse drive and truly open the door to the stars.

Hyams's name remains common in Imperial science thousands of years later. Warp fields are generally divided into natural fields and artificial fields called Hyams fields. The strength of a warp field is often measured in hyams units. The original equations used by Hyams to predict the interaction of natural and artificial warp fields remain in use into modernity, relatively unchanged.

It must be noted that the difference between natural warp fields and Hyams fields are not based solely upon what causes them. Natural warp fields (such as gravity) generally have infinite range, albeit reducing intensity as that range extends. Hyams fields by contrast typically have finite range but a more constant strength throughout their limited influence.

3B
MASSLESS IMPULSE DRIVE

THE FIRST MASSLESS IMPULSE drive was developed by Albert Müller and Zhang Tsu. Müller was regarded as a visionary in his time as an accomplished engineer, businessman, and all-around eccentric. He was the man best suited to take the theories of the Hyams Effect and put them into practical applications. Dr. Zhang was regarded as a brilliant physicist and, as a youth, studied under Hyams himself. Together, with funding from the wealthy Wagner family, the pair designed and built the *Spirit of Humanity*, the first ship to fly under the power of a functional MID. The *Spirit of Humanity* is one of the few pre-Empire historic artifacts that survives into the modern era. The Müller-Zhang MID was such a simple design that after the vessel was already a museum ship, it was easily restored to working order. This allowed the ship to escape the destruction of Earth in the Therican War. The vessel remains intact and on display in the Imperial History Museum within the Solar Cathedral.

In the ensuing millennia, the technology of the MID has improved considerably, and modern drives are exponentially more powerful than those that came before. Despite its age, the MID remains the primary method of faster-than-light travel. No other propulsion method invented has been able to do the job as efficiently or simply. The drives themselves are not massless—far from it. A MID functions by dramatically warping space-time around the traveling ship. This is what enables the ship to exceed light-speed relative to anything beyond the resulting warp bubble. The ability to cause such a pronounced warping effect on space-time is normally the domain of hyper-massive objects such as black holes. By comparison, the mass of the typical MID may as well be nothing.

A ship traveling on the power of a MID has its own reference point in space-time and does not experience time dilation like an object accelerating close to *c* through more conventional means. Any time dilation the ship experiences will be based on its speed *within* the warp bubble, which is often too low to matter. There are two main types of MID in common use, with literally hundreds of specialized subtypes. This entry will focus only on the two primary families of which all other systems are variations. These are the compression drive and the longitudinal drive.

The compression drive is essentially a realization of the device first envisaged by Miguel Alcubierre ages ago. The drive functions by compressing a volume of space-time to the ship's nose while dilating space-time at the rear. Compression drives favor designs that minimize the distance between the points of compression and dilation, and are responsible for the distinctive "flying wing" shape of Armadas ships. The size of the ship has less of an effect on attainable speeds in compression drives. Smaller ships will accelerate more quickly, but larger ships with more powerful drives can often equal or even exceed them in top speed.

Longitudinal drives, known more commonly as rotary drives, were a much later development than the compression drive. Of the two systems, rotary drives are the more high performance. Rotary drives function by twisting space-time around the ship, enabling it to travel through space-time in a manner not too unlike a drill bit through a piece of wood or a propeller through fluid. While a MID enables a ship to move faster than light, the components of the drive, like everything else, are subject to basic physics. For most MID systems, their sustainable speed is limited by the speed at which its parts move while in operation. The advantage of a rotary drive is that all its moving parts operate in a single, sustained circular motion. This is in opposition to a compression drive with many reciprocating parts. This enables rotary drives to spool up and sustain higher rates of operation, allowing for both greater acceleration and top speed. Rotary drives favor ship designs where their greatest dimension is length.

When comparing the two systems, a rotary drive will generally always be faster than a compression drive made with a similar technological proficiency. This rule can break down when comparing drives from different origins. The Interstellar Combine uses rotary drives on its warships because that civilization cannot build compression drives fast enough to be militarily useful. Imperial compression drives are routinely faster than Combine rotaries due to the more advanced design and construction.

The Solar Armadas has long preferred compression drives for their warships. The components of a compression drive are well distributed throughout a ship's body. While a compression drive is much more likely to sustain damage, its distributed nature means it is less likely for a single hit to destroy it. Compression drives can function while damaged and are easy to repair. Buried at the heart of its host ship, a rotary drive is more difficult to damage. However, any damage to the delicately timed and balanced parts can render the drive inoperable. Rotary systems also require more maintenance to be kept in normal operation than do compression drives. The Empire primarily limits the use of rotary drives to applications where speed is paramount, as well as where the greater maintenance is a non-issue. One example is in missiles, which require high speed, and due to their single-use nature, make the maintenance imposed by time spent in operation moot.

All ships carry a main drive and at least one backup drive in the event the main should fail. Some ships even carry multiple drives for different functions. An example of this can be found in the Commando Corps's *Phantom*-class ships. These ships carry both a compression and a rotary drive with a hull that physically reconfigures itself depending on which is used. The compression drive is used when the ships must remain stealthy, and the rotary when speed is paramount. From time to time, the idea is raised of building a ship with multiple drives designed to operate simultaneously with each other, but such ideas rarely leave the concept stage of development. A ship operating multiple drives simultaneously would need to maintain an unparalleled level of synchronicity between them. Any failure to do so could have disastrous consequences, including the ship disrupting itself as conflicting warp fields create catastrophic interference.

What is unknown to most is that such a ship has already been built and deployed. The *Rook*-class sloop was one of the most expensive research and development products ever undertaken by Galaxy Staryards Corporation. The Rook utilizes four MIDs, two compression and two rotary, to enable the ship to reach unmatched speeds. In this instance, however, each of the two compression drives is dedicated to a specific task. The forward MID only compresses space-time and serves a function not unlike the air intake of a jet engine. The second MID serves solely to dilate space-time behind the ship, and rapidly disperse the resultant warp-wake. The twin rotaries operate concurrently with each other and, due to the effect of the forward compression drive, can manipulate a much larger volume of space-time with each cycle than would normally be possible.

This incredibly complex system is one of the most precise pieces of engineering ever created. The operations of the quad-MIDs are synchronized to within a zeptosecond of each other. Their resulting warp frequencies are held to a uniformity of less than one ten-trillionth of a difference. This system is so precise and so maintenance-intensive that two Rooks are assigned to every mission. One in case maintenance keeps the first from being able to deploy.

To hide a ship at warp from warp sensors is a technological challenge comparable to building a ship with concurrently operating MIDs. A warp bubble creates a massive reflection when interacting with such sensors. To warp sensors, the concept of speed is one that is largely moot, and their effective range is limited primarily by how much clutter they must see through. A ship moving at warp will create a sensor return approximately the same size as a star, yet moving at FTL. The only effective stealth ships to be built and deployed are the *Phantom*-class ships of the Solar Commando Corps and their *Intruder*-class shuttles. While these ships are far from undetectable, they can generally hide in the clutter so long as they remain within the plane of a galaxy. If detected, they are more likely to appear as a sensor glitch than a legitimate target.

Imperial MID systems are generally fueled by using xenomatter. Xenomatter itself is an extremely complex subject, which will not be detailed in full here. In short, it is one of the densest forms of exotic matter ever produced, dwarfing even kilosteel. Under ordinary conditions, xenomatter is stable and inert. However, under specialized conditions, it can be made to undergo rapid decay. When xenomatter decays, it does so into an almost even split of particles and antiparticles, which can then be annihilated for energy. This enables xenomatter to function as an extremely compact antimatter fuel source without the catastrophic risks of containment failure. The actual production of xenomatter itself is both expensive and dangerous. Civilian MIDs by contrast generally incorporate fusion systems. While the Empire's fusion technology is exceptionally efficient, this forces civilian ships to dedicate far more of their internal volume to reactor space and fuel storage.

Massless impulse drives tend to "snag" interstellar detritus such as radiation and gas within the ship's warp bubble. While experiments have often been made to weaponize the effect, in practice it is generally not worth the effort. The accumulation of large amounts of excited matter within a warp bubble can both collapse the field and potentially endanger the ship or missile. To mitigate this problem, all MID-equipped ships and devices utilize an oscillation matrix. The oscillation matrix constantly reshapes or even cycles the operation of the field to eject any "hitchhikers."

If one needs to get somewhere faster than a MID can take them, they have entered the domain of the transpatial drive.

Table 5 — Speed Comparison Chart

Speed Comparison Chart		
Ship	**Drive Type**	**Speed Cruise/Maximum (Multiples of *c*)**
Civilian Freighter (typical)	Compression (fusion powered)	105,000/210,000
Majestic-class VIP Shuttle	Compression	455,641/686,920
Longrunner-class rapid deployment transport	Compression	500,490/721,000
Interstellar Combine, Type-II Frigate	Combine-type Rotary	667,852/696,141

Legacy-class battlecruiser	Compression	555,041/0.94 million
Hurricane-class supercruiser	Compression	536,207/1.1 million
Commando Corps's *Phantom*-class	Multi-channel Compression (stealth)	576,000/1.015 million
	Rotary	4.5 million/5.1 million
Arc-5 Anti-Ship Missile	Forced-Cycle Rotary	6.4 million/7.4 million
Rook-class Reconnaissance Sloop	Quad-MID System	7.7 million/12.4 million

The cruising speeds listed here represent a ship's economic cruise. That is the speed at which the ship is managing the best balance of speed to rate of fuel consumption. Ships will often travel at this speed to minimize the amount of time they must stop to take on or synthesize more fuel. Maximum speed in this context represents the highest speed the ship can attain without risk of damage to its locomotive systems.

As with many things, raw numbers can sometimes be misleading. The Arc-5 missile is often cited as having a maximum range of 100,000 light-years. However, this assumes ideal launch conditions, such as the target moving toward the launch platform at warp, making no attempt to evade, and the missile being able to follow a straight trajectory to the target. Similarly, navigation concerns, threats from nearby enemies, and more can all force ships to maintain higher or lower speeds depending on circumstance. These numbers reflect only ideal conditions.

3C
TRANSPATIAL DRIVE

THE DEVELOPMENT OF THE transpatial drive heralded the end of the Long Morning in the Solar Empire. At least as significant, it was the transpatial drive that made intergalactic travel a practical reality. Prior to the drive's development, a few intergalactic voyages had been made to the Solar Galaxy's satellites. These expeditions were purely to prove it could be done, and yielded little tangible benefit. A massless impulse drive consumes power and fuel throughout its operation. In the intergalactic void, there is little opportunity for a ship to synthesize and replenish its fuel supplies. To make intergalactic travel practical required a more direct means.

Some historians have pointed to the development of the transpatial drive as the cause of the first real schism between the Rhinegrave and Mandrake dynasties. Through their company, Galaxy Staryards Corporation, the Rhinegraves had spent a generation and countless sums of money developing the drive for their own purposes. Eventually, the Rhinegraves reported their progress to the Solar Armed Forces as required by Obligation 3 of sovereign dominion. The Mandrakes ordered that the development project be opened to the rest of the royal families and their scientists.

The Rhinegraves were reluctant to oblige. The family had hoped to keep the technology exclusive to themselves, and units sold to the Solar Armed Forces. To force the issue, the Mandrakes shared the information that had been provided to the SAF with the rest of the families. The throne then created Project Andromeda as an Imperial program and ordered all families to contribute. In the end, this delayed progress of the drive's development. The Rhinegraves had been the only family actively researching the technology. Years were required for scientists in service to the other families to catch up before they could contribute. To the Mandrakes, this was acceptable. The throne did not want any family to have a monopoly on the technology. Additionally, it hoped that the development could serve as a point of unity between families growing increasingly competitive with one another.

The first successful transpatial trip was made by the ship *H.M.S. Spirit of Discovery*, which traveled to the Andromeda Galaxy and returned. With the mission's success, all families would redouble their efforts to further the transpatial drive's development and expand to Andromeda. This would eventually result in the War of Kings but would also eventually turn the Empire into an intergalactic superpower.

Gravity is one of the few forces in the universe with infinite range. Warp fields are capable of merging with each other even when those fields come from different sources. This means that Hyams fields can be merged with gravity. This is the principle behind the transpatial drive. Space itself is deluged with layers upon layers of weak but present natural warp fields given off by massive bodies. The transpatial drive identifies such a field, isolates it from the rest, and then merges it with a Hyams field to create a bridge across space-time to the source. The resulting bridge is often known (not quite accurately) as a wormhole.

The resulting transpatial bridge is then used to warp space-time and merge the entry and exit points together, or at least to bring them in extremely close proximity. This allows the ship to pass through the resulting bridge (either conventionally or on a MID) and travel to the distant destination almost immediately. On a theoretical level, this would enable one to travel anywhere in the universe given the billions of years gravity has had to propagate through the cosmos. One should be able to jump anywhere within the infinite gravitational reach of the target object.

The transpatial drive does not allow one to travel anywhere in the universe whenever they want. The more distant the source of the target warp field, the more difficult it is to identify and isolate it. Even once the target field has been identified, a multitude of calculations must be made or disaster is inevitable. One possible result is the exit-point intersecting the target, which could cause situations such as a ship plunging itself into a black hole, rather than arriving in proximity to one. The arrival point must be relatively close to the target. If a ship tries to arrive too far from its gravitational target, it may become lost, emerging at some unknown point in the universe from which return may be impossible. The more distant the jump, the closer to the target the ship must emerge to make the trip safely and accurately.

The first transpatial drives were only capable of locking in on the gravity of supermassive black holes in neighboring galaxies, or black holes in a local galaxy. Modern drives are much more capable but still have limitations. Intergalactic travel generally requires a black hole or neutron star to serve as the target and point of arrival. Intragalactic jumps can generally target stars or even massive planets. Jump buoys, large space stations producing powerful warp fields, can also be constructed to serve as the navigation point. These buoys are the most effective but are obvious high-value targets in warfare.

Another weakness of transpatial drives is found in the combination of their size and required power. Beyond the drive itself, an enormous amount of sensor and computing equipment is necessary, which limits useful drives to larger ships. Drives require enormous amounts of power to jump intergalactic distances, thus placing greater size restriction due to the need to store all the necessary fuel. Even large ships can require minutes or hours to perform all scans, calculations, and power generation depending on the distance of the jump. Often most of the time spent on an intragalactic jump will be spent making calculations rather than moving. This forces military commanders to plot their jumps carefully. If a ship or fleet jumps into battle and the battle goes sideways, it may not be possible to use the drive to escape quickly. Moreover the effects a transpatial drive have on space-time are instantly detectable for thousands of light-years to warp sensors. To jump covertly and without detection is difficult.

As of the year 100,016, the only known civilizations to have developed functional transpatial drives are the Solar Empire, Interstellar Combine, Kaurken, and Praetheen Unity.

(i)
Transpatial Gateway

THE TRANSPATIAL GATEWAY IS designed primarily to provide the means for travel across distances too vast for the standard transpatial drive to bridge. They are also used to allow ships that do not have their own transpatial drives to make long-distance trips at smaller scales. Transpatial gateways take the shape of giant rings, one at the departure and another at the arrival point. Depending on how vast a distance two gates are, bridging travel through them can be instant or take weeks.

Across extremely vast distances such as the crossing between the Local and Virgo Clusters, gates are linked through buoy-telescoping. This method is also used to enable ships to cross these vast distances. Transpatial buoys are sent on an automated ship traveling via its massless impulse drive. When the ship runs out of fuel, the buoy is laid. The next ship jumps to the buoy and repeats the process until the destination is reached. A construction ship will then jump from one buoy to the next until arriving at the terminus where it then constructs the gate. A gate at the arrival point is either constructed beforehand or simultaneously. Once each gate is completed, they lock onto the closest buoy. Each buoy passes the signal to the next until the bridges meet at the center and the connection is complete.

A gateway can be shut down and its direction reversed, but while a gate is active, it is a one-way transit. Any ship attempting to go the wrong direction through a gate on a MID will find it impossible as warp interference strips their warp field away. Ships attempting to go through via more mundane means will find the tidal forces at work impossible and dangerous to move against.

Transpatial gateways are designed for "always on" operation, which is more energy efficient than the standard point-to-point jumps made by ships. The process remains energy intensive, and gates are usually placed in regions where they can be easily supplied, or can easily synthesize their own fuel. Because they are priority targets in war, gateways are typically well defended.

If a gateway is destroyed, ships can still potentially use the buoys for transit, assuming they have their own transpatial drives. Depending upon the distance, however, this may not be practical as every jump requires considerable energy, and a ship may run out of fuel before completing the trip. The Empire has a policy to *never* abandon an intact gateway. A civilization is not likely to gain transpatial technology through reverse-engineering if they don't already have it. However, the Armadas does not leave it to chance. Nor is there a reason to leave the gate intact for an enemy with the capability to study, and in doing so gain a handle on how sophisticated the Empire's transpatial technology is.

3D
ALCHEMIC PRINTER

EVEN MORE THAN THE massless impulse drive, the alchemic printer would have to hold the distinction of being the most important piece of technology in the known universe. The device is named for the alchemists of old who tried to transmute lead to gold. Though they failed in that endeavor, they made the greater contribution of establishing the scientific method. Generations later, Imperial scientists would complete the work of the alchemists. The development of the alchemic printer is one of the best-known science and engineering stories of the Empire. The project had hundreds of contributors of coequal importance. Many of the contributors were killed by individuals who feared what the device could do. But in the end, the technology made it to reality.

Alchemy occurs quite often in nature—every moment that a star fuses hydrogen into helium. Nuclear weapons perform alchemy, splitting heavy atoms or fusing lighter substances. But the Hyams Effect offered a means to perform alchemy in less severe circumstances. By using Hyams fields to compress the space-time matter occupied, it could be made to fuse without requiring the enormous heat and temperature of more conventional nuclear mechanisms.

One thing the universe has no shortage of is hydrogen, and by compressing larger amounts of it, an alchemic printer can transmute hydrogen into any other element. This technology was soon combined with other more mature fields such as 3-D printing. The alchemic compressor would turn hydrogen into the raw materials, and the printer would fabricate the finished product.

The technology of alchemic printing has come a long way since its introduction. Modern printers often dispense with 3-D printing, shaping the created materials as they are transmuted. Many modern printers can work in reverse, pulling atoms apart into lighter particles. As such a prolific technology, it is also an extremely complicated subject. Not all printers compress hydrogen, as the fusion of hydrogen into helium releases a great deal of energy that cannot be ignored. Fusion only produces net energy with materials lighter than iron, and the amount drops sharply when simply making the jump from hydrogen to helium fusion.

The food printers in a soldier's mess kit to provide field rations do not use hydrogen but can make use of many other elements such as oxygen, nitrogen, silicon, and others. Civilian printers are deliberately designed so that they cannot make use of hydrogen, helium, or heavy elements such as uranium—to prevent them from being weaponized. Only some printers are high-energy systems. The wall-mounted units most people think of as their home printer is not the printer itself but simply the dispensing terminal. Imperial engineers are not fools. These high-energy devices are not only laden with safety features but are generally placed in locations that minimize damage if the unthinkable should occur.

The alchemic printer has enormous cultural and economic impacts, as portended by those who feared the technology's development. Alchemic printers did not lead to a post-scarcity society. That is impossible. There are some things one cannot simply make more of on an arbitrary basis. If, for example, people wish to see a live performance, only so many seats can be added to an arena. The alchemic printer did create a post-essentials society. Together with the Empire's technology for cheaply producing power, it soon became trivial to ensure that all persons had enough food, water, medicine, and shelter to live their lives. Soon the measure of wealth became how much one had that printers could not produce. When combined with automation, the technology turned the Empire into an ever-growing land of plenty.

Printers would also lead to what is known as the Horvat Effect. Jon Horvat was a celebrity chef at a time when alchemic printers were first being used to mass-produce food. He was made somewhat of a mockery when, in a blind taste test, he failed to distinguish a meal he had cooked from one that had been alchemically printed. He continued to insist that printed food could never taste as good as "real" food. The Horvat Effect has morphed into the perceived greater value of "real" food, grown or butchered, versus printed food. While there are indeed some dishes that printers have trouble getting right, this is not true for most. Most agree that the real value in the Horvat Effect is that a printed dish will always taste the same unless programmed to taste otherwise. A naturally grown meal may have variation based on the history of the dish from farm to table.

Alchemic printing also created a nightmare for intellectual property, royalties, and similar concepts. In modernity, one often patents a printer pattern. If one wishes to print a patented design, they will be charged a royalty at the time of printing. One example of this concept in action can be found in restaurants. If one wishes to eat a quintuple cheeseburger for dinner, the alchemic printer can provide. If one wishes to eat a Derf's Five-Decker, they must either pay a royalty to Derf's or go to a Derf's and order. Many restaurants do not allow printing of their recipes. Most restaurants aren't in business to sell food but to sell space. Since most of the Empire's population is unemployed, they need something to do. Restaurants provide a place for people to meet, gather, socialize, spend the day in astranet virtual reality, and avoid having to clean up after themselves. Other restrictions on printers also exist. In most jurisdictions, the law forbids the sale or distribution of any printer not designed to refuse a request for weaponry. Weapons must be limited to purpose-designed and licensed-weapons printers.

The more complex the end product, the more work that must go into it. Printers can minimize this work, but they cannot do all of it. One of the reasons Armadas warships are flying factories is that a lot of military matériel requires more to make. To build a functional coil for a disrupter rifle requires an entire laboratory. To print bond-forged matter is an enormously more complicated process and requires much more complex and expensive equipment than something like the average person's food printer.

3E
BOND-FORGING

THROUGHOUT HISTORY, SCIENTISTS HAVE often postulated many concepts from the exceptional to the mundane, all made impossible by the fundamental limits of the matter in the universe that can be used for any task. The advent of bond-forging technology would change this situation forever. While Dr. Hyams pontificated on what this technology might make possible, it fell to two other scientists to lay the groundwork that made it a reality: the husband-and-wife team of Lewis and Renee Lombardo, the father and mother of the technology.

The Lombardo team began their work with a single premise: that all things in the universe came into being in the universe. This meant that all matter and energy, their formation, interactions, and expressions, were determined by the nature of the universe. If one could change the nature of the universe, one could achieve different results. The Hyams Effect offered the opportunity to do exactly that, to alter the universe at a local level through the direct and controlled manipulation of space-time. The couple spent their lives on the project and succeeded in their twilight years. Together they successfully managed the interaction between fluorine and potassium atoms to create new particles. The result of their labor was the Lombardo particle, which has absolutely no practical use. Their experiments, however, opened the door for scientists who came later to do the rest. Though their end product was not useful, it proved that the Hyams Effect could be used to create exotic matter.

In the following generations, scientists would build heavily on the Lombardos' work. New particles eventually spelled new interactions, and even new forces beyond the fundamental forces of nature. Imperial science now recognizes the elementary forces. These are made up of the natural forces—strong, weak, electromagnetic, and gravity, as well as the exotic X, Y, Z, AA, BB, and CC forces, which have been exhibited by exotic matter.

In time, Imperial scientists and engineers successfully impregnated mundane matter with lab-created synthetic matter, allowing overlap and combination of these two sets of forces. The X-force for example is carried by particles, which will orbit atomic nuclei just like electrons, but the X-force is in fact stronger than the strong nuclear force while acting much like electromagnetism in forming chemical bonds. The X-force is carried by a particle named the magnetotron. If a magnetotron is slammed into a neutron, it creates a neutron-Y. The neutron-Y carries the Y-force.

The Y-force magnifies the effect of the strong force many times over. The AA, BB, and CC forces are relatively recent additions, and are found only in the exotic matter used to manufacture both Reichsylvannian steel and astranium. It is because of these three forces that those materials are the most and second most resilient materials known to Imperial science.

It would be nearly impossible to overstate how important the development of bond-forging would become. Materials for use in building things ranging from cutlery to buildings to ships could now be strengthened to levels that were impossible, even preposterously so before this technology existed. While not everything is bond-forged, the Empire simply would not have the capabilities it possesses without this technology.

Bond-forging created some problems for military planners early on when the technology first began to proliferate. The bond-forging process can take simple, abundant iron and turn it into something so resilient, even the heat and pressure of a nuclear blast will do little to damage it. If an enemy armors himself in such a material, how does one bear enough force to kill him without utterly obliterating the environment he is in at the same time? The answer to this question would come with the proliferation of disrupter technology, though a sort of never-ending arms race would begin between the two technologies. Bond-forging and density are the only material properties that can affect a material's resistance to disrupter weaponry. Thus the race continues of better disrupters and better bond-forging.

One of the most interesting traits of bond-forged material is that it does not react with antimatter unless the antimatter itself has been bond-forged. Bond-forged antimatter will not react with mundane matter. This quality became a vital element in solving some of the Empire's energy problems prior to the development of xenomatter and more efficient fusion systems. The Hyams Effect had yielded economic means to produce antimatter for use as fuel, but it was only after bond-forging greatly simplified the process of containing the antimatter that it became a truly viable fuel source for all the applications demanding it.

3F
SHIELD TECHNOLOGY

SHIELD TECHNOLOGY IS AS varied as the objects it is used to protect. In general, the Empire defines active shielding as a system that generates an artificial barrier, distinct from armor, and which can be activated or deactivated at will. Shield technology falls into two basic families.

(i)
Ship Shielding

IMPERIAL WARSHIPS AND OBJECTS of similar scale rely on high-intensity warp-shielding in order to defend themselves from enemy fire. Such powerful shielding is the closest thing in this universe to invulnerability, and it effectively immunizes a ship against any non-disrupter type of weapon. While the execution is complicated, the concept is rather simple. For an incoming attack to strike a ship, it must cross space to get there. High-intensity warp-shielding makes this impossible.

Imagine a mouse on a carpet with a piece of cheese in front of it. Naturally, the mouse will cross the carpet to eat the cheese. But what if the cheese is placed under the carpet? Now there is no path the mouse can take to reach the cheese. The principle behind warp-shielding is effectively the same. Any laser beam, plasma bolt, missile, bullet, or similar attack must cross space-time to reach the ship it targets. Warp-shielding warps the space-time around the ship to such a degree that there is literally no path through space or time that will allow an incoming attack to intersect the ship's position. The effect is similar to the warping of space-time beyond the event horizon of a black hole, where trapped matter finds space-time so warped that there is no path away from the singularity.

If one were to ride a laser beam fired at an Imperial ship, they would experience traveling only in a straight line. The observer would see the beam approaching the ship until it disappeared and reappeared behind them. An outside observer would see the laser beam arc around the ship's position. While photons and the like can survive the trip, impacting masses are generally obliterated as the highly warped space-time rips them apart. Consequently, this type of shielding renders a ship impervious to light-based detection. This however is generally irrelevant as Imperial ships move and do battle at FTL.

Disrupter-type weapons are the only real threat to a ship, space station, or planet protected by such shielding as they are themselves warps in space-time and will react with the shield itself. Going back to the analogy of the mouse, a disrupter is the mouse tunneling through the carpet to seize the cheese. Whenever a disrupter meets a warp-shield, local intensity rules. If a thirty-millimeter-diameter warp pulse strikes the shield, it will penetrate unless the thirty-millimeter section of affected shield is more intense than the disrupter pulse. This forces shields to have many orders of magnitude more energy to have any ability to stand up to concentrated fire. Most warp-shields are multi-layered to help dilate disrupter attack in stages and hasten the drop in intensity.

Warp-shielding on a warship is tied closely to the warp field generated by the ship's MID. A ship generally has much more powerful shielding at warp because the shield system can augment the warp field created by the MID and enable it to double as its own shield layer.

Planetary shielding has many similarities but is also a much more complex issue. Such a powerful warp field will interfere with the natural gravitational attraction between a planet and its host star. This will inevitably result in the planet beginning to drift away from its host. While self-correcting shielding exists to prevent such an effect, the cost and complexity typically see it limited to high-priority worlds.

(ii)
Infantry/Vehicle Shielding

FOR THOSE FIGHTING A ground war, the super-intense shielding used on warships is both impractical and undesirable. The Hyams Effect allows for the extremely energy-efficient warping of space-time, but the process still requires considerable power. Most ground vehicles let alone infantry cannot carry systems of sufficient strength. Even if they could, creating such a powerful warp field on a planet's surface would be little different from establishing a massive gravity sink in that location. It does an infantryman no favors to have everything in his environment falling toward him at terminal velocity.

Ground units do use warp-shielding, but it is far less intense. Warp-shielding for these units is designed to help redirect incoming fire and to sandwich other types of shielding between these warped layers rather than mimicking the "hole in reality" effect of ship shielding. The main defense for ground units is in the form of barrier fields.

Barrier fields are fields of charged particles kept in containment around the protected object by using sandwiched layers of warp fields to confine their movement into a circuit rather than venting into the environment. The charged particles used in this situation are known as MMPs or Magnetic-Momentum Particles. MMPs were one result of scientific experiments to use Hyams fields to create negative-mass particles. While a failure in that regard, MMPs demonstrated that if contained in an electromagnetic field, rather than acting with an equal/opposite or equal/alike force, they would always move in the direction that current flowed. The movement of one group of MMPs within a field would then cause others within that field to move with them. This allows a barrier field of MMPs to direct the force of any incoming attack in a preselected direction regardless of the actual angle of impact. By alternating the strength of the magnetic field, MMP fields could be calibrated to allow or deny the passage of incoming objects based on their velocity, enabling something like an infantryman to pick up a can of soda without damaging it.

MMP barriers are usually multi-layered with streams flowing in multiple directions. When an object such as a bullet strikes, its momentum transfers to the MMPs, while some MMPs will be pushed in a direction perpendicular to the bullet's line of travel. This will have a deflecting effect on the bullet similar to striking a spinning wheel. Meanwhile other MMPs will be rammed into the bullet further accelerated as a result of its own momentum. It is not uncommon for such colliding projectiles to be melted or vaporized from the resulting impact. Less dense impactors such as a plasma bolt usually fare more poorly as they are scattered by the collision. MMPs offer minimal defense against lasers as they are designed to be transparent. Other defenses such as magnetic screens, the containment warp fields, and armor are generally more than adequate at defending against such threats. When subject to a force such as a blast wave, the momentum is transferred to the MMPs, which often does little more than cause a spinning wheel to spin faster. An exceptionally powerful blast, however, can overwhelm the MMP field, allowing some of the blast wave to reach the target.

MMPs are one of the few defenses that are effective against disrupters, albeit far less so than warp-shielding. A disrupter field will dilate as it accumulates matter. The unusual behavior of MMPs causes them to behave within a disrupter field as if they were much more massive and voluminous than they actually are, enhancing the effect of dilation. When combined with layers of warp-shielding, this provides enough of a defense that a soldier is not completely helpless against incoming disrupter fire. However the best defense still remains to avoid being hit in the first place. MMPs simply cannot stand up to disrupter fire in the way true warp-shielding can.

The biggest disadvantage of MMP shielding is that it will invariably lose strength when subjected to significant attack. Some MMPs will leech out of their magnetic field and into the warp fields where they will be ejected. This means that unlike high-intensity warp-shielding, which will maintain a constant strength so long as the equipment is undamaged, MMP fields will lose strength as they are subjected to sustained attack. If this loss exceeds the rate at which new MMP particles can be synthesized, the field will degrade to the point it becomes irrelevant.

Further defense for ground units is found in armor and concussion fields. Concussion fields are an adaptation of inertial damping technology designed to diffuse changes in momentum that could harm the protected person or object.

3G
WARP WEAPONRY (DISRUPTERS)

HISTORICALLY ANY NEW TECHNOLOGY or scientific discovery has existed for all of five minutes before the military tries to find a use for it. The Hyams Effect was no exception. Beyond its potential to get troops to the battlefield, attempts to weaponize the effect began almost immediately. It would take many years to make warp weaponry a reality, but once the work was done, the technology was here to stay. Some have called the disrupter the last weapon anyone will ever need. While many weapons have been developed after it, even after tens of thousands of years, none have supplanted it.

Most other weapon systems—whether they are bullets, laser beams, explosives, or heavy rocks—function on the same basic principle. That is to force energy and momentum into the target until something bad happens. The disrupter is the exception. Disrupters function by affecting the space-time in and around an object. Many material properties that have great influence on the effectiveness against other weapons such as hardness, tensile strength, melting point, and more, are reduced to irrelevance.

Matter is held together by the elementary forces. These include the fundamental forces: strong, weak, electromagnetic, and gravity, as well as the exotic forces at work in exotic and bond-forged matter. Other weapon systems generally must contend with these forces to break an object. Disrupters instead disrupt the ability of particles to exchange forces between one another. A simple analogy would be to imagine two magnets working to attract each other. A conventional weapon is equivalent to grabbing these magnets and pulling them apart. A disrupter expands the actual distance between them until they are no longer attracted, rather than acting on the magnets themselves.

It is an oversimplification to say that disrupters are more powerful than other weapons. Disrupters are more effective. Perhaps the greatest advantage disrupters offer is that they can penetrate defenses such as armor and shielding while requiring only a fraction of the power that a conventional weapon would need. Technology such as bond-forging allows the Empire and other civilizations to create materials of truly astounding resilience. Disrupters are often the best and sometimes only practical means to defeat these defenses.

One of the most notable advantages of disrupters is that they are inherently faster-than-light weapons. While no massive object can travel beyond *c*, this does not apply to space-time itself, which lacks substance. At relatively close ranges such as within a planetary atmosphere, this largely obviates the need to compensate for things such as distance or movement. It was this type of weaponry that obsoleted aircraft from the modern battlefield. A modern army is full of cybernetically enhanced soldiers carrying FTL weaponry with smart-targeting assistance. To be in the sky, where everyone has a line of sight over a great distance, is generally a very bad idea.

There are many types of disrupters, and each is given its own explanation below. The general principle to keep in mind is a simple one. When space moves, matter within it moves as well. At least relative to everything else.

(i)
Pulse Gun

WHEN MOST HEAR THE word "disrupter," their first thought is of the pulse gun. Pulse guns are by far the most common type of disrupter weapon in existence. They range in size from tiny concealable pistols to massive battleship guns capable of striking targets light-years away. The pulse gun functions by creating a highly distorted volume of space-time and then projecting it at the target. As this pulse travels, it will effectively snag any matter in its path. This process happens so quickly that atoms and molecules will generally be torn apart, though most will remain intact and are taken along for the ride.

The warp pulse fired from a pulse gun is essentially a sphere turning itself inside out so rapidly that it takes on the shape of a toroid. Each pulse has three effective parts. These are the event horizon, the volume, and the zero point. The event horizon of a disrupter pulse was named due to some passing similarities to that of a black hole. For a disrupter pulse, the event horizon is a mathematically derived point surrounding the pulse. Objects that intersect the event horizon will be pulled into the volume of the pulse. That which lies beyond the event horizon will not. The thickness of the event horizon is extremely small, less than that of a single electron. Atomic nuclei bisected by the event horizon can and will be split.

Particles separated from each other by the event horizon of a disrupter pulse can no longer exchange the electromagnetic, strong, weak, or gravity forces with one another. This contrasts with the exotic X, Y, Z, AA, BB, and CC forces, which can. This essentially means that anything relying on the fundamental forces to hold it together is helpless to prevent being separated by the pulse's event horizon. The exotic forces can continue to function across the event horizon, albeit at greatly reduced levels of influence. The fact that they can do so at all is one of the primary reasons all armor meant to withstand disrupter fire is bond-forged.

Matter that crosses the pulse's event horizon will then enter the volume. For all intents and purposes, this highly distorted region of space-time might as well be a pocket universe unto itself. It maintains spatial dimensions but can exceed the three-spatial dimensions of "normal" space-time, a concept that is hard to visualize or explain without the conversation becoming more about arithmetic than language. Objects drawn into this region are routinely ripped into smaller and smaller (though macroscopic) pieces as it is shifted around within the maelstrom.

The zero point is the absolute center of the pulse, the gap at the middle of the toroid. The size of this gap is so small that it is difficult to visualize. There is no known particle small enough to enter it. Matter that crosses the volume of the zero point is obliterated as surely as if subject to a matter-antimatter reaction.

While a disrupter pulse produces a lot of dramatic effects such as annihilation and nuclear fission, this does not lead to the consequences one might expect. While a pulse gun can indeed cause nuclear fission, it is highly unlikely to cause an atomic blast. Only the fission of materials heavier than iron will produce a net release of energy. Even then, extremely heavy elements such as uranium are required for this effect to become pronounced. Even if one were to shoot a block of uranium-235 with a pulse gun, the odds of a fission explosion are small enough to be regarded as zero. While nuclear fission will occur, it is highly unlikely to produce the type of chain reaction needed for an atomic detonation. Similarly, while some of the matter drawn into a pulse will be annihilated by contact with the zero point, the total amount that suffers this fate is quite small. In infantry-scale weapons, it is barely enough to produce a noticeable effect. At most, such guns produce a sudden spike of light and radiation. Though by the time one reaches the scale of warship weapons, the effect can become prodigious enough to create secondary damaging effects.

Unlike the event horizon of a black hole, the event horizon of a disrupter pulse is not a point of no return. Matter can and will be ejected from the pulse as the volume continuously turns itself inside out. In these ejections, lighter objects rule. A single oxygen atom freed by the reaction is likely to escape. A thimble-sized piece of intestine is not.

As a pulse travels it begins to dilate, expanding in diameter perpendicular to its line of travel. This effect is exasperated as more matter is drawn into the pulse's volume. For a pulse to be effective, it must be highly concentrated and localized. This is the primary limitation on the range of pulse guns. Eventually the pulse will dilate so rapidly that it will dissipate. Any matter trapped within will be released, and the effect will end. Most infantry weapons can generally retain their lethality out to the visual horizon. For starship guns, this can be measured in light-years.

Generating a disrupter pulse requires a considerable amount of energy. Most Imperial disrupters meant to be wielded in the user's hands function on micro-fusion power cores. These cores pull double duty as heat sinks. When their hydrogen fuel is exhausted, the cores are ejected, carrying heat with them. Larger guns like those mounted on tanks, warmechs, or ships generally have dedicated reactors and cooling systems. The sheer power required in generating a disrupter pulse is one of the factors that keeps infantry-sized weapons out of reach for most civilizations.

Beyond their ability to rip holes in things, disrupters can cause wounding or damage through a number of secondary mechanisms. The passage of a disrupter pulse often results in the release of free electrons. Many an individual who has received what might have been a nonlethal wound from the hole left by a pulse has been electrocuted as a result. Additional effects come in the form of burns and exposure to radiation.

The most mass-produced pulse gun in the Empire is Reichsylvannia Armaments' model-117. The RA-117 assault rifle is considered by many to be the most ideal blend of power, weight, expense, and simplicity that can be practically achieved. It is as simple a design as one can have and still pose as a functional pulse gun. It is used extensively by the Solar Armed Forces, noble guard, law enforcement, and civilians where it can be legally owned.

(ii)
Wave Gun

TO MANY, THE WAVE gun is the bad idea that simply refuses to die. It is an attempt to create a disrupter gun more powerful than a pulse gun without resorting to the single-use ammunition of the ordnance gun. Rather than project a disrupter pulse, the wave gun generates and holds the pulse within its barrel before attempting to stretch it out toward the target.

As the wave gun is providing constant power, the resulting space-time distortion it creates can be much more powerful. Additionally, the gun can make constant adjustments in the frequency of the beam, helping it to more rapidly eject accumulated matter. The downside is that this causes the resulting beam to dissipate far more rapidly than would a disrupter pulse. This makes a wave gun extremely deadly at short-range but vastly limits that range. Whereas the simple RA-117 pulse gun can kill a foe on the horizon, even a tank-sized wave gun is rarely effective beyond a kilometer's distance.

Equally damning, wave guns require far more power than an equivalent pulse gun and burn out their systems far more quickly.

Beyond these differences, there is little to differentiate the effects of a pulse gun from that of a wave gun. They are considered niche weapons at best. The technology had been all but abandoned by the Empire prior to hostilities with the Interstellar Combine. That conflict would see the Empire bring wave guns back into service, in anticipation of using them to repel mass waves of enspa attackers. While enspa pose little real threat even to light infantry, they can create a deadly distraction from more dangerous Vaar attackers.

(iii)
Ordnance Gun

WHEN ONE WISHES TO maximize the shot-for-shot power of a disrupter, the ordnance gun is generally the ticket. The term *ordnance gun* is applied to warp weapons that rely on firing a field-generating projectile rather than projecting a field created by the gun itself. This projectile is the literal ordnance and is generally referred to as a warp shell, or simply *shell* for short. Warp shells are nothing less than a rotary MID used to ferry the target to the afterlife rather than their preferred destination. Rotary MIDs can be built extremely large or small, down to the size of ammunition that can be employed by infantry. While the tiny infantry-sized MIDs will burn themselves out long before they can cross an interstellar distance, they are plenty sufficient for the ranges involved in ground combat. Starship ordnance guns are, effectively, medium-ranged weapons capable of striking over light-years, but they are inferior to missiles in their ability to do so.

A warp shell has four primary components. These are the shell, the launch pack, sabot, and casing. The shell is the rotary MID, which is used to inflict damage on the target. The launch pack is a micro-fusion battery that fits beneath the shell as they are contained in the casing. Nearly all warp shells utilize a multi-piece sabot composed of 343-neodymium. This is a synthetic form of neodymium that has been atomically ordered to maximize its natural magnetic properties. The final portion is the casing into which all these components fit and are protected.

As mentioned, the shell is the literal MID, which upon clearing the barrel, will generate a warp field around itself. This confers a number of advantages over a standard pulse gun, the most significant of which is power. Unlike a pulse gun, which must contain its own pulse before it is fired at the target, a shell will not begin to generate a warp field until it clears the launching weapon. This allows the generation of a much more powerful field without endangering the operator. The presence of physical equipment and a dedicated fusion cell within the shell itself allows it to generate an extremely powerful field. Unlike a pulse, this field can be continually refurbished by the shell, making it far more resistant to the dilation and dissemination of the field.

Like ships, which utilize oscillation matrices to avoid collecting interstellar dust, a shell can use a similar system to more rapidly dispose of matter it accumulates within its warp field. This further enhances the shell's ability to penetrate any given target. The MID itself allows for the shell to make course corrections as it travels. In interstellar combat, this affords shells a limited homing capability. While ground combat takes place at too short a distance for this to be possible, it allows shells to be pre-programmed to follow a given flight path. This can allow for capabilities such as firing over obstructions.

Most ordnance guns rely on a device known as a gauss magnatron to launch the shell. This is an evolution of the gauss gun concept. The primary difference between the two is that the gauss magnatron is a frictionless system. A shell propelled by such a system is completely suspended in a magnetic field and never makes physical contact with the barrel of the weapon firing it. Interestingly, while modern terminology generally refers to any two-handed firearm as a "rifle," weapons with a gauss magnatron are one of the few examples where the term is used in a manner more true to its origin. Gauss magnatrons generally incorporate hundreds or even thousands of micromagnets arranged in sequence through a series of grooves in the barrel. These magnets grip the sabot and eject it along with the shell from the barrel. The sabot will be discarded upon exit, often destroyed by the activation of the shell.

The power pack takes the form of a fusion cell and is responsible for powering the gauss magnatron. This pack also provides a kickstart to the battery within the shell to prime it for firing. The casing is the final component, the majority of which are Messer-type thermal converters. The casing not only cools the firing weapon but uses the waste heat of the fusion cell to recharge the onboard systems of the gun itself. When fully assembled into its casing, a complete warp shell often bears a superficial resemblance to the ammunition of ancient autocannons.

Some ordnance guns utilize "bombshell" ammunition. Bombshells are warp shells that are fitted with a vortex or inflation charge within the body of the shell. These weapons are designed to penetrate the target before detonating for maximum destructive potential. Bombshells are generally utilized in larger ordnance guns, as there are few cases where an infantry-grade weapon would need this ability to defeat legitimate targets.

When considering weapons of the same size, an ordnance gun will always be more powerful than a pulse gun. The ubiquitous RA-117 assault rifle can punch an 11.45-millimeter-diameter hole through 5 meters of solid uranium. The Titan Works D-500, which is of similar physical dimensions, can use one of its shells to put a 12mm hole through 23 meters of the same test media. The large guns found on warships designed to kill other kilosteel-hulled warships are inherently weapons of mass destruction and can completely perforate any habitable planet.

While ordnance guns have a clear advantage in power, they have disadvantages that limit their use. The most notable of these is the weight and volume of the shells themselves. A pulse gun operated by a power pack can generally provide dozens or even hundreds of shots to its gun before it must be replaced. Larger guns, like those on vehicles, often have their own generators, allowing them to fire until the generators run dry. A warp shell is inherently a single-use item, and a unit utilizing an ordnance gun will only be able to fire as many shots as the number of shells it carries. Shells cannot be produced via alchemic printer, whereas simple fusion cells can.

Ordnance guns also tend to be much heavier than pulse guns. An ordnance gun is generally designed to launch its shells out of the barrel at extreme velocities. In infantry weapons, this can be at ranges of twenty-five to fifty kilometers per second. In warship guns, this can be 3 to 5 percent of c. This adds weight both in the form of the gauss magnatron and for infantry in the form of anti-recoil systems. Even the RA-117, which is considered a "featherweight" rifle, has a mass of ten kilograms. That weight would have made the weapon too heavy to be practical to pre-Solar humans, if they lacked cybernetics or powered armor, but the Titan Works CC-500 has a mass of twenty kilograms.

The largest and most powerful ordnance gun in general production is made by Titan Works's subsidiary Titan Ordnance. The TO-N-6666 is mounted only on battleships, battlecruisers, and supercruisers. This colossal autocannon fires kilosteel-encased shells measuring 508x2,200 meters. The fact that these shells are larger than the warships of many civilizations is not lost on the Empire. Images of these shells superimposed over those of foreign warships are often used for propaganda value. The more limited range and maneuverability of these shells against missiles somewhat limit their use to slow and stationary targets. Only the strongest warp-shielding provides an impediment to this weapon, and even it will quickly be overwhelmed. All loading is performed by machinery.

Though rare, some ordnance guns can be mounted with hypercoils if the operator is unsatisfied with the levels of overkill he is achieving. A hypercoil is effectively the disrupter coil of a pulse gun designed to generate a pulse and merge it with the field generated by the shell as it activates. A process that can be expected to enhance the short-range power of the shell by around 15–20 percent. Hypercoils are an enthusiast piece of equipment. Not only is the added power rarely needed, but it requires a great deal of special care in calibration and maintenance to function properly.

(iv)
Warp Charge

WARP CHARGES ARE USED to fulfill the mission of an explosive device even though they themselves do not explode. Warp charges come in three varieties: inflation charges, compression charges, and vortex charges.

Due to their hyper-destructive nature, inflation charges are used only in space combat. The detonation of an inflation charge creates an expanding bubble of space-time that proves devastating to everything in its influence. The nature of Hyams waves allows them to dilate space-time at a rate which exceeds c. In a sort of microcosm of the "Big Rip" theorized as a possible end to the universe, the matter in which space occupies expands so much quicker that matter is torn apart. A cornucopia of reactions occurs within and on the perimeter of the blast. These include nuclear fusion, fission, decay, and even annihilation resulting from the spontaneous creation of matter-antimatter pairs. While the shredding of matter via expanding space-time is the primary damage mechanism, the sheer energy released as a byproduct creates a powerful secondary mechanism. Inflation charges are not used by ground forces. Even the smallest such devices could pose hazards to the operator, and would unavoidably cause catastrophic damage to the local environment.

Vortex charges are the preferred warp charge for ground combat. Vortex charges create a rotating vortex of space-time similar to the activation of a rotary-MID. This has the effect of stretching and pulling matter apart, though in a much less fantastic fashion than an inflation charge. Most of the effects of a vortex charge are macroscopic rather than microscopic. While a large object such as a person will be torn apart by the detonation, most of their constituent atoms will survive and be violently dispersed.

Compression charges are the last and rarest form of disrupter charge even though they were the first to be developed. Compression charges came about as a result of the Mojave Project, which bore many parallels with the Manhattan Project of ages past. Compression charges magnify the effects of warp fields, such as gravity within their influence many times over. The Mojave Project was designed to create an efficient but also terrifying weapon of mass destruction. The detonation of a compression charge will create a black hole by compressing matter beyond its Schwarzschild Radius. The magnified effects of gravity will continue for some time, allowing this black hole to consume matter and grow at an unnatural rate. The Empire has turned stars into black holes with compression charges both to test them and to demonstrate their power. These weapons have never actually been used in warfare, however. Modern weapons such as inflation charges have effectively rendered them obsolete. If the Empire needs to do something like destroy a planet, every single warship in the Armadas has more than enough firepower to do so.

3H
CELLULAR NANITES

THE TERM *CELLULAR NANITES* refers to the tiny nanomachines that inhabit the cells of modern humans. In the end, these nanites are the primary difference between modern homo solaris, and earlier homo sapiens. These nanites first became a part of the human anatomy as a result of the nanosingularity and have remained since. There are many types and subtypes of these nanites either living in cells or cocooning them. In any case, they are integral and inseparable from the body of the host. To list every function of these nanites and how they perform their work would create a text that makes most medical journals light reading in comparison. Therefore only a summary is offered here.

Cellular nanites are self-replicating and self-configuring. They inhabit every cell of the body, and as new cells are produced, so too are new nanites. Children of sexual reproduction gain their nanites from those inhabiting the sperm and egg cells of their parents. Those created through genetic engineering will generally have nanites removed from their parents and introduced in manners dependent upon the actual engineering that occurs. These nanites are controlled by software called nanoware, though this is often conflated with cyberware, which is used in other types of cybernetics.

These nanites can acquire a great deal of the material and energy they require through the body heat and diet of the host. However, the machines do have some needs that a normal diet has difficulty providing. To meet the needs of the machines, most Solar routinely ingest nanite sustenance substance or NSS. To the average person, NSS is more commonly referred to as "goo." As with food, there are many types of goo, ingested in various ways. Most commonly, goo is combined with artificial flavorings and used as a garnish on food. Special goo such as "red goo," which is designed to double as a stimulant, is common.

Solar humans are effectively impervious to disease thanks to their nanites. The small machines can identify any viral or bacterial agent in the body that poses a threat to the host. The nanites will physically attack these agents while stimulating the immune system to better combat them. Similarly, the machines can generally counteract the effects of poisons and other toxins by stimulating the necessary responses in the body. Even chemical agents such as nerve gases are functionally useless against Solars.

On the rare occasion such a weapon does prove effective, its effectiveness soon ends when a nanoware update is released, prepping the machines to deal with the toxin. Even foreign nanites can and will be attacked and destroyed by those of the body. The nanites will actively recognize and destroy developing cancers and can even counteract DNA damage from effects such as ionizing radiation. The nanites can even turn obesity into a rare cosmetic choice by blocking the body's ability to store excess calories as fat.

It is the health-maintaining effects of these nanites that allow Solars to routinely live in excess of three thousand years. The leading cause of death for Solar humans is a condition known as Neuro-Nanite Entropic Decay. Many people refer to this syndrome as the dreaded "Uncle Ned." Just as the body is controlled by the brain, the nanites within the body are controlled by those conjoined to brain cells. Over time the connections between brain cells and neural nanites can degrade. Bit-rate errors in nanite communication and other effects can compound to disrupt the linkage between the two systems. As time goes on, this can interfere with the nanites' ability to maintain the body and results in physical aging.

Uncle Ned can take centuries to result in death. One of the most visible signs of a person suffering late-stage N-NED is the graying of hairs and eventually the onset of albinism. The body's mechanisms that control pigment take a very low priority in the nanites' list of bodily maintenance. As the nanites' ability to repair the body degrades, maintenance of factors such as pigment is dropped to focus on more important functions. N-NED typically does not begin to manifest until close to a person's three thousandth birthday. Even then a person can typically live on for several more centuries. N-NED is not a death sentence per se. There exist numerous prospects for a person to enhance their longevity. This reaches an intersectional point, which concerns matters of morality, ethics, and sometimes what constitutes life. As with all things concerning human beings, some will choose to age and accept their eventual passing while others will seek means to live on.

Thanks to their nanites, members of homo solaris are much stronger and more resilient than were homo sapiens beyond longevity. The nanites' ability to heal damage to the body is so great that "medical science" often boils down to providing additional resources to the nanites. Whereas homo sapiens could not regenerate lost limbs, homo solaris can. In such an event, the nanites will synthesize stem cells and rebuild the limb that was lost. To kill a Solar often requires enormous levels of trauma to be inflicted within a short time. Other injuries are less common and less serious. The nanites enhance bone density to the point that a Solar's bones are roughly nine times less likely to be broken by something like a fall than were those of homo sapiens.

By affecting muscles, tendons, and ligaments, the nanites provide enhanced strength to the host. This is perhaps the most "unfair" portion of their benefits in terms of who benefits and how much. The nanites increased the strength disparity between men and women, as well as large and small individuals. The average Solar female has only 35 percent the upper-body, and 40 percent the lower-body strength of the average Solar male. The more muscle cells a person has, the more they benefit from this strength enhancement. A larger man will have even more of a strength advantage over a smaller man than their size alone would suggest.

However, the true extent to which the nanites can enhance strength will be found only in those who actively work to build their might. Naturally, muscle cells will increase in size when the body determines that more muscle is necessary. The nanites can not only enhance how large the muscle cells will grow but can stimulate the development of new muscle cells, which the body cannot do on its own after puberty. The nanites cannot work from nothing—the host must maintain sufficient calorie intake—but the result can be quite prodigious.

As part of their physical exam for entry into Hell's Gate, Solars wishing to enter the program must perform several exercises. At a minimum, candidates must be able to bench press 1,500 kilograms, deadlift 1,800 kilograms, and power-clean 600 kilograms, each for ten reps. These are weights that were functionally impossible for homo sapiens without cybernetic strength enhancement. These lifts can be performed by Solars who are noticeably fit but are by no means muscle-bound. Solars who seek to maximize their physical might can go well beyond these numbers.

Cellular nanites provide numerous mental and cognitive benefits as well as physical boons. The nanites have processing power and storage space to spare. The average Solar will never actually need a computer, calculator, smartphone, or similar device. All these functions can be handled by the nanites. Math proficiency is a poor means to judge a Solar's mental acumen. If a Solar is exposed to a math problem and their own brain requires more than a second to devise the solution, the nanites will perform the calculation. The host will generally experience the answer "popping into their head" as if they had memorized the answer beforehand. By the time one has reached math that the nanites cannot handle, one has entered the realm of supercomputing.

Solars have three distinct levels of consciousness. These are consciousness, subconsciousness, and digital consciousness. The digital consciousness is a result of the brain-nanite interface and exists between the prior two. In general, a Solar will never be aware of what goes on in their digital consciousness. It is at this layer that commands are sent from neural-nanites to the rest of the body, and where calculations are performed.

While many functions of the nanites are autonomous and not normally within the user's control, others are. Every Solar has a NOD or Neuro-Optic Display. The NOD is created by the neural nanites and is projected to the visual cortex of the brain so that the host sees a virtual screen within their field of vision. The host can use this to control their nanites, listen to music, play games, or handle other computing functions.

The modern astranet was designed primarily for compatibility with human nanites, as were many other technologies. Tools for aliens are generally "NOD-compliant" to allow them to interface with the same systems. Solars are born with the ability to wirelessly uplink with the astranet whenever they wish so long as they are within its footprint. Outside of the astranet, Solars can still communicate wirelessly over short distances via radio waves produced by nanites in the skin of the host, and received by those in the skin of the target.

While it is a popular subject in Imperial fiction, there is no real risk of a Solar being "hacked." Control over systems such as autonomic functions and motor control are standalone and not connected directly to parts such as the NOD, which can access outside networks. Chemical signals from the brain are checked for all commands as a sort of master control. If one tried to hack a Solar and force them to uppercut themselves, they would first have to access inaccessible networks. Ignoring the fact that this is impossible, one would then have to direct the host to perform the action. When the host attempts to physically resist, the nanites would obey the commands sourced from the brain and ignore the intrusive command. To hack a Solar, one would need not only a god-like hacker but an extremely powerful telepath capable of remote control. Such a telepath, however, would make the hacker redundant.

Contrary to the belief of many aliens, Solars do not have perfect memory. It is debatable if this would be beneficial from a psychological standpoint. What the nanites will do is index all memories of their host. If a Solar cannot remember something, they can use their NOD to run a search of their memory index and pull otherwise forgotten memories from their minds. This has limits. Memory indexing can help the host with something like remembering the time and place of the appointment. It still falls on the Solar to either remember the appointment exists or set a reminder for themselves.

Memory indexing has led to some new psychological maladies that Imperial medical personnel must deal with. One of these is Post-Traumatic Re-engagement Syndrome. Individuals with PTRS compulsively use their indexing abilities to relive traumatic events with which they are having difficulty coping.

This skims only the basics of what the nanites can do for a person. The machines can self-reconfigure and accept new nanoware to alter their functions. A person who wants to build more muscle can simply run a program in their NOD, which will direct the nanites to stimulate the muscles while they sleep. While combining this with exercise would be more effective, it makes it possible for a person to develop strength without having to do the exercise. A person who wishes for better reflexes can run commands in their NOD, which will direct the nanites to modify their brain's signal-processing abilities. In any case, while some benefit can be gained, *more* will be gained if the host does more than rely on the nanites alone. Forcing the nanites to work without actively helping them is more likely to induce side effects that the host may find undesirable.

Just as most people will never truly try to push themselves to their limits, few will take full advantage of everything their nanites can do for them. Often, those who seek more than the default array of abilities, do so for professional reasons. But for those who are so motivated, the nanites can in many ways turn the body into a configurable machine. Imperial scientists routinely use nanoware routines that modify their brain so that they can better and more directly integrate with external computers for high-level processing. Soldiers utilize a host of enhancements to increase their survivability. Models can use specialized programs to help maintain their figures into whatever they consider an idealized image. These capabilities do have limits; the nanites are not magic, and pushing for too much enhancement in one area can force sacrifices in another.

3I
MILITARY CYBERIZATION

IN THE ORGANIC ARMS race, it can be said that humans for the most part won the brain competition. Humans were heavily shafted in the physical categories. There are many species that are far tougher and more able to survive the rigors of combat than can a natural human. There is very little on the battlefield that an organic being of any kind can do, that a machine can't do better. For humans, the nanosingularity helped to narrow the gap between man and machine, but it did not close it. When a soldier joins the Solar Armed Forces, he will be heavily augmented. Soldiers must be there to supervise the machines, but they must be capable enough that they are not a liability. Both humans and aliens will receive augmentation in some form. This entry focuses primarily on that to which human soldiers are subject. While aliens will be augmented as well, their augmentations are highly dependent on their needs and anatomy. This entry covers only that augmentation to which *all* human soldiers are subject. A crewman in the Solar Armadas will receive different augmentation than an infantryman in the Solar Legionnaires. This entry covers what they share.

For a human soldier, the first step of augmentation is nanite replacement. The original design of cellular nanites was such a good one that little could be done to improve it. Military nanites are not necessarily better—they are more specialized. These nanites have enhanced capabilities to improve the host's reflexes, ability to survive and heal from trauma, enhance cardiovascular fitness, and augment muscular strength. They also serve an important role in facilitating the next stages of the process. Nanite replacement occurs with a simple injection. The new nanites enter the body, are met by the old nanites, and the new begins to replace the old. This process typically lasts about six weeks.

Step two of military cyberization is bone replacement. Soldiers' bones are not the flimsy calcium-phosphate bones of a natural human but bond-forged titanium. Some bones will be surgically replaced with the new cybernetics, while others are manufactured within the body by the soldier's new nanites. These cybernetics are fully capable of performing all the bones' functions, including the tasks of marrow. If these bones are broken, they can either be replaced or repaired within the body by the nanites.

Step three of military cyberization is organ replacement. Almost every organ in the soldier's body is replaced by a lab-grown model that is both more capable and more resistant to trauma. A soldier's lungs provide an excellent example. An ordinary human's lungs are fragile bags that, if perforated, become useless. Each of a soldier's lungs is essentially a collection of hundreds of microlungs bound together. These smaller lungs are not only more efficient, but if something like a bullet penetrates the lung, the damaged sub-lungs will simply be closed off while the rest continue doing their job. The veins and arteries are replaced with new versions that are full of sphincters. If an artery is severed, the sphincters can close to prevent the soldier from bleeding out. While this system is not perfect, it takes a very massive and sudden trauma to make a soldier bleed out.

The final phase of organ replacement is skin replacement. Soldiers' skin is far more resistant to cuts, abrasions, and penetration. Imperial soldiers do not even need armor to be safe from primitive weapons like arrows and spears. Even most gunpowder weapons are incapable of penetrating, and the bullet will at best lodge itself in the skin. A soldier's skin is also fireproof, though it can melt if subject to sufficient heat. The concept itself can be somewhat relative. While the skin will not catch fire, if one is covered in a flaming substance (such as hydraulic fluids) the difference can be one of semantics. This does enable a soldier the potential to save himself from an incendiary weapon if he can remove it from his skin.

By the time organ replacement is complete, the soldier can survive extremes of heat and temperature that no ordinary human could endure. While not comfortable, Imperial soldiers can survive exposure to temperatures below -90 degrees Celsius and as high as 150 without risk of hypothermia or heat stroke. Their ability to survive extremes of pressure is better than ten times that of an un-augmented human. The average soldier's ability to survive even in a vacuum is limited primarily to how long he can hold his breath. For the average soldier, thirty minutes is uncomfortable but doable.

After organ replacement, a soldier will receive what is likely the most important upgrade. Organic soldiers must be able to think and react at a speed on par with machines. However, soldiers are people too. When they are not fighting the enemies of the Empire, they need to be able to socialize with other people. To trap them in a mental state where normal people seem to take weeks to finish a sentence would be incredibly cruel. And a soldier needs to be able to do things like embrace his wife without ripping her into bloody fabric. To bring all these factors together is the task of the Neuro-Central Processor.

The corpus callosum of the soldier's brain is removed and the NCP is put in its place. The NCP handles all the functions of the replaced brain matter, and much more. With an NCP, the brain effectively becomes a multi-core processor. In combat, a soldier's ability to think, reason, and act are elevated to be handled by the much faster NCP. At this point, the NCP is what the soldier is using to do his thinking and acting. The NCP scans the input from the soldier's senses constantly and looks for certain markers to decide when to activate this enhanced processing. For the average soldier, the transition is so seamless that they are not consciously aware it has occurred. The NCP is so effective that soldiers have been known to literally dodge bullets. The NCP detects the gunshot, engages, and the soldier can move out of the bullet's path.

The NCP includes other features such as a dedicated gyroscope to help fight disorientation. Some of the most important features are those that do things such as enable a soldier to control his greatly augmented strength. Nerve heighteners were installed specifically so that soldiers can do things like cradle their loved ones safely. Nerve heighteners enhance the soldier's sense of touch so he is more aware of the pressure he is exerting. This, however, must be activated by the soldier.

It is not true that Imperial soldiers do not feel pain. The sense of touch cannot be separated from the sense of pain. Pain serves an important function in the body, namely to alert the person to injury. The NCP enhances the soldier's task persistence—their ability to continue acting despite pain. While Imperial soldiers do feel pain, it is far less likely to debilitate them. The NCP helps the soldier to process the mental trauma of injury quicker in order to break the initial shock. Simultaneously, there are other mental benefits such as augmented spatial reasoning. Few ground troops need a rangefinder to approximate distance within the visual horizon.

Further augmentation will be given to a soldier based on his actual military specialty. Solar Legionnaires and Army personnel receive specialized stomachs that expand the list of materials they are capable of digesting. This grants them a greater chance of survival if they end up cut off and somehow without their mess kit. Armadas personnel receive additional augmentations to help cope with the effects of a vacuum as they are at greater risk of exposure due to battle damage inflicted on a ship.

3J
THE ASTRANET

THE CORNERSTONE OF SOLAR civilization is the Imperial astranet. Most of the Empire lies within its footprint. The astranet enables lag-free communication anywhere within its influence, the ability to teleport across the Empire, and even for primitive species to reach the stars. The astranet is composed of three layers, each with a dedicated function.

Layer 1 of the astranet is the communications layer. This layer relies on the teleportation of data from point to point in order to facilitate instantaneous communication. This takes the form of personal messages, ship navigation, and more. Layer 1 of the astranet is considered vital to the Empire's ability to defend itself. Though not outright impossible, it is exceedingly difficult for a ship to move within the astranet's influence and not be seen. The Armadas monitor the sensory capabilities of the net constantly, looking for any sign of hostile encroachment.

Layer 1 is also the most heavily regulated by Imperial law. As the astranet covers the entire Empire, the Mandrake Dynasty has rejected claims by national sovereigns to regulate it. Thanks largely to the Mandrakes, the Empire has extremely aggressive privacy laws. Companies and governments alike are strictly limited with how much of a person's information can be gathered via the astranet. It is technically possible to locate any person at any given time if they have an astranet connection. Imperial law, however, requires a high standard of cause to do so, though a person can sever the astranet connection if they wish to remain hidden.

Layer 2 is the transportation layer. This layer is what enables a person to stand on an astranet router on one planet and arrive almost instantly on another even in a faraway galaxy. Experiments in using the Hyams Effect to achieve teleportation date all the way back to Hyams himself. Hyams conducted several experiments in which he could use the effect to instantly transport small things such as protons between one point and another. He found that the teleportation of living beings could not be achieved in the same way. An attempt to do so led to the tragic redistribution of a lab mouse throughout his lab. Said mouse was quite difficult to locate as all its pieces were at the atomic scale. Living beings are simply too fragile and complex to be teleported in this way. Layer 2 relies on transpatial technology. An astranet router is, in essence, a tiny transpatial gateway capable of being linked to other gateways on demand. Astranet routers come in forms large and small and take on many variations. One of the most prolific is the astranet highway. These always-on gateways are built into roads for individuals using vehicles such as conveyors. One can literally drive to another planet or star hive by taking the highways.

Layer 2 also houses the critical junctures of the astranet power grid. This system enables those with the proper equipment to wirelessly tap into the astranet and distribute power across interstellar distances. It supports the convenient harvesting of energy from sources such as singularity power plants or other similarly exotic and high-output installations. The astranet itself requires an immense amount of energy to operate, and without Layer 2's power-distribution capabilities, it would not be viable in its modern form. The Solar Armed Forces consider the astranet highways vital to the Empire's defense. It is because of these highways that most consider an invasion of the Empire to be impossible. By using these highways, the Solar Army can quickly move and concentrate enormous levels of force without having to pack their troops on ships to get them to the fighting. It was the development of astranet highways in the Hourglass Galaxy, which was among the primary motives of the Interstellar Combine to declare war. The Combine was well aware that allowing these highways to be completed could have made the Empire impossible to dislodge.

The existence of mobile routers is considered a technological impossibility by most. The fact that they exist is a closely guarded secret by the handful of organizations that possess them. Mobile routers are some of the most complex and advanced pieces of equipment in existence. Even for the Commando Corps, the regulations pertaining to their use are many. Above all is to maintain the secrecy. These devices are so secret that even most members of the royal family do not know they exist. Mobile routers only allow one to travel from any given point, and they must still arrive at a fixed and established router. Requiring such a demanding task from such a small device carries a high cost. Mobile routers are good for only a handful of uses before they must be replaced. They will only function within the astranet's influence.

Layer 3 of the astranet is the railroad layer, named for the ancient railroads of Earth. The Empire builds up Layer 3 primarily for the benefit of primitive civilizations. Many civilizations are not capable of building massless impulse drives for themselves, and the Empire is not always interested in sharing a technology with so many military applications. But if a species can build a ship that can get into space, the rails can enable them to reach the stars.

The rails are made up of fixed installation, which broadcast traversable warp fields between each other. A ship can ride on a traversable field much like an ocean-going vessel on the water's waves. These rails are constructed to link points of interest and economic activity and are actively patrolled by the Solar Armadas. In times of peace, it is typically the Second Armada that patrols these rails both to monitor for incursion and to assist travelers in distress. While any ship with a MID can make interstellar travel on its own, many who have the capability choose to use the rails to save on fuel costs. The Empire encourages this as it makes space activity easier to monitor. It has always been the Mandrake Dynasty's stance that the astranet exists for the public benefit, and therefore must be available for easy use by said public.

While the astranet is vast, it does not cover the entire Empire. There are still remote regions that lack astranet coverage for reasons ranging from political to economic to isolationism. The astranet takes considerable time to build up once a new area is colonized. This would be a contributing factor in leading the Empire to believe there was no risk of war with the Vaar. Imperial planners correctly assumed that the Vaar would see any war with the Empire as being impossible once the astranet had been fully established in the Virgo Cluster. However, they incorrectly assumed that the Vaar would be unable to muster and mobilize in time to prevent the Empire from completing the task. This led to the false sense of security that the Vaar would believe they could do nothing before it was too late.

The Vaar were engaged in a massive counter-intelligence campaign to mislead the Empire about their capabilities while working to mobilize their forces. The Empire was correct in their belief that the Vaar assumed victory would be impossible if the astranet were to come online.

APPENDIX 4

METAPSIONICS

THE FIRST OFFICIAL METAPSION recognized by Imperial science was Prince David Mandrake in the year 646. Prince David demonstrated empathy, telepathy, and very limited psionic abilities to Imperial researchers. Later, David would often demonstrate his abilities publicly. In the following years, many more individuals would come forward to demonstrate that they too possessed these talents. The initial reception these people found from the general public was decidedly mixed. Paranoia about telepaths stealing secrets from people's minds or planting thoughts in their heads quickly rose to a point that bordered on mass hysteria. While telepaths were never placed in concentration camps or faced with genocide, the matter was seriously proposed in some circles. If not for the fact that by the year 654, six members of the Mandrake family demonstrated these abilities, it may well have happened. It was not until 4CM systems became widely available three hundred years later that social discrimination against metapsions declined.

There are three recognized forms of metapsionics. These are telepathy, psionics, and providence. Empathy is the weakest form of telepathy and is not counted as its own ability. All these abilities are related on a scaling basis. All telepaths have the full range of empathic abilities. All psions are telepaths. Providents are almost too rare to measure, but all are quite powerful in terms of both telepathy and psionics.

Correlation does not equal causation. Metapsionics first appeared shortly after the nanosingularity, leading many to assume that it was the cause. But even after thousands of years of research, no causal relationship between the two has ever been demonstrated. For that matter, no actual cause of these abilities has been identified. While theories abound, none have enough evidence to support them. Scientists have conclusively detected warp effects when a psion moves an object, but the effect is just barely on the side of being measurable. This leads most scientists to believe that metapsionics operate at such small scales that their mechanism of action cannot be observed directly. Further that if they do occur at such small scales, direct observation may never be possible.

In any case, metapsions are relatively rare. Humans are the only species known to possess these abilities. Most children are tested early by the education system. Metapsions have special needs when it comes to learning how to interact with others, and they are often placed in special schools for that purpose. Metapsionic ability is highly distributed and is anything but fair. Again, correlation is not causation, but in these cases, the correlation is too high to assume there is not an underlying if unidentified reason. Differences correlate to gender, nationality, socioeconomic status, applied intelligence score, and psychological factors. Some of these can be unified or taken out.

Members of the noble and royal aristocracy are *far* more likely to demonstrate these abilities than common persons. Wealthy individuals demonstrate these abilities more often than those on a stipend. Most correlate this to AIS. The aristocracy and the wealthy tend to have a higher AIS than the rest, and this is likely the root cause of the economic difference. AIS is short for Applied Intelligence Score, the method the Empire uses to test cognitive abilities in humans.

Reichsylvannians are roughly ten times more likely to be born with some kind of metapsionic ability than those of other nations. This is likely a result of AIS, as the average Reichsylvannian scores higher than the rest of the Solar population. Those with above-average AIS not only demonstrate metapsionic ability more often, but the two factors seem to be related.

There is a very clear and unexplained gender disparity in these abilities. In terms of total metapsions, men and women are roughly equal. However, the upper ranks of both telepathic and psionic ability are dominated by men. Men account for approximately 90 percent of those with T-scores above 5, and 100 percent of those with T-scores of 10 or higher. Similarly, men account for nearly all psions with P-scores above 5.

Annabelle Chriss of Miss Empire fame was not well-known simply because she was pretty. Miss Empire exists to provide young trophy wives for noblemen, no matter what those who run the contest may claim. The contest is arranged so that the winner each year will be crowned the same year she is old enough to marry. The fact that Annabelle Chriss was a P-6, a woman, and not yet a full adult makes her an extreme statistical outlier. The fact that all Commando officers are men is due solely to the fact that no woman has ever met their metapsionic requirements. The organization itself would be extremely interested in finding a woman who can meet the qualifications, as her gender alone would go a long way in disguising her affiliation.

While it was not often reflected upon by her children, the fact that Empress Marianne Mandrake was a provident makes her one of only a handful of women who ever demonstrated the ability. But the total extent of her metapsionic abilities and the fact that she was a provident were a closely guarded secret by the Mandrake family. Only a handful of people outside the Solar Court even knew that she was a psion, let alone the strongest in the family. As far as the general public knew, she was a weak telepath. The royal dynasties have long hidden and under-reported their abilities to keep that knowledge from potential foes. Sometimes they hid their true abilities from their own family. Mason Mandrake was an exception purely due to the political capital it afforded him to be the emperor who could see the future. The Rhinegraves were really the first people to gain these abilities but kept them secret so as to exploit them via covert use of telepathy. When David Mandrake went public so long ago, it was a warning to the public.

Much of the gender disparity can be found in other correlations. Just as intelligence correlates, so too does a ratio of brain mass. This ratio is visible in both sexes. Men in general have more brain mass than women even when accounting for differences in body size. Metapsionic men with physically larger brains generally have higher scores than those with smaller brains. Similarly, metapsionic women with larger brains routinely score better than women with smaller brains.

Another and perhaps the most important factor is psychological. The strongest metapsions demonstrate a number of psychological traits. These include much greater predispositions to domineering, possessive, and aggressive behavior. While some are better at controlling these impulses than others, they are far too prevalent in the top ranks to be ignored. Some studies have gone so far to suggest that possessing these psychological dispositions may be more important than intelligence or brain mass, but these studies are disputed. Most empaths have laid-back, docile, or even outright submissive personalities.

A final overall correlation is one of lineage. Studies have shown that the child of two metapsions has a roughly 50 percent chance of developing at least T-0 abilities. But this is a question of *lineage*, not genetics. There seems to be minimal change in the odds if only one parent is a metapsion. Meanwhile clones of metapsionic individuals seem no more likely to inherit these abilities than a child with one, or no metapsionic parent. No clone created through spin-genesis has ever demonstrated metapsionic abilities. This leads to speculation of a biological, if not genetic, factor that is handed down—one that seems to be independent of conception with those conceived naturally, having no higher or lower odds than one created through various means of genetic engineering.

As with much else in life, metapsions do not escape regulation by the law. It is illegal in most jurisdictions to read a person's mind without their consent. Similarly, the use of psionics to inflict violence on another person is often considered assault with a deadly weapon. Passive empathy is the exception and is generally unregulated. Passive empathy is limited to observation of emotions. This is an ability that can be accomplished in other, more mundane ways such as reading facial expressions or body language.

4A
TELEPATHY

TELEPATHIC ABILITY IS GENERALLY regarded as a set parameter. Those born with the ability will usually demonstrate empathy early in childhood. Their powers will not meaningfully develop until adolescence. Once those abilities develop, they seem to be an upper limit. No amount of practice has ever shown potential to allow a telepath to raise their T-score. At most, it allows telepaths to affect more than one person at a time. But in any case, once their abilities develop, those they have are the only abilities they will have. Telepathic strength is measured on the T-scale. To measure telepathic ability is not so simple as to measure psionics, where force can be calculated on an object. Telepathic strength can only be measured relative to other telepaths rather than as an absolute value. That said, the scale recognizes a logarithmic effect. While telepaths can compete and interfere with each other, a higher-ranking telepath will almost always overcome resistance by a lower-ranking one. If a T-6 wanted to stop a T-7 from reading his mind, he would need as many as nine other T-6s to level the playing field.

T-0: **Simple Empath.** An individual with a T-score of zero can identify emotions of other humans with 100 percent accuracy. They do not possess any other abilities.

T-0.5: **Sensing Empath:** An individual with a T-score of 0.5 can not only sense emotions with 100 percent accuracy but is capable of experiencing the feelings of others.

T-0.75: **Projecting Empath:** An individual with a T-score of 0.75 can sense emotions with 100 percent accuracy and can experience the feelings of others. This is arguably the weakest point of true telepathy as projecting empaths can project their emotions onto others but with considerable difficulty. Famous example—Princess Simmonne Mandrake.

T-1: **Basic telepath.** In addition to the full range of empathic abilities, a basic telepath is capable of projecting thoughts to others. A T-1's ability to do so is generally poor, however, lacking any capacity for conveying concepts such as tone or cadence. A basic telepath could send a message like "That shirt looks good on you," but could not convey sarcasm while doing so. All telepaths of T-1 and above have a "telepathic voice," which the target experiences much the same as a spoken voice in their mind. A person's spoken voice is determined by other factors such as the shape and size of their vocal cords. Most telepaths have to put in considerable practice to make their telepathic voice match their spoken voice.

T-2: Subtle Telepath. As with T-1 but can convey tone and attitude.

T-3: Listening Telepath. T-3 is the lowest rank at which a telepath is capable of reading thoughts in the minds of others. This is limited to "surface thoughts," as in what the subject happens to be focused on at that point in time. The ability remains limited and can generally be focused on one mind at a time. Just as a T-1 cannot convey something like tone in a message, a T-3 cannot pick up on many of these subtle details in thoughts they read.

T-4: Adept Telepath. At T-4, a telepath can easily read surface thoughts and may be able to do so from more than one person at a time with great difficulty. Unlike the T-3, the T-4 can pick up subtle details in the thoughts they read. All psions have T-scores of at least this rank.

T-5: Memory Telepath. A T-5 telepath can go beyond surface thoughts and can delve into the memories of another person. To do this, the telepath begins by scanning surface thoughts, while simultaneously thinking of specific events, places, people, or things, which may conjure appropriate memories from the target as if the telepath were the one remembering the events. The more recent the memory, the more expedient the recall. T-5s can sense emotions tied to memories, but accuracy in identifying the emotions is often low.

T-6: Accurate Memory Telepath. The primary differences between a T-5 and T-6 are twofold. A T-6 can accurately identify emotions connected to a memory. A T-6 can also spot "false memories" with a high degree of accuracy. T-6s are readily hired by the criminal justice system. They can establish guilt by pulling the memory of committing the crime from the mind of the accused then identifying attempts to use technological means to remove or alter these memories. They can also establish innocence by confirming that no memory of the crime does or ever did exist. They are also extremely useful in examining witnesses. Eye-witness accounts are notoriously unreliable, and a T-6 can often bring a more accurate memory of events than the witness can account for on their own. Their ability to identify false memories implanted by another telepath is far less accurate.

T-7: **Programmer Telepath.** A programmer telepath is capable of implanting false memories in the mind of another person, but the ability is limited. While the telepath can plant a false memory, the subject will know the memory is false and more akin to the memory of a dream or imagined event.

T-8: **Flawless Programmer Telepath.** A T-8 can implant false memories and do so with such high precision that, to the subject, the memory is indistinguishable from those of actual events.

T-9: **Remote Telepath.** A telepath with a T-score of 9 or better is capable of "remote viewing." A telepath using remote viewing can substitute a target's sensory input for their own or vice versa. They can see through their target's eyes and hear through their ears. They can perform the reverse as well, substituting input from the subject's senses for their own. Famous example—Emperor Mason Mandrake.

T-10: **Puppeteer Telepath.** A puppeteer telepath can control the body of a target, making them move, talk, and engage in other voluntary motor functions. The individual will be fully aware that they are being compelled by an outside force. The ability of the subject to resist seems to be predicated on psychology. Those with more domineering and aggressive mindsets are far more difficult to control than those with more compliant personalities. Some individuals cannot be controlled unless they voluntarily allow it. Famous example—Empress Marianne Mandrake.

T-11: **Control Telepath.** A control telepath can not only take physical control of another person's motor functions but can affect autonomic functions as well. A control telepath can alter the target's heart rate, their breathing, and other factors over which the target may have limited to no control. While less of an influence, the psychology of the target still imposes a limiting effect. T-11 is the minimum T-score one must possess to be eligible for recruitment as a Solar Commando.

T-12: **Illusory Telepath.** An illusory telepath has all the abilities of a T-11, but the psychological disposition of the target becomes irrelevant to any target who does not have similar telepathic abilities.

A T-12 can not only exert remote control over both voluntary and involuntary functions, but they can also create a phantom sensation by using their imaginations. Lower-ranking telepaths can only create "illusions" by tampering with short-term memory and are hard-pressed to do so in a convincing way. A T-12 can force a target to see, hear, smell, taste, or touch things that do not actually exist, substituting the target's actual sensory input for their own imagination. But even for a T-12, a great deal of practice is generally required to do so in a way that results in a "flawless" illusion for the target.

T-13: Gestalt Telepath. The T-13 is the upper limit of the T-scale. By this point, an individual has the full range of all telepathic abilities to have ever been demonstrated. Above this rank, additional ranks would only be useful in comparing the "strongest of the strongest" against each other. Not all T-13s are created equal, and some can overpower others. However, as the sample size for T-13s at any given time is extremely small, it makes little sense to try to increase the scale further to account for outliers in a group of extreme outliers.

Gestalt telepaths are the only telepath capable of mental assimilation. This is the ability to effectively absorb the conscious and subconscious mind of the target into their own. In this state, the gestalt telepath has perfect knowledge of all thoughts, memories, and sensations of the target. The target effectively becomes an extension of the telepath until the bond is broken. A gestalt telepath is perfectly capable of performing mental assimilation, killing the subject, and retaining the full breadth of the subject's life experience.

The strongest T-13 in the Empire is generally considered to be Commandant of the Solar Commando Corps Nicolae Espada. At least in so far as those who know he exists. Because one of the commandant's responsibilities is to hunt down any commando who goes renegade, a T-score of 13 is considered mandatory to take the position.

4B
PSIONICS

THOUGH MORE RARE THAN telepathy, psionics is far easier to gauge and measure. While numerous methods for gauging psionic strength exist, the most common is the Newton Equivalence Scale. This scale measures the ability of a psion to accelerate an object and correlates it to the amount of newton force that would be required to achieve a similar effect. This scale can be somewhat misleading, however. For one, psions are not applying force in a conventional sense. They are warping space-time in a way that exerts force, mimicking the ability of gravity to do so. Second, this measures only peak force equivalent. Some of the stronger psions can exert peak force equivalence greater than the thrust of the Saturn-V rocket, which carried the first men to Earth's moon. But even those psions would have a difficult time actually sending an object into orbit. Finally, personal psychology does come into play. Just as a powerlifter may need to "psych himself up" to perform a difficult lift, a psion may need several tries to hit his peak. While this scale has flaws, it is the most simple when it comes to comparing one psion to another.

The common P-scale measures two numbers. The first is the Newton Equivalence Scale given above. The second is the Object Total. There is a disparity among psions between maximum force and total force. A psion may not be able to exceed a total force of an arbitrary amount on a single test object, yet they may be capable of exerting that same amount of force on multiple test objects at once. For example, a psion may have a maximum force of one thousand newtons and be unable to accelerate a single object with any greater force. But at the same time, that psion may be able to exert two or more objects at one thousand newtons each. For this reason, a psion is tested for both their peak force and how many objects they can simultaneously subject to that force.

Typical test conditions involve one-kilogram bond-forged lead spheres in an environment with 1G gravity, one atmosphere of pressure, and 10 percent humidity. The subject is then tested for the peak force achieved while accelerating the lead sphere over a distance of five meters. It must also be reiterated that the P-scale is measuring *peak* force, as opposed to sustained force. A P-10 can exceed the peak thrust of the ancient Saturn-V rocket (approximately 34 meganewtons). However that same P-10 would be hard-pressed to sustain that force long enough to propel an object of similar mass to escape velocity of a habitable planet. The longer a psion attempts to exert force, the more difficult it becomes to sustain their peak.

Psionic proficiency is a bit different from telepathic proficiency. Telepathic proficiency seems to be predetermined. While it may take years or even centuries before a telepath can master the full spectrum of their abilities, it will be clear early what abilities they have the potential to obtain. No amount of practice or dedication will enable them to climb the T-scale. Psions can, however, increase their P-score through considerable dedication. But there is a lot of gray area here. The weakest psions seem to gain very little advancement from practice. Those who begin with higher scores seem to be much more capable of advancing their numbers over time.

Psions also have many more technologies available that can augment the person's abilities. One of the most important is multitasking software for a person's NOD. A psion's Object Total is as much a function of their ability to focus on multiple objects as anything else. NOD software can expand a person's ability to focus on multiple objects. Formal evaluation requires such accessories be deactivated while a person is being evaluated. As Object Total varies greatly from one person to the next and does not seem to be correlated to newton equivalence, they are not listed below.

P-0   0.1 newton or less

P-1   < 1 newton

P-2   1 newton

P-3   10 newton

P-4   100 newton

P-5   1 kilonewton

P-6   10 kilonewton

P-7   100 kilonewton

P-8   1 meganewton

P-9   10 meganewton

P-10   100 meganewton

4C
PROVIDENCE

PROVIDENCE IS DEFINED AS the ability to sense, perceive, or possibly even interact with persons, places, and events across the axis of time. Providence is by far the rarest form of metapsionics, so rare that it has proven extremely difficult to study. Far less than one percent of metapsions will ever demonstrate this ability.

Half of those who have the gift are effectively mentally disabled, often having great difficulty in trusting that they are in the "now" at any given moment. Even among the Mandrake Dynasty, which has more metapsion members than not, Mason Mandrake was one of only three provident emperors. His wife, the late Empress Marianne, was one of the only female providents known to have existed.

The gift of providence relates directly to persons, places, and things. If a provident wants to see into the past or future of a place, he generally needs to be *in* that place. To see the past or future of a person, they generally need to be near that person. This can lead to interlinked ripple effects. A provident may see a person's past or future by being in the place that person is, was, or will one day be.

It is not known whether the ability to perceive the future is a separate ability from the ability to perceive the past, or if it is simply easier for providents to see into the past than the future. What is known is that all true providents can see the past almost at will. Very few have ever been able to look into the future when they wish. Often, visions of the future are random and unsolicited. Whereas schools and curriculum exist for telepaths and psions, providents are so rare that no such organizations or programs exist. For an individual with provident ability, it often falls solely on their shoulders to learn how to use their gift. Even the counsel of another provident is rarely helpful, as how one experiences providence seems to vary considerably from one individual to another.

What is known is that providence, when true, has an accuracy of 100 percent. When a provident looks into the past, they see things as they happened. When a provident sees the future, they see things that will happen. There is no confirmed record of a provident ever being able to alter the events of a future vision. This has opened some debate into the nature of free will, causality, and other concepts.

Providence is so rare that there is no objective system to measure the relative abilities of one provident to the next. The only real academic text on the subject useful to a provident is in the writings of Arthur Wells, one of the most gifted providents on record. Wells himself would eventually disappear, which most suspect was to escape the flocks of followers who gathered around him hoping for guidance in how to live their lives. Part of his legacy is that he is the one who canonized the term *providence*.

Wells identified four distinct types of provident vision:

Empathic Clairvoyance. Likely what empathy is to telepathy, clairvoyance does not manifest as visions, sights, sounds, or smells. Clairvoyance manifests as feelings either of anticipation or even dread corresponding to events that the individual does not yet know are going to occur.

Echo Sight. Echo Sight is quite simply looking into the past and experiencing it in a way similar to how one hears an echoing sound. How accurately one can perceive events during echo sight is rather low. Many since Wells have conjectured that the providents who have great difficulty with the gift likely do as a result of this ability. Echo sight can be muddled, indistinct, and indistinguishable from a hallucination.

True Clairvoyance. Wells identified true clairvoyance as the ability to know information such as the outcome of events from either the past or future, that the individual in question had no other possibility to know. A person experiencing true clairvoyance might know the identity of a murderer without ever having been exposed to the planning or commission of the crime.

Foresight. The most famous ability, foresight, was the ability of some providents to see future events anywhere from minutes to years before they transpired. Wells was said to be particularly skilled with this ability and noted that the further into the future he tried to see, the more difficult it became. In his writing, he speculated that it might be impossible for a provident to see events that would occur after the seer's death. Whether or not he was correct in this speculation is unknown.

Transcendence. Wells speculated that it might be possible for an individual to do more than see across time, but to use telepathy and psionics to *act*. This action could be in the form of sending messages to people in visions or using psionics to manipulate objects. His personal journals note that he had experimented with doing exactly that and may have even found some success. Since his disappearance thousands of years ago, some have speculated that he sequestered himself to pursue further study. Many conspiracy theories have been raised on this point, with some even suggesting that he was so successful that the Commando Corps or some other organization was responsible for his disappearance. No provident since him has ever had any success at using telepathy or psionics to influence past or future events.

Wells strongly suggested that telepathy was already at work. He noted that whenever he experienced a vision, it was always from a first-person perspective. He was either seeing through his own eyes at a future time or through the eyes of another person in the past or future. This led him to conclude that in that latter case, telepathy in some form had to be involved.

4D
4CM TECHNOLOGY

ALMOST AS SOON AS metapsionics were proven to exist, the Commando Corps began actively recruiting men with those talents to join their ranks. So too did the organization provide much of the capital to fund research into finding ways to hinder or obstruct metapsionics. It would take nearly three hundred years, but the research would eventually pay off. It was first noted that the presence of anti-gravity systems has an extremely slight but measurable ability to interfere with metapsionics. This is where the research would begin and eventually lead to a finished product. While 4CM technology is based on anti-gravity technology, the two are highly distinct. The amount by which anti-gravity systems interfere with metapsionics is negligible. A functioning 4CM system is no longer suited to work as an anti-gravity device.

In the modern Empire, the term *4CM* is an orphan initialism. When the first anti-psion tools were made, they were part of a suite of jamming systems meant to protect against mundane threats as well. Over time, however, the term *4CM* came to refer specifically to those systems used to hinder telepathy and psionics.

One of the few things that are known about metapsions is that they create non-Hyams, non-gravity warp fields that can be measured, barely. This led researchers to conclude that Hyams fields might cause interference. This is exactly how 4CM systems work. A telepath attempting to project a message or read a mind across a 4CM field will experience interference. Read thoughts will come across as gabbled, muted, or nonsensical. Psions who attempt to move objects across the influence of a 4CM field are generally left nauseous by the experience, in some cases even becoming dizzy and disoriented.

In the modern Empire, 4CM systems are a common and easily obtained technology for anyone who wants them. They come in many forms that can be worn inconspicuously from being woven into clothing or worn as jewelry. Essentially all VIPs rely on 4CM systems of some kind to protect their minds. The members of the Mandrake Dynasty have long installed 4CM systems in their crowns. But 4CMs works both ways. A telepath wearing a 4CM system to protect their mind from a stronger telepath would first have to deactivate their system if they wanted to use their own abilities without interference.

4CM systems are an effective but imperfect defense. Some telepaths, particularly those of T-6 ranking or higher, are far less inhibited. T-9 telepaths can generally act across a 4CM field without any meaningful effect. Psions, by contrast, are always affected, and even the strongest psions typically feel some disorientation trying to act in or through a 4CM field. Having 4CM equipment is considered mandatory for soldiers and law enforcement across the Empire. Many private citizens have 4CM systems of their own in discreet forms. That said, the odds of meeting a telepath or psion are rare, and the odds of encountering one strong enough to negate such a protective field are even smaller.

These systems have some common-sense limitations. 4CM protects objects within its influence, not beyond. A 4CM system could protect a person from being psionically thrown off a bus, but it won't help much if the psion throws the bus at them.

Humans are the only species to have ever demonstrated metapsionic abilities. The fact that the Vaar had 4CM technology when the Empire first encountered them was a cause for concern. It led many to conclude that the Vaar knew a lot more about the Empire and humanity than they would admit.

www.TheEncephalon.com
www.Facebook.com/SolarWindsSeries

www.ingramcontent.com/pod-product-compliance
Lightning Source LLC
Chambersburg PA
CBHW060240030726
47493CB00024B/1426